NORA ROBERTS

THE
PAGAN
STONE

JOVE
New York

A JOVE BOOK
Published by Berkley
An imprint of Penguin Random House LLC
375 Hudson Street, New York, New York 10014

Copyright © 2008 by Nora Roberts
Excerpt from *Naked in Death* by J. D. Robb copyright © 1995 by Nora Roberts
Penguin Random House supports copyright. Copyright fuels creativity, encourages
diverse voices, promotes free speech, and creates a vibrant culture. Thank you for buying
an authorized edition of this book and for complying with copyright laws by not
reproducing, scanning, or distributing any part of it in any form without permission.
You are supporting writers and allowing Penguin Random House to continue to
publish books for every reader.

A JOVE BOOK, BERKLEY, and the BERKLEY & B colophon
are registered trademarks of Penguin Random House LLC.

ISBN: 9780515144666

First Edition: December 2008

Printed in the United States of America
19   21   22   20

Cover photograph by Raymond K. Gehman / Getty
Cover design by Rich Hasselberger
Text design by Kristin del Rosario

Years ago, after their blood brother ritual, Gage, Fox, and Caleb emerged from the woods, each with a piece of bloodstone. Now, it will become their weapon in the final fight against the demon they awakened. Winner take all . . .

Shared nightmares, visions of blood and fire, and random violence plague the longtime friends *and* Quinn, Layla, and Cybil, the women bound to them by Fate. None of them can ignore the fact that, this year, the demon has grown stronger—feeding off the terror it creates. But now the three pieces of the bloodstone have been fused back together. If only they could figure out how to use it.

A gambling man like Gage has no trouble betting on his crew to find a way. And though he and Cybil share the gift of seeing the future, that's all they have in common. Were they to take their flirtation to the next level, it would be on their own terms, not because Fate decreed it. But Gage knows that a woman like Cybil—with her brains and strength and devastating beauty—can only bring him luck. Whether it's good or bad has yet to be determined—and could mean the difference between absolute destruction or an end to the nightmare for Hawkins Hollow.

**Third in the Sign of Seven trilogy
from the #1 *New York Times* bestselling author**

**Turn the page for a complete list of titles by
Nora Roberts and J. D. Robb from Berkley . . .**

Nora Roberts

Series

Nora Roberts & J. D. Robb

REMEMBER WHEN

J. D. Robb

NAKED IN DEATH
GLORY IN DEATH
IMMORTAL IN DEATH
RAPTURE IN DEATH
CEREMONY IN DEATH
VENGEANCE IN DEATH
HOLIDAY IN DEATH
CONSPIRACY IN DEATH
LOYALTY IN DEATH
WITNESS IN DEATH
JUDGMENT IN DEATH
BETRAYAL IN DEATH
SEDUCTION IN DEATH
REUNION IN DEATH
PURITY IN DEATH
PORTRAIT IN DEATH
IMITATION IN DEATH
DIVIDED IN DEATH
VISIONS IN DEATH
SURVIVOR IN DEATH
ORIGIN IN DEATH
MEMORY IN DEATH
BORN IN DEATH
INNOCENT IN DEATH
CREATION IN DEATH
STRANGERS IN DEATH
SALVATION IN DEATH
PROMISES IN DEATH
KINDRED IN DEATH
FANTASY IN DEATH
INDULGENCE IN DEATH
TREACHERY IN DEATH
NEW YORK TO DALLAS
CELEBRITY IN DEATH
DELUSION IN DEATH
CALCULATED IN DEATH
THANKLESS IN DEATH
CONCEALED IN DEATH
FESTIVE IN DEATH
OBSESSION IN DEATH
DEVOTED IN DEATH
BROTHERHOOD IN DEATH
APPRENTICE IN DEATH

Anthologies

FROM THE HEART
A LITTLE MAGIC
A LITTLE FATE

MOON SHADOWS
(with Jill Gregory, Ruth Ryan Langan, and Marianne Willman)

The Once Upon Series
(with Jill Gregory, Ruth Ryan Langan, and Marianne Willman)

ONCE UPON A CASTLE
ONCE UPON A STAR
ONCE UPON A DREAM

ONCE UPON A ROSE
ONCE UPON A KISS
ONCE UPON A MIDNIGHT

SILENT NIGHT
(with Susan Plunkett, Dee Holmes, and Claire Cross)

OUT OF THIS WORLD
(with Laurell K. Hamilton, Susan Krinard, and Maggie Shayne)

BUMP IN THE NIGHT
(with Mary Blayney, Ruth Ryan Langan, and Mary Kay McComas)

DEAD OF NIGHT
(with Mary Blayney, Ruth Ryan Langan, and Mary Kay McComas)

THREE IN DEATH

SUITE 606
(with Mary Blayney, Ruth Ryan Langan, and Mary Kay McComas)

IN DEATH

THE LOST
(with Patricia Gaffney, Mary Blayney, and Ruth Ryan Langan)

THE OTHER SIDE
(with Mary Blayney, Patricia Gaffney, Ruth Ryan Langan, and Mary Kay McComas)

TIME OF DEATH

THE UNQUIET
(with Mary Blayney, Patricia Gaffney, Ruth Ryan Langan, and Mary Kay McComas)

MIRROR, MIRROR
(with Mary Blayney, Elaine Fox, Mary Kay McComas, and R. C. Ryan)

DOWN THE RABBIT HOLE
(with Mary Blayney, Elaine Fox, Mary Kay McComas, and R. C. Ryan)

Also available . . .

THE OFFICIAL NORA ROBERTS COMPANION
(edited by Denise Little and Laura Hayden)

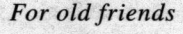
For old friends

Where there is no vision,
the people perish.

—PROVERBS 29:18

I have nothing to offer but blood,
toil, tears, and sweat.

—WINSTON CHURCHILL

Prologue

~◊~

Mazatlán, Mexico
April 2001

SUN STREAKED PEARLY PINK ACROSS THE SKY, splashed onto blue, blue water that rolled against white sand as Gage Turner walked the beach. He carried his shoes—the tattered laces of the ancient Nikes tied to hang on his shoulder. The hems of his jeans were frayed, and the jeans themselves had long since faded to white at the stress points. The tropical breeze tugged at hair that hadn't seen a barber in more than three months.

At the moment, he supposed he looked no more kempt than the scattering of beach bums still snoring away on the sand. He'd bunked on beaches a time or two when his luck was down, and knew someone would come along soon to shoo them off before the paying tourists woke for their room-service coffee.

At the moment, despite the need for a shower and a shave, his luck was up. Nicely up. With his night's winnings hot in his pocket, he considered upgrading his ocean-view room for a suite.

Grab it while you can, he thought, because tomorrow could suck you dry.

Time was already running out: it spilled like that white, sun-kissed sand held in a closed fist. His twenty-fourth birthday was less than three months away, and the dreams crawled back into his head. Blood and death, fire and madness. All of that and Hawkins Hollow seemed a world away from this soft tropical dawn.

But it lived in him.

He unlocked the wide glass door of his room, stepped in, tossed aside his shoes. After flipping on the lights, closing the drapes, he took his winnings from his pocket, gave the bills a careless flip. With the current rate of exchange, he was up about six thousand USD. Not a bad night, not bad at all. In the bathroom, he popped off the bottom of a can of shaving cream, tucked the bills inside the hollow tube.

He protected what was his. He'd learned to do so from childhood, secreting away small treasures so his father couldn't find and destroy them on a drunken whim. He might've flipped off any notion of a college education, but Gage figured he'd learned quite a bit in his not-quite-twenty-four years.

He'd left Hawkins Hollow the summer he'd graduated from high school. Just packed up what was his, stuck out his thumb and booked.

Escaped, Gage thought as he stripped for a shower. There'd been plenty of work—he'd been young, strong, healthy, and not particular. But he'd learned a vital lesson while digging ditches, hauling lumber, and most especially during the months he'd sweated on an offshore rig. He could make more money at cards than he could with his back.

And a gambler didn't need a home. All he needed was a game.

He stepped into the shower, turned the water hot. It sluiced over tanned skin, lean muscles, through thick black hair in need of a trim. He thought idly about ordering some coffee, some food, then decided he'd catch a few hours' sleep first. Another advantage of his profession, in Gage's mind. He came and went as he pleased, ate when he was hungry, slept when he was tired. He set his own rules, broke them whenever it suited him.

Nobody had any hold over him.

Not true, Gage admitted as he studied the white scar across his wrist. Not altogether true. A man's friends, his true friends, always had a hold over him. There were no truer friends than Caleb Hawkins and Fox O'Dell.

Blood brothers.

They'd been born the same day, the same year, even—as far as anyone could tell—at the same moment. He couldn't remember a time when the three of them hadn't been . . . a unit, he supposed. The middle-class boy, the hippie kid, and the son of an abusive drunk. Probably shouldn't have had a thing in common, Gage mused as a smile curved his mouth, warmed the green of his eyes. But they'd been family, they'd been brothers long before Cal had cut their wrists with his Boy Scout knife to ritualize the pact.

And that had changed everything. Or had it? Gage wondered. Had it just opened what was always there, waiting?

He could remember it all vividly, every step, every detail. It had started as an adventure—three boys on the eve of their tenth birthday hiking through the woods. Loaded down with skin mags, beer, smokes—his contribution—with junk food and Cokes from Fox, and the picnic basket of sandwiches and lemonade Cal's mother had packed. Not that Frannie Hawkins would've packed a picnic if she'd known her son planned to camp that night at the Pagan Stone in Hawkins Wood.

All that wet heat, Gage remembered, and the music on the boom box, and the complete innocence they'd carried along with the Little Debbies and Nutter Butters they would lose before they hiked out in the morning.

Gage stepped out of the shower, rubbed his dripping hair with a towel. His back had ached from the beating his father had given him the night before. As they'd sat around the campfire in the clearing those welts had throbbed. He remembered that, as he remembered how the light had flickered and floated over the gray table of the Pagan Stone.

He remembered the words they'd written down, the words they'd spoken as Cal made them blood brothers. He remembered the quick pain of the knife across his flesh, the feel of Cal's wrist, of Fox's as they'd mixed their blood.

And the explosion, the heat and cold, the force and fear when that mixed blood hit the scarred ground of the clearing.

He remembered what came out of the ground, the black mass of it, and the blinding light that followed. The pure evil of the black, the stunning brilliance of the white.

When it was over, there'd been no welts on his back, no pain, and in his hand lay one-third of a bloodstone. He carried it still, as he knew Cal and Fox carried theirs. Three pieces of one whole. He supposed they were the same.

Madness came to the Hollow that week, and raged through it like a plague, infecting, driving good and ordinary people to do the horrible. And for seven days every seven years, it came back.

So did he, Gage thought. What choice did he have?

Naked, still damp from the shower, he stretched out on the bed. There was time yet, still some time for a few more games, for hot beaches and swaying palms. The green woods and blue mountains of Hawkins Hollow were thousands of miles away, until July.

He closed his eyes, and as he'd trained himself, dropped almost instantly into sleep.

In sleep came the screams, and the weeping, and the fire that ate so joyfully at wood and cloth and flesh. Blood ran warm over his hands as he dragged the wounded to safety. For how long? he wondered. Where was safe? And who could say when and if the victim would turn and become attacker?

Madness ruled the streets of the Hollow.

In the dream he stood with his friends on the south end of Main Street, across from the Qwik Mart and its four gas pumps. Coach Moser, who'd guided the Hawkins Hollow Bucks to a championship football season Gage's senior year, gibbered with laughter as he soaked himself, the ground, the buildings with the flood of gas from the pumps.

They ran toward him, the three of them, even as Moser held up his lighter like a trophy, as he splashed in the pools of gas like a boy in rain puddles. They ran even as he flicked the lighter.

It was flash and boom, searing the eyes, bursting in the ears. The force of heat and air flung him back so he landed in a bone-shattering heap. Fire, blinding clouds of it, spewed skyward as hunks of wood and concrete, shards of glass, burning twists of metal flew.

Gage felt his broken arm try to knit, his shattered knee struggle to heal with pain worse than the wound itself. Gritting his teeth, he rolled, and what he saw stopped his heart in his chest.

Cal lay in the street, burning like a torch.

No, no, no, no! He crawled, shouting, gasping for oxygen in the tainted air. There was Fox, facedown in a widening pool of blood.

It came, a black smear on that burning air that formed into a man. The demon smiled. "You don't heal from death, do you, boy?"

Gage woke, sheathed in sweat and shaking. He woke with the stench of burning gas scoring his throat.

Time's up, he thought.

He got up, got dressed. Dressed, he began to pack for the trip back to Hawkins Hollow.

One

~◆~

THE DREAM WOKE HIM AT DAWN, AND THAT WAS A pisser. From experience, Gage knew it would be useless to try to find sleep again with images of burning blood in his brain. The closer it got to July, the closer it got to the Seven, the more vivid and vicious the dreams. He'd rather be awake and doing than struggling with nightmares.

Or visions.

He'd come out of the woods that long-ago July with a body that healed itself, and with the gift of sight. Gage didn't consider the precognition wholly reliable. Different choices, different actions, different outcomes.

Seven years before, come July, he'd turned off the pumps at the Qwik Mart, and had taken the added precaution of locking Coach Moser in a cell. He'd never known, not for certain, if he'd saved his friends' lives by those actions, or if the dream had been just a dream.

But he'd played the odds.

He continued to play the odds, Gage supposed as he grabbed a pair of boxers in case he wasn't alone in the house.

He was back, as he was every seventh year. And this time he'd thrown his lot in with the three women who'd turned his, Fox's, and Cal's trio into a team of six.

With Cal engaged to Quinn Black—blond bombshell and paranormal writer—she often spent the night at Cal's. Hence the inadvisability of wandering downstairs naked to make coffee. But Cal's attractive house in the woods felt empty to Gage, of people, of ghosts, of Cal's big, lazy dog, Lump. And that was all to the good, as Gage preferred solitude, at least until after coffee.

He assumed Cal had spent the night at the house the three women rented in town. As Fox had done the headfirst into love with the sexy brunette Layla Darnell, they might've bunked at the house, or Fox's apartment over his law offices. Either way, they'd stay close, and with Fox's talent for pushing into thoughts, they had ways of communicating that didn't require phones.

Gage put coffee on, then went out to stand on the deck while it brewed.

Leave it to Cal, he thought, to build his home on the edge of the woods where their lives had turned inside out. But that was Cal for you—he was the type who took a stand, kept right on standing. And the fact was, if country charm rang your bell, this was the spot for it. The green woods with the last of the spring's wild dogwoods and mountain laurel gleaming in slants of sunlight offered a picture of tranquility—if you didn't know any better. The terraced slope in front of the house exploded with color from shrubs and ornamental trees, while at the base the winding creek bubbled along.

It fit Cal to the ground, just as his lady did. For himself, Gage figured the country quiet would drive him crazy within a month.

He went back for the coffee, drank it strong and black. He took a second mug up with him. By the time he'd showered and dressed, restlessness nipped at him. He tried to quell it with a few hands of solitaire, but the house was too . . . settled. Grabbing his keys, he headed out. He'd hunt up his friends, and if nothing was going on, maybe he'd zip up to Atlantic City for the day and find some action.

It was a quiet drive, but then the Hollow was a quiet place, a splat on the map in the rolling western Maryland countryside that got itself juiced up for the annual Memorial Day parade, the Fourth of July fireworks in the park, the occasional Civil War reenactment. And, of course, the madness that flowed into it every seven years.

Overhead, the trees arched over the road; beside it, the creek wound. Then the view opened to rolling, rock-pocked hills, distant mountains, and a sky of delicate spring blue. It wasn't his place, not the rural countryside nor the town tucked into it. Odds were he'd die here, but even that wouldn't make it his. And still, he'd play the long shot that he, his friends, and the women with them would not only survive, but beat down the thing that plagued the Hollow. That they would end it this time.

He passed the Qwik Mart where foresight or luck had won the day, then the first of the tidy houses and shops along Main. He spotted Fox's truck outside the townhouse that held Fox's home and law office. The coffee shop and Ma's Pantry were both open for business, serving the breakfast crowd. A hugely pregnant woman towing a toddler stepped out of the bakery with a large white bag. The kid talked a mile a minute while Mom waddled down Main.

There was the empty gift shop Fox's Layla had rented with plans to open a fashion boutique. The idea made Gage shake his head as he turned at the Square. Hope sprang, he supposed, and love gave it a hell of a boost.

He gave a quick glance at the Bowl-a-Rama, town institution and Cal's legacy. And looked away again. Once upon a time he'd lived above the bowling center with his father, lived with the stench of stale beer and cigarettes, with the constant threat of fists or belt.

Bill Turner still lived there, still worked at the center, reputedly five years sober. Gage didn't give a flying fuck, as long as the old man kept his distance. Because the thought burned in his gut, he shut it down, tossed it aside.

At the curb, he pulled up behind a Karmann Ghia—property of one Cybil Kinski, the sixth member of the team. The sultry gypsy shared his precog trait—just as Quinn shared Cal's ability to look back, and Layla shared Fox's reading of what was hidden in the now. He supposed that made them partners of sorts, and the supposing made him wary.

She was a number, all right, he thought as he started up the walk to the house. Smart, savvy, and sizzling. Another time, another place, it might've been entertaining to deal a few hands with her, see who walked away the winner. But the idea that some outside force, ancient powers, and magic plots played a part in bringing them together had Gage opting to fold his hand early.

It was one thing for both Cal and Fox to get twisted up with their women. He just wasn't wired for the long-term deal. Instinct told him that even the short-term with a woman like Cybil would be too complicated for his taste and style.

He didn't knock. They used the rental house and Cal's as bases of sorts, so he didn't see the need. Music drifted—something New Agey—all flutes and gongs. He turned toward the source, and there was Cybil. She wore loose black pants and a top that revealed a smooth, tight midriff and sleekly muscled arms. Her wild black curls spilled out of their restraining band.

The toes of her bare feet sported bright pink polish.

As he watched, she braced her head on the floor while her body lifted up. Her legs spread, held perpendicular to the floor, then somehow twisted, as if her torso were a hinge. Fluidly, she lowered one leg until her foot was flat on the floor, forming her into some erotic bridge. With movements that seemed effortless, she shifted herself, tucking one leg against her hip while the other cocked up behind her. And reaching back, she gripped her foot to bring it to the back of her head.

He considered the fact that he didn't drool a testament to his massive power of will.

She bent, twisted, flowed, *arranged* herself into what should have been impossible positions. His willpower wasn't so massive he didn't imagine that any woman that flexible would be amazing in bed.

She'd arched back, foot hooked behind her head when a flicker in those deep, dark eyes told him she'd become aware of him.

"Don't let me interrupt."

"I won't. I'm nearly done. Go away."

Though he regretted missing how she ended such a session, he wandered back to the kitchen, poured himself a cup of coffee. Leaning back on the counter, he noted the morning paper was folded on the little table, the dog bowl Cal left there for Lump was empty, and the water bowl beside it half full. The dog might've already had breakfast, but if anyone else had, the dishes had already been stowed away. Since the news didn't interest him at the moment, he sat and dealt out a hand of solitaire. He was on his fourth game when Cybil strolled in.

"Aren't you a rise-and-shiner this morning."

He laid a red eight on a black nine. "Cal still in bed?"

"It seems everyone's up and about. Quinn hauled him off to the gym." She poured coffee for herself, then reached in the bread bin. "Bagel?"

"Sure."

After cutting one neatly in half, she dropped it in the toaster. "Bad dream?" She angled her head when he glanced up at her. "I had one, woke me at first light. So did Cal and Quinn. I haven't heard, but I imagine Fox and Layla— they're at his place—got the same wake-up call. Quinn's remedy, weights and machines. Mine, yoga. Yours . . ." She gestured to the cards.

"Everybody's got something."

"We kicked our Big Evil Bastard in the balls a few days ago. We have to expect him to kick back."

"Nearly got ourselves incinerated for the trouble," Gage reminded her.

"*Nearly* works for me. We put the three pieces of the

bloodstone back together, magickally. We performed a blood ritual." She studied the healing cut across her palm. "And we lived to tell the tale. We have a weapon."

"Which we don't know how to use."

"Does it know?" She busied herself getting out plates, cream cheese for the bagels. "Does our demon know any more about it than we do? Giles Dent infused that stone with power more than three hundred years ago in the clearing, and—theoretically—used it as part of the spell that pulled the demon, in its form as Lazarus Twisse, into some sort of limbo where Dent could hold it for centuries."

Handily, she sliced an apple, arranged the pieces on a plate while she spoke. "Twisse didn't know or recognize the power of the bloodstone then, or apparently hundreds of years later when your boyhood ritual released it, and the stone was split into three equal parts. If we follow that logic, it doesn't know any more about it now, which gives us an advantage. We may not know, yet, how it works, but we know it does."

Turning, she offered him his plated bagel. "We put the three pieces into one again. The Big Evil Bastard isn't the only one with power here."

Just a bit fascinated, Gage watched Cybil cut her half bagel in half before spreading what he could only describe as a film of cream cheese over the two quarters. While he loaded his own half, she sat and took a bite he estimated consisted of about half a dozen crumbs.

"Maybe you should just look at a picture of food instead of going to all the trouble to fix it." When she only smiled, took another minuscule bite, he said, "I've seen Twisse kill my friends. I've seen that countless times, in countless ways."

Her eyes met his, dark with understanding. "That's the bitch of our precog, seeing the potentials, the possibilities, in brutal Technicolor. I was afraid when we went into the clearing to perform the ritual. Not just of dying, though I don't want to die. In fact, I'm firmly against it. I was afraid of living and watching the people closest to me die, and worse, somehow being responsible for it."

"But you went in."

"We went in." She chose an apple slice, took a stingy bite. "And we didn't die. Not all dreams, not all visions are . . . set in stone. You come back, every Seven, you come back."

"We swore an oath."

"Yes, when you were ten. I'm not discounting the validity or the power of childhood oaths," she continued, "but you'd come back regardless. You come back for them, for Cal and Fox. I came for Quinn, so I understand the strength of friendship. We're not like them, you and I."

"No?"

"No." Lifting her coffee, she sipped slowly. "The town, the people in it, they're not ours. For Cal and Fox—and now in a very real sense for Quinn and Layla—this is home. People go to great lengths to protect home. For me, Hawkins Hollow is just a place I happen to be. Quinn's my home, and now so is Layla. And by extension, by connection, so are Cal and Fox. And so, it seems, are you. I won't leave my home until I know it's safe. Otherwise, while I'd find all this fascinating and intriguing, I wouldn't shed blood for it."

The sun beamed in the kitchen window, haloed over her hair, set the little silver hoops at her ears glinting. "I think you might."

"Really?"

"Yeah, because the whole thing pisses you off. Wanting to kick its ass weighs on the side of you staying, seeing it through."

She took another tiny bite of bagel and smiled at him. "Got me. So here we are, Turner, two pairs of itchy feet planted for love and general pissiness. Well. I want my shower," she decided. "Would you mind staying at least until Quinn and Cal get back? Ever since Layla had her 'snakes in the bathroom' event, I've been leery about showering when I'm alone in the house."

"No problem. You going to eat the rest of that?"

Cybil pushed the untouched quarter bagel toward him. As she rose to go to the sink to rinse out her coffee mug, he studied the black-and-blue cloud on the back of her shoulder. It reminded him they'd taken a beating on the night of the full moon at the Pagan Stone, and that she—unlike Cal, Fox, and himself—didn't heal within moments of an injury.

"That's a bad bruise on your shoulder there."

She shrugged it. "You should see my ass."

"Okay."

With a laugh, she glanced over her shoulder. "Rhetorically speaking. I had a nanny who believed that a good paddling built character. Every time I sit down I'm reminded of her."

"You had a nanny?"

"I did. But paddling aside, I like to think I built my own character. Cal and Quinn should be back soon. You might want to make another pot of coffee."

As she walked out he gave the ass in question a contemplative study. Top of the line, he decided. She was an interesting, and to his mind, complicated mix in a very tidy package. While he had a fondness for tidy packages, he preferred simple contents when it came to fun and games. But for life and death, he thought Cybil Kinski was just what the doctor ordered.

She'd brought a gun along on their hike to the Pagan Stone. A little pearl-handled .22, which she'd used with the cold, calculated skill of a veteran mercenary. She'd been the one to do the research on the blood rituals—and she'd done the genealogies that had proven she, Quinn, and Layla were descendants of the demon known as Lazarus Twisse and Hester Deale, the girl it had raped over three centuries before.

And the woman could cook. Bitched about it, Gage mused as he rose to put on another pot of coffee, but she knew her way around the kitchen. He respected the fact that she generally said what was on her mind, and kept a cool head in a crisis. This was no weak-kneed female needing to be rescued.

She smelled like secrets and tasted like warm honey.

He'd kissed her that night in the clearing. Of course, he'd thought they were all about to die in a supernatural blaze and it had been a what-the-hell kind of gesture. But he remembered exactly how she'd tasted.

Probably not smart to think about it—or to think about the fact that she was upstairs right now, wet and naked. But a guy had to have some entertainment during a break from fighting ancient evil. And strangely, he was no longer in the mood for Atlantic City.

He heard the front door open, and the quick burst of Quinn's bawdy laughter. As far as Gage could see, Cal had hit the jackpot in Quinn for the laugh alone. Then you added in the curvy body, the big baby blues, the brain, the humor, the guts, and his friend rang all the bells, blew all the whistles.

Gage topped off his coffee, and hearing only Cal's footsteps approach, got down another mug.

Cal took the mug Gage held out, said, "Hey," then opened the refrigerator for milk.

For a man who'd likely been up since dawn, Cal looked pretty damn chipper, Gage noted. Exercise might release endorphins, but if Gage was a betting man—and he was—he'd put money on the woman putting the spring in his friend's step.

Cal's gray eyes were clear, his face and body relaxed. His dark blond hair was damp and he smelled of soap, indicating he'd showered at the gym. He doctored his coffee, then took a box of Mini-Wheats out of a cupboard.

"Want?"

"No."

With a grunt, Cal shook cereal into a bowl, dumped in milk. "Team dream?"

"Seems like."

"Talked to Fox." Cal ate his cereal as he leaned back against the counter. "He and Layla had one, too. Yours?"

"The town was bleeding," Gage began. "The buildings, the streets, anyone unlucky enough to be outside. Blood bubbling up from the sidewalks, raining down the buildings. And burning while it bled."

"Yeah, that's the one. It's the first time the six of us shared the same nightmare, that I know of. That has to mean something."

"The bloodstone's back in one piece. The six of us put it back together. Cybil puts a lot of store in the stone as a power source."

"And you?"

"I guess I'd have to agree, for what it's worth. What I do know is we've got less than two months to figure it out. If that."

Cal nodded. "It's coming faster, it's coming stronger. But we've hurt it, Gage, twice now we've hurt it bad."

"Third time better be the charm."

HE DIDN'T HANG AROUND. IF ROUTINE HELD, THE women would spend a good chunk of the day looking for answers in books and on the Internet. They'd review their charts, maps, and graphs, trying to find some new angle. And talking it all to death. Cal would head over to the Bowl-a-Rama, and Fox would open his office for the day. And he, Gage thought, was a gambler without a game.

So he had the day free.

He could head back to Cal's, make some calls, write some e-mails. He had his own research lines to tug. He'd been studying and poking into demonology and folklore for years, and in odd corners of the world. When they combined his data with what Cybil, Quinn, and Layla had dug up, it meshed fairly well.

Gods and demons warring with each other long before man came to be. Whittling the numbers down so that when man crawled onto the scene, he soon outnumbered them. The time of man, Giles Dent had called it, according to the journals written by his lover, Ann Hawkins. And in the time of man only one demon and one guardian remained—not that he was buying that one, Gage thought. But there was only one who held his personal interest. Mortally wounded, the guardian passed his power and his mission to a young human boy, and so the line continued through the centuries until there was Giles Dent.

Gage considered it as he drove. He accepted Dent, accepted that he and his friends were Dent's descendants through Ann Hawkins. He believed, as did the others, that Dent found a way, twisting the rules to include a little human sacrifice, to imprison the demon, and himself. Until hundreds of years later, three boys released it.

He could even accept that the act had been their destiny. He didn't have to like it, but he could swallow it. It was their Fate to face it, fight it, to destroy it or die trying. Since the ghost of Ann Hawkins had made a few appearances this time out, her cryptic remarks indicated this Seven was the money shot.

All or nothing. Life or death.

Since most of his visions featured death, in various unpleasant forms, Gage wasn't putting money on the group victory dance.

He supposed he'd driven to the cemetery because death was on his mind. When he got out of the car, he thrust his hands into his pockets. It was stupid to come here, he thought. It was pointless. But he began to walk across the grass, around the stones and monuments.

He should've brought flowers, he thought, then immediately shook his head. Flowers were pointless, too. What good did flowers do the dead?

His mother and the child she'd tried to bring into the world were both long dead.

May had greened the grass and the trees, and the breeze stirred the green. The ground rolled, gentle slopes and dips where somber gray markers or faithful white monuments rose, and the sun cast their shadows. His mother and his sister who'd died inside her had a white marker. Though it had been years, many years, since he'd walked this way, he knew where to find them.

The single stone was very simple, small, rounded, with only names and dates carved.

CATHERINE MARY TURNER
1954–1982
ROSE ELIZABETH TURNER
1982

He barely remembered her, he thought. Time simply rubbed the images, the sounds, the *feel* of her to a faded blur. He had only the vaguest memory of her laying his hand against her swollen belly so he could feel the baby kick. He had a picture, so he knew he favored his mother in coloring, in the shape of his eyes, his mouth. He'd never seen the baby, and no one had ever told him what she looked like. But he remembered being happy, remembered playing with trucks in the sunsplash through a window. And yes, even of running to the door when his father came home from work, and screaming with fun as those hands lifted him up high.

There'd been a time, a brief time, when his father's hands had lifted him instead of knocking him down. The sunsplashed time, he supposed. Then she'd died, and the baby with her, and everything had gone dark and cold.

Had she ever shouted at him, punished him, been impatient? Surely, she must have. But he couldn't remember any of that, or chose not to. Maybe he'd idealized her, but what was the harm? When a boy had a mother for such a brief time, the man was entitled to think of her as perfect.

"I didn't bring flowers," he murmured. "I should have."

"But you came."

He spun around, and looked into eyes the same color, the same shape as his own. As his heart squeezed, his mother smiled at him.

Two

SHE'S SO YOUNG. THAT WAS HIS FIRST THOUGHT. Younger, he realized, than he as they stood studying each other over her grave. She had a calm and quiet beauty, a kind of simplicity he thought would have kept her beautiful into old age. But she hadn't lived to see thirty.

And even now, a grown man, he felt something inside him ache with that loss.

"Why are you here?" he asked her, and her smile bloomed again.

"Don't you want me to be?"

"You never came before."

"Maybe you never looked before." She shook her dark hair back, breathed deep. "It's such a pretty day, all this May sunshine. And here you are, looking so lost, so angry. So sad. Don't you believe there's a better place, Gage? That death is the beginning of the next?"

"It was the end of before, for me." That, he supposed, was the black and white of it. "When you died, so did the better."

"Poor little boy. Do you hate me for leaving you?"

"You didn't leave me. You died."

"It amounts to the same." There was sorrow in her eyes, or perhaps it was pity. "I wasn't there for you, and did worse than leave you alone. I left you with him. I let him plant death inside me. So you were alone, and helpless, with a man who beat you and cursed you."

"Why did you marry him?"

"Women are weak, you must have learned that by now. If I hadn't been weak I would have left him, taken you and left him and this place." She turned, just a bit, so she looked back toward the Hollow. There was something else in her eyes now—he caught a glint of it—something brighter than pity. "I should have protected you and myself. We would have had a life together, away from here. But I can protect you now."

He watched the way she moved, the way her hair fell, the way the grass stirred at her feet. "How do the dead protect the living?"

"We see more. We know more." She turned back to him, held out her hands. "You asked why I was here. I'm here for that. To protect you, as I didn't during life. To save you. To tell you to go, go away from here. Leave this place. There's nothing but death and misery here, pain and loss. Go and live. Stay and you'll die, you'll rot in the ground as I am."

"Now see, you were doing pretty well up till then." The rage inside him was cold, and it was fierce, but his voice was casual as a shrug. "I might've bought it if you'd played more Mommy and Me cards. But you rushed it."

"I only want you safe."

"You want me dead. If not dead, at least gone. I'm not going anywhere, and you're not my mother. So take off the dress, asshole."

"Mommy's going to have to spank you for that." With a wave of its hand the demon blasted the air. The force knocked Gage off his feet. Even as he gained them, it was changing.

Its eyes went red, and shed bloody tears as it howled with laughter. "Bad boy! I'm going to punish you the most of all the bad boys. Flay your skin, drink your blood, gnaw your bones."

"Yeah, yeah, yeah." In a show of indifference, Gage hooked his thumbs in his front pockets.

The face of his mother melted away into something hideous, something inhuman. The body bunched, the back humping, the hands and feet curling into claws, then sharpening into hooves. Then the mass of it twisted into a writhing formless black that choked the air with the stink of death.

The wind blew the stench into Gage's face, but he planted his feet and stood. He had no weapon, and after a quick calculation, decided to play the odds. He bunched his hand into a fist and punched it into the fetid black.

The burn was amazing. He wrenched his hand free, jabbed again. Pain stole his breath, so he sucked more of it and struck out a third time. It screamed. Fury, Gage thought. He recognized pure fury even when he was flying over his mother's gravestone and slamming hard to the ground.

It stood over him now, stood atop the gravestone in the form of the young boy it so often selected. "You'll beg for death," it told him. "Long after I've torn the others to bits, you'll beg. I will dine on you for years."

Gage swiped blood from his mouth, smiled, though a wave of nausea rolled over him. "Wanna bet?"

The thing that looked like a boy dug its hands into its own chest, ripped it open. On a mad roll of laughter, it vanished.

"Fucking crazy. The son of a bitch is fucking crazy." He sat a moment, catching his breath, studying his hand. It was raw and red with blisters, pus seeping from them and the shallow punctures he thought came from fangs. He could feel it healing as the pain was awesome. Cradling his arm, he got to his feet and swayed as dizziness rocked the ground under him.

He had to sit again, his back braced on the gravestone of his mother and sister, until the sickness passed, until the world steadied. In the pretty May sunshine, with only the dead for company, he breathed his way through the pain, focused his mind on the healing. As the burning eased, his system settled again.

Rising, he took one last look at the grave, then turned and walked away.

* * *

HE STOPPED BY THE FLOWER POT AND BOUGHT A splashy spring arrangement that had Amy, who worked the counter, speculating on who the lucky lady might be. He left her speculating. It was too hard to explain—and none of Amy's damn business—that he had flowers and mothers on the brain.

That was one of the problems—and in his mind they were legion—with small towns. Everybody wanted to know everything about everyone else, or pretend they did. When they didn't know enough, they were just as likely to make it up and call it God's truth.

There were plenty in the Hollow who'd whispered and muttered about him. Poor kid, bad boy, troublemaker, bad news, good riddance. Maybe it had stung off and on, and maybe that sting had gone deep when he'd been younger. But he'd had what he supposed he could call a balm. He'd had Cal and Fox. He'd had family.

His mother was gone, and had been for a very long time. That, he thought as he drove out of town, had certainly come home to him today. So he'd make a gesture long overdue.

Of course, she might not be home. Frannie Hawkins didn't hold a job outside the home—exactly. Her work *was* her home, and the various committees she chaired or participated in. If there was a committee, society, or organization in the Hollow, it was likely Cal's mother had a hand in it.

He pulled up behind the clean and tidy car he recognized as hers in the drive of the tidy house where the Hawkinses had lived as long as Gage remembered. And the tidy woman who ran the house knelt on a square of bright pink foam as she planted—maybe they were petunias—at the edges of her already impressive front-yard garden.

Her hair was a glossy blond under a wide-brimmed straw hat, and her hands were covered with sturdy brown gloves. He imagined she thought of her navy pants and pink T-shirt as work clothes. She turned her head at the sound of the car, then her pretty face lit with a smile when she saw Gage.

That was, always had been, a small wonder to him. That she smiled, and meant it, when she saw him. She tugged off her gloves as she rose. "What a nice surprise. And look at those flowers! They're almost as gorgeous as you are."

"Coals to Newcastle."

She touched his cheek, then took the offered flowers. "I can never have too many flowers. Let's go in so I can put them in water."

"I interrupted you."

"Gardening is a constant work in progress. I can't stop fiddling."

The house was the same for her, he knew. She upholstered, sewed, painted, made crafty little arrangements. And still the house was always warm, always welcoming, never set and stiff.

She led him back through the kitchen and into the laundry room where, being Frannie Hawkins, she had a sink for the specific purpose of flower arranging. "I'm just going to put these in a holding vase, then get us something cold to drink."

"I don't want to hold you up."

"Gage." She waved off his protest as she got down a holding vase, filled it. "Go, sit out back on the patio. It's too pretty to be inside. I'll bring us out some iced tea."

He did as she asked, mostly because he needed to figure out exactly what he'd come here to say to her, and how he wanted to say it. She'd been busy in the back garden as well, and with her container pots. All the color, the shapes, the textures seemed somehow magically perfect and completely natural. He knew, because he'd seen her, that she routinely sketched out her plans for her beds, her pots every year.

Unlike Fox's mother, Frannie Hawkins absolutely never allowed other hands to weed. She trusted no one to tug out bindweed instead of petunias, or whatever. But he'd hauled his share of mulch for her over the years, his share of rocks. He supposed, in some way, that made her magazine-cover gardens his, in a very limited sense.

She stepped out. There was iced tea with sprigs of mint in a fat green glass pitcher, the tall coordinating glasses, and a plate of cookies. They sat at her shaded table, looking out over trim grass and flowing flowers.

"I always remember this backyard," he told her. "Fox's farm was like Adventure World, and this was . . ."

She laughed. "What? Cal's mom's obsession?"

"No. Somewhere between fairyland and sanctuary."

Her smile faded into quiet warmth. "What a lovely thing to say."

He knew what he wanted to say, Gage realized. "You always let me in. I was thinking about things today. You and Fox's mother, you always let me in. You never once turned me away."

"Why in the world would I?"

He looked at her then, into her pretty blue eyes. "My father was a drunk, and I was a troublemaker."

"Gage."

"If Cal or Fox had trouble, I probably started it."

"I think they started plenty of their own and dragged you into that."

"You and Jim, you made sure I had a roof over my head—and you made it clear I could have this one, I could have yours whenever I needed it. You kept my father on at the center, even when you should've let him go, and you did that for me. But you never made me feel like it was charity. You and Fox's parents, you made sure I had clothes, shoes, work so I had spending money. And you never made me feel it was because you felt sorry for that poor Turner kid."

"I never thought of you, and I don't imagine Jo Barry ever thought of you, as 'that poor Turner kid.' You were, and are, the son of my friend. Your mother was my friend, Gage."

"I know. Still, you could've discouraged Cal from hanging out with me. A lot of people would have. I'm the one who had the idea of going into the woods that night."

The look she gave him was pure *mother*. "And neither one of them had anything to do with it?"

"Sure, but it was my idea, and you probably figured that out twenty years ago. You still kept the door open for me."

"None of that was your fault. I don't know a lot of what

you're doing now, the six of you, what you've discovered, what you plan to do. Cal keeps a lot of it from me. I guess I let him. But I know enough to be certain what happened at the Pagan Stone when the three of you were boys wasn't your fault. And I know without the three of you, and all you've done, all you've risked, I wouldn't be sitting here on my patio on this pretty day in May. There'd be no Hawkins Hollow without you, Gage. Without you, Cal, and Fox, this town would be dead."

She laid a hand over his, squeezed. "I'm so proud of you."

With her, maybe particularly with her, he couldn't be less than honest. "I'm not here for the town."

"I know. For some odd reason, it only makes me prouder that you're here. You're a good man, Gage. You are," she said, with some heat when she saw the denial on his face. "You'll never convince me otherwise. You've been the best of friends to my son. You've been the best of brothers. My door isn't just open to you. This is your home, whenever you need it."

He needed a moment to settle himself. "I love you." He looked back into her eyes. "I guess that's what I came here to say. I can't remember my mother very well, but I remember you and Jo Barry. I guess that's made the difference."

"Oh. That's done it." So she cried a little as she got up to wrap her arms around him.

To make it two for two, Gage hit the nursery just outside of town. Figuring Joanne Barry would appreciate a plant even more than flowers, he found a flowering orchid that fit his bill. He drove out to the farm, and when he found no one at home, left the orchid on the big front porch with a note under the pot.

The gestures, the talk with Frannie had smoothed out the rough edges from his visit to the cemetery. He considered heading home and doing some solo research, but reminded himself—for better or worse—he was part of a team. His first choice was Fox, but when he drove by the office, Fox's truck was no longer parked out front. In court, Gage assumed, or off meeting a client. With Cal at the bowling center, and the old man working there, that avenue simply wasn't an option.

Gage swung around and made the turn toward the rental house. It appeared it would be ladies' day for him.

Both Cybil's and Quinn's cars were out front. He walked into the house as he had that morning, without knocking. With coffee on his mind, he started back to the kitchen as Cybil appeared at the top of the steps.

"Twice in one day," she said. "Don't tell me you're becoming sociable."

"I want coffee. Are you and Quinn in the office up there?"

"We are, just a couple of busy demon-researching worker bees."

"I'll be up in a minute."

He caught the sexy arch of her eyebrow before he continued back. Armed with a mug of coffee, he backtracked and headed up the stairs. Quinn sat at the keyboard, her quick fingers tapping. They continued to tap even as she glanced up and sent him her big, bright smile. "Hi. Have a seat."

"That's okay." Instead he wandered over to the town map tacked to the wall, studied all the colored pins ranged over it that represented incidents involving paranormal activity.

The graveyard wasn't a favorite, he noted, but it got some play. He moved on to the charts and graphs Layla had generated. There, too, he noted the graveyard wasn't a usual *haunt*, for lack of a better term. Maybe it was too clichéd to meet the Big Evil Bastard's standards.

Behind him, Cybil sat studying her own laptop screen. "I've found a source that claims the bloodstone was originally part of the great Alpha—or Life Stone. It's interesting."

"Does it tell us how to use it to kill the fucker?"

Cybil glanced up briefly, spoke to Gage's back. "No. It does, however, speak of wars between the dark and the light—the Alpha and the Omega, the gods and the demons—depending on which version of the mythology I've found. And during these wars, the great stone exploded into many fragments, infused with the blood and the power of the gods. And these fragments were given to the guardians."

"Hey now." Quinn stopped typing, swiveled to face Cybil.

"That's hitting close to home. If so, the bloodstone was passed down to Dent as a guardian. And he, in turn, passed it to our guys here in three equal fragments."

"I've got other sources that cite the bloodstone's use in magickal rituals, its ability to stimulate physical strength and healing."

"Another bingo," Quinn said.

"It's also reputed to aid in regulating the female menstrual cycle."

Gage turned at that. "Do you mind?"

"Not a bit," Cybil said easily. "But more to our purposes, the bloodstone is, by all accounts, a healing stone."

"We already knew that. Cal and Fox and I did our home-work on the stone years ago."

"All of this comes to blood," Cybil went on. "We know that, too. Blood sacrifice, blood ties, bloodstone. And also fire. Fire's played a role in many of the incidents, and was a major factor the night Dent and Twisse tangled, and the night you and Cal and Fox first camped at the Pagan Stone. Cer-tainly on the night the six of us fused the stone back into one whole. So think about this—what do you get when you strike stones together? A spark, and sparks lead to fire. The cre-ation of fire was, arguably, the first magickal act of man. Bloodstone—fire and blood. Fire not only burns, it purifies. Maybe it's fire that will kill it."

"What, you want to stand around banging stones together and hope a magic spark lands on Twisse?"

"Aren't you in a cheery mood?"

"If fire could kill it, it would already be dead. I've seen it ride on flames like they were a damn surfboard."

"*Its* fire, not ours," Cybil pointed out. "Fire created from the Alpha Stone, from the fragment of that stone passed to you, through Dent, by the gods. Fusing it that night made one hell of a blaze."

"How do you propose to light a magic fire with a single stone?"

"I'm working on it. How about you?" Cybil countered. "Any better ideas?"

This wasn't why he was here, Gage reminded himself. He hadn't come to debate magic stones and conjuring the fire of gods. He wasn't even sure why he was baiting her. She'd come through, he reminded himself, all the way through in fusing the three parts of the stone into one.

"I had a visit today, from our resident demon."

"Why didn't you say so?" All business, Quinn reached for her tape recorder. "Where, when, how?"

"In the cemetery, shortly after I left here this morning."

"What time was that?" Quinn looked at Cybil. "Around ten, right? So between ten and ten thirty?" she asked Gage.

"Close enough. I didn't check my watch."

"What form did it take?"

"My mother's."

Immediately, Quinn went from brisk to sympathetic. "Oh, Gage, I'm sorry."

"Has it ever done that before?" Cybil asked. "Appeared in a form of someone you know?"

"New trick. That's why it had me conned for a minute. Anyway, it looked like her, like I remember her. Or, actually, I don't remember her that well. It looked like pictures I've seen of her."

The picture, he thought, his father had kept on the table beside his bed.

"She—it—was young," he continued. "Younger than me, and wearing one of those summer dresses."

He sat now, drinking his cooling coffee as he related the event, and the conversation nearly word for word.

"You *punched* it?" Quinn demanded.

"Seemed like a good idea at the time."

Saying nothing, Cybil rose, crossed to him, held out her hand for his. She examined his, back, palm, fingers. "Healed. I'd wondered about that. If you'd heal completely if it was able to wound you directly."

"I didn't say it wounded me."

"Of course it did. You punched your fist into the belly of the beast, literally. What kinds of wounds were there?"

"Burns, punctures. Fucker bit me. Fights like a girl."

She cocked her head, appreciating his grin. "I'm a girl, and I don't bite . . . in a fight. How long did it take to heal?"

"A while. Maybe an hour altogether."

"Longer, considerably, than if you'd sustained burns from a natural source. Any side effects?"

He started to shrug that off, then reminded himself every detail mattered. "A little nausea, a little dizziness. But it hurt like a mother, so you'll have that."

She cocked her head, sent him a speculative look. "What did you do afterward? There's a couple of hours between then and now."

"I had some things I needed to do. We punching time clocks now?"

"Just curious. We'll write it up, log it in. I'm going to make some tea. Do you want any, Quinn?"

"I want a root beer float, but . . ." Quinn held up her bottle of water. "I'll stick with this."

When Cybil walked out, Gage drummed his fingers on his thigh a moment, then pushed to his feet. "I'm going to top off my coffee."

"You do that." Quinn held her own speculative look until he'd left. Rocks weren't the only things that shot off sparks when they slapped together, she mused.

Cybil put the kettle on, set out the pot, measured her tea. When Gage stepped in, she plucked an apple from the bowl, cut it neatly in quarters, then offered him one.

"So here we are again." After getting a plate, she quartered a second apple, added a few sprigs of grapes. "When Quinn starts talking root beer floats, she needs a snack. If you're looking for something more substantial, there're sandwich makings or cold pasta salad."

"I'm good." He watched her as she added a few crackers, a handful of cubed cheese to the snack plate. "There's no need to get pissy."

She cocked that brow at him. "Why would I be pissy?"

"Exactly."

Taking one of the apple slices, she leaned back against the counter, and took a tiny bite. "You're misreading me. I came down because I wanted tea, not because I was annoyed with you. Annoyance wasn't what I felt. You probably won't like what I was feeling, what I do feel."

"What's that?"

"Sorry that it used your personal grief against you."

"I don't have any personal grief."

"Oh, shut up." She took another, and this time angry, bite out of the apple. "That *is* annoying. You were in the cemetery. As I sincerely doubt you go there for nature walks, I have to conclude you went to visit your mother's grave. And Twisse defiled—or tried to—your memory of her. Don't tell me you don't have grief for the loss of your mother. I lost my father years ago, too. And he chose to leave me, chose to put a bullet in his brain, and still I have grief. You didn't want to talk about it, so I gave you your privacy, then you follow me down here and tell me I'm pissy."

"Which is obviously off," he said dryly, "as you're not in the least pissy."

"I wasn't," she muttered. She let out a breath, then nibbled on the apple again as the kettle began to sputter. "You said she looked very young. How young?"

"Early twenties, I guess. Most of my impressions of her, physically, are from photographs. I . . . Shit. Shit." He dug out his wallet, pulled a small picture from under his driver's license. "This, this is the way she looked, down to the goddamn dress."

After turning off the burner, Cybil moved to him, stood side-by-side to study the photo in his hand. Her hair was dark and loose, her body slim in the yellow sundress. The little boy was about a year, a year and a half, Cybil judged, and propped on her hip as both of them laughed into the camera.

"She was lovely. You favor her."

"He took this out of my head. You were right about that. I haven't looked at this in . . . I don't know, a few years maybe. But it's my clearest memory of her because . . ."

"Because it's the one you carry with you." Now Cybil laid her hand on his arm. "Be annoyed if that's how you have to handle it, but I'm so sorry."

"I knew it wasn't her. It only took a minute for me to know it wasn't her."

And in that minute, she thought, he must have felt unbearable grief and joy. She turned back to pour the water into the pot. "I hope you hit a couple of vital organs, if organs it has, when you punched it."

"That's what I like about you, that healthy taste for violence." He slipped the picture of his mother back into his wallet.

"I'm a fan of the physical, in a lot of areas. It's interesting, isn't it, that in this guise, its first push was to try to convince you to leave. Not to attack, not even to taunt as it has before, but to use a trusted form to tell you to go, to save yourself. I think we have it worried."

"Yeah, it looked really concerned when it knocked me on my ass."

"Got up again, didn't you?" She arranged the plate, the pot, a cup on a tray. "Cal should be here in another hour, and Fox and Layla shortly after. Unless you've got a better offer, why don't you stay for dinner?"

"Are you cooking?"

"That is, apparently, my lot in this strange life we're leading at the moment."

"I'll take that offer."

"Fine. Carry this up for me, and we'll put you to work in the meantime."

"I don't make charts."

She shot him that smug look over her shoulder as she started out ahead of him. "You do today if you want to eat."

LATER, GAGE SAT ON THE FRONT STEPS, ENJOYING the first beer of the evening with Fox and Cal. Fox had changed out of his lawyer suit into jeans and a short-sleeved sweatshirt. He looked, as Fox habitually did, comfortable in his own skin.

How many times had they done just this? Gage wondered. Sat, sharing a beer? Countless times. And often when he was in another part of the world, he might sit, sip a beer, and think of them in the Hollow.

And there were times he came back, between the Seven, because he missed them as he'd miss his own legs. Then they could sit like this, in the long evening sunlight without the weight of the world—or at least this corner of it—on their shoulders.

But the weight was there now with less than two months left before what they all accepted was do or die.

"We could go back to the cemetery, the three of us," Fox suggested. "See if it wants another round."

"I don't think so. It had its fun."

"Next time you go wandering around, don't go unarmed. I don't mean that damn gun," Cal added. "You can pick up a decent and legal folding knife down at Mullendore's. No point letting it try to take a chunk out of your hand."

Idly, Gage flexed the hand in question. "Felt good to punch the bastard, but you're right. I didn't even have a damn penknife on me. I won't make that mistake again."

"Can it just come back as the dead—sorry," Fox added, laying a hand on Gage's shoulder.

"It's okay. Quinn brought that up earlier. If it can take the form of the living, it's a big skill. The dead's hard enough. Cybil thinks not. She had some convoluted, intellectual theory, which I stopped listening to after she and Quinn started the debate. But I'm leaning toward Cybil's end of it. It had substance. But the image, the form—that was like a shell, and the shell was . . . borrowed, was the gist of Cybil's long, involved lecture on corporeal changes and shape-shifting. It can't borrow from the living because they're still wearing the shell, so to speak."

"Whatever," Fox said after a moment. "We know Twisse has a new twist. If he wants to play that game again, we'll be ready."

Maybe, Gage thought, but the odds were long. And getting longer every day.

Three

~⌇~

IN LOOSE COTTON PANTS AND A TANK SHE
considered suitable only for sleeping, Cybil followed the
life-affirming scent of coffee toward the kitchen. It was
lovely to know someone in the household woke before she
did and had a pot going. The chore, all too often, fell to her
as she was up and about before any of the others.

Of course, none of the others slept alone, she thought, so
they got coffee *and* sex. Didn't seem quite fair, she decided,
but that's the way the cookie crumbled. Still, the cookie
meant she wasn't required to make precaffeine conversation,
and had a quiet interlude with the morning paper until the
frisky puppies rolled out of bed for the day.

Halfway between the stairs and the kitchen, she stopped,
sniffed the air. That, she realized, was more than coffee. Bacon scented the air, which made it a red-letter day. Someone
besides Cybil was cooking.

At the doorway, she saw Layla busy at the stove, humming away as she fried and flipped, her dark hair pulled
back in a little stub at the nape of her neck. She looked so

happy, Cybil thought and wondered why she felt this big-sister affection for Layla.

They were of an age, after all, and while Layla might not be as well-traveled as she was, her housemate had lived in New York for several years, and even in cropped pants and a T-shirt wore urban polish. With Quinn, there'd been an instant connection for Cybil—a click the moment they'd met in college. And now, there was Layla.

She'd never had that same affinity, that *click* with her own sister, Cybil thought. But then she and Rissa never fully understood each other, and her younger sister tended to get in touch primarily when she needed something or was embroiled in yet another mess.

Cybil decided she should count herself lucky. There was Quinn, who'd been like a missing piece of herself, and now Layla sliding smoothly into the slot, to make the three of them a unit.

With the bacon set aside to drain, Layla turned for a carton of eggs and jolted when she saw Cybil. "God!" On a laugh, she clutched at her heart. "You scared me."

"Sorry. You're up early."

"And with a yen for bacon and eggs." Before Cybil could do it herself, Layla got down a cup and poured coffee. "I made plenty of bacon. I figured you'd be down before I finished, and Fox is always up for a meal."

"Hmm," Cybil said, and dumped milk into the coffee.

"Anyway, I hope you're hungry because I seem to have fried up half a pig. And the eggs are fresh from the O'Dell farm. I got the paper." Layla gestured toward the table. "Why don't you sit down and have your coffee while I finish this up?"

Cybil took that first mind-clearing sip. "I'm forced to ask. What are you after, Darnell?"

"Transparent as Saran Wrap." With a wince, Layla broke the first egg in the bowl. "There is this little favor, and I'd be bribing Quinn with breakfast if she were here instead of at Cal's. I have the morning off, and a fistful of paint samples.

I was hoping I could talk you and Quinn into going over to the shop with me this morning, helping me decide on my color scheme."

Cybil pushed her hair back, drank more coffee. "Here's a question. Why would you think either of us would let you get away with deciding on the color scheme for your own boutique without us badgering you with our opinion?"

"Really?"

"Nobody escapes my opinion, but I'll be eating bacon and eggs."

"Good. Good. It just seems crazy, worrying about paint chips when we've got life-and-death issues to worry about."

"Color schemes are life-and-death issues."

Layla laughed, but shook her head. "We've got a demon who wants us dead, coming into full power in about six weeks, and I'm pursuing the wild hare of opening my own business in the town it wants for its personal playground. Meanwhile Fox has to interview and train—or I have to train—my replacement as his office manager while we figure out how to stay alive and destroy ancient evil. And I'm going to ask Fox to marry me."

"We can't stop living because . . . Whoa." Cybil held up a hand, and waited for her morning-fuzzy brain to clear. "In my journalism classes, that's what we called burying the lead. Big time."

"Is it crazy?"

"Of course, you never bury the lead." Since it was there, Cybil reached over and took a slice of bacon. "And yes, of course, marriage is insane—that's why it's human."

"I don't mean marriage, I mean asking him. It's so unlike me."

"I would hope so. I'd hate to think you go around proposing to men all willy-nilly."

"I always thought when everything was in place, when the time was right, that I'd wait for the man I loved to set the scene, buy the ring, and ask." Sighing, Layla went back to breaking eggs in the bowl. "*That's* like me—or was. But

I don't care about everything being in place, and how the hell can anybody know, especially us, if the time's right? And I don't want to wait."

"Go get him, sister."

"Would you—I mean under the circumstances?"

"You're damn right I would."

"I feel . . . Here he comes," Layla whispered. "Don't say anything."

"Damn, I was planning to blurt it all out, then toss a few handfuls of confetti."

"Morning." Fox sent Cybil a sleepy smile, then turned a dazzling one on Layla. "You're cooking."

"My boss gave me the morning off, so I've got time to spare."

"Your boss should always give you whatever you need." He reached in the fridge for his usual Coke. And, popping the top, looked from one woman to the other. "What? What's going on?"

"Nothing." And thinking of his ability to read thoughts and feelings, Layla pointed her whisk at him. "And no peeking. We were just talking about the boutique, paint chips, that sort of thing. How many eggs do you want?"

"A couple. Three."

Layla sent Cybil a satisfied smile when Fox leaned in to nuzzle her and cop some bacon behind her back.

THE BUILDING THAT WOULD HOUSE LAYLA'S BOU-tique had an airy feel to it, good light, good location. Important pluses, to Cybil's mind. Layla had years of experience in fashion retail, as well as an excellent eye for style—other major advantages. Added to them was her shared ability with Fox to sense thoughts, and that sense of what a customer really wanted would be an enormous advantage.

She wandered the space. She liked the old wood floors, the warm tones of it and the wide trim. "Charming or slick?" Cybil asked.

"Charming, with slick around the edges." Standing at the

front window with Quinn, Layla held one of the paint chips up in the natural light. "I want to respect the space, and jazz it up with little touches. Female, comfortable, but not cozy. Accessible, but not altogether expected."

"No pinks, roses, mauves."

"None," Layla said decisively.

"A couple of good chairs for customers to sit in," Quinn suggested, "to try on shoes, or wait for a friend in the changing area, but no floral fabrics, no chintz."

"If this were a gallery, we'd say your stock would be your art."

"Exactly." Layla beamed over at Cybil. "That's why I'm thinking neutral tones for the walls. Warm neutrals, because of the wood. And I'm thinking instead of a counter"—she waved the flat of her hand waist-high—"I might find a nice antique desk or pretty table for the checkout area. And over here—" She pushed the chips into Quinn's hand, crossed the bare floor. "I'd have clear floating shelves in a random pattern, to display shoes, smaller bags. And then here . . ."

Cybil followed as Layla moved from section to section, outlining her plans for the layout. The image formed clearly— open racks, shelves, pretty glass-fronted curios for accessories.

"I need Fox's father to build in a couple of dressing rooms back here."

"Three," Cybil said. "Three's more practical, is more interesting to the eye and it's a magickal number."

"Three then, with good, flattering lighting, and the tortuous triple mirror."

"I hate those bastards," Quinn muttered.

"We all do, but they're a necessary evil. And see, the little kitchen back here." With a come-ahead gesture, Layla led the way. "They kept that, through its various retail incarnations. I thought I could do quirky little vignettes every month or so. Like, ah, candles and wine on the table, some flowers— and a negligee or a cocktail dress tossed over the back of the chair. Or a box of cereal on the counter, some breakfast dishes in the sink—and a messenger- or briefcase-style handbag on the table, a pair of pumps under it. You know what I mean?"

"Fun. Clever. Yes, I know what you mean. Let me see those chips." Cybil snatched them from Quinn, then headed back to the front window.

"I've got more," Layla told them. "I've sort of whittled it down to those."

"And have your favorite," Quinn finished.

"Yeah, I do, but I want opinions. Serious opinions, because I'm as scared as I am excited about this, and I don't want to screw it up by—"

"This. Champagne Bubbles. Just the palest gold, really just the impression of color. Subtle, neutral, but with that punch, that fun factor. And any color you put against this will pop."

Lips pursed, Quinn studied the chip over Cybil's shoulder. "She's right. It's great. Female, sophisticated, warm."

"That was my pick." Layla closed her eyes. "I swear, that was my pick."

"Proving the three of us have excellent taste," Cybil concluded. "You're going in to apply for the business loan this week?"

"Yeah." Layla blew out a breath that fluttered her bangs. "Fox says it's a slam dunk. I have references from him, Jim Hawkins, my former boss from the boutique in New York. My finances are—hah—modest, but in good order. And the town wants and needs businesses. Keep revenue local instead of sending it out to the mall and so on."

"It's a good investment. You've got prime location here— Main Street only steps from the Square. You were raised in the business, as your parents owned a dress shop. Work experience, a canny sense of style. A very good investment. I'd like a piece of it."

Layla blinked at Cybil. "Sorry?"

"My finances are healthy—not bank-loan healthy, but healthy enough to invest in a smart enterprise. What have you projected as your start-up costs?"

"Well . . ." Layla named a figure, and Cybil nodded and wandered. "I could manage a third of that. Quinn?"

"Yeah, I could swing a third."

"Are you kidding?" was all Layla could say. "Are you *kidding*?"

"Which would leave you to come up with the final third out of your modest finances or the bank loan. I'd go with the loan, not only to give yourself breathing room, but for tax purposes." Cybil brushed back her hair. "Unless you don't want investors."

"I want investors if they're you. Oh God, this is—wait. You should think about it awhile. Seriously. You need to take some time, think about it. I don't want you to—"

"We have been thinking about it."

"And talking about it," Quinn added. "Since you decided to go for it. Christ, Layla, look what we've already invested in each other, and in this town. This is only money—and as Gage would probably say, we want to ante up."

"I'll make it work. I will." Layla brushed away a tear. "I will. I know what we are to each other, but if you do this, I want it all legal and right. Fox will . . . He'll fix it, he'll take care of that part. I know I can make it work. Now, especially, I know I can."

She threw her arms around Quinn, then opened up to pull Cybil into the hug. "Thank you, thank you, thank you."

"Not necessary. Remember what else Gage might say," Cybil reminded her.

"What?"

"We could all be dead before August." With a laugh, Cybil gave Layla a pat on the butt, then stepped back. "Have you thought of any possible names for the place yet?"

"Again, are you kidding? This is me, here. I have a list. In fact I have three lists, and a folder. But I'm tossing them because I just thought of the perfect name." Layla held her hands out to the sides, palms up. "Welcome to Sisters."

THEY SEPARATED, LAYLA TO THE OFFICE, QUINN to have lunch with Cal's mother to discuss wedding plans, Cybil back home. She wanted to pursue the bloodstone-as-weapon angle, and push deeper into the idea of it being a fragment of a larger mystical power source.

She liked the quiet and the solitude. It was good for thinking, reshuffling thoughts, for moving them around like puzzle pieces until she found a better fit. Because she wanted a change of venue, she brought her laptop and the file of notes she'd printed out that dealt specifically with the bloodstone down to the kitchen. With the back door and windows open to the spring air, she made iced tea, fixed a small bowl of salad. Over lunch, she reviewed her notes.

July 7, 1652. Giles Dent (the Guardian) wore the bloodstone amulet on the night Lazarus Twisse (the Demon) led the mob it had infected to the Pagan Stone in Hawkins Wood, where Giles had a small cabin. Prior to that night, Dent had spoken of the stone, and shown it to Ann Hawkins, his lover and the mother of his triplet sons (who would be born on 7/7/1652). Ann wrote of it, briefly and cryptically, in the journals she kept after Dent sent her away (to what would become the O'Dell farm) in order to birth their sons in safety.

When next documented, the stone had been divided into three equal parts, and was clutched in Cal Hawkins's, Fox O'Dell's, and Gage Turner's fists, after they had performed their blood brother ritual, at the Pagan Stone at midnight on their shared tenth birthday (7/7/1987). The ritual—blood ritual—freed the demon for a period of seven days, every seven years, during which time it infected certain people in Hawkins Hollow, said infection causing them to perform acts of violence, even murder.

However, as the demon was freed, the three boys gained specific powers of self-healing and psychic gifts. *Weapons*.

Cybil nodded at the word she'd underscored. "Yeah, these are weapons, these are tools that kept them alive, kept them in the fight. And those weapons sprang from, or are certainly connected to, the bloodstone."

She reviewed her notes on Ann Hawkins's journal entry about bringing three back to one, and her conversations—such as they'd been—with Cal, with Layla. One into three,

three into one, Cybil mused and found herself mildly annoyed Ann hadn't elected to appear to her.

She thought she'd like to interview a ghost.

She began to type her thoughts, using the stream-of-consciousness method that served her best, and could and would be refined later. From time to time she paused to make a quick handwritten note to herself on her pad, on some point she wanted to dig into later, or a reference area that needed a closer look.

When she heard the front door open, she kept working—thought fleetingly: Quinn's back early. Even when the door slammed, sharp as a shot moments later, she didn't stop the work. Wedding tension, she supposed.

But when the door behind her slammed, and the thumb bolt on the lock snicked, it got her attention. She saved the work—it was second nature to save the work, and her mind barely registered the automatic gesture. Over the sink, the window slid down, the slow movement somehow more threatening than the slammed door.

She could hurt it, she reminded herself, as she rose to sidestep to the knife block on the counter. They'd hurt it before. It felt pain. Drawing the chef's knife out of the block, she promised herself if it was in the house with her, she would damn well cause it some pain. Still, her instincts told her she'd do better outside than locked in. She reached for the thumb bolt.

The shock ripped up her arm, had her loosing a breathless scream as she stumbled back. On a sudden, thunderous burst, the kitchen faucet gushed blood. She stepped toward the phone—help, should she need it, was only two minutes away. But when she reached for the phone, a second, more violent shock jolted her.

Scare tactics, she told herself as she began to edge out of the kitchen. Trap the lone woman in the house. Make a lot of noise, she added when the booming shook the walls, the floor, the ceiling.

She saw the boy through the living room window. Its face was pressed against it. It grinned.

I can't get out, but it can't get in, she thought. Isn't that interesting? But as she watched, it crawled up the glass, across it, down, like some hideous bug.

And the glass bled until it was covered with red, and with the buzzing black flies that came to drink.

They smothered the light until the room, the house, was dark as pitch. Like being blind, she thought as her heart began to buck and kick. That's what it wanted her to feel. It wanted to claw through her to that old, deep-seated fear. Through the booming, the buzzing, she braced a hand on the wall to guide her. She felt the warm wet run over her hand, and knew the walls bled.

She would get out, she told herself. Into the light. She'd take the shock, she'd handle it, and she *would* get out. Wall gave way to stair banister, and she shuddered with relief. Nearly there.

Something flew out of the dark, knocking her off her feet. The knife clattered uselessly across the floor. So she crawled, hands and knees. When the door flew open, the light all but blinded her. She came up like a runner off the mark.

She plowed straight into Gage. Later, he'd think she would have gone straight through him if she could've managed it. He caught her, fully expecting to have a clawing, kicking, hysterical female in his hands. Instead, she looked into his eyes with her own fierce and cold.

"Do you see it?" she demanded.

"Yeah. Your neighbor out sweeping her front walk doesn't. She's waving."

Cybil kept a viselike grip on Gage's arm with one hand, turned, and waved with the other. On the front window, the boy scrabbled like a spider. "Keep it up." Cybil spaced her words evenly. "Waste all the energy you like on today's matinee." Deliberately she released Gage and sat on the front steps. "So," she said to Gage, "out for a drive?"

He stared at her for a moment, then shaking his head, sat down beside her. The boy leaped down to race around the lawn. Where it ran, blood flowed like a river. "Actually, I'd stopped in to see Fox. While I was there, he got this little buzz in the brain. A lot of static, he said, like a signal just off channel. Since Layla said you were the only one on your own, I came up to check."

"I'm very glad to see you." Fire sprang up from the bloody river. "I wasn't sure I was getting through, with our psychic Bat Signal." To help keep herself steady, she reached out, took Gage's hand.

On the lawn, the thing screamed in fury. It leaped, and it dived into the stream of flaming blood.

"Impressive exit."

"You've got balls of fucking steel," Gage murmured.

"A professional gambler should be able to read a bluff better than that."

As every inch of her began to shake, Gage took her chin in his hand, turned her face to his. "It takes balls of fucking steel to bluff like that."

"It feeds on fear. I was damned if I was going to give it lunch. But I'm double damned if I'm going back in the house alone, right at the moment."

"Do you want to go back in, or do you want to go somewhere else?"

His tone was casual, almost careless, without a trace of *there, there, honey.* The last hard knot in her belly loosened, and she realized that last little one had been pride, not fear. "I want to be in Bimini, sipping a bellini on the beach."

"Let's go."

When she laughed, he went with instinct rather than judgment, and took her mouth with his.

Stupid, he knew it was stupid, but smart couldn't be half as satisfying. She tasted like she looked—exotic and mysterious. She didn't feign surprise or resistance, and instead took as he did. When he released her, she kept her eyes on his as she leaned back.

"Well, that was no bellini in Bimini, but it was very nice."

"I can do better than nice."

"Oh, I have no doubt. But . . ." She gave his shoulder a

companionable pat as she rose. "I think we'd better go inside, make sure everything's all right in there." She looked out over the lush green lawn, toward the front window sparkling now in the afternoon sunlight. "It probably is, but we should check."

"Right." He got up to go inside with her. "You should call Fox's office, let them know you're okay."

"Yeah. In the kitchen. That's where I was when it started." She gestured to the living room chair lying on its side. "That must've been what flew across the room and knocked me down. The little bastard threw a chair at me."

Gage righted it, then picked up the knife. "Yours?"

"Yeah, too bad I didn't get to use it." She stepped into the kitchen with him, let out a slow breath. "The back door's closed and locked, and so's the window. It did that. That was real. It's best to know what's real and what isn't." After rinsing the knife and sliding it back into the block, she picked up the phone to call Layla.

Assuming she'd want it the way it was, Gage unlocked and opened both door and window.

"I'm going to cook," Cybil announced when she hung up the phone.

"Fine."

"It'll keep me calm and centered. I'll need a few things, so you can drive me to the market."

"I can?"

"Yes, you can. I'll get my purse. And since I now have bellinis on the brain, we'll stop by the liquor store and pick up some champagne."

"You want champagne," he said after a beat.

"Who doesn't?"

"Anything else on our list of errands?"

She only smiled. "You can bet I'm getting a pair of rubber gloves. I'll explain on the way," she said.

SHE BROWSED, STUDIED, EXAMINED THE OFFER-ings in produce. She selected tomatoes with the care and deliberation he imagined a woman might use when selecting an important piece of jewelry. In the brightly lit market with its mind-melting Muzak and red dot specials, she looked like some fairy queen. Titania, maybe, he decided. Titania had been no pushover either.

He'd expected to be irritated, or at least impatient with the household task of food shopping, but she was fascinating to watch. She had a fluid way of moving, and a look in her eyes that said she noticed everything. He wondered how many people could be terrorized by a demon, then coolly stroll behind a grocery store shopping cart.

He had to admire that.

She spent a full fifteen minutes over poultry, examining, rejecting chickens until she found one that somehow met her standards.

"We're having chicken? All this for chicken?"

"Not just chicken." She tossed back her hair, gave him that sidelong smile of hers. "It's a roasted chicken made with wine, sage, garlic, balsamic—and so on. You'll weep with joy at every bite."

"I don't think so."

"Your tastebuds will. Your travels have probably taken you to New York a time or two over the years."

"Sure."

"Ever dined at Piquant?"

"Fancy French place, Upper West."

"Yes, and a New York institution. The chef there was my first serious lover. He was older, French, absolutely perfect for the first serious lover of a woman of twenty." That smile turned knowing, and just a little sultry. "He taught me quite a bit—about cooking."

"How much older?"

"Considerably. He had a daughter my age. Naturally, she despised me." She poked at a baguette. "No, I'm not settling for the bread here, not this late in the day. We'll stop by the bakery in town. If nothing there works, I'll just bake some."

"You'll just bake some bread."

"If necessary. If I'm in the mood to, it can be therapeutic and satisfying."

"Like sex."

Her smile was quick and easy. "Exactly." She rolled the cart into line. Leaned on the handle. "So, who was your first serious lover?"

She didn't notice, or didn't appear to care, that the woman ahead of them in line looked back over her shoulder with wide eyes. "I haven't had one yet."

"Well, that's a shame. You've missed all the wild passion, the bitter arguments, the mad yearnings. Sex is fun without it, but all the rest adds intensity." Cybil smiled at the woman ahead of them. "Don't you agree?"

The woman flushed, moved her shoulders. "Ah, yeah, I guess. Sure." And developed a sudden—and to Gage's eyes, bogus—interest in the tabloids on the rack before the belt.

"Still, women are more prone to look for all that emotion. It's genetic—hormonal," Cybil continued conversationally. "We're more sexually satisfied, as a gender, when we let our emotions engage, and believe—even if the belief is false— our lover's emotions are as well."

When the belt cleared enough, she began to load her purchases on. "I cook," she told Gage, "you pay."

"That wasn't mentioned."

She gave the bird a pat as she set it on the belt. "If you don't like the chicken, I'll give you a refund."

He watched her load. Long fingers, palely painted nails, a couple of sparkling rings. "I could lie."

"You won't. You like to win, but like women and emotion and sex, the win isn't as satisfying for you unless you play it straight."

He watched the items ring up, and total. "It better be damn good chicken," he said as he pulled out his wallet.

Four

SHE'D BEEN RIGHT ABOUT THE CHICKEN; HE'D
never had better. And he thought she'd been right to decree
no discussion of her experience, or any demon-related topic
during the group meal.

It was fascinating how much *other* the six of them had to
talk about, even though they'd been in one another's pockets
for months. Wedding plans, new business plans, books,
movies, celebrity scandals, and small-town gossip bounced
around the table like tennis balls. At any other time, in any
other place, the gathering would have been exactly as it
appeared—a group of friends and lovers enjoying each other
and a perfectly prepared meal.

And how did he fit into the mix? His relationship with
Cal and Fox had changed and evolved over the years as
they'd gone from boys to men, certainly when he'd yanked
out his roots in the Hollow to move on. But at its base it was
what it had always been—the friendship of a lifetime. They
simply were.

He liked the women they'd chosen, for their own sakes, and for the way they'd meshed with his friends into couples. It took unique women to face what they were all facing and stick it out. It told him that if any of them survived, the four of them would buck the odds and make the strange entity of marriage work.

In fact, he believed they'd thrive.

And if they survived, he'd move on again. He was the one who left—and who came back. That's how he made his life work, in any case. There was always the next game, and another chance to play. That's where he fit in, he supposed. The wild card that turned up after the cut and shuffle.

That left Cybil, with her encyclopedic brain, her genius in the kitchen, and her nerves of steel. Only once since they'd come together had he seen her break down. Twisse had triggered the deepest personal fear in all of them, Gage remembered, and for Cybil that was blindness. She'd wept in his arms when that was over. But she hadn't run.

No, she hadn't run. She'd stick it out, all of them would. Then if they lived through it, she'd move on. There wasn't a single cell of small-town girl in that interesting body of hers. Adaptable she was, he thought. She'd settled smoothly enough into the Hollow, the little house, but it was . . . like Frannie Hawkins's holding vase, he realized. This was just a temporary stop before she moved on to something more suited to her style.

But where, and to what would she move? He wondered that, wondered about her more than was wise.

She caught his glance, arched a brow. "Looking for a refund?"

"No."

"Well then. I'm going for a walk."

"Oh, but, Cyb—" Quinn began.

"Gage can come with me, while the four of you deal with the dishes."

"How come he gets out of kitchen duty?" Fox wanted to know.

"He shopped, he paid. I want a little air before we bring

the Big Evil Bastard to the table. How about it, big guy? Be my escort?"

"Take your phone." Quinn caught Cybil's hand. "Just in case."

"I'll take my phone, and I'll put on a jacket. And I won't take candy from strangers. Relax, Mommy."

When she breezed out, Quinn turned to Gage. "Just don't go far, okay? Keep her close."

"This is Hawkins Hollow, everything in it's close."

She put on a light sweater and slipped black skids onto feet that were so often bare. The minute she stepped outside, she breathed deep. "I like spring nights. Summer's even better. I like the heat, but under the circumstances, I'm hoarding spring."

"Where do you want to go?"

"Main Street, of course. Where else? I like knowing my ground," she continued as they walked. "So I walk around town, drive around the area."

"And could probably draw a detailed map of both by now."

"Not only could, have. I do have an eye for detail." She took another breath, this one loaded with the scent of peonies rioting pink in someone's front garden. "Quinn's going to be happy here. It's so absolutely right for her."

"Why?"

He saw the question surprised her—or, he thought more accurately, the fact he'd asked surprised her.

"Neighborhood. That's Quinn. Developments, suburbia, no, not so much. Too . . . formed. But neighborhood, where she knows the tellers at the bank, the clerks at the market by name? That's all Q. She's a social creature who needs her alone time. So, the town—that gives her the neighborhood. And the house outside town—that gives her the alone. She gets it all," Cybil decided. "And the guy, too."

"Handy Cal falls in there."

"Very. I admit, when she first talked about Cal, I thought Bowling Alley Guy? Q's gone deep end." Laughing, she shook back her hair. "Shame on me for assuming a cliché.

Of course, the minute I met him, I thought, oh, Really Cute Bowling Alley Guy! Then seeing them together clinched it. From my standpoint, they're both getting it all. I'll enjoy coming back here to visit them, and Fox and Layla."

They turned at the Square, and onto Main Street. One of the cars stopped at the light had its windows open and Green Day blasting. While Ma's Pantry and Gino's remained open—and a few teenagers loitered outside the pizza joint— the shops were closed for the night. By nine, Ma's would be dark, and just after eleven, Gino's would lock it up. The Hollow's version, Gage thought, of rolling up the sidewalks.

"So, no yen to build yourself a cabin in Hawkins Wood?" he asked her.

"A cabin in the woods might be nice for the occasional weekend. And the small-town charm," she added, "is just that—charming for visits. I love visiting. It's one of my favorite things. But I'm an urbanite at heart, and I like to travel. I need a base so I have somewhere to leave from, to come back to. I have a very nice one in New York, left to me by my grandmother. How about you? Is there a base, a headquarters, for you?"

He shook his head. "I like hotel rooms."

"Me, too—or to qualify, a room in a well-run hotel. I love the service, the convenience of my well-appointed chamber in a hive where I can order up Do Not Disturb and room service at my whim."

"Twenty-four hours a day," he added. "And somebody comes in and cleans it all up while you're out doing something a lot more interesting."

"That can't be overstated. And I like looking out the window at a view that doesn't belong to me. Still, there are other types in the world, like many of the people in this town Twisse is so hell-bent to destroy. And they like looking out at the familiar. They need and want the comfort of that, and they're entitled to it."

That brought it back to square one, Gage thought. "And you'd bleed for that?"

"Oh, I hope not—at least not copiously. But it's Quinn's

town now, and Layla's. I'd bleed for them. And for Cal and Fox." She turned her head, met his eyes. "And for you."

There was a jolt inside him at that, at the absolute truth he felt from her. Before he could respond, her phone rang.

"Saved by the ring tone," Cybil murmured, then drew out her phone, glanced at the display. "Hell. Damn. Fuck. Sorry, I'd better deal with this." She flipped the phone open. "Hello, Rissa."

She took a few steps away, but Gage had no trouble with the logistics or the ethics of eavesdropping on her end of the conversation. He heard a lot of "no"s between long, listening pauses. And several chilly, "I've already told you"s and "not this time"s followed by an "I'm sorry, Marissa" that spoke of impatience rather than apology. When she closed the phone, that impatience was clear on her face.

"Sorry. My sister, who's never quite grasped the concept that the world doesn't actually revolve around her. Hopefully she's pissed enough at me now to lay off for a few weeks."

"This would be flat-tire sister?"

"Sorry? Oh." And when she laughed, he could see her click back to the night they'd met when they'd nearly run into each other on a deserted county road as each of them traveled toward Hawkins Hollow. "Yes, the same sister who'd borrowed my car and left a flat spare in my trunk. The same who routinely 'borrows' what she likes, and if she remembers to return it, generally returns it damaged or useless."

"Then why did you lend her your car?"

"Excellent question. A weak moment. I don't have many, at least not anymore." Annoyance darkened her eyes now, the steely kind.

"I bet."

"She's in New York, flitting back from wherever she flitted off to this time and doesn't see why she and whatever leeches currently sucking on her can't stay at my place for a couple weeks. But golly, the locks and the security code have been changed—which was necessary because the last time she stayed there with a few friends, they trashed the place, broke an antique vase that had been my great-grandmother's, borrowed several items of my wardrobe—including my cashmere coat, which I'll never see again—and had the cops drop by at the request of the neighbors."

"Sounds like a fun gal," he commented when Cybil ran out of breath.

"Oh, she's nothing but. All right, I'm venting. You have the option of listening or tuning out. She was the baby, and she was pampered and spoiled as babies often are, especially when they're beautiful and charming. And she is, quite beautiful, quite charming. We were children of privilege for the first part of our lives. There was a lot of family money. There was an enormous and gorgeous home in Connecticut, a number of pied à terres in interesting places. We had the best schools, traveled to Europe regularly, socialized with the children of wealthy and important people, and so on. Then came my father's accident, his blindness."

She said nothing for a moment, only continued to walk, her hands in her pockets, her eyes straight ahead. "He couldn't cope. He couldn't see, so he wouldn't see. Then one day, in our big gorgeous home in Connecticut, he locked himself in the library. They tried to break down the door when we heard the shot—we still had servants then, and they tried to break it down. I ran out, and around. I saw through the window, saw what he'd done. I broke the glass, got inside. I don't remember that very well. It was too late, of course. Nothing to be done. My mother was hysterical, Marissa was wild, but there was nothing to be done."

Gage said nothing, but then she knew him to be a man who often said nothing. So she plowed on.

"It was afterward we learned there'd been what they like to call 'considerable financial reversals' since my father's accident. As his untimely death gave him no time to reverse the reversals, we would have to condense, so to speak. My mother dealt with the shock and the grief, which were very real for her, by fleeing with us to Europe and squandering great quantities of money. In a year, she'd married an operator who squandered more, conned her into funnelling most of what was left to him, then left her for greener pastures."

The bitterness in her tone was so ripe, he imagined she could taste it.

"It could've been worse, much worse. We could've been destitute and instead we simply had to learn how to live on more limited resources and earn our way. My mother's since married again, to a very good man. Solid and kind. Should I stop?"

"No."

"Good. Marissa, as I did, came into a—by our former standards—modest inheritance at twenty-one. She'd already been married lavishly, and divorced bitterly, by this time. She blew through the money like a force-five hurricane. She toys with modeling, does very decently with magazine shoots and billboards when she bothers. But what she wants most is to be a celebrity, of any sort, and she continues to pursue the lifestyle of one—or what she perceives to be the lifestyle of one. As a result, she's very often broke and can only use her charm and beauty as currency. Since neither has worked on me for a long time, we're usually at odds."

"Does she know where you are?"

"No, thank God. I didn't tell her, and won't, first because as big a pain in my ass as she is, she remains my sister and I don't want her hurt. Second, more selfishly, I don't want her in my hair. She's very like my mother, or as my mother was before this third marriage settled and contented her. People always said I took after my father."

"So he was smart and sexy?"

She smiled a little. "That's a nice thing to say after I've unloaded on you. I've wondered if being like my father meant I wouldn't be able to face the worst life threw at me."

"You already did. You broke the window."

She let out a breath that trembled in a way that warned him there were tears behind it. But she held them back—major points for her—and turning, looked up at him with those deep, dark eyes. "All right, you've earned this for listening, and I've earned it for being smart enough to dump it on a man who would."

She gripped his shirt front, rose on her toes. Then she slid her hands over his shoulders, linked her arms around his neck.

Her mouth was silk and heat and promise. It moved over his, a slow glide that invited him in, to sample or to taste fully. The flavors of her wound through him, strong and sweet, beckoning like a crooked finger.

Come on, have a little more.

When she started to ease away, he gripped her hips, brought her back up to her toes. And had a little more.

She didn't regret it. How could she? She'd offered, he'd answered. How could she regret being kissed on a quiet spring night by a man who knew exactly how she wanted to be kissed?

Hard and deep, with just a hint of bite.

If her pulse tripped, if her belly fluttered, if this sample caused her system to yearn, to burn, she chose to ride the excitement, not step away with regret. So when she stepped back, it wasn't with regret, it wasn't with caution, but with the clear understanding that a man like Gage Turner respected a challenge. And giving him one would undoubtedly prove more satisfying to both of them.

"That might've been a slight overpayment," she decided. "But you can keep the change."

He grinned back at her. "That *was* your change."

She laughed, and on impulse held out a hand for his. "I'd say our after-dinner walk did both of us good. We'd better get back."

In the living room, Cybil sat with her feet tucked up, a mug of tea in her hand as she relayed the incident from that afternoon for the group, and Quinn's recorder.

She didn't skimp on the details, Gage noted, and she didn't flinch from them.

"There was blood in the house," Quinn prompted.

"The illusion of blood."

"And the flies, the noise. The dark. You saw and heard all that, too?" Quinn asked Gage.

"Yeah."

"The doors and windows were locked from the inside."

"The front door opened when I tried it, from the outside," Gage qualified. "But when we went back in, the kitchen door was still locked, so was the window over the sink."

"But it—the boy," Layla said slowly, "was outside, on the window. It never came in."

"I think it couldn't." Cybil took a thoughtful sip of tea. "How much more threatened would I have felt if it was locked in here with me? If it could have gotten in, I think it would have. It could cause me to see and hear—even feel things that weren't real inside the house. It could lock the door, the window in the room where I was when it started. Not the front," she said. "Maybe it used up that area of its power on the back of the house. It could only make me *think* the front door was locked. Stupid. I never thought of it when it was happening."

"Yeah." Cal shook his head at her. "It's pretty stupid of you not to cop to that when the house was bleeding and shaking and you were stuck in the dark with demon boy crawling on the window."

"Now that we've established Cybil completely loses her head in a crisis, we should ask ourselves why it couldn't come in." Fox sat on the floor, scratching Lump on his big head. "Maybe it's like the vampire deal. Has to be invited."

"Or, keeping Dracula inside of fiction where he belongs, it just wasn't up to full power. And won't be," Gage reminded them, "for a few more weeks."

"Actually . . ." Cybil frowned. "If we consider vampyric lore, it's not impossible the undead, drinker of blood, and so forth, doesn't have its legitimate roots in this demon. Some of that lore speaks of the vampire's ability to hypnotize its victims or foes—mind control. It feeds off human blood. This is more your area, Quinn, than mine."

"You're doing fine."

"All right, to stick with this channel, vampires are often said to have the ability to turn into a bat, a wolf. This demon certainly shape-shifts—which adds the possibility of the shape-shifter, of which the lycanthrope is a subset, found in various lore. To some extent, these might be bastardizations of this demon."

She picked up her own notebook, scribbled in it as she continued. "Undead. We know now that it can take the form of someone who's died. What if this isn't, as we thought, a new trick, but an ability it had before Dent imprisoned it, and is only now, as what we're told is the final Seven approaches, able to pull that out of its hat again?"

"So it kills Uncle Harry," Fox proposed, "then for fun, it comes back as Uncle Harry to terrorize and kill the rest of the family."

"It does have a sick sense of fun." Quinn nodded. "Should we start sharpening stakes?"

"No. But we'd better figure out how the weapon we do have works. Still, this is interesting." Thoughtfully, Cybil tapped her pencil on the notepad. "If it couldn't come in, that might give us a little more security, and peace of mind. Have any of you ever seen it inside a home?" Cybil asked.

"It just gets the people in it to kill themselves, or each other, or burn the place down." Gage shrugged. "Often all of the above."

"Maybe there's a way to block it, or at least weaken it." Layla slid off her chair to sit on the floor beside Fox. "It's energy, right? And energy that feeds on, or at least seems to prefer, negative emotions. Anger, fear, hate. At every Seven, or the approach of one, it targets birds and animals first— smaller brains, less intellect than humans. And it recharges on that, then moves, usually, to people who're under some influence. Alcohol, drugs, or those emotions again. Until it's stronger."

"It's coming out stronger this time," Cal pointed out. "It's already moved past animals, and was able to infect Block Kholer to the point he nearly beat Fox to death."

As Layla took Fox's hand, Cybil considered. "That was target specific, and it wasn't able to infect the chief of police when he got there and dragged Block off. Target specific might be another advantage."

"Unless you're the target," Fox pointed out. "Then it seriously sucks."

Cybil smiled at him. "True enough. It doesn't just feed off hate, it hates. Us especially. As far as we know, everything it's done or been able to do since February targets one of us, or the group as a whole."

She set her notebook on the arm of the sofa. "It's expending a lot of energy to scare us, hurt us. That's a thought I had today when it had me trapped in here. Well, before it went dark and I wasn't so cocky. That it was using up energy. Maybe we can taunt it into using more. It's stronger, yes, and it's getter stronger yet, but anytime it puts on a big show, there's a lull afterward. It's still recharging. And while there might not be a way to block or weaken it, there might be a way to divert it. If it's aiming at us, its ability to infect the Hollow may be diminished."

"I'm pretty sure I can state categorically it's been aimed at us plenty, and still managed to wreak havoc in the Hollow."

Cybil nodded at Fox. "Because you've always been in the Hollow trying to save lives, fight it off."

"What choice do we have?" Cal demanded. "We can't leave people unprotected."

"I'm suggesting they might not need as much protection if we were able to draw it away."

"How? And where?"

"How might be a challenge," Cybil began.

"But where would be the Pagan Stone. Tried that," Gage continued. "Fourteen years ago."

"Yes, I've read that in Quinn's notes, but—"

"Do you remember our last trip there?" Gage asked her. "That was a walk on the beach compared to getting through Hawkins Wood anywhere close to the Seven."

"We made it that time, two Sevens ago. Barely," Fox added.

"We thought maybe we could stop it by repeating the ritual at the same time, the same place. Midnight, our birthday—the dawn of the Seven, so to speak. Didn't work, obviously. By the time we got back to town, it was bad. One of the worst nights of this ever."

"Because we weren't here to help anyone," Cal finished. "We'd left the town unprotected. How can we risk that again?"

Cybil started to speak, then decided to let it go for now. "Well, back to the bloodstone then. That's one of the new elements on our side of the scoreboard. I've got some avenues I'm exploring. And was about to push a little deeper earlier today when I was so rudely interrupted. I'll get back on that tomorrow. I was also going to suggest, if you're up for it, Gage, that you and I try what Cal and Quinn have, and Fox and Layla."

"You want to have sex? Always up for it."

"That's so sweet, but I was staying on topic and speaking of combining abilities. We have past." She gestured to Cal and Quinn. "We have now, with Fox and Layla. You and I see forward. Maybe it's time to find out if we see further, or clearer, together."

"I'm game if you are."

"How about tomorrow then? I'll drive out to Cal's, maybe about one."

"Ah, about that." Cal cleared his throat. "After today, I think we have to limit solo time as much as possible. Nobody should be staying here or at my place alone at night, for one thing. We can split that up, so there's at least two—better three—in one place. And during the day, we should use the buddy system whenever possible. You shouldn't drive out to my place alone, Cybil."

"I'm not going to disagree about safety and strength in numbers. So, who's going to buddy up with Fox whenever he has to drive up to Hagerstown, to the courthouse? Or with Gage when he's zipping from here to there?"

Fox shook his head sadly at Cal. "Warned you, didn't I?"

"For the record, I'm not the least bit insulted that you'd

want to protect me and my fellow females." Cybil smiled at Cal. "And I agree we should stick together as much as possible. But it's not practical or feasible that we can avoid basic alone time or tasks for the duration. We're six weeks out. I think we can all promise to be sensible and cautious. I, for one, won't be lighting the candle and creeping down to the basement at midnight to investigate strange noises."

"I'll come here," Gage told her.

"No, because now it's a matter of principle. And I think we'd have more luck with this at Cal's. This house still feels . . ."

"Smudged," Quinn finished. She reached over to rub Cybil's knee. "It'll fade."

"Yes, it will. Well, while you all work out who's sleeping where tonight, I'm going to bed." Rising, she glanced at Gage. "I'll see you tomorrow."

She wanted a long hot soak in the tub, but that struck her as too close to going down into a dark basement. Both were horror-movie clichés for a reason, after all. She settled on the nightly routine of cleanser, toner, moisturizer. As she started to turn down the bed, Quinn came in.

"Cal and I are staying here tonight."

"All right, but wouldn't it make more sense for you two to go home, with Gage?"

"Fox and Layla are bunking at Cal's. I wanted to be here tonight."

Because she understood, Cybil's eyes stung. She sat on the side of the bed, took Quinn's hand, laid it against her cheek as Quinn sat beside her.

"I was all right until the lights went out. More interested, even intrigued than scared. Then they went out, and I couldn't see. Nothing was as horrible as that."

"I know. I can sleep in here with you tonight."

Cybil shook her head, tipped it to Quinn's shoulder. "It's enough to know you're across the hall. We all felt it, didn't we? That smudge like you said, that smear it left on the house. I was afraid it was just me, just being paranoid."

"We all felt it. It'll fade, Cyb. We won't give ground."

"It'll never understand how we are together, or what we are together. It would never understand that you knew I'd sleep better tonight with you in the house, or that I'd be better talking to you for a few minutes alone."

"It's one of the ways we'll beat it."

"I believe that." She sighed. "Marissa called."

"Crap."

"Yeah, and it was—the usual crap. 'Can't you do this, can't I have that? Why are you so mean?' It just added to an upsetting day. I dumped a good chunk of my unfortunate family history on Gage's head."

"Really?"

"Yes, I know, not my usual style. It was a weak moment, but he handled it well. He didn't say much, but he said exactly the right thing. Then I kissed his brains out."

"Well." Quinn gave her a friendly shoulder bump. "It's about damn time."

"Maybe it is, I don't know. I don't know if it would complicate things, simplify them, or make no damn difference at all. But while I'm sure the sex would be good—in fact superior—I'm equally sure it would be as risky as going down in the basement to see what the banging's about."

"It could be, but since there'd be two of you involved, you wouldn't be going down to the basement alone."

"True." Pursing her lips, Cybil studied her own toes. "And there would be some comfort when we were both hacked to death by the ax murderer."

"At least you'd've had sex first."

"Superior sex. I'll sleep on it." She gave Quinn a squeeze. "Go on, go snuggle up with your adorable guy. I'm going to do a little yoga to help me relax before I go to bed."

"Just call if you need me."

Cybil nodded. That was the thing, she thought when Quinn left her. That was a constant in her life. If she needed Quinn, all she had to do was call.

Five

~⟆~

SHE'D BEEN IN HIS DREAMS, AND IN HIS DREAMS, she came to his bed. In his dreams her lips, soft and seeking, yielded to his. Her body, sleek and smooth, arched up, long arms, long legs wrapping him in warmth, in fragrance. In female.

The wild glory of her hair, dark against white sheets, spilled away from her face while those deep, seductive eyes watched him.

She rose. She opened. She took him in.

In his dreams, his blood beat like a heart, and his heart pounded its fist in his chest. Inside him, joy and desperation rolled into one mad tangle of need. Locked, lost, he took her lips again. The taste, the taste that burned through him like a fever while their bodies raced together. Faster. Faster.

While around them the room began to bleed, and to burn.

She cried out, her nails biting like teeth into his back

while the sea of bloody flames rolled over them. And the word she cried as they were consumed was *bestia*.

HE WOKE, ONCE AGAIN AT FIRST LIGHT. AND THAT, Gage thought, had to stop. He had no particular affinity for mornings, and now it seemed he was doomed to deal with them. There'd be no going back to sleep after the little movie clip his subconscious had drummed up. It was too damn bad such a promising dream had taken a turn so far south at the—ha—climax.

He could pick apart the symbolism, he thought, staring at the ceiling of Cal's guest room. But then, it was easy to identify the springboard for the lion's share of tonight's entertainment.

He was a guy. He was horny.

Moreover, it suited his fantasy to have her come to him rather than him pursuing her. They'd made a pact not that long ago on this very topic. How had she put it? *You won't try to seduce me, and I won't pretend to be seduced.*

Remembering made him smile into the dim, dawn light. But if she made the moves, all bets were off as far as he was concerned. The challenge would be to con her into making those moves so she believed it was her idea in the first place.

Then again, the interlude in the dream had ended badly. He could ascribe that to his own cynical, pessimistic nature, or he could consider it a portent. Or, third option, a warning. If he let himself become involved with her—because it hadn't just been sex in the dream, he'd been *involved*—they could both pay the ultimate price. Blood and fire, he thought—as usual. And it hadn't been her lover's name she'd cried out when she'd been consumed by passion and flame, but *bestia*.

Latin for beast. A dead language used by dead gods and guardians.

Simply put, the distraction of sex would blur their focus, and the Big Evil Bastard would strike when they were defenseless. Meaning, any of the three options indicated the smart money was on keeping it in his pants, at least as far as Cybil Kinski was concerned.

He rolled out of bed. He'd shower off the dream, and the urges it stirred. He was damn good at controlling his urges. If he was restless and horny, it meant he needed a game and sex. So he'd make it a point to find both. A quick trip to AC would meet both needs, eliminate any possible complications or consequences.

And he and Cybil would use the sexual tension between them as an energy source for the greater good. Of course, if they won, if they lived, he'd make damn sure he found a way to get her naked. Then he'd find out if her skin was as soft as it looked, her body as limber, her . . .

That line of thinking wasn't going to help him control his urges.

He toweled off, opted out of shaving (what the hell for?), then pulled on jeans and a black T-shirt because they were the handiest. As he started downstairs he heard the murmur of voices, and a quick, sexy giggle behind the closed bedroom door. So the lovebirds were up early and already cooing, he mused. Odds were they'd be at it long enough for him to have a quiet, solitary cup of coffee.

In the kitchen, he started the first pot of the day, and while he brooded, he walked out of the house to hike down to the road and the paper box. Cal's front slope was a riot of blooms. The azaleas—one of the few ornamentals Gage actually recognized—were in full, showy bloom. Some sort of delicate weeper arched over, dripping pink. All that color and shape tumbled down toward the gravel lane, cheerful as children, while the woods stood along the edges with its thickening green hiding its secrets. Its joy and its terrors.

Birds trilled, the winding creek murmured, and his footsteps crunched. Some of Cal's blooms were fragrant, so their perfume fluttered in the air while dappled sunlight played over the ribbon of the creek.

Soothing, he thought, the sounds, the scents, the scene. And for a man like Cal, unquestionably satisfying. He enjoyed it himself for short stretches, Gage admitted, as he

reached into the blue box and pulled out the morning paper.
And he needed, again unquestionably, infusions of Cal and
Fox. But if those stretches played out too long, he'd start
jonesing for neon, for green baize, for horns and crowds.
For the action, the energy, the anonymity of a casino or a
city.

If they killed the bastard and lived through it, he thought
he'd buzz off somewhere for a few weeks. Cal's wedding in
September would bring him back, but in the meantime, there
was a big world out there, and a lot of cards to be dealt.
Maybe Amsterdam or Luxembourg for a change of pace.

Or, if he was in the get-Cybil-naked mode, he might suggest Paris. Romance, sex, gambling, and fashion all in one
shot. He thought she'd like the idea. After all, she shared his
affection for travel and a good hotel. Finding out how they
traveled together might be a nice way to celebrate living beyond his thirty-first birthday.

She was bound to bring him luck—good or bad was yet to
be seen—but a woman like that tipped scales. He was willing to gamble they'd tip his way.

A couple of weeks, pure fun, no strings, then they'd come
back, watch their friends get hooked up, and part ways. It
was a good blueprint, he decided, one that could easily be
adjusted to whim and circumstance.

With the paper tucked under his arm, he started back the
way he came.

The woman stood just over the other side of the little
wooden bridge that spanned the creek. Her hair fell loose and
free around her shoulders, and glowed pale gold in the delicate
sunlight. Her long dress was a quiet blue, high at the neck. His
heart gave one hard thump as he knew her to be Ann Hawkins,
dead for centuries.

But just for an instant, for one quick beat when she
smiled, he saw his mother in her.

"You are the last of the sons of the sons of my sons. You
are what came from me and my love, what came from passion, cold blood, and bitter sacrifice. Faith and hope came
before you, and must remain steadfast. You are the vision.

You and she who came from the dark. Your blood, its blood, our blood. With this, the stone is whole once more. With this, you are blessed."

"Blah, blah, blah," he said, and wondered if the gods struck you dead for mouthing off to a ghost. "Why don't you tell me how to use it, and we'll finish this thing and get on with our lives?"

Ann Hawkins tilted her head, and damned if he didn't see the *mother* look on her face. "Anger is a weapon as well, if used judiciously. He did all that he could, gave you all you would need. You have only to see, to trust what you know, to take what is given. I wept for you, little boy."

"Appreciate it, but tears didn't do me a lot of good."

"Hers will, when they come. You are not alone. You never were. From blood and fire came the light and the dark. With blood and fire, one will prevail. The key to your vision, to the answers, is in your hand. Turn it, and see."

When she faded, he stood where he was. Typical, he thought, typical female. They just couldn't make things simple. Irritated now, he crossed the bridge and climbed the slope of the lane to the house.

The lovebirds were in the kitchen, so he'd lost his chance for that quiet and solitary cup of coffee. They were wrapped around each other, naturally, lip-locked in front of the damn coffeepot.

"Break it up." Gage bumped Fox with his shoulder to nudge him clear of the pot.

"Hasn't had his first cup yet." Fox gave Layla a last squeeze before picking up the Coke he'd already opened. "He's bitchy until."

"Do you want me to fix you some breakfast?" Layla offered. "We've got time before we have to leave for the office."

"Aren't you Mary Sunshine?" On this grouchy pronouncement, Gage pulled a box of cereal out of the cupboard, then dug in for a handful. "I'm good." Then he narrowed his eyes as Fox opened the paper. "I walked down for that, I get it first."

"I'm just checking the box scores, Mr. Happy. Any Pop-Tarts around here?"

"God, you're pathetic."

"Man, you're eating Froot Loops out of the box. Pot, kettle."

With a frown, Gage glanced down. So he was. And since the coffee kicked the worst of his crabbiness down, he looked back at Layla with an easy smile. "Hey, good morning, Layla. Did you say something about fixing breakfast?"

She laughed. "Good morning, Gage. I believe I did mention that, in a weak moment. But since I am feeling pretty sunny, I'll follow through."

"Great. Thanks. While you are, I'll tell you guys about the visitor I had on my morning stroll."

Layla froze with her hand on the handle of the refrigerator. "It came back?"

"Not it. She. Though technically maybe a ghost is an it. I haven't given it much thought."

"Ann Hawkins." Fox tossed the paper aside. "What's the word?"

Topping off his coffee, Gage told them.

"Everyone's seen her now, one way or the other, but Cybil." Layla set a platter of French toast on the breakfast bar.

"Yeah, I bet that'll tick her off. Cybil, that is," Gage added as he forked up two slices.

"Blood and fire. There's sure been a lot of that, in reality and in dreams. And that's what put the bloodstone back together. That was Cybil's brainstorm," Fox remembered. "Maybe she'll have one about this."

"I'll fill her in when she gets here later today."

"Sooner's better." With a generous hand, Fox poured syrup on his stack of French toast. "Layla and I will swing by the house before we go to the office."

"She's just going to want me to go through it all again when she gets here."

"Still." Fox sampled a bite, grinned at Layla. "This is great."

"Well, it's not Pop-Tarts."

"Better. Are you sure you don't want me to go into the bank with you this afternoon? Being you, your paperwork's in order, but—"

"I'm fine. You've got a busy schedule today. Plus, with my two investors, I'm not applying for a big, fat loan. More of a slim, efficient one."

So they segued, Gage thought, from ghosts to interest rates. He tuned them out, started to scan the headlines in the paper he'd stolen back from Fox. Then caught a stray comment.

"Cybil and Quinn are investing in your shop?"

"Yeah." Layla's smile radiated like sunlight. "It's great. I hope it's great for them—I'm going to make it great for them. It's just wonderful, and staggering, that they'd have that kind of faith in me. You know what that's like. You and Fox and Cal have always had that."

He supposed he did, just as he supposed this was one more tangible aspect of how the six of them were entwined. Ann had said he wasn't alone. None of them were, he realized. Maybe it was that, just that, that would weigh the odds in their favor.

When he had the house to himself, he spent an hour answering and composing e-mails. He had a contact in Europe, a Professor Linz, whose expertise was demonology and lore. He was full of theories and a lot of verbose rhetoric, but he had come through with what Gage considered salient information.

And the more data you tossed into the hat, the better the chance the winning ticket was in there. It wouldn't hurt to get Linz's take on Cybil's newest hypothesis. Was the bloodstone—*their* bloodstone—a fragment of some larger whole, some mythical, magickal power source?

Even as he wrote the post, he shook his head. If anyone outside of his tight circle of friends knew he spent a great deal of his time searching out information on demons, they'd laugh their asses off. Then again, those outside that circle who knew him, only saw what he let them see. Not one of them reached the level he'd call friend.

Acquaintances, players, bedmates. Sometimes they won his money, sometimes he won theirs. Maybe he'd buy them a drink, or they'd stand him a round or two. And the women—away from the tables—they'd give each other a few hours, maybe a few days if it suited both of them.

Easy come, easy go.

And why did that suddenly seem more pathetic than a grown man wanting a Pop-Tart for breakfast?

Annoyed with himself, he combed his hands through his hair, tipped back in the chair. He did as he pleased, and lived as he wanted. Even coming here, facing this, was a choice he'd made. If he didn't make it past the first week of July, that would be too damn bad. But he couldn't complain. He'd had thirty-one years, and he'd seen the world on his own terms. From time to time, he'd lived pretty damn high. He'd rather live, and work his way back up to that high a few more times. A few more rolls of the dice, a few more hands dealt. But if not, he'd take his losses.

He'd already accomplished the most important goal of his life. He'd gotten out of the Hollow. And for fifteen years and counting, when someone raised a fist to him, he hit back, harder.

The old man had been drunk that night, Gage remembered. Filthy drunk after falling face-first off the shaky wagon he'd managed to ride for a handful of months. The old man was always worse when he fell off than when he waved that wagon on and kept stumbling down the road.

Summer, Gage thought. The kind of August night where even the air sweated. The place was clean, because the old man had been since April. But being up on the third floor of the bowling center meant that sweaty air just rose and rose until it squatted there, laughing at the constant whirl of the window AC. Even after midnight, the whole place felt wet, so the minute he stepped in, he wished he'd crashed at Cal's or Fox's.

But he'd had a sort of a date, the sort where a guy had to peel off from his pals if he wanted any kind of a chance to score.

He figured his father was in bed, sleeping or trying to, so he toed off his shoes before heading into the kitchen. There was a pitcher half full of iced tea, the instant crap that always tasted too sweet or too bitter no matter how you doctored it up. But he drank down two glasses before looking for something to kill the aftertaste.

He wished he had pizza. The alley and the grill were closed, so no chance there. He found a half a meatball sub, surely several days old. But small matters such as these didn't concern teenage boys.

He ate it cold, standing over the sink.

He cleaned up after himself. He remembered too clearly what the apartment smelled like when his father was drinking heavily. Bad food, old garbage, sweat, stale whiskey and smoke. It was nice that, despite the heat, the place smelled normal. Not as good as Cal's house or Fox's. There were always candles or flowers or those girly dishes of petals and scent there. And the female aroma he guessed was just skin touched with lotions and sprayed with perfume.

This place was a dump compared, not the kind of place he'd want to bring a date, he thought with a glance around. But it was good enough, for now. The furniture was old and tired, and the walls could use some new paint. Maybe when it cooled off in the fall, he and the old man could slap some on.

Maybe they could swing a new TV, one that had been manufactured in the last decade. Things were pretty solid right now with them both working full-time for the summer. He was squirreling away some of his take for a new headset, but he could kick in half. He had a couple more weeks before school started up, a couple more paychecks. A new TV would be good.

He put his glass away, closed the cupboard. He heard his father's step on the stairs. And he knew.

The optimism drained out of him like water. What was left in him hardened like stone. Stupid, he thought, stupid of him to let himself believe the old man would stay sober. Stupid to believe there'd ever be anything decent in this rat trap of an apartment.

He started to cross to his room, go inside, shut the door. Then he thought the hell with it. He'd see what the drunken son of a bitch had to say for himself.

So he stood, hip-shot, thumbs in the front pockets of his jeans, a defiant red flag eager to wave at the bull. His father pushed open the door.

Weaving, Bill Turner gripped the jamb. His face was red from the climb, from the heat, from the liquor. Even across the room, Gage could smell the whiskey sweat seeping out of his pores. His T-shirt was stained with it under the arms, down the front in a sodden vee. The look in his eyes when they met Gage's was blurry and mean.

" 'Fuck you looking at?"

"A drunk."

"Had a couple beers with some friends, don't make me a drunk."

"I guess I was wrong. I'm looking at a drunken liar."

The meanness intensified. It was like watching a snake coil. "You watch your fucking mouth, boy."

"I should've known you couldn't do it." But he *had* done it, for nearly five months. He'd stayed sober through Gage's birthday, and that, Gage knew, had been when he'd started to believe. For the first time since his father had stumbled down the drunken path, he'd stayed on that wagon over Gage's birthday.

This disappointment, this betrayal was a sharper slash than any lash of the belt had ever been. This killed every small drop of his hope.

"None of your goddamn business," Bill shot back. "This is *my* house. You don't tell me what's what under my own roof."

"This is Jim Hawkins's roof, and I pay rent on it just like you. You drink your paycheck again?"

"I don't answer to you. Shut your mouth, or—"

"What?" Gage challenged. "You're so drunk you can barely stand. What the hell are you going to do? And what the hell do I care," he finished in disgust. Turning, he started toward his room. "I wish you'd drink yourself dead and finish the job."

He was drunk, but he was fast. Bill lunged across the room, slammed Gage back against the wall. "You're no good, never been any damn good. Never should've been born."

"That makes two of us. Now take your hands off me."

Two quick slaps, front and back, set Gage's ears ringing, split his bottom lip. "Time you learned some goddamn *respect*."

Gage remembered the first punch, remembered plowing his fist into his father's face, and the shock that fired in his father's eyes. Something crashed—the old pole lamp—and someone cursed viciously over and over. Had that been him?

The next clear memory was standing over his father as the old man sprawled on the floor, his face bruised and bleeding. His own fists had screamed from the pounding, and the healing of his swollen, bloody knuckles. His breath wheezed in and out of his lungs, and sweat soaked him like water.

How long had he beaten on the old man with his fists? It was a hot red haze. But it cleared now, and behind it was ice cold.

"If you ever touch me again, if you ever lay a fucking hand on me again in your life, I'll kill you." He crouched down to make sure the old man heard him. "I swear an oath on it. In three years, I'm gone. I don't care if you drink yourself to death in the meantime. I'm past caring. I've got to live here at least most of the time the next three years. I'll give my share of the rent straight to Mr. Hawkins. You don't get a dime. I'll buy my own food, my own clothes. I don't want anything from you. But however drunk you are, you'd better be able to think this one thought. Hit me again, you motherfucker, you're a dead man."

He rose, walked into his room, shut the door. He'd buy a lock for it the next day, he thought. Keep the bastard out.

He could go. Exhausted, he sat on the side of the bed and dropped his head in his hands. He could pack up what was his and if he showed up on Cal's doorstep or at Fox's farm, they'd take him in.

That's the kind of people they were.

But he needed to stick this out, needed to show the old man and, more, show himself, that he could stick it out. Three years till his eighteenth birthday, he thought, then he'd be free.

Not quite accurate, Gage thought now. He'd stuck it out, and the old man had never raised a hand to him again. And he'd taken off when his three years were up. But freedom? That was another story.

You carried the past with you, he thought, dragging it behind you on a thick, unbreakable chain no matter how far you looked ahead. You could ignore it for good long stretches of time, but you couldn't escape it. He could drag that chain ten thousand miles, but the Hollow, the people he loved in it, and his goddamn destiny just kept pulling him back.

He pushed away from the computer, went down to get himself more coffee. Sitting at the counter, he dealt out a hand of solitaire. It calmed him, the feel of the cards, the sound of them, their colors and shapes. When he heard the knock on the door, he glanced at his watch. It appeared Cybil was early. He left the cards where they were, grateful the simple game had kept his mind off the past, and off the woman as well.

When he pulled open the door, it was Joanne Barry on the front deck. "Well, hey."

She only looked at him for a moment. Her dark hair was braided back, as she often wore it. Her eyes were clear in her pretty face, her body slim in jeans and a cotton shirt. Then she touched his face, laid her lips on his forehead, his cheeks, his lips in her traditional greeting when there was love.

"Thank you for the orchid."

"You're welcome. Sorry I missed you when I dropped it off. Do you want to come in? Do you have time?"

"Yes, I'd like to come in, for a few minutes."

"Probably something to drink back here." He led the way back toward the kitchen.

"Cal's got a nice place here. It's always a surprise."

"Really?"

"That he—all of you—are grown men. That Cal's a grown man with this very nice home of his own, with its beautiful gardens. Sometimes still, just every so often, I wake up in the morning and think: I've got to get those kids up and off to school. Then I remember, the kids are grown and gone. It's both a relief and a punch in the heart. I miss my little guys."

"You'll never be rid of us." Knowing Jo, he skipped right over all the sodas, whittled her choices down to juice or bottled water. "I can offer you water or what I think might be grapefruit juice."

"I'm fine, Gage. Don't bother."

"Could make some tea—or you could. I'd probably—" He broke off when he turned and saw a tear sliding down her cheek. "What is it? What's wrong?"

"The note you left me, with the plant."

"I'd hoped to be able to talk to you. I stopped by Cal's mom's, but—"

"I know. Frannie told me. You wrote: 'Because you were always there for me. Because I know you always will be.'"

"You were. I do."

With a sigh, she put her arms around him, laid her head on his shoulder. "All of your life, as a parent, you wonder and you worry. Did I do that right? Should I have done that, said this? Then, suddenly, in a fingersnap it seems, your children are grown. And still you wonder and you worry. Could I have done this, did I remember to say that? If you're very lucky, one day one of your children . . ." She leaned back to look into his eyes. "Because you're mine and Frannie's, too. One of your children writes you a note that arrows straight into your heart. All that worry goes away." She gave him a watery smile. "For a moment anyway. Thank you for the moment, baby."

"I wouldn't have gotten through without you and Frannie."

"I think you're wrong about that. But we damn sure helped." She laughed now, gave him a hard squeeze. "I have to go. Come and see me soon."

"I will. I'll walk you out."

"Don't be silly. I know the way." She started out, turned. "I pray for you. Being me, I cover my bases. God, the Goddess, Buddha, Allah, and so on. I pretty much tap on them all. I just want you to know that a day doesn't go by that I don't have all of you in my prayers. I'm nagging the hell out of every higher power there is. You're going to come through this, all of you. I'm not taking no for an answer."

Six

❧

HE SHOULD HAVE KNOWN SHE'D BE EXACTLY ON time. Not late, not early, but on the button. Cybil had that preciseness about her. She wore a shirt the color of ripe, juicy peaches with bark brown pants that cropped off a couple inches above her ankles, and sandals with a couple of thin straps that showed off those intriguing narrow feet with their toes painted to match the shirt. She'd scooped that mass of curling hair back at the temples so he could see the trio of tiny hoops on her left ear, the duet of them on her right.

She carried a brown handbag the size of a bull terrier.

"I heard you had a visitor. I'll need you to tell me about it so we're sure nothing gets lost in translation."

And right to business, he thought. "Fine." He started back toward the kitchen. If he had to run through it again, he wanted his coffee.

"Mind if I get something cold?"

"Help yourself."

She did. He watched as she pulled out the grapefruit juice

and the diet ginger ale. "I'm a little put out she hasn't talked to me yet," Cybil said as she filled a glass with ice then proceeded to mix the two liquids in the glass. "But I'm trying to be big about it." She glanced over, cocked an eyebrow as she lifted the glass. "Do you want some?"

"Absolutely not."

"If I drank coffee all day the way you do, I'd be doing cartwheels off the ceiling." She glanced at the cards spread out on the counter. "I interrupted your game."

"Just passing the time."

"Hmm." She studied his card layout. "It's often called *Réussite*—or Success—in France, where some historians believe it originated. In Britain, it's Patience, which I suppose you have to have to play it. The most interesting theory I've come across is that in its early origins the outcome was a form of fortune-telling. Mind?" she asked, tapping the deck, and he shrugged his go-ahead.

She turned up the card, continued the play. "Computer play's given the game a major boost in the last couple decades. Do you play online?"

"Rarely."

"Online poker?"

"Never. I like to be in the same room as my opponents. Winning's no fun if it's anonymous."

"I tried it once. I like to try most everything once."

His mind took a sidetrip into the possibilities of "most everything." "How'd you do?"

"Not bad. But, like you, I found it lacked the zip of the real thing. Well, where should we do this?" She set her drink down to pull a notebook from the massive area of her purse. "We can start with you giving me the details of this morning's visitation, then—"

"I had a dream about you."

Her head angled slightly. "Oh?"

"Given the X rating, you can have the option of sharing it with the others, if you think it applies, or keeping it to yourself."

"I'd have to hear it first." Her lips curved. "In minute detail."

"You came to my bedroom upstairs. Naked."

She flipped open the notebook, began to write. "That was brazen of me."

"There was some moonlight; it gave the room a blue wash. Very sexy, very black-and-white movie. It didn't feel like the first time; there was a sense of familiarity when I touched you. The kind that said, maybe the moves would be a bit different, maybe we'd change up the rhythm, but we'd danced before."

"Did we speak?"

"Not then." There was interest in her eyes, he noted, and amusement—both on the cool side. And no pretense of embarrassment. "I knew how you'd taste, knew the sounds you'd make when I put my hands on you. I knew where you like to be touched, and how. When I was inside you, when we were . . . locked, taking each other, the room began to bleed, and burn." The interest sharpened; the amusement died. "It rolled over us, that fire, that blood. Then you spoke. Right as it took us, right as you came, you said *bestia*."

"Sex and death. It sounds more like an erotic or stress dream than foresight."

"Probably. But I thought I should pass it on." He tapped a finger on her book. "For your notes."

"It would be hard not to have sex and death on the brain, considering. But—"

"Do you have a tattoo?" He watched her eyes narrow in consideration, and knew. "About this big," he continued, holding his thumb and forefinger a couple inches apart. "At the small of your back. It looks like a three with a small wavy line coming out of the bottom curve, then a separate symbol above—a curved line with a dot in the center."

"That would be Sanskrit for the Hindu mantra of *ohm*. The four parts stand for the four stages of concentration, which are awake, asleep, dreaming, and the transcendental state."

"And here I thought it was just sexy."

"It is." Turning, Cybil lifted the back of her shirt a few inches to reveal the symbols at the small of her back. "But it also has meaning. And since you obviously saw it, we'll have to consider your dream had some meaning."

She let her shirt drop, turned back. "We both know that what we see is potential, not absolute. And that often what we see is crowded with symbolism. So, going by your dream, we have the potential to become lovers."

"Didn't need to dream to get that one."

"And as lovers we have the potential to pay a high price for the enjoyment." She kept her gaze steady on his as she spoke. "We could further speculate that while you want me on a physical level, on the emotional and mental levels, you don't. The idea of us pairing off strikes too close to following suit behind our friends, and you don't care to fall in line. Can't blame you, as I don't either. It's also irritating—an irritation I share—to consider this pairing up could be part of a larger plan put into place hundreds of years ago. How am I doing so far?"

"You're hitting the highlights."

"Then to finish up, I'd include the fact that your pessimistic nature—which I don't share—would sway your subconscious, or your gift, over to the get in, get off, get dead arena."

He let out a short laugh. "Okay."

"For me, I don't make decisions on lovers based on the possibility that orgasm might include being consumed by evil forces. It just takes all the romance out of it."

"You looking for romance, Cybil?"

"Everyone is. It's the personal definitions thereof that vary. Why don't we take this outside, on the deck? I like spring, and it doesn't last long. We might as well grab some of it while it's around."

"All right." Taking his coffee, he opened the door to the back deck. "Are you afraid?" he asked as she moved by him.

"Every day since I've come here. Aren't you?"

He left the door open behind them. "I used to be. I used to

spend a lot of my life being afraid and pretending not to be. Then, along the way, I got to the fuck-it stage. Just fuck it. Now, mostly, the whole business just annoys me. It doesn't annoy you."

"Fascinates." She took sunglasses out of her purse, slid them on. "I think it's good all of us don't have the same re-action. This way we cover more ground." She sat at one of the tables on Cal's deck, facing his back gardens, and the green woods that stood along their edges. "Tell me about Ann Hawkins."

So he did, and she took her notes. "Three," she began. "Three boys, descended from her and Dent. Faith, that's Cal's area. Believing not only in himself, in you, in the town, but having the faith to accept what he can't literally see. The past, what happened before him. Hope falls to Fox, and his opti-mism that he can and will make a difference. His understand-ing and trust in what is. Which leaves the vision to you—what can be—for better or worse. A second three—Q, Layla, me—falls in with that, forming subsets. Cal and Q, Fox and Layla, and now you and me. Three into one—three men, three women, three subsets, into one unit. We've accomplished that in a very real sense. Just as we accomplished re-forming the three pieces of the bloodstone into one whole."

"Still doesn't tell us how to use it."

"But she made it clear, at least to me it's clear, that we have what we need. There's no other tangible element. That's something. Tears." Frowning, Cybil drummed her fin-gers on her notebook. "She wept for you, and if I'm inter-preting correctly, she's saying I will. I'm happy to shed a few if it sends the Big Evil Bastard back to hell. Tears," she repeated, and closed her eyes. "They're often an ingredient used in magickal arts. I think they're usually female tears. You'll have your tears of a virgin, of a pregnant woman, of a mother, of an ancient, blah blah blah, depending. I don't know that much about it."

"There's something you don't know that much about?"

She shot him an answering smirk, tipped down her sun-glasses to peer at him over them. "There are worlds I don't know much about, but almost nothing I can't find out everything about. We need to see. She appears to be saying that while the other subsets may certainly be called on to do more in their specific areas, they've done the bulk of their job there. It's time to look ahead, and that's up to you and me, partner."

"I can't whistle it up like a German shepherd."

"Of course you can. It takes practice, concentration, and attention. All of which you're capable of or you wouldn't be able to make a living playing cards. What may be more problematic is both of us being capable of calling it up together, and narrowing in on one potential future event."

She dug into her voluminous handbag again, and this time pulled out a deck of Tarot cards.

"Are you kidding me?"

"Tools," she said, and began to shuffle the oversized cards with some skill. "I also have runes, several types of crystal balls, a scrying mirror. At one point in my life I studied witchcraft very seriously, looking for answers as to why I could foretell. But like any religion or organization there are a lot of rules. The rules began to crowd me, so after a while, I simply accepted I had this gift, and my studies spread out in wider circles."

"When did you first know?"

"That I could foretell? I'm not altogether sure. It wasn't like you, in a blinding flash. I've always had vivid dreams. I used to tell my parents about them, when I was a little girl. Or cry for them in the middle of the night if the dreams scared me. They often did. Or there would be what I'd have called déjà vu if I'd known the term as a child. My paternal grandmother, who had Romany blood, told me I had the sight. I did my best to learn how to refine it, control it. There were still dreams, some good, some bad. I often dreamt of fire. Of walking through it, of dying in it, of causing it."

She did a quick spread. The colorful illustrations on the cards drew him closer to the table. "I think I dreamed of you," she said, "long before I met you."

"Think?"

"I never saw your face. Or if I did, I couldn't keep it in my head when I woke. But in the dreams, or the visions, I knew someone was waiting for me. A lover, or so it seemed. I had my first orgasm at about fourteen during one of those dreams. I'd wake from those dreams, aroused or satisfied. Or quaking with terror. Because sometimes it wasn't a lover—or not a human one—waiting for me. I never saw its face either, not even when it burned me alive." She looked up at him now. "So I learned all I could, and I learned how to keep my mind and body centered with yoga, meditation, herbs, trances—any and everything to stave off the beast in the dreams. It works most of the time. Or did."

"Harder to keep that center here in the Hollow?"

"Yes."

He sat, waved a finger at the spread. "So, what does the future hold?"

"This? Just a little personal Q and A. As to the rest . . ." She scooped the cards together, shuffled again. "Let's find out."

She set them down, said, "Cut," and when he did she fanned the deck facedown on the table. "Let's try a simple pick-a-card. You first."

Willing to play, he slid one out of the fan, and at her nod, turned it over. On the card, the couple was twined together, with her dark hair wound around their naked bodies.

"The Lovers," Cybil announced. "Shows where your mind's lodged."

"They're your cards, sugar."

"Mmm-hmm." She chose one for herself. "The Wheel of Fortune—more in your line, if we're speaking literally. Symbolizing change, chance, for good or for ill. Take another."

He turned over the Magician.

"Major Arcana, three for three." The faintest of frowns marred her brows. "It's actually one of my favorite cards, not only the art, but it stands for imagination, creativity, magic, of course. And in this case, we could say it stands for Giles Dent, your ancestor." She drew out another card, slowly turned it over. "And mine. The Devil. Greed, destruction, obsession, tyranny. Go again."

He drew the High Priestess. And without waiting, Cybil chose the Hanged Man.

"Our maternal ancestors, despite the male figure in mine. Understanding and wisdom in yours, martyrdom in mine. And still all Major Arcanas, all absolutely apt. Again."

He slid out and turned the Tower, and she Death.

"Change, potential disaster, but with the other cards you've chosen, the possibility of change for the positive, the potential to rebuild. Mine, obviously an end, and not so sunny when viewed with my other picks. Though it rarely stands for literal death, it does symbolize an absolute end."

She lifted her glass. "I need a refill."

He rose before she did, took the glass. "I'll get it. I saw how you made it."

It would give her time to settle down, Gage thought as he stepped inside. However fascinating she found the process, the results of this particular experiment had shaken her. He knew something about Tarot himself—there was no area of the occult he hadn't poked into for answers over the years. And if he'd been betting on the pulls, he wouldn't have put money on two people drawing eight Major Arcana in a row out of a deck.

He fixed her drink, switched for his next round from coffee to water. When he went outside again, she stood at the rail looking out toward the woods.

"I reshuffled, recut. And I drew eight cards at random. Only two were Major Arcana, but oddly enough they were the Devil and Death again." When she turned he noted she'd settled herself. "Interesting, isn't it? You and I together pull the most powerful and pointed cards. Because we were meant to, or because we, without direct purpose, foresaw where those cards were in the fan, and instinctively chose them."

"Why don't we try another tool? Have you got your crystal ball in that duffel bag of yours?"

"No, and it happens to be Prada. Are you willing to try to look forward, to link our ability and see what happens?"

"What did you have in mind?"

"Accepting and exploiting, hopefully, the connection. I'm better able to focus during or after meditation, but—"

"I know how to meditate."

"With all that caffeine in your system?"

He only tipped back his water bottle. "We'd better take it back inside."

"Actually, I was thinking of out here, on the grass. The gardens, the woods, the air." She took off her sunglasses, set them down on the rail, then wandered down the steps. "What do you do to relax, body and mind?"

"I play cards. I have sex. We could play strip poker, and after you lose I'll make sure we're both relaxed."

"Interesting, but I was thinking more of yoga." She slid out of her shoes, and into Prayer Position. With fluid grace she moved into a basic Sun Sign.

"I'm not doing that," Gage said as he followed her into the yard. "But I'll watch you."

"It'll just take me a minute. And on your suggestion? We made a deal. We weren't going to have sex."

"The deal was I wouldn't try to seduce you, not that we wouldn't have sex."

"Semantics."

"Specifics."

From the Down Dog position, she turned her head to look up at him. "I suppose you're right. In any case." She finished, then lowered to the grass to sit in the Lotus position.

"I'm not doing that either." But he sat across from her.

Where normally she would have rested the back of her hands on her knees, she reached out to take his. "Can you clear your mind like this?"

"I can if you can."

She smiled. "All right. Do whatever you do that works for you—other than cards and sex."

He didn't have any objections to sitting on the grass on a May afternoon with a beautiful woman. Not that he expected anything to happen. He expected her to close her eyes and float off on whatever mantra (the *ohm* symbol at the base of her spine, that intriguing symbol on flesh the color of gold dust, right at the subtle dip from smooth back to firm ass).

Don't think about it, he warned himself. That wasn't the way to relax.

In any case, she didn't close her eyes, so he stared straight into them. A man couldn't ask for a more appealing focal point than that rich velvet brown. He timed his breathing to hers—or she to his, he wasn't sure. But in a matter of seconds they were in tune, perfectly in rhythm.

Her eyes were all he could see. Drowning pools. Her fingertips were so light on his, yet he felt weightless, as if he'd float up and away without that tenuous contact.

And he felt, for a moment, absolutely *right*, and completely connected to her.

It slammed and screamed through him, so fast, image after image ramming into the next. Fox lying by the side of the road in the rain. Cal sprawled, his shirt blood-soaked, on the floor of his office. Quinn screaming in terror, beating her hands on a locked door, and the knife that sliced down to cut her throat. Layla, bound and gagged, eyes wild with fear as flames snaked across the floor toward her.

He saw himself, by the Pagan Stone, with Cybil lying lifeless on the altar flames. And heard himself scream with rage an instant before it leaped out of the woods and took him to the dark.

Then it all jumbled together, image and sound, blurring, changing. The bloodstone fired in his hand, and voices rose with words he couldn't understand. And he was alone, alone as those flames rose from his hand toward the hot summer moon. Alone as it came out of the shadows, grinning.

He didn't know who broke contact, but the visions snapped off into a red haze of pain. He heard Cybil say his name, once, twice, and the third time with the kind of verbal slap that made him snarl.

"What?"

"Pay attention. Pay attention to the points I'm pressing. I

need you to do this for me when I'm done. Are you hearing me?"

"Yeah, yeah, yeah." He could hear her, nagging at him, while his head fucking exploded. Like drilling holes in the back of his neck with her fingers was going to . . .

The pain eased from hot, stabbing knives to a dull misery. And when she took his hand, pressing, pressing on the web between his thumb and forefinger, the misery downshifted to annoying ache.

He risked opening his eyes and looked straight into hers, and saw that rich velvet was clouded. Saw her face was bone white, while she took slow, even breaths. "Okay, okay."

He pulled his hand from hers, placed his on the back of her neck. "Is this right?"

"A little to the . . . Yes. Yes. Firm, you won't hurt me."

He couldn't do worse than the visions had, so he pressed hard on the knots that pain and tension had built under her skin while she addressed the accupressure points on her own hand.

She'd tended to him first, Gage realized, and wasn't sure whether to be embarrassed or grateful. He watched those clouds of pain dissolve until she closed her eyes on a relief he understood perfectly.

"All right, that's better. That'll do. I just need to . . ." She slid back, lay down on the grass with her face to the sun, eyes closed.

"Good idea." He did exactly the same.

"We didn't control it," she said after a moment. "It just dragged us along like dogs on a leash. I couldn't stop it, or slow it down. I couldn't block the fear out."

"Proving you're a complete failure."

He heard her muffled laugh, knew her lips would be curved. "That makes two of us, tough guy. We'll do better. We have to. What did you see?"

"You first."

"All of us dead or dying. Fox, bleeding on the side of the road, in the dark and the rain. Headlights, I think the headlights from his truck." She went through them all, her voice shaking a little.

"The same for me. Then it changed."

"It was all so fast, then it got faster, more blurred, images overlapping. Ordinary things rolling into nightmares, so fast it was impossible to tell one from the other. Everything so fractured. But in the end, you had the stone."

"Yeah, everyone's dead, and I've got the stone. And the bastard killed me while it was burning in my hand."

"Did it, or was that an interpretation? What I know is that the stone was there, right through the end, that you had it, and that it held power." She rolled to her side to face him. "And I know that what we saw were possibilities. Foresight is forearmed. So we tell the others the possibilities, and we all strap it on."

"Strap what on?"

"Whatever it takes. What?" she demanded when he pressed his fingers to his eyes and shook his head.

"I just got a picture of you strapping that little pearl-handled .22 to your thigh. I must be feeling better."

"Hmm. What was I wearing?"

He dropped his hands and grinned at her. "We both must be feeling better. Why don't we . . ." This time he rolled on top of her.

"Hold on there, cowboy. A deal's a deal."

"No seduction intended."

She gave him a casual smile. "None taken."

"You're a hard case, Cybil." Testing, he took her hands, then drew her arms up over her head. Positive energy—she was big on positive energy. And Christ knew he could use some now.

She didn't resist, only continued to watch him with that half smile on her face.

"I was thinking the two of us deserve a little payoff," he told her.

"Which would be rolling around naked in Cal's backyard?"

"You read my mind."

"Not gonna happen."

"Okay. Just say when."

He took her mouth, and there was nothing testing or teasing about it. He went for the heat, and what he found spiked like a fever. Her fingers curled on his and held as her lips parted. It was more demand than invitation, more challenge than surrender. Under him, her body seemed to ripple— rising waves of energy.

Very positive.

No seduction, she thought, no persuasion, and her body responded, rejoiced, in the possession. The honesty of sheer and undisguised lust meant equal terms. Needs trapped inside her for months raced free. She'd take more, just a little more, before herding them back into the pen.

Hooking a leg around him, she arched her hips, deliberately pressing center to center before she pushed to reverse their positions. Now her mouth took command, took its fill as his hands fisted in her hair. When she heard the growl, she laughed against his lips. But when it sounded again, she felt ice slide down her spine.

Slowly, she drew her lips a breath from his. "Did you hear that?"

"Yeah."

She lifted her head another inch, and that ice floe spread. "We've got an audience."

The dog was massive, its brown fur matted and stained. Frothy drool dripped from its jowls as it lurched drunkenly out of the woods.

"That isn't Twisse," Cybil whispered.

"No."

"Meaning it's real."

"Real, and rabid. How fast can you run?"

"As fast as I need to."

"Get into the house. My gun's upstairs, on the table beside the bed. Get it, get back, and shoot the damn dog. I'll keep it off you."

Cybil ignored the rise of gorge at the thought of killing a dog. "My .22's in my bag on the deck. We can both make it."

"Go, get *inside*. Don't stop."

He dragged her up, gave her one hard shove toward the house. And the dog gathered itself, and charged.

He didn't run with her, and she didn't allow herself to think, not even when she heard the horrible sounds behind her. With her heart slamming, she flew onto the deck, shoved her hand into her bag and closed it around the butt of her revolver.

The scream she loosed when she turned was as much terror as an attempt to draw the dog's attention to her. But it only continued to roll, snap, to clamp its teeth into Gage as they fought a vicious war on Cal's pretty green grass.

She raced back, releasing the safety as she ran.

"Shoot it! Shoot the fucker!"

"I can't get a clear shot!"

His arms, his hands, were torn and bleeding. "Goddamn it, shoot!" As he shouted, he wrenched the dog's head up, looked straight into those madly snapping jaws. The dog's body jerked, once, twice, as bullets plowed into its flank, and still it tried to go for the throat. On the next shot it let out a high shriek of pain, and those mad eyes went glassy. Panting, Gage shoved the weight aside, crawled over the blood-slicked grass.

Through the haze of pain he heard weeping. Through the haze of pain he saw Cybil step up to the dying dog and fire the coup de grace into its head.

"It wasn't dead. It was suffering. Let me get you inside. God, you're torn up."

"I'll heal." But he put his arm around her shoulders, let her take his weight. He made it as far as the steps before his legs gave out. "Give me a minute. I need a minute."

She left him slumped on the steps to dash inside. Minutes later, she rushed out again with a fresh bottle of water, a basin filled with more, and several cloths. "Should I call Cal and Fox? When Fox was hurt it helped him to have you both."

"No. Not that bad."

"Let me see. I need to see." Quickly, efficiently, she drew off what was left of his shirt. Her breath might have shuddered at the tears and rips in his flesh, but she washed the wounds with a steady hand. "The shoulder's bad."

"Unnecessary information seeing as it's my shoulder." He hissed as she pressed the cool, wet cloth to the wound. "Anyway, nice shooting, Tex."

She used the bottled water to dampen a fresh cloth, then wiped it gently over his face. "I know it hurts. I know the healing hurts almost as much as the need for it."

"It's no spring picnic. Do me a favor? Get me a whiskey?"

"All right."

Inside, she braced her hands on the counter a moment. She wanted to be sick, badly wanted to be sick. But she pushed down the need, shuddered her way past it. And pulling down the bottle of Jameson, poured him a generous three fingers.

When she came back out with it, she saw that most of his surface injuries had healed, and the more serious ones had begun to close. He downed two-thirds of the whiskey she handed him in one pull, then, studying her face, held out the glass. "Down the rest, sweetheart. You look like you could use it."

She nodded, downed it. Then she did what she'd avoided doing. She turned and looked at what lay on the blood-stained grass. "I've never killed anything before. Clay pigeons, targets, shooting gallery bears. But I never put bullets into a living thing."

"If you hadn't, I might be dead. That dog weighs a good eighty pounds, mostly muscle, and it was shithouse crazy."

"It has a collar, tags." Steeling herself, she crossed the lawn, crouched. "An up-to-date rabies tag. It wasn't rabid, Gage, not in the usual sense. But I guess we both knew that."

She straightened when Gage limped over to join her. "What do we do now?" she asked him.

"We bury it."

"But . . . Gage, this was someone's dog. This wasn't a stray, he belonged to someone. They must be looking for him."

"Getting him back dead isn't going to help. Trying to explain why you put four bullets in a household pet—one who won't show rabies on any test—isn't going to help." Gage gripped her shoulders, fingers digging in for emphasis. "This is a goddamn war, do you understand? One we've been fighting a long time. More than dogs die, Cybil, so you're going to have to man up. Telling some kid that Fido won't be home for dinner because a demon infected him isn't on the boards. We bury it, we move on."

"It must help not to have any feelings, any guilt or remorse."

"That's right, it does. Go home. We're done for the day."

"Where are you going?" she demanded when he turned away.

"To get a damn shovel."

Gritting her teeth, she marched to the garden shed ahead of him, wrenched open the door.

"I said go home."

"I say go to hell; we'll see who gets where first. I put that dog down, didn't I? So I'll help bury him." She wrenched down a shovel, all but threw it at Gage before grabbing another. "And here's something else, you son of a bitch, we're *not* done for the day. What happened here needs to be shared with the others. Whether you like it or not you're part of a team. This whole ugly business has to be reported, documented, charted. Burying it isn't enough. It's not enough. It's not."

She pressed the back of her hand to her mouth, choked back a sob as the cracks in her composure widened. When she would have pushed by him, Gage grabbed her, pulled her against him.

"Get away from me."

"Shut up. Just shut up." He held firm, ignoring her struggles, and when she gave up, gave in and clung, he held her

THE PAGAN STONE
91

still. "You did what you had to do," he murmured. "You did fine. You held up. Go on inside, let me finish this. You can call the others."

She leaned against him another moment. "We'll finish it. We'll bury him together. Then we'll go call the others."

Seven

~⌇~

SHE'D ASKED QUINN TO BRING HER A CHANGE OF clothes. After the horrible business of burying the dog, Cybil was filthy, sweaty, and stained. Rather than think about what stained her pants and shirt, she simply shoved them into a plastic bag, and once she'd showered, intended to shove *that* into Cal's trash.

She'd gone to pieces, she admitted as she stepped under the spray. She'd done what needed to be done, true enough, but then her shaky wall of control had broken down into emotional rubble.

So much for cool, clearheaded Cybil Kinski.

Now, if she couldn't manage cool, she could at least make a stab at the clearheaded.

Was it worse or better that she'd melted down in front of Gage? Two ways of thinking, she supposed. Worse—much— for her pride, but for the overall picture, it was best they knew what made each other tick. In order to handle their end of this successfully, knowing each other's strengths, weaknesses, and breaking points was essential.

It was a pisser she'd broken first, but she'd accept that. Eventually.

It was a tough swallow, she supposed, when she'd always perceived herself as the strong one. As the one who made the choices—the tough choices when necessary—and followed them through. Other people fell apart—her mother, her sister—but she held it together. She'd made damn sure of it.

Second swallow, she admitted, was accepting that Gage was right. A dead dog wasn't going to be the worst of it. If she couldn't handle that, she'd be useless to the others. So she'd handle it.

Bury it, as he said, and move on.

When the door opened, she felt a flash of temper along with the chilly air. "Just turn around, hotshot, and go back the way you came."

"It's Q. You okay?"

The sound of her friend's voice had tears flooding her throat again. Ruthlessly, she swallowed them down. "Better. You were quick."

"We headed right over. Cal and I. Fox and Layla will be along as soon as they can. What can I do?"

Cybil turned off the spray. "Hand me a towel." She shoved back the shower curtain and took the one Quinn held out.

"God, Cyb, you look exhausted."

"It was my first day on the job as grave digger. I'm in damn good tune, but Jesus, Q, that's awful work. On every possible level."

As Cybil wrapped the first towel around herself, Quinn handed her a second for her hair. "Thank God you weren't hurt. You saved Gage's life."

"I'd say it was a mutual lifesaving affair." She glanced in the steamy mirror. Both emotional and physical weariness crumbled under the sheer weight of vanity. Who *was* that pale, drawn woman with the dull, bruised-looking eyes? "Oh my God. Please tell me you had the good sense to bring my makeup along with a change of clothes."

Reassured by the reaction, Quinn leaned a hip against the door. "How long have we been friends?"

"I should never have doubted you."

"Everything's on the bed. I'm going down to pour you a glass of wine while you get changed. Do you want anything else?"

"I think you've just covered the essentials."

Alone, Cybil brushed, dabbed, and blended away the signs of fatigue. She changed into the fresh clothes, did a final check, then gathered up the bag holding her soiled shirt and pants. Downstairs, she shoved the bag into the kitchen garbage, then backtracked to the front deck where Quinn sat with Cal and Gage.

Nobody, she imagined, wanted to sit on the back deck just at the moment.

She picked up her glass of wine, sat, then smiled at Cal. "So. How was your day?"

He answered her smile in kind, even as his patient gray eyes searched her face. "Not as eventful as yours. The Memorial Day committee met this morning to go over the final schedule for the day's events. Wendy Krauss, who'd had a couple of glasses of wine during today's birthday party for a league-mate, dropped a bowling ball on her foot. Broke her big toe, and a couple of teenagers got into a pushy-shovey over a dispute during a game of Foosball in the arcade."

"It's constant drama in Hawkins Hollow."

"Oh yeah."

Sipping her wine, Cybil looked out over the terraced slope, the curvy land, the winding creek. "It's a nice spot to sit after such a busy day. Your gardens are beautiful, Cal."

"They make me happy."

"Secluded spot, yet connected to the whole. You know almost everyone around here."

"Pretty much."

"You know who that dog belonged to."

He hesitated only a moment. "The Mullendores over on Foxwood Road. Their dog went missing day before yesterday." As if he needed the contact, Cal leaned down to stroke a hand on Lump's side as his dog snored at his feet. "Their place is in town. It's a long walk for a dog from there to here, but the way Gage described him, I'd say it was the Mullendores' Roscoe."

"Roscoe." Rest in peace, she thought. "Infecting animals is a usual pattern. And I know we have a list of documented attacks by pets and wildlife in the files. Still, as you say, it's a long way from town to here, on foot—even on four feet. No reports of sightings or attacks by a rabid dog?"

"None."

"So, logically, this today was, again, target specific. The Big Evil Bastard not only infected that poor dog, but directed him here. You're often here alone during the day," she said to Gage. "Twisse couldn't know I'd be here, certainly not before he infected that dog if it's been missing for two days. So you go out, maybe take a nap in that appealing hammock Cal's got between those maple trees, or maybe Cal goes out to cut the grass. Or Quinn takes a walk through the gardens."

"Any one of us could've been alone out there," Cal agreed. "And it might not have been a dog you buried."

"A clever way to do it," Cybil mused, "or try it, with little effort or energy on its part."

"Handy, having a woman with a gun around." Gage took a slow sip of his own wine.

"And one," Cybil added, "who eventually comes around to the simple truth that she didn't kill that dog. Twisse did. Just one more thing to add to the list of payback he's earned." She glanced toward the road. "Here come Fox and Layla."

"And dinner." Quinn touched a hand to Cybil's. "I ordered up a big salad and a couple of pizzas from Gino's, figuring we'd want to stick with the simple and the staple tonight."

"Good thinking. We've got a lot of ground to cover."

THEY DIDN'T, AS THEY OFTEN DID, TALK OF ORDINary and easy things over the meal. The day had been too full, and the mood too urgent.

"You'll need to record this, Q," Cybil began, then turned to Gage. "Gage had a dream."

He held her gaze another few seconds, then relayed the dream of passion and death.

"Symbolism," Quinn decided quickly. "That doesn't go into the prophetic column. Obviously, no matter how good the sex might be, neither of you would just keep at it while the room burst into flame around you."

"Good point," Cybil murmured.

"Maybe it was such hot sex, they self-combusted." Fox shrugged. "Just trying to add a little levity."

"Really little." Layla poked his ribs. "We're all stressed, so violent or, ah, sexual dreams aren't surprising. And if you consider that . . . well, if you factor in that you, Gage, that you might be feeling somewhat—"

"Sexually frustrated," Quinn broke in, "and attracted to Cybil. We're all big boys and girls, and this isn't the time to be delicate. Sorry. But the fact is you and Cyb are healthy adults, not to mention really pretty, and you share an ability during a time of extreme stress. It'd be amazing if there weren't some sexual vibes buzzing about."

"Satisfy an urge, burn in hellfire?" Cal chewed on the thought as he chewed on pizza. "I don't think it's that simple, even symbolically speaking. Connect on intimate levels, there are consequences. And connect to forge another separate link in the chain the six of us have already created, increases the consequences and the power."

"I agree with that, exactly." With a nod of approval, Cybil smiled at Cal. "Too bad Q's in the way, or you and I could have hooked up."

"Staying in the way, sister."

"You're so selfish. Anyway, prophetic dreams, in my experience, are often clouded with symbolism. I think this one could go into that column, or at least be penciled into it."

"We could go upstairs now," Gage suggested. "Test the theory."

"That's a generous offer. Heroic really." Pausing, Cybil sipped her wine. "I'll pass. While I might be willing to sacrifice my body to sex for the good of the cause, I don't think it's necessary at this point."

"Just let me know when we've reached that point."

"You'll be the first. What?" she demanded as Quinn slapped a hand at the air.

"Just swatting at these damn buzzing vibes."

"Aren't you the funny one? But moving on," Cybil continued, "as the astute and handsome Caleb theorized, it's about connections, links. And there are links every bit as intimate as sex."

"Still tops my scoreboard," Fox commented. He grinned at Cybil's stony look and reached for more pizza. "But you were saying."

"Gage and I experienced one of those links when we combined our particular gifts. There was power, and there were consequences. Before that shared experience, he had another on his own. Ann Hawkins."

Cybil paused again, but this time to watch the iridescent flash of a hummingbird outside the window as it dived to the heart of a bold red blossom. "Before I left to come here, Quinn and I logged that incident, charted and mapped it. Gage went through it again for me, for my notes, in case there were any details that dropped out in the relay. There weren't, that I found."

"I thought about that off and on today," Layla put in. "She said she'd wept for him, for Gage, and that you would, Cybil. At least that's my interpretation. That it would matter."

"Tears should matter." Cybil continued to watch as the jeweled bird darted to another blossom.

"I wonder if tears are literal, like a magickal ingredient we'll need, or if they're symbolic again. Grief, joy—emotion. If it's the emotional connection that's important."

"And again, I agree exactly," Cybil added.

"We know emotions are part of it," Quinn continued. "Twisse feeds on the negative—fear, hate, anger. And it seems pretty likely the positive is one of the things that kept us all from being crisped at the Pagan Stone last trip."

"In other words, she wasn't telling us anything we don't already know."

"Positive reinforcement," Quinn said to Gage. "And she said, clearly, we have everything we need to win this. Figuring out what that everything is, and how to use it—that's the problem."

"Weaknesses versus strengths." Fox took a swig of his beer. "Twisse knows our weaknesses, and plays on them. We need to counter that, and in fact, negate that, with our strengths. Basic strategy."

"That's good." Layla nodded. "We need to make lists."

"My girl's hell on lists."

"Seriously. Our strengths and weaknesses as a group, and as individuals. It's war, isn't it? Our strengths are our weapons, and weaknesses are the gaps in our defense. Shore up the defense, or at least recognize where the gaps are, and we build up the offensive position."

"I've been teaching her chess," Fox told the group. "She catches on quick."

"It's a little late in the day for lists," Gage said.

Unoffended, Layla shook her head. "It's never too late for lists."

As Cybil picked up her wine, the hummingbird shot away like a sparkling bullet. "Next on mine is cards."

"You want to play cards?" Cal asked her. "Aren't we a little busy for a game?"

"You're never too busy for a game," Gage corrected. "But I think the lady's referring to her Tarot deck."

"I brought it with me today, and Gage and I conducted an experiment."

Though she trusted her memory, Cybil took out her notes to relate the result to the others. "All Major Arcana, all with meanings specific to both of us," she concluded. "As our resident gambler would agree, the odds of that being coincidence are in the astronomical range. The cards are open to various interpretations depending on the reader, the question, the surrounding cards, and so on. But it *feels* as though, in this case, they spoke of connection—physical, emotional, psychic connection. Then the symbol of each ancestry, and the potential for dramatic change, and consequence. I'd like to do a series of this same experiment. Cal and Quinn, Fox and Layla, all three men, all three women, and lastly, all six of us together."

"You always had a hand with Tarot," Quinn said.

"My Romany forebears. But this today was more than that."

"You did the card trick before the dog came on the scene," Fox commented. "Before the attack."

"Yeah." As the memory still unsettled her, Cybil reached for her wine. "Before."

"Maybe it was part of the trigger. That," Fox continued, "and you and Gage linking up. We still need the details on that, but if the cards weren't coincidence, and the linking generates energy and power, it doesn't seem like another co-incidence that the attack came right on the heels."

"No," Cybil said slowly. "No, it really doesn't."

"You were outside," Quinn prompted. "In the backyard."

"Yeah." Cybil glanced at Gage. "Why don't you take this part?"

He didn't particularly care to give reports, but he assumed it was still difficult for her to speak of it. He ran it through, from the moment they'd sat and linked fingertips on the grass, to the moment Cybil fired the kill shot.

"Oh, honey." Her face filled with concern, Layla reached for Cybil's hand.

"Excuse me?" Gage held up a finger. "Teeth, claws, rended flesh, spilled blood. Crazy Roscoe took a chunk out of my shoulder the size of a—"

"Oh, honey." Layla rose and surprised and amused Gage by rounding the table to plant a kiss on his cheek.

"That's more like it. Anyway, that covers it."

"Gage has neglected to add that I fell apart. If we're mak-ing lists, that one has to go under weakness. I had a serious meltdown afterward. I can't guarantee it won't happen again, but I don't think it will."

"Said meltdown was intense, but brief," Gage continued.

"And went into effect *after* the job was done. Personally, I don't give a rat's ass how much anybody gnashes their teeth or freaks after the job's done."

"Point well taken," Cybil decided.

"It made a mistake." Quinn spoke quietly, but her eyes were a vivid and burning blue. "It made a big goddamn mistake."

"How?" Cal asked her.

"For three of us here, a crucial element of this has all been theory before today. We've talked about what happens to people during the Seven, what they're capable of doing when infected. But only you, Fox, and Gage have ever dealt with it face-to-face. Only the three of you have ever had to defend yourselves or someone else from an attack of another living thing. An ordinary living thing that's turned into a threat. How could we know, how could we be sure, how we'd react, if we'd really be able to do what needed to be done when we were faced with it? Now we do.

"That dog today wasn't one of Twisse's nasty illusions. It was flesh and blood. Meltdown, my ass, Cyb. You didn't panic, you didn't run, you didn't freeze. You got a gun and you put it down. You saved a life. So the bastard made a big mistake with his preview of coming attractions. Because now four of us have had face-offs, and I'll be damned if Layla and I aren't just as able to stand up the way Cybil did. My vote? That's a big red check in the plus column."

"That's telling him, Blondie." Cal leaned over, kissed her.

"You're right." Fox lifted his beer in toast. "It wanted to show off, and got shot down. Literally. Psych."

Cybil continued to stare at Quinn for another moment, as the last knots of shock and grief inside her untangled. "You've always been able to cut through the bullshit, haven't you? So, okay then." She took her first truly clear breath in hours. "Let's take a moment to congratulate ourselves . . . And that's the moment. Somebody start clearing the table, and I'll get my cards."

As she left the room, Gage pushed away from the table and followed her.

"Look, you've already proved a lot today."

Reaching in her purse she hunted for her cards.

"There's no need to deal from your magic deck tonight. You're tired."

"You're right, I am tired." But it was annoying to be told so when she'd gone to the trouble to mask it. "I imagine in the days before the Seven, and during it, you and Cal and Fox function at a state well beyond tired."

"When it comes to that, choices are limited to none. It hasn't come to that yet."

"But it will. And while I'm not above needing or wanting to prove something, this isn't about that. I appreciate the concern, but—"

She broke off when he took her arm. "I don't like being concerned."

The look on his face was one of barely restrained frustration. "No, I bet you don't. I can't help you with that, Gage."

"Look. Look." The frustration rippled again, more visibly. "Let's just get something straight, right from the jump."

"By all means."

"The way the others have hooked up, that's not in the cards. Not those," he said pointing at the Tarot deck. "Not mine, not any. It's not about love songs and playing house for me."

She angled her head, kept an easy, reasonable smile on her face. "Are you under the impression I want you to sing to me, and play house?"

"Cut it out, Cybil."

"No, you cut it out, you arrogant ass. If you've got some jitters that I'm somehow going to spin you in my web until you're serenading under my window and picking out china patterns, that's your problem." She shot a finger at him and her smile was no longer easy and reasonable, but had hardened to a sneer. "If you actually have it in your tiny brain that I would want that, you're just stupid. Which is redundant due to tiny brain, and I *hate* being annoyed enough to be redundant."

"Are you going to stand there and try to tell me that when

the rest of them are falling off the cliff like lemmings, you haven't given a thought to grabbing hold and dragging me off with you?"

"What a lovely image, and quite the testament to your views on our friends' feelings for each other."

"It's apt enough," he muttered. "Add in Quinn's buzzing vibes and it strikes me as pretty damn reasonable to lay it out."

"Then let me lay this out. If and when I decide I want a man for the long term, it won't be because Fate crammed him down my throat. If and when," she repeated, "and contrary to what you with your sexist stupidity might believe— not every woman is looking for long-term—I won't need to grab or drag. If I did, I wouldn't want the son of a bitch. You're safe from my wiles and whims, you narcissistic jerk. If that doesn't reassure you, you can kiss my ass."

She shoved by him, marched into the dining room to slap the deck on the table. "I need to clear my head first," she said to no one in particular, then sailed out into the kitchen and through the back door.

After a quick glance at Cal, Quinn headed out after her. "She's mighty pissed," Quinn commented when Layla stepped out behind her.

"So I see."

After a rapid stride up the deck and down again, Cybil whirled to them. "Even in my current state of blind rage, I'm not going to say all men are arrogant, ignorant pigs who deserve a good kick in their precious balls."

"Just one particular man," Quinn translated.

"One particular, who just had the *nerve* to warn me that any secret, cherished dreams I might have regarding him are held in vain."

"Oh God." The hands Quinn put to her face muffled a sound caught between a groan and a snorting laugh.

"I shouldn't mistake the fact that the four of you, who've run over the cliff like lemmings, I may add, are a precursor of my future bliss with him."

"As I'm not certain his healing powers are a match for the Wrath of the Cyb, do we need to call nine-one-one?"

"If so," Layla considered, "we should let him suffer a little while longer first. Lemmings?"

"To be fair, though God knows why I should be, I'd say that remark was more due to his concern over his own situation than his opinion of any of you."

Quinn cleared her throat. "Ah, just to throw a wrench at the monkey, it's also possible he went asshat because he's projecting somewhat, due to complicated feelings for and about you."

Cybil merely shrugged at Quinn. "That would be his problem."

"Absolutely. But in your position I'd take some satisfaction from that. The possibility that he's not as worried you'll fall for him as he is he'll fall for you."

Now Cybil pursed her lips. Temper throttled back to give consideration room on the road. "Hmm. I was too mightily pissed to see that angle. I like it. I ought to give him the Treatment."

"Dear God, Cyb." With exaggerated horror on her face, Quinn gripped her friend's arm. "Not the Treatment."

"What's the Treatment?" Layla demanded. "Does it hurt?"

"The Treatment, designed and implemented by Cybil Kinski, is many faceted and multilayered," Quinn told her. "No man can hold against it."

"It's approach, attitude, response." Absently, Cybil brushed at her hair. "Knowing the quarry and adjusting that approach, attitude, and response to his specific qualifications. You can add in seduction and sex if that's acceptable to you, but it's really more about luring them to exactly where you want them. Eye contact, body language, conversation, wardrobe—all of that specifically tailored toward the man in question."

She let out a huff of breath. "But this isn't the time for that sort of thing. No matter how much he deserves it. But after this is over . . ."

"Okay, I have to know," Layla decided. "How would you tailor the Treatment for Gage?"

"It's elemental, really. He prefers sophisticated women with some style. Though he probably thinks otherwise, he's more truly attracted to—because he respects—women of strength. She shouldn't be coy about sex, but if she's sure, buddy, let's roll, he's not going to think about her twice afterward. He likes brains, leavened with humor."

"Ah, don't hit me," Layla said, "but it sounds like you're describing yourself."

That put a momentary hitch in Cybil's stride, but she continued. "Unlike Fox, we'll say, he isn't inclined to nurture. Unlike Cal, he isn't drawn to his roots, or to putting them down. He gambles, and a woman who knows how to play the game well would draw his attention. One who knows how to win, and how to lose. He can be drawn in physically—but what man can't—but only to a point. He has excellent control under most circumstances, so control would be key in drawing him."

"She'd have notes on all of this if she were going to do it." Like a proud mama, Quinn beamed at Cybil. "Then she'd do a detailed outline."

"Of course, but since this is just hypothetical . . ." Moving her shoulders, Cybil continued. "He requires challenge, so you'd have to walk the line between interest and disinterest, giving him just enough of both. No running hot and cold, which, oddly enough, some men can't resist, but finding just the right temperature—then varying it at unexpected moments to keep him just a bit off balance. And—"

She stopped, shook her head. "Doesn't matter, as I'm not going to do it. The stakes are too high to play that kind of game."

"When we were in college, she used it on this guy who cheated on me, *then* suggested we have a threesome with the girl he cheated on me with. Oink." After slinging an arm around Cybil's shoulders, Quinn gave Cybil a hard squeeze. "Cyb wound that fuckhead up like a clock, then just when he thought his alarm was going to go off, slapped him off the nightstand. It was beautiful. But yeah, probably inappropriate under our current circumstances."

"Oh well." With a shrug, Cybil shook back her hair. "It

was fun thinking about it. And it calmed me down. We'd better go back in, get started."

Layla tugged Quinn back as Cybil went inside. "Am I really the only one who noticed that she just kept describing herself as the kind of woman Gage would fall for?"

"Nope. But isn't it interesting that Cyb didn't appear to get that?" Quinn draped an arm around Layla's shoulders now. "Even though, in my opinion, she was right on target. She's exactly the woman he'd fall for. Won't this be fun to watch?"

"Is it Fate, Quinn, or choice? For all of us?"

"I vote choice, but you know what?" She gave Layla a pat. "I don't much care, not as long as we all live happy-ever-after."

Thinking of just that, Layla looked at Fox as she walked into the kitchen. He popped the top on a Coke, laughing at something Cal said. As his tawny eyes glanced her way, they warmed like suns.

"Ready for a little fortune-telling?" He held out a hand for hers.

"I want to ask you a question first." It was important to ask now, she realized, before those cards were turned.

"Sure, what do you need?"

"I need to know if you'll marry me."

The conversations around them stopped. For several long seconds there was no sound as he stared at her. "Okay. Now?"

"Fox."

"Because I was thinking more like February. You know what a crappy month February is? Why shouldn't there be something really great to look forward to in the mostly crappy month of February?" He took a slug of his Coke, then set it down as she stared back at him. "Plus, it was February when I saw you for the first time. But not Valentine's Day because, you know, complete cliché and way too traditional."

"You've been thinking?"

"Yeah, I've been thinking, seeing as I'm completely in love with you. But I'm glad you asked me first. Takes the pressure off." With a laugh, he lifted her off her feet. "February work for you?"

"February's perfect." She laid her hands on his cheeks, kissed him. Then lifting her head, she grinned. "Fox and I are getting married in February."

Amid the congratulations and hugs, Cybil caught Gage's eye. "Don't worry," she said quietly. "I won't propose."

She put on the kettle for tea, to keep her calm and centered when they went back to work.

Eight

~

GAGE SLEPT POORLY, AND THE INSOMNIA HAD
nothing to do with dreams or visions. He wasn't used to making serious mistakes, or worse—certainly more mortifying—
clumsy missteps. Particularly with women. He made his
living not just reading cards and the odds, but out of reading
people, what went on behind the eyes, the words, the gestures.

It was small comfort to understand, at about three a.m.,
that he hadn't read Cybil incorrectly. She was just as intrigued and attracted as he, just as interested—and probably
just as wary—of acting on those now-famous buzzing sexual
vibes.

No, he wasn't wrong about the sexual connection between them.

His monumental mistake had been knee-jerking off a
disquiet inside himself and kicking it right into her face.
The second layer of the mistake being—and Christ, it was
lowering—he'd been after *reassurance*. He'd wanted her to
agree with him, to tell him there wasn't anything to worry

about. She wasn't any more willing to get dicked around by
Fate than he was.

With that all tidied up, they'd work together, sleep together, fight together, hell, maybe die together, and no
problem.

All that talk about emotion and emotional connection had
spiced the stew he'd already had simmering inside him.
Hadn't he watched both his closest friends, his brothers, fall
in love? And weren't they both heading toward the altar?
Any man in his right mind would take a hard look at the
hand being dealt and fold before the draw.

And, with hindsight flashing like neon, he had to admit he
should've kept that move, that thought, that opinion to himself. Instead, he'd fumbled it, gone on the defensive. And
had, essentially, accused her of setting him up. She'd been
right to kick his ass over it. No question about it. Now the
question was how to put things back on a level field without
having to wade through the sticky waters of an apology first.
He could use the greater-good ploy, but however true it
might be, it was weak.

In the end, he decided to play it by ear, and walked into
the rental house. Quinn was halfway down the steps, and
paused when he came in. After the briefest of hesitations,
she jogged the rest of the way down. "Hi. You wouldn't be
here to work, would you?"

"Actually—"

She plowed right over him with a rush of words and
movement. "Because we're very shorthanded. Fox and Cal
are both in meetings, and Fox's dad had a couple hours, so
Layla's over at the boutique with him going over plans. It's
down to me and Cyb, and actually, I need to run out to the
place to get the thing. I came down to get Cyb some coffee,
there's fresh in the kitchen. Get that, will you? I'll be back in
twenty."

She nipped straight out the door before he could get in a
word. At least half of what she'd said was bullshit manufactured on the spot. A man recognized bullshit when he was
standing knee deep in it. But since it served his purposes, he

just walked back to the kitchen and poured two coffees, then carried them upstairs.

That curly mass of hair tumbled this way and that out of pins Cybil had used to secure it to the top of her head. A new look for her, he thought—at least that he'd seen—and a damn sexy one. She worked with her back to him, on the big dry erase board. Another chart, he noted, and recognized the names of the cards they'd all chosen in the various rounds the night before. The music, he assumed, came from one of the laptops set up in the room. Melissa Etheridge soared.

"Wouldn't logging those into the computer be faster?"

He saw the quick jolt, and the quick recovery before she turned. The look she spared him was what he thought of as beige. Absolutely neutral. "They are logged, but this is easier on the eyes, and more accessible to the whole group. Would one of those be my coffee, or do you plan to drink both?"

He stepped over, held one out to her. "Quinn said she had to go to the place to get the thing, and would be back in twenty."

Irritation flickered over Cybil's face before she turned back to the board. "In that case, you ought to go downstairs, or outside until you have a chaperone to protect you from my wiles."

"I can handle you."

She glanced back. No beige now, Gage mused. This look was all smoke, with the faintest tinge of hot blue at the edges. "Others have thought the same. Their mistake."

Screw it, he decided as she continued to print her perfectly formed letters. When a man played his hand poorly, he had to take his losses. "I was out of line."

"Yes, we've established that much already."

"Then no problem."

"I never imagined you had one."

He drank some coffee. He watched her. He tried to figure out why her cool disinterest just pissed him off. So he set the coffee down, and took her arm to get her attention. "Look—"

"Careful." The warning dripped like molten sugar. "The last time you started a statement that way you ended up with both feet jammed in your mouth. I imagine you'd find it as boring as I do to make the same mistake twice."

"I never said I made a mistake."

When she met this with silence, and a long, bland stare, it occurred to him she'd be a killer at the poker table. "Okay. All right. The whole day was over the top. Since I don't see you as a tease, it's pretty clear we're going to end up in bed together."

The sound she made wasn't quite a laugh, and was all insult. "I wouldn't place my bets on that just yet."

"I like the odds. But the point is, I thought we'd both want the rules laid out beforehand. The over-the-line part was making it sound as if you were looking for something more."

"That was the over-the-line part?"

"You could cut me a small break here, Cybil."

"Actually, I already have." She thought of the Treatment, and smiled. "You just don't know about it. Let me ask you something. Do you really believe you're so irresistible, so appealing, that I'll fall in love with you and start dreaming of white picket to fence you in?"

"No, I don't. That's part two of the over-the-line. Straight out?"

"Oh, yes, please."

"All the hookups, the link-ups, the subsets like you called them," he said, gesturing to her board, "started to make me uneasy. Added in the more we're in this, the more I've got an urge for you—which I know damn well is mutual—I overreacted."

And that, Cybil decided, was as close to an apology as he'd come up with, unless she beat him with a stick. All in all, it wasn't half bad. "Okay," she said, mimicking him, "all right. I'll cut you a slightly bigger break than I already have. I'll also toss in the fact that I think both of us are old enough and smart enough to resist our *urges* should we have concerns that acting on them will result in driving the other party into mad and hopeless love. Does that work for you?"

"Yeah, that works for me."

"In that case, you can either run along and do whatever it is you do, or you can stay and pitch in."

"Define 'pitch in.'"

"Lend a fresh eye with the charts, the graphs, the maps. Maybe you'll see something we're missing, or at least the potential of something. I need to finish this one, then it needs to be analyzed." She began to write again. "Then, if you're still around, it might be a good idea to try another link-up—of the psychic variety—when at least one other person's around. It occurred to me if the timing had been different yesterday, and that dog had gotten there sooner—"

"Yeah, it occurred to me, too."

"So, I think at least until we have a better handle on it, we shouldn't try that sort of thing alone, or outside."

He couldn't argue with that. "Tell me about this first, the cards."

"All right. Start with me. I've listed my cards, in the succession they were picked, and the subsets I picked with. Yours and mine here, then with Q and Layla, then with the group as a whole. There are twenty-two Major Arcana in a Tarot deck. You and I chose five cards each, all ten of them Major Arcana."

He scanned the board, nodded. "Got that."

"My female subset, five cards each, and a total of fifteen of Major Arcana. When I picked with the group as a whole, the first three were again Major Arcana, the last three—and as I elected to pull from the deck last, all twenty-two were already pulled—were the Queen of Swords, the Ten of Rods, and the Four of Cauldrons.

"Now, when you look at my three rounds, you see that in the first, and the last, I pulled both Death and the Devil. Other repeats, first and second rounds, the Hanged Man, and in all three rounds, I drew the Wheel of Fortune. Second and third, Strength."

"All of us drew repeat cards."

"That's right, so those repetitions add weight to our individual columns. And, tellingly, each woman picked a queen, each man a king. Mine, Queen of Swords, represents someone on guard. An intelligent woman who uses that intellect to gain her own way. Which I'm certainly prone to do. This queen is usually seen as a dark-haired, dark-eyed woman. Ten of Rods, a burden, a determination to succeed. Four of Cauldrons, help from a positive source, new possibilities and/or relationships."

She stepped back, frowned at the board. "My take here is, the cards from the Lesser Arcana represent not only who we are, but what we need to do individually to aid the whole. With the repeat cards representing what was set before us— individually again—what's come to be or is coming, and the eventual outcome."

"How about my king?"

"Again Swords. Represents a man of action who has an analytical mind. And though it might be seen more as Fox, as it's often someone in the legal profession, it means this man is fair, a good judge and basically, nobody's patsy. Next, you have the Six of Rods, triumph after a struggle. And last, Nine of Cauldrons. Someone who enjoys the good life, and has found material success.

"So . . ." She blew out a breath. "As Q and I are most familiar with the Tarot and its meanings, we'll work this. Shuffle it around, analyze, dig into meanings in each subset and in the order of individual picks, repeats, and so on."

"Which will tell us . . . ?"

"Strengths and weaknesses—that's a key, isn't it? For each of us, for each subset, and for the whole. And speaking of Q," Cybil continued when Quinn stepped to the doorway. "Did you get the thing from the place?" Cybil asked sweetly.

"What? Oh, that thing from that place. They were out. So, what are we up to?"

"You and I are on cards. Gage will be putting his analytical mind and his judgment into charts, maps, and graphs."

"Cool. Isn't it sweet how Cal and I picked King and Queen of Rods?" She beamed her smile at Gage. "Both prefer country living, are loyal with strong ties to family."

"Handy." With that, Gage decided the maps needed his attention.

He wondered how many hours they'd put into all this—their pushpins and computer printouts. He understood and valued the need for research and prep work, but honestly couldn't see what help color-coded index cards were against the forces of evil.

As he studied the map of the Hollow, his mind automatically filled in houses, buildings, landmarks. How many times had he cruised those streets—on a bike, then in a car? There was the place where the dog had drowned at the dawn of the second Seven. But the summer before, he and Fox and Cal had snuck out and gone skinny-dipping in that pool one hot summer night.

The bank would be there, corner of Main and Antietam. He'd opened an account there when he'd been thirteen, to hoard money where the old man couldn't find it. And that asshole Derrick Napper had jumped Fox there one night, just for the hell of it, as Fox cut through on his way from ball practice to the Bowl-a-Rama. The Foster house had been right about there, on Parkside, and in the basement family room, he'd lost his virginity and taken that of the pretty Jenny Foster one memorable night when her parents had been out celebrating their anniversary.

Less than eighteen months later, long after he and pretty Jenny had parted ways, her mother had set the bed on fire while her father slept. There had been many fires during that Seven, and Mr. Foster one of the lucky ones. He'd awakened, put the fire out, then managed to subdue his wife before she lit up their children.

There was the bar where he and Cal and Fox had all gotten ridiculously drunk when he'd come back to celebrate their twenty-first birthday. A few years before, he recalled Lisa Hodges had stumbled out of that same bar and shot at anything that moved—and some that didn't. She'd put a bullet in his arm that Seven, Gage thought, then offered him a blow job.

Strange times.

He scanned the graphs, but as far as he could see, it didn't appear that any one area, or sector, of the Hollow experienced more episodes of violence or paranormal activity. Main Street, of course, but you had to factor in that Main got more traffic, more people used it than any of the other streets or roads in and around town. It was the primary route, with the Square the hub.

He visualized it that way, as a wheel, then as a grid, with the Square as the central point. But no particular pattern emerged. Waste of time, he thought. They could play at this for weeks, and nothing could change. All it proved was that at one time or another, nearly every place within the town limits had been hit.

The park, the ball field, the school, the old library, bowling alley, bars, shops, private homes. Documenting wasn't going to stop them from being hit again when . . .

He stepped back, used both his eyes and his memory to build Hawkins Hollow on its map. Maybe it meant nothing, but hell, the stupid pushpins were right there. Picking up the box, he began adding blue ones to the map.

"What are you doing?" Cybil demanded. "Why—"

He cut her off simply by holding up a finger as he shuffled through his memory, added more pins. There had to be more, he thought. How the hell was a man supposed to remember every applicable incident in some wild theory? And not all of them would involve him. He and Cal and Fox had been tight, but they hadn't been joined at the hip.

"Those locations were already marked," Cybil pointed out when he paused.

"Yeah, that would be the point. And these particular locations have all been hit more than once, some at each Seven. And some of those have already had an incident this time."

"Multiple hits would be logical." Quinn moved forward to study the map. "A town the size of Hawkins Hollow is limited. Other than Main Street, it's fairly spread out, but that's logical, too, as Main has more activity, more people per square foot."

"Yeah, yeah. Interesting, isn't it?"

"It might be, if we knew what the blue pins represented," Cybil said.

"Places, memories, highlights, lowlights. The bowling center. The three of us spent a hell of a lot of time there as kids. I lived on the third floor, worked there—so did Cal and Fox—for spending money. The first violent incident, at least the first we know about, happened in the center on the night of our tenth birthday. At least one act of violence happened there every Seven. Already this time, you had the mess on Valentine's Day, and Twisse shot me back to the apartment— illusion or not, it felt pretty damn real. I got the shit kicked out of me plenty of times up there."

"Violence drawing violence," Cybil murmured. "It returns to locations where you, or one of you, had a violent experience."

"Not just. See this." He tapped the map. "I had sex for the first time in the house that sits here. I was fifteen."

"Precocious," Quinn commented.

"The opportunity presented itself. Next Seven, the lady of the house tried to burn it down, with everyone in it. Didn't work out for her, fortunately. By the next Seven, my first conquest had married her college sweetheart and moved away, and the rest of the family moved to a bigger house well out of town. But the guy who bought the place broke every mirror in the place—that would be July of '01, and according to his wife, whom he attacked, started screaming about devils in the glass. The school—God knows we put in time at all three levels—we got in our share of fights there, copped our share of feels and long, wet kisses once we hit high school."

"Violent or sexual energy. Yours," Cybil added. "You, Cal, and Fox. Yes, that is interesting."

"There's bound to be more. There's also some interest in the fact that up until last month, there was never an incident of any kind at Fox's farm. It wasn't real, but it happened. Nothing ever happened at Cal's parents' place either. But it's something we should watch out for."

"I'm going to call him right now." Quinn dashed out of the room.

"Well, King of Swords, your observant and analytical mind may be on to something." Cybil tapped a finger on the map. "This is our house. No incidents here before we moved into it."

"There might have been something we didn't know about."

"No major incidents, because if there had been, you'd know. But after we move in, it starts here. Aimed at us, very likely using our own energy as part of the fuel. The first incident you're aware of happened at the bowling center when the three of you were there. This time around, the center was the scene of the first major illusionary incident, when four of the group were there. Quinn saw the demon here, when she was driving to Cal's house to meet him for the first time, which put four of the six of us in the area—for the first time."

"What are you looking for?"

"A pattern in the pattern. The second Seven, one of the first major occurrences involved a woman coming out of this bar, and firing a gun. You were hit."

"Yeah, then hit on."

"The three of you on the scene, and of course, the alcohol making the woman more susceptible. But as you were just seventeen, it's doubtful any of you spent appreciable time at that bar, or had any sort of experience there that would—"

"The old man spent plenty of time there." Understanding where she was headed, Gage checked the urge to keep that area buried. "Kicked me out, literally, when I went in looking for him. I was around seven. It was the first time he seriously laid into me. That's what you're looking for?"

"Yes."

When she offered no sympathy, no gesture of comfort, his stomach muscles relaxed again. "The last Seven we tried the ritual again, so we were at the Pagan Stone at midnight. I don't know where the first incident took place, but it was the worst of them. That year was the worst of all."

"All right, let's backtrack. You knew it was coming; you were prepared. Things happened, as they are now, before that stroke of midnight on July seventh. What do you remember happening first?"

"The dreams always come first. I came back early spring that year. We bunked in this apartment Cal had back then. I saw the little fucker crouched right on the Welcome to Hawkins Hollow sign when I first drove into town. Forgot about that. And the first night, or early morning, the three of us stayed in Cal's place, the crows hit."

"Where?"

"Main Street, that's where they like it best. But heavier on the building where we were. Yeah, that took the biggest hit. And there were a lot of fights at the high school. People put it down to end-of-year tempers and stress, but there were a lot of fights at the school."

"We can work with this, I think," Cybil responded as she swung back to her computer and began peppering the keys. "A lot of inputting, cross-referencing, and so on, but we can work this." She glanced up briefly when Quinn came back. "Is he coming?"

"As soon as he sees his parents."

"Get Fox and Layla over here, too."

"She got something?" Quinn asked Gage.

"Apparently."

"Defense is as integral to any war as offense."

"Integral," Gage repeated.

"We pinpoint the highest-risk locations, then take the necessary defensive steps."

"Which would be?"

"Evacuation, fortification." She waved the question off as she might a persistent fly. "One thing at a time."

Gage didn't put much stock in evacuation or fortification, but he followed Cybil's line of thinking. He saw the pattern within the pattern. He edged back as the others arrived, as the six of them crammed into the little office.

"We've agreed we're catalysts," Cybil began. "We know the three men released the entity we call Twisse, as that was the name it was last known by, by performing a blood ritual. We know that Quinn's first sighting was in February, the earliest we have on record—when she arrived. Layla and Quinn, both staying at the hotel, had their first shared sighting there. It's escalated since, faster and stronger. In the bowling center at the Sweetheart Dance when four of the six of us were there. The attack on Lump at Cal's when all six of us stayed there. We've logged the individual and mutual sightings this time. Again the bowling center, the Square, Fox's office and apartment, this house. So when we go back to previous Sevens, there's a locational pattern."

"Bowling center's a major site." Quinn studied the updated map. "The high school, the bar, what was the Foster house, the area around the Square. Obvious reasons for all that. But it's interesting that before this year, neither Fox's building nor this house had any incidents. We're on to something here."

"Why didn't we see this before?" Cal wondered. "How the hell did we miss it?"

"We never did charts and graphs," Fox pointed out. "We wrote stuff down, sure, but we never put it all together this way. The logical, visual way."

"And you see it every day," Cybil added. "You and Cal live here. You see the town every day, the streets, the buildings. Gage doesn't. So when he looks at the map, he sees it in a different way. And doing what he does for a living, he instinctively looks for patterns."

"What do we do with this?" Layla asked.

"We add as much data as possible from these guys' memories," Cybil began. "We input that, study and analyze the resulting pattern, and . . ."

"We calculate the odds on the first strike or strikes," Gage finished when she looked at him. "Bowling center year one, the bar year two. We don't know, because we were at the Pagan Stone, what took the first hit year three."

"We might." Frowning at the map, Cal pinned a finger to a spot. "My father stayed in town. He knew we were going to the clearing, to try to stop this, so he stayed in case . . . I didn't know it. He didn't tell me until after it was all over. He planted himself in the police station. A couple of guys in the bank parking lot, going at each other's cars—and each other—with tire irons."

"Did anything significant happen to any of you there?"

"Yeah." Fox hooked his thumbs in his front pockets. "Napper jumped me there once, beat half the snot out of me before I got my second wind and beat the rest of it out of him."

"Just what I'm after," Cybil told him. "Where'd you lose your virginity, Cal?"

"Well, Jesus."

"Don't be shy." Muffling laughter, Quinn bumped his shoulder.

"Backseat of my car, like any self-respecting high school senior."

"He was a late bloomer," Gage pointed out.

Cal hunched his shoulders, then deliberately straightened them again. "I've since made up for it."

"So I hear," Cybil said, and Quinn laughed again. "Where were you parked?"

"Up on Rock Mount Lane. There weren't many houses along there back then. They'd just started to develop, so . . ." He angled his head, and once again laid a finger on the map. "Here, right about here. And last Seven, two of those houses burned to the ground."

"Fox?"

"Alongside of the creek. Well outside town limits. There are a few houses tucked in there now, but they're not part of the Hollow. I don't know if that plays in this."

"We should log them in anyway. What we'll need you to do, all of you, is dig back, think back, note down anything, anywhere, that might be significant. A violent episode, a traumatic one, a sexual one. Then we'll correlate. Layla, you're a hell of a correlator."

"All right. My shop, or what will be my shop," Layla corrected. "It's been hit hard every Seven, and already took damage this time. Did anything happen there?"

"It used to be a junk shop."

The tone of Gage's voice, the quality of silence from both Cal and Fox told Cybil this wasn't only significant. It was monumental. "A kind of low-rent antique store. My mother worked there part-time off and on. We were all in there—I think maybe our mothers got together to have lunch in town, or poke around. I don't remember. But we were all in there when . . . She got sick, started to hemorrhage. She was pregnant, I can't remember how far along. But we were all in there when whatever went wrong started going wrong."

"They got an ambulance." Cal finished it so Gage wouldn't have to. "Fox's mother went with her, and mine took the three of us back to the house with her. They couldn't save her or the baby."

"The last time I saw her, she was lying on the floor of that junk shop, bleeding. I guess that's pretty fucking significant. I need more coffee."

Downstairs, he bypassed the pot and went straight out on the porch. Moments later, Cybil stepped out behind him.

"I'm sorry, so sorry this causes you pain."

"Nothing I could do then, nothing I can do now."

She moved to him, laid a hand on his arm. "I'm still sorry it causes you pain. I know what it is to lose a parent, one you loved and who loved you. I know how it can mark your life into before and after. However long ago, whatever the circumstances, there's still a place in the child that hurts."

"She told me it was going to be all right. The last thing she said to me was, 'Don't worry, baby, don't be scared. It's going to be all right.' It wasn't, but I hope she believed it."

Steadier, he turned to her. "If you're right about this, and I think you are, I'm going to find a way to kill it. I'm going to kill it for using my mother's blood, her pain, her fear to feed on. I swear a goddamn oath right here and now on that."

"Good." With her eyes on his, she held out a hand. "I'll swear it with you."

"You didn't even know her. I barely—"

She cut him off, taking his face in her hands, pulling so

that his mouth met hers in a quick and fierce kiss that was more comforting than a dozen soft words. "I swear it."

Even as she drew back, her hands stayed on his face. And a single tear spilled out of her eyes to trail down her cheek. Undone, he lowered his forehead to hers.

Grateful, he took the comfort of her tears.

Nine

∽ꝫ∾

INSIDE WHAT WOULD BE SISTERS, CYBIL STUDIED the swaths of paint on the various walls. Fresh color, she thought, to cover old wounds and scars. Layla, being Layla, had created a large chart of the interior on the wall—to scale—with the projected changes and additions in place. It took little effort to visualize what could be.

And for Cybil, it took little effort to visualize what had been. The little boy, scared and confused as his mother bled on the floor of a junk shop. From that moment, Gage's life snapped, she thought. He'd glued the pieces back together, but the line of them would be forever changed by those moments in this place, the loss suffered.

She knew, as the line of her life had forever changed at the moment of her father's suicide.

Another snap in Gage's, she realized, the first time his father had raised a hand to him. Another patch, another change in the line. Then another break on his tenth birthday.

A great deal of damage and repair for one young boy. It

would take a very strong and determined man not only to accept all that damage, but to build a life on it.

Because the chatter behind her had stopped, she turned to see Layla and Quinn watching her.

"It's perfect, Layla."

"You're thinking about what happened here, about Gage's mother. I've thought about it, too." Layla's eyes clouded as she looked around the shop. "I spent a lot of time thinking about it last night. There's another property a few blocks up. It might be better if I looked into renting that instead—"

"No, no, don't. This is your place." Cybil touched a hand to the chart.

"He never said a thing. Gage never said a thing, and all the times I babbled on about my plans here. Fox never . . . Or Cal. And when I asked Fox about it, he said the point was to make things what they should be, or preserve what they were meant to be. You know how he gets."

"And he's right." Fresh paint, Cybil thought again. Color and light. "If we don't keep what's ours, or take it back, we've already lost. None of us can change what happened to Gage's mother, or whatever ugliness happened since. But you can make this place live again, and to me, that's giving Twisse a major ass-kicking. As for Gage, he said his mother liked coming here. I think he'd appreciate seeing you make it somewhere she'd have enjoyed."

"I agree with that, and not just because this place is going to rock," Quinn added. "You'll put a lot of positive energy here, and that shoves it right up the ass of negative energy. That's a powerful symbol. More than that, it's damn good physics. What we're dealing with breaks down, on a lot of levels, to basic physics."

"Nature abhors a vacuum," Cybil decided, nodded. "So don't give it one. Fill it up, Layla."

Layla sighed. "As I'm about to be officially unemployed, again, I'll have plenty of time to do that. But right now, I've got to get to the office. It's the first full day of training my replacement."

"How's she working out?" Quinn wondered.

"I think she's going to be perfect. She's smart, efficient, organized, attractive—and happily married with two teenagers. I like her; Fox is a little bit afraid of her. So, perfect." As they started out, Layla looked at Cybil. "If you talk to Gage today, would you ask him? Physics and ass-kickings aside, if it's too hard for him to have this place a part of his life—and it would be because Fox is—I can take a closer look at that other property."

"If I talk to him, I will."

After Layla locked up and turned in the opposite direction to walk to the office, Quinn hooked an arm through Cybil's. "Why don't you go do that?"

"Do what?"

"Go talk to Gage. You'll work better when you're not wondering how he's doing."

"He's a big boy, he can—"

"Cyb. We go back. First, you're involved. Even if you just thought of the guy as part of the team, you'd be involved. But it's more than that. Just you and me here," she said when Cybil stayed silent.

"All right, yes, it's more. I'm not sure how more might be defined, but it's more."

"Okay, there's the nebulous more. And you're thinking of the little boy who lost his mom, and whose father picked up the bottle instead of his son. Of the boy who took more knocks than he should have, and the man who didn't walk away when he could have. So there's the sympathy and respect elements mixed into that more."

"You're right."

"He's smart, loyal, a little bit of a hard-ass and just rough enough around some of the edges to be intriguing. And, of course, he's extremely hot."

"We do go back," Cybil agreed.

"So, go talk to him. Relieve Layla's mind, maybe get a better handle on the more, then you can concentrate on what we have to do next. Which is a lot."

"Which is why I can and should talk to him later. We've

barely skimmed the surface of what we're thinking of as the hot spots. And I need a fresh look at the Tarot card draws. Most important, I'm not leaving you alone in that house. Not for anything."

"That's why laptops were invented. I'm taking mine over to the bowling center." Quinn gestured back toward the Square. "Further proof why I made the right choice in men and home base. I'll set up in Cal's office, or the vicinity, and you can swing by and get me when you're finished talking to Gage."

"Maybe that's not such a bad idea."

"Pal of mine," Quinn said as they walked into the house, "not such bad ideas are my stock and trade."

AT CAL'S KITCHEN COUNTER, GAGE DUG INTO HIS memories, and with coffee at his elbow, documented them on his own laptop. Shit happened, he thought, and a lot of it had been monumentally bad shit. But in writing it down, he began to see there were a handful of locations where it happened repeatedly.

Still, it didn't all make sense. He'd experienced the worst of his life—pain, fear, grief, and fury—in that damn apartment over the bowling alley. Though incidents occurred there during every Seven, he couldn't recall a single major one. No loss of life, no burning, no looting.

And that itself was odd, wasn't it? A town institution, his childhood home, Cal's family's center in a very true sense, Fox's favorite hangout. Yet when the infection raged, and people were burning, breaking, beating hell out of each other, the old Bowl-a-Rama stood almost untouched.

That earned a big *why* in his book, with a secondary, *how can we use it.*

There was the old library, and the three of them had certainly put in time there. Cal's great-grandmother had run the place. Ann Hawkins had lived there, and died there during the early days of the Hawkins Hollow settlement. Fox had suffered a major tragedy during the previous Seven when his fiancée took a header off the roof.

But . . . But, he mused, sipping coffee, it was the only tragedy he could remember in that location. No burning or pillaging there either. And with all those books as fuel.

The middle and high schools, hit every time, and the elementary virtually untouched. Interesting.

He shifted to study his drawing of the town map and began to speculate not only on the hot spots, but the cold ones.

The mild irritation of the knock on the front door turned into another kind of speculation when he found Cybil on the other side.

"Why don't you just come in?" he asked her. "Nobody else knocks."

"Superior breeding." She closed the door herself then tilted her head as she gave him a slow once-over. "Rough night?"

"I'd've put on a suit and tie if I'd been expecting company of superior breeding."

"A shave wouldn't hurt. I'm charged with discussing something with you. Should we discuss it standing here?"

"Is it going to take long?"

The amused glint in her eye struck a chord with him. "Aren't you the gracious host?"

"Not my house," he pointed out. "I'm working in the kitchen. You can come on back."

"Why, thank you. I believe I will." She strolled ahead of him in what he thought of as her sexy queen glide. "Mind if I make tea?"

He shrugged. "You know where everything is."

"I do." She took the kettle off the stove, walked to the sink.

He wasn't particularly annoyed that she'd come by. The fact was, it wasn't exactly a hardship to have a beautiful woman making tea in the kitchen. And that was the sticky part, he admitted. Not just any beautiful woman, but Cybil. Not just any kitchen, but for all intents and purposes right at the moment, his kitchen.

There'd been something intense between them the night

before, when she'd kissed him, when she'd shed tears for him. Not sexual, or not at its core, he admitted. Sexual he could work with, he could handle. Whatever was going on between them was a hell of a lot more dangerous than sex.

She glanced over her shoulder and he felt that instant and recognizable punch of physical attraction. And there the ground held firmer under his feet.

"What are you working on?" she asked him.

"My homework assignment."

She wandered over, then gave his map an approving nod. "Nicely done."

"Do I get an A?"

Her gaze flicked up to his. "I appreciate bad moods. I have them often myself. Why don't I skip the tea, get right to the point, then I can leave you alone to enjoy yours?"

"Finish making the tea, it's no skin off mine. You can top off my coffee while you're at it. And what is the point?"

Wasn't it fascinating to watch her face while she debated between being pissed and flipping him off, or being superior and doing what she'd come to do.

She turned, got out a cup and saucer—and, he noted, ignored his request to top off his coffee. She leaned back against the opposite counter while she waited for the water to boil. "Layla's considering an alternate location for her boutique."

He waited for the rest, lifting his hands when it didn't come. "And this needs to be discussed with me because . . . ?"

"She's considering an alternative because she's concerned about your feelings."

"My feelings regarding ladies' boutiques are pretty much nonexistent. Why would she . . ."

With a nod, Cybil turned to turn off the burner under the sputtering kettle. "I see your brain's able to engage even through your bad mood. She's worried that opening her business there will hurt you. As her cards indicated, compassion and empathy are some of her strengths. You're Fox's brother in the truest sense of the word, so she loves you. She'll adjust her plans."

"There's no need for that. She doesn't have to . . . It's not . . ." He couldn't put the words together; they simply wouldn't come.

"I'll tell her."

"No, I'll talk to her." Christ. "It's just a place where something bad happened. If they boarded up all the places where something bad happened in the Hollow, there wouldn't be a town. I wouldn't give a good damn about that, but there are people I give a good damn about who do."

And loyalty, Cybil thought, was one of his strengths. "She'll make it shine. I think it's what she's meant to do. I saw her there. Two separate flashes. Two separate potentials. In one the place was burned out, the windows broken, the walls scorched. She stood alone inside the shell of the place. There was light coming through the broken front window, and that made it worse somehow. The way it beamed and burned over the ruin of her hopes."

Turning again, she poured out a cup of tea. "In the other, the light was beaming and burning in through sparkling glass, over the polished floor. She wasn't alone. There were people inside, looking at the displays, the racks. There was such movement and color. I don't know which may happen, if either. But I do know she needs to try to make that second version the truth. She'll be able to try if you tell her you're okay with it."

"Fine."

"Well, since I've completed my mission, I'll just go and leave you alone."

"Finish your damn tea."

She carried her cup over, leaned on the counter so they were face-to-face. A little sympathy shone in those big, brown eyes of hers. "Love's a weight, isn't it? And here you are loaded down with Cal and Fox, with the Hawkinses and the Barry-O'Dells. Now Layla goes and drops a big stone on the pile. There's Quinn, too, you might as well shoulder that one because she's the type who'll just keep picking it back up and dropping it on again. No wonder you're in such a sour mood."

"That's your take. To me, this just feels normal."

"In that case." She strolled around the counter to study his laptop screen over his shoulder. "My, my, you *are* doing your homework."

She smelled like the woods, he thought. Autumn woods. Nothing fragile and pastel like spring, but rich and vivid, with just a hint of distant smoke.

"A lot of locations here," she commented. "I think I get the basic idea of your groupings, but why don't you explain your—"

He didn't think about the move, he just made it. Usually a mistake, he knew, but it didn't feel like one. It didn't taste like one. He had his mouth on hers, his hands fisted in her hair before either one of them knew it was coming.

He'd jerked her off balance—he hoped in more ways than one—so her hands braced on his shoulders. She didn't shy back or pull away, but sank in. Not surrender, but like a woman who chose to enjoy.

"No seduction," he said with his mouth an inch from hers. "I don't welch on a deal, so this is straight-out. We can keep dancing around this, or we can go upstairs."

"You're right. That's definitely not seduction."

"You named the terms," he reminded her. "If you want to change them—"

"No, no. A deal's a deal." This time her mouth took his, just as hot, just as greedy. "And while I do like to dance, it's . . ." She trailed off at the knock on the door. "Why don't I see who that is? You probably need a moment or two to . . . settle down."

And so, Cybil thought as she walked out of the kitchen, did she. She had no objections to jumping into the deep end of the pool. She was, after all, a skilled and sensible swimmer. But it didn't hurt to take a couple of good, head-clearing breaths first, then decide if she wanted to jump into this particular pool at this particular time.

She took one of those breaths and opened the door. It took her a moment to recognize the man she'd seen a few times in the bowling center. She thought again that Gage favored his mother, as there was no resemblance she could see between father and son.

"Mr. Turner, I'm Cybil Kinski." He stood, Cybil thought, looking embarrassed, and a little scared. His hair had gone thin and gray. He had Gage's height, but a scrawnier build. It would be the years of drinking, she assumed, that had dug the lines in his face and webbed the broken capillaries over it. His eyes were a watered-down blue that seemed to struggle to meet hers.

"Sorry. I thought if Gage was here, I could . . ."

"Yes, he is. Come in. He's back in the kitchen. Why don't you have a seat and I'll—"

"He won't be staying." Gage's voice was brutally neutral when he stepped in. "You need to go."

"If I could have just a minute."

"I'm busy, and you're not welcome here."

"I asked Mr. Turner in." Cybil's words dropped like stones into the deep well of silence. "So I'll apologize to both of you. And I'm going to leave you alone to deal with each other. Excuse me."

Gage didn't so much as glance at her as she walked back toward the kitchen. "You need to go," he repeated.

"I just got some things to say."

"That's not my problem. I don't want to hear them. I'm living here for now, and as long as I am, you don't come around here."

Bill's jaw tightened; his mouth firmed. "I put this off since you came back to town. I can't put it off anymore. You give me five minutes, for Chrissake. Five minutes, and I won't bother you no more. I know you only come around the bowling center when I'm off. You hear me out, I'll make myself scarce anytime you want to come in, see Cal. I won't come around you, you got my word."

"Because your word always meant so much?"

Color came and went in Bill's face. "It's all I got. Five minutes, and you're rid of me."

"I've been rid of you." But Gage shrugged. "Take your five."

"Okay then." Bill cleared his throat. "I'm an alcoholic. I've been sober five years, six months, and twelve days. I let drink take over my life. I used it as an excuse to hurt you. I should've looked after you. I should've taken care of you. You didn't have nobody—anybody else, and I made it so you had nobody." His throat moved as he swallowed hard. "I used my hands and my fists and my belt on you, and I'da kept using them if you hadn't gotten big enough to stop me. I made you promises, and I broke them. Over and over again. I wasn't no kind of father to you. I wasn't no kind of man."

His voice wavered, and he looked away. While Gage said nothing, Bill took several audible breaths, then looked back into his son's face. "I can't go back and change that. I could tell you I'm sorry from now until the day I die, and it won't make up for it. I'm not going to promise you I won't drink again, but I'm not going to drink today. When I wake up tomorrow, I'm not going to drink. That's what I'm going to do, every day. And every day I'm sober, I know what I did to you, how I shamed myself as a man, and as a father. How your ma must've looked down and cried. I let her down. I let you down. I'll be sorry for that the rest of my life."

Bill took another breath. "I guess that's what I had to say. 'Cept, you made yourself into something. You did that on your own."

"Why?" If this would be the last time they faced each other, Gage wanted the answer to the single question that had haunted him most of his life. "Why did you turn on me that way? Drinking was the excuse. That's a true thing. So why?"

"I couldn't take the belt to God." Emotion gleamed in Bill's eyes, and though his voice wavered, he continued on. "I couldn't beat God with my fists. But there you were. Had to blame someone, had to punish someone." Bill looked down at his hands. "I wasn't anything special. I could fix things, and I didn't mind hard work, but I wasn't anything special. Then she looked at me. Your ma, she made me a better man. She loved me. I'd wake up every morning, go to bed every night amazed that she was there, and she loved me. She . . . I got a couple minutes left of my five, right?"

"Finish it then."

"You oughta know . . . She was—we were—so happy when she got pregnant with you. You probably don't remember how it was . . . before. But we were happy. Cathy . . . Your ma had some problems with the pregnancy, and then it happened so fast, you coming. We didn't even get to the hospital. You come out of her heading up the pike in the ambulance."

Bill glanced away again, but this time—whether Gage wanted to see it or not—it was grief vivid in those faded blue eyes. "And there were some problems, and the doctor, he said there shouldn't be any more kids. That was okay, that was fine with me. We had you, and, Jesus, you looked just like her. I know you don't remember, but I loved you both more'n anything in the world."

"No," Gage said when Bill stopped. "I don't remember."

"I guess you wouldn't. After a while, she wanted another. She wanted another baby so bad. She'd say: Look, Bill, look at our Gage. Look what we made. Isn't he beautiful? He needs a brother or sister. And well, we started another, and she was careful. She took such good care of herself, did everything the doctor said, and no complaint. But it went wrong. They came and got me from work, and . . ."

He pulled out a bandanna, mopped at tears without any sign of shame. "I lost her, and the little girl we'd tried to make. Jim and Frannie, Jo and Brian, they helped all they could. More than most would. I started drinking, just a little here and there to get through, to get by. But it wasn't enough, so I drank more, and more yet."

His eyes dry again, he shoved the cloth back in his pocket. "I started thinking how it was my fault she died. I should've gone and gotten myself fixed, and not told her, that's all. She'd be alive if I had. Then that hurt too much, so I'd drink some more. Till I started thinking how she'd be alive if we hadn't had you. Hadn't had you, whatever messed her up inside wouldn't be, and she'd still be there when I woke in the morning. Blaming you didn't hurt so much, so I talked myself into seeing that as God's truth instead of a damned lie. Everything was your fault. Lost my job because

I was drunk, but I turned that around so I lost my job because I had to look after you on my own. Anything went wrong, it was because of you, then I could drink some more, whale on you, and I wouldn't have to face the truth.

"There was nobody to blame, Gage." He let out a long sigh. "It wasn't anybody's fault. Things just went wrong, and she died. And when she died, I stopped being a man. I stopped being your daddy. What was left of me, your ma, she'd never have looked at twice. So that's the why. That's the long way around the why. I'm not asking you to forgive me. I'm not asking you to forget. I'm just asking for you to believe that I know what I did, and I'm sorry for it."

"I believe you know what you did, and you're sorry for it. You're well over your five minutes."

With a nod, Bill cast his eyes down, turned to open the door. "I won't get in your way," he said with his back to Gage. "You want to come in and see Cal, or have a beer at the grill, I won't get in your way."

When Bill closed the door behind him, Gage stood where he was. How was he supposed to feel? Was all that supposed to make a difference? All the sorry in the world didn't erase one minute of the years he'd lived in fear, of the years he'd lived in bitter anger. It did nothing to negate the shame or the sorrow.

So the old man got it off his chest, Gage thought as he strode back to the kitchen. That was fine. That was the end between them.

He saw Cybil through the window as she sat on Cal's back deck drinking her tea. He shoved open the door.

"Why the hell did you let him in? Is that your superior breeding?"

"I suppose. I've already apologized for it."

"It's the day for goddamn apologies." The anger he hadn't let himself feel for his father—the old man wasn't entitled to it—sparked now. And flared. "You're sitting out here thinking I should forgive and forget. Poor old guy's sober now, and just trying to mend fences with his only son, the one he used to kick the shit out of regularly. But that was the booze, and the booze was the answer to grief and guilt. Besides, alcoholism's a disease, and he caught it like cancer. Now he's in remission, he's in his one fucking day at a time, so all's fucking forgiven. I should break out the poles and see if he wants to go down to the fishing hole and drown some worms. Did your father ever punch you in the face before he blew his brains out?"

He heard her breath hitch in, release. But her voice was rock steady when she spoke. "No, he did not."

"Did he ever take a belt to your back until it bled?"

"No, he did not."

"That being the case, I'd say you lack the experience to sit out here thinking I should shrug all that off and have myself a real *Oprah* moment with the old man."

"You'd be right, absolutely. But here's another thing. You're putting thoughts in my head that aren't there, and words in my mouth I have no intention of saying. And I don't appreciate it. I imagine that talking with your father just now has left you feeling both raw and prickly, so I'll give you some room. In fact, I'll give you plenty of room and leave you alone to have your tantrum in private."

She made it all the way to the door before she whirled back. "No, I will not. I'll be damned if I will. Do you want to know what I think? Are you at all interested in hearing my own opinion rather than the one you've projected on me?"

He waved a hand, a gesture so brittle with sarcasm, it all but cracked the air. "Go right ahead."

"I think you're under no obligation whatsoever to forgive anything, to forget anything. You're not required to push away the years of abuse because the abuser now chooses to be sober and in his sobriety regrets his actions. And while it may be small and unforgiving of *me*, I think people who do so at the snap of a damn finger are either liars or are in need of serious therapy. I assume you heard him out, so in my personal opinion, any debt you might owe for your existence is now paid in full. It may be fashionable to hold the opinion that terrible actions are indeed terrible, but that the person inflicting them isn't responsible due to alcohol, drugs, DNA, or goddamn PMS. He damn well *was* responsible, and if you decide to loathe him for the rest of your life, I wouldn't blame you for it. How's that?"

"Unexpected," Gage said after a moment.

"I believe the strong have an obligation to protect the weak. It's why they're the strong. I believe a parent has an obligation to protect the child. It's why they're the parent. As for my father—"

"I'm sorry." A day for apologies, he thought again. And this one might qualify as the most sincere of his lifetime. "Cybil, I'm very sorry I threw that at you."

"Regardless, he never raised a hand to me. If he were able to stand where you are right now and apologize to me for killing himself, I don't know if I'd forgive him. He ripped my life in two with that single, selfish, self-pitying act, so I think it would take more than an apology. Which would be useless since he'd still be dead. Your father's alive, and he's taken a step toward making amends. Good for him. But for my money, you can't forgive without trust, and he hasn't earned that from you. He may never, and that's not on you. His actions, his consequences. End of story."

She'd said it all, he thought. She might have said it all in the heat of temper and resentment. But everything she'd said was a comfort. "Can I start over?"

"With what?"

"I'd like to thank you for stepping out and letting me deal with that."

"You're welcome."

"And to thank you for not leaving."

"No problem."

"And last, to thank you for the kick in the ass."

She huffed out a breath, almost smiled. "That part was my pleasure."

"I bet."

He stepped to her, held out a hand. "Come upstairs."

She looked down at his hand, up into his eyes. "All right," she said, and put her hand in his.

Ten

~❧~

"YOU SURPRISE ME."

Cybil tipped her head, gave him that long, slanted stare as they walked through the house. "I hate to be predictable. What's the current surprise?"

"I figured, especially after the mood-breaker, you'd say no thanks."

"That would be shortsighted and self-defeating. I like sex. I'm fairly sure I'm going to like sex with you." She gave a quick, careless shrug, while that half-smile stayed in place. "Why shouldn't I have something I like?"

"I can't think of a single reason."

"Neither can I. So." At the top of the stairs she pushed him back against the wall, crushed her mouth against his. And the easy, the expected glide of arousal inside him banked hard, then shot straight through him.

She bit lightly on his bottom lip once, then spoke against them—each word a separate stroke. "Let's both have something we like."

She stepped back, gestured toward a bedroom doorway.

"That one's yours, isn't it?" With one last glance over her shoulder, one that literally caused the breath to back up in his lungs, she strolled to it, and through.

This, Gage thought as he pushed off the wall, was going to be pretty damn interesting.

She was bent over the bed, straightening his disordered sheets when he came in. "I wasn't planning on using that again before tonight."

She flicked a look back at him, eyes wicked. "Isn't it nice when plans change? I'm a bed-maker myself. I like everything all . . . smooth when I slide in at night. Or . . ." She gave the sheets a last pat, turned. "Whenever."

"I don't mind a few tangles." He moved to her, gripped her hips to lift her onto her toes.

"That's good, because there's bound to be more than a few when we're finished with it, and I won't be making the bed for you." Sinuously, she hooked her arms around his neck, met his mouth in a long, slow burn of a kiss.

In one lazy glide, his hands slid up, under her shirt, over her sides with a teasing brush of thumbs over her breasts. Her shirt slithered up with the movement as he drew her arms over her head.

"Nice move," she said when her shirt dropped away.

"I've got more."

"Me, too." Smiling, she flipped open the button of his jeans, eased the zipper down barely an inch. Watching him, she grazed her nails over his belly, up to his chest. "Nice definition, for a cardplayer," she added as she pulled his shirt up and off.

She was a killer, he thought. "Thanks."

Both of them, he knew, understood the steps of the dance, had practiced its variations, its changing rhythms. But for this dance, their first together, he intended to take the lead.

He took her mouth again, a playful meeting of lips and tongues while he unhooked her pants. Then he lifted her off her feet in a sudden and casual show of strength that had her breath snagging even as the cotton slid down her legs to the floor. *Gotcha*, he thought, and lowered her just enough to bring her mouth to his. And when her sound of pleasure warmed his lips, when the hands on his shoulders tensed, he released her with just enough force to have her falling onto the bed.

She lay on her back, hair tumbled. Dusky skin and frothy black lace.

"You didn't get that muscle shuffling cards."

"You'd be surprised." He eased down, planted his hands on either side of her head. "Fast or slow?"

"Let's try some of both." Fisting her hands in his hair, she pulled him to her. The kiss spun out, rolls of white satin, then darkened and fired with the first hungry nips of teeth. Her hands stroked down his back, slid under his loosened jeans to ride over taught muscles. And like lightning her legs hooked around him, her body bowed up pressing them urgently center to center in a move that yanked furiously at his chain of control.

A killer, he thought again, and ravished her neck.

He had a fantastic mouth, an amazing mouth. She let her head fall back so it could sample her wherever it chose. Her skin hummed under it, and under her skin her blood began to beat. His body—long, hard, with the ripple of muscle, pressed down on hers in exactly the right way so that need gathered into tight knots that set pulses drumming.

Heat. Hunger. Hurry.

She shoved the jeans down his hips, pushing them clear as she rolled over to straddle him. He countered by levering up, fixing his mouth on hers as he flicked open the clasp of her bra.

Even as the kiss spoke of speed, of urgency, his hands skimmed, stroked, in a kind of lazy torture that kindled low fires in her belly. When his mouth lowered to taste, to possess what his hands had aroused, she bowed back to offer more.

She flowed, was all he could think, agile and eager. The beautiful lines of her, the lovely curves all in pale gold, an exotic feast for the taking. And she took, grasping her own pleasure, gliding on it. Nothing could have been more provocative to him than Cybil steeped in that inevitable rise of passion.

Had he wanted her this much? Had this clenched fist of desire been inside him all along—waiting, just waiting, to punch through caution and control? It pounded in him now, beating down all reason so he wanted to feel her tremble, to see her writhe. To hear her scream. Pinning her beneath his weight he used his hands to plunder, to loose that slow rise into a hot, fast flood.

She came, quaking under him, her skin sheened from the heat glowing in the sunlight. Those dark eyes, those gypsy eyes seemed to hold a world of secrets when they locked on his.

"All of you," she said and closed her hand around him. "All of you now." Wrapping her legs around him, she took him into her.

A flash, a wire sparking in the blood. She let it burn through her, crying out when it brought release, moaning as it whipped her into need again, wildly. She yielded when he shoved her legs back to go deeper, and her nails bit into his hips like spurs to urge him on. Even as the pleasure, dark and intense, battered her breathless, she rushed toward that next swamping wave.

She erupted under him, and dragged him with her into the fire.

They lay flat on their backs, side by side on the bed. He felt as if he'd been kicked off a cliff, doing the tumble down through screaming air to land in a hot river. He'd barely had the strength or the brainpower to roll off her so they could both try to get their breath back.

That hadn't been sex, he thought. Sex was anything from an enjoyable pastime to a good, sweaty bout. That had been a revelation of near-biblical proportions.

"Well, okay," he managed. "The surprises just keep coming."

"I think I saw God." Cybil's breath streamed out in something between sigh and moan. "She was pleased."

He laughed, closed his eyes. "You're like a live, female version of Gumby. Without the green."

She was silent a moment. "Since I believe that was a compliment, thanks."

"You're welcome."

"And since we're handing them out, you—" She broke off, and her hand clamped on his. "Gage."

He opened his eyes. The walls bled. Long rivers of red gushed down the walls, swam over the floor. "If that were real, Cal would be sincerely pissed off. Blood's a bitch to clean."

"It doesn't like what went on here." She took a breath, rolled to nudge him back when he started to rise. Eyes hard, face pale, she spoke in a steady voice. "Peeping Toms are so disgusting. But, we might as well give this one something to write home about. Tell me, is it true what I hear from my housemates?"

"What would that be?"

"That your healing powers include impressively fast recovery?"

He grinned at her. "Are you up for a demonstration?"

"More to the point, are you?" She tossed a leg over him, mounted him. Her head fell back, her breath shuddered out. "It's comforting to know my friends are honest. Oh God. Wait." Her hands gripped his as sensation clawed through her.

"Take your time."

"Brace yourself," she warned. "This is going to be a wild ride."

Later, though the walls and floor showed no signs of demon tantrums, he took her again in the shower. Hair damp, eyes sleepy, she dressed.

"Well, what an interesting day. Now I've got to get back to work and swing by and get Q from the bowling center."

"Maybe I'll ride in with you."

"Oh?"

"You want input, and I figure I'll cop lunch out of the deal."

"That might be arranged." When she started to walk by him, out of the room, he took her arm.

"Cybil. I'm not nearly done with you."

"Cutie." She gave his cheek a very deliberate pat. "They never are."

When she kept on going, he shook his head. He'd walked into that one, he admitted. By the time he got downstairs she'd dug a lipstick out of her cavernous bag and was sliding it, with perfect accuracy, over her lips. "How do you do that without looking?"

"Oddly, my lips remain in exactly the same place day after day, year after year. Are you going to want your laptop?"

"Yeah." He'd never considered a woman applying lipstick particularly sexy. Before. "If it gets too irritating working with you and the blonde, I'll set up somewhere."

"Gather it up then. The train's about to pull out." While he did she took out blusher, stroked a bit over her cheeks. In seconds, she'd done something with a minute mirror and a pencil to soot up her eyes. As they walked toward the door she spritzed something from a silver tube about the size of his thumb onto her throat. And that scent, that autumn woods scent reached out and grabbed him by his.

So he grabbed her, rubbed his lips over hers. "We could blow off the day." And had the satisfaction of feeling her heart kick against his.

"Tempting. Seriously tempting, but no. I'd have to call Quinn and explain I'm not picking her up because I've decided spending the day naked in bed with you is more important than trying to find the way to destroy a demon who wants us all dead. Not that she wouldn't understand, but still."

She opened the door, stepped out on the deck.

The boy crouched on the roof of her car, a grinning gargoyle. As it flashed its teeth, Gage pushed Cybil behind him. "Get back in the house."

"Absolutely not."

With a flourish, the boy raised its hands, then chopped them down like a mad conductor. The dark fell; the wind rose.

"It's just show," Cybil shouted. "Like the walls upstairs."

"More than that this time." He could feel it in the bite of

the wind. Inside in surrender, Gage thought, or out here, in challenge? If he'd been alone, it wouldn't be a question. "My car's faster."

"All right."

They started forward, pushing into the wind that shoved them back. Gage kept his eyes on the boy as it whirled in wild circles over the slope of hill, the curve of road. Debris flew, chunks of garden mulch, falling twigs, and peppering gravel. He used his body in an attempt to shield her from the worst of it. Then the boy leaped down.

"Fuck the whore while you can." The words were only uglier when shouted in that young, childish voice. "Before long, you'll watch as I make her scream in pleasure and pain. Want a taste, bitch?"

Crying out in shock, Cybil doubled over, clutching herself. Gage made the choice quickly, and letting her fall to her knees, he pulled out his knife. On a howling laugh, the boy flipped out of range in a gleeful handspring. Gage gripped Cybil's arm, wrenched her to her feet. One look at her face had her horror, her helplessness stabbing through him like his own knife.

"Get in the car. Get in the damn car." He shoved her inside, fighting off the rage as the thing in a boy's form pumped its hips obscenely. The rage pushed at him, screamed at him to go after the thing, to hack and slice. But she was curled into a ball inside the car, shaking.

Gage pulled himself in, fought to slam the door against the wind. Ruthlessly now, he shoved Cybil back, yanked the seat belt around her. Shock and pain turned her face to white marble.

"Hold on. Just hold on."

"It's in me." She gasped it out while her body jerked. "It's in me."

Gunning the engine, Gage shot into reverse, then whipped the wheel. The car bucked in the force of the wind as he sped over the bridge toward the road. Blood spat out of the sky, splatting the windshield, hissing like acid on the roof, the hood. The boy's head appeared at the top, its eyes slanted like a snake's. As it ran its tongue through the blood, Cybil moaned.

It laughed when Gage flipped the wipers on full speed, pumped the washer to spray. Laughed as though it was a fine, fine joke. Then it squealed, either with humor or with surprise, when Gage wrenched the car into a vicious three-sixty. The windshield erupted with fire.

He cut his speed rather than risk a wreck, blocked out everything but the need for a steady hand on the wheel. Slowly, the dark ebbed, the fire sputtered.

When the sun flashed on again with a gentle spring breeze, he pulled to the side of the road. She slumped back in the seat, staring up as her shoulders shook with each breath.

"Cybil."

She cringed away. "Please don't. Don't touch me."

"Okay." Nothing to say, he thought. Nothing to do but get her home. She'd been raped right in front of his eyes, and there was nothing to say, nothing to do.

When they got to the house he didn't help her inside. Don't touch me, she'd said, so he only held the door, closed it after her. "Go upstairs, lie down or . . . I'll call Quinn."

"Yes, call Quinn." But she didn't go upstairs. Instead she walked back toward the kitchen. When he went in moments later, she had a glass of brandy in her shaking hands.

"She's on her way. I don't know what you need, Cybil."

"Neither do I." She took a long drink, then a long breath. "God, neither do I, but that's a start."

"I can't leave you alone, I can't give you that. But if you want to go up and lie down, I'll stay outside the bedroom." When she shook her head, everything about her seemed to tremble. "Goddamn it, god*damn* it, scream, cry, throw something, punch me."

She shook her head again, drank the rest of the brandy. "It wasn't real, physically. But it felt real, physically, and every other way there is to feel. I'm not going to scream; I might never stop. I want Quinn, that's all. I want Quinn."

When the front door slammed open, Gage thought Quinn must have run every step. She was still running when she reached the kitchen. "Cyb."

Cybil made a sound, a mix of moan and whimper that sliced straight through Gage's belly. Even as she turned into Quinn's arms, Quinn led her away. "Come on, baby, let's go upstairs. I'll take you upstairs."

Quinn sent Gage one long grieving look, then they were gone. Gage picked up the glass, smashed it in the sink. Changed nothing, he thought, looking down at the shards. Just a broken glass, and that changed nothing, fixed nothing, helped nothing.

Cal came in to find him standing at the sink, staring out at the sunny afternoon. "What happened? After Quinn got your call she told me to call Layla, get her here, and she ran out. Cybil, is she hurt?"

"Christ knows." His throat burned, Gage realized. Burned as if he'd swallowed flame. "It raped her. The son of a fucking bitch, and I didn't stop it."

Cal stepped up to him, laid a hand on his shoulder. "Tell me what happened."

He began coldly, almost clinically, beginning with the blood on the walls. He didn't stop or acknowledge Fox when Fox came in, but he picked up the beer Fox opened and set in front of him.

"About a mile, mile and a half from your place it stopped. It all went away. Except for Cybil. I don't know if that kind of thing ever goes away."

"You got her away," Cal pointed out. "You got her back home."

"Give me a medal and call me hero."

"I know how you feel." Fox met Gage's hot and bitter look quietly. "It's happened to Layla, so I know how you feel. Layla's upstairs now. That's going to help. And Cybil will get through it because that's the way they're made. We'll get through it because it's all we can do. We'll all get through it because we're going to make the bastard pay. That's what the fuck we're going to do."

He held out a hand. After a moment, Gage gripped it, and Cal laid his over theirs. "We'll make the bastard pay," Gage repeated. "That's what the fuck we're going to do. I swear an oath."

"We swear an oath," Cal and Fox agreed, then Cal blew out a breath and rose.

"I'll make her some tea. Tea's the thing she likes."

"Put some whiskey in it," Fox suggested.

They put it together, and after some discussion and debate, put a pony of whiskey on the side. Gage carried it up, then hesitated outside the closed bedroom door. Before he could knock, Layla opened it, jumped a little.

"Cal made this tea," Gage began.

"Perfect. I was just coming down to do exactly that. Is that whiskey?"

"Yeah. Fox's contribution."

"Good." Layla took the tray. Then studied Gage with weary eyes. "She'll be all right, Gage. Thanks for bringing this up." She closed the door and left him staring at the blank panel.

In the bathroom that linked the two bedrooms, Cybil lay in the tub. She'd had her jag, and that had left her exhausted. Oddly, the fatigue helped. Not as much as her friends, she thought, but some.

As did the hot water, and the fragrance and froth Layla had added to it. Quinn rose from the little stool beside the tub when Layla brought in the tea tray.

"That was really fast, like superpower fast."

"Gage brought it up. Cal made it, so it's probably just fine. Honey, there's whiskey here. Do you want it in the tea?"

"Oh yeah. Thanks. God." Shifting up, Cybil squeezed her burning eyes, breathed through the threatening flood of tears. "No, no, done with that."

"Maybe not." Layla doctored the tea. "I have a moment every now and again. It's okay. We're allowed."

With a nod, Cybil accepted the tea. "It wasn't the pain, though, oh Jesus, nothing's ever hurt like that. It was feeling it in me, pounding and pushing, and not being able to stop it, or fight it. It was the boy. Why is that worse? That it made me see the boy while it—" She broke off, made herself drink the spiked tea.

"It's a kind of torture, isn't it? A kind of physical and psychological torture designed to break us down." Quinn brushed a hand over Cybil's hair. "We won't be broken."

"No, we won't." She held out a hand, and in a gesture that mirrored the one made in the kitchen, Quinn took it, and Layla closed hers over theirs. "We won't break."

She dressed, and took some comfort in grooming. She wouldn't break, Cybil vowed, nor would she look like a victim. When she stepped out of the bedroom she heard the murmur of voices from the office. Not yet, she thought. Not quite ready for that. She moved quietly past, and down the stairs. Maybe after another ocean or two of tea.

In the kitchen she took the kettle to the sink and saw Gage outside, alone. Her first inclination was to back away, to slink away into some dark corner and hide. And the urge both surprised and embarrassed her. In defense, she took the opposite tact, and went outside.

He turned, stared at her. In his eyes she saw the rage and the ruin.

"Absolutely nothing I can say would sound remotely right. I thought you might want me to take off, but I didn't want to leave until I was sure you . . . What?" he said in disgust. "I don't have a clue what."

She considered for a moment. "You're not far wrong. I guess a part of me hoped you'd be gone so I didn't have to talk about this now."

"You don't have to."

"I don't like that part of me," she continued. "So let's just get this done. It came at me, the attack that's a woman's nightmare. The big fear. It made me feel that violation, and the helplessness. That horror that drove Hester Deale mad."

"I should've gone after it."

"And left me? Would you, *could* you leave me when I was completely defenseless, completely terrorized? I couldn't stop it; that's not my fault. You got me away, and getting away made it stop. You defended me when I couldn't defend myself. Thank you."

"I'm not looking for—"

"I know you're not," she interrupted. "I probably wouldn't feel as grateful if you were. Gage, if either of us feel guilty about what happened, it wins a kind of victory. So let's don't."

"Okay."

But he would, for a while yet anyway, she realized. A man would. *This* man would. Maybe she could do something to soothe them both. "Would it complicate our straightforward and mature relationship if you just held on to me for a minute?"

He put his arms around her with the wary caution of a man handling thin and priceless crystal. But when she sighed, laid her head on his shoulder, it was he who broke. His hold tightened. "Christ, Cybil. Good Christ."

"When we destroy it." She spoke clearly now, steadily now. "If it comes in a form with a dick, I will personally castrate it."

His grip tightened again, and he kissed her hair. Complicated, he realized, didn't begin to cover whatever was going on inside him. But right at that moment, he didn't give a damn.

To avoid having everyone tiptoeing around her, Cybil voted for work. The small second-floor office might've been cramped with six people inside, but she had to admit, it felt safe.

"Gage found what may be another pattern dealing with locations," she began, "that springs off the one we talked about before. We can look at them as hot spots and safe zones. The bowling center. While that was the location of the first known infection and violence and has seen other incidents, it's never sustained any damage. No fires, no vandalism. Right?"

Cal nodded. "Not really. Some fights, but most of the trouble's been outside."

"This house," Cybil continued. "Incidents since we moved in, and there may have been some during previous Sevens, but no deaths here, no fires. The old library." She paused to look at Fox. "I know you lost someone important to you there, but before Carly's death, there'd been no major incident there. And again, the building itself has never been attacked. There are several other locations, including Fox's family farm and Cal's family home that have proven to be safe zones. Fox, your office building's another. It can get in, but not physically. Only to create its illusions, so nothing it's been able to do in those places is real. Nor, more importantly, I think, have any of those locations been attacked by those infected during the Seven."

"So the questions are why, and how do we use it." Fox scanned the map. "The old library was Ann Hawkins's home, and my family farm was where she stayed and gave birth to her sons. If we go back to energy, it may be that enough of hers remains as a kind of shield."

"There you go." Quinn planted her hands on her hips. "So we dig and find out what connection the safe zones, or even those places that see less violence, have."

"I can tell you that the land the center sits on was the site of the home Ann Hawkins's sister and her husband built." Cal puffed out his cheeks. "I can check the books, and with my grandmother, but what I remember is it was originally a house, then converted to a market. It morphed and evolved over the years until my grandfather opened the original Bowl-a-Rama. But the land was always Hawkins's land."

"I think that's going to be our why," Layla commented. "But we need to remember that the old library was, well, breached, during the last Seven. It could happen to any of these locations this time."

"There wasn't a Hawkins in the library over the last Seven." Gage continued to study the map, the pattern. "Essie'd retired by then, hadn't she?"

"Yeah, she had. She still went in most every day, but . . . It wasn't hers anymore." Cal stepped up to look more closely. "They'd already started building the new library, and approved plans to make the old one a community center. It belonged to the town then. Technically, it had for years, but . . . "

"But emotionally, essentially." Cybil nodded. "It was Essie's. How long has your family owned this house, Cal?"

"I don't know. I'll find out."

"I bought my building from your dad," Fox reminded Cal. "Yeah, that's going to be the why. So how do we use it?"

"Sanctuaries," Layla said.

"Prisons," Gage corrected. "The question will be how do we hold a couple thousand infected people bent on murder and mayhem in a bowling alley, on a farm, and in a law office, to start."

"We can't. I'm not talking about the legal crap," Cal added.

"Hey, if anyone's going to talk about legal crap, it should be me." Fox took a pull from his beer. "And I'm not going to deny trampling over civil liberties isn't a big issue with me during the Seven, but the logistics won't hold."

"How many could we convince to camp out at your farm before they were infected?" Cybil met Fox's eyes as he turned to her. "And yes, I realize what an enormous risk this would be, but if a few hundred people could be talked into going there before the Seven, staying there through it—or until we kill this bastard—then others might be convinced to leave altogether for that period, or hole up in what we'll designate as safe zones, or as close to safe as we can define."

"Some leave anyway," Cal pointed out. "But the majority don't remember, don't get it, not until it's too late."

"It's different this time," Quinn added. "It's been showing itself, showing off. This is all or nothing for both sides. Even if only ten percent of the town moves out or holes up, it's a stand, isn't it?"

"Every step we take toward the positive counts," Cybil agreed.

"But doesn't kill it."

Cybil turned to Gage. "No, but it uses tactics to try to

weaken us. We'll counter with those that may weaken it."
She gestured toward the board with the Tarot outline. "We
all have our strengths, too. Knowing who and what we are is
a positive step. We have a weapon in the bloodstone, another
positive. We know more, are more, and have more to work
with than the three of you did before."

"If we're going to try moving anyone out who's willing,
Fox needs to talk to his family. If you want to ditch the idea
from the get," Cal continued, "no arguments."

"Yeah, I want to ditch it, but I'm stuck with the old free
will, make your own choices song and dance I was raised on.
They'll decide for themselves if they want to start a damn
refugee camp. Which they will because that's how they're
made. Damn."

"I'll need to talk to mine, too." Cal blew out a breath.
"First, people in town tend to listen to my father, give what
he says some weight. Second, we'll figure if their house or
the center should be a secondary camp, or if they should stay
out at the farm to help Fox's family. And we're going to need
to push, and push hard on finding out how to use the stone.
Having a weapon's no damn good if we don't know how to
trigger it."

"We've built on the past," Quinn began, "and we have a
handle on the now."

"We need to look again." Cybil nodded. "We've started
on that, but—"

"We're not going there tonight." Gage's statement came
cold and firm. "No point in pushing on that," he said before
Cybil could argue. "It's nothing you mess with when you're
already worn down. Go back to that positive energy crap
you're hyping. I'd say you're running low on that tonight."

"You'd be right. Rude, which is no surprise, but accurate.
In fact, I'd probably be better off hunkering down with some
research, solo, for tonight. I'll do more digging on the stone
because Cal's right, too."

Eleven

◆~◆~

SHE DIDN'T DREAM, AND THAT SURPRISED HER. Cybil had fully expected to be dogged by nightmares, portents, imagery, but instead had slept straight through the night.

Something accomplished, she supposed, as she'd gotten nowhere on the evening research. Hopefully, she'd do better today, rested and focused. Rising, she walked over to take a good, hard look at herself in the mirror.

She looked the same, she thought. She was the same. What had happened to her wasn't a turning point in her life. It didn't make her less, and it hadn't broken her down. If anything, the attack had given her more incentive, made her more *involved* and more determined to win.

It may feed on humans, she realized. But it didn't understand them. And that, she supposed, could be another weapon in their arsenal.

Now, she wanted a session at the gym to kick her energy level up. Sweating out the toxins, she thought, would be a kind of ritual cleansing. With any luck Quinn would be available for gym buddy. She pulled on a sports bra, bike pants, tossed what she'd need in a small tote. Stepping out, she noted Quinn's bedroom door was open, and the room empty. So, she'd grab a bottle of water out of the kitchen, and catch up with Quinn and Cal at the health club in the basement of the old library.

She strode into the kitchen, pulling up short when she saw Gage at the table with a mug of coffee and a deck of cards.

"You're out early."

"Never left." As she'd done herself, he gave her a long, hard look. "Bunked on the couch."

"Oh." It gave her a quiver in the belly. "You didn't need to do that."

"Do what?" His eyes never left her face, adding another quiver. "Stay, or bunk on the couch?"

She opened the refrigerator, got out the water. "Either. But thanks. I'm going over to the gym. I want some cardio. I assume that's where Quinn is?"

"Noises were made. Why don't you stick with the Gumby routine?"

"It's not what I'm after. Yoga relaxes me. I need to pump."

"Crap."

"What?" she demanded as he rose.

"Cal's got half his gear here. I'll find something. Wait," he ordered and strode out.

If she was going to wait, she wanted coffee, so she picked up Gage's mug and finished his off. He came back wearing a pair of gray sweats that had seen much better days, and a Baltimore Orioles T-shirt. "Let's go," he ordered.

"Am I correct in assuming you're going to the gym with me?"

"Yeah, get it moving."

She opened the fridge, took out a second bottle of water and shoved it in her tote. She doubted he could have done or said anything at that particular moment that would have meant more to her. "I'm not going to argue or tell you I can get to the gym fine by myself. First, because it would be stupid after yesterday. And second, I want to see what you've got."

"You've already seen what I've got."

She laughed, and felt better than she'd have believed possible. "Good point."

She got a solid hour in, and had the bonus of watching Gage work up a nice sweat lifting weights. It was more than the very appealing view, she realized. Watching him gave her just a little more insight into him. He didn't want to be there, particularly, but since he was, he put his time to use. Focused, thorough, patient, she thought. It might have been more the cat-at-the-mouse-hole kind of patience than the altruistic sort, but the results were the same. He waited.

Looser and energized, she walked back with him. "Where will you go when this is over?" she asked, then moved her shoulders at his quiet look. "That's optimism, which is positive energy. Any particular destination in mind?"

"I've kicked around a couple. Probably Europe, unless there's something happening in the States. I'll come back for the wedding—Jesus, weddings now. You?"

"I'll go back to New York, I think, at least briefly. I miss it, and that's God's truth, so I'll give myself an infusion of crowds and noise and pace. Plus, I'll need to get back to work that pays. But I expect I'll put in considerable time here. The girl part of the weddings will be more demanding than your boy part of them. If I can swing it after Quinn's, I thought a few days on a nice island—palm trees and margaritas, and balmy, tropical nights."

"That's a plan."

"A flexible one, which is my favorite kind." As they turned at the Square, she gestured to the Bowl-a-Rama. "I admire people like that. Cal and his family, who dig in and build and make a genuine mark on a place. I'm grateful they exist, and glad of the fact that by existing and digging in and building, they allow me to make flexible plans and visit lots of those genuine marks someone else has made."

"No burning desire to make a mark?"

"I like to think I do make them, in my own fashion. I find things out. You need information to write a book, make a movie, rehab a house, build a shopping center, and I can get that for you. And I can get you information you didn't realize you needed or wanted. Maybe all of those projects would have gotten done without me, but I can promise you they're better with me. That's enough of a mark for me. How about you?"

"I just like to win. I can settle for having played if the game's solid, but winning's always better."

"Isn't it just," she agreed.

"But if I leave a mark, it gives the other players too much information, too much they might use if we faced each other over a pile of chips again. Better to have a blank slate, as much as possible. They don't know you, it's harder for them to read you."

"Yes." She spoke quietly. "Yes, that's exactly right. And to bring this into our situation, I had a similar thought this morning. It doesn't understand us. It can't really know us. It can anticipate some. What it did to me, what it did to Fox years ago by killing Carly right in front of him. It knows how to hurt, how to use specific weapons to harm and to undermine. But it still doesn't get it. It doesn't seem to comprehend that the opposite side of fear is courage. Every time it uses our fears, it only pushes us to find more courage. It can't read us, not accurately."

"Wouldn't flip to a bluff."

"A bluff? What bluff?"

"I don't know yet, but it's worth thinking about because you've got a point. I want a shower and my own clothes," he added the minute they stepped into the house, and headed straight upstairs.

Cybil considered. She heard the voices from the kitchen. Quinn and Cal had left the gym a good twenty minutes before, and were probably finishing up breakfast and talking with Fox and Layla. She could go back, grab some coffee before going up. Or . . .

Since the shower was already running, she stripped in the

bedroom before strolling in. Hair dripping, Gage narrowed his eyes when she tugged back the curtain and stepped in with him.

"Mind?"

His gaze skimmed over her, then stayed steady on hers. "There's probably enough water for both of us."

"That's what I thought." Casually, she picked up her tube of gel, squirted a generous amount into her hand. "And twofers are more efficient. Plus." Watching him, she soaped her breasts in slow circles. "I could pay you back for the night spent on the couch, and the stint at the gym."

"I don't see any money on you."

"Barter system." Slick and soapy, she pressed against him. "Unless you'd rather take an IOU."

He plunged his hand into her hair, got a good grip to jerk her face up to his. "Pay up," he demanded, then closed his mouth over hers.

There it was, she thought, outrageously grateful. There was the instant thrill, the response, the need. It had taken nothing from her. His body moved wet and hard against hers, his mouth took from hers, and there was nothing, nothing but pleasure.

"Touch me." She demanded it, using her teeth, her nails. Nothing fragile here, nothing damaged or in need of tending. Touch me, she thought, take me. Make me feel utterly, utterly human.

He'd wanted to give her time, had been prepared to give her room. And perhaps to give both to himself as well. But her need, the challenge and raw edges of it spoke to his own. So he touched, hands sliding over that sleek skin as the steam plumed and the water pounded.

And he took, pressing her back to the wet tiles, keeping his eyes on hers as he thrust into her. What he saw in hers was dark delight. He gripped her hips to anchor her, drove them both to peak.

Winded, she dropped her head to his shoulder. "Just hang on a minute."

"Same goes."

"Okay. All right. Thanks for getting into the spirit so quickly."

"Same goes."

She laughed, stayed where she was. "This might be a good time to say that I didn't like you, particularly, when we first met."

He let his eyes close, let himself steep in her scent. "I'm going to repeat myself again. Same goes."

"My first instincts are generally very accurate. Not this time. I do like you, and not just because you're very talented in bed, and in the shower."

Idly, hardly realizing he did so, he traced the tattoo at the base of her spine with a fingertip. "You're not as annoying as I initially thought."

"Here we are, all wet and naked and sentimental." Sighing now, she eased back to study him through the steam. "I trust you. That's an important issue for me. I can work with someone I don't completely trust, it just makes it a little more of a challenge. I can sleep with someone I don't completely trust, it just means it's going to be a very brief encounter. But the work's more productive, and the sex more satisfying, when I trust."

"You want to shake on that?"

She laughed again. "A superfluous gesture, under the circumstances." She lifted the gel again, turned his hand over and poured some into his palm. And turned. "But you could wash my back."

AN HOUR LATER, CYBIL POURED HER FIRST FULL cup of coffee, and had to admit she felt well-buzzed without it. She went upstairs to the office where Quinn and Layla sat at laptops. On the chart, her rape was documented.

Good, Cybil thought. It was good to see it there, straight-out, and know she'd survived it intact. "I'm going to keep the setup in my room this morning," she told them. "But I asked Gage to come back later. It's time we tried another link. I'm hoping one or both of you will hang around, act as an anchor."

"We'll be here," Quinn said.

"Did you know Gage stayed, slept on the couch downstairs?"

"We talked about going back with him, to Cal's." Layla swiveled away from the keyboard. "He said he was staying. The fact is, none of us wanted to leave in case you had a bad night."

"Maybe because none of you left, I didn't have one. Thanks."

"I've got something that might perk you up, too. This house." Quinn spread her hands. "Or the land this house is on—considerably more of it at one time, but this particular plot? Ann Hawkins's grandson Patrick Hawkins, son of Fletcher, owned it. Fox is checking on his building, but I'd say we're well on the way to proving another theory."

"If this is right, and even if Gage's definition of it as prison is more accurate than mine as sanctuary," Layla continued, "it could give us a viable way to protect people. At least some people."

"The more we can protect or at least give a fighting chance to, the more we'll be able to focus on attack." Cybil nodded. "I agree. And we are going to have to attack. It's going to have to be at the Pagan Stone. I know we haven't discussed it, not in detail since the men are resistant, but whatever we do to end it is going to have to be done there. We can't be here, in town, putting out fires, trying to stop people from hurting themselves or each other. We all know when and where we'll take our stand."

"Midnight," Quinn said with a sigh. "As July seventh begins. As this Seven begins, in full. I know you're right. I think we all know it, but it feels like we're deserting the field."

"And it's going to be harder on them, the guys," Layla added. "Because they tried it before, and failed."

"We're not deserting the field. We're taking the game to ours. We won't fail this time, because we can't." Cybil looked back at the chart. "It doesn't know us. It thinks it understands, and part of its understanding is that we're weak, fragile, vulnerable. It's got reason to think that. It comes, and in a very real way, it wins. Every time. Getting stronger, every time."

"Dent took it down," Layla reminded her. "For centuries."

"Dent broke the rules, sacrificed himself. And he was a guardian." Quinn angled her head as she studied Cybil's face. "And still, it was a stopgap, still the burden and some of the power had to be passed on. Diluted, fractured. It took the six of us to reform that power and we still don't know how to use it. But . . ."

"Yes, but. We have it now, and the means to learn. We know the time and the place," Cybil said again. "We're complete with the six of us. Those images I had, of something happening to each of us. I think they were warnings. It has to try to fracture us again, to dilute what we have. We can't and we won't let that happen."

"I'll talk to Cal about ending this at the Pagan Stone. Part of him knows it has to be that way already."

"The same with Fox," Layla said. "I'll talk to him."

"Which leaves me with Gage." Cybil let out a breath.

GAGE PACED CAL'S OFFICE. "SHE WANTS TO TRY the link again. Today."

"Not that many todays left, son, before the big one. No point wasting any."

"You know what it's like, even pushing that on your own. It's a fucking sucker punch. She had a bad experience yesterday. The worst."

"Are you looking out for her?"

Gage stopped, baffled, annoyed. "No more than I would anybody. Plus, I'm looking out for myself. If she can't handle it—"

"Too late for that, you already put her first. Don't bother bullshitting me. You've got a thing. Why wouldn't you have a thing?"

"The thing is sex," Gage insisted. "And, sure, a mutual dependency given the circumstances. We're in this together, so we look out for each other. That's all I'm doing."

"Uh-huh."

Gage turned back with a stony look that did nothing to break Cal's grin. "Look, it's different for you."

"Sex is different for me?"

"For one thing." Frustrated, Gage jammed his hands in his pockets. "For a lot of things. You're dead-normal guy."

"Don't use the word *dead,* under the circumstances."

Jingling the change in his pocket, Gage worked it out in his head. "You're Bowl-a-Rama boy, Cal. House-in-the-country guy, with the tight family ball, the big, stupid dog—no offense," he added, glancing down at Lump, who snored away with all four feet in the air.

"None taken."

"You're a Hawkins of the Hollow, and always will be. You've got the sexy blonde who's happy to plunk her particularly fine ass down here with you and your big, stupid dog in your house in the country, and raise a brood of kids."

"Sounds about right."

"As for Fox, he's as mired here as you. Hippie kid turned town lawyer with his sprawling and interesting family who snags the pretty brunette who turns out to have a spine of steel—enough of one to open a business in this town because that works for them. Like the house with a garden and a bunch of kids will work for them. The four of you will probably be happy as lunatics."

"That's the plan."

"That's if we live, and you know, I know, we all know some of us might not make it."

"If and might." Cal nodded. "Well, life's a gamble."

"For me, gambling's life. If I get through, it's on to the next. There's no house in the country, no nine-to-five or what's for dinner, honey in me."

"And you figure that's what Cybil's looking for?"

"I don't know what she's looking for. It's not my business to know, that's the *point.*" Uneasy, he raked his fingers through his dark hair. Then stopped, annoyed, knowing the gesture was one of his tells. "We're having sex," he continued. "We've got a mutual goal to kill this bastard and live to talk about it. That's it."

"Fine." Obligingly, Cal spread his hands. "Then what are you so worked up about?"

"I . . . Damned if I know," Gage admitted. "Maybe I don't want to be responsible, and linking up that way makes me responsible. They can claim equal shares all they want, but you know how it is, you know how it feels."

"Yeah, I do."

"What happened . . . What it did to her, how am I supposed to get that out of my head, Cal? How am I supposed to put that aside?"

"You can't, you don't. But that doesn't mean we can stop. We all know that, too."

"Maybe she gets to me." He let out a breath. "Okay, she gets to me, no maybe about it. Hardly a surprise, considering." His fingers itched to drag through his hair again, and he kept them firmly at his side. "This is all fucking intense."

"Caring about her doesn't equal house in the country and big, stupid dog, son."

"No." Gage let himself relax. "No, it doesn't. I could spell that out for her. Diplomatically this time."

"Sure, you do that. I'll bring the platter so your head has somewhere to sit after she knocks it off and hands it to you."

"Point," Gage muttered. "So we let it ride, that's all. But when we do the link-up, I want you and Fox there."

"Then we will be."

HE STILL DIDN'T LIKE IT, BUT GAGE WAS REALISTIC enough to know a lot of things needed doing he didn't like. He'd offset that by setting the time and place. His ground— and Cal's house was the closest to his ground as any in the Hollow—and late enough in the day to have his brothers with him.

If anything went wrong, he'd have backup.

"Even considering Crazy Roscoe, I'd rather do this outside." Cybil glanced around the room, then zeroed in on Gage. "The fact is, we might need to do this later on, and in the open, so we might as well figure out how to defend ourselves if necessary."

"Fine. Hold on." Gage walked out of the room, returning moments later with his Luger.

"Don't even think about handing that to me," Fox told him.

"So grab a garden tool like last time." Gage turned to Cal.

"Okay. Shit." With considerable care, Cal took the gun.

"Safety's on."

Cybil opened her bag, took out her .22 and handed it to Quinn. Quinn flipped open the cylinder, examined the chamber, then smoothly locked it back in place. "Okay," she said while Cal stared at her.

"Well, the things you learn about the love of your life. Maybe you should take the big one."

"That's okay, cutie, you can handle it."

"Quinn's an excellent shot," Cybil commented. "So, are we ready for this?"

As they headed out the back, through the kitchen, Fox pulled two knives from the block on Cal's counter. "Just in case," he said when he gave one to Layla.

"Just in case."

Clouds were edging in, Gage noted, but for now there was enough light and the breeze was easy. Like Cybil, he sat on the grass while their friends circled around them.

"Why don't we try to focus on a specific place?" she suggested.

"Such as?"

"Right here. Cal's house. It's a good starting point. We can work our way out from there. Ease into it this time, and we might lessen the side effects."

"Okay." He took her hands. He looked into her eyes. This place, he thought. This grass, this wood, this glass, this dirt.

He saw it in his mind, the lay of the land, the slopes and rises, the lines of the house. Colors and shapes. As he let it form, the greens of spring, the blooms of it faded, withered, browned. White crept in until snow covered the ground, layered on the branches. It fell still, in fat, fast flakes. He felt them, cold and wet against his skin. In his hands, Cybil's hands chilled.

Smoke spiraled from the chimney, and a cardinal, a bright red splash, winged through the falling snow to land in the bird feeder.

Inside, he thought. Who was inside? Who'd built the fire, filled the feeder? Gripping Cybil's hand, he walked through the walls, into the kitchen. A bowl he recognized as Fox's mother's work sat on the counter holding fruit. Music drifted in, something classical that struck the first uneasy note in him. Cal wasn't the classical type, and he'd never known Quinn to go for it.

Who was listening to the music? Who'd bought the apples, the oranges in the bowl? The thought of strangers in Cal's house pushed him forward, lit a spark of anger in him. Cybil's hands tightened on his, nudged him back. He sensed, almost heard her.

No anger. No fear. Wait and see.

Locking down emotion, he moved with her.

A fire crackled in the hearth. Tulips spilled out of a clear glass vase on the mantel. And on the couch, Quinn slept under a colorful blanket. As he watched, Cal stepped to her, leaned over, and kissed her cheek. Even as the restrained tension eased out of Gage, Quinn stirred.

She smiled as her eyes opened. "Hi."

"Hi, Blondie."

"Sorry. Mozart may be good for the kid, but it puts me to sleep every time."

As she shifted, as the blanket slid down, Gage saw she was hugely pregnant. Her hands crossed over her belly, and Cal's closed over them.

It flicked off, the sounds, the images, the scents, and he was back on the grass staring into Cybil's eyes.

"It's nice to have a positive possibility for a change," she managed.

"Headache?" Quinn asked immediately. "Nausea?"

"Not really. It was easier, smoother. And the vision was a quiet one. I think that makes a difference, too. A happy one. You and Cal, in the house. It was winter, and you were sitting in front of the fire."

She squeezed Gage's hand, shot him a look. He took both as a warning, and shrugged. She didn't want to bring up the bun in the oven, fine.

"I like that better than the last one you had of us," Quinn decided. "So, how'd I look? Any disfiguring scars from demon battles?"

"Actually, you looked fabulous. Both of you did. Let's try again. Not a place this time, but people." Cybil looked up at Fox and Layla. "If that's okay with you?"

"Yeah." Layla reached for Fox's hand. "Okay."

"The same way." Cybil met Gage's eyes, settled her breathing. "Slow."

He brought them into his mind as he had Cal's house, shapes, colors, textures. He envisioned them as they were now, standing hand-in-hand behind him. Again, what was faded into what might be.

The shop, he decided. Layla's future boutique with the counters, the displays, the racks. She sat at a fancy little desk, typing something on a laptop. When the door opened, she glanced up and stood as Fox strolled in.

"Good day?" he asked.

"Good day. September's looking great, and I got more fall stock in this afternoon."

"Then congratulations and happy anniversary." He brought a bouquet of pink roses from behind his back.

"They're gorgeous! Happy anniversary."

"One month since your official grand opening."

She laughed, and as she took the flowers, the diamond on her finger caught the light and sizzled. "Then let's go home and celebrate. I'll have my one glass of wine a week."

"You're on." He put his arms around her. "We made it."

"Yes, we did."

When they came back, Cybil's hands once again squeezed his. "You take this one," she suggested.

"Your shop looks pretty slick, and so did you," he added when Layla let out a shaky breath. "That one looked pretty much like he always did. So considering these are possibilities, you've still got time to dump him."

He looked up at the sky. "We're going to get rained on before much longer."

"We've got time for another," Cybil insisted. "Let's go for the gold. The Pagan Stone."

He'd expected her to want to see herself, specifically, or the two of them. As he'd thought before, she surprised him. "We do this, that's it for tonight."

"Agreed. I've got some ideas for other avenues. Another time. Ready?"

It came too fast. He knew it the moment he opened to it, to her. Not a drift this time, but the sensation of being the pebble flying from the slingshot. The flight flung him straight into the holocaust. It rained blood and fire, each striking the scorched ground of the clearing to flash, to burn. The stone boiled with both.

He saw Cybil, her face pale as wax. Her hand bled, as did his. His lungs strained as he fought to breathe in the smoke-thickened air. He heard the shouts around him, and braced.

For what? For what? What did he know?

It came from everywhere at once. Out of the dark, the smoke, out of the ground, the air. When he reached for his gun, his hand came up empty. When he reached for Cybil, it struck, knocking her to the ground where she lay still as death.

He was alone with his own fear and fury. The thing that surrounded him roared in a sound of greedy triumph. Whatever sliced out at him carved a burning gash across his chest. The pain all but swallowed him whole.

Staggering, he tried to drag Cybil away. Her eyes flickered open, latched on to his. "Do it now. You have to do it now. There's no other choice."

He leaped toward the Pagan Stone, fell painfully against it. And he grasped the burning bloodstone atop it in his bare hand. With it closed in his fist, with its flames licking between his clenched fingers, he plunged with it into absolute black.

There was nothing, there was nothing, there was nothing but pain. Then he lay on the Pagan Stone as its fire consumed him.

He clawed his way back, head ringing, nausea a wretched churn in his belly. Swiping blood from his nose, he looked into Cybil's glassy eyes. "So much for slow and easy."

Twelve

~✦~

IT DIDN'T TAKE MUCH OF A PUSH TO CONVINCE
Cybil to throttle back to research mode for a few days. They'd
have to look again, she and Gage, but she couldn't claim to
look forward to the experience.

Had she seen Gage's death? Had she felt her own? The
question played through her mind over and over. Had it been
death, or another kind of end when the black had dropped
around her, leaving her blind. Had the screams she'd heard
been her own?

She'd seen herself at the Pagan Stone before, and every
time she did, death came for her there. Not life, not like Quinn
and Layla, she mused, no celebration. Only the blood and the
black.

She'd have to go back, she knew. In vision and in reality.
Not only to seek answers, but to accept them. When she
did, she had to go back strong. But not today. Today was a holiday with red, white, and blue bunting, with marching bands
and little girls in sparkling costumes. Today's Memorial Day
parade was, in her opinion, a little slice of the Hawkins

Hollow pie, and sampling it helped remind her why she would go back.

And the view from the steps of Fox's office building was one of the best in the house.

"I love a parade," Quinn said beside her.

"Main Street, U.S.A. Hard to resist."

"Aw, look, there's some of the Little League guys." Quinn bounced on her toes while the pickup carting kids in the back inched by. "Those are the Blazers, proudly sponsored by the Bowl-a-Rama. Cal's dad coaches, too. They're on a three-game streak."

"You're really into all this. I mean, seriously into small-town mode."

"Who knew?" With a laugh, Quinn snaked an arm around Cybil's waist. "I'm thinking of joining a committee, and I'm going to do a discussion and signing at the bookstore. Cal's mom offered to teach me how to make pie, but I'm dodging that. There are limits."

"You're in love with this place," Cybil observed. "Not just Cal, but the town."

"I am. Writing this book changed my life, I guess. Bringing me here, realizing I was part of the lore I was researching. It brought me to Cal. But the process of writing it—beyond the hard stuff, the ugly stuff we've faced and have to face—it pulled me in, Cyb. The people, the community, the traditions, the pride. It's just exactly what I want. Not your style, I know."

"I've got nothing against it. In fact, I like it very much."

She looked out over the crowds lining the sidewalks, the fathers with kids riding their shoulders, long-legged teenage girls moving in their colorful packs, families and friends hunkered down in their folding chairs at the curbs. The air was ripe with hot dogs and candy, spicy with the heliotrope from the pots Fox had stacked on his steps. Everything was bright and clear—the blue sky, the yellow sun, the patriotic bunting flying over the streets, the red and white petunias spilling out of baskets hanging on every lamppost along Main.

Young girls in their spangles tossed batons, executed

cartwheels on their way toward the Square. In the distance she heard the sound of trumpets and drums from an approaching marching band.

Most days she might prefer the pace of New York, the style of Paris, the romance of Florence, but on a sunny Saturday afternoon while May readied to give over to June, Hawkins Hollow was the perfect place to be.

She glanced over when Fox held out a glass. "Sun tea," he told her. "There's beer inside if you'd rather."

"This is great." Looking over his shoulder, she lifted an eyebrow at Gage as she sipped. "Not a parade fan?"

"I've seen my share."

"Here comes the highlight," Cal announced. "The Hawkins Hollow High School Marching Band."

Majorettes and honor guards twirled and tossed silver batons and glossy white rifles. The squad of cheerleaders danced and shook pom-poms. Crowd favorites, Cybil thought as cheers and applause erupted. And with the pair of drum majors high-stepping, the band rocked into "Twist and Shout."

"Bueller?" Cal said from behind her, and Cybil laughed.

"It's perfect, isn't it? Just absolutely."

The sweetness of it made her eyes sting. All those young faces, the bold blue and pure white of the uniforms, the tall hats, the spinning batons all moving, moving to the sheer fun of the music. People on the sidewalk began to dance, to call out the lyrics, and the sun bounced cheerfully over the bright, bright brass of instruments.

Blood gushed out of trumpets to splash over the bold blue and pure white, the fresh young faces, the high hats. It splatted from piccolos, dripped from flutes, rained up from the beat of sticks on drums.

"Oh God," Cybil breathed.

The boy swooped over the street, dropped to it to dance. She wanted to cringe back, to cower away when its awful eyes latched on to hers. But she stood, fighting off the quaking and grateful when Gage's hand dropped firmly onto her shoulder.

Overhead the bunting burst into flame. And the band played to the cheers of the crowd.

"Wait." Fox gripped Layla's hand. "Some of them see it or feel it. Look."

Cybil tore her gaze away from the demon. She saw shock and fear on some of the faces in the crowd, paleness or puzzlement on others. Here and there parents grabbed young children, pushed through the onlookers to drag them away while others only stood clapping hands to the beat.

"Bad boy! Bad boy!" A toddler screamed from her perch on her father's shoulders. And began to cry in harsh, horrible sobs. Batons flamed as they spiraled in the air. The street ran with blood. Some of the band broke ranks and ran.

Beside her, Quinn coolly, efficiently snapped pictures.

Cybil watched the boy, and as she stared, its head turned, turned, turned impossibly on its neck until its eyes met hers again. It grinned madly, baring sharp and glistening teeth.

"I'll save you for last, keep you for a pet. I'll plant my seed in you. When it ripens, when it blooms, I'll cut it from you so it can drink your blood like mother's milk."

Then it leaped, springing high into the air on a plate of fire. Riding it, it shot toward her.

She might have run, she might have stood. She'd never know. Gage yanked her back so violently she fell. Even as she shoved to her feet, he was planted in front of her. She saw the thing burst into a mass of bloody black, and vanish with the horrible echo of a boy's laughter.

Her ears rang with it, and with the brass and drums as the band continued its march up Main Street. When she pushed Gage aside to see, the buntings waved red, white, and blue. The sun bounced cheerfully off the instruments.

Cybil stepped back again. "I think I've had enough of parades for one day."

IN FOX'S OFFICE, QUINN USED HIS COMPUTER TO load and display the photographs. "What we saw doesn't come through." She tapped the screen.

"Because it wasn't real. Not all the way real," Layla said.

"Blurs and smears," Quinn noted. "And this cloudy area on each where the little bastard was. There, but not there."

"There are opposing schools of thought on paranormal photography." Calm now with something tangible to study, Cybil pushed her hair back as she leaned closer to the screen. "Some claim that digital cameras have the advantage, able to record light spectrums not visible to the human eye. Others discount them, as they can pick up refractions and reflections, dust motes and so on that cloud the issue. So a good thirty-five millimeter is recommended. But . . ."

"It's not light, but dark," Quinn finished, following the line. "An infrared lens might do better. I should've gotten my recorder out of my purse," she added, scrolling slowly through the series of photos. "It happened so fast, and I was thinking pictures not sound until . . ."

"We heard what it said," Cybil stated.

"Yeah." Quinn laid a hand over hers. "I'd like to see if and how its voice records."

"Isn't it more to the point that we weren't the only ones to see something?"

Quinn looked up at Gage. "You're right. You're right. Does it mean it's strong enough now to push through to the edges of reality, or that those who saw something, even just felt something, are more sensitive? More connected?"

"Some of both gets my vote." Fox ran a hand up and down Layla's back as they watched the photos scroll. "What Layla said about it not being completely real? That's how it felt to me. And that means it wasn't completely *not* real. I didn't see everyone who reacted, but those I noticed were part of families that've been in the Hollow for generations."

"Exactly," Cal confirmed. "I caught that, too."

"If we're able to move people out, that would be where we'd start," Fox said.

"My dad's talked to a few people, felt some of them out." Cal nodded. "We'll make it work." He glanced at his watch. "We're supposed to be heading over to my parents' pretty

soon. Big backyard holiday cookout, remember? If anybody's not up for it, I'll explain."

"We should all go." Straightening, Cybil looked away from
the photos. "We should all go, drink beer, eat burgers and potato salad. We've said it before. Living, doing, being normal,
especially after something like this, it's saying: Up yours."

"I'm with Cybil on that. I need to run back to the house,
file this memory card. Then Cal and I can head over."

"We'll lock up and ride with you." Fox looked at Gage.
"Cool?"

"Yeah, we'll follow."

"Why don't you go ahead?" Cybil suggested. "We'll lock
up."

"Good enough."

Gage waited until he and Cybil were alone. "What do you
need to say you didn't want to say in front of them?"

"Reading people that well must come in handy, professionally. Despite the optimistic possibilities we saw, we've
seen the other side of that. There are two things, actually. I
realize that the last time out you tried to fight this at the Pagan Stone and it didn't work. People died. But—"

"But we have to finish this at the Pagan Stone," he interrupted. "I know it. There's no way around it. We've seen it
enough times, you and I, to understand it. Cal and Fox know
it, too. It's harder for them. This is their town, these are their
people."

"Yours, too. At the base of it, Gage," she said before he
could disagree. "It's where you come from. Whether or not
it's where you end up, it's where you started. So it's yours."

"Maybe. What's the second thing?"

"I need to ask you for a favor."

He lifted his eyebrows in question. "What's the favor?"

She smiled a little. "I knew you weren't the type to just
say: Name it. If things don't go the way we hope, and if
you're sure we wouldn't be able to turn it around—and one
more if, if I'm not able to do it myself, which would be my
first choice—"

"You're going to stand there and ask me to kill you."

"You do read well. I've seen you do just that in other dreams, other visions. The other side of the coin. I'm telling you, Gage, standing here with clear mind, cool blood, that I'd rather die than live through what that thing just promised me. I need you to know that, understand that, and I'm asking you not to let it take me, whatever has to be done."

"I won't let it take you. That's all you get, Cybil," he added when she started to speak. "I won't let it take you."

She stared into his eyes—green and direct—until she saw what she needed to see. "Okay. Let's go eat potato salad."

BECAUSE HE FELT HE NEEDED A DISTRACTION, Gage hunted up a poker game just outside of D.C. The stakes weren't as rich as he might have liked, but the game itself served. So, he could admit, did the temporary distance from Hawkins Hollow and from Cybil. Couldn't escape the first, he thought as he drove back on a soft June morning. But he'd let himself get much too involved with the woman.

It was stepping-back time.

When a woman looked to you to take her life to save her from worse, it was past stepping-back time. Too much responsibility, he thought as he traveled the familiar road. Too intense. Too damn real. And why the hell had he promised he'd take care of her—because that's just what he'd done. Something in the way she'd looked at him, he decided. Steady, calm as she'd asked him to end her life. She'd meant what she'd said, flat-out meant it. More, she'd trusted him to know she meant it.

Time for a conversation, he decided. Time to make sure they both understood exactly what was on the table, and what wasn't. He didn't want anyone depending on him.

He could ask himself why he hadn't stayed over after the game, used the hotel room he'd booked. Why he hadn't moved on the signals sent by the very appealing redhead who'd given him a good run for his money at the table. All things being equal, he should be enjoying a post-sex room-service breakfast with the redhead right about now. Instead he was, again, heading for the Hollow.

So he wouldn't ask himself why. No point in asking when he didn't want the answer.

He glanced in the rearview at the sound of the sirens, then took a casual glance down at the speedometer. Only about five over the posted limit, he noted, as he wasn't in any hurry. He pulled over to the shoulder. He wasn't surprised that the view in his side mirror showed him Derrick Napper climbing out of the cruiser.

Fucking Napper, who'd hated him, Cal, and Fox since childhood. And had made it his life's work, so it seemed, to cause them trouble. Fox, particularly, Gage mused. But none of the three of them were immune.

Asshole likes to strut, Gage thought, as Napper did just that to cover the distance from the cruiser to Gage's Ferrari. How the hell did they allow such a complete bastard to strap on a weapon and pin on a badge?

Cocking a hip, Napper leaned down, gave Gage a wide, white smile. "Some people think having a fancy machine gives them the right to break the law."

"Some might."

"You were speeding, boy."

"Maybe." Without being asked, Gage offered license and registration.

"What'd this thing set you back?"

"Just write the ticket, Napper."

Napper's eyes narrowed to slits. "You were weaving."

"No," Gage said with the same dead calm, "I wasn't."

"Driving erratically, speeding. You been drinking?"

Gage tapped the to-go cup in its holder. "Coffee."

"I believe I smell alcohol on your breath. We take driving drunk serious around here, fuckhead." He smiled when he said it. "I need you to step out of the car, take a test."

"No."

Napper's hand dropped to the butt of his sidearm. "I said step out of the car, fucker."

Baiting the hook, Gage thought. It was the sort of thing

that too often worked on Fox. For himself, he'd just let Deputy Asshole play it out. Slowly, Gage took the keys out of the ignition. He stepped out, clicked the locks, all the while staring into Napper's eyes. "I'm not taking a Breathalyzer, and it's within my rights to refuse."

"I say you stink of alcohol." Napper jammed a finger into Gage's chest. "I say you're a lousy drunk, just like your old man."

"Say anything you want. The opinions of dickheads don't weigh much with me."

Napper shoved Gage back against the car. Though Gage's hands curled into fists, he kept them at his sides. "I say you're drunk." To punctuate it, Napper slammed his hand on Gage's chest. "I say you resisted arrest. I say you assaulted an officer. We'll see how much that weighs when you're behind bars." He shoved Gage again, grinned. "Chicken-shit bastard." He pushed Gage around. "Spread 'em."

Coolly, Gage laid his hands on the roof of the car as Napper frisked him. "You get off on that? Is that part of the perks?" He hissed in a breath, but stayed as he was when Napper rabbit-punched him.

"You shut the fuck up." Wrenching Gage's arms behind his back, Napper cuffed him. "Maybe we'll take a little ride, you and me, before I put you in jail."

"It'll be interesting to hear you explain that, when I call in the six witnesses who drove by while you were rousting me. While you put hands on me while mine were at my sides. License numbers are in my head. I'm good with numbers." He didn't flinch when Napper pushed him violently against the car again. "And look, here comes another one."

The approaching car slowed. Gage recognized it as Joanne Barry's little hybrid. She stopped the car, rolled down the windows, and said, "Oh-oh."

"You just drive on, Ms. Barry. This is police business."

The disgusted look she sent Napper spoke volumes. "So I see. Need a lawyer, Gage?"

"Looks like. Why don't you have Fox meet me at the police station."

"I said you drive *on*!" Once again Napper's hand went to the butt of his weapon. "Or do you want me to arrest you for interfering with an officer?"

"You always were a nasty little prick. I'll call Fox, Gage." She pulled her car to the shoulder, staring at Napper as she took out her cell phone.

On an oath, Napper pushed Gage in the back of the cruiser. Gage saw his eyes latch on to the rearview as he got behind the wheel. And saw the fury in them as Joanne followed the cruiser into town, and all the way to the police station.

Gage's first twinge of fear came when both Joanne and Napper stepped out of their cars at the station, and he himself was locked inside the cruiser. No, no, he thought, witnesses here, too. Napper wouldn't lay a hand on her and if he did . . .

But he saw only a brief exchange of words before Napper unlocked the backseat and hauled him out. Joanne marched straight inside, skirted Dispatch with a "Hey, Carla," for the woman who sat there, then clipped to chief of police Wayne Hawbaker's office. "I need to file a complaint against one of your deputies, Wayne. And you need to come out here, now."

Just look at her, Gage thought. Wasn't she something?

Hawbaker came out, looked from Joanne to Gage to Napper. "What seems to be the trouble?"

"I tagged this *individual* for speeding, reckless driving. I suspected he was driving under the influence. He refused to take a Breathalyzer, resisted, and took a swing at me."

"Bullshit!"

"Joanne," Hawbaker said quietly. "Gage?"

"I'll cop to the speeding. I was about five over the limit. Joanne gave you the rest. It's bullshit."

Hawbaker's steady stare gave nothing away. "You been drinking?"

"I had a beer about ten o'clock last night. That's, what, about twelve hours ago?"

"He was driving erratically. Had an open container in the car."

"I wasn't driving erratically, and the open container was a goddamn go-coffee from Sheetz. Your boy here baited me, manhandled me, rabbit-punched me, cuffed me, and suggested we take a ride before he brought me in."

Red flags of fury rode Napper's cheeks. "He's a lying sack."

"My car's on the side of the road," Gage continued in the same even tone. "Just before Blue Mountain Lane, in front of a two-story redbrick house, white shutters, front garden. White Toyota hatchback in the driveway, Maryland vanity license plate reads Jenny4. Nice-looking brunette was out front gardening and saw it go down. You ought to check it out." He looked back at Napper now, smiled easily. "You're not very observant for a cop."

"That'd be Jenny Mullendore." Hawbaker studied Napper's face. Whatever he saw in it had his jaw tightening. Before he could speak, Fox pushed through the door.

"Quiet," he said, pointing a finger at Gage. "Why is my client in handcuffs?" he demanded.

"Derrick, uncuff him."

"I'm booking him on the aforesaid charges, and—"

"I said uncuff him. We're going to sit down and hash this out now."

Napper whirled on his chief. "You're not standing by me?"

"I want to speak to my client," Fox interrupted. "In private."

"Fox." Hawbaker dragged his hands over his bristly, graying hair. "Give me a minute here. Derrick, did you strike Gage?"

"Hell, no. I had to take him in hand when he resisted."

"Is that what Jenny Mullendore's going to tell me when I ask her?"

Napper's eyes went to furious slits. "I don't know what she's going to tell you. For all I know she's screwing him and she'll say any damn thing."

"You're quite the lover, Gage," Joanne said with a smile. "According to Deputy Napper, I'm screwing you, too."

Fox rounded on Napper, and currently cuffed, Gage could only body-bump him back. "What did you say to my mother?"

"Don't worry." Knowing her son, Joanne stepped forward, took a firm grip on his arm. "I'm filing a complaint. He told me to fuck off when I followed him in, and I followed him in because I saw him shoving Gage, who was already handcuffed. He suggested that I put out for Gage, and half the men in town."

"Jesus Christ, Derrick."

"She's lying."

"Everyone's lying but you." Gage shook his head. "That must be tough. If these cuffs aren't off in the next five seconds, I'm authorizing my attorney to file a civil suit against the deputy, and the Hawkins Hollow police department."

"Uncuff him. Now, Deputy! Carla." Chief Hawbaker turned to the wide-eyed woman at Dispatch. "Get ahold of Jennifer Mullendore."

"Um, actually, Chief, she's on the line. She just called in about, ah, an incident in front of her house."

Fox beamed a smile. "Isn't it nice when private citizens do their public duty? Are you filing charges against my client, Chief?"

This time Hawbaker scrubbed his hands over his face. "I'd appreciate it if you'd give me a few minutes on that. I'm going to take this call in my office. Deputy, come with me. If y'all would just have a seat?"

Fox sat, stretched out his legs. "Just can't stay out of trouble, can you?" he said to Gage.

"Apparently not."

"You either," he said to his mother.

"My boyfriend and I are badasses."

"He crossed the line with this," Fox said quietly. "Hawbaker's good police, he's a good chief, and he's not going to take it, not going to let it ride. If Jenny corroborates your statement, you've got grounds for those civil suits, and

Hawbaker knows it. More, he knows he's got a loose cannon on his hands in Napper."

"My girlfriend hadn't come along, he would've done more. He was working himself up to it." Gage leaned over, kissed Joanne's cheek. "Thanks, honey."

"Cut that out or I'm telling my father." Fox leaned closer to Gage. "Was it just Nap the Prick, or was it more?"

"I can't say for certain, but we all know Napper doesn't need demonic help being a violent bastard. Just him, I think. He got worried when I mentioned I had plate numbers for about six cars that went by while he was shoving me around."

Gage glanced toward the closed office door when Napper's voice boomed out. "Fuck you, then. I quit." He burst out a moment later, rage burning in his eyes.

Gage noted his sidearm was missing. "There won't always be a slut around for you bastards to hide behind." He slammed out the front door of the station.

"Did he mean me or Jenny Mullendore was a slut?" Joanne wondered. "Because honestly, I don't see how she has time for slut activities with those two preschoolers of hers. Me, I've got lots of time."

"Okay, Mom." Fox patted her arm, then rose when Hawbaker stepped out of his office.

"I want to apologize to you, Joanne, for the unacceptable behavior of one of my deputies. I'd appreciate it if you'd file that complaint. I'd like to apologize to you, Gage, on behalf of my department for the harassment. Mrs. Mullendore's statement jibed with what you told me. I realize you're within your rights to file a civil action. I will tell you that due to the circumstances, I suspended Deputy Napper, with the intention of conducting a full investigation of this matter. He has elected to resign from the department."

"That works for me." Gage got to his feet.

"Unofficially, I'm going to tell you, all of you—and you can pass this to Cal, because it seems to me Derrick sees you as one. You be careful. You watch your backs. He's . . . volatile. I can have you taken back to your car, Gage, if you want."

"I've got that covered," Fox told Hawbaker. "You watch your back, too. Napper holds grudges."

GAGE PLANNED TO HEAD STRAIGHT BACK TO CAL'S, grab a shower, some food, maybe some sleep. But impulse pushed him to the rental house. Cybil stood out front, in shorts and a tank that showed off long legs and long arms, and watered the pots and baskets of flowers scattered around the entrance.

She lowered the big, galvanized can, and strolled down to meet him. "I heard you had a busy morning."

"No secrets in the Hollow."

"Oh, a few. Is everything all right now?"

"I'm not in jail and Napper no longer works for the town police."

"Both good news." She angled her head. "How pissed off are you? It's difficult to tell."

"Only mildly at this point. During? I wanted to kick his ass out into the road and stomp on his face. It's hard to resist that kind of pleasure. But . . ."

"A man who controls himself has a better chance of winning."

"Something like that."

"Well, you won this one. Are you coming in, or passing by?"

Step back, go home, Gage told himself. "Any chance of getting a meal around here?"

"There might be. I guess you've earned it."

When she turned, Gage took her arm. "I wasn't going to come here today. I don't know why I did."

"For a meal?"

He pulled her to him, took her lips with a hunger that had nothing to do with food. "No. I don't know what this is, this you and me. I don't know if I like it."

"At least we're in step there because neither do I."

"If we're alive come mid-July, I'm gone."

"So am I."

"Okay then."

"Okay. No strings on you, no strings on me." But she brushed her hands through his hair and kissed him, warmly, again. "Gage, there are a lot more important things to worry about here than what this you-and-me thing might be."

"I don't lie to women, and I don't like to misdirect them either. That's all."

"So noted. I don't like to be lied to, but I have a habit of picking my own direction. Do you want to come in and have that meal?"

"Yeah. Yeah, I do."

Thirteen

HE PUT FLOWERS ON HIS MOTHER'S GRAVE, AND she reached up, a slim hand spearing through earth and grass, to take them. As Gage stood in the flood of sunlight, in the quiet cemetery with its somber stones, his heart slammed into his throat. Draped in innocent white, she ascended—pretty and pale from the maw of dirt—clutching the bouquet like a bride her wedding roses.

Had they buried her in white? He didn't know.

"You used to bring me dandelions, and the wild butter-cups and violets that colored the little hill near our house in the summer."

His throat ached, straining to hold his trembling heart. "I remember."

"Do you?" She sniffed the roses, red as blood against her white dress. "It's hard to know what little boys remember, what little boys forget. We used to take walks in the woods, and in the fields. Do you remember that?"

"Yes."

"There are houses in the fields now, where we used to walk. But we could walk here, for a little while."

Her skirts billowed as she turned, and with his flowers cradled in the crook of her arm, began to walk. "There's so little time left," she said. "I was afraid you wouldn't come back, not after what happened when you were here last." She looked into his eyes. "I couldn't stop it. It's very strong, and getting stronger."

"I know that, too."

"I'm proud of you for staying, for being brave. Whatever happens, I want you to know I'm proud of you. If . . . If you fail, I'll be waiting for you. I don't want you to be afraid."

"It feeds on fear."

She looked at him again. A sleek black hornet crawled out from the delicate petals of a rose, but she looked nowhere but at him. "On many things. It's had an eternity to develop its appetites. If you could stop it . . ."

"We will stop it."

"How? There are only a few weeks left, such a little bit of time. What can you do this time you didn't do before? Except be brave. What do you plan to do?"

"Whatever it takes."

"You're still looking for answers, with time running out." Her smile was soft as she nodded, soft as a second hornet, then a third squirmed, black on red. "You were always a brave and stubborn boy. All those years your father had to punish you."

"Had to?"

"What choice did he have? Don't you remember what you did?"

"What did I do?"

"You killed me, and your sister. Don't you remember? We were walking in the fields, just like this, and you ran. Even when I told you not to, you ran and ran, and fell. You cried so hard, poor little boy." Her smile was full, and somehow luminous, as the roses disgorged hornets. And the hornets began to hum.

"Your knees were all scraped and scratched. So I had to

carry you, and the weight of you, the strain of it, was too much for me. You see?"

She spread her arms and the white gown blossomed with blood. Hornets swarmed in buzzing black clouds until even the roses bled. "Only a few days later, the blood and the pain. From you, Gage."

"It's a lie." It was Cybil who spoke, who was suddenly at his side. "You're a lie. Gage, it's not your mother."

"I know."

"She's not so pretty now," it said. "Want to see?"

The white dress thinned to filthy rags over rotted flesh. It laughed and laughed as fat worms writhed through the flesh, as the flesh gave way to bone.

"How about you?" it said to Cybil. "Want to see Daddy?"

The bones re-formed into a man with sightless eyes and a charming grin. "There's my princess! Come give Daddy a kiss!"

"More lies."

"Oh, I can't see! I can't see! I can't see what a worthless shit I am." It laughed uproariously. "I chose death over you." Hornets stabbed out to crawl at the corners of its grin. "Death was better than your constant *need*, your unrelenting, sickening love. Didn't have to think twice before . . ." It mimed shooting a gun with its hand. And the side of its head exploded into a ruin of blood, bone, brain.

"That's the truth, isn't it? Remember, bitch?" Its single blind eye rolled in its socket, then the image burst into flame. "I'm waiting for you, for both of you. You'll burn. They all burn."

He woke with his hand clutching Cybil's, and her eyes staring into his.

"Are you okay?"

She nodded, but stayed as she was when he sat up. Dawn spread milky light into the room as her breath shuddered in and out.

"It wasn't them," she managed. "It wasn't them, and it wasn't the truth."

"No." Because he thought they both needed it, he took her hand again. "How did you do that? Get into my dream?"

"I don't know. I could see you, hear you, but at first I was removed from it—not part of it. It was almost like watching a movie, or a play, but through a film, or a curtain. Like gauze. Then I was in it. I pushed . . ." Dissatisfied, she shook her head. "No, that's not right, not really. It was less deliberate than that, more visceral. More like a flick, the way you'd give a curtain in your way an annoyed flick. I was so angry because I thought you believed what it was saying."

"I didn't. I knew what it was from the start. Bluff me once," Gage murmured.

"You were playing it." Cybil closed her eyes a moment. "You're good."

"It's looking for our hole card, wants to know what we've got. And it told us more than we told it."

"That there's still time." Now, she sat up beside him. "However strong it's getting, however much it might be able to do, it still has to wait for the seventh for the real show."

"Give the lady a cigar. It's about time for our bluff. Time to make the bastard believe we have more than we do."

"And we'd do that by . . . ?"

Gage rose, went to the dresser, opened a drawer. "Bait."

Cybil stared at the bloodstone he held. "That's supposed to be in a safe place, not knocking around in . . . Wait. Let me see it."

Gage tossed it casually in the air, then over to her.

"This isn't our bloodstone."

"No, I picked it up at a rock shop a few days ago. But it fooled you for a minute."

"It's the same basic size, not quite the same shape. It might have power, too, Gage. The research I've done points to bloodstones as part of the Alpha Stone."

"It's not ours. Not the one it's worried about. It might be worthwhile finding out just how worried it is, and what it might do to get its hands on what it thinks is Dent's bloodstone."

"And to see how pissed off it gets when it realizes—if it does—this is a substitute."

"Can't be overstated. It's used our pain against us, our tragedies. Let's return the favor. The bloodstone helped Dent keep that thing under for three centuries. Stopped it in its tracks a good long while and set the stage for what we're doing. That's got to be one of the big losses."

"Okay. How do we con a demon?"

"I've got some ideas."

She had some of her own, but they were down avenues her research had taken her, avenues she didn't want to travel. So she kept her silence, and listened to his.

A COUPLE HOURS LATER, CYBIL STORMED OUT OF Cal's back door with sharp lashes of fury whipping from her. She spun around when Gage slammed out after her. "You've got no right, no *right* to make these plans, to make these decisions on your own."

"The hell I don't. It's my life."

"It's all our lives!" she tossed back. "We're supposed to work as a team. We're meant to work as a team."

"Meant? I'm sick to death of this destiny crap you're so high on. I make my own choices, and I deal with the results. I'm not going to let some ancient guardian make them for me."

"Oh, for God's sake." Everything about her snapped out in angry frustration, voice, hands, eyes. "We all have choices. Aren't we fighting, risking our lives, because Twisse takes away choice? But that doesn't mean any of us can just forget why we were brought together like this and go off on his own."

"I am on my own. Always have been."

"Oh, screw that! You're sick of destiny talk? Fine, *I'm* sick of your 'I'm a loner and I don't belong' refrain. It's boring. We're bound by blood, all of us."

"Is that what you think?" In contrast to her heat, his tone was brittle and cold. "You think I'm bound to you, by anything? Didn't we just cover this a little while ago? We're having sex. That's the beginning and the end of it. If you're looking for more—"

"You conceited ass. I'm talking about life and death and you're worried about me trying to get my hooks in you? Believe me, outside of the bedroom, I wouldn't have you on a bet."

Something flashed in his eyes. It might have been insult or challenge. It might have been hurt. "I'd take that bet, sister. I know your type."

"You don't know—"

"You want it all your way. You figure you're so damn smart you can run the show and everyone in it. Nobody runs me. And when this is over, you think you can keep me on the line or cut me loose, at your whim. You've got the looks, the brains, the style, what man could resist you? Well, you're looking at one."

"Is that so?" she said, her tone frigid. "Is what you were doing in bed with me last night your definition of resisting?"

"No, that's my definition of banging a willing and convenient woman."

Her angry color drained, but she inclined her head, regally. "In that case, you can consider me now unwilling and inconvenient, and do your substandard banging elsewhere."

"Part of the point. I go my way on this because this has all played out long enough for me. This fight, this town, you. All of it."

Her hands curled at her sides. "I don't care how selfish you are, how stupid you are, after this is done. But before it is, you're not going to jeopardize all the work we've done, all the progress we've made."

"Progress, my ass. Since you and your girl pals got here, we've been bogged down in charts, graphs, exploring our emotional thresholds, and other bullshit."

"Before we got here, you and your idiot brothers fumbled around on this for twenty years."

He backed her against the rail. "You haven't lived through a Seven. You think you know? What you've dealt with so far's been nothing. A few chills and spills. Wait until you see some guy disembowel himself, or try to stop some teenage girl from lighting the match after she's poured gas all over herself and her baby brother. Then you talk to me about what I can do, what I can't. You think seeing your old man put a bullet in his ear makes you some kind of expert? That was quick and clean, and you got off easy."

"You son of a bitch."

"Suck it up." His words were a slap, quick and careless. "If Twisse isn't offed before the next Seven, you're going to be dealing with a lot worse than a father who'd rather kill himself than stand up with his family."

She swung out, and there was enough behind the blow to have his head jerking back. With his ears ringing from it, he gripped her arms to ward off a second attack. "Do you want to talk about fathers, Gage? Do you really want to bring up fathers, considering your own?"

Before he could respond, Quinn rushed out. "Hold it, hold it, hold it!"

"Go back inside," Cybil ordered, "this doesn't concern you."

"The hell it doesn't. What the hell's wrong with you? Both of you?"

"Step back, Gage." Cal pushed through the door, with Fox and Layla behind him. "Just step back. Let's go inside and talk this out."

"Back off."

"Okay, okay, that's not the way to win friends and influence people." Fox moved up, put a hand on Gage's arm. "Let's take a breath here and—"

Gage shoved him off, knocked him back a step. "The back off goes for you, too, Peace and Love."

"You want to go a round with me?" Fox challenged.

"Jesus!" Layla fisted her hands in her hair. "Stop! Just because Gage is being an idiot doesn't mean you have to be one."

"Now I'm an idiot?" Fox rounded on Layla. "He shoves Cybil around, tells me to back off, and *I'm* an idiot."

"I didn't say you were an idiot, I said you didn't have to be an idiot. But apparently I'm wrong about that."

"Don't start on me. I didn't get this stupid ball rolling."

"I don't care who got it rolling." Cal held up his hands. "It stops here."

"Who gave you the gold star and put you in charge?" Gage demanded. "You don't tell me what to do. We wouldn't be in this mess in the first place without you and your ridiculous blood brothers ritual with your pussy Boy Scout knife."

It erupted then, the shouts, the accusations, each rolling over the next into an ugly mass of anger, resentment, and hurt. Words struck like fists, and none of them paid attention to the darkening sky or the oncoming rumble of thunder.

"Oh, just stop! Stop it. Shut the hell up!" Cybil pitched her voice over the chaos, silencing it to a ragged and humming silence. "Can't you see he doesn't give a damn what the rest of you think or feel? It's all about him, maybe it always has been. If he wants to go his own way, he'll go. I, for one, am done." She looked dead into Gage's eyes. "I'm done here."

Without a backward glance, she walked back into the house.

"Cyb. Shit." Quinn scalded the men with one long stare. "Nice job. Come on, Layla."

When Quinn and Layla slammed in behind Cybil, Cal swore again. "Who the hell are you to lay all this on me? Not who I thought, that's for damn sure. Maybe Cybil's right. Maybe it's time to be done with you."

"You'd better cool off," Fox managed as Cal left them. "You'd better take some time and cool the hell off unless you really do like being alone."

And alone, Gage let his mind seethe with resentment, let his thoughts travel on the stony road of blame and grievances. They turned on him, all of them, because he had the balls to take a step, because he'd decided to stop sitting around scratching his ass and studying charts. The hell with them. All of them.

He took the bloodstone out of his pocket, studied it. It meant absolutely nothing. None of it. The risks, the effort, the work, the *years*. He'd come back, time after time. He'd bled time after time. And for what?

He laid the stone on the porch rail, stared bitterly out at Cal's blooming backyard. For what? For whom? What had the Hollow ever given him? A dead mother, a drunk for a father. Pitying or suspicious looks by the *good* townspeople. And oh yeah, just recently, it got him handcuffed and shoved around by an asshole the town deemed worthy to wear a badge.

She was done? He sneered, thinking of Cybil. No, *he* was done. Hawkins Hollow and everyone in it could go straight to hell.

He turned, slammed back into the house to get his things.

It oozed out of the woods, a miasma of black. Inside the house, angry voices rang out again, and it seemed to shudder with pleasure. As it flowed over grass, pretty beds of flowers, it began to take shape. Limbs, torso, head writhing into form through the murk. Fingers, feet, eyes glowing unearthly green took shape as it crept closer to the pretty house with its generous deck and cheerful flowers raining out of glossy pots.

Ears and chin, and a grinning mouth that flashed its teeth. The thrill it felt was terrible. It smeared blood over the green of the grass, the bright petals of flowers, because it could.

Soon all would burn, all, and it would dance on the bloody ashes. The boy danced now, in greedy delight, then hopped up to crouch on the rail beside the stone. A small thing, it thought. Such a small thing to have caused so much trouble, so much time.

It cocked its head. What secrets did it hold? What power? And why were those secrets, that power blocked so that in no form could it see? Blocked from them, too, it thought. Yes, yes, the guardian had given them the key, but not the lock.

It wanted to touch the deep green and dark red of it. To steal whatever waited inside. It reached out, drew its hand back. But no, better to destroy. Always better to destroy. And it spread its hands over the stone.

"Yo," Gage said from the doorway, and shot the boy dead center of the forehead.

It screamed, and what poured from the wound was thick and black, and reeked like death. It leaped, even as Gage continued to fire, as the others rushed out of the house with him. Perched on the roof, it snarled like a mad dog.

Wind and rain erupted in a horrific gush. Taking position in the yard, Gage reloaded, prepared to fire again.

"Try not to shoot my house," Cal told him.

It leaped again, and as it slammed its fists into the air, the bloodstone exploded into dozens of fragments, into clouds of dust. The boy screamed, in triumph now, even as the blood ran from it. It spun, then it swooped, snake-fast, to latch its teeth into Gage's shoulder. As Gage dropped helplessly to his knees, it vanished.

Dimly, Gage heard voices, but they were smothered by a drowning fog of pain. He saw the sky, saw it was going blue again, but the faces that leaned over him were blurred and indistinct.

Had it killed him? If so, he wished to Christ death would get a damn move on so the agony would end. It burned, burned, boiling blood, searing bone, and inside his head he screamed. But he had no breath to make a sound, no strength even to writhe in the torment that squeezed, that clawed like flaming talons.

So he closed his eyes.

Enough, he thought. Enough now. Time to go.

So, in surrender, he began to float away from the pain.

The sharp slap to his face irritated him. The second pissed him off. Couldn't he die in relative peace?

"You come back, you son of a bitch! Do you hear me? You come back. You fight, you fucking coward. You are *not* going to die and let that bastard win."

The pain—goddamn it—the pain flooded back. When he opened his eyes in defense, Cybil's face filled his blurry vision, and her voice just kept badgering, hammering. Those dark eyes of hers were drenched with fury and tears.

He wheezed in an agonizing breath. "I wish you'd shut up."

"Cal. Fox."

"We've got him. Come on, Gage." Cal's voice came from some strange distance—miles off, it seemed, and buried in mud. "Focus. Right shoulder. It's your right shoulder. We're with you. Focus on the pain."

"How the fuck am I supposed to do anything else?"

"He's saying something." Fox's face edged into Gage's view. "Can you hear him? He's trying to tell us something."

"I am telling you something, you asshole."

"His pulse is weak. It's getting weaker."

Who was that? Gage wondered. Layla? He saw her words as pale blue lights, drifting at the corner of his eye.

"The bleeding's stopped. It's already stopped. The punctures aren't that deep now. It has to be something else. Some sort of poison."

And Quinn chimed in, Gage thought. Gang's all here. Just let me go, for God's sake. Just let me go.

"We won't. We can't." Cybil leaned closer, but this time her lips rather than her hand laid over his cheek. Blessedly cool. "Please. You have to stay. You have to come back. We can't lose you."

Tears spilled out of her eyes, dropped gently onto the wound. They washed through his blood, into the bite, and eased the burn.

"I know it hurts." She stroked his cheeks, his hair, his screaming shoulder, and wept. "I know it hurts, but you have to stay."

"He moved. His hand moved." Fox's fingers tightened on Gage's as Gage's flexed. "Cal?"

"Yeah. Yeah. Right shoulder, Gage. Start there. We've got you."

He closed his eyes again, but not in surrender this time. Bearing down, he concentrated on the source of the pain, followed it as it spread from his shoulder, down his arm, across his chest. He felt his lungs open again as if the hands that had squeezed them closed now slipped away.

"His pulse is stronger!" Layla called out.

"His color's coming back, too. He's coming back, Cyb," Quinn said.

From where she sat on the ground, cradling his head in her lap, Cybil leaned back down, watched his eyes. "It's almost over," she crooned. "Just a little more."

"Okay. Okay." He saw her clearly now, felt the grass under him, the grip of his friends' hands over his. "I've got it. Did you call me a fucking coward?"

Her breath drew in on a watery laugh. "It worked."

"Welcome back, man," Fox said to him. "The wound's closing. Let's get you inside."

"I got it," Gage repeated, but couldn't so much as lift his head. "Okay, maybe I don't."

"Give him another minute," Quinn suggested. "The wound's closed now, but . . . there's a scar."

"Let's go inside." Cybil sent looks to Quinn and Layla that said more than her words. "We'll make Gage some tea, get his bed ready."

"I don't want tea. I don't want a bed."

"You're getting both." Cybil shifted his head from her lap, patted his cheek, then rose. If she understood men at all—and Gage in particular—he'd prefer the women out of sight when his friends helped him into the house.

"I want coffee," Gage said, but the women were already headed back to the house.

"Bet you do. Quinn's right about the scar," Fox added. "Nothing's ever scarred us since the blood brothers ritual."

"None of us had a demon try to take a bite out of us either," Cal put in. "It's never been able to do anything like that before, not even during the Seven."

"Times change. Give me a hand, will you? Let's just start with sitting up." With his friends on either arm, Gage managed to make it to sitting. Where his head spun for three wicked revolutions. "Jesus." He sat, with his head braced by his updrawn knees. "I've never felt pain like that and I've had plenty of pain. Did I scream?"

"No. You went white, dropped like a stone." Cal swiped sweat off his own face.

"Inside I was screaming like a little girl. Where's my

shirt?" he demanded when he lifted his head and realized he was naked to the waist.

"We had to rip it off you, get to the wound," Fox told him. "You didn't move, not a flicker, Gage. You were barely breathing. I swear to God, I thought you were gone."

"I was. Or nearly." Cautiously, Gage turned his head, pressed fingers to the scar on his shoulder. "It doesn't even ache now. I feel pretty weak, a lot shaky, but there's no pain."

"You need to sleep. You know how it goes," Cal added. "It sucks you dry, that intense a healing."

"Yeah, maybe. Get me up, will you?"

With an arm slung around each of his friends, Gage gained his rubbery legs. When half a dozen steps toward the house left him kitten-weak, he accepted he'd need that bed. But there was satisfaction in his belly as he looked at the empty porch rail.

"Bastard blew that rock to hell and back."

"Yeah, he did. Can you make the steps?"

"I can make them." In fact, he was smiling through gritted teeth when Cal and Fox all but carried him into the house.

Since he was too tired to fight off a trio of females, he drank the tea Cybil foisted on him. And he dropped onto the bed with its freshly smoothed sheets and plumped pillows.

"Why doncha lie down with me, sugar?"

"That's sweet, honey."

"Not you." Gage waved off Fox, pointed to Cybil. "Big brown eyes there. Fact, maybe all the pretty women oughta lie down here with me. Plenty of room."

"What the hell did you put in that tea?" Cal demanded.

"Secret ingredient. Go ahead." Cybil sat on the side of the bed. "I'll stay with him until he drops off."

"Come on over here and say that."

Smiling, Cybil waved off the others, then angling her head, studied Gage's face.

"Hello, gorgeous," he mumbled.

"Hello, handsome. You've had a busy morning. Go to sleep."

"Pissed you off."

"Pissed you off back. That was the plan."

"Damn good plan."

"Risky, potentially stupid plan."

He smirked. "Worked."

"You have me there."

"Didn't mean that shit about your father."

"I know. Shh." She bent down, kissed his cheek.

"Maybe meant some of the other shit—can't remember. Did you?"

"We'll talk about it later."

"She said—Ann Hawkins said—you'd cry for me. That it would matter. You did. It did. You brought me back, Cybil."

"I gave you a jumpstart. You did the rest. Gage." Shuddering once, she laid her cheek against his. "I thought you'd die. Nothing's ever scared me like that, or torn at me like that. I thought you'd die. That we'd lose you. That I would. You were dying in my arms, and until that moment, I didn't realize that I—"

She lifted her head, broke off when she saw he'd fallen asleep. "Well." She drew a long breath, then another. "Well, that's probably excellent timing for both of us. No point in humiliating myself or putting you on the spot by telling you, at a weak moment for both of us, that I've been stupid enough to fall in love with you."

Taking his hand, she sat with him a little while longer as he slept. And she wondered if she'd find the way to be smart enough to get over him.

"Do you think you must?"

Slowly, Cybil lifted her gaze from Gage's face, and looked into Ann Hawkins's. "Well, last but not least." It didn't surprise her she was so calm. She'd been waiting for this, and she'd seen much more shocking things now than a ghost by a bedside on a June morning.

"Do you think you must?" Ann repeated.

"Must what?"

"Close your heart to what you feel for him. Deny yourself the joy and the pain of it."

"I'm not a fan of pain."

"But it's life. Only the dead feel nothing."

"What about you?"

Ann's lips curved. "It is not death. My own love told me that. There is more than the dark and the light. So many shades between. I feel yet, because it is not finished. When it is, one thing ends, another begins. You are young, and may have many years in this life, in this body, in this time. Why would you live it with a closed heart?"

"Easy for you to say. Your love was returned. I know what it is to live loving someone who can't or won't love you back, or not enough."

"Your father was consumed by despair. He lost his sight, and couldn't see love."

What's the difference? Cybil thought, but shook her head. "This would be a fascinating conversation over a drink sometime, just us girls, but at the moment we're more into the life-or-death mode around here. You may have noticed."

"You are angry."

"Of course I'm angry. He nearly died today, nearly died in my arms trying to find a way to stop something that was pushed on him, on all of us. He may die yet, any or all of us might. I've seen how it might be."

"You haven't told them all you've learned, all you've seen."

Cybil looked down at Gage again. "No, I haven't."

"You will see more before it is done. Child—"

"I'm not your child."

"No, but neither are you its. Life or death, you say, and so it is. Either the light or the dark will end with the Seven. My love will either be freed, or be damned."

"And mine?" Cybil demanded.

"He will make his choice, and so will you all. I have no one but you, my hope, my faith, my courage. Only today, you used all of those. And he sleeps," Ann murmured, looking down at Gage. "Alive. More than alive, he brought back from death's shadow another answer. Another weapon."

Cybil got to her feet. "What answer? What weapon?"

"You are an educated woman with a strong and seeking mind. Find it. Use it. All is in your hands now. Yours, his, and the others'. And it fears you. His blood, its blood," she said as she began to fade, "our blood, your blood. And theirs."

Standing alone, Cybil again looked down at Gage. "His blood," she said quietly, and hurried out of the room.

Fourteen

∿

WHEN GAGE WOKE HE DIDN'T JUST WANT COFFEE, he wanted it desperately. He sat up first, testing, and when the room stayed steady, stood. No weakness, no nausea, no dizziness. All good news. And no odd euphoria, he realized as his mind tracked back.

What the hell had she put in that tea?

As much as he craved coffee, he wanted a shower more, so walked into the bathroom and stripped. In the mirror, he studied his shoulder, poked at the puckered crescent marring the skin. It was odd having a scar after all these years, a tangible reminder of those keen, feral teeth tearing into him. He'd broken bones, been stabbed, shot, burned, and not a mark to show for it. But Twisse, in the form of that little bastard, manages to get a quick bite, and it appeared he'd be carrying the scar from it for the rest of his life.

However long that might be.

He showered, dressed, and headed out in search of coffee. He stopped at Cal's home office where both Layla and Quinn were hunkered at a computer. Both looked up, both gave him the let's-have-a-look-at-you once-over.

"How are you feeling?" Layla asked him.

"I want coffee."

"Back to normal then." Quinn's look brightened into a smile. "Should be some downstairs. Cyb's down there, and you might be able to sweet-talk her into fixing you something to eat if you want it."

"Where's everybody else?"

"They ran into town. Various errands." Quinn glanced down at the computer, and the clock in the bottom corner. "They should be back any minute. Maybe I should call Cal, just have them bring food back. Cyb's burrowed, and might not be sweet-talked into cooking all that easy."

"I want coffee," he repeated, and walked away.

She didn't seem especially burrowed, Gage thought when he saw Cybil at Cal's kitchen counter. She had her laptop, her notebook, a bottle of water, but she sat right out in the open. And whatever she was doing, she stopped when he came in.

"You look better."

"Feel better. Couldn't have felt much worse." He poured the last cup of coffee, wished someone else would make a fresh pot. And so thinking, turned to study her. "How about making fresh coffee since I almost died?"

"Doing ordinary, routine things, such as making fresh coffee, would probably make you appreciate life more."

So much for sweet talk, he decided. Since there was a bag of Fritos on the counter, he dug in. "What was in the tea?"

She only smiled. "About four hours' sleep, apparently. Someone dropped by to see you while you were out."

"Who?"

"Ann Hawkins."

He considered, sipped coffee. "Is that so? Sorry I missed her."

"We had a nice chat while you sawed a few off."

"Cute. What about?"

"Life, love, the pursuit of happiness." She picked up her bottle of water. "Death, demons. You know, the usual."

"More cute. You're on a roll." And on edge, he mused. However well she masked it, he sensed nerves.

"I'm working on something that popped into my head when we talked. We'll go over it when I nail it down a bit more. She loves you."

"Sorry?"

"She loves you. I could see it in the way she looked at you while you were sleeping. And by the expression on your face now, I see that kind of talk is uncomfortable for a big he-man like you. But that's what I saw on her face, heard in her voice. For what it's worth. Now, go find something else to do and somewhere else to do it. I'm working."

Instead, he crossed over, grabbed a fistful of her hair and tugged her head back so he could crush his mouth to hers. The moment flashed, then spun, then held. He felt another hint of dizziness, another taste of euphoria before he released her.

Her eyes opened, slow and sleepy. "What was that about?"

"Just another ordinary, routine thing to help me appreciate life."

She laughed. "You're cute, too. Oh the hell with it," she said and pulled him against her to hold on, to lay her head on his shoulder where the demon's mark rode. "Scared me. Really, really scared me."

"Me, too. I was going. It didn't seem so bad, all in all." He tipped her head back again. This face, he thought, these eyes. They'd filled his vision, his head. They'd brought him back. "Then I heard you bitching at me. You slugged me, too."

"Slapped, that time. I slugged you before, during our brilliant performance on the deck."

"Yeah. And about that. I don't remember us talking about punching."

"What can I say. I'm a genius at improv. Plus, it seriously and genuinely pissed you off and we needed plenty of anger to sucker the Big Evil Bastard in. Your plan, remember? And you said we'd all have to get rough and real to make it work."

"Yeah." He picked up her hand, studied it. "You've got a decent right jab."

"That may be, but I believe it hurt my hand more than it hurt your face."

He closed her hand into a loose fist, then brought it to his lips. Over her knuckles he saw those gorgeous eyes go wide with shock. "What? I'm not allowed to make a romantic gesture?"

"No. Yes. Yes," she said again. "It was just unexpected."

"I've got a few more, but we made a deal early on." Intrigued by her reaction, he rubbed his thumb over the knuckles he'd just kissed. "No seduction. Maybe you want to close that deal off, consider it old, finished business."

"Ah . . . maybe."

"Well then, why don't we . . ." He trailed off at the sound of the front door opening, slamming. "Continue this later?"

"Why don't we."

Fox strode in first, carting a couple of bags. "Look who's back from the dead. Got food, got stuff, got beer. Couple of twelve-packs in the car. You ought to go out, give Cal a hand bringing the rest in."

"Got coffee?" Gage demanded.

"Two pounds of beans."

"Grind and brew," Gage ordered and walked out to help Cal.

Cybil looked at Fox, who was already pulling a Coke out of the fridge. "I don't suppose you'd take that and go away, and take the rest of your kind with you for an hour."

"Can't. Perishables." He pulled milk out of one of the grocery bags. "Plus, starving."

"Oh well." Cybil pushed away from the laptop. "I'll help you put those away. Then I guess we'll eat, and talk."

SHE WASN'T REQUIRED TO COOK, WHICH CYBIL felt she was often cornered into doing. Apparently Cal and Fox had decided it was time for their own backyard barbecue. There were worse ways to spend a June afternoon than watching three good-looking men standing over a smoking grill.

And just look at them, she thought as she and the other women set bowls of deli potato salad, coleslaw, pickles, and condiments on the picnic table. As united over patties as they were over war. Just look at all of us. She paused a moment to do just that. They were about to have a backyard picnic, and in the same backyard hours before, one of them had bled, had suffered. Had nearly died. Now there was music pumping out of Cal's outdoor speakers, burgers sizzling on the grill, and beer frosty in the cooler.

Twisse thought he could beat them, beat *this*? No. Not in a century of Sevens. It would never beat what it could never understand, and constantly underestimated.

"You okay?" Quinn rubbed a hand over Cybil's back.

"Yes." A weight of stress and doubts dropped away. She might have to pick them up again, but for now, it was a beautiful day in June. "Yes, I am."

"Quite a view," Quinn added, nodding toward the men at the grill.

"Camera worthy."

"Excellent idea. Be right back."

"Where's she going?" Layla asked.

"I have no idea. Just as I have no idea why it apparently takes three grown men to cook some hamburgers."

"One to cook, one to kibitz, and one to insult the other two."

"Ah. Another mystery solved." Cybil lifted her brow when Quinn dashed out with her camera.

"Aren't those dogs and burgers done yet?" Quinn called out, and putting the camera on the deck rail, peered through the viewer, adjusted angles. "Hurry up. This is a photo op."

"If you were going to take pictures, you might have given us some warning so we could fix ourselves up," Cybil complained.

"You look great, Miss Fussy. Stand more over there. Cal! Come *on*."

"Just hold your pixels, Blondie."

"Fox, he doesn't need you. Stand over here between Layla and Cyb."

"I can have both?" Strolling over, Fox wrapped arms around each of their waists.

For the next five minutes, Quinn directed, ordered, adjusted until the five of them were arranged to her satisfaction. "Perfect! Set. I'll take a couple by remote." She hurried down, positioned herself between Cal and Gage.

"Food's going to get cold," Cal complained.

"Smile!" She clicked the remote. "Don't move, don't move. I want a backup."

"Starving," Fox sang out, then laughed when Layla dug her fingers into his ribs. "Mom! Layla's picking on me."

"Don't make me come over there," Quinn warned. "On three. One, two, three. Now just *stay* put while I check to make sure I got a good one."

The mutters and complaints apparently held no sway as she hurried up to the deck, bent down to call back the last two shots. "They're great. Go, Team Human!"

"Let's eat," Cal announced.

As they sat, as food was grabbed, conversation rolled, beers were uncapped, Cybil knew one true thing. They called themselves a team, and they were. But they were more than that. They were family.

It was a family who would kill the beast.

So they ate, as the June afternoon slipped into June evening, with the flowers blooming around them, and the lazy dog—sated with handouts—snoring on the soft green grass. At the edges of that soft green grass, the woods stayed silent and still. Cybil nursed a single beer through the lazy meal. When the interlude passed, she wanted her head clear for the discussion that had to follow.

"We got cake," Fox announced.

"What? Cake? What?" Quinn set down her own beer. "I can't eat cake after eating a burger and potato salad. It's against my lifestyle change. It's just not . . . Damn it, what kind of cake?"

"The kind from the bakery with the icing and the little flowers."

"You bastard." She propped her chin on her fist and looked pitifully at Fox. "Why is there cake?"

"It's for Gage."

"You got me a cake?"

"Yeah." Cal sent Gage a sober and serious nod. "We got you a Glad You Didn't Die cake. Betts at the bakery wrote that on it. She was confused, but she wrote it on. She had cherry pie, which was my first choice, but O'Dell said it had to be cake."

"We could've bought both," Fox pointed out.

"Somebody brings cake *and* pie into this house," Quinn said darkly, "somebody *will* die. By my hand."

"Anticipating that," Cal said, "we just went for the cake."

Gage considered a minute. "You guys are idiots. The appropriate Glad You Didn't Die token is a hooker and a bottle of Jack."

"We couldn't find a hooker." Fox shrugged. "Our time was limited."

"You could give him an IOU," Layla suggested.

Gage grinned at her. "All markers cheerfully accepted."

"Meanwhile, I guess we'd better clear this up, clean it up, and take a little time before we indulge in celebratory cake—of which I can have a stingy little sliver," Quinn said.

Cybil rose first. "I've been working on something, and need to explain it. After we clear the decks here, do you all want to have that explanation, and the inevitable ensuing discussion, inside or out here?"

There was another moment of silence before Gage spoke. "It's a nice night."

"Out here then. Well, as the men hunted, gathered, and cooked, I guess the cleanup's on us, ladies."

As the women cleared and carried, Gage walked over to the edge of the woods with his friends and watched Lump sniff, lift his leg, sniff, lift his leg.

"Dog's got wicked bladder control," Fox commented.

"He does that. Good instincts, too. He won't go any farther

into the woods than that anymore, not without me. Wonder where the Big Evil Bastard is now," Cal asked.

"The hits it took today?" Fox's smile was fierce. "It'll need some alone time, you bet your ass. Jesus, Gage, I thought you had the bastard. Nailed it right between the eyes, ripped holes all over it. I thought: Fucking A, we're taking it out right here and now. If I hadn't gotten so goddamn smug, it might not have gotten by us and bitten you."

"I didn't die, remember? The cake says so. It's not on you," Gage continued. "Or you," he added to Cal. "Or any of us. It got under our guard and took me down. Temporarily. But it showed us something we didn't know. It's not all illusion anymore, or infection. It can take on corporeal form, or enough of one to do damage now. It's evolved. In the who-did-damage-to-who department today, I'd say we broke even. But in the strategy department? We kicked its ass."

"It was fun, too. Yelling at each other." Fox dipped his hands in his pockets. "Like therapy. I did worry that Layla was going to take a page out of Cybil's playbook and punch me. Man, she really clocked you."

"She hits like a girl."

Fox snorted. "Not from my angle. You had little X's in your eyes for a couple seconds there."

"Bullshit."

"Birdies circling over your head," Cal put in. "I was embarrassed for you and all mankind."

"You want to see some birdies?"

Cal grinned, then sobered. "Cybil was pretty quiet during dinner." He glanced over his shoulder. "I guess we'd better go find out what she's got on her mind."

Cybil switched to sun tea, and noted Gage had gone back to coffee. Though she'd been sorry to cut back on the mood, she'd turned the music off herself. It was time Team Human, as Quinn had called it, got back to business.

"I suppose it wouldn't hurt to do a quick roundup of today's events," she began. "Gage's brainstorm about using a substitute bloodstone and drawing Twisse in with our own negative and violent emotions worked."

"Points for us," Quinn commented.

"Points for us. More points for us because we have to assume that it believes it destroyed the bloodstone. It believes it's destroyed our best weapon against it. Still, our ambush had mixed results. We hurt it. Nothing screams like that unless there's pain. It hurt us. It was able to solidify its form, at least temporarily, but long enough to sink its teeth into Gage. We all saw the wound, and it looked nasty, but hardly life-threatening. And we all know he nearly died from it. We thought venom, poison. Gage, I don't know if you have a sense of what happened to you."

"It burned," he said. "I've been burned, all three of us have. But I've never felt anything like this. Felt like my goddamn bones were cooking. I could feel it spreading, closing me down. I could think, I could feel, but I couldn't move or speak. So yeah, I'd go with venom, some sort of paralytic."

Nodding absently, Cybil scribbled some notes. "There are a number of creatures both in nature and in lore that poison and paralyze their prey. Several species of marine animals and fish, arachnids, reptiles. In lore, the Din, a magical catlike beast, possesses an extra claw that holds paralytic poison. The vampire, and so on."

"We've always known it could infect the mind," Cal put in. "Now we've seen it can poison the body."

"And may have killed humans and guardians just that way," Cybil agreed. "Everything in our research, everything we've learned tells us that this demon left the last guardian for dead, but the guardian lived long enough to pass the power and the burden to a human boy. So it's very possible the guardian was poisoned, its injuries more severe and the poison more concentrated and powerful than in Gage's bite today. It's talked about devouring us, consuming us, eating us. Those may not be colorful euphemisms."

Quinn winced. "May I just say: Eewwww."

"I'll second that eewwww and add an Oh God," Layla said.

"The missing," Cybil continued. "In our documented and anecdotal evidence, there are always people missing after the demon sweeps through. We've assumed they've gone off insane, or died, killed each other—and that's very likely true for some, maybe even most. But there were likely others who it used for . . ."

"Munchies," Fox added.

"Somehow this discussion isn't making me feel more optimistic and cheerful."

"Sorry." Cybil offered Cal a smile. "I'm hoping to change that. Ann Hawkins finally decided to pay me a visit, in Gage's room while he was sleeping. I've given you the highlights of our conversation—the pep talk, we'll say. But not all the highlights, because I wanted to check some things out first. She said Gage was alive, more than alive. That he'd brought something back. Another weapon."

"I was a little out of it, but I'm pretty sure I came back empty-handed."

"Not in your hands," Cybil told him. "Its blood, our blood, their blood. And now, Gage, your blood."

"What about my blood?"

"Oh! Oh well, *shit!*" Quinn's grin spread.

"Hardly a wonder we've been friends so long." Cybil nodded at her. "You survived," she said to Gage. "Your body fought off the poison, the infection. Antibodies, immunoglobulins."

Layla raised a hand. "Sorry, science isn't my strong suit."

"Antibodies are produced by the immune system, in response to an antigen—bacteria, toxins, viruses. Basically, we've got hundreds of thousands of blood cells capable of producing a single type of antibody, and its job would be to bind with the invading antigen, and that triggers a signal for the body to manufacture more of the antibody. It neutralizes the effect of the toxin."

"Gage's blood kicked the poison's ass," Fox said. "He's got an advantage on that, like me and Cal. Our healing gifts."

"Yes. It helped him survive, and because he survived, his blood produced the antibodies that destroyed the toxin, and his blood now contains the basis for immunity. It bit you before," Cybil reminded Gage. "At the cemetery."

"I didn't have a reaction to that like I did today."

"It barely nipped you, and on the hand. Did it burn?"

"Yeah, some. Yeah, a lot, but—"

"Did you feel any nausea or dizziness?"

He started to deny it, then considered. "Maybe a little. Maybe it took longer than I expected to heal."

"You've survived two bites—one minor, and one serious—and closer to the heart. It's speculative," she hurried on, "it's not a hundred percent. But antibodies can recognize and neutralize toxins. It's a leap of faith from the science to taking what Ann said to me as what I'm suggesting now. But we don't have the time, the means, or the ability to test Gage's blood, analyze it. We don't have a sample of the poison."

"I don't think anyone's going to volunteer to get one," Fox added.

"You could be immune," Cybil said to Gage. "The way some people are to certain venoms after being bitten, or diseases after recovery from them. And your blood may be a kind of antivenom."

"You're not suggesting you send some of my blood off to the lab and have it made into a serum."

"No, first because serology is complicated and again, we don't have the means or the know-how. But this isn't just about science. It's also about parascience. It's about magicks."

Cybil laid her hands on her notebook as the moon made its slow rise through the trees. "You and Cal and Fox mixed your blood twenty-one years ago and opened the door for Twisse, as we believe Dent planned all along. The six of us mixed blood, ritualistically, and fused the three sections of the bloodstone you were given into one."

"You're banking that another blood ritual, mixing mine with all of yours, will transfer this immunity—if I have it—to the rest of you."

"Yes. Yes, I do."

"Then let's do it."

Just like that, she thought, relieved. Just like that. "I'd like to do a little more research on the ritual itself—when, how, where it should be performed."

"Don't hedge your bets, sugar. It happened here, so it should be here. It happened today, so it should be today."

Layla spoke before Cybil could. "I agree with Gage and not just because of the *eewwww, oh God*. Though that's a factor. Twisse is hurt, but it won't stay that way. We don't know how long we have before it comes back. If you think this is a defense, then let's put up the shield now."

"Cyb, you researched blood rituals inside and out before our last trip to the Pagan Stone. You know we can do this." Quinn looked around the table. "We know we can do it."

"We need words, and—"

"I'll handle it." Quinn pushed to her feet. "Writing under pressure is one of my best things. Set it up, and give me five," she added before she walked into the house.

"Well." Cybil blew out a breath. "I guess it's here and now."

She scouted through Cal's gardens for specific flowers and herbs, and continued to snip when Gage crossed the lawn to her. They stood in the wash of moonlight.

"Making a bouquet?"

"Candles, herbs, flowers, words, movements." She moved a shoulder. "Maybe they're trappings, maybe they're largely symbolic, but I believe in symbols. They're a sign of respect, if nothing else. Anytime you shed blood, anytime you ask a higher power for a favor, it should be with respect."

"You're a smart woman, Cybil."

"I am."

He took her arm, held it until she'd turned to face him. "If this works, it's because you were smart enough to put it together."

"If it doesn't?"

"It won't be because of the lack of brainpower."

"Are you seducing me by flattering my mind?"

"No." He smiled, trailed a finger over her cheek. "I'll seduce you by clouding your mind. I'm telling you this is going to work."

"Optimism? From you?"

"You're not the only one who's looked into rites and rituals. I've spent a lot of the time I'm away from here looking
into those areas. Some of it's show. But some? It's faith and
respect, and it's truth. It's going to work because between
the six of us, we cover those bases. It's going to work because it's not just my blood, not just antibodies and science.
Your tears are in me now. I felt them. So whatever I brought
back, part of it's you. Get your symbols, and let's do this
thing."

She stood where she was when he walked away, stood in
the moonlight with flowers in her hands, and closed her eyes.
Close her heart? she thought. Get over him? No, no, not if
she lived a dozen lifetimes.

It was life, Ann Hawkins had told her. The joy and the
pain. It was time to accept she'd have to feel both.

They lighted the candles, and sprinkled the flowers and
herbs over the ground where Gage had fallen. Over them, in
the center of the circle they formed, Quinn laid the photograph she'd taken of them. All six of them linked—hands or
arms—with the big dog leaning adoringly against Cal's leg.

"Nice touch," Cybil commented, and Quinn smiled.

"I thought so. I kept the words simple. Pass it around,"
she suggested.

Cybil took the page first, and read. "You do good work."
She passed it to Gage, and so the words went from hand to
hand. "Everybody got it?"

Gage took Cal's Boy Scout knife, skimmed the blade
across his palm. Cal took the knife, mirrored the gesture. As
with the words, the knife passed from hand to hand.

And they spoke together as hands clasped, and blood
mixed.

"Brother to brother, brother to sister, lover to lover. Life
to life for the then, for the now, for the to be. Through faith,
through hope, in truth. With blood and tears to shield light

from black. Brother to brother, brother to sister, lover to lover."

Though there was no wind, the candle flames swayed and rose higher. Cal crouched. "Friend to friend," he said and taking Lump's paw, scored a shallow cut. Lump stared, dark eyes full of trust as Cal closed his hand over the cut. "Sorry, pal." He straightened, shrugged. "I couldn't leave him out."

"He's part of the team." Quinn bent, picked up the photograph. "I don't feel any different, but I believe it worked."

"So do I." Layla crouched to gather up the flowers and herbs. "I'm going to put these in water. It just . . . seems like the right thing to do."

"It's been a good day." Fox took Layla's hand, brushed his lips over her palm. "I've got one thing to say. Who wants cake?"

Fifteen

~⌐~

BECAUSE IT WAS A QUIET PLACE WHERE THE THREE
of them could meet in private, Gage and Fox joined Cal in
his office in the bowling center. Time was ticking by. Gage
could all but feel the days draining away. None of them had
seen Twisse, in any form, since the day Gage had shot it. But
there had been signs.

The increase in animal attacks, or the bloated bodies of
animals on the sides of the road. Unexplained power outages
and electrical fires. Tempers grew shorter, it seemed, every
day. Accidents increased.

And the dreams became a nightly plague.

"My grandmother and cousin are moving into my parents'
place today," Cal told them. "Somebody threw a rock through
Grand's next-door-neighbor's window yesterday. I'm trying
to convince them all to move out to the farm, Fox. Safety in
numbers. The fact is, the way things are, we'll need to get
those who're willing out there soon. I know it's earlier than
we thought, I know it's a lot, but—"

"They're ready. My mom and dad, my brother and his

family, my sister and her guy." Fox rubbed the back of his neck. "I had a fight with Sage over the phone last night," he added, speaking of his older sister. "She started talking about making plans to come back, to help. She's staying in Seattle—pissed at me, but she's staying. I used the fact that Paula's pregnant as leverage there."

"That's good. Enough of your family's involved in this. My two sisters are staying where they are, too. People are heading out of town every day. A couple here, a couple there."

"I stopped by the flower shop yesterday," Fox told them. "Amy told me she's closing up the end of the week, taking a couple weeks' vacation up in Maine. I've had three clients cancel appointments for next week. I'm thinking I might just close the office until after this is done."

"Find out if there's anything your family needs out at the farm. Supplies, tents. I don't know."

"I'm going to head out there later, give them a hand with some of it."

"You need help?" Gage asked.

"No, we've got it covered. I might be late heading back to Cal's if that's where we'll all bunk tonight. One of you could make sure Layla's not on her own, and gets there."

"No problem. Anybody getting any sleep?" Cal asked them, and Gage merely laughed. "Yeah. Me, too." Cal nudged the bloodstone over the desk. "I took this out of the safe when I got here this morning. I thought maybe if I just sit here, stare at the damn thing, something will come."

"We've got so much going." Fox pushed to his feet to pace. "I can feel it. Can't you feel it? We're right on the edge of it, but we just can't push over. It seems like it's all there, all the pieces of it. Except that one." He picked up the stone. "Except this one. We've got it, but we don't know how the hell to use it."

"Maybe what we need is a howitzer instead of a hunk of rock."

With a half smile, Fox turned to Gage. "I'm at the point a howitzer doesn't sound so bad. But this is what'll do the bastard. The women are spending nearly every waking hour—which is most of the time these days—trying to find the answer to this hunk of rock. But . . ."

"We can't see past that edge," Cal put in.

"Cybil and I have tried the link-up, but it's either a really crappy vision, or nothing. That interference, that static the bastard can jam things with. It's working overtime on blocking us."

"Yeah, and Quinn's working overtime to find a way around the block. This paranormal stuff's her deal," Cal said with a shrug. "Until then, we keep doing what we can do to protect ourselves, protect the town, and figure out how to use the weapons we have."

"If we can't take it down . . ." Gage began.

Fox rolled his eyes. "Here goes our Pollyanna with a penis."

"If we can't take it down," Gage repeated, "if we know it's going south, is there a way to get the women clear? To get them out? I know you've both thought the same."

Fox slumped back into a chair. "Yeah."

"I've gone around with it," Cal admitted. "Even if we could convince them, which I don't see happening, I don't see how they'd get out, not if we have to take this stand at the Pagan Stone."

"I don't like it." Fox's jaw tightened. "But that's where it has to be. The middle of Hawkins Wood, in the dark. I wish I didn't know in my gut that it has to be there, that they have to go in there with us. But I do know it. So we can't let it go south, that's all."

IT HAD BEEN EASIER, GAGE ADMITTED, WHEN IT had just been the three of them. He loved his friends, and part of him would die if either of them did. But they'd been in it together since day one. Since minute one, he corrected, as he started downstairs.

It had been easier, too, when the women had first gotten involved. Before any of them really mattered to him. Easier before he'd seen the way Quinn meshed with Cal, or the way Fox lit up when Layla was in the room.

Easier before he'd let himself have feelings for Cybil, because, goddamn it, he had feelings. Messy, irritating, impossible feelings for Cybil. The kind of feelings that pushed him into having thoughts. Messy, irritating, impossible thoughts.

He didn't want a relationship. He sure as hell didn't want a long-term relationship. And by God, he didn't want a long-term relationship that involved plans and promises. He wanted to come and go as he pleased, and that's just what he did. Except for every seventh year. And so far, so good.

You didn't mess with a streak.

So the feelings and the thoughts would just have to find another sucker to . . . infect, he decided.

"Gage."

He stopped, saw his father at the base of the steps. Perfect, Gage thought, just one more thing to give a shine to his day.

"I know I said I wouldn't get in your way when you came in to see Cal. And I won't."

"You're standing in it now."

Bill stepped back, rubbed his hands on the thighs of his work pants. "I just wanted to ask you—I didn't want to get in the way, so I wanted to ask you . . ."

"What?"

"Jim Hawkins tells me some of the towners are going to camp out at the O'Dell farm. I thought it might be I could help them out. Haul people and supplies out and such, do runs back and forth when needs be."

In Gage's memory his father had spent every Seven skunk drunk upstairs in the apartment. "That'd be up to Brian and Joanne."

"Yeah. Okay."

"Why?" Gage demanded as Bill backed away. "Why don't you just get out?"

"It's my town, too. I never did anything to help before. I never paid much mind to it, or to what you were doing about it. But I knew. Nobody could get drunk enough not to know."

"They could use help out at the farm."

"Okay then. Gage." Bill winced, rubbed his hands over his face. "I should tell you, I've been having dreams. Last few nights, I've been having them. It's like I wake up, but I'm asleep, but it's like I wake up 'cause I hear your ma out in the kitchen. She's right there, it's so real. She's at the stove cooking dinner. Pork chops, mashed potatoes, and those little peas I always liked, the way she made them. And she . . ."

"Keep going."

"She talks to me, smiles over. She had some smile, my Cathy. She says: Hey there, Bill, supper's almost ready. I go on over, like I always did, put my arms around her while her hands are busy at the stove and kiss her neck till she laughs and wiggles away. I can smell her, in the dream, and I can taste . . ."

He yanked out his bandanna, mopped his eyes. "She tells me, like she always did, to cut that out now, unless I want my supper burned. Then, she says why don't you have a drink, Bill? Why don't you have a nice drink before supper? And there's a bottle on the counter there, and she pours the whiskey into the glass, holds it out to me. She never did that, your ma never did that in her life. And she never looked at me the way she does in the dreams. With her eyes hard and mean. I gotta sit down here a minute."

Bill lowered to the steps, wiped at the sweat that pearled on his forehead. "I wake up, covered in sweat, and I can smell the whiskey she held out to me. Not Cathy, not anymore, just the whiskey. Last night, when I woke up from it, I went on out in the kitchen to get something cold 'cause my throat was so dry. There was a bottle on the counter. It was right there. I swear to Christ, it was there. I didn't buy a bottle." His hands shook now, and fresh sweat popped out above his top lip. "I started to pick it up, to pour it down the sink. I pray to God I was going to pour it down the sink, but there was nothing there. I think I'm going crazy. I know I'll go crazy if I pick up a bottle again and do anything but pour it down the sink."

"You're not going crazy." Another kind of torture, Gage thought. The bastard didn't miss a trick. "Have you ever had dreams like this before?"

"Maybe, a few times over the years. It's hard to say because I wasn't picking up bottles to pour them down the sink back then." Bill sighed now. "But maybe a few times, around this time of year. Around the time Jim says you boys call the Seven."

"It fucks with us. It's fucking with you. Go on out to the farm, give them a hand out there."

"I can do that." Bill pushed back to his feet. "Whatever it is, it's got no right using your ma that way."

"No, it doesn't."

When Bill started to walk away, Gage cursed under his breath. "Wait. I can't forget, and I don't know if I can ever forgive. But I know you loved her. I know that's the truth, so I'm sorry you lost her."

Something came into Bill's eyes, something Gage reluctantly recognized as gratitude.

"You lost her, too. I never let myself think that, not all those years. You lost her, too, and me with her. I'll carry that the rest of my life. But I won't drink today."

Gage went straight to the rental house. He walked in, and right up the stairs. As he reached the top, Quinn stepped out of her bedroom draped in a towel.

"Oh. Well. Hi, Gage."

"Where's Cybil?"

Quinn hitched the towel a little higher. "Probably in the shower or getting dressed. We hit the gym. I was just going to . . . never mind."

He studied her face. Her cheeks seemed a little flushed, her eyes a little overbright. "Something wrong?"

"Wrong? No. Everything's good. Great. Thumbs-up. I, ah, better get dressed."

"Pack, too."

"What?"

"Pack up what you need," he told her as she stood frowning and dripping. "Seeing as you're three women, it's going to take more than one trip. Cal and Fox can come by at some point and haul more. There's no point in the three of you staying here—and by the way, do any of you ever *think* about locking the door? It's getting dangerous in town. Everyone can bunk at Cal's until this is over."

"You're making that decision for everyone involved?" Cybil asked from behind him.

He turned. She was dressed and leaning against the jamb. "Yeah."

"That's fairly presumptuous, to put it mildly. But I happen to agree with you." She looked over at Quinn. "It's just not practical to have three bases—here, Cal's, Fox's—anymore. We'd be better to consolidate. Even assuming this house is a cold spot, and safe, we're too spread out."

"Who's arguing?" Quinn adjusted her towel again. "Layla's at the boutique with Fox's dad, but Cyb and I can put some of her things together."

Cybil continued to look at Quinn. "It might be helpful if you went by there now, Gage, let her know. It's going to take a little time for us to pack up the research equipment any-way. Then you could borrow Cal's truck, and we could take the first load."

He knew when he was getting the brush-off. Cybil wanted him gone, for now. "Get it together then. And once we're at Cal's, you and I have to try the link-up again."

"Yes, we do."

"I'll be back in twenty, so get a move on."

Cybil ignored him. She stood in her doorway and Quinn in hers, watching each other until they heard the front door close behind him.

"What's up, Q?"

"I'm pregnant. Holy shit, Cyb, I'm pregnant." Tears flooded her eyes even as she moved her feet and hips into what could only be interpreted as a happy dance. "I'm knocked up, I'm on the nest, I am with child and have a bun in the oven. Holy shit."

Cybil crossed the hallway, held out her arms. They stood holding each other. "I didn't expect to be expecting. I mean, we weren't trying for it. All this going on, and planning the wedding. After, we both figured."

"How far along?"

"That's just it." Drawing back, Quinn used the towel to dry her face, then turned naked to dig out clothes. "I'm not even late, but the last few days, I've just felt sort of . . . different. And I had this feeling. I thought, *ppffit*, no, but I couldn't shake the feeling. So I bought a—okay five—I bought five early response pregnancy tests because I went a little crazy. At the pharmacy in the next town," she said, laughing now, "because, you know—small towns."

"Yes, I know."

"I only took three—came down from crazy to obsessed. I just took them. Three of them. Pink, plus sign, and the no-frills pregnant all came up. I'm probably only a couple of weeks in, if that, but . . ." She looked down at her belly. "Wow, somebody's in there."

"You haven't told Cal."

"I didn't want to say before I knew. He'll be happy, but he'll be worried, too." She pulled on capris. "Worried because of what's coming, what we have to do, and I'm, well, in the family way."

"How do you feel, about that part of it?"

"Scared, protective. And I know nothing will ever be right for us, any of us, or for this baby if we don't end it. If we don't follow through, and I'm part of that follow-through. I guess I have to believe that this—" Quinn laid a hand on her belly. "This is a sign of hope."

"I love you, Q."

"Oh God, Cyb." Once more, Quinn went into Cybil's arms. "I'm so glad you were here. I know Cal should've been the first I told, but—"

"He'll understand. He has brothers." Gently, Cybil smoothed Quinn's damp hair back. "We're going to get through this, Q, and you and Cal? You're going to be amazing parents."

"We are. Both counts." Quinn let out a breath. "Whew.

You know, maybe I'll go all hormonal on the Big Evil Bastard. That might do it."

Cybil laughed. "It just might."

WHEN GAGE RETURNED, THEY LOADED CAL'S truck. "I'm going to need my car," Quinn said, "so I'll toss some stuff in there, and I'll pick up Layla. I need to go see Cal first." She glanced at Cybil. "So I might be a while."

"Take your time. We'll unpack this load, get things organized. Well . . . See you later." Quinn gave Cybil a hard squeeze then puzzled Gage by giving him the same. "Bye."

Gage got in the truck, started the engine. Then sat, drumming his fingers on the wheel while it ran. "What's up with Quinn?"

"Quinn's fine."

"She seems a little nervy."

"We're all a little nervy, which is why I agree with you about all of us staying at the same place now."

"Not that kind of nervy." He turned in his seat, met her eyes. "Is she pregnant?"

"Well, aren't you the insightful one? Yes, she is, and I'm only confirming that because she's going to tell Cal right now."

He sat, rubbed his hands over his face. "Christ."

"You can look at it as the glass is half empty, as you obviously are. Or that it's half full. Personally, I see the glass as overflowing. This is good, strong, positive news, Gage."

"Maybe for normal people under normal circumstances. But try to look at this from Cal's angle. Would you want the woman you love, who's carrying your child, risking her life, the life of the kid? Or would you wish her a hundred miles away from this?"

"I'd wish her a thousand miles away. Do you think I can't understand how he'll feel? I love her, enormously. But I know she can't be a thousand miles away. So I'm going to look at this, as Quinn is, as a sign of hope. We knew this was coming—or the possibility of this, Gage. We saw it. We saw her and Cal together, alive and together, with Quinn pregnant. I'm going to believe that's what will be. I have to."

"We also saw her killed."

"Please don't." Cybil closed her eyes as her belly twisted. "I know we have to prepare for the worst, but please don't. Not today."

He pulled away from the curb, let her have silence for the next several minutes. "Fox is going to close his office in a couple days anyway. If Layla wants to keep on with the rehab—"

"She will. It's another positive."

"He can go back and forth with her, work with his father some. Between them, Cal and his father, we'll have eyes and ears on the town. There's no reason for Quinn—or you for that matter—to go back into the Hollow until this is over."

"Maybe not." A reasonable compromise, she mused. Surprise.

"My old man's been having dreams," Gage said, and told her.

"Feeding on fears, pain, weaknesses." Cybil closed her hand over his a moment. "It's good that he told you. That's another positive, Gage, however you feel about him. You can feel it in town now, can't you? It's like raw nerves on the air."

"It'll get worse. People coming into the Hollow for business or whatever else will suddenly change their minds. Others who planned to drive through on their way to somewhere else will decide to take a detour. Some of the locals will pack up and go away for a couple weeks. Some of those who stay will hunker down like people do to ride out a hurricane."

He scanned the roads as he drove, braced for any sign. A black dog, a boy. "People who decide they want out after July seventh, well, they won't be able to find their way out of town. They'll drive around in circles, scared, confused. If they try to call for help, mostly the calls won't go through."

He turned onto Cal's lane. "There's a burning in the air, even before the fires start. Once they do, nobody's safe."

"They will be this time. Some will be safe out at Fox's family's farm. And when we end it, the air won't burn, Gage. And the fires will go out."

He shoved open the door of the truck, then looked back at her. "We'll get this stuff inside. Then—" He grabbed her hand, jerked her back as she opened her own door. "Stay in the truck."

"What? What is it? Oh my God."

She followed his direction and saw what slithered and writhed over Cal's front deck.

"Copperheads," Gage told her. "Maybe a dozen or so."

"Poisonous. And that many? Yes, the truck's an excellent place to be." She drew her .22 out of her purse, but shook her head. "I don't suppose we can shoot them from here, especially with this."

He reached under the seat, took out his Luger. "This would do the job, but not from here. And shit, Cal will burn my ass if I put bullet holes in his house. I've got a better idea. Stay in the truck. I get bit, it'll piss me off. You get bit, you'll be out of commission—at the least."

"Good point. What's the better idea?"

"First, trade." He handed her the Luger, took the pistol. "Any other surprises, use it."

She tested the weight and feel of the gun in her hand as he stepped out of the truck. Since she had no choice but to trust him, she watched the snakes, and tried to remember what she knew about this specific species.

Poisonous, yes, but the bite was rarely fatal. Still, a few dozen bites might prove to be. They preferred rocky hillsides, and weren't especially aggressive. Of course, they weren't usually driven mad by a demon either.

These would attack. She had no doubt of that.

On cue, several of the snakes lifted their triangular heads as Gage came around the house with a shovel.

A shovel? Cybil thought. The man had a gun but decided to use a damn shovel against a nest of crazed snakes. She started to lower the window, call out her opinion of his strategy, but he was striding up the steps, and straight into the slithering nest.

It was ugly. She'd always considered herself in possession of a strong stomach, but it rolled now as he smashed and beat and sliced. She couldn't count the number of times they struck at him, and knew despite his healing gift there was pain as fang pierced flesh.

When it was over, she swallowed hard and got out of the truck. He looked down at her, his face glistening with sweat. "That's it. I'll clean this up and bury them."

"I'll give you a hand."

"I've got it. You look a little green."

She passed a hand over her brow. "I'm embarrassed to admit I feel a little green. That was . . . Are you okay?"

"Got me a few times, but that's no big."

"Thank God we got here before Layla. I can help. I'll get another shovel."

"Cybil. I could really use some coffee."

She struggled a moment, then accepted the out he offered. "All right."

She didn't suppose there was any shame in averting her eyes from the mess of it as she went into the house. Why look if she didn't have to? In the kitchen she drank cold water, splashed a little on her face until her system re-settled. When the coffee was brewed, she carried it out to him where he dug a hole just inside the edge of the woods.

"This is turning into a kind of twisted pet cemetery," she commented. "Crazy Roscoe, and now a battalion of snakes. Take a break. I can dig. Really."

He traded her the shovel for the coffee. "More of a practical joke."

"What?"

"This. Not a big show. More of an elbow in the ribs."

"I'm still laughing. But yes, I see what you mean. You're right. Just a casual little psyche-out."

"Snakes come out during the Seven. People find them in their houses, the basement, closets. Even in their cars if they're stupid enough not to close the windows when they park. Rats, too."

"Lovely. Yes, I've got the notes." The summer heat and exertion dewed her skin. "Is this deep enough?"

"Yeah, it'll do. Go on back in the house."

She glanced toward the two drywall compound buckets, and thought about what he'd had to put inside them. "I'm going to see worse than this. No pandering to the delicate female."

"Your choice."

When he dumped the contents in—and her gorge rose—she could only think she hoped she didn't see much worse. "I'll wash these out." She picked up the empty buckets. "And clean off the deck while you finish here."

"Cybil," he said as she walked away. "Delicate's not how I think of you."

Strong, he thought as he dumped the first shovelful of dirt. Steady. The kind of woman a man could trust to stick, through better or worse.

When he'd finished, he walked around the house, and stopped short when he saw her on her hands and knees, scrubbing the deck. "Okay, here's another way I haven't thought of you."

She blew hair out of her eyes, looked over. "As?"

"A woman with a scrub brush in her hand."

"While I may prefer to pay someone else to do it, I've scrubbed floors before. Though I can say this is the first time I've ever scrubbed off snake guts. It's not a pleasant, housewifely task."

He climbed up, leaned on the rail out of range of the soap and water. "What would be a pleasant, housewifely task?"

"Cooking a pretty meal when the mood strikes, arranging flowers, setting an artistic table. I'm running out, that's the short list." With sweat sliding down her back, she sat back on her heels. "Oh, and making reservations."

"For dinner?"

"For anything." Rising, she started to lift the bucket, but he put his hand over hers. "I need to dump this out, then hose this off."

"I'll take care of it."

With a smile, she tipped her head. "A not-altogether-unpleasant manly task?"

"You could say."

"Then have at it. I'll clean up and we can start unloading the truck."

They worked quickly, and in tandem. That was another thing, he thought. He couldn't remember ever working in tandem with a woman. He couldn't think of a single sane reason cleaning up with her after dealing with the mangled bodies of snakes should start up those messy thoughts and feelings.

"What do you want when this is over?" he asked as he washed up at the sink.

"What do I want when this is over?" She repeated it thoughtfully as she poured him another cup of coffee. "About twelve hours' sleep in a wonderful bed with 450 thread count sheets, followed by a pitcher of mimosas along with breakfast in bed."

"All good choices, but I meant what do you want?"

"Ah, the more philosophical and encompassing want." She poured grapefruit juice and ginger ale over ice, rattled it, then took a long drink. "A break initially. From the work, the stress, this town—not that I have anything against it. Just a celebratory break from all of it. Then I want to come back and help Quinn and Layla plan their weddings, and now help Q plan for her baby. I want to see Hawkins Hollow again. I want the satisfaction of seeing it when there's no threat hanging over it, and knowing I had a part in that. I want to go back to New York for a while, then back to work, wherever that takes me. I want to see you again. Does that surprise you?"

Everything about her surprised him, he realized. "I was thinking we might catch that twelve hours' sleep and breakfast in bed together. Somewhere that's not here."

"Is that an offer?"

"It sounds like it."

"I'll take it."

"Just like that?"

"Life's short or it's long, Gage. Who the hell knows. So, yes, just like that."

He reached out, touched her cheek. "Where do you want to go?"

"Surprise me." She lifted her hand to cover his.

"What if I said—" He broke off when they heard the front door open. "Never mind," he said. "I'll surprise you."

Sixteen

~ᴎⵜ~

Layla came into the dining room, which was currently in the process of morphing into their main research area. Laptops, stacks of files, charts, maps covered the table. The dry-erase board stood wedged in a corner, and Cal crouched on the floor hooking up a printer.

"Fox says he grabbed dinner at the farm, and we should probably start without him—Gage and Cybil should start without him, that is. He might be a couple hours yet. I didn't tell him the news." She beamed at Quinn. "I had to saw my tongue off a couple times, but I thought you and Cal would want to tell him in person about the baby."

"I think I still need somebody to tell me again, a few times."

"How about if I just call you Daddy?" Quinn suggested.

He let out the breathless laugh of a man caught between the thrill and the terror. "Wow." Then shifted to where Quinn sorted the files. "Wow." When he took Quinn's hand, and the two of them just stared at each other, Layla eased out of the room.

"They're basking," she told Gage and Cybil in the kitchen.

"They're entitled." Cybil closed a cupboard door, put her hands on her hips, and did a survey of the room. "I think this'll have to do. All the perishables from our place are stowed, and we'll have to live with the spill-over in dry goods."

"I'll get what makes sense out of Fox's apartment tomorrow," Layla said. "Is there anything else I can do?"

"Flip for the guest room." Gage took a quarter out of his pocket. "Loser takes the pullout in the office."

"Oh." Layla frowned at the coin. "I want to be gracious and say you're already in there, but I've slept on that pullout. Heads. No . . . tails."

"Pick one, sweetheart."

She fisted her hands on either side of her head, wiggled her hips, squeezed her eyes tight. Gage had seen people invent stranger rituals for luck.

"Tails."

Gage flipped it, snagged it, slapped it on the back of his hand. "Should've gone with your first instinct."

She sighed over the eagle. "Oh well. Fox is going to be a while, so . . ."

"We'll try the link as soon as the dining room's set up." Cybil glanced out the window. "I guess we stick inside. It's starting to rain."

"Plus, snakes. Well, enough basking for them." Layla walked back in the dining room to help organize.

"YOU'RE TAKING A LOT ON." FOX STOOD BY HIS FAther on the back porch of the farmhouse, staring out through the steady, soaking rain.

"I was at Woodstock, kid of mine. We'll be fine."

In the distant field a handful of tents stood already pitched. He and his father, along with his brother, Ridge, and Bill Turner, had put together a wooden platform, hung a canopy over it on poles to serve as a kind of cook tent.

That wasn't so weird, Fox thought, but the line of bright blue Porta Potties along the back edge of the field? That was a strange sight.

His parents would take it in stride, Fox knew. That's what they did.

"Bill's going to hook up a few shower areas," Brian went on, adjusting the bill of his ball cap as he stood in his old work boots and ancient Levi's. "He's a handy guy."

"Yeah."

"They'll be pretty rude and crude, but it'll serve for a week or two, and supplement the schedule your mom and Sparrow are going to make up for people to use the house."

"Don't just let people have the run of the place." Fox looked into his father's calm eyes. "Come on, Dad, I *know* you guys. Not everybody's honest and trustworthy."

"You mean there are dishonest people in the world who aren't in politics?" Brian lifted his eyebrows high. "Next thing you're going to tell me there's no Easter Bunny."

"Just lock up at night for a change. Just for now."

Brian made a noncommittal sound. "Jim expects some people to start heading over within the next couple of days."

Fox surrendered. His parents would do what they would do. "Could he give you any idea how many?"

"A couple hundred. People listen to Jim. More if he can manage it."

"I'll help as much as I can."

"You don't worry about that. We'll take care of this. You do what you have to do, and goddamn it, you take care of yourself. You're the only oldest son I've got."

"That's true." He turned, gave Brian a hug. "I'll see you later."

He jogged out to his truck, through the soft summer rain. Hot shower, dry clothes, beer, he thought. In that order. Better, maybe he could talk Layla into the shower with him. He started the truck, backed around his brother's pickup to head out to the road.

He hoped Gage and Cybil had some luck, or were having some if they were into the link-up. Things had started to . . .

pulse, he decided. He could feel it. The town had taken on shadows, he thought, that had nothing to do with summer rain or wet, gloomy nights. Just a couple more answers, he thought. Just a couple more pieces of the puzzle. That's all they needed.

He caught the flash of headlights, well behind him, in his rearview mirror, and made the next turn. His windshield wipers swished, and Stone Sour rocked out of the radio. Tapping his hands on the wheel, thinking of that hot shower, he drove another mile before his engine clicked and coughed.

"Oh, come on! Didn't I just give you a tune-up?" Even as he spoke, the truck shuddered, slowed. Annoyed, he eased to the side of the road, coasting when the engine simply died on him like a sick dog.

"The rain just makes it perfect, doesn't it?" He started to get out, considered. As his tawny eyes shifted to his rearview mirror, he pulled out his phone. And cursed when he saw the No Service display. "Yeah, yeah, can you hear me now?"

The road behind him was dark and fogged with rain when he closed his fingers on the handle of the door.

IN THE LIVING ROOM, GAGE AND CYBIL SAT ON THE floor, facing each other. And facing each other, reached out to clasp hands. "I think we should try focusing on the three of you," she said to Gage, "and the bloodstone. It came to the three of you. So we could start there. The three of you, then the stone."

"Worth a shot. Ready?"

She nodded, leveled her breathing as he did. He came first to her mind. The man, the potential. She focused on what she saw in him as much as his face, his eyes, his hands. And moved on to Cal, putting him shoulder-to-shoulder with Gage inside her head. The physical Cal, and what she considered the spiritual Cal, before pulling Fox into her head.

Brothers, she thought. Blood brothers. Men who stood for each other, believed in each other, loved each other.

The drumming of the rain increased. It all but roared in

her ears. A dark road, the splatting rain. A swath of lights turning the wet pavement to black glass. Two men stood in the rain on the black glass of the pavement. For a flash, she saw Fox's face clearly, just as she saw the gun glistening as it pointed at him.

Then she was falling, cut loose so that her breath gasped in and out, so that she fumbled for a moment for the support that wrenched away. She heard Gage's voice dimly.

"It's Fox. He's in trouble. Let's go."

Dizzy, Cybil pushed to her knees as Layla rushed toward Gage, grabbed his arm. "Where? What's happening? I'm coming with you."

"No, you're not. Let's move!"

"He's right. Let them go. Let them go now." Flailing out with a hand, Cybil gripped Layla's. "I don't know how much time there is."

"I can find him. I can find him." Clutching Cybil's hand, and now Quinn's, Layla pushed everything she had toward Fox. Her eyes darkened, went glassy green. "He's close. Only a couple of miles . . . He's pushing back, pushing toward us. The first bend, the first bend on White Rock Road, heading here from the farm. Hurry. Hurry. It's Napper. He's got a gun."

FOX HUNCHED AGAINST THE RAIN AND LIFTED the hood of the truck. He knew how to build things. Ask him to make a table, stud out a wall, no problem. Engines? Not so much. Basic stuff, sure—change the oil, jump the battery, go wild and replace a fan belt.

As he stood in the rain with headlights approaching, the basic stuff, and his own gift, was all he needed to assess the situation. Getting out of it in one piece? That might not be as simple.

He could run, he supposed. But it just wasn't in him. Fox shifted, angled his body, and watched Derrick Napper swagger toward him through the rain.

"Got trouble, don't you?"

"Looks like." Fox didn't see the gun Napper held in the hand he kept down at his side so much as he sensed it. "How much sugar did it take?"

"Not as stupid as you look." Now Napper raised the gun. "We're going to take a little walk back into the woods here, O'Dell. We're going to have a talk about you getting me fired."

Fox didn't look at the gun but kept his gaze level on Napper's "I got you fired? I thought you pulled that one off all by yourself."

"You don't have your slut of a mother, or your two faggot friends around to protect you now, do you? Now you're going to find out what happens to people who fuck with me, like you've been fucking with me my whole life."

"You really see it that way?" Fox spoke almost conversationally. He changed his stance slightly, planting his feet. "I was fucking with you every time you jumped me on the playground when we were kids? When you ambushed me in the parking lot of the bank? Funny how that works. But I guess you could loosely define it as me fucking with you every time you tried to kick my ass and failed."

"You're going to wish I only beat down on you by the time I'm done."

"Put the gun down and walk away, Napper. I'd say I don't want to hurt you, but what's the point in lying? Put it down and walk away while you can."

"While I can?" Napper pressed the gun to Fox's chest and pushed him back a step. "You really are stupid. You're going to hurt me, is that what you think?" His voice rose to a shout. "Who's got the gun, asshole?"

Watching Napper's eyes, Fox swung up the baseball bat he'd held behind his back. He felt it crack against bone, just as he felt the vicious punch of the bullet in his arm. The gun skittered off into the wet dark. "Nobody. Asshole." Fox swung again for insurance, this time plowing the bat into Napper's belly. And holding it like a batter preparing to swing for the fences, he looked down at the man sprawled at his feet. "Pretty sure I broke your arm. I bet that hurts."

He glanced up briefly as another set of headlights cut through the rain. "I told you to walk away." Crouching, he jerked Napper's head up by the hair, stared into the pasty white face. "Was it worth it?" Fox demanded. "Jesus, was it ever worth it?"

He let Napper go, rose to wait for his friends.

They came out of Gage's car fast—like bullets, Fox thought, since bullets were on his mind. "Thanks for coming. One of you needs to call Hawbaker. I can't get cell service right here."

Cal scanned the situation, heaved out a breath. "I'll take care of it." Pulling out his cell phone, he walked a few yards down the road.

"You're bleeding," Gage commented.

"Yeah. The gun went off when I broke his arm. The bullet went right through the meat. Hurts like a mother." He stared down at Napper, who sat wheezing on the wet pavement. "His arm's going to hurt a lot longer. Don't touch that," he added as Gage bent to pick up the gun. "Let's not screw up the evidence by getting your fingerprints on his weapon."

Fox yanked out his bandanna, offered it. "Wrap it up in this, will you? And for God's sake be careful with it."

"Walk on down with Cal."

Gage's flat, frigid tone had Fox's head jerking back up, and his eyes met Gage's. He shook his head. "No. No reason for that, Gage."

"He shot you. And you know damn well he meant to kill you."

"He meant to. He wanted to. You know, I've been carrying this bat around in the truck ever since you and Cybil had that preview of me lying on the side of the road. I'm a lucky guy." He laid a hand on his arm, grimaced at the smear of red he took away. "Mostly. We're going to do this straight, according to the law."

"He doesn't give a damn about the law."

"We're not like him."

Cal walked back to them. "The chief's on his way. I called the house, too. Layla knows you're okay."

"Thanks." Fox cradled his injured arm. "So, did either of you catch any of the game? O's in New York?"

They stood in the rain, waiting for the cops, and talked baseball.

LAYLA STREAKED OUT OF THE HOUSE, LAUNCHING herself at Fox as he levered himself out of the car he, Cal, and Gage had squeezed into. As Cybil and Quinn stood on the porch, Gage walked up. "He's fine."

"But what happened? What— You're all soaked." Quinn drew in a breath. "Let's get inside so you all can get into dry clothes. We'll suck it up until you are."

"All but this one thing," Cybil interrupted. "Where is he? Where is that son of a bitch?"

"In police custody." With his arm snug around Layla, Fox climbed the steps to the deck. "Getting his broken arm treated and being booked on a nice variety of charges. Christ, I want a beer."

A short time later, dry, a beer in hand, Fox filled them in. "At first I was just irritated, started to get out of the truck, pop the hood. Then I remembered what Gage and Cybil had seen, which is why I had my trusty Louisville Slugger under the seat."

"Thank God," Layla breathed, then turned her head to press her lips to his healed arm.

"I had nearly a full tank, and I'd had the truck tuned up a couple weeks ago, so I focused on the engine."

"You know zero about engines," Gage pointed out.

Fox shot up his middle finger. "Sugar in the gas tank. Engine'll run for a couple miles or so, then it coughs up and dies. Now my truck's DOA."

"That's urban myth." Cal gestured with his own beer. "It sounds like the sugar got through, clogged your fuel filter or your injectors, and that's what stopped your engine. You just need your mechanic to change the filters a few times, and drop the tank, clean it out. Cost you a couple hundred."

"Really? That's it? But I thought—"

"You're questioning MacGyver?" Gage asked him.

"Lost my head for a minute. Anyway, I got the sabotage, and it wasn't a stretch to who. I just angled myself with the bat behind me when Napper showed up."

"With a gun," Layla added.

Fox squeezed her hand. "Bullets bounce off me. Almost. And we think of it this way. Napper's going to be behind bars and out of our hair. I was prepared because of Gage and Cybil, so instead of lying by the side of the road, I'm sitting here. It's all good."

"Positive," Cybil said. "A positive outcome, and one more in the plus column for us. That's important. Over and above the fact our Fox is sitting here, he was able to turn a potentially negative outcome into a positive one. Destiny has more than one road."

"I'm real happy to be off the road for the moment. In other news . . ." Fox told them about the progress at the farm. He grinned over at Quinn when she yawned. "Boring you?"

"No. Sorry. I guess it's part of the baby thing."

"What baby thing?"

"Oh God, we didn't tell you. With all the bullets bouncing off you and Porta Potties, we forgot. I'm pregnant."

"What? Seriously? I'm busy getting shot and digging latrines, and the next thing I know we're having a baby." He pushed out of the chair to cross over and kiss her, then punched Cal in the shoulder. "Take the woman to bed. Obviously you know how."

"He does, but I can get myself there. And I think I will." Rising, Quinn laid her hands on Fox's cheeks. "Welcome home."

"I'll be right up." Cal got to his feet. "We could all use some sleep. We didn't get very far with the link, being rudely interrupted. Tomorrow?"

"Tomorrow," Gage agreed.

"I think I'll go up, too." Cybil stepped over to Fox, kissed him. "Nice work, cutie."

She heard Quinn's laugh as she passed Cal's bedroom

door, and smiled. Talk about positive energy, she thought. Q
had always had it in abundance. Now, it would likely be pouring off her like light. And light was just what they needed.

She was a little tired herself, Cybil admitted. She supposed
they all were, with the bombarding dreams and restless nights.
Maybe she'd try a little yoga, or a warm bath, something to
soothe her system into relaxation.

Gage came up behind her, and as she started to glance
back, he took her hips, turned her. He moved her back against
the door to close it, held her there.

"Well, hello."

His hands moved from her hips to her wrists, then drew
her arms over her head. The system she'd thought to relax
went on high alert. Braced for, anticipating the demand she
saw in his eyes, she could only sigh when his mouth descended to hers. Then could only tremble when instead of
demand there was tenderness.

Soft, quiet, the kiss soothed even as it aroused. While his
hands held hers prisoner, adding an excited kick to her
heartbeat, his mouth took its time exploring and exploiting
hers. She sank into the pleasure of it, with a purr in her
throat when he cuffed her wrists with one hand and stroked
her body with the other.

The light, almost delicate touch stirred desire in her belly,
weakened her knees. And all the while his lips slid and
skimmed against hers. He flipped open the button at her
waistband, danced his fingers under her skirt, closed his
teeth lightly, very lightly over her jaw.

She imagined herself pouring into his hands like cream.

Then he hooked his hand in the neck of her shirt, and tore
it down the center.

He saw the shock in her eyes, heard it in her quick gasp.
Once again, his fingers played lightly over her skin. "Seduction shouldn't be predictable. You think you know." His
mouth took hers again in a long, drugging kiss. "But you
don't. You won't."

His hand tightened on her wrists, a kind of warning while

the kiss shimmered like silk. He felt her melt into it, degree by degree, that lovely body yielding, those lovely limbs going limp. So he shot his hand between her legs and drove her to a fast, almost brutal peak and muffled her shocked cries with his mouth.

"I want you in ways you can't imagine."

Her breath shuddered out; her eyes stayed on his. "Yes, I can."

And he smiled. "Let's find out."

He whipped her around so she was forced to brace her hands against the door, then fist them there as he did things to her body, to her mind, things that pushed her past desperation into surrender, then ripped her back again. Then he slowed, and once again he soothed, and he lifted her into his arms. At the bed she would have turned into him, curled into him in absolute bliss, but he pinned her beneath him.

"Not quite finished."

"Oh God." She shuddered when he lowered his head to flick his tongue over her nipple. "Do we have a crash cart?"

His lips curved against her breast. "I'll bring you back." And he took her hungrily into his mouth.

She shivered under him, and she gave. She yielded under him, and she surrendered. Her body lifted, held trembling before it fell again. And always, always, he knew she was with him, bound with him, need fused to need. She was strength and beauty, beyond any he'd thought to possess, and she was with him.

When he was inside her again, hard against soft, he knew her blood pounded as his did. Knew when she said his name, they were lost. Lost together.

She floated, what else could she do but float on the warm lake of pleasure? No stress, no fatigue, no fears for tomorrow. Exhaustion was bliss, she thought. Gliding on it, she opened her eyes, and found him watching her.

She had enough energy to smile. "If you're even thinking about going again, you must've suffered brain damage the last round."

"It was a knockout." How could he explain what happened inside him when they came together? He didn't have the words. Instead, he lowered his head to touch his lips to hers. "I thought you were asleep."

"Better than asleep. In the lovely, lovely between."

He took her hand, and she saw what was in his eyes. "Oh. But—"

"When better?" he asked her. "What's more relaxing than sex? What releases more positive energy, if it's done right? And, sweetheart, we did it right. But we both have to want to try it."

She let herself breathe. He was right. Linking now when they couldn't be any closer in mind and body might break through the block that had frustrated them the last several attempts.

"All right." She shifted so they lay on the bed face-to-face, heart-to-heart. "The same way we were going to try it earlier. Focusing on you, Cal, Fox, then the stone."

Her eyes. He could see himself in them. Feel himself in them. He let himself sink, then drew himself out until he stood in the clearing with the Pagan Stone. Alone.

He thought the air smelled of her—secret, seductive. The sunlight glowed gold; the trees massed with thick green. Cal moved to his side, fully formed, his gray eyes quiet, serious. And an ax held in his hands. Fox flanked him, face fierce. He held a glistening scythe.

For a moment they stood, only the three, facing the stone atop the stone.

Then hell came.

The dark, the wind, the blood-soaked rain attacked like animals. Fire roared in bellowing walls and sheathed the stones like blazing skin. He knew, in that instant, the war they'd believed they'd fought for twenty-one years had been only skirmishes, only feints and retreats.

This was war.

Soaked with sweat and blood, the women fought with them. Blades and fists and bullets whipping through a sea of screams. The iced air choked with smoke as they fell, fought back. Something sliced across his chest like claws, ripping flesh, spilling more blood. His blood stained the ground, and sizzled.

Midnight. He heard himself think it. Nearly midnight. And smearing his hands over the wound, he reached for Cybil. With tears glistening in her eyes, she gripped his hand, reached for Cal.

In turn, one by one, they joined until their hands, their blood, their minds, their will joined as well. Until the six were one. The ground split, the fire ripped its way closer. And the mass of black took form. Once again, he looked into Cybil's eyes, and taking what he found there, he broke the chain.

Reaching into the flames, he pulled the burning stone out with his bare hand. Closing it into his fist, he leaped, alone, into the black.

Into the belly of the beast.

"Stop, stop, stop." Cybil knelt beside him on the bed, beating her hands on his chest. "Come back, come back. Oh God, Gage, come back."

Could he? Could anyone come back from that? That cold, that burn, that pain, that terror? When he opened his eyes, it rolled through him, all of it, to center like a swarm of wasps in his head.

"Your nose is bleeding," he managed.

She made a sound, something between a sob and a curse before she slid off the bed, stumbled to the bath. She came back with a cloth for each of them, pressed her own against her bone-white face. "Where . . . Where's that spot?" He fumbled for the accupressure points on her hand, her neck.

"Doesn't matter."

"It does if your head feels like mine. Might be sick." He laid still, closed his eyes. "Really hate being sick. Let's just take a minute."

Shaking, shaking, she lay beside him, wrapped close. "I thought . . . I didn't think you were breathing. What did you see?"

"That it's going to be worse than anything we've come up against, anything we imagined we would. You saw it. I felt you right there with me."

"I saw you die. Did you see that?"

The bitterness in her tone surprised him enough for him to risk sitting up. "No. I took the stone, I've seen that before. The blood, the fire, the stone. I took it, and I went right into the bastard. Then . . ." He couldn't describe what he'd seen, what he'd felt. He didn't want to. "That's it. You were punching me and telling me to come back."

"I saw you die," she repeated. "You went into it, and you were gone. Everything went mad. Everything was mad, but it got worse. And the thing, form after form after form, twisting, screaming, burning. I don't know how long. Then, the light was blinding. I couldn't see. Light and heat and sound. Then silence. It was gone, and you were lying on the ground, covered with blood. Dead."

"What do you mean it was gone?"

"Did you *hear* what I said. You were dead. Not dying, not unconscious or floating in some damn limbo. When we got to you, you were dead."

"We? All of you?"

"Yes, yes, yes." She covered her face with her hands.

"Stop it." He yanked them back down. "Did we kill it?"

Her tearful eyes met his. "We killed you."

"Bullshit. Did we destroy it, Cybil? Did taking the bloodstone into it destroy it?"

"I can't be sure—" But when he gripped her shoulders, she closed her eyes, dug for strength. "Yes. There was nothing left of it. You took it back to hell."

The light on his face burned like the fires that waited there. "Now we know how it's done."

"You can't be serious. It *killed* you."

"We saw Fox dead on the side of the road. Right now he's on the lumpy pullout sleeping like a baby or banging Layla. Potential, remember. It's one of your favorites."

"None of us are going to let you do this."

"None of you makes decisions for me."

"Why does it have to be you?"

"It's a gamble." He shrugged. "It's what I do. Relax, sugar." He gave her arm an absent stroke. "We've made it this far. We'll hash it out some yet, look at the angles, options. Let's get some sleep."

"Gage."

"We'll sleep on it, kick it around tomorrow."

But as he lay in the dark, knowing she lay wakeful beside him, Gage had already made up his mind.

Seventeen

HE TOLD THEM IN THE MORNING, AND TOLD THEM straight-out. Then he drank his coffee while the arguments and the alternatives swarmed around him. If it had been any of them proposing to jump into the mouth of hell without a parachute, Gage thought, he'd be doing the same. But it wasn't any of them, and there was a good reason for that.

"We'll draw straws." Fox stood scowling, hands jammed in his pockets. "The three of us. Short straw goes."

"Excuse me." Quinn jabbed a finger at him. "There are six of us here. We'll *all* draw straws."

"Six and a fraction." Cal shook his head. "You're pregnant, and you're not playing short straw with the baby."

"If the baby's father can play, so can its mother."

"The father isn't currently gestating," Cal shot back.

"Before we start talking about stupid straws, we need to *think*." At her wit's end, Cybil whirled around from her blind stare out of the kitchen window. "We're not going to stand around here saying one of us is going to die. Gee, which one should it be? None of us is willing to sacrifice one for the whole."

"I agree with Cybil. We'll find another way." Layla rubbed a hand over Fox's arm to soothe him. "The bloodstone is a weapon, and apparently *the* weapon. It has to get inside Twisse. How do we get it inside?"

"A projectile," Cal considered. "We could rig up something."

"What, a slingshot? A catapult?" Gage demanded. "A freaking cannon? This is the way. It's not just about getting it into Twisse, it's about *taking* it there. It's about jamming it down the bastard's throat. About blood—our blood."

"If that's true, and without more we can't say it is, we're back to straws." Cal shoved his own coffee aside to lean toward Gage. "It's been the three of us since day one. You don't get to decide."

"I didn't. It's the way it is."

"Then why you? Give me a reason."

"It's my turn. Simple as that. You jammed a knife into that thing last winter, showed us we could hurt it. A couple months later, Fox showed us we could kick its ass back and live through it. We wouldn't be sitting here, this close to ending it, if the two of you hadn't done those things. If these three women hadn't come here, stayed here, risked all they've risked. So it's my turn."

"What next?" Cybil snapped at him. "Are you going to call time-out?"

He looked at her calmly. "We both know what we saw, what we felt. And if we all look back, step by step, we can see this one coming. I was given the future for a reason."

"So you wouldn't have one?"

"So, whether I do or not, you do." Gage shifted his gaze from Cybil to Cal. "The town does. So wherever the hell Twisse plans to go next when he's done here has a future. I play the cards I'm dealt. I'm not folding."

Cal rubbed the back of his neck. "I'm not saying I'm on board with this, but say I am—we are—there's time to think of a way for you to do this without dying."

"I'm all for that."

"We pull you out," Fox suggested. "Maybe there's a way to pull you out. Get a rope on you, some sort of harness rig?" He looked at Cal. "We could yank him back out."

"We could work with something like that."

"If we could get Twisse to take an actual form," Layla put in. "The boy, the dog, a man."

"And get it to hold form long enough for me to ram the stone up its ass?"

"You said down his throat."

Gage grinned at Layla over his coffee. "Metaphorically. I'm going to check with my demonologist friend, Professor Linz. Believe me, I'm not going into this unprepared. All things being equal, I'd like to come out of this alive." He shifted his gaze to Cybil. "I've got some plans for after."

"Then we'll keep thinking, keep working. I've got to get into the office," Fox said, "but I'm going to cancel or reschedule all the appointments and court dates I can for the duration."

"I'll give you a ride in."

"Why? Shit, right. Napper, truck. Which means I've got to swing by and see Hawbaker again this morning and check with the mechanic about my truck."

"I want in on the first part," Gage said. "I'll follow you in. I can run you by the mechanic if you need to go."

Cal got to his feet. "We're going to figure this out," he said to the group at large. "We're going to find the way."

With the men gone, the women sat in the kitchen.

"This is so completely stupid." Quinn rapped the heel of her hand on the counter. "Draw straws? For God's *sake*. As if we're going to say sure, one of us falls on the damn grenade while the rest of us stand back and twiddle our thumbs."

"We weren't twiddling," Cybil said quietly. "Believe me. It was horrible, Q. Horrible. The noise, the smoke, the *stink*. And the cold. It was everything, this thing. It was mammoth. No evil little boy or big, bad dog."

"But we fought it. We hurt it." Layla closed a hand around

Cybil's arm. "If we hurt it enough, we'll weaken it. If we weaken it enough, it can't kill Gage."

"I don't know." She thought of what she'd seen, and of her own research. "I wish I did."

"Possibilities, Cyb. Remember that. What you see can be changed, has been changed *because* you see it."

"Some of it. We need to go upstairs. We need one of your spare pregnancy tests."

"Oh, but I took three." Distressed, Quinn pressed a hand to her belly. "And I even felt queasy this morning, and—"

"It's not for you. It's for Layla."

"Me? What? Why? I'm not pregnant. My period's not even due until—"

"I know when it's due," Cybil interrupted. "We're three women who've been living in the same house for months. Our cycles are on the same schedule."

"I'm on birth control."

"So was I," Quinn said thoughtfully. "But that doesn't explain why you think Layla's pregnant."

"So pee on a stick." Cybil rose, gave the come-ahead sign. "It's easy."

"Fine, fine, if it makes you feel better. But I'm not pregnant. I'd know. I'd sense it, wouldn't I?"

"It's harder to see ourselves." Cybil led the way upstairs, strolled into Quinn's room, sat on the bed while Quinn opened a drawer.

"Take your pick." She held out two boxes.

"It doesn't matter because it doesn't matter." Layla took one at random.

"Go pee," Cybil told her. "We'll wait."

When Layla went into the bathroom, Quinn turned to Cybil. "You want to tell me why she's in there peeing on a stick?"

"Let's just wait."

Moments later Layla came back with the test stick. "There, done. And no plus sign."

"It's been about thirty seconds since you flushed," Quinn pointed out.

"Thirty seconds, thirty minutes. I can't be pregnant. I'm getting married in February. I don't even have the ring yet. After February, and if we buy this house we're thinking about, and I decorate it, after my business is up and running smoothly, *then* I can be pregnant. Next February—our first anniversary—would be the perfect time to conceive. Everything should be in place by then."

"You really are an anal and organized soul," Cybil commented.

"Absolutely. And I know my own body, my own cycle, my own . . ." She trailed off when she glanced down at the test stick. "Oh."

"Let me see that." Quinn snatched it out of her hand. "That's a really big, really clear, really unmistakable plus for positive Miss I Can't Be Pregnant."

"Oh. Oh. Wow."

"I said holy shit a lot." Quinn passed the stick to Cybil. "Give yourself a minute. See how you feel after the shock clears."

"That might take more than a minute. I . . . I had a sort of loose schedule worked out, for when this would happen. We want kids. We talked about it. I just thought . . . Let me see that again." Taking it from Cybil, Layla stared. "Holy shit."

"Good shit or bad shit?" Quinn asked.

"Another minute, and that one sitting down." Layla dropped onto the bed and just breathed. Then she laughed. "Good, really, really good. About a year and a half ahead of schedule, but I can adjust. Fox is going to be over the moon! I'm pregnant. How did you know?" She swiveled to Cybil. "How did you know?"

"I saw you." Moved by the radiant smile, Cybil stroked Layla's hair. "Both you and Quinn. I've been expecting this. We saw you, Quinn, Gage and I. In the winter—next winter. You were napping on the couch when he came in. And when you turned over, well, you were unmistakably pregnant."

"How'd I look?"

"Enormous. And beautiful, and wonderfully happy. You both did. And I saw Layla. You were in your boutique, which looked terrific, by the way. Fox brought you flowers. They were for your first month in business. It was sometime in September."

"We think I could open in mid-August, if . . . I'm going to open in mid-August," she corrected.

"You weren't showing yet, not really, but something you said . . . I don't think Gage caught that. A man probably wouldn't. You were all so happy." Remembering what else she'd seen, only the night before, Cybil pressed her lips together. "That's how it should be. I believe now that's how it will be."

"Honey." Quinn sat beside her, draped an arm over Cybil's shoulder. "You think Gage has to die for all this to happen for the rest of us."

"I've seen it happen. I've seen all of it happen. So has he. How much is destiny, how much is choice? I just don't know anymore." She took Layla's hand, laid her head on Quinn's shoulder. "Some of the research, it talks about the need for sacrifice, for balance—destroy the dark, the light must die, too. The stone—the power source—must be taken into the dark, by the light. I didn't tell you."

Cybil lifted her hands, held them over her face, dropped them. "I didn't tell any of you because I didn't want to believe it. Didn't want to face it. I don't know why I had to fall in love with him to lose him. Not this way."

Quinn hugged harder. "We'll find another."

"I've tried."

"We'll all be trying now," Layla reminded her. "We'll find it."

"We don't give up," Quinn insisted. "That's the one thing we don't do."

"You're right. You're right." Hope wasn't something to dismiss, Cybil reminded herself. "And this isn't the moment for gloom and doom. Let's get out of this house. Let's just get out of this house for a few hours."

"I want to tell Fox. We could drive into town, and I could tell him face-to-face. Make his day."

"Perfect."

WHEN THEY LEARNED FROM FOX'S PEPPY NEW office manager that Fox was with a client, Layla decided to multitask.

"I'll run upstairs, get some more clothes, clean out the perishables from the kitchen. If he's not done by that time, well, I'll just wait."

"I'll let him know you're here as soon as he's free," the new office manager sang out as the three women started up the stairs.

"I'll start in the kitchen," Cybil said.

"I'll give you a hand with that. As soon as I pee." Quinn shifted from foot to foot. "It's probably psychological pee, because I know I'm pregnant. But my bladder thinks otherwise. Wow," she continued when Layla opened the door to Fox's apartment to the living room. "This place is . . ."

"The word is *habitable*." With a laugh, Layla shut the door behind them. "It's amazing what a regular cleaning woman can do."

They separated, Cybil to the kitchen, Quinn to the bathroom. Layla stepped into the bedroom, and froze with a knife point at her throat.

"Don't scream. It'll go right through you, right through, and that's not the way it has to be."

"I won't scream." Her gaze latched on to the bed—and the rope, the roll of duct tape on it. On the can of gasoline. Cybil's vision, she thought. Cybil and Gage had seen her bound and gagged, on the floor with fire crawling toward her.

"You don't want to do this. Not really. It's not you."

He eased the door shut. "It needs to burn. It all needs to burn. To purify."

She looked up at his face. She knew that face. Kaz. He

delivered pizza for Gino's. He was only seventeen. But now his eyes gleamed with a kind of jittery madness she thought was ancient. And his grin was wild as he backed her toward the bed. "Take off your clothes," he said.

In the kitchen Cybil pulled milk, eggs, fruit out of the refrigerator, set them on the counter. When she turned toward a broom closet, hoping for a box or bag, she saw the broken pane in the back door. Instantly she pulled her .22 from her purse and reached for a knife in the block.

One missing, she thought, fighting panic. A knife already out of the block. Gripping hers, she spun back toward the living room just as Quinn opened the bathroom door. Cybil put her finger to her lips, pushed the knife into Quinn's hand. She gestured toward the bedroom door.

"Go get help," Cybil whispered.

"Not leaving you. Not leaving either one of you." Instead, Quinn pulled out her phone.

Inside, Layla stared at the boy who delivered the pizza, who liked to talk with Fox about sports. Keep his eyes on yours, she told herself while her heart made odd piping sounds in her chest. Talk. Keep talking to him. "Kaz, something's happened to you. It's not your fault."

"Blood and fire," he said, still grinning.

She took another backward step as he jabbed out with the knife, nicked her arm. And the hand fumbling in her purse behind her back finally clamped on its target. She did scream now, and so did he, as she spewed the pepper spray in his eyes.

At the screams, both Quinn and Cybil rushed the bedroom door. They saw Layla scrambling for a knife on the floor, and the boy they all recognized howling with his hands over his face. Whether it was instinct, panic, or simply rage, Cybil followed through. She kicked the boy in the groin, and when he doubled over, his hands leaving his streaming eyes for his crotch, shoved him into the closet. "Quick, quick, help me push the dresser in front of the door," she ordered when she slammed the closet door.

He screamed, he wept, he battered the door.

Though her hand trembled, Quinn retrieved her phone.

Within fifteen minutes, Chief Hawbaker pulled the weeping boy out of the bedroom closet.

"What's going on?" Kaz demanded. "My eyes! I can't see. Where am I? What's going on?"

"He doesn't know," Cybil said as she stood clutching Quinn's hand. He was nothing but a hurt and confused teenage boy now. "It let him go."

After cuffing Kaz, Hawbaker nodded to the can on the floor. "That what you used on him?"

"Pepper spray." Layla sat on the side of the bed, clinging to Fox. Cybil wasn't sure if she held him to stop him from leaping at the pitiful boy, or to ground herself. "I lived in New York."

"I'm going to take him in, deal with his eyes. You need to come in, all of you, make your statements."

"We'll be in later." Fox leveled his gaze on Kaz. "I want him locked up until we get there, sort this out."

Hawbaker studied the rope, the knives, the can of gas. "He will be."

"My eyes are burning. I don't understand," Kaz wept as Hawbaker guided him out. "Fox, hey, Fox, what's *up* with this?"

"It wasn't him." Layla pressed her face to Fox's shoulder. "It wasn't really him."

"I'm going to get you some water." Cybil started out, stopped as Cal and Gage rushed through the apartment door. "We're all right. Everyone's all right."

"Don't touch anything," Fox warned. "Come on, Layla, let's get you out of here."

"It wasn't him," she repeated, and took Fox's face in her hands. "You know it wasn't his fault."

"Yeah, I know. Doesn't mean I don't want to beat him into a bloody pulp right at the moment, but I know."

"Somebody want to fill us in?" Cal demanded.

"He was going to kill Layla," Gage said tightly. "The kid. What Cybil and I saw. Strip her down, tie her up, light the place up."

"But we stopped it. The way Fox stopped Napper. It didn't happen. That's twice now." Layla let out a breath. "That's two we've changed."

"Three." Cybil gestured toward Fox's front door. "That's it, isn't it?" She turned to Gage. "That's the door we saw Quinn trying to get out of when a knife was stabbing down at her. The knife Kaz had. The one from out of the block in the kitchen. Neither of those things happened because we were prepared. We changed the potential."

"More weight on our side of the scale." Cal drew Quinn to him.

"We need to go down to the police station, deal with this. Press charges."

"Fox."

"Unless," he continued over Layla's distress, "he gets out of town. Out to the farm, or just out, until after the Seven. We'll talk to him, and his parents. He can't stay in the Hollow. We can't risk it."

Layla let out another breath. "If the rest of you could go ahead? I want a few minutes to talk to Fox."

LATER, BECAUSE IT SEEMED LIKE THE THING TO do, Cybil dragged Gage back to Fox's apartment to load up the food.

"What's the big fucking deal about a quart of milk and some eggs?"

"It's more than that, and besides, I don't approve of waste. And it saves Layla from even thinking about coming back up here until she's steadier. And why are you so irritable?"

"Oh, I don't know, maybe it has something to do with having a woman I like quite a lot being held at knifepoint by some infected pizza delivery boy."

"You could always tip that and be happy Layla was carrying pepper spray and between her quick reflexes and Quinn and me, we managed to handle it." As a tension headache turned her shoulders into throbbing knots of concrete, Cybil bagged the milk. "And the pizza delivery boy, who was being used, is on his way to stay with his grandparents in Virginia along with the rest of his family. That's five people out of harm's way."

"I could look at it that way."

His tone made her lips twitch. "But you'd rather be irritable."

"Maybe. And we can factor in that now we've got two pregnant women instead of one to worry about."

"Both of whom have proven themselves completely capable, particularly today. Pregnant Layla managed to keep her head, to reach into her very stylish handbag and yank out a can of pepper spray. Then to blast same in that poor kid's eyes. Saving herself, potentially saving both Quinn and me from any harm. Certainly saving that boy. I would have shot him, Gage."

She sighed as she packed up food. The tension, she realized, wasn't simply about what had happened, but what might have happened. "I would have shot that boy without an instant's hesitation. I know this. She saved me from having to live with that."

"With that toy you carry, you'd have just pissed him off."

Because her lips twitched again, she turned to him. "If that's an attempt to make me feel better, it's not bad. But Jesus, I could use some aspirin."

When he walked away, she continued bagging food. He returned with a bottle of pills, poured her a glass of water. "Medicine cabinet in the bathroom," he told her.

She downed the pills. "Back to our latest adventure, both Layla and Quinn came out of this with barely a scratch—unlike the potential outcome we saw. That's a big."

"No argument." He went behind her, put his hands on her shoulders and began to push at the knots.

"Oh God." Her eyes closed in relief. "Thanks."

"So not everything we see will happen, and things we don't see will. We didn't see pregnant Layla."

"Yes, we did." She gave his hands more credit than the

aspirin for knocking back the leading edge of the headache. "You didn't recognize what you saw. We saw her and Fox in her boutique, this coming September. She was pregnant."

"How do you—never mind. Woman thing," Gage decided. "Why didn't you mention it at the time?"

"I'm not really sure. But what it tells me is that some things are meant, and some things can be changed." She turned now so they were eye-to-eye. "You don't have to die, Gage."

"I'd rather not, all in all. But I won't back off from it."

"I understand that. But the things we've seen played some part in helping our friends stay alive. I have to believe they'll help you do the same. I don't want to lose you." Afraid she might fall apart, she pushed the first of two grocery bags into his arms and spoke lightly. "You come in handy."

"As a pack mule."

She shoved the second bag at him. "Among other things." Because his arms were full, she toed up, brushed her lips over his. "We'd better get going. We'll need to stop by the bakery."

"For?"

"Another Glad You're Not Dead cake. It's a nice tradition." She opened the door, let him pass through ahead of her. "I'll tell you what, for your birthday—when you're still alive—I'll bake you one."

"You'll bake me a cake if I live."

"A spectacular cake." She closed Fox's door firmly, glanced at the plywood Gage had put up where the glass pane was broken. "Six layers, one for each of us." When her eyes stung and welled inexplicably, she pulled her sunglasses out of her bag, put them on.

"Seven," Gage corrected. "Seven's the magic number, right? It should be seven."

"July seventh, a seven-layer cake." She waited for him to put the bags in the trunk of his car. "That's a deal."

"When's your birthday?"

"November." She slid into the car. "The second of November."

"I'll tell *you* what. If I get to eat a piece of your famous seven-layer cake, I'll take you anywhere you want to go on your birthday."

Despite the ache in her belly, she sent him an easy smile. "Careful. There are a lot of places I want to go."

"Good. Same here."

THAT WAS JUST ONE OF THE THINGS ABOUT HER, Gage thought, that kept pushing at his mind. There were a lot of places they wanted to go. When had it stopped being he and she in his mind, and become they? He couldn't pinpoint it, but he knew that he wanted to go to all of those places with her.

He wanted to show her his favorite spots, to see hers. And he wanted to go to places neither of them had ever been, and experience them together for the first time.

He didn't want just to follow the game any longer. To simply go wherever and whenever alone. He wanted to go, to see, to do, and God knew he wanted to play, but the idea of *alone* didn't have the appeal it once had.

Irritable, she'd called him. Maybe that was part of the reason why. It was, in his opinion, a damn good reason for being irritable. It was ludicrous, he decided, and started to pace the guest room instead of checking his e-mail as he'd intended. It was absolutely insane to start thinking about long-term, about commitment, about being part of a couple instead of going solo.

But he *was* thinking about it. That was the kicker. And he could imagine it, could see how it might be—the potential of it—with Cybil. He could imagine the two of them exploring the world together without the weight of it on their shoulders. He could even imagine having a base with her somewhere. New York, Vegas, Paris—wherever.

A home with her, somewhere to come back to.

The only place he'd ever had to come back to was Hawkins Hollow. And not by choice, not really by choice.

But this could be, if he took the bet.

It might be fun talking her into it.

There was time left, he thought, enough time left for him to work out a game plan. Have to be cagey about it, he mused as he sat down at his laptop. He'd have to find just the right way to tie her up in those strings they'd both agreed they didn't want. Then once he had, he could just tie a knot here, tie a knot there. She was a smart one, but then so was he. He'd lay odds he could have her wrapped up before she realized he'd changed the game—and the rules.

Pleased with the idea, he opened an e-mail from Professor Linz. And as he read, his belly tightened; his eyes chilled.

So much, he thought, fatalistically, for planning futures. His was already set—and it had less than two weeks to run.

Eighteen

❧

ONCE AGAIN, GAGE CALLED FOR A MEETING AT Cal's office. Just his brothers. He'd made certain he'd been up and out of the house that morning before Cybil so much as stirred. He'd needed time to think, time alone, just as he needed time now with his two friends.

He laid out what he'd learned from Linz in calm and dispassionate terms.

"Screw that," was Fox's opinion. "Screw that, Gage."

"It's how it ends."

"Because some demon academic we don't *know*, who's never been here, never dealt with what we've dealt with says so?"

"Because it's how it ends," Gage repeated. "Everything we know, everything we've found out, everything we've dealt with leads right up to it."

"I'm going to have to go with the lawyer's technical terminology on this," Cal said after a moment. "Screw that."

Gage's eyes were green and clear; he'd made his peace with what had to be. "I appreciate the sentiment, but we all know better. None of us should have made it this far. The only reason we have is because Dent broke the rules, gave us abilities, gave us a power source. Time to pay up. Don't say 'why you.'" Gage tapped a finger in the air at Fox. "It's all over your face, and we've been over that part. It's my turn, and it's my goddamn destiny. It stops this time. This is when and how. Upside is I'm not going to have to haul my ass back here every seven years to save you guys."

"Screw that, too," Fox said, but without heat as he pushed to his feet. "There's going to be another way. You're looking at this in a straight line. You're not checking out the angles."

"Brother, angles are my business. It's either destroyed this time, or it *becomes*. Fully corporeal, fully in possession of all its former power. We've already seen that begin to happen."

Absently, Gage rubbed his shoulder where the scar rode. "I've got a souvenir. To destroy it, absolutely take it out, requires a life from our side. Blood sacrifice, to pay the price, to balance the scales. One light for the dark, and blah blah blah. I'm going to do this thing one way or the other. It'd be a hell of a lot easier if I had you behind me."

"We're not just going to sit back and watch you take one for the team," Cal told him. "We keep looking for another way."

"And if we don't find one? No bullshit, Cal," Gage added. "We've been through too much to bullshit each other."

"If we can't, can I have your car?"

Gage glanced over at Fox and felt the weight drop off his shoulders. They'd do what needed to be done. They'd stand behind him, just like always. "The way you drive? Hell no. Cybil gets it. That woman knows how to handle a car. I need you to lawyer up that kind of thing for me. I'd have that off my head."

"Okay, no problem." He shrugged off Cal's curse. "And my fee's a bet. One thousand says we not only off the Big Evil Bastard, but you walk away from the Pagan Stone with the rest of us after we do."

"I want in on that," Cal said.

"That's a bet then."

Cal shook his head, absently rubbed Lump under his desk as the dog stirred from sleep. "Only a sick son of a bitch bets a thousand he's going to die."

Gage only smiled. "Dead or alive, I like to win."

"We need to take this back to the women," Fox put in, then narrowed his eyes at Gage. "Problem?"

"Depends. If we take it back to the women—"

"There's no if," Cal interrupted. "There are six of us in this."

"*When* we take it back to the women," Gage qualified, "the three of us go in as a unified front. I'm not going to be arguing with you *and* them. The deal is, we look for another way until time runs out. When time runs out and there's no other way, it's my way. Nobody welshes."

Cal rose, preparing to come around the desk to shake on the deal. The office door burst open. Cy Hudson, one of the fixtures of the Bowl-a-Rama's leagues, rushed in, teeth bared, and madly firing a .38. One of the bullets plowed into Cal's sternum, took him down even as Gage and Fox dove at Cy.

His enormous bulk didn't topple, and his sheer madness flung them off like flies. He aimed at Cal again, shifted the gun at the last moment as Gage shouted, and Lump bunched to attack. Gage braced for the bullet, caught Fox rising up like a runner off the mark out of the corner of his eye.

Bill Turner came through the door like fury. He leaped onto Cy's back, fists pounding even as Fox went in low and the dog sprang, jaw snapping. The four of them went down in a bone-breaking tangle. The gun went off again even as Gage shoved up and grabbed a chair. He brought it down, brutally, twice on Cy's exposed head.

"Okay?" he said to Fox as Cy went limp.

"Yeah, yeah. Hey, boy, good dog." Fox hooked an arm around Lump's big neck. "Cal?"

Pushing up again, Gage dropped down beside Cal. Cal's face was bone white, his eyes glassy, and his breath came in short pants. But when Gage ripped his shirt open, he saw the spent bullet pushing up through the wound. Sidling over, Lump licked Cal's face and whined.

"It's okay, you're okay. You're pushing it out." He gripped Cal's hand, sent him all he could. "Give me something."

"Smashed a rib, I think," Cal managed. "Ripped hell out of me in there." He struggled to even his breathing as Lump nosed his shoulder. "I can't exactly tell."

"We've got it. Fox, for Christ's sake, give me a hand."

"Gage."

"What! Can't you see he's . . ." Furious, Gage whipped his head around. He saw Fox kneeling on the floor pressing the blood-soaked wad of his own shirt to Bill's chest.

"Call for an ambulance. I've got to keep the pressure on."

"Go. God." Cal pushed breath out, drew more in. He fisted his hand in Lump's fur. "I've got this. I've got this. Go."

But Gage kept Cal's hand tight in his, drew out his phone. And with his eyes locked on his father's pale face, called for help.

CYBIL WOKE GROGGY, HEADACHY. THE GROGGY wasn't much of a surprise. Mornings weren't her finest hour, particularly after a restless night, and the dreams were a plague now. More, Gage had been closed in the night before. Barely speaking, she thought, as she grabbed a robe in case there were men in the house.

Well, his moods weren't her responsibility, she decided, and felt fairly closed in herself. She'd take her coffee out on the back deck—alone. And sulk.

The idea perked her up a little, or would have if she hadn't found both Layla and Quinn holding a whispered conference in the kitchen.

"Go away. Nobody talk to me until I've had two solid hits of caffeine."

"Sorry." Quinn blocked her path to the stove. "You'll have to put that off."

Warning flashed into her eyes. "Nobody tells me to put off my morning coffee. Move it or lose it, Q."

"No coffee until after this." She picked the pregnancy test off the counter, waved it in front of Cybil's face. "Your turn, Cyb."

"My turn for what. *Move!*"

"To pee on a stick."

Cybil's jones for coffee tripped over sheer shock. "What? Are you crazy? Just because sperm met egg for the two of you doesn't mean—"

"Isn't it funny I have this on hand just like I had one for Layla."

"Ha ha."

"And it's interesting," Layla continued, "how you pointed out yesterday the three of us are on the same cycle."

"I'm not pregnant."

Layla looked at Quinn. "Isn't that what I said?"

Nearly desperate for coffee, Cybil rolled her eyes. "I *saw* you pregnant. Both of you. I didn't see me that way."

"It's always harder to see ourselves," Quinn returned. "You've told me that a few times. Let's make it simple. You want coffee? Go pee on a stick. You won't get past both of us to the goal, Cyb."

Fuming, Cybil snatched the box. "Pregnancy's made both of you bossy and bitchy." She stalked off to the first-floor powder room.

"It has to mean something." Layla rubbed her hands over her arms, ridiculously nervous. "If we're right, or if we're wrong, it has to mean something. I just wish I could figure out what."

"I've got some ideas, but . . ." Worried, Quinn paced to the kitchen doorway. "We'll think about that later. After. And either way, we have to be with her on this."

"Well, of course. Why wouldn't . . . Oh. You mean if she is, and she doesn't want to be." With a nod, Layla stepped up so she stood beside Quinn. "No question about it. Whatever it is, whatever she needs."

They waited a few more minutes, then Quinn dragged both hands through her hair. "That's it. I can't stand it."

She marched to the door, knocked for form, then pushed

the door open. "Cyb, how long does— Oh, Cybil." She knelt down immediately to gather Cybil up as her friend sat on the floor.

"What am I going to do?" Cybil managed. "What am I going to do?"

"Get off the floor to start." Briskly, Layla leaned down to help her up. "I'm going to make you some tea. We'll figure this out."

"I'm so stupid. So *stupid*." Cybil pressed her hands to her eyes as Quinn led her to the kitchen and a chair. "I should've seen it coming. All three of us. It's a perfect goddamn fit. It was right there in front of my face."

"It didn't click for me," Quinn told her. "The possibility of it didn't click in for me until the middle of the night. It's going to be all right, Cybil. Whatever you want or need, whatever you decide, Layla and I are going to be right there to make sure it's all right."

"It's not the same for me as it is for the two of you. Gage and I . . . We don't have any plans. We're not . . ." She managed a weak smile. "Linked the way you are with Cal and Fox."

"You're in love with him."

"Yes, I am." Cybil looked into Quinn's eyes. "But that doesn't mean we're together. He's not looking for—"

"Forget what he's looking for." Layla's voice was so sharp, Cybil blinked. "What are *you* looking for?"

"Well, it certainly wasn't this. I was looking to finish what we started here, and to have some time with him outside of this. If I looked further than that, and I'm not so strong and coolheaded that I didn't look further and hope that we might make something together. And not so wide-eyed and optimistic that I expect to."

"You know you don't have to decide right away." Quinn stroked Cybil's hair. "This is between the three of us, and we'll keep it that way as long as you want."

"You know we can't do that," Cybil replied. "There's a purpose in this, and that purpose might be the difference between life and death."

"Gods, demons, Fate—," Layla snapped. "None of them have a right to make this choice for you."

When Layla set the tea on the table, Cybil took her hand, squeezed fiercely. "Thanks. God. Thanks. The three of us, the three of them. Ann Hawkins had three sons and they were her hope, her faith, her courage. Now there are three more—the possibilities of three more inside us. There's a symmetry there that can't be ignored. In many cultures, in much lore, the pregnant woman holds particular power. We'll use that power."

She took a deep breath, reached for the tea. "I could, when it's finished, choose to end this possibility. My choice, and yes, screw gods and demons. *My* choice. And I don't choose to end this possibility. I'm not a child, and I'm not without resources. I love the father. Whatever happens between Gage and me, I absolutely believe this was meant."

She took another breath. "I know this is the right thing for me. And I know I'm officially scared to death."

"We'll all be going through it together." Quinn took Cybil's hand, took a good, strong hold. "That's going to help."

"Yes, it is. Don't say anything yet. I need to work out the best way to tell Gage. The best time, the best method. Meanwhile, the three of us need to try to figure out how we can use this surprising bout of mutual fertility. I can contact—"

"Hold that thought," Quinn said when the phone rang. After glancing at the display, she smiled. "Hello, lover. You—" The smile dropped away, and so did her color. "We're coming. I—" She shot alarmed glances at Cybil and Layla. "All right. Yes, all right. How bad? We'll meet you there."

She hung up. "Bill Turner—Gage's father—he's been shot."

THEY'D TAKEN HIS MOTHER AWAY IN AN AMBU-lance, Gage thought. All the lights, the sirens, the rush. He hadn't gone with her, of course. Frannie Hawkins had bundled him away, given him milk and cookies. Kept him close.

Now it was his father—the lights, the sirens, the rush. He

wasn't entirely sure how it was he was speeding behind the ambulance, wedged in between Fox and Cal in the cab of Fox's truck. He could smell the blood. Cal's, the old man's.

There had been a lot of blood.

Cal was still pale, and the healing wasn't complete. Gage felt Cal tremble—quick, light shivers—as his body continued the pain and the effort of healing itself. But Cal wasn't dead, wasn't lying in a pool of his own blood as he'd been in the vision. They'd changed that . . . potential, as Cybil would call it.

Score another for the home team.

But they hadn't seen the old man. There'd been no vision of his father—dead or alive. No foresight of the old man leaping through the door and onto crazed Cy Hudson's back. No preview of that hot, determined look in his eyes. There sure as hell hadn't been any quick peek through the window to show him the way the old man lay on the floor, bleeding through Fox's wadded-up shirt.

He'd looked broken, Gage realized. Broken and frail and old when they'd loaded him into the ambulance. It wasn't right, it wasn't the right image. It didn't match the picture of Bill Turner that Gage carried around in his head the way, he supposed, he carried the picture of his mother in his wallet.

In that, she was forever young, forever smiling.

In Gage's head, Bill Turner was a big man, hefting the sway of a beer belly. He was hard eyes, hard mouth, hard hands. That was Bill Turner. As soon backhand you as look at you Bill Turner.

Who the hell was that broken bleeding man in the ambulance up ahead? And why the hell was he following him?

It blurred on him. The road, the cars, the buildings as Fox swung toward the hospital. He couldn't quite solidify it, couldn't quite bring it into focus. His body moved—getting out of the truck, climbing out when Fox slammed to the curb of the emergency entrance, striding into the ER. Part of his brain registered odd details. The change in temperature from June warmth to the chill of air-conditioning, the different sounds, voices, the new rush as medical people descended on the broken, bleeding man. He heard phones ringing—a tinny, irritatingly demanding sound.

Answer the phone, he thought, answer the goddamn phone.

Someone spoke to him, peppering him with questions. *Mr. Turner, Mr. Turner*, and he wondered how the hell they expected the old man to answer when they'd already wheeled him off. Then he remembered *he* was Mr. Turner.

"What?"

What was his father's blood type?

Did he have any allergies?

His age?

Was he on any medications, taking any drugs?

"I don't know," was all Gage could say. "I don't know."

"I'll take it." Cal took Gage's arm, gave him a quick shake. "Sit down, get coffee. Fox."

"I'm on that."

There was coffee in his hand. How had that happened? Surprisingly good coffee. He sat with Cal and Fox in a waiting room. Gray and blue couches, chairs. A TV set on some morning show with a man and a woman laughing behind a desk.

Surgical waiting room, he remembered, as if coming out of a dream. The old man was in surgery. GSW—that's what they called it. Gunshot wound. The old man was in surgery because he had a bullet in him. Supposed to be in me, Gage remembered as his mind replayed that quick whip of the gun toward him. That .38 slug should be in me.

"I need to take a walk." As Fox started to stand with him, Gage shook his head. "No, I just need some air. I'm just . . . have to clear my head."

He rode down in the elevator with a sad-eyed woman with graying roots and a man with a seersucker blazer buttoned tight over a soccer ball belly.

He wondered if they'd left anyone broken and bleeding upstairs.

On the main level, he passed the gift shop with its forest of shiny balloons (Get Well Soon! It's a Boy!) and cold case

of overpriced floral arrangements, racks of glossy magazines and paperback novels. He went straight out the front
doors, turned left, and walked without any thought of destination.

Busy place, he thought idly. Cars, trucks, SUVs jammed the
lots, while others circled, searching for a spot to park. Some of
them would stop by the gift shop for glossy magazines and
balloons. A lot of sick people around, he supposed, and wondered how many of them had a GSW. Was there an appropriate
tagline on a balloon for a GSW?

He heard Cybil call his name. Though the sound of it
seemed absurdly out of place, he turned. She hurried down
the sidewalk toward him, at just short of a run. All that dark,
curling hair was sunstruck, flying around that fabulous face.

Gage had the odd thought that if a man had to die, he
could go happier knowing a woman like Cybil Kinski had
once run to him.

She caught him, grabbed both his hands. "Your father?"

"In surgery. How'd you get here?"

"Cal called. Quinn and Layla went in. I saw you so . . .
Can you tell me what happened?"

"Cy brought his .38 into Cal's office, shot up the place.
Cal, too."

"Cal—"

"He's okay. You know how it goes."

An ambulance roared into the lot hot, sirens, lights.
Someone else in trouble, Gage thought. Another balloon on
a string.

"Gage. Let's find a place to sit down."

He brought himself back to her, to Cybil with the gypsy
eyes. "No, I'm . . . walking. It happened fast. Couple of fin-
gersnaps. Let's see. Bang, bang, Cal's down. Cy aims for
him again, so I yelled out. No . . ." Not quite right, he remembered.

"It doesn't matter." She hooked her arm around his waist.
If she could have taken his weight, she would have. But the
weight he carried wasn't physical.

"It does. It all matters."

"You're right." Gently, she guided him around so they were walking back toward the hospital. "Tell me what happened."

"We went for him first, for Cy, but the guy's built like a mountain, and you add in the infection. Shook us right off. Then I yelled. He turned the gun at me."

In his mind, it replayed in slow motion, every detail, every movement. "The dog had been asleep, as usual, under the desk. He came up like vengeance. I wouldn't have believed it if I hadn't seen it. Fox is about to charge Cy again, might've had enough time. We'll never know. The old man, he comes through the door like a freight train, jumps Cy, and the three of them go down—and the dog, too. The gun went off. Fox was okay, so I got over to Cal. Never gave the old man a thought. Fox was okay, Cal was bleeding and working on pushing the goddamn bullet out. I never gave the old man a thought."

Cybil stopped, turned to him. She said nothing, only watched his face, held his hands.

"I looked over. Fox must've pulled his shirt off. He was using it to put pressure on the wound. Chest wound. GSW. The old man, he can't push the goddamn bullet out like we can."

She released his hands to put her arms around him.

"I don't know how I'm supposed to feel."

"You don't have to decide."

"I could've taken the bullet. Odds are it wouldn't have killed me."

"Cal could've taken another, on the same scale. But you tried to stop it. That's what people do, Gage. They try to stop it."

"We didn't see this, Cybil."

"No, we didn't."

"I changed it. I called a meeting with Cal and Fox, so we were there. Instead of Cal being alone in his office when Cy came in shooting, we were there."

"Gage, listen to me." She brought their hands together between them, looked over the joining directly into his eyes. "You're asking yourself, you're wondering if being there makes you to blame for what happened. You know in your heart, in your head—you *know* after twenty-one years of fighting this what's to blame."

"Cal's alive. I know that matters to me more—"

"This isn't about more, or about less."

"He—the old man—it's the first time in my life I remember him stepping up for me. It's hard knowing it might be the last."

Standing in the June sunshine, as the scream of another ambulance hacked through the air, her heart broke for him. "We could look now, look at your father, if that would help you."

"No." He laid his cheek on the top of her head. "We'll wait."

HE THOUGHT IT WOULD BE HOURS. THE WAITING and the wondering and second-guessing that went with it. But Gage had barely reached the waiting room when a doctor in surgical scrubs came in. Gage knew as soon as their eyes met. He saw death in them. Inside his belly something twisted viciously, like a clenched fist jerking once, hard. Then it let go, and what was left behind was numb.

"Mr. Turner."

Gage rose, waved his friends back. He walked out to listen to the doctor tell him the old man was dead.

HE'D BURY THE OLD MAN BESIDE HIS WIFE AND daughter. That Gage could do. He wasn't having any damn viewing, or what he thought of as the after-graveside buffet. Short, simple, done. He let Cal handle the arrangements for a graveside service as long as it was brief. God knew Cal knew Bill Turner better than he did. Certainly the Bill Turner who died on the operating table.

He retrieved his father's one good suit from the apartment and delivered it to the funeral home. He ordered the headstone, paid for it and the other expenses in cash.

At some point, he supposed, he'd need to clean out the apartment, donate everything to Goodwill or the Salvation

Army. Something. Or, as the odds were Cal would be making arrangements for his own graveside service before much longer, Gage figured he could leave that little chore to Cal and Fox.

They lied to the police, which wouldn't keep Gage from sleeping at night. With Jim Hawkins's help, they'd tampered with evidence. Cy remembered nothing, and Gage figured if the old man had to die, that shouldn't be for nothing either.

He came out of the funeral home, telling himself he'd done all he could. And he saw Frannie Hawkins standing beside his car.

"Cybil said you'd be here. I didn't want to come in, to intrude."

"You've never intruded."

She put her arms around him—one good, hard hug. "I'm sorry. I know how things were between you and Bill, but I'm sorry."

"I am, too. I'm just not sure what that covers."

"However things were, however he was, in the past, in the end he did everything he could to protect you—and my boy, and Fox. And in the end, you've done exactly the right thing for them, for the Hollow, and for Bill."

"I'm laying the rap for his own death on him."

"You're saving a good man, an innocent man from a murder charge and prison." Frannie's face radiated compassion. "It wasn't Cy who shot Cal or Bill—and we know that. It isn't Cy who should spend, potentially, the rest of his life behind bars, leave his wife alone, his kids and grandkids."

"No. We talked about that. The old man's not in a position to put his two cents in, so . . ."

"Then you should understand Bill considered Cy a friend, and it was mutual. After Bill quit drinking, Cy was one of the ones who'd sit around with him, drinking coffee or Cokes. I want you to know I feel absolutely certain this is what Bill would want you to do. As far as anyone knows, Bill came in with the gun, God knows why because none of us do, and when Cy and the rest of you tried to stop him, there was an accident. Bill wouldn't want Cy punished for what was beyond his control. And nothing can hurt Bill now. You know what happened, what Bill did in the end. It doesn't matter what anyone else knows."

It helped hearing it, helped rub dull the sharper edges of guilt. "I can't feel—the grief, the anger. I can't feel it."

"If and when you need to, you will. All you need to know now is you've done what can and should be done. That's enough."

"Would you do something for me?"

"Just about anything."

"When I'm not around, will you put flowers out there now and again? For the three of them."

"Yes. I will."

He stepped over to her car, opened the door for her. "Now I'm going to ask you something."

"Ask away."

"If you knew you had a week or two to live, what would you do?"

She started to speak, stopped, and Gage understood she'd smothered her instinctive response—for his sake. Instead, she smiled. "How am I feeling?"

"Good."

"In that case, I'd do exactly as I pleased, particularly if it was something I'd normally deny myself or hesitate over. I'd grab everything I wanted, needed. I'd make sure the people who annoyed me knew just what I thought. And more important, that everyone I loved knew how much they meant to me."

"No confessing your sins, making amends?"

"If I haven't confessed and amended by that point, screw it. It's all about me now."

Laughing, he leaned down and kissed her. "I really love you."

"I know you do."

AS USUAL, IN GAGE'S OPINION, FRANNIE HAD HER sensible finger on the heart of the matter. But first things first. He knew too well that death—anyone's death—

wouldn't stop the approach of the Seven. The meeting they'd held in Cal's office now had to be open to all six.

"The deal's pretty straightforward," he began. They sat, all of them, in Cal's living room on the night before his father's burial. "Some of the books and folklore Linz accessed have fancy or fanciful language, but it boils down to this: The bloodstone—our stone—is the key. Part of the Alpha Stone, just as Cybil theorized. A power source. And oddly enough, in some of Linz's studies, this fragment is called the Pagan Stone. I don't see that as coincidence."

"What's the lock?" Quinn asked.

"Its heart. The black, festering heart of our own Big Evil Bastard. Insert key, turn, the lock opens and the Evil Bastard goes back to hell. Simple as that."

"No," Cybil said slowly, "it's not."

"Actually it is. But you've got to ante up first."

"And you're saying you're what we ante up?"

"The stakes are a little too rich for me," Layla added. "Why play its game? We'll find one of our own, and use our rules."

"It's not its game," Gage corrected. "It's the only game we've got. And one it's been trying to delay and destroy for eons. The bloodstone destroys it, which is why it came to us in threes, why we weren't able to put it together until now. Until we were old enough, until we were all a part of it. It took all six of us. The rest of it will, too. But only one of us turns the key. That's for me."

"How?" Cybil demanded. "By going inside it? By dying and going to hell with it?"

" 'Into the black.' You already know this," he said, watching her face. "You've already found what Linz did."

"Some sources theorize the bloodstone—or Pagan Stone—this particular fragment of the Alpha, will destroy the dark, the black, the demon, if it pierces its heart. Can," she said quickly, "may—if it's been imbued with the blood of the chosen, if it's taken in at exactly the right time. *If, can, may.*"

"You didn't share this?"

"I'm still verifying. I'm still checking sources. No," she added after a moment of silence. "I didn't share it."

" 'Into the black,' " Gage repeated. "All the lore uses that phrase or a close variation. The dark, the black. The heart of the beast, and only when it's in its true form. *Bestia*. And every living thing around it, not protected, dies when it dies. Its death requires equal sacrifice. Blood sacrifice. A light to smother the dark. And you'd found that, too," he added to Cybil.

"I found some sources that speak of sacrifice, balance." She started to qualify, to argue—*anything*—then stopped. They were all entitled to hear it. "Most of the sources I've found claim that to pierce the heart, the demon must be in his true form, and the stone must be taken into it by the guardian, by the light. And that light must go in with full knowledge that, by destroying, he will, in turn, be destroyed. The sacrifice must be made with free will."

Gage nodded. "That jibes with Linz."

"Isn't that handy? Doesn't that just tie it up in a bow?"

For a moment, as Gage and Cybil watched each other, no one spoke. Then Quinn made an *ahem* sound. "Okay, question." Quinn held up a finger. "If the bloodstone and a sacrifice does the job, why didn't Dent kill it?"

Still watching Cybil, Gage answered. "First, it came as Twisse, not in its true form."

"I think there's more," Cal said. "I've been thinking about this since Gage ran it by us. Dent had broken the rules, and intended to break more. He couldn't destroy it. It couldn't be done by his hand. So he paved the way for us. He weakened it, made certain it couldn't become, as Linz says. Not fully corporeal, not in full power. He bought time, and passed all he could down to his ancestors—to us—to finish it."

"I'll go with that. But I don't think it's the whole story." Quinn glanced at Cybil, and her eyes held sorrow and apology. "Destroying the demon was—is—Dent's mission. His reason to exist. His sacrifice—his life—wouldn't be enough. True sacrifice involves choice. We all have choices in this. Dent isn't wholly human. Despite our heritages, all of us are. This is the price, the choice to sacrifice life for the whole. Cyb—"

Cybil held up a hand. "There's always a price." She spoke steadily. "Historically, gods demand payment. Or in more pedestrian terms, nothing's free. That doesn't mean we have to accept the price is death. Not without trying to find another way to pay the freight."

"I'm all for coming up with an alternate payment plan. But," Gage added, "we all have to agree, right here and now so we get this behind us, that if we can't, I take point on this. Agree or not, that's how it's going to be. It'd be easier for me if we agreed."

No one spoke, and everyone understood Cybil had to be the first.

"We're a team," she began. "None of us would question just how completely we've become one. Within that team we've formed various units. The three men, the three women, the couples. All of those units play into the dynamics of the team. But within those units we're all individual. We're all who we are, and that's the core of what makes us what and who we are together. None of us can make a choice for another. If this is yours, I won't be responsible for making it harder, for adding to the stress, for possibly distracting you, or any of us so we make a mistake. I'll agree, believing we'll find a way where all of us walk away whole. But I'll agree, more importantly, because I believe in you. I believe in you, Gage.

"That's all I have to say. I'm tired. I'm going up."

Nineteen

〜〜

HE GAVE HER SOME TIME. HE WANTED SOME HIM-
self. When he walked to the door of the bedroom they
shared, Gage thought he knew exactly what he needed to
say, and how he intended to say it.

Then he opened the door, saw her, and it all slipped away
from him.

She stood at the window in a short white robe, with her
hair loose, her feet bare. She'd turned the lights off, lighted
candles instead. Their glow, the shifting shadows they created suited her perfectly. The look of her, what he felt for
her, were twin arrows in the heart.

He closed the door quietly at his back; she didn't turn.

"I was wrong not to pass along the research I found."

"Yeah, you were."

"I can make excuses, I can tell you I felt I needed to dig
deeper, gather more data, analyze it, verify, and so on. It's
not a lie, but it's not altogether true."

"You know this is the way. You know it in your gut, Cybil,

the same as I do. If I don't do this thing, and do it right, it takes us all—and the Hollow with us."

She said nothing for a moment, but only stood in the candlelight, looking out at the distant hills. "There's still a smear of sunlight at the very tips of the mountains," she said. "Just a hint of what's dying. It's beautiful. I was standing here, looking out and thinking we're like that. We still have that little bit of light, the beauty of it. A few more days of that. So it's important to pay attention to it, to value it."

"I paid attention to what you said downstairs. I value that."

"Then you might as well hear what I didn't say. If you end up being the hero and dying out there in those woods, it's going to take me a long time to stop being angry with you. I will, eventually, but it's going to take a good, long time. And after I stop being angry with you—after that . . ." She drew a long breath. "It's going to take me even longer to get over you."

"Would you look at me?"

She sighed. "It's gone now," she murmured as that smear of light faded into the dark. Then she turned. Her eyes were clear, and so deep he thought they might hold worlds inside them.

"I have things I need to say to you," he began.

"I'm sure. But there's something I need to tell you. I've been asking myself if it would be better for you if I didn't tell you, but—"

"You can decide after I say what I have to say. I got an answer on this earlier today from someone whose opinion I respect. So . . ." He slipped his hands into his pockets. If a man had the guts to die, Gage thought, he ought to have the guts to tell a woman what he felt for her.

"I'm not telling you—or not just telling you—because I may not come through this. That's kind of the springboard for saying it now. But I'd've landed here sooner or later. No getting around it."

"Getting around what?"

"A deal's a deal for me. But . . . the hell with that." Annoyance ran over his face, heated his eyes to a burning green. "All bets are off. I like my life. It works for me. What's the point of changing what works? That's one thing."

Intrigued, she angled her head. "I suppose it is."

"Don't interrupt."

Her eyebrows winged up. "Pardon me. I assumed this was a conversation, not a monologue. Should I sit down?"

"Just shut up for two damn minutes." Frustration only kicked up the annoyance factor. "I've got this push-pull thing with the whole destiny deal. No denying it pulls me in, or I'd be a few thousand miles away from here right now. But I'm damned if it pushes me where I don't want to go."

"Except you're here, and not wherever else. Sorry." She waved a hand when his eyes narrowed in warning. "Sorry."

"I make up my own mind, and I expect other people to do the same. That's what I'm saying." And all at once, he knew exactly what he was saying.

"I'm not here with you because of some grand design dictated before either of us were born. I don't feel what I feel for you because somebody, or something, decided it would be for the greater good for me to feel it. What's inside me is mine, Cybil, and it's in there because of the way you are, the way you sound, the way you smell, you look, you think. It wasn't what I was after, it's not what I was looking for, but there it is."

She stood very still while the candlelight played gold over the dark velvet of her eyes. "Are you trying to tell me you're in love with me?"

"Would you just be quiet and let me manage this on my own?"

She walked to him. "Let me put it this way. Why don't you lay your cards on the table?"

He'd had worse hands, he supposed, and walked away a winner. "I'm in love with you, and I'm almost through being annoyed about it."

Her smile bloomed, beautifully. "That's interesting. I'm in love with you, and I'm almost through being surprised by it."

"That is interesting." He took her face in his hands, said her name once. His lips brushed hers, softly at first, like a wish. Then the kiss deepened. And as her arms hooked around him, there was the warmth, and the *rightness* of her. Of them. Home, he thought, wasn't always a place. Sometimes, home was a woman.

"If things were different," he began, then tightened his grip when she shook her head. "Hear me out. If things were different, or I get really lucky, would you stick with me?"

"Stick with you?" She tipped her head back to study him. "You're having a hard time with your words tonight. Are you asking me if I'd marry you?"

Obviously thrown off, he drew back a little. "I wasn't. I was thinking of something less . . . formal. Being together. Traveling, because it's what we both do. Maybe having a base. You've got one already in New York and that could work for me. Or somewhere else. I don't think we need . . ."

He wanted to be with her, to have her not just in his life, but *of* his life. Wasn't marriage putting the chips on the line and letting them ride?

"On the other hand," he thought out loud, "what the hell, it's probably not going to be an issue. If I get really lucky, do you want to marry me?"

"Yes, I do. Which probably surprises me as much as it does you. But yes, I do. And I'd like to travel with you—and have you travel with me. I'd like to have a base together, maybe a couple of them. I think we'd be good at it. We'd be good together. Really good."

"Then that's a deal."

"Not yet." She closed her eyes. "You need to know something first. And that I won't hold you to your hypothetical proposal if it changes your mind." She stepped back until they were no longer touching. "Gage. I'm pregnant." He said nothing, nothing at all. "Sometimes destiny pushes, sometimes it pulls. Sometimes it kicks you in the ass. I've had a couple of days to think about this, and—"

Thoughts tumbled inarticulately through his head.

Emotions stumbled drunkenly inside his heart. "A couple days."

"I found out the morning your father was shot. It just . . . I couldn't tell you." She took another step back from him. "Chose not to tell you when you were dealing with so much."

"Okay." He drew a breath, then walked to the window to stand as she had been. "You've had a couple days to think about it. So what do you think?"

"We'll start globally, because somehow that's easier. There's a reason the three of us conceived so closely together—very likely on the same night. You, Cal, and Fox were born at the same time. Ann Hawkins had triplets."

Her tone was brisk. In his head he saw her standing at a podium, efficiently lecturing the class. What the hell *was* this?

"Q, Layla, and I share branches on the same family tree. I believe this has happened for a purpose, an additional power that we'll need to end Twisse."

When he didn't speak, she continued. "Your blood, our blood. What's inside me, Q, Layla, combines that. Part of us, part of the three of you. I believe this is meant."

He turned then, his face unreadable. "Smart, logical, a little cold-blooded."

"As you were," she returned, "when you talked about dying."

He shrugged. "Let's shift down from global, Professor. What do you think about two weeks from now, a month from now? When this is over?"

"I don't expect—"

"Don't tell me what you expect." Sparks of anger sizzled along the edges of control. "Tell me what you want. Goddamn it, Cybil, save the lectures and tell me what the hell you want."

She didn't flinch at his words, at the tone of them—not outwardly. But he sensed her flinch, sensed her draw back, and away from him.

Let it ride, he told himself. See where the ball drops.

"All right, I'll tell you what the hell I want." Though she'd drawn back, it didn't lessen the power of her punch. "First, what I didn't want. I didn't want to find myself pregnant, to deal with something this personal, this important when the rest of *everything* is in upheaval. But that's what's happened. So."

She angled her head so their eyes were level. "I want to experience this pregnancy. I want to have this child. To give it the best life I possibly can. To be a good mother, hopefully an interesting and creative one. I want to show this child the world. I want to bring my son or daughter back here so he or she knows Quinn's and Layla's children, and sees this piece of the world we helped preserve."

Her eyes gleamed now, tears and anger. "I want you to live, you idiot, so you can have a part of that. And if you're too stupid or selfish to want a part, then I'd not only expect but demand you peel off some of your winnings every goddamn month so you help support what you helped create. Because I'm carrying part of you, and you're just as responsible as I am. I don't just want to make a family, I'm going to. With or without you."

"You're going to have the kid whether I live or die."

"That's right."

"You're going to have it if I happen to live and don't want any part of being its father, except for a check every month."

"Yes."

He nodded. "You've had a couple days to think about it. That's a lot of thinking in a short amount of time."

"I know my own mind."

"Tell me about it. Now, do you want to know mine?"

"I'm riveted."

His lips quirked. If words were fists, he'd be flat on his ass. "I'd like to send you away, tonight. This minute. Get you and what we've started in you as far away from here as possible. I've never given much thought to having kids. A lot of good reasons for that. Add on that I'm not quite finished being annoyed to find myself in love with you, and handing out hypothetical marriage proposals, and it's a jam."

"Tant pis." She shrugged at his blank stare. "Too bad."

"Okay. But I can do a lot of thinking in short amounts of time, too. It's one of my skills. Right now? Right at this moment? I don't give a flying fuck about global thinking, greater good, destiny. None of it. This is you and me, Cybil, so listen up."

"It was easier to do that when you didn't talk so damn much."

"Apparently I've got more to say to you than I used to. That kid—or whatever they call it at this stage—is as much mine as it is yours. If I happen to live past midnight on July seventh, you're both going to have to deal with that. It's not going to be you, it's going to be we. As in, we show him the world, we bring him back here. We give him the best life we can. We make a family. That's how it's going to work."

"Is that so?" Her voice trembled a little, but her eyes stayed level on his. "That being the case, you're going to have to do better than a hypothetical marriage proposal."

"We'll get to that after midnight, July seventh." He walked to her, touched her cheek, then cautiously laid his hand on her belly. "I guess we didn't see this one coming."

"Apparently we didn't look in the right place."

He pressed his hand a bit firmer against her. "I'm in love with you."

Understanding he meant both her and what they'd begun, she laid her hand over his. "I'm in love with you."

When he lifted her up, she released a watery laugh. And when he sat on the side of the bed, cradling her, she curled in, held on. They both held on.

IN THE MORNING, HE STOOD BY HIS FATHER'S grave. It surprised him how many people had come. Not just his own circle, but people from town—those he knew by name or face, others he couldn't place. Many came up to speak to him, so he went through the motions, got through it on autopilot.

Then Cy Hudson reached for his hand, shook it hard

while giving him a shoulder pat that was a male version of an embrace. "Don't know what to say to you." Cy stared at Gage out of his battered face. "I talked to Bill just a couple days before . . . I don't know what happened. I can't remember exactly."

"It doesn't matter, Cy."

"The doctor says it's probably getting hit in the head, and the shock and all scrambled it up in my brain or something. Maybe Bill, maybe he had a brain tumor or something like that, you know? You know how sometimes people do things they wouldn't, or—"

"I know."

"Anyway, Jim said how I should take the family on out to the O'Dell place. Seemed like a screwy thing to do, but things are screwy. I guess I will then. If you, well, you know, need anything . . ."

"Appreciate it." Standing by the grave, Gage watched his father's killer walk away.

Jim Hawkins stepped up, slid an arm around Gage's shoulders. "I know you had it rough, for a long time. Rougher and longer than you should've. All I'm going to say is you've done the right thing here. You've done right for everybody."

"You were more father to me than he was."

"Bill knew that."

They drifted away, the people from town, the ones he knew by name or face, or couldn't quite place. There were businesses to run, lives to get back to, appointments to keep. Brian and Joanne stood by him a moment longer.

"Bill was helping out at the farm the last week or two," Brian said. "I've got some of his tools, some of his things out there, if you want them."

"No. You should keep them."

"He did a lot to help us with what we're doing," Joanne told Gage. "With what you're doing. In the end, he did what he could. That counts." She kissed Gage. "You take care."

Then it was only the six of them, and the dog who sat patiently at Cal's feet.

"I didn't know him. I knew, a little, who he was before

she died. I knew, too much, who he was after. But I didn't know the man I just buried. And I don't know if I'd have wanted to, even if I'd had the chance. He died for me—for us, I guess. Seems as if that should even it all out."

He felt something. Maybe it was some shadow of grief, or maybe it was just acceptance. But it was enough. He reached out for a handful of dirt, then let it fall out of his hand onto the casket below. "So. That's that."

CYBIL WAITED UNTIL THEY WERE BACK AT CAL'S. "I have something we need to discuss and deal with."

"You're all having triplets." Fox dropped into a chair. "That would put a cap on it."

"Not so far as I know. I've been doing a lot of research on this, but I've hesitated to bring it up. Time's too short for hesitation. We need Gage's blood."

"I'm using it right now."

"You'll have to spare some. What we did for us after the attack, we need to do for Cal's and Fox's families. In their way, they'll be on the front line. Your antibodies," she explained. "You survived the demon bite, and there's a very decent chance you're immune to its poison."

"So you're going to mix up a batch of antidemon venom in the kitchen?"

"I'm good. Not quite that good. We'd use the ritual we used before—the basic blood brothers ritual. Protection," she reminded Gage. "Your Professor Linz spoke of protection. If Twisse gets past us, or if it's able to breach the town, or worse, the farm, protection may be all we can offer."

"There are a lot of other people besides our families," Cal pointed out. "And I don't see them circling up to hold bloody hands with Gage."

"No. But there's another way. Taking it internally."

Gage sat up, leaned forward. "You want the population of Hawkins Hollow to drink my blood? Oh yeah, I bet the mayor and town council will jump right on that."

"They won't know. There was a reason I put off bringing

this up, and this is it." She sat on the arm of the sofa. "Hear me out. The town has a water supply. The farm has a well. People drink water. The Bowl-a-Rama's still doing business, selling beer on tap. We wouldn't cover everyone, but this is the best shot at a broad-based immunization. I think it's worth a try."

"We're down to days left now," Fox considered. "When we go into the woods we'll be leaving the Hollow, the farm, all of it. The last time we did that, it was damn near a massacre. I'd feel easier if I knew my family had something—a chance at something. If that something's Gage's blood, let's start pumping."

"Easy for you to say." Gage rubbed the back of his neck. "The whole immune thing is a theory."

"A solid one," Cybil said, "based on science, and magicks. I've looked into both elements, studied all the angles. It could work. And if it doesn't, we're no worse off."

"Except me," Gage muttered. "How much blood?"

Cybil smiled. "Going with a magickal number, I think three pints ought to do it."

"Three? And just how are you going to get it out of me?"

"I've got that covered. I'll be right back."

"My dad gives blood to the Red Cross a few times a year," Fox commented. "He says it's no big, and after he gets OJ and a cookie."

"What kind of cookie?" Gage wanted to know, then looked dubiously at Cybil when she came back in with a shipping carton. "What's that?"

"Everything we need. Sterile needles, tubing, container bags with anticoagulant, and so on."

"What?" The thought of what was in the box had his stomach doing a long, slow roll. "Did you go to some vampire site online?"

"I have my sources. Here." She handed Gage the bottle of water she'd set on top of the box. "It's better for you if you drink plenty of water before we draw the blood, particularly as we're going to draw about three times what's usually taken in a donation."

He took the bottle, then glanced into the box and winced.

"If I'm going to have to slice some part of me open again for the ritual, why can't we just take it from there."

"This is more efficient, and tidier." She smiled at him. "You're willing to punch a hole in a demon and die, but you're afraid of a little needle?"

"*Afraid* is a strong word. I don't suppose you ever jabbed anyone else with one of those."

"No, but I've been jabbed and I studied the procedure."

"Oh, oh! Let me do it." Fox waved a hand.

"No way in hell. She does it." Gage pointed at Layla, whose mouth dropped open in shock.

"Me? Why? Why?"

"Because of everyone here you'll worry most about hurting me." He smiled thinly at Cybil. "I know you, sweetheart. You like it rough."

"But . . . I don't want to."

"Exactly." Gage nodded at Layla. "Neither do I. That makes us the perfect team."

"I'll talk you through it," Cybil told Layla, and held up a pair of protective gloves.

"Oh, well. Shit. I'm going to go wash my hands first."

It was surprisingly simple, though Layla—whom he'd seen literally crawl through fire—squealed breathlessly as she slid the needle into his arm. He munched on macadamia nut cookies and drank orange juice—though he'd requested a beer—while Cybil efficiently stowed the three filled bags.

"Thanks to your recuperative powers, we could do this all at once. We'll give you a little while, then go ahead and do the rituals."

"The farm should be first. We could swing by there," Fox calculated, "take care of that."

"That works. I want to take Lump out there." Cal glanced at the dog sprawled under the coffee table. "He's not going in with us this time."

"We'll take him out, then go by the Hawkinses'," Fox said, "then into town. Head out to the water supply from there." When he reached for a cookie, Gage slapped his hand aside.

"I don't see your blood in the bag, bro."

"He's good," Fox proclaimed. "Who's driving?"

IT MIGHT HAVE BEEN A WASTE OF THEIR TIME, efforts, and Gage's blood. Cybil gnawed on that in the days—and nights—that followed. Everything that had seemed logical, everything she'd been able to document, verify, research, speculate on now seemed completely useless. What had begun for her months before as a fascinating project was now the sum total of everything that mattered. What good was intellect, she thought as she rubbed her exhausted eyes, when Fate twisted what should be into the impossible?

How had time run out? How could that be? Hours now, essentially, she could count in hours the time they had left. Everything she learned, everything she saw, told her that at the end of those hours she would lose the man she loved, the father of her child. She would lose the life they might have made together.

Where were the answers she'd always been so good at finding? Why were they all the wrong ones?

She glanced up as Gage came into the dining room, then put her fingers back on the keyboard though she had no idea what she'd been typing.

"It's three in the morning," he told her.

"Yes, I know. There's a handy little clock in the bottom corner of the screen."

"You need sleep."

"I have a pretty good idea what I need." When he sat down, stretched out his legs, she shot him a single hot look. "And what I *don't* need is you sitting there staring at me while I'm trying to work."

"You've been working pretty much around the clock for days now. We've got what we've got, Cybil. There isn't any more."

"There's always more."

"One of the things I tripped over when it came to you was

your brain. That's one Grade-A brain you've got. The rest of the package gets the big thumbs-up, too, but the brain's what started the fall for me. Funny, I never gave a damn, before you, if the woman I was hooked up with had the IQ of Marie Curie or an Idaho potato."

"IQ scales are considered controversial by many, and skewed toward white and middle-class."

"See." He tapped a finger in the air. "There you go. Facts and theories at the fingertips. It just kills me. Whatever the scale, you're one smart woman, Cybil, and you know we've got what we've got."

"I also know it ain't over till the fat lady sings. I'm trying to gather more information about a lost tribe in South America that may have been descended from—"

"Cybil." He reached out, laid his hand over hers. "Stop."

"How can I stop? How can you ask me to stop? It's July fourth, for God's sake. It's three hours and twelve minutes into July fourth. We only have *now*. Tonight, tomorrow, tomorrow night, before we start back to that godforsaken place, and you . . ."

"I love you." When she covered her face with her free hand and struggled with sobs, he continued to speak. Calm and clear. "That's a damn big deal for me. Never looked for it, and I sure as hell never expected it to slap me in the face like a two-by-four. But I love you. The old man told me my mother made him a better man. I get that because you make me a better man. I'm not going back to the Pagan Stone for the town. I'm not doing it just for Cal and Fox, or Quinn and Layla. I'm not doing it just for you. I'm doing it for me, too. I need you to understand that. I need you to know that."

"I do. Accepting it is the problem. I can walk into that clearing with you. I just don't know how I can walk out without you."

"I could say something corny about how I'll always be with you, but neither one of us would buy that. We've got to see how the cards fall, then we've got to play it out. That's all there is."

"I was so sure I'd find the way, find *something*." She stared blindly at the computer screen. "Save the day."

"Looks like that's going to be my job. Come on. Let's go to bed."

She rose, turned into him. "Everything's so quiet," she murmured. "The Fourth of July, but there weren't any fireworks."

"So we'll go up and make some, then get some sleep."

THEY SLEPT, AND THEY DREAMED. IN THE DREAMS, the Pagan Stone burned like a furnace, and flaming blood spat from the sky. In the dreams, the writhing black mass scorched the ground, ignited the trees.

In the dreams, he died. Though she cradled him in her arms and wept over him, he did not come back to her. And even in dreams, her grief burned her heart to ashes.

SHE DIDN'T WEEP AGAIN. CYBIL SHED NO TEARS AS they packed and prepared throughout the day of July fifth. She stood dry-eyed as Cal reported there were already some fires, some looting and violence in town, that his father, Chief Hawbaker, and a handful of others were doing all they could to keep order.

All that could be done had been done. All that could be said had been said.

So on the morning of July sixth, she strapped on her weapons, shouldered her pack like the others. And with the others left the pretty house on the edge of Hawkins Wood to strike out on the path to the Pagan Stone.

It was all familiar now, the sounds, the scents, the way. More shade than there had been weeks before, of course, Cybil thought. More wildflowers, and a thicker chatter from birds, but still much the same. It wouldn't have been so very different in Ann Hawkins's time. And the feelings clutched tight inside Ann as she'd left these woods, left the man she loved to his sacrifice, not so different, Cybil imagined, than what was tight in her walking into them.

But at least she would be there, with him, to the end of it.

"My knife's bigger than yours." Quinn tapped the scabbard hooked at Cybil's waist.

"Yours isn't a knife, it's a machete."

"Still, bigger. Bigger than yours, too," Quinn said to Layla.

"I'm sticking with my froe, just like last time. It's my lucky froe. How many people can say that?"

They were trying to take her mind off things, Cybil knew.

"Cybil." The word came in a conspirator's whisper, and from the left, from the deep green shadows.

When she looked, when she saw, Cybil's heart simply broke.

"Daddy."

"It's not." Gage stepped back to her, gripped her arm. "You know it's not."

When he reached for his gun, Cybil stilled his hand. "I know, I know it's not my father. But don't."

"Don't you want to come give Daddy a hug?" It spread its arms wide. "Come on, princess! Come give Daddy a great, *big* kiss!" It bared its sharklike teeth, and laughed. And laughed. Then it raked its own claws down its face, its body, to vanish in a waterfall of black blood.

"That's entertainment," Fox said under his breath.

"Poorly staged, overplayed." Shrugging it off, Cybil took Gage's hand. Nothing, she promised herself, would shake her. "We'll take point for a while," she said, and with Gage walked to the front of the group.

Twenty

꩜

THEY'D PLANNED TO STOP FOR REST AT HESTER'S Pool, where the young, mad Hester Deale had drowned herself weeks after giving birth to the child Twisse put inside her. But the water there bubbled red. On its agitated surface, bloated bodies of birds and some small mammals bobbed and floated.

"Not exactly the right ambiance for a quick picnic," Cal decided. With his hand on Quinn's shoulder, he leaned over to brush his lips at her temple. "You okay to go another ten minutes before we break?"

"Hey, I'm the three-miles-a-day girl."

"You're the pregnant girl. One of them."

"We're good," Layla said, then dug her fingers into Fox's arm. "Fox."

Something rose out of the churning water. Head, neck, shoulders, the dirty red sludge of the pond, dripping, running. Torso, hips, legs, until it stood on the churning surface as it might a platform of stone.

Hester Deale, bearer of the demon's seed, damned by madness, dead centuries and by her own hand, stared out of wild and ravaged eyes.

"You'll birth them screaming, demons all. You are the damned, and his seed is cold. So cold. My daughters." Her arms spread. "Come, join me. Spare yourselves. I've waited for you. Take my hand."

What she held out was brittle with bone, stained with red.

"Let's go." Fox put his arm firmly around Layla's waist, drew her away. "Crazy doesn't stop with death."

"Don't leave me here! Don't leave me here alone!"

Quinn glanced back once, with pity. "Was it her, or another of Twisse's masks?"

"It's her. It's Hester." Layla didn't look back. Couldn't. "I don't think Twisse can take her form—or Ann's. They're still a presence, so it can't mimic them. Do you think when we finish this, she'll be able to rest?"

"I believe it." Cybil looked back, watched Hester—weeping now—sink back into the pool. "She's part of us. What we're doing is for her, too."

They didn't stop at all. Whether it was nerves, adrenaline, or the Nutter Butters and Little Debbies Fox passed around, they kept hiking until they'd reached the clearing. The Pagan Stone stood silent. Waiting.

"It didn't try to stop us," Cal pointed out. "Barely messed with us."

"It didn't want to waste the energy." Cybil peeled off her pack. "Storing it up. And it thinks it destroyed the one weapon we had. Bastard's feeling cocky."

"Or like the last time we came here on the eve of a Seven, it's hitting the town." Cal pulled out his cell phone, punched the key for his father's. His face, his eyes were grim when he flipped it back closed. "Nothing but static."

"Jim Hawkins will kick demon ass." Quinn put her arms around Cal. "Like father, like son."

"Fox and I could try to see," Layla began, but Cal shook his head.

"No, nothing we can do. Not there, not at the farm. And

there's something to be said for saving our energies. Let's set up."

In short order Gage dumped an armload of wood near Cybil as she unpacked provisions. "Seems superfluous. If we wait a few hours, there'll be plenty of fire."

"This is our fire. An important distinction." Cybil lifted a thermos. "Want some coffee?"

"For once, no. I'm going to have a beer." He looked around as he opened one. "Funny, but I'd feel a lot better if it had come after us, like last time. Bloody rain, lashing wind, bone-snapping cold. That bit with your father—"

"Yes, I know. It was like a tip of the hat. Have a nice walk, catch you later. Arrogance is a weakness, one we'll make sure it regrets."

He took her hand. "Come here a minute."

"We need to build the fire," she began as he drew her to the edge of the clearing.

"Cal's the Boy Scout. He'll do it. There's not a lot of time left." He put his hands on her shoulders, ran them down her arms, up again. "I've got a favor to ask you."

"It's a good time to ask for one. But you'll have to live to make sure I followed through."

"I'll know. If it's a girl . . ." He saw the tears swim into her eyes, watched her will them back. "I want Catherine for her middle name—for my mother. I always felt first names should belong to the kid, but the middle one . . ."

"Catherine for your mother. That's a very easy favor."

"If it's a boy, I don't want you to name him after me. No juniors or any crap like that. Pick something, and put your father's name in the middle. That's it. And, make sure he knows—or she, whichever—not to be a sucker. You don't draw to an inside straight, don't bet what you can't afford to lose and—"

"Should I be writing this down?"

He gave her hair a tug. "You'll remember. Give him these." Gage pulled a deck of cards out of his pocket. "The last hand I played with this deck? Four aces. So it's lucky."

"I'll hold them, until after. I have to believe—you have to let me believe—you'll be able to give them to him yourself."

"Fair enough." He put his hands on her face, skimmed his fingers up into her hair, curled them there as he brought his lips down to hers. "You're the best thing that ever came my way." He kissed her hands, then looked into her eyes. "Let's get this done."

Step by step, Cybil told herself. The fire, the stone, the candles, the words. The circle of salt. Fox had turned on a little boom box so there was music. That, too, was a step in Cybil's opinion. We whistle while we work, you bastard.

"Tell me what you need from me." Quinn spoke quietly as she helped Cybil arrange more candles on the table of the stone.

"Believe we'll end it—that he'll end it. And live."

"Then I will. I do. Look at me, Cybil. No one, not even Cal knows me like you. I believe."

"So do I." Layla stepped up, laid her hand over Cybil's. "I believe it."

"There, you see." Quinn closed her hand over the two of theirs. "Three pregnant women can't be . . . Whoa, what was that?"

"It . . . moved." Layla glanced up at both of them. "Didn't it?"

"Shh. Wait." Spreading her fingers over the stone under Layla's and Quinn's, Cybil fought to *feel*. "It's heating, and it's vibrating. Like it's breathing."

"The first time Cal and I touched it together, it warmed," Quinn said. "And then we were slapped back a few hundred years. If we could focus, maybe there's something we're supposed to see."

Without warning, the wind lashed out, hard, slapping hands, and knocked all three of them to the ground.

"Show time," Fox called out as black, pulsing clouds rolled across the sky toward the setting sun.

IN TOWN JIM HAWKINS HELPED CHIEF HAWBAKER drag a screaming man into the Bowl-a-Rama. Jim's face was bloody, his shirt torn, and he'd lost one of his shoes in the scuffle out on Main Street. The alleys echoed with the screams, wails, the gibbering laughter of more than a dozen they'd already pulled in and restrained.

"We're going to run out of rope." Favoring his throbbing arm where the man who'd taught his son U.S. history sank his teeth, Hawbaker secured the rope and the now-giggling teacher to a ball return. "Christ Jesus, Jim."

"A few more hours." Air wheezed in and out of Jim's lungs as he dropped down, mopped at his streaming face. They had half a dozen people locked into the old library, a scattering of others secured in what Cal told him were other safe zones. "We've just got to hold things a few more hours."

"There are hundreds of people left in town. And a handful of us still in our right mind that aren't burrowed in somewhere, hiding. Fire at the school, another in the flower shop, two more residential."

"They got them out."

"This time." Outside something crashed. Hawbaker gained his feet, drew out his service revolver.

Inside Jim's chest, his already laboring heart sprinted. Then Hawbaker turned the gun, holding it butt first toward Jim. "You need to take this."

"Shit fire, Wayne. Why?"

"My head's pounding. Like something's beating on it trying to get in." As he spoke, Hawbaker wiped at his face, shiny with sweat. "If it does, I want you holding the weapon. I want you to take care of it. Take care of me if you have to."

Jim got slowly to his feet and with considerable care, took the gun. "The way I look at it? Anybody doing what we've been doing the last couple hours is bound to have the mother of all headaches. I've got some Extra-Strength Tylenol behind the grill."

Hawbaker stared at Jim, then burst out laughing, laughed until his sides ached. "Sure, hell. Tylenol." Laughed until his eyes ran wet. Until he felt human. "That'll do her." At the next crash, he looked toward the doors and sighed. "You'd better bring the whole bottle."

"IT BROUGHT THE NIGHT," CAL SHOUTED AS THE wind tore at them with frozen hands. Outside the circle, snakes writhed, biting, devouring each other until they burned to cinders.

"Among other things." Quinn hefted the machete, ready to slice at anything that got through.

"We can't move on it yet." Gage watched a three-headed dog pace the clearing, snapping, snarling. "It's trying to draw us out, to sucker us in."

"It's not really here." Fox shifted to try to block Layla from the worst of the wind, but it came from everywhere. "This is just . . . echoes."

"Really loud echoes." Layla clamped a hand on the handle of her froe.

"It's stronger in the dark. Always stronger in the dark." Gage watched the huge black dog pace, wondered if it was worth a bullet. "And stronger during the Seven. We're nearly there."

"Stronger now than ever. But we don't take sucker bets." Cybil bared her teeth in a grin. "And we're going to draw it in."

"If it's in town now, if it's this strong and in town . . ."

"They'll hold it." Cybil watched a rat, plump as a kitten, leap on the dog's ridged back. "And we'll reel it in."

Fox's phone beeped. "Can't read the display. It's black. Before he could flip it open, the voices poured out. Screaming, sobbing, calling his name. His mother's, his father's, dozens of others.

"It's a lie," Layla shouted. "Fox, it's a lie."

"I can't tell." He lifted desperate eyes to hers. "I can't tell."

"It's a *lie*." Before he could stop her, Layla snatched the phone, hurled it away.

With a long, appreciative whistle, Bill Turner walked out of the woods. "Sign her up! Bitch's got an arm on her. Hey, you useless little piece of shit. I got something for you." He snapped the belt held in his hands. "Come on out and take it like a man."

"Hey, asshole!" Cybil elbowed Gage aside. "He died like a man. You won't. You'll die squealing."

"Don't taunt the demon, sugar," Gage told her. "Positive human emotions, remember."

"Damn. You're right. I'll give you a positive human emotion." She spun around and in the mad wind yanked Gage to her for a deep, drowning kiss.

"I'm saving you for dessert!" The thing in Bill's form shifted, changed. She heard her father's voice boom out now. "What I plant in you will rip and claw to be born."

She closed her mind to it, poured the love she felt—so strong, so new—into Gage. "It doesn't know," she whispered against his mouth.

The wind died; the world fell silent. She thought: Eye of the storm, and took a breath. "It doesn't know," she repeated, and touched her fingers lightly to her belly. "It's one of the answers we never found. It has to be. Another way, if we can figure out how to use it."

"We've got a little over an hour left until eleven thirty—that hour of light before midnight." Cal looked up at the pure black sky. "We have to get started."

"You're right. Let's light the candles while we can." And she'd pray the answer would come in time.

Once again the candles burned. Once again the knife that had joined three boys as brothers drew blood, and those wounded hands clasped firm. But this time, Cybil thought, they weren't three, they weren't six—but the potential of nine.

On the Pagan Stone six candles burned, one to represent each other, and a seventh to symbolize their single purpose. Inside that ring of fire three small white candles flickered for the lights they'd sparked.

"It's coming." Gage looked into Cybil's eyes.

"How do you know?"

"He's right." Cal glanced at Fox, got a nod, then leaned over to kiss Quinn. "No matter what, stay inside the circle."

"I'll stay in as long as you do."

"Let's not fight, kids," Fox said before Cal could argue. "Time's a wasting."

He leaned over, kissed Layla hard. "Layla, you're my it. Quinn, Cybil, you go into the small and exclusive club of the best women I know. You guys? I wouldn't change a minute of the last thirty-one years. So when we come through the other side of this, we'll exchange manly handshakes. I'm going for big, sloppy kisses from the women, with a little something extra from my it."

"Is that your closing?" Gage demanded. The stone tucked in his pocket weighed like lead. "I'm taking big, sloppy kisses all around. One in advance." He grabbed Cybil. If his life had come down to minutes, he was taking the taste of her into the dark. He felt her hand fist on his shirt—a strong, possessive grip. Then she let him go.

"Just a down payment," she told him. With her face pale and set, she drew both her weapons. "I feel it now, too. It's close."

From somewhere in the bowels of the black woods, it roared. Trees trembled, then lashed at each other like enemies. At the edges of the clearing, fire sputtered, sparked, then spewed.

"Bang, bang, on the door, baby," Quinn murmured, and had Cal gawking at her.

" 'Love Shack'?"

"I don't know why that popped in my head," she began, but Fox started laughing like a loon.

"Perfect! Knock a little louder, sugar," he sang out.

"Oh God. Bang, bang, on the door, baby," Layla repeated, and unsheathed her froe.

"Come on," Fox demanded, "put something *behind* it. I can't *hear* you."

As the fire gushed, as the stench of what came poured over the air, they sang. Foolish, maybe, Gage thought. But it was so in-your-face, so utterly and humanly defiant. Could do worse, he decided, could do a hell of a lot worse as a battle cry.

The sky hemorrhaged bloody rain that spat and sizzled on the ground, casting up a fetid haze of smoke. Through that smoke it came, while in the woods trees crashed and the wind howled like a thousand tortured voices.

The boy stood in the clearing.

It should have been ludicrous. It should, Gage thought, have been laughable. Instead it was horrible. And when the smiling child opened its mouth, the sound that ripped from it filled the world.

Still, they sang.

Gage fired, saw the bullets punch into flesh, saw the black-ened blood ooze. Its scream tore gullies in the ground. Then it flew, spinning in blurry circles that spiraled smoke and dirt into a choking cloud. It changed. Boy to dog, dog to snake, snake to man, all whirling, coiling, screaming. Not its true form. The stone was useless until it took its true form.

"Bang, bang, bang," Cal shouted, and leaped out of the circle to slash, and slash, and slash with his knife.

Now it shrieked, and however inhuman the sound, there was both pain and fury in it. With a nod, Gage slipped the bloodstone out of his pocket, set it in the center of the burn-ing candles.

As one, they rushed out of the circle, and into hell.

Blood and fire. One fell, one rose. The fierce cold bit like teeth, and the stinking smoke scored the throat. Behind them, in the center of the circle, the Pagan Stone flashed, then boiled in flame.

He saw something strike out of the smoke, rip across Cal's chest. Even as his friend staggered, Fox was rushing in, hacking at what was no longer there. Fox called out to Layla, shoved her down. This time Gage *saw* claws slice out of the smoke, and miss Layla's face by inches.

"It's playing with us," Gage shouted. Something leaped onto his back, sank its teeth into him. He tried to buck it off, to roll. Then the weight was gone and Cybil stood with her knife black with blood.

"Let it play," she said coldly. "I like it rough, remember?"

He shook his head. "Fall back. Everybody, back inside!"

Shoving to his feet, he all but dragged her into the circle where the Pagan Stone ran with fire.

"We're hurting it." Layla dropped to her knees to catch her breath. "I can *feel* its pain."

"Not enough." They were all bloody, Gage thought. Every one of them splashed or stained with blood—its and their own. And time was running out. "We can't take it this way. There's only one way." He put his hand on Cybil's until she lowered her knife. "When it takes its true form."

"It'll kill you before you have a chance to kill yourself! At least when we're fighting it, we're giving it pain, we're weakening it."

"No, we're not." Fox rubbed his stinging eyes. "We're just entertaining it. Maybe distracting it a little. I'm sorry."

"But . . ." Distracting it. Cybil looked back at the Pagan Stone. That was *theirs*. She believed that. Had to believe it. It had responded when she, Quinn, and Layla had laid hands on it together.

Dropping her knife—what good was it now?—she spun to the Pagan Stone. Holding her breath, she plunged a hand through the flame to lay it on the burning altar. "Quinn! Layla!"

"What the hell are you doing?" Gage demanded.

"Distracting it. And I sincerely hope pissing it off." In the fire was heat, but no burn. This, she thought, wild with hope, was an answer. "It doesn't know." She placed her free hand on her belly as the spearing fire illuminated her face. "This is *power*. It's light. It's *us*. Q, please."

Without a moment's hesitation, Quinn shot her hand through the fire, laid it on Cybil's. "It's moving!" Quinn called out. "Layla."

But Layla was already there, and her hand closed over theirs.

It sang, Cybil thought. In her head she heard the stone sing in thousands of pure voices. The flame that shot up from the center of the stone was blinding white. Beneath them, the ground began to shake, a sudden and furious violence.

"Don't let go," Cybil called out. What had she done? she

thought as her eyes blurred with tears. Oh God, what had she done.

Looking through that white shaft of flame, she met Gage's eyes. "You're one smart cookie," he said.

In the clearing, through the smoke, in the smoke, *of* the smoke, the black formed—and its hate of the light, its fury toward its radiance spewed into the air. Arms, legs, head—it was impossible to know—bulged. Eyes, eerily green, rimmed with red blinked open by the score. It grew, rolling and rising until it consumed both earth and sky. Grew until there was only the dark, the red walls of flames. And its hungry wrath.

She heard its scream of rage in her head, knew the others did, too.

I'll rip it squalling from your belly and drink it like wine.

Now, Cybil thought, *now* it knew.

"It's time. Don't let go." The stone shook under her hand, but her eyes never left Gage. "Don't let go."

"I don't plan to." He shot his hand through the fire, clutched the flaming bloodstone.

Then he turned away from her. Even then her face was in his mind. For one last moment, he stood linked with Cal and Fox. Brothers, he thought, start to finish. "Now or never," he said. "Take care of what's mine."

And with the bloodstone vised in his fist, he leaped into the black.

"No. No, no, no." Cybil's tears fell through the flame to pool on the stone.

"Hang on." Quinn clutched her hand tighter, locked an arm around her for support. On the other side, Layla did the same.

"I can't see him," Layla called out. "I can't see him. Fox!"

He came to her, and with nothing left but instinct and grief, both he and Cal laid hands on the stone. The black roared, its eyes rolled with what might have been pleasure.

"It's not going to take him, not like this." Cal shouted over the storm of sound. "I'm going after him."

"You can't." Cybil choked back a sob. "This is what he needs to finish it. This is the answer. Don't let go, of the stone, of each other. Of Gage. Don't let go."

Through the rain sliced a bolt of light. And the world quaked.

IN THE HOLLOW, JIM HAWKINS COLLAPSED ON THE street. Beside him, Hawbaker shielded his eyes from a sudden burst of light. "Did you hear that?" Jim demanded, but his voice was swallowed in the din. "Did you hear that?"

They knelt in the center of Main Street, washed in the brilliance, and clutched each other like drunks.

At the farm, Brian held his wife's hand as hundreds of people stood in his fields staring at the sky. "Jesus, Jo, Jesus. The woods are on fire. Hawkins Woods."

"It's not fire. Not just fire," she said as her throat throbbed. "It's . . . something else."

At the Pagan Stone, the rain turned to fire, and the fire turned to light. Those sparks of light struck the black to sizzle, to smoke. Its eyes began to wheel now, not in hunger or pleasure, but in shock, in pain, and in fury.

"He's doing it," Cybil murmured. "He's killing it." Even through her grief, she felt stunning pride. "Hold on to him. We have to hold on to him. We can bring him back."

SENSATION WAS ALL HE HAD. PAIN, SOMETHING SO far above agony it had no name. Ferocious cold bound by intolerable heat. Thousands of claws, thousands of teeth tore and ripped at him—each wound a separate, searing misery. His own blood burned under his broken skin, and its blood coated him like oil.

Around him, the dark closed in, squeezing him in a terrible embrace so he waited to feel his own ribs snap. In his ears sounds seemed to boil—screeches, screams, laughter, pleas.

Was it eating him alive? Gage wondered.

Still he crawled and shoved through the quivering wet mass, gagging on the stench, wheezing for what little dirty air was left to him. In the heat, what was left of his shirt smoked. In the cold, his fingers numbed.

This, he thought, was hell.

And there, up there, that pulsing black mass with its burning red eye, was the heart of hell.

With his strength draining, with it simply leaking out of him like water through a sieve, he struggled for another inch, still another. Dozens of images tumbled through his brain. His mother, holding his hand as they walked across a green summer field. Cal and Gage plowing toy cars through the sand of a sandbox Brian had built at the farm. Riding bikes with them along Main Street. Pressing bloody wrists together by the campfire. Cybil, casting that sultry look over her shoulder. Moving to him. Moving under him. Weeping for him.

Nearly over, he thought. Life flashing in front of my eyes. So fucking tired. Going numb. Going out. Nearly done. And the light, he mused, dizzy now. Tunnel of light. Fucking cliché.

Cards on the table now. He felt—thought he felt—the bloodstone vibrate in his hand. As he reared back, it shot fire through his clutched fingers.

The light washed white, blinding him. In his mind, he saw a figure. The man closed his hands over his. Eyes, clear and gray, looked into his.

It is not death. My blood, her blood, our blood. Its end in the fire.

Their joined hands plunged the stone into the heart of the beast.

In the clearing, the explosion knocked Cybil off her feet. The rush of heat rolled over her, sent her tumbling like a pebble in an angry surf. The light blazed like the sun, dazzling her eyes before throwing everything into sharp relief. For a moment the woods, the stone, the sky were a single sheet of fire, and in the next stood utterly still, like the negative of a photograph.

At the edge of the clearing two figures shimmered—a man and a woman locked in a desperate embrace. In a fingersnap they were gone, and the world moved again.

A rush of wind, a last throaty call of flame, the smoke that crawled along the ground, then faded as that ground burgeoned up, swallowed it. When the wind died to a quiet breeze, the fire guttering out, she saw Gage lying motionless on that ruined earth.

She pushed up to run to him, dropping down to lay her trembling fingers at his throat. "I can't find a pulse!" So much blood. His face, his body looked as if he'd been torn to pieces.

"Come on, goddamn it." Cal knelt, gripped one of Gage's hands as Fox took the other. "Come back."

"CPR," Layla said, and Quinn was already straddling Gage, crossing her hands over his chest to pump.

Cybil started to tip his head back to begin mouth-to-mouth. And saw the Pagan Stone was still sheathed in fire, pure and white. There. She had seen him there.

"Get him on the stone. On the altar. Hurry, hurry."

Cal and Fox carried him—bloodied and lifeless—to lay him on the simmering white flames. "Blood and fire," Cybil repeated, kissing his hand, then his lips. "I had a dream—I got it wrong, that's all. All of you on the stone, like I'd killed you, and Gage coming out of the dark to kill me. Ego, that's all. Please, Gage, please. Just my ego. Not me, not about me. All of us *around* the stone, and Gage coming out of the dark after killing *it*. "Please come back. Please."

She pressed her lips to his again, willing him to breathe. Her tears fell on his face. "Death isn't the answer. Life's the answer."

She laid her lips on his again and his moved against hers.

"Gage! He's breathing. He's—"

"We've got him." Cal squeezed his hand on Gage's hand. "We've got you."

His eyes fluttered open, and met Cybil's. "I—I got lucky."

On a shudder, Cybil laid her head on his chest, listened to the beat of his heart. "We all did."

"Hey, Turner." With his grin huge, Fox leaned over so Gage could see his face. "You owe me a thousand dollars. Happy fucking birthday."

Epilogue

~∿~

HE WOKE ALONE IN BED, WHICH HE FIGURED WAS a damn shame since he felt nearly normal again. The sun blasted through the windows. He'd probably been out for hours, Gage thought. And small wonder. Dying took a lot out of a man.

He couldn't remember much of the trip back. The entire trip had been one of those "one foot in front of the other" ordeals, and with several stints of that made with his arms slung around Fox's and Cal's shoulders. But he'd wanted to get the hell back—all of them had.

He'd been weak as a baby, that much he remembered. So weak even after they'd gotten back to the house that Cal and Fox had had to help him shower off the blood and dirt, and Christ only knew what he'd brought back from hell with him.

But it no longer hurt to breathe—a good sign. And when he sat up, nothing spun. When he got to his feet, the floor stayed steady and nothing inside him wept with pain. Taking a moment to be sure he remained upright, he glanced at the scar across his wrist, then explored the one on his shoulder with his fingertips.

The light, and the dark. He'd carried both in with him.

He pulled on jeans and a shirt to go downstairs.

The front door was open, letting in more sunshine and a nice summer breeze. He spotted Cal and Fox on the front deck, with Lump laid out between their chairs. When he stepped out, both of them grinned at him—and Fox flipped the top of the cooler that sat beside him, took out a beer, offered it.

"Read my mind."

"Can do." Fox rose, as did Cal. They tapped bottles, drank.

"Kicked its ass," Fox said.

"That we did."

"Glad you're not dead," Cal added.

"So you said a couple dozen times on the way back."

"I wasn't sure you remembered. You were in and out."

"I'm in now. The Hollow?"

"My dad, Hawbaker, a few others, they held it during the worst. It got bad," Cal added, staring out at his front gardens. "Fires, looting—"

"Your usual random acts of violence," Fox continued. "There are some people in the hospital, others who'll have to decide if they want to rebuild. But Jim Hawkins. Hero time."

"He's got a broken hand, some cuts, and a lot of bruises, but he came through. The farm, too," Cal told him. "We went out to check on things, pick up Lump, and swung through town while you were getting your beauty sleep. It could've been a lot worse. Hell, it has been a lot worse. No new fatalities. Not a single one. The Hollow owes you, brother."

"Shit, it owes all of us." Gage tipped back his beer. "But yeah, especially me."

"Speaking of owing," Fox reminded him. "That'll be a grand—for each of us."

Gage lowered his beer, grinned. "It's one bet I don't mind

losing." Then staggered back when Fox threw an arm around him, and kissed him square on the mouth.

"Changed my mind about the manly handshake."

"Jesus, O'Dell." Even as Gage lifted a hand, Cal moved in and repeated the gesture. Laughing now, Gage swiped a hand over his mouth. "Good thing nobody saw that, or I'd have to deck you both."

"Twenty-one years is a long time to say this, and mean it." Cal lifted his beer again. "Happy birthday to us."

"Fucking A." Fox lifted his.

As Gage tapped bottles, Quinn and Layla stepped out. "There he is. Pucker up, handsome."

When Quinn grabbed him, planted one on, Gage nodded. "Now that's what I'm talking about."

"My turn." Layla elbowed Quinn aside, pressed her lips to Gage's. "Are you up for a party?"

"Could be."

"We've got Fox's family and Cal's on hold. We'll give them a call if you're up for it."

A birthday party, he thought. Yeah, it had been a hell of a long time. "That'd be good."

"Meanwhile, there's someone in the kitchen who'd like to see you."

She wasn't in the kitchen, but out on the back deck, alone. When he walked out, she turned. And everything he needed bloomed on her face. Then she was in his arms, hers locked tight around him as he swung her in a circle.

"We did okay," he told her.

"We did just fine."

When he lowered her, he kissed the bruise on her temple. "How banged up are you?"

"Not very, which is another small miracle in a streak of them. I've become a fan of Fate again."

"Dent. It was Dent in there with me."

She brushed back his hair, traced her fingers over his face, his shoulders. "You told us a little. You were pretty weak, a little delirious at times."

"I was going to make it—I mean finish it. I felt that. I *knew* that. But that was going to be it, that was all I had left. Then there was the light—a shaft of it, then, Jesus, an explosion of it. A nova of it."

"We saw it, too."

"I saw Dent—in my head. Or I think in my head. I had the stone in my hand. It was on fire, flames just shooting between my fingers. It started to—it sounds crazy."

"Sing," she finished. "It sang. Both stones sang."

"Yeah, it sang. A thousand voices. I felt Dent's hand close over mine. Mine over the stone, his over mine. I felt . . . linked. You know what I mean."

"Yes, exactly."

" 'It is not death.' That's what he said to me, then we punched the stone right into the heart. I heard it scream, Cybil. I heard it scream, and I felt it . . . implode. From the heart out. Then that's it until I came back. Not like last time, when the bastard bit me. This was like cruising on a really good drug."

"The light tore through it," she told him. "I'd have to say vaporized it. It's the closest I can come. Gage, I saw them, for just a moment—less than a moment. I saw Giles Dent and Ann Hawkins holding each other. I saw them together, I *felt* them together. And I understood."

"What?"

"It was to be his sacrifice all along. He needed us, and he needed you to willingly offer. For you to take the stone in, knowing it would be your life. Because we did what we've done, because you were willing to give your life, he could give his instead. It is not death, he told Ann, and us, and you. He existed still, all these years. And last night, through us, through you, he was the sacrifice demanded to end it. He could finally let go. He's with Ann now, and they're—cliché time—at peace. We all are."

"It's going to take a while to get used to. But I'm all about trying." He took her hand. "I figure this. We stick around for a couple of days, until everything settles down. Then we'll take off for a couple of weeks. The way my luck's running, I figure I can win enough to buy you a ring the size of a door-knob, if you like the idea."

"I do, if that's an actual proposal rather than a hypothe-tical."

"How's this for actual? Let's get married in Vegas. We can talk everyone who matters into going out for it."

"In Vegas." She cocked her head, then laughed. "I don't know why, but that sounds absolutely perfect. You're on." She took his face in her hands, kissed him. "Happy birthday."

"I keep hearing that."

"Expect to hear it more. I baked you a cake."

"No joke?"

"A seven-layer cake—as promised. I love you, Gage." She slid into his arms. "I love everything about you."

"I love you, too. I've got a woman who's ready to get mar-ried in Vegas, bakes cakes, *and* has brains. I'm a lucky guy."

He laid his cheek on the top of her head, holding on while he looked out to the woods where the beaten path led to the Pa-gan Stone.

And at the end of the path, past Hester's Pool, where the water flowed cool and clean, the once-scorched earth of the clearing greened again. On the new ground, the Pagan Stone stood silent in the streaming sun.

Can't get enough of Nora Roberts?
Try the #1 *New York Times* bestselling
In Death series, by Nora Roberts
writing as J. D. Robb.

Turn the page to see where it began . . .

NAKED IN DEATH

SHE WOKE IN THE DARK. THROUGH THE SLATS ON the window shades, the first murky hint of dawn slipped, slanting shadowy bars over the bed. It was like waking in a cell.

For a moment she simply lay there, shuddering, imprisoned, while the dream faded. After ten years on the force, Eve still had dreams.

Six hours before, she'd killed a man, had watched death creep into his eyes. It wasn't the first time she'd exercised maximum force, or dreamed. She'd learned to accept the action and the consequences.

But it was the child that haunted her. The child she hadn't been in time to save. The child whose screams had echoed in the dreams with her own.

All the blood, Eve thought, scrubbing sweat from her face with her hands. Such a small little girl to have had so much blood in her. And she knew it was vital that she push it aside.

Standard departmental procedure meant that she would spend the morning in Testing. Any officer whose discharge of weapon resulted in termination of life was required to undergo emotional and psychiatric clearance before resuming duty. Eve considered the tests a mild pain in the ass.

She would beat them, as she'd beaten them before.

When she rose, the overheads went automatically to low setting, lighting her way into the bath. She winced once at her reflection. Her eyes were swollen from lack of sleep, her skin nearly as pale as the corpses she'd delegated to the ME.

Rather than dwell on it, she stepped into the shower, yawning.

"Give me one oh one degrees, full force," she said and shifted so that the shower spray hit her straight in the face.

She let it steam, lathered listlessly while she played through the events of the night before. She wasn't due in Testing until nine, and would use the next three hours to settle and let the dream fade away completely.

Small doubts and little regrets were often detected and could mean a second and more intense round with the machines and the owl-eyed technicians who ran them.

Eve didn't intend to be off the streets longer than twenty-four hours.

After pulling on a robe, she walked into the kitchen and programmed her AutoChef for coffee, black; toast, light. Through her window she could hear the heavy hum of air traffic carrying early commuters to offices, late ones home. She'd chosen the apartment years before because it was in a heavy ground and air pattern, and she liked the noise and crowds. On another yawn, she glanced out the window, followed the rattling journey of an aging airbus hauling laborers not fortunate enough to work in the city or by home 'links.

She brought the *New York Times* up on her monitor and scanned the headlines while the faux caffeine bolstered her system. The AutoChef had burned her toast again, but she ate it anyway, with a vague thought of springing for a replacement unit.

She was frowning over an article on a mass recall of droid cocker spaniels when her telelink blipped. Eve shifted to communications and watched her commanding officer flash onto the screen.

"Commander."

"Lieutenant." He gave her a brisk nod, noted the still-wet hair and sleepy eyes. "Incident at Twenty-seven West Broadway, eighteenth floor. You're primary."

Eve lifted a brow. "I'm on Testing. Subject terminated at twenty-two thirty-five."

"We have override," he said, without inflection. "Pick up your shield and weapon on the way to the incident. Code Five, Lieutenant."

"Yes, sir." His face flashed off even as she pushed back from the screen. Code Five meant she would report directly to her commander, and there would be no unsealed interdepartmental reports and no cooperation with the press.

In essence, it meant she was on her own.

BROADWAY WAS NOISY AND CROWDED, A PARTY that rowdy guests never left. Street, pedestrian, and sky traffic were miserable, choking the air with bodies and vehicles. In her old days in uniform she remembered it as a hot spot for wrecks and crushed tourists who were too busy gaping at the show to get out of the way.

Even at this hour steam was rising from the stationary and portable food stands that offered everything from rice noodles to soy dogs for the teeming crowds. She had to swerve to avoid an eager merchant on his smoking Glida-Grill, and took his flipped middle finger as a matter of course.

Eve double-parked and, skirting a man who smelled worse than his bottle of brew, stepped onto the sidewalk. She scanned the building first, fifty floors of gleaming metal that knifed into the sky from a hilt of concrete. She was propositioned twice before she reached the door.

Since this five-block area of West Broadway was affectionately termed Prostitute's Walk, she wasn't surprised. She flashed her badge for the uniform guarding the entrance.

"Lieutenant Dallas."

"Yes, sir." He skimmed his official CompuSeal over the door to keep out the curious, then led the way to the bank of elevators. "Eighteenth floor," he said when the doors swished shut behind them.

"Fill me in, Officer." Eve switched on her recorder and waited.

"I wasn't first on the scene, Lieutenant. Whatever happened upstairs is being kept upstairs. There's a badge inside waiting for you. We have a homicide, and a Code Five in number eighteen-oh-three."

"Who called it in?"

"I don't have that information."

He stayed where he was when the elevator opened. Eve stepped out and was alone in a narrow hallway. Security cameras tilted down at her, and her feet were almost soundless on the worn nap of the carpet as she approached 1803. Ignoring the hand plate, she announced herself, holding her badge up to eye level for the peep cam until the door opened.

"Dallas."

"Feeney." She smiled, pleased to see a familiar face. Ryan Feeney was an old friend and former partner who'd traded the street for a desk and a top-level position in the Electronics Detection Division. "So, they're sending computer pluckers these days."

"They wanted brass, and the best." His lips curved in his wide, rumpled face, but his eyes remained sober. He was a small, stubby man with small, stubby hands and rust-colored hair. "You look beat."

"Rough night."

"So I heard." He offered her one of the sugared nuts from the bag he habitually carried, studying her, and measuring if she was up to what was waiting in the bedroom beyond.

She was young for her rank, barely thirty, with wide brown eyes that had never had a chance to be naive. Her doe-brown hair was cropped short, for convenience rather than style, but suited her triangular face with its razor-edge cheekbones and slight dent in the chin.

She was tall, rangy, with a tendency to look thin, but Feeney knew there were solid muscles beneath the leather jacket. But Eve had more—there was also a brain, and a heart.

"This one's going to be touchy, Dallas."

"I picked that up already. Who's the victim?"

"Sharon DeBlass, granddaughter of Senator DeBlass."

Neither meant anything to her. "Politics isn't my forte, Feeney."

"The gentleman from Virginia, extreme right, old money. The granddaughter took a sharp left a few years back, moved to New York and became a licensed companion."

"She was a hooker." Dallas glanced around the apartment. It was furnished in obsessive modern—glass and thin chrome, signed holograms on the walls, recessed bar in bold red. The wide mood screen behind the bar bled with mixing and merging shapes and colors in cool pastels.

Neat as a virgin, Eve mused, and cold as a whore. "No surprise, given her choice of real estate."

"Politics makes it delicate. Victim was twenty-four, Caucasian female. She bought it in bed."

Eve only lifted a brow. "Seems poetic, since she'd been bought there. How'd she die?"

"That's the next problem. I want you to see for yourself."

As they crossed the room, each took out a slim container, sprayed their hands front and back to seal in oils and fingerprints. At the doorway, Eve sprayed the bottom of her boots to slicken them so that she would pick up no fibers, stray hairs, or skin.

Eve was already wary. Under normal circumstances there would have been two other investigators on a homicide scene, with recorders for sound and pictures. Forensics would have been waiting with their usual snarly impatience to sweep the scene.

The fact that only Feeney had been assigned with her meant that there were a lot of eggshells to be walked over.

"Security cameras in the lobby, elevator, and hallways," Eve commented.

"I've already tagged the discs." Feeney opened the bedroom door and let her enter first.

It wasn't pretty. Death rarely was a peaceful, religious experience to Eve's mind. It was the nasty end, indifferent to saint and sinner. But this was shocking, like a stage deliberately set to offend.

The bed was huge, slicked with what appeared to be genuine satin sheets the color of ripe peaches. Small, soft-focused spotlights were trained on its center where the naked woman was cupped in the gentle dip of the floating mattress.

The mattress moved with obscenely graceful undulations to the rhythm of programmed music slipping through the headboard.

She was beautiful still, a cameo face with a tumbling waterfall of flaming red hair, emerald eyes that stared glassily at the mirrored ceiling, long, milk-white limbs that called to mind visions of *Swan Lake* as the motion of the bed gently rocked them.

They weren't artistically arranged now, but spread lewdly so that the dead woman formed a final X dead-center of the bed.

There was a hole in her forehead, one in her chest, another horribly gaping between the open thighs. Blood had splattered on the glossy sheets, pooled, dripped, and stained.

There were splashes of it on the lacquered walls, like lethal paintings scrawled by an evil child.

So much blood was a rare thing, and she had seen much too much of it the night before to take the scene as calmly as she would have preferred.

She had to swallow once, hard, and force herself to block out the image of a small child.

"You got the scene on record?"

"Yep."

"Then turn that damn thing off." She let out a breath after Feeney located the controls that silenced the music. The bed flowed to stillness. "The wounds," Eve murmured, stepping closer to examine them. "Too neat for a knife. Too messy for a laser." A flash came to her—old training films, old videos, old viciousness.

"Christ, Feeney, these look like bullet wounds."

Feeney reached into his pocket and drew out a sealed bag. "Whoever did it left a souvenir." He passed the bag to Eve.

"An antique like this has to go for eight, ten thousand for a legal collection, twice that on the black market."

Fascinated, Eve turned the sealed revolver over in her hand. "It's heavy," she said half to herself. "Bulky."

"Thirty-eight caliber," he told her. "First one I've seen outside of a museum. This one's a Smith and Wesson, Model Ten, blue steel." He looked at it with some affection. "Real classic piece, used to be standard police issue up until the latter part of the twentieth. They stopped making them in about twenty-two, twenty-three, when the gun ban was passed."

"You're the history buff." Which explained why he was with her. "Looks new." She sniffed through the bag, caught the scent of oil and burning. "Somebody took good care of this. Steel fired into flesh," she mused as she passed the bag back to Feeney. "Ugly way to die, and the first I've seen it in my ten years with the department."

"Second for me. About fifteen years ago, Lower East Side, party got out of hand. Guy shot five people with a twenty-two before he realized it wasn't a toy. Hell of a mess."

"Fun and games," Eve murmured. "We'll scan the collectors, see how many we can locate who own one like this. Somebody might have reported a robbery."

"Might have."

"It's more likely it came through the black market." Eve glanced back at the body. "If she's been in the business for a few years, she'd have discs, records of her clients, her trick books." She frowned. "With Code Five, I'll have to do the door-to-door myself. Not a simple sex crime," she said with a sigh. "Whoever did it set it up. The antique weapon, the wounds themselves, almost ruler-straight down the body, the lights, the pose. Who called it in, Feeney?"

"The killer." He waited until her eyes came back to him. "From right here. Called the station. See how the bedside unit's aimed at her face? That's what came in. Video, no audio."

"He's into showmanship." Eve let out a breath. "Clever bastard, arrogant, cocky. He had sex with her first. I'd bet my badge on it. Then he gets up and does it." She lifted her arm, aiming, lowering it as she counted off, "One, two, three."

"That's cold," murmured Feeney.

"He's cold. He smooths down the sheets after. See how neat they are? He arranges her, spreads her open so nobody can have any doubts as to how she made her living. He does it carefully, practically measuring, so that she's perfectly aligned. Center of the bed, arms and legs equally apart. Doesn't turn off the bed 'cause it's part of the show. He leaves the gun because he wants us to know right away he's no ordinary man. He's got an ego. He doesn't want to waste time letting the body be discovered eventually. He wants it now. That instant gratification."

"She was licensed for men and women," Feeney pointed out, but Eve shook her head.

"It's not a woman. A woman wouldn't have left her looking both beautiful and obscene. No, I don't think it's a woman. Let's see what we can find. Have you gone into her computer yet?"

"No. It's your case, Dallas. I'm only authorized to assist."

"See if you can access her client files." Eve went to the dresser and began to carefully search drawers.

Expensive taste, Eve reflected. There were several items of real silk, the kind no simulation could match. The bottle of scent on the dresser was exclusive, and smelled, after a quick sniff, like expensive sex.

The contents of the drawers were meticulously ordered, lingerie folded precisely, sweaters arranged according to color and material. The closet was the same.

Obviously the victim had a love affair with clothes and a taste for the best and took scrupulous care of what she owned.

And she'd died naked.

"Kept good records," Feeney called out. "It's all here. Her client list, appointments—including her required monthly health exam and her weekly trip to the beauty salon. She used the Trident Clinic for the first and Paradise for the second."

"Both top-of-the-line. I've got a friend who saved for a

NAKED IN DEATH   317

year so she could have one day for the works at Paradise. Takes all kinds."

"My wife's sister went for it for her twenty-fifth anniversary. Cost damn near as much as my kid's wedding. Hello, we've got her personal address book."

"Good. Copy all of it, will you, Feeney?" At his low whistle, she looked over her shoulder, glimpsed the small gold-edged palm computer in his hand. "What?"

"We've got a lot of high-powered names in here. Politics, entertainment, money, money, money. Interesting, our girl has Roarke's private number."

"Roarke who?"

"Just Roarke, as far as I know. Big money there. Kind of guy that touches shit and turns it into gold bricks. You've got to start reading more than the sports page, Dallas."

"Hey, I read the headlines. Did you hear about the cocker spaniel recall?"

"Roarke's always big news," Feeney said patiently. "He's got one of the finest art collections in the world. Arts and antiques," he continued, noting when Eve clicked in and turned to him. "He's a licensed gun collector. Rumor is he knows how to use them."

"I'll pay him a visit."

"You'll be lucky to get within a mile of him."

"I'm feeling lucky." Eve crossed over to the body to slip her hands under the sheets.

"The man's got powerful friends, Dallas. You can't afford to so much as whisper he's linked to this until you've got something solid."

"Feeney, you know it's a mistake to tell me that." But even as she started to smile, her fingers brushed something between cold flesh and bloody sheets. "There's something under her." Carefully, Eve lifted the shoulder, eased her fingers over.

"Paper," she murmured. "Sealed." With her protected thumb, she wiped at a smear of blood until she could read the protected sheet.

ONE OF SIX

"It looks hand printed," she said to Feeney and held it out. "Our boy's more than clever, more than arrogant. And he isn't finished."

EVE SPENT THE REST OF THE DAY DOING WHAT would normally have been assigned to drones. She interviewed the victim's neighbors personally, recording statements, impressions.

She managed to grab a quick sandwich from the same Glida-Grill she'd nearly smashed before, driving across town. After the night and the morning she'd put in, she could hardly blame the receptionist at Paradise for looking at her as though she'd recently scraped herself off the sidewalk.

Waterfalls played musically among the flora in the reception area of the city's most exclusive salon. Tiny cups of real coffee and slim glasses of fizzling water or champagne were served to those lounging on the cushy chairs and settees. Headphones and discs of fashion magazines were complimentary.

The receptionist was magnificently breasted, a testament to the salon's figure-sculpting techniques. She wore a snug, short outfit in the salon's trademark red, and an incredible coif of ebony hair coiled like snakes.

Eve couldn't have been more delighted.

"I'm sorry," the woman said in a carefully modulated voice as empty of expression as a computer. "We serve by appointment only."

"That's okay." Eve smiled and was almost sorry to puncture the disdain. Almost. "This ought to get me one." She offered her badge. "Who works on Sharon DeBlass?"

The receptionist's horrified eyes darted toward the waiting area. "Our clients' needs are strictly confidential."

"I bet." Enjoying herself, Eve leaned companionably on the U-shaped counter. "I can talk nice and quiet, like this, so we understand each other—Denise?" She flicked her gaze

down to the discreet studded badge on the woman's breast.
"Or I can talk louder, so everyone understands. If you like the
first idea better, you can take me to a nice quiet room where
we won't disturb any of your clients, and you can send in
Sharon DeBlass's operator. Or whatever term you use."

"Consultant," Denise said faintly. "If you'll follow me."

"My pleasure."

And it was.

Outside of movies or videos, Eve had never seen anything so lush. The carpet was a red cushion your feet could
sink blissfully into. Crystal drops hung from the ceiling and
spun light. The air smelled of flowers and pampered flesh.

She might not have been able to imagine herself there,
spending hours having herself creamed, oiled, pummeled,
and sculpted, but if she were going to waste such time on
vanity, it would certainly have been interesting to do so under such civilized conditions.

The receptionist showed her into a small room with a
hologram of a summer meadow dominating one wall. The
quiet sound of birdsong and breezes sweetened the air.

"If you'd just wait here."

"No problem." Eve waited for the door to close then, with
an indulgent sigh, she lowered herself into a deeply cush-
ioned chair. The moment she was seated, the monitor beside
her blipped on, and a friendly, indulgent face that could only
be a droid's beamed smiles.

"Good afternoon. Welcome to Paradise. Your beauty
needs and your comfort are our only priorities. Would you
like some refreshment while you wait for your personal consultant?"

"Sure. Coffee, black, coffee."

"Of course. What sort would you prefer? Press C on your
keyboard for the list of choices."

Smothering a chuckle, Eve followed instructions. She
spent the next two minutes pondering over her options, then
narrowed it down to French Riviera or Caribbean Cream.

The door opened again before she could decide. Re-
signed, she rose and faced an elaborately dressed scarecrow.

Over his fuchsia shirt and plum-colored slacks, he wore an open, trailing smock of Paradise red. His hair, flowing back from a painfully thin face, echoed the hue of his slacks. He offered Eve a hand, squeezed gently, and stared at her out of soft doe eyes.

"I'm terribly sorry, Officer. I'm baffled."

"I want information on Sharon DeBlass." Again, Eve took out her badge and offered it for inspection.

"Yes, ah, Lieutenant Dallas. That was my understanding. You must know, of course, our client data is strictly confidential. Paradise has a reputation for discretion as well as excellence."

"And you must know, of course, that I can get a warrant, Mr.—?"

"Oh, Sebastian. Simply Sebastian." He waved a thin hand, sparkling with rings. "I'm not questioning your authority, Lieutenant. But if you could assist me, your motives for the inquiry?"

"I'm inquiring into the motives for the murder of DeBlass." She waited a beat, judged the shock that shot into his eyes and drained his face of color. "Other than that, my data is strictly confidential."

"Murder. My dear God, our lovely Sharon is dead? There must be a mistake." He all but slid into a chair, letting his head fall back and his eyes close. When the monitor offered him refreshment, he waved a hand again. Light shot from his jeweled fingers. "God, yes. I need a brandy, darling. A snifter of Trevalli."

Eve sat beside him, took out her recorder. "Tell me about Sharon."

"A marvelous creature. Physically stunning, of course, but it went deeper." His brandy came into the room on a silent automated cart. Sebastian plucked the snifter and took one deep swallow. "She had flawless taste, a generous heart, rapier wit."

He turned the doe eyes on Eve again. "I saw her only two days ago."

"Professionally?"

"She had a standing weekly appointment, half day. Every other week was a full day." He whipped out a butter yellow scarf and dabbed at his eyes. "Sharon took care of herself, believed strongly in the presentation of self."

"It would be an asset in her line of work."

"Naturally. She only worked to amuse herself. Money wasn't a particular need, with her family background. She enjoyed sex."

"With you?"

His artistic face winced, the rosy lips pursing in what could have been a pout or pain. "I was her consultant, her confidant, and her friend," Sebastian said stiffly and draped the scarf with casual flair over his left shoulder. "It would have been indiscreet and unprofessional for us to become sexual partners."

"So you weren't attracted to her, sexually?"

"It was impossible for anyone not to be attracted to her sexually. She . . ." He gestured grandly. "Exuded sex as others might exude an expensive perfume. My God." He took another shaky sip of brandy. "It's all past tense. I can't believe it. Dead. Murdered." His gaze shot back to Eve. "You said murdered."

"That's right."

"That neighborhood she lived in," he said grimly. "No one could talk to her about moving to a more acceptable location. She enjoyed living on the edge and flaunting it all under her family's aristocratic noses."

"She and her family were at odds?"

"Oh definitely. She enjoyed shocking them. She was such a free spirit, and they so . . . ordinary." He said it in a tone that indicated ordinary was more mortal a sin than murder itself. "Her grandfather continues to introduce bills that would make prostitution illegal. As if the past century hasn't proven that such matters need to be regulated for health and crime security. He also stands against procreation regulation, gender adjustment, chemical balancing, and the gun ban."

Eve's ears pricked. "The senator opposes the gun ban?"

"It's one of his pets. Sharon told me he owns a number of nasty antiques and spouts off regularly about that outdated right to bear arms business. If he had his way, we'd all be back in the twentieth century, murdering each other right and left."

"Murder still happens," Eve murmured. "Did she ever mention friends or clients who might have been dissatisfied or overly aggressive?"

"Sharon had dozens of friends. She drew people to her, like . . ." He searched for a suitable metaphor, used the corner of the scarf again. "Like an exotic and fragrant flower. And her clients, as far as I know, were all delighted with her. She screened them carefully. All of her sexual partners had to meet certain standards. Appearance, intellect, breeding, and proficiency. As I said, she enjoyed sex, in all of its many forms. She was . . . adventurous."

That fit with the toys Eve had unearthed in the apartment. The velvet handcuffs and whips, the scented oils and hallucinogens. The offerings on the two sets of colinked virtual reality headphones had been a shock even to Eve's jaded system.

"Was she involved with anyone on a personal level?"

"There were men occasionally, but she lost interest quickly. Recently she'd spoken about Roarke. She'd met him at a party and was attracted. In fact, she was seeing him for dinner the very night she came in for her consultation. She'd wanted something exotic because they were dining in Mexico."

"In Mexico. That would have been the night before last."

"Yes. She was just bubbling over about him. We did her hair in a gypsy look, gave her a bit more gold to the skin— full body work. Rascal Red on the nails, and a charming little temp tattoo of a red-winged butterfly on the left buttock. Twenty-four-hour facial cosmetics so that she wouldn't smudge. She looked spectacular," he said, tearing up. "And she kissed me and told me she just might be in love this time. 'Wish me luck, Sebastian.' She said that as she left. It was the last thing she ever said to me."

NORA ROBERTS

THE HOLLOW

JOVE
New York

A JOVE BOOK
Published by Berkley
An imprint of Penguin Random House LLC
375 Hudson Street, New York, New York 10014

ISBN: 9780515144598

First Edition: May 2008

Printed in the United States of America
21   23   22   20

Cover design by Rich Hasselberger
Text design by Kristin del Rosario

In memory of my parents

Keep the home fires burning.

—LENA GUILBERT FORD

The natural flights of the human mind are not from
pleasure to pleasure, but from hope to hope.

—SAMUEL JOHNSON

Prologue

∾

Hawkins Hollow
June 1994

ON A BRIGHT SUMMER MORNING, A TEACUP poodle drowned in the Bestlers' backyard swimming pool. At first Lynne Bestler, who'd gone out to sneak in a solitary swim before her kids woke, thought it was a dead squirrel. Which would've been bad enough. But when she steeled herself to scoop out the tangle of fur with the net, she recognized her neighbor's beloved Marcell.

Squirrels generally didn't wear rhinestone collars.

Her shouts, and the splash as Lynne tossed the hapless dog, net and all, back into the pool, brought Lynne's husband rushing out in his boxers. Their mother's sobs, and their father's curses as he jumped in to grab the pole and tow the body to the side, woke the Bestler twins, who stood screaming in their matching My Little Pony nightgowns. Within moments, the backyard hysteria had neighbors hurrying to fences just as Bestler dragged himself and his burden out of the water. As, like many men, Bestler had developed an

attachment to ancient underwear, the weight of the water was too much for the worn elastic.

So Bestler came out of his pool with a dead dog, and no boxers.

The bright summer morning in the little town of Hawkins Hollow began with shock, grief, farce, and drama.

Fox learned of Marcell's untimely death minutes after he stepped into Ma's Pantry to pick up a sixteen-ounce bottle of Coke and a couple of Slim Jims.

He'd copped a quick break from working with his father on a kitchen remodel down Main Street. Mrs. Larson wanted new countertops, cabinet doors, new floors, new paint. She called it freshening things up, and Fox called it a way to earn enough money to take Allyson Brendon out for pizza and the movies on Saturday night. He hoped to use that gateway to talk her into the backseat of his ancient VW Bug.

He didn't mind working with his dad. He hoped to hell he wouldn't spend the rest of his life swinging a hammer or running a power saw, but he didn't mind it. His father's company was always easy, and the job got Fox out of gardening and animal duty on their little farm. It also provided easy access to Cokes and Slim Jims—two items that would never, never be found in the O'Dell-Barry household.

His mother ruled there.

So he heard about the dog from Susan Keefaffer, who rang up his purchases while a few people with nothing better to do on a June afternoon sat at the counter over coffee and gossip.

He didn't know Marcell, but Fox had a soft spot for animals, so he suffered a twist of grief for the unfortunate poodle. That was leavened somewhat by the idea of Mr. Bestler, whom he *did* know, standing "naked as a jaybird," in Susan Keefaffer's words, beside his backyard pool.

While it made Fox sad to imagine some poor dog drowning in a swimming pool, he didn't connect it—not

then—to the nightmare he and his two closest friends had lived through seven years before.

He'd had a dream the night before, a dream of blood and fire, of voices chanting in a language he didn't understand. But then he'd watched a double feature of videos— *Night of the Living Dead* and *The Texas Chainsaw Massacre*—with his friends Cal and Gage.

He didn't connect a dead French poodle with the dream, or with what had burned through Hawkins Hollow for a week after his tenth birthday. After the night he and Cal and Gage had spent at the Pagan Stone in Hawkins Wood—and everything had changed for them, and for the Hollow.

In a few weeks he and Cal and Gage would all turn seventeen, and that was on his mind. Baltimore had a damn good chance at a pennant this year, so that was on his mind. He'd be going back to high school as a senior, which meant top of the food chain at last, and planning for college.

What occupied a sixteen-year-old boy was considerably different from what occupied a ten-year-old. Including rounding third and heading for home with Allyson Brendon.

So when he walked back down the street, a lean boy not quite beyond the gangly stage of adolescence, his dense brown hair tied back in a stubby tail, golden brown eyes shaded with Oakleys, it was, for him, just another ordinary day.

The town looked as it always did. Tidy, a little old-timey, with the old stone townhouses or shops, the painted porches, the high curbs. He glanced back over his shoulder toward the Bowl-a-Rama on the Square. It was the biggest building in town, and where Cal and Gage were both working.

When he and his father knocked off for the day, he thought he'd head on up, see what was happening.

He crossed over to the Larson place, walked into the unlocked house where Bonnie Raitt's smooth Delta blues slid

smoothly out of the kitchen. His father sang along with her in his clear and easy voice as he checked the level on the shelves Mrs. Larson wanted in her utility closet. Though the windows and back door were open to their screens, the room smelled of sawdust, sweat, and the glue they'd used that morning to install the new Formica.

His father worked in old Levi's and his Give Peace a Chance T-shirt. His hair was six inches longer than Fox's, worn in a tail under a blue bandanna. He'd shaved off the beard and mustache he'd had as long as Fox remembered. Fox still wasn't quite used to seeing so much of his father's face—or so much of himself in it.

"A dog drowned in the Bestlers' swimming pool over on Laurel Lane," Fox told him, and Brian stopped working to turn.

"That's a damn shame. Anybody know how it happened?"

"Not really. It was one of those little poodles, so they think it must've fallen in, then it couldn't get out again."

"You'd think somebody would've heard it barking. That's a lousy way to go." Brian set down his tools, smiled at his boy. "Gimme one of those Slim Jims."

"What Slim Jims?"

"The ones you've got in your back pocket. You're not carrying a bag, and you weren't gone long enough to scarf down Hostess Pies or Twinkies. I'm betting you're packing the Jims. I get one, and your mom never has to know we ate chemicals and meat by-products. It's called blackmail, kid of mine."

Fox snorted, pulled them out. He'd bought two for just this purpose. Father and son unwrapped, bit off, chewed in perfect harmony. "The counter looks good, Dad."

"Yeah, it does." Brian ran a hand over the smooth eggshell surface. "Mrs. Larson's not much for color, but it's good work. I don't know who I'm going to get to be my lapdog when you head off to college."

"Ridge is next in line," Fox said, thinking of his younger brother.

"Ridge wouldn't keep measurements in his head for two minutes running, and he'd probably cut off a finger dreaming while he was using a band saw. No." Brian smiled, shrugged. "This kind of work isn't for Ridge, or for you, for that matter. Or either of your sisters. I guess I'm going to have to rent a kid to get one who wants to work with wood."

"I never said I didn't want to." Not out loud.

His father looked at him the way he sometimes did, as if he saw more than what was there. "You've got a good eye, you've got good hands. You'll be handy around your own house once you get one. But you won't be strapping on a tool belt to make a living. Until you figure out just what it is you want, you can haul these scraps on out to the Dumpster."

"Sure." Fox gathered up scraps, trash, began to cart them out the back, across the narrow yard to the Dumpster the Larsons had rented for the duration of the remodel.

He glanced toward the adjoining yard and the sound of kids playing. And the armload he carried thumped and bounced on the ground as his body went numb.

The little boys played with trucks and shovels and pails in a bright blue sandbox. But it wasn't filled with sand. Blood covered their bare arms as they pushed their Tonka trucks through the muck inside the box. He stumbled back as the boys made engine sounds, as red lapped over the bright blue sides and dripped onto the green grass.

On the fence between the yards, where hydrangeas headed up toward bloom, crouched a boy that wasn't a boy. It bared its teeth in a grin as Fox backed toward the house.

"Dad! Dad!"

The tone, the breathless fear had Brian rushing outside. "What? What is it?"

"Don't you—can't you see?" But even as he said it, as he pointed, something inside Fox knew. It wasn't real.

"What?" Firmly now, Brian took his son's shoulders. "What do you see?"

The boy that wasn't a boy danced along the top of the chain-link fence while flames spurted up below and burned the hydrangeas to cinders.

"I have to go. I have to go see Cal and Gage. Right now, Dad. I have to—"

"Go." Brian released his hold on Fox, stepped back. He didn't question. "Go."

He all but flew through the house and out again, up the sidewalk to the Square. The town no longer looked as it usually did to him. In his mind's eye Fox could see it as it had been that horrible week in July seven years before.

Fire and blood, he remembered, thinking of the dream.

He burst into the Bowl-a-Rama where the summer afternoon leagues were in full swing. The thunder of balls, the crash of pins pounded in his head as he ran straight to the front desk where Cal worked.

"Where's Gage?" Fox demanded.

"Jesus, what's up with you?"

"Where's Gage?" Fox repeated, and Cal's amused gray eyes sobered. "Working the arcade. He's . . . he's coming out now."

At Cal's quick signal, Gage sauntered over. "Hello, ladies. What . . ." The smirk died after one look at Fox's face. "What happened?"

"It's back," Fox said. "It's come back."

One

～⌒～

Hawkins Hollow
March 2008

Fox REMEMBERED MANY DETAILS OF THAT LONG-
ago day in June. The tear in the left knee in his father's
Levi's, the smell of coffee and onions in Ma's Pantry, the
crackle of the wrappers as he and his father opened Slim
Jims in Mrs. Larson's kitchen.

But what he remembered most, even beyond the shock
and the fear of what he'd seen in the yard, was that his father had trusted him.

He'd trusted him on the morning of Fox's tenth birthday, too, when Fox had come home, bringing Gage with
him, both of them filthy, exhausted, and terrified, with a
story no adult would believe.

There'd been worry, Fox reflected. He could still see the
way his parents had looked at each other as he told them
the story of something black and powerful and *wrong* erupting out of the clearing where the Pagan Stone stood.

They hadn't brushed it off as overactive imagination,
hadn't even come down on him for lying about spending

the night at Cal's and instead trooping off with his friends to spend the night of their tenth birthday in the woods west of town.

Instead they'd listened. And when Cal's parents had come over, they'd listened, too.

Fox glanced down at the thin scar across his wrist. That mark, one made when Cal had used his Boy Scout knife nearly twenty-one years before to make him, Cal, and Gage blood brothers, was the only scar on his body. He'd had others before that night, before that ritual—what active boy of ten didn't? Yet all of them but this one had healed smooth—as he'd healed from any injury since. Without a trace.

It was that mark, that mixing of blood, that had freed the thing trapped centuries before. For seven nights it had stormed through Hawkins Hollow.

They thought they'd beaten it, three ten-year-old boys against the unholy that infected the town. But it came back, seven years later, for seven more nights of hell. Then returned again, the week they'd turned twenty-four.

It would come back again this summer. It was already making itself known.

But things were different now. They were better prepared, had more knowledge. Only it wasn't just him, Cal, and Gage this time. They were six with the three women who'd come to the Hollow, who were connected by ancestry to the demon, just as he, Cal, and Gage were connected to the force that had trapped it.

Not kids anymore, Fox thought as he pulled up to park in front of the townhouse on Main Street that held his office and his apartment. And if what their little band of six had been able to pull off a couple weeks before at the Pagan Stone was any indication, the demon who'd once called himself Lazarus Twisse was in for a few surprises.

After grabbing his briefcase, he crossed the sidewalk. It had taken a lot of sweat and considerable financial juggling for Fox to buy the old stone townhouse. The first couple of

years had been lean—hell, they'd been emaciated, he thought now. But they'd been worth the struggle, the endless meals of PB and J, because every inch of the place was his—and the Hawkins Hollow Bank and Trust's.

The plaque at the door read FOX B. O'DELL, ATTORNEY AT LAW. It could still surprise him that it had been the law he'd wanted—more that it had been small-town law.

He supposed it shouldn't. The law wasn't just about right and wrong, but all the shades between. He liked figuring out which shade worked best in each situation.

He stepped inside, and got a jolt when he saw Layla Darnell, one of that little band of six, behind the desk in his reception area. His mind went blank for a moment, as it often did if he saw her unexpectedly. He said, "Um . . ."

"Hi." Her smile was cautious. "You're back sooner than expected."

Was he? He couldn't remember. How was he supposed to concentrate with the hot-looking brunette and her mermaid green eyes behind the desk instead of his grandmotherly Mrs. Hawbaker? "I—we—won. The jury deliberated less than an hour."

"That's great." Her smile boosted up several degrees. "Congratulations. That was the personal injury case? The car accident. Mr. and Mrs. Pullman?"

"Yeah." He shifted his briefcase to his other shoulder and kept most of the pretty parlorlike reception area between them. "Where's Mrs. H?"

"Dentist appointment. It's on your calendar."

Of course it was. "Right. I'll just be in my office."

"Shelley Kholer called. Twice. She's decided she wants to sue her sister for alienation of affection and for . . . Wait." Layla picked up a message pad. "For being a 'skanky, no-good ho'—she actually said 'ho.' And the second call involved her wanting to know if, as part of her divorce settlement, she'd get her cheating butt-monkey of a soon-to-be-ex-husband's points for some sort of online NASCAR

contest because she picked the jerkwad's drivers for him. I honestly don't know what that last part means except for jerkwad."

"Uh-huh. Well, interesting. I'll call her."

"Then she cried."

"Shit." He still had a soft spot for animals, and had a spot equally soft for unhappy women. "I'll call her now."

"No, you'll want to wait about an hour," Layla said with a glance at her watch. "Right about now she's getting hair therapy. She's going red. She can't actually sue her skanky, no-good ho of a sister for alienation of affection, can she?"

"You can sue for any damn thing, but I'll talk her down from it. Maybe you could remind me in an hour to call her. Are you okay out here?" he added. "Do you need anything?"

"I'm good. Alice—Mrs. Hawbaker—she's a good teacher. And she's very protective of you. If she didn't think I was ready to fly solo, I wouldn't be. Besides, as office manager in training, I should be asking you if you need anything."

An office manager who didn't jump-start his libido would be a good start, but it was too late for that. "I'm good, too. I'll just be . . ." He gestured toward his office, then walked away.

He was tempted to shut the pocket doors, but it felt rude. He never closed the doors of his office unless he was with a client who needed or wanted privacy.

Because he never felt quite real in a suit, Fox pulled off the jacket, tossed it over the grinning pig that served as one of the hooks. With relief, he dragged off his tie and draped it over a happy cow. That left a chicken, a goat, and a duck, all carved by his father, whose opinion had been that no law office could be stuffy when it was home to a bunch of lunatic farm animals.

So far, Fox figured that ran true.

It was exactly what he'd wanted in an office, something part of a house rather than a *building*, with a view of

neighborhood rather than urban streets. Shelves held the law books and supplies he needed most often, but mingled with them were bits and pieces of him. A baseball signed by the one and only Cal Ripken, the stained-glass kaleidoscope his mother had made him, framed snapshots, a scale model of the Millennium Falcon, laboriously and precisely built when he'd been twelve.

And, in a place of prominence sat the big glass jar, and its complement of dollar bills. One for every time he forgot and said *fuck* in the office. It was Alice Hawbaker's decree.

He got a Coke out of the minifridge he kept stocked with them and wondered what the hell he was going to do when Mrs. Hawbaker deserted him for Minneapolis and he had to deal with the lovely Layla not only as part of the defeat-the-damn-demon team, but five days a week in his office.

"Fox?"

"Huh?" He spun around from his window, and there she was again. "What? Is something wrong?"

"No. Well, other than Big Evil, no. You don't have any appointments for a couple of hours, and since Alice isn't here, I thought we could talk about that. I know you've got other work, but—"

"It's okay." Big Evil would give him focus on something other than gorgeous green eyes and soft, glossy pink lips. "Do you want a Coke?"

"No, thanks. Do you know how many calories are in that can?"

"It's worth it. Sit down."

"I'm too jumpy." As if to prove it, Layla rubbed her hands together as she wandered the office. "I get jumpier every day that nothing happens, which is stupid, because it should be a relief. But nothing's happened, nothing at all since we were all at the Pagan Stone."

"Throwing sticks and stones and really harsh words at a demon from hell."

"That, and Gage shooting at it. Or Cal . . ." She stopped, faced Fox now. "I still get shaky when I remember how Cal stepped right up to that writhing mass of black and shoved a knife into it. And now nothing, in almost two weeks. Before, it was nearly every day we saw it, felt it, dreamed of it."

"We hurt it," Fox reminded her. "It's off wherever demons go to lick their wounds."

"Cybil calls it a lull, and she thinks it's going to come back harder the next time. She's researching for hours every day, and Quinn, well, she's writing. That's what they do, and they've done this before—this kind of thing if not this precise thing. First-timer here, and what I'm noticing is they're not getting anywhere." She pushed a hand through her dark hair, then shook her head so the sexy, jagged ends of it swung. "What I mean is . . . A couple of weeks ago, Cybil had what she thought were really strong leads toward where Ann Hawkins might have gone to have her babies."

His ancestors, Fox thought. Giles Dent, Ann Hawkins, and the sons they'd made together. "And they haven't panned out, I know. We've all talked about this."

"But I think—I feel—it's one of the keys. They're your ancestors, yours, Cal's, Gage's. Where they were born may matter, and more since we have some of Ann's journals, we're all agreed there must be others. And the others may explain more about her sons' father. About Giles Dent. What was he, Fox? A man, a witch, a good demon, if there are such things? How did he trap what called itself Lazarus Twisse from that night in sixteen fifty-two until the night the three of you—"

"Let it out," Fox finished, and Layla shook her head again.

"You were meant to—that much we agree on, too. It was part of Dent's plan or his spell. But we don't seem to know any more than we did two weeks ago. We're stalled."

"Maybe Twisse isn't the only one who needs to recharge.

We hurt it," he repeated. "We've never been able to do that before. We scared it." And the memory of that was enough to turn his gilded brown eyes cool with satisfaction. "Every seven years all we've been able to do is try to get people out of the way, to mop up the mess afterward. Now we know we can hurt it."

"Hurting it isn't enough."

"No, it's not." If they were stalled, he admitted, part of the reason was his fault. He'd pulled back. He'd made excuses not to push Layla on honing the skill—the one that matched his own—that had been passed down to her.

"What am I thinking now?"

She blinked at him. "Sorry?"

"What am I thinking?" he repeated, and deliberately recited the alphabet in his head.

"I told you before I can't read minds, and I don't want—"

"And I told you it's not exactly like that, but close enough." He eased a hip onto the corner of his sturdy old desk, and brought their gazes more level. His conservative oxford-cloth shirt was open at the throat, and his bark brown hair waved around his sharp-featured face and brushed the back of his collar. "You can and do get impressions, get a sense, even an image in your head. Try again."

"Having good instincts isn't the same as—"

"That's bullshit. You're letting yourself be afraid of what's inside you because of where it came from, and because it makes you other than—"

"Human?"

"No. Makes you 'other.'" He understood the complexity of her feelings on this issue. There was something in him that was other as well. At times it was more difficult to wear than a suit and tie. But to Fox's mind, doing the difficult was just part of living. "It doesn't matter where it came from, Layla. You have what you have and are what you are for a reason."

"Easy to say when you can put your ancestry back to some bright, shining light, and mine goes back to a demon who raped some poor sixteen-year-old girl."

"Thinking that's only letting him score points off you. Try again," Fox insisted, and this time grabbed her hand before she could evade him.

"I don't—stop pushing it at me," she snapped. Her free hand pressed against her temple.

It was a jolt, he knew, to have something pop in there when you weren't prepared. But it couldn't be helped. "What am I thinking?"

"I don't know. I just see a bunch of letters in my head."

"Exactly." Approval spread in his smile, and reached his eyes. "Because I was thinking of a bunch of letters. You can't go back." He spoke gently now. "And you wouldn't if you could. You wouldn't just pack up, go back to New York, and beg your boss at the boutique to give you your job back."

Layla snatched her hand away as color flooded her cheeks. "I don't want you prying into my thoughts and feelings."

"No, you're right. And I don't make a habit of it. But, Layla, if you can't or won't trust me with what's barely under the surface, you and I are going to be next to useless. Cal and Quinn, they flash back to things that happened before, and Gage and Cybil get images, or even just possibilities of what's coming next. We're the now, you and me. And the now is pretty damn important. You said we're stalled. Okay then, let's get moving."

"It's easier for you, easier for you to accept because you've had this thing . . ." She waved a finger beside her temple. "You've had this for twenty years."

"Haven't you?" he countered. "It's more likely you've had it since you were born."

"Because of the demon hanging on my family tree?"

"That's right. That's an established fact. What you do

about it's up to you. You used what you have a couple of weeks ago when we were on our way to the Pagan Stone. You made that choice. I told you once before, Layla, you've got to commit."

"I have. I lost my job over this. I've sublet my apartment because I'm not going back to New York until this is over. I'm working here to pay the rent, and spending most of the time I'm *not* working here working with Cybil and Quinn on background, research, theories, solutions."

"And you're frustrated because you haven't found the solution. Commitment's more than putting the time in. And I don't have to be a mind reader to know hearing that pisses you off."

"I was in that clearing, too, Fox. I faced that thing, too."

"That's right. Why is that easier for you than facing what you've got inside you? It's a tool, Layla. If you let tools get dull or rusty, they don't work. If you don't pick them up and use them, you forget how."

"And if that tool's sharp and shiny and you don't know what the hell to do with it, you can do a lot of damage."

"I'll help you." He held out his hand.

She hesitated. When the phone in the outer office began to ring, she stepped back.

"Let it go," he told her. "They'll call back."

But she shook her head and hurried out. "Don't forget to call Shelley."

That went well, he thought in disgust. Opening his briefcase, he pulled out the file on the personal injury case he'd just won. Win some, lose some, Fox decided.

As he figured it was the way she wanted it, he stayed out of her way for the rest of the afternoon. It was simple enough to instruct her through interoffice e-mail to generate the standard power-of-attorney document with the specific names his client required. Or to ask her to prepare and send out a bill or pay one. He made what calls he needed to make himself rather than asking Layla to place them first.

That kind of thing had always struck him as stupid in any case.

He knew how to use the damn phone.

He managed to calm Shelley down, catch up on paperwork, and win a game of online chess. But when he considered sending Layla another e-mail to tell her to go ahead and knock off for the day, he realized that came under the heading of avoidance, not just keeping the peace.

When he walked out to reception, Mrs. Hawbaker was manning the desk. "I didn't know you were back," he began.

"I've been back awhile. I've just finished proofing the papers Layla took care of for you. Need your signature on these letters."

"Okay." He took the pen she handed him, signed. "Where is she? Layla?"

"Gone for the day. She did fine on her own."

Understanding it was a question as much as an opinion, Fox nodded. "Yeah, she did fine."

In her brisk way, Mrs. Hawbaker folded the letters Fox had signed. "You don't need both of us here full-time and can't afford to be paying double either."

"Mrs. H—"

"I'm going to come in half days the rest of the week." She spoke quickly now, tucking letters into envelopes, sealing them. "Just to make sure everything runs smoothly for you, and for her. Any problems, I can come in, help handle them. But I don't expect there to be. If there aren't problems, I won't be coming in after Friday next. We've got a lot of packing and sorting to do. Shipping things up to Minneapolis, showing the house."

"Goddamn it."

She merely pointed her finger at him, narrowed her eyes. "When I'm gone you can turn the air blue around here, but until I am, you'll watch your language."

"Yes, ma'am. Mrs. H—"

"And don't give me those puppy dog eyes, Fox O'Dell. We've been through all this."

They had, and he could feel her sorrow, and her fear. Dumping his own on her wouldn't help. "I'll keep the F-word jar in my office, in memory of you."

That made her smile. "The way you toss it around, you'll be able to retire a rich man on the proceeds of that jar. Even so, you're a good boy. You're a good lawyer, Fox. Now, you go on. You're clear for the rest of the day— what's left of it. I'm just going to finish up a couple things, then I'll lock up."

"Okay." But he stopped at the door, looked back at her. Her snowy hair was perfectly groomed; her blue suit digni- fied. "Mrs. H? I miss you already."

He closed the door behind him, and stuck his hands in his pockets as he walked down to the brick sidewalk. At the toot of a horn, he glanced over and waved as Denny Moser drove by. Denny Moser, whose family owned the local hardware store. Denny, who'd been a balletic third base- man for the Hawkins Hollow Bucks in high school.

Denny Moser, who during the last Seven had come after Fox with a pipe wrench and murder on his mind.

It would happen again, Fox thought. It would happen again in a matter of months if they didn't stop it. Denny had a wife and a kid now—and maybe this time during that week in July, he'd go after his wife or his little girl with a pipe wrench. Or his wife, former cheerleader and current licensed day-care provider, might slit her husband's throat in his sleep.

It had happened before, the mass insanity of ordinary and decent people. And it would happen again. Unless.

He walked along the wide brick sidewalk on a windy March evening, and knew he couldn't let it happen again.

Cal was probably still at the bowling alley, Fox thought.

He'd go there, have a beer, maybe an early dinner. And maybe the two of them could figure out which direction to try next.

As he approached the Square, he saw Layla come out of Ma's Pantry across the street, carrying a plastic bag. She hesitated when she spotted him, and that planted a sharp seed of irritation in his gut. After she sent him a casual wave, they walked to the light at the Square on opposite sides of the street.

It might have been that irritation, or the frustration of trying to decide to do what would be natural for him—to wait on his side of the corner for her to cross and speak to her. Or to do what he felt, even with the distance, she'd prefer. For him to simply keep going up Main so they didn't intersect. Either way, he was nearly at the corner when he felt the fear—sudden and bright. It stopped him in his tracks, had his head jerking up.

There, on the wires crossing above Main and Locust, were the crows.

Dozens of them crowded together in absolute stillness along the thin wire. Hulking there, wings tucked and—he knew—watching. When he glanced across the street, he saw that Layla had seen them, too, either sensing them herself or following the direction of his stare.

He didn't run, though there was an urgent need to do just that. Instead he walked in long, brisk strides across the street to where she stood gripping her white plastic bag.

"They're real." She only whispered it. "I thought, at first, they were just another . . . but they're real."

"Yeah." He took her arm. "We're going inside. We're going to turn around, and get inside. Then—"

He broke off as he heard the first stir behind him, just a flutter on the air. And in her eyes, wide now, huge now, he saw it was too late.

The rush of wings was a tornado of sound and speed. Fox shoved her back against the building, and down. Push-

ing her face against his chest, he wrapped his arms around her and used his body to shield hers.

Glass shattered beside him, behind him. Brakes squealed through the crash and thuds of metal. He heard screams, rushing feet, felt the jarring force as birds thumped into his back, the quick sting as beaks stabbed and tore. He knew the rough, wet sounds were those flying bodies smashing into walls and windows, falling lifeless to street and sidewalk.

It was over quickly, in no more than a minute. A child shrieked, over and over—one long, sharp note after another. "Stay here." A little out of breath, he leaned back so that Layla could see his face. "Stay right here."

"You're bleeding. Fox—"

"Just stay here."

He shoved to his feet. In the intersection three cars were slammed together. Spiderwebs cracked the safety glass of windshields where the birds had flown into them. Crunched bumpers, he noted as he rushed toward the accident, shaken nerves, dented fenders.

It could have been much worse.

"Everybody all right?"

He didn't listen to the words: *Did you see that? They flew right into my car!* Instead he listened with his senses. Bumps and bruises, frayed nerves, minor cuts, but no serious injuries. He left others to sort things out, turned back to Layla.

She stood with a group of people who'd poured out of Ma's Pantry and the businesses on either side. "The damnedest thing," Meg, the counter cook at Ma's, said as she stared at the shattered glass of the little restaurant. "The damnedest thing."

Because he'd seen it all before, and much, much worse, Fox grabbed Layla's hand. "Let's go."

"Shouldn't we do something?"

"There's nothing to do. I'm getting you home, then we'll call Cal and Gage."

"Your hand." Her voice was awe and nerves. "The back of your hand's already healing."

"Part of the perks," he said grimly, and pulled her back across Main.

"I don't have that perk." She spoke quietly and jogged to keep up with his long, fast stride. "If you hadn't blocked me, I'd be bleeding." She lifted a hand to the cut on his face that was slowly closing. "It hurts though. When it happens, then when it heals, it hurts you." Layla glanced down at their clasped hands. "I can feel it."

But when he started to let her go, she tightened her grip. "No, I want to feel it. You were right before." She glanced back at the corpses of crows scattered over the Square, at the little girl who wept wildly now in the arms of her shocked mother. "I hate that you were right and I'll have to work on that. But you were. I'm not any real help if I don't accept what I've got in me, and learn how to use it."

She looked back at him, took a bracing breath. "The lull's over."

Two

~<~

HE HAD A BEER SITTING AT THE LITTLE TABLE with its fancy iron chairs that made the kitchen in the rental house distinctly female. At least to Fox's mind. The brightly colored minipots holding herbs arranged on the windowsill added to that tone, he supposed, and the skinny vase of white-faced daisies one of the women must have picked up at the flower shop in town finished it off.

The women, Quinn, Cybil, and Layla, had managed to make a home out of the place in a matter of weeks with flea market furniture, scraps of fabric, and generous splashes of color.

They'd managed it while devoting the bulk of their time to researching and outlining the root of the nightmare that infected the Hollow for seven days every seven years.

A nightmare that had begun twenty-one years before, on the birthday he shared with Cal and Gage. That night had changed him, and his friends—his blood brothers. Things

had changed again when Quinn had come to town to lay the groundwork for her book on the Hollow and its legend.

It was more than a book to her now, the curvy blonde who enjoyed the spookier side of life, and who had fallen for Cal. It was more than a project for Quinn's college pal Cybil Kinski, the exotic researcher. And he thought it was more of a problem for Layla Darnell.

He and Cal and Gage went back to babyhood—even before, as their mothers had taken the same childbirth class. Quinn and Cybil had been college roommates, and had remained friends since. But Layla had come to the Hollow, come into this situation, alone.

He reminded himself of that whenever his patience ran a bit thin. However tightly the friendship was that had formed between her and the other two women, however much she was connected to the whole, she'd come into this alone.

Cybil walked in carrying a legal pad. She tossed it on the table, then picked up a bottle of wine. Her long, curling hair was pinned back from her face with clips that glinted silver against the black. She wore slim black pants and an untucked shirt of candy pink. Her feet were bare, with toenails painted to match the shirt.

Fox always found such details particularly fascinating. He could barely remember to match up a pair of socks.

"So . . ." Her deep brown eyes tracked over to his. "I'm here to get your statement."

"Aren't you going to read me my rights?" When she smiled, he shrugged. "We gave you the gist when we came in."

"Details, counselor." Her voice was smooth as top cream. "Quinn particularly likes details in the notes for her books and we all need them to keep painting the picture. Quinn's getting Layla's take upstairs while Layla changes. She had blood on her shirt. Yours, I'm assuming, as she didn't have a scratch on her."

"Neither do I, now."

"Yes, your super-duper healing power. That's handy. Run it through for me, will you, cutie? I know it's a pain, because when the others get here, they'll want to hear it, too. But isn't that what they say on the cop shows? Keep going over it, and maybe you'll remember something more?"

Since she had a point, he began at the moment he'd looked up and seen the crows.

"What were you doing right before you looked up?"

"Walking up Main. I was going to drop in and see Cal. Buy a beer." Lips curved in a half smile, he lifted the bottle. "Came here and got one free."

"You bought them, as I recall. It just seems if you were walking toward the Square, and these birds were doing their Hitchcock thing above the intersection, you'd have noticed before you said you did."

"I was distracted, thinking about . . . work, and stuff." He raked his fingers through hair still damp from being stuck under the faucet to wash the bird gunk out. "I guess I was looking across the street more than up the street. Layla came out of Ma's."

"She walked over to get some of Quinn's revolting two percent milk. Was it luck—good or bad—that both of you were there, right on the spot?" Her head cocked to the side; her eyebrow lifted. "Or was that the point?"

He liked that she was quick, that she was sharp. "I lean toward it being the point. If the Big Evil Bastard wanted to announce it was back to play, it makes a bigger impact if at least one of us was on the scene. It wouldn't be as much fun if we'd just heard about it."

"I lean the same way. We agreed before that it's able to influence animals or people under some kind of impairment easier, quicker. So, crows. That's happened before."

"Yeah. Crows or other birds flying into windows, into people, buildings. When it does, even people who were here when it happened before are surprised. Like it was the

first time they'd seen anything like it. That's part of the symptoms, we'll call it."

"There were other people out—pedestrians, people driving by."

"Sure."

"And none of them stopped and said: Holy crap, look at all those crows up there."

"No." He nodded, following her. "No. No one saw them, or no one who did found them remarkable. That's happened before, too. People seeing things that aren't there, and people not seeing things that are. It's just never happened this far out from the Seven."

"What did you do after you saw Layla?"

"I kept walking." Curious, he angled his head in an attempt to read her notes upside down. What he saw were squiggles of letters and signs he didn't understand how anyone could decipher right-side up. "I guess I stopped for a second the way you do, then I kept walking. And that's when I . . . I felt it first, that's what *I* do. It's a kind of awareness. Like the hair standing up on the back of your neck, or that tingle between the shoulder blades. I saw them, in my head, then I looked up, and saw them with my eyes. Layla saw them, too."

"And still, no one else did?"

"No." Again, he scooped a hand through his hair. "I don't think so. I wanted to get her inside, but there wasn't time."

She didn't interrupt or question when he ran through the rest of it. When he was done, she set down her pencil, smiled at him. "You're a sweetheart, Fox."

"True. Very true. Why?"

She continued to smile as she rose, skirted the little table. She took his face in her hands and kissed him lightly on the mouth. "I saw your jacket. It's torn, and it's covered with bird blood and God knows what else. That could've been Layla."

"I can get another jacket."

"Like I said, you're a sweetheart." She kissed him again.

"Sorry to interrupt this touching moment." Gage strode in, his dark hair windblown, his eyes green and cynical. He stored the six-pack he carried in the fridge, then pulled out a beer.

"Moment's over," Cybil announced. "Too bad you missed all the excitement."

He popped the top. "There'll be plenty more before it's over. Doing okay?" he asked Fox.

"Yeah. I won't be pulling out my DVD of *The Birds* anytime soon, but other than that."

"Cal said Layla wasn't hurt."

"No, she's good. She's upstairs changing. Things got a little messy."

At Fox's glance, Cybil shrugged. "Which is my cue to go up and check on her and leave you two to man talk."

As she walked out, Gage followed her with his eyes. "Looks good coming or going." Taking a long pull on the beer, he sat across from Fox. "You looking in that direction?"

"What? Oh, Cybil? No." She'd left a scent in the air, Fox realized, that was both mysterious and appealing. But . . . "No. Are you?"

"Looking's free. How bad was it today?"

"We've seen a lot worse. Property damage mostly. Maybe some cuts and bruises." Everything about him hardened, inside and out. "They'd've messed her up, Gage, if I hadn't been there. She couldn't have gotten inside in time. They weren't just flying at cars and buildings. They were heading right for her."

"It could've been any one of us." Gage pondered on it a moment. "Last month, it went after Quinn when she was alone in the gym."

"Targeting the women," Fox said with a nod, "most specifically when one of them is alone. From the

viewpoint—the faulty viewpoint—that a woman alone is more vulnerable."

"Not entirely faulty. We heal, they don't." Gage kicked back in his chair. "There's no way to keep three women under wraps while we try to come up with how to kill a centuries-old and very pissed-off demon. Besides that, we need them."

He heard the front door open and close, then shifted in his chair to watch Cal come in with an armload of take-out bags. "Burgers, subs," Cal announced. He dumped them on the counter as he studied Fox. "You're okay? Layla's okay?"

"The only casualty was my leather jacket. What's it like out there?"

Getting out his own beer, Cal sat with his friends. His eyes were a cold and angry gray. "About a dozen broken windows on Main Street, and the three-car pileup at the Square. No serious injuries, this time. The mayor and my father got some people together to clean up the mess. Chief Hawbaker's taking statements."

"And if it goes as it usually does, in a couple of days, nobody will think any more about it. Maybe it's better that way. If things like this stuck in people's minds, the Hollow'd be a ghost town."

"Maybe it should be. Don't give me the old hometown cheer," Gage said to Cal before Cal could speak. "It's a place. A dot on the map."

"It's people," Cal corrected, though this argument had gone around before. "It's families, it's businesses and homes. And it's ours, goddamn it. Twisse, or whatever name we want to call it, isn't going to take it."

"Doesn't it occur to you that it would be a hell of a lot easier to take him down if we didn't have to worry about the three thousand people in the Hollow?" Gage tossed back. "What do we end up doing through most of the Seven, Cal? Trying to keep people from killing themselves

or each other, getting people medical help. How do we fight it when we're busy fighting what it causes?"

"He's got a point." Fox lifted a hand for peace. "I know I've wished we could just clear everybody the hell out, have a showdown. Fucking get it done. But you can't tell three thousand people to leave their homes and businesses for a week. You can't empty out an entire town."

"The Anasazi did it." Quinn stepped in from the doorway. She went to Cal first. Her long blond hair swung forward as she leaned over his chair to kiss him. "Hi."

When she straightened, her hands stayed on his shoulders. Fox wasn't sure the gesture was purely out of affection or to soothe. But he knew when Cal's hand came up to cover one of hers, it meant they were united.

"Towns and villages have emptied out before, for mysterious and unexplained reasons," she continued. "The ancient Anasazi, who built complex communities in the canyons of Arizona and New Mexico, the colonial village of Roanoke. Causes might have been warfare, sickness, or something else. I've been wondering if some of those cases might be the something else we're dealing with."

"You think Lazarus Twisse wiped out the Anasazi, the settlers of Roanoke?" Cal asked.

"Maybe, in the case of the Anasazi, before he took any name we know. Roanoke happened after sixteen fifty-two, so we can't hang that on our particular Big Evil Bastard. Just a theory I've been kicking around." She turned to poke into the bags on the counter. "In any case, we should eat."

While food and plates were transferred to the dining room, Fox managed to get Layla aside. "Are you okay?"

"Yeah." She took his hand, turned it over to study the unbroken skin. "I guess you are, too."

"Listen, if you want to take a couple of days off, from the office, I mean, it's fine."

She released his hand, angled her head as she took a

long study of his face. "Do you really think I'm that . . .
lily-livered?"

"No. I just meant—"

"Yes, you do. You think because I'm not sold on this
idea of the—the Vulcan Mind Meld, I'm a coward."

"I don't. I figured you'd be shaken up—anyone would
be. Points for the Spock reference, by the way, even though
it's inaccurate."

"Is it?" She brushed past him to take her seat at the
table.

"Okay." Quinn gave Cal's burger one wistful glance before she started on her grilled chicken. "We're all up to
date on what happened at the Square. Bad birds. We'll log
it and chart it, and I'm planning on talking to bystanders
tomorrow. I wondered if it might be helpful to get one of
the bird corpses and send it off for analysis. Maybe there'd
be a sign of some physical change, some infection, something *off* that would come out in an autopsy."

"We'll just leave that to you." Cybil made a face as she
nibbled on the portion of the turkey sub she'd cut into
quarters. "And let's not discuss autopsies over dinner.
Here's what I found interesting about today's event. Both
Layla and Fox sensed and saw the birds, as far as I can tell,
simultaneously. Or near enough to amount to the same.
Now, is that simply because all six of us have some connection to the dark and the light sides of what happened,
and continues to happen in Hawkins Hollow? Or is this because of the specific ability they share?"

"I'd say both," was Cal's opinion. "With the extra click
going to shared ability."

"I tend to agree. So," Cybil continued, "how do we use
it?"

"We don't." Fox scooped up fries. "Not as long as Layla
pulls back from learning how to use what she's got. That's
the way it is," he continued when Layla stared at him. "You
don't have to like it, but that's how it is. What you have

isn't any good to you, or to the team, if you won't use it, or learn how to use it."

"I didn't say I wouldn't, but I'm not going to have you shove it down my throat. And trying to shame me into it isn't going to work either."

"What will?" Fox countered. "I'm open to suggestions."

Cybil held up a hand. "Since I opened this can of worms, let me try. You've got reservations about this, Layla. Why don't you tell us what they are?"

"I feel like I'm losing pieces of myself, or who I thought I was. Adding this in, I'm never going to be who I was again."

"That may be," Gage said easily. "But you're probably not going to live past July anyway."

"Of course." On a half laugh, Layla picked up her glass of wine. "I should look on the bright side."

"Let's try this." Cal shook his head at Gage. "The odds are you'd have been hurt today if something hadn't clicked between you and Fox. And it clicked without either one of you purposely trying. What?" he asked as Quinn started to speak, then stopped herself.

"No. Nothing." Quinn exchanged a quick look with Cybil. "Let's just say I think I understand where everyone's coming from, and everyone makes a point. So I want to say, Layla, that maybe you could consider looking at it another way. Not that you're losing something with this, but you could be gaining something. Meanwhile, we're still going through Ann Hawkins's journals, and the other books Cal's great-grandmother gave us. And Cybil's working on finding where Ann might have gone the night Giles Dent faced down Lazarus Twisse at the Pagan Stone, where she stayed to have her sons, where she lived until she came back here when they were about two. We're still hopeful that if we find the place, we may find more of her journals. And Cybil also verified her branch of the family tree."

"A younger branch than all of yours, so far as I can tell," Cybil continued. "One of my ancestors, a Nadia Sytarskyi, traveled here with her family, and with others in the mid-nineteenth century. She married Jonah Adams, a descendent of Hester Deale. I actually get two branches, as about fifty years later, one of my other ancestors—Kinski side—also came here, and hooked up with Nadia and Jonah's grandchild. So, like Quinn and Layla, I'm a descendent of Hester Deale, and the demon who raped her and got her with child."

"Making us all one big happy family," Gage put in.

"Making us something. It doesn't sit well with me," Cybil added, speaking directly to Layla, "to know that part of what I have, part of what I am, comes down from something evil, something neither human or humane. In fact, it pisses me off. Enough that I intend to use everything I have, everything I am to kick its ass."

"Does it worry you that it may be able to use what you have and are?"

Cybil lifted her glass again, her dark eyes cool as she sipped. "It can try."

"It worries me." Layla scanned the table, the faces of the people she'd come to care for. "It worries me that I have something in me I can't fully understand or control. It worries me that at some point, at any point, it may control me." She shook her head before Quinn could speak. "Even now I don't know if I chose to come here or if I was directed here. More disturbing to me is not being sure anymore if anything I've done has been a choice, or just some part of a master plan created by these forces—the dark and the light. That's what's under it for me. That's the sticking point."

"Nobody's chaining you to that chair," Gage pointed out.

"Ease off," Fox told him, but Gage only shrugged.

"I don't think so. She's got a problem, we've all got a

problem. So let's deal with it. Why don't you just pack up and go back to New York? Get your job back selling—what is it—overpriced shoes to bored women with too much money?"

"Step back, Gage."

"No." Layla put a hand on Fox's arm as he started to rise. "I don't need to be rescued, or protected. Why don't I leave? Because it would make me a coward, and up until now I've never been one. I don't leave because what raped Hester Deale, what put its half-demon bastard in that girl, drove her mad, drove her to suicide, would like nothing better than for me to cut and run. I know better than anyone here what it did to her, because it made me experience it. Maybe that makes me more afraid than the rest of you; maybe that was part of the plan. I'm not going anywhere, but I'm not ashamed to admit that I'm afraid. Of what's out there, and of what's inside me. Inside all of us."

"If you weren't afraid you'd be stupid." Gage lifted his glass in a half toast. "Smart and self-aware are harder to manipulate than stupid."

"Every seven years good people in this town, ordinary people, smart, self-aware people hurt each other, and themselves. They do things they'd never consider doing at any other time."

"You think you could be infected?" Fox asked her. "That you could turn, hurt someone? One of us?"

"How can we be sure I'm immune? That Cybil and Quinn are? Shouldn't we consider that because of our line of descent we could be even more vulnerable?"

"That's a good question. Disturbing," Quinn added, "but good."

"Doesn't fly." Fox shifted so Layla met his eyes. "Things didn't go the way Twisse planned or expected, because Giles Dent was ready for him. He stopped him from being around when Hester delivered, stopped him from potentially siring more offspring, so the line's been diluted.

You're not what he was after, and in fact, according to what we know, what we can speculate, you are part of what's going to give me, Cal, and Gage the advantage this time around. You're afraid of him, of what's in you? Consider Twisse is afraid of you, of what's in you. Why else has he tried to scare you off?"

"Good answer." Quinn rubbed her hand over Cal's.

"Part two," Fox continued. "It's not just a matter of immunity to the power he has to cause people to commit violent, abnormal acts. It's a matter of having some aspect of that power, however diluted, that when pooled together is going to end him, once and for all."

Layla studied Fox's face. "You believe that?"

He started to answer, then took her hand, tightening his grip when she started to pull it free. "You tell me."

She struggled—he could see it, and he could feel it, that initial and instinctive shying away from accepting the link with him. He had to resist the urge to push, and simply left himself open. And even when he felt the click, he waited.

"You believe it," Layla said slowly. "You . . . you see us as six strands braided together into one rope."

"And we're going to hang Twisse with it."

"You love them so much. It's—"

"Ah . . ." It was Fox who pulled away, flustered and embarrassed that she'd seen more, gone deeper than he'd expected. "So, now that we've got that settled, I want another beer."

He headed into the kitchen, and as he turned from the refrigerator with a beer in his hand, Layla stepped in.

"I'm so sorry. I didn't mean to—"

"It's nothing. No big."

"It *is*. I just . . . It was like being inside your head, or your heart, and I saw—or felt—this wave of love, that connection you have to Gage and Cal. It wasn't what you asked me to do, and it was so intrusive."

"Okay, look, it's a tricky process. I was a little more

open than I should've been because I figured you needed me to be. The fact is, you don't need as much help as I thought. As you thought."

"No, you're wrong. I do need help. I need you to teach me." She walked to the window to look out at the dark. "Because Gage was right. If I keep letting this be a problem for me, it's a problem for all of us. And if I'm going to use this ability, I have to be able to control it so I'm not walking into people's heads right and left."

"We'll start working on it tomorrow."

She nodded. "I'll be ready." And turned. "Would you tell the others I went on up? It's been a very strange day."

"Sure."

For a moment, she just stood, looking at him. "I want to say, and I'm sorry if it embarrasses you, but there's something exceptional about a man who has the capacity to love as deeply as you do. Cal and Gage are lucky to have a friend like you. Anyone would be."

"I'm your friend, Layla."

"I hope so. Good night."

He stayed where he was after she'd gone, reminding himself to stay her friend. To stay what she needed, when she needed it.

Three

~◊~

IN THE DREAM IT WAS SUMMER. THE HEAT GRIPPED with sweaty hands, squeezing and wringing out energy like water out of a rag. In Hawkins Wood, leaves spread thick and green overhead, but the sun forced its way through in laser beams to flash into his eyes. Berries ripened on the thorny brambles, and the wild lilies bloomed in unearthly orange.

He knew his way. It seemed Fox had always known his way through these trees, down these paths. His mother would have called it sensory memory, he thought. Or past-life flashes.

He liked the quiet that was country woods—the low hum of insects, the faint rustle of squirrels or rabbits, the melodic chorus of birds with little more to do on a hot summer day but sing and wing.

Yes, he knew his way here, knew the sounds here, knew even the feel of the air in every season, for he had walked here in every season. Melting summers, burgeoning springs,

brisk autumns, brutal winters. So he recognized the chill in
the air when it crawled up his spine, and the sudden change
of light, the gray tinge that wasn't the simplicity of a stray
cloud over the sun. He knew the soft growl that came from
behind, from in front, and choked off the music of the
chickadees and jays.

He continued to walk the path to Hester's Pool.

Fear walked with him. It trickled along his skin like
sweat, urged him to run. He had no weapon, and in the
dream didn't question why he would come here alone, unarmed. When the trees—denuded now—began to bleed, he
kept on. The blood was a lie; the blood was fear.

He stopped only when he saw the woman. She stood at
the small dark pond, her back to him. She bent, gathering
stones, filling her pockets with them.

Hester. Hester Deale. In the dream he called out to her,
though he knew she was doomed. He couldn't go back
hundreds of years and stop her from drowning herself. Nor
could he stop himself from trying.

So he called out to her as he hurried forward, as the
growling turned to a wet snicker of horrible amusement.

*Don't. Don't. It wasn't your fault. None of it was your
fault.*

When she turned, when she looked into his eyes, it
wasn't Hester, but Layla. Tears streaked her face like bitter
rain, and her face was white as bone.

*I can't stop. I don't want to die. Help me. Can't you
help me?*

Now he began to run, to run toward her, but the path
stretched longer and longer, the snickering grew louder
and louder. She held out her hands to him, a final plea before she fell into the pool, and vanished.

He leaped. The water was viciously, brutally cold. He
dove down, searching until his burning lungs sent him up
to gulp in air. A storm raged in the woods now, wild red
lightning, cracking thunder, sparking fires that engulfed

entire trees. He dove again, calling for Layla with his mind.

When he saw her, he plunged deeper.

Once again their eyes met, once again she reached for him.

She embraced him. Her mouth took his in a kiss that was as cold as the water. And she dragged him down to drown.

HE WOKE GASPING FOR AIR, HIS THROAT RAW AND burning. His chest pounded with pain as he fumbled for the light, as he shoved up and over to sit on the side of the bed and catch his laboring breath.

Not in the woods, not in the pond, he told himself, but in his own bed, in his own apartment. As he pressed the heels of his hands to his eyes he reminded himself he should be used to the nightmares. He and Cal and Gage had been plagued by them every seven years since they'd turned ten. He should be used, too, to pulling aspects of the dream back with him.

He was still chilled, his skin shivering spasmodically over frigid bones. The iron taste of the pool's water still coated his throat. Not real, he thought. No more real than bleeding trees or fires that didn't burn. Just another nasty jab by a demon from hell. No permanent damage.

He rose, left the bedroom, crossed his living room, and went into the kitchen. He pulled a cold bottle of water out of the fridge and drank half of it down as he stood.

When the phone rang, he felt a fresh spurt of alarm. Layla's number was displayed on the caller ID. "What's wrong?"

"You're okay." Her breath came out in a long, jerky whoosh. "You're okay."

"Why wouldn't I be?"

"I . . . God, it's three in the morning. I'm sorry. Panic attack. I woke you up. Sorry."

"You didn't wake me up. Why wouldn't I be okay, Layla?"

"It was just a dream. I shouldn't have called you."

"We were at Hester's Pool."

There was a moment of silence. "I killed you."

"As attorney for the defense, I have to advise that's going to be a hard case to prosecute, as the victim is currently alive and well and standing in his own kitchen."

"Fox—"

"It was a dream. A bad one, but still a dream. He's playing on your weakness, Layla." And mine, Fox realized, because I want to save the girl. "I can come over. We'll—"

"No, no, I feel stupid enough calling you. It was just so real, you know?"

"Yeah, I do."

"I didn't think, I just grabbed the phone. All right, calmer now. We'll need to talk about this tomorrow."

"We will. Try to get some sleep."

"You, too. And Fox, I'm glad I didn't drown you in Hester's Pool."

"I'm pretty happy about that myself. Good night."

Fox carried the bottle of water back to the bedroom. There, he stood looking out the window that faced the street. The Hollow was quiet, and still as a photograph. Nothing stirred. The people he loved, the people he knew, were safe in their beds.

But he stood there, watchful in the dark, and thought about a kiss that had been cold as the grave. And still seductive.

"CAN YOU REMEMBER ANY OTHER DETAILS?" CYBIL wrote notes on Layla's dream as Layla finished off her coffee.

"I think I gave you everything."

"Okay." Cybil leaned back in the kitchen chair, tapped

her pencil. "The way it sounds, you and Fox had the same dream. It'll be interesting to see if they were exact, or how the details vary."

"Interesting."

"And informative. You could've woke me, Layla. We all know what it's like to have these nightmares."

"I felt steadier after I'd spoken to Fox, and he wasn't dead." She managed a small smile. "Plus, I don't need to be shrink-wrapped to figure out that part of the dream was rooted in what we talked about last night. My fear of hurting one of you."

"Especially Fox."

"Maybe especially. I'm working for him, for now. And I need to work with him. You and I and Quinn, we're, well, fish in the same pool. I'm not as worried about the two of you. You'll tell Quinn about the dream."

"As soon as she's back from her workout. Since I assume she dragged Cal to the gym with her, she'll probably talk him into coming back here for coffee. I can tell them both, and someone will fill Gage in. Gage was a little rough on you last night."

"He was."

"You needed it."

"Maybe I did." No point in whining about it, Layla thought. "Let me ask you something. You and Gage are going to have to work together, too, at some point. How's that going to work?"

"I'll cross that bridge when. And I think we'll figure out a way to handle it without shedding each other's blood."

"If you say so. I'm going to go up and get dressed, get to work."

"Do you want a ride in?"

"No, thanks. The walk'll do me good."

Layla took her time. Alice Hawbaker would be manning the office, and there would be little to do. With Alice there, Layla didn't think it would be wise to huddle with Fox over a

shared dream. Nor would it be the best time to have a lesson on honing and, more important to her, controlling her ability.

She'd handle busywork for a couple of hours, run whatever errands Alice might have on tap. It had taken her only a few days to understand the rhythm of the office. If she had any interest or aspirations toward managing a law office, Fox's practice would have been just fine.

As it was, it would bore her senseless within weeks.

Which wasn't the point, Layla reminded herself as she deliberately headed to the Square. The point was to help Fox, to earn a paycheck, and to keep busy.

She stopped at the Square. And that was another point. She could stand here, she thought, she could look at the broken or boarded windows straight-on. She could tell herself to face what had happened to her the evening before, promise herself she would do all she could to stop it.

She turned, started down Main Street to cover the few blocks to Fox's office.

It was a nice town if you just overlooked what happened to it, in it, every seven years. There were lovely old houses along Main, pretty little shops. It was busy in the way small towns were busy. Steady, with familiar faces running the errands and making the change at the cash registers. There was a comfort in that, she supposed.

She liked the wide porches, the awnings, the tidy front yards and bricked sidewalks. It was a pleasant, quaint place, at least on the surface, and not quite postcardy enough to make it annoying.

The town's rhythm was another she'd tuned to quickly. People walked here, stopped to have a word with a neighbor or a friend. If she crossed the street to Ma's Pantry, she'd be greeted by name, asked how she was doing.

Halfway down the block she stopped in front of the little gift shop where she'd picked up some odds and ends for the house. The owner stood out front, staring up at her broken windows. When she turned, Layla saw the tears.

"I'm sorry." Layla walked to her. "Is there something—"

The woman shook her head. "It's just glass, isn't it? Just glass and things. A lot of broken things. A couple of those damn birds got through, wrecked half my stock. It was like they wanted to, like they were drunks at a party. I don't know."

"I'm so sorry."

"I tell myself, well, you've got insurance. And Mr. Hawkins'll fix the windows. He's a good landlord, and those windows will be fixed right away. But it doesn't seem to matter."

"I'd be heartbroken, too," Layla told her, and laid a hand on her arm for comfort. "You had really pretty things."

"Broken now. Seven years back a bunch of kids—we think—busted in and tore the place up. Broke everything they could, wrote obscenities on the walls. It was hard coming back from that, but we did it. I don't know if I've got the heart to do it again. I don't know if I have the heart." The woman walked back to her shop, went inside behind the broken glass.

Not just broken glass and broken things, Layla thought as she walked on. Broken dreams, too. One vicious act could shatter so much.

Her own heart was heavy when she walked into the reception area. Mrs. Hawbaker sat at the desk, fingers clicking away at the keyboard. "Morning!" She stopped and gave Layla a smile. "Don't you look nice."

"Thanks." Layla slipped off her jacket, hung it in the foyer closet. "A friend of mine in New York packed up my clothes, shipped them down for me. Can I get you some coffee, or is there anything you want me to get started on?"

"Fox said to ask you to go on back when you got in. He's got about thirty minutes before an appointment, so you go ahead."

"All right."

"I'll be leaving at one today. Be sure to remind Fox he's

in court in the morning. It's on his calendar, and I sent him a memo, but it's best to remind him at the end of the day, too."

"No problem."

From her observations, Layla thought as she walked down the hall, Fox wasn't nearly as forgetful or absent-minded as he and Alice liked to think. Since the pocket doors to his office were open, she started to knock on the edge as she entered. Then she just stopped and stared.

He stood in back of his desk in front of the window in his no-court-today jeans and untucked shirt, juggling three red balls. His legs were spread, his face absolutely relaxed, and those tiger eyes of his following the circle as his hands caught and tossed, caught and tossed.

"You can juggle."

She broke his rhythm, but he managed to catch two balls in one hand, one in the other before they went flying around the room. "Yeah. It helps me think."

"You can juggle," she repeated, dazed and delighted.

Because it was rare to see her smile just that way, he sent the balls circling again. "It's all timing." When she laughed, he shot them high, began to walk and turn as he tossed the balls. "Three objects, even four, same size and weight, not really a challenge. If I'm looking for a challenge I mix it up. This is just think juggling."

"Think juggling," she repeated as he caught the balls again.

"Yeah." He opened his desk drawer, dropped them in. "Helps clear my head when I'm . . ." He got a good look at her. "Wow. You look . . . good."

"Thanks." She'd worn a skirt and a short, cinched jacket and now wondered if it was too upscale for her current position. "I got the rest of my clothes, and I thought since I had them . . . Anyway, you wanted to see me."

"I did? I did," he remembered. "Wait." He crossed to the doors, slid them closed. "Do you want anything?"

"No."

"Okay." His juggling-clear head was fogged up again thanks to her legs, so he went to his minifridge and took out a Coke. "I thought, since there's some time this morning, we should compare notes about the dream. Let's sit down."

She took one of the visitors' chairs, and Fox took the other. "You go first," she told him.

When he'd finished, he got up, opened his little fridge, and took out a bottle of Diet Pepsi. When he put it into her hand and she just stared at it, he sat again. "That's what you drink, right? That's what's stocked in the fridge at your place."

"Yes. Thanks."

"Do you want a glass?"

She shook her head. The simple consideration shouldn't have surprised her, and yet it did. "Do you keep Diet Sprite in there for Alice?"

"Sure. Why not?"

"Why not," she murmured, then drank. "I was in the woods, too," Layla began. "But it wasn't just me. She was in my head, or I was in hers. It's hard to tell. I felt her despair, her fear, like they were mine. I . . . I've never been pregnant, never had a child, but my body felt different." She hesitated, then told herself she'd been able to give Cybil the details. She could give them to Fox. "My breasts were heavy, and I understood, I *knew*, I'd nursed. In the same way I'd experienced her rape. It was that same kind of awareness. I knew where I was going."

She paused again, shifted so she could look at his face. He had a way of listening, she thought, so that she knew he not only heard every word, but also understood what came behind them. "I don't know those woods, have only been in them that one time, but I knew where I was, and I knew I was going to the pond. I knew why. I didn't want to go. I didn't want to go there, but I couldn't stop myself. I couldn't stop her. I was screaming inside because I didn't want to die, but she did. She couldn't stand it anymore."

"Couldn't stand what?"

"She remembered. She remembered the rape, how it felt, what was in her. She remembered, Fox, the night in the clearing. He—it—controlled her so that she accused Giles Dent of her rape, denounced him and Ann Hawkins as witches, and she assumed they were dead. She couldn't live with the guilt. He told her to run."

"Who?"

"Dent. In the clearing, just before the fire, he looked at her—he pitied her, he forgave her. He told her to run. She ran. She was only sixteen. Everyone thought the child was Dent's, and pitied her for that. She knew, but was afraid to recant. Afraid to speak."

It pierced her as she spoke of it. That fear, that horror and despair. "She was afraid all the time, Fox, and mad with that fear, that guilt, those memories by the time she delivered the child. I felt it all, it was all swimming inside her—and me. She wanted to end it. She wanted to take the child with her, and end that, too, but she couldn't bring herself to do it."

Those alert and compassionate eyes narrowed on Layla's face. "She thought about killing the baby?"

As she nodded, Layla drew air in slowly. "She feared it, and hated it, and still she loved it. It, not she. I mean—"

"Hester thought of the baby as 'it.'"

"Yes. Yes. But still, she couldn't kill the baby. If she had—I thought, when I understood that, if she had, I wouldn't be here. She gave me life by sparing the child, and now she was going to kill me because I was trapped with her. We walked, and if she heard me she must've thought I was one of the voices driving her mad. I couldn't make her listen, couldn't make her understand. Then I saw you."

She paused to drink again, to steady herself. "I saw you, and I thought, Thank God. Thank God, he's here. I could feel the stones in my hand when she picked them up, feel the weight of them dragging down the pockets of the dress we wore. There was nothing I could do, but I thought—"

"You thought I'd stop her." So had he, Fox mused. Save the girl.

"You were calling out, telling her it wasn't her fault. You ran to her—to me. And for an instant, I think she heard you. I think, I felt, she wanted to believe you. Then we were in the water, going down. I couldn't tell if she fell or jumped, but we were under the water. I told myself not to panic. Don't panic. I'm a good swimmer."

"Captain of the swim team."

"I told you that?" She managed a small laugh, wet her throat again. "I told myself I could get to the surface, even with the weight, I'm a strong swimmer. But I couldn't. Worse, I couldn't even try. It wasn't just the stones weighing me down."

"It was Hester."

"Yes. I saw you in the water, diving down, and then . . ." She closed her eyes, pressed her lips hard together.

"It's okay." Reaching over, he closed a hand over hers. "We're okay."

"Fox, I don't know if it was her, or if I . . . I don't know. We grabbed on to you."

"You kissed me."

"We killed you."

"We all came to a bad end, but it didn't actually happen. However vivid and sensory, it wasn't real. It was a hard way for you to get inside Hester Deale's head, but now we know more about her."

"Why were you there?"

"Best guess? We've got this link, you and me. I've shared dreams with Cal and Gage before. Same thing. But there was more this time, another level of connection. In the dream, I saw you, Layla. Not Hester. I heard you. That's interesting. Something to think about."

"When you juggle."

He grinned. "Couldn't hurt. We need to—"

His intercom buzzed. "Mr. Edwards is here."

Fox rose, flipped the switch on his desk. "Okay, give me a minute." He turned back to Layla as she rose. "We need some more time on this. My last appointment today's at—"

"Four. Mrs. Halliday."

"Right. You're good. If you're not booked, we could go upstairs after my last appointment, do some work on this."

It was time, Layla thought, to suit up. "All right."

He walked to the doors with her, slid them open. "We could have some dinner," he began.

"I don't want you to go to any trouble."

"I have every delivery place within a five-mile radius on speed dial."

She smiled a little. "Good plan."

He walked out with her to where two hundred and twenty pounds of Edwards filled a chair in reception. His belly, covered in a white T-shirt, pillowed over the waistband of his jeans. His scrubby gray hair was topped by a John Deere gimme cap. He pushed to his feet, held out a hand to clasp the one Fox offered.

"How you doing?" Fox asked.

"You tell me."

"Come on back, Mr. Edwards. We'll talk about it."

Works outside, Layla decided as Fox led his client back. A farmer maybe, or a builder, a landscaper. A couple clicks over sixty, and discouraged.

"What's his story, Alice? Can you tell me?"

"Property dispute," Alice said as she gathered up envelopes. "Tim Edwards has a farm a few miles south of town. Developers bought some of the land that runs with it. Survey puts some eight acres of Tim's land over the line. Developer wants it, so does Tim. I'm going to run to the post office."

"I can do that."

Alice wagged a finger. "Then I wouldn't get the walk or the gossip. I've got notes here on a trust Fox is putting together. Why don't you draft that out while I'm gone?"

Alone, Layla sat, got to work. Within ten minutes, she wondered why people needed such complicated, convoluted language to say the straightforward. She picked her way through it, answered the phone, made appointments. When Alice came back, she had questions. She noted that Edwards walked out looking considerably less discouraged.

By one o'clock, she was on her own and pleased to print out the trust Alice had proofed for her. By page two, the printer signaled its cartridge was out of ink. She went to the supply closet across from the pretty little law library hoping Fox stocked backups. She spotted the box on the top shelf.

Why was it always the top shelf? she wondered. Why were there top shelves anyway when not everyone in the world was six feet tall? She rose to her toes, stretched up and managed to nudge a corner of the carton over the edge of the shelf. With one hand braced on a lower shelf, she wiggled it out another inch.

"I'm going out to grab some lunch," Fox said from behind her. "If you want anything— Here, let me get that."

"I've almost got the damn thing now."

"Yeah, and it's going to fall on your head."

He leaned in, reached up, just as she turned.

Their bodies brushed, bumped. Her face tipped up, filled his vision as her scent slid around him like satin ribbons. Those sea-siren eyes made him feel a little drunk and a lot needy. He thought: Step back, O'Dell. Then he made the mistake of letting his gaze drop down to her mouth. And he was done.

He angled down, another inch, heard her breath draw in. Her lips parted, and he closed that last whisper of distance. A small, soft taste, then another, both feather light. Then her lashes swept down over those seductive eyes; her mouth brushed his.

The kiss went deeper, a slow slide into heat that tangled

his senses, that filled them with her until all he wanted was to sink and sink and sink. And drown.

She made some sound, pleasure, distress, he couldn't tell with the blood roaring in his ears. But it reminded him where they were. How they were. He broke the kiss, realized he was essentially shoving her into the storage closet.

"Sorry. I'm sorry." She was working for him, for God's sake. "I shouldn't have. That was inappropriate. It was—" Amazing. "It was . . ."

"Fox?"

He jerked back an entire foot at the voice behind him. When he whirled around, he could feel his stomach drop straight to his knees. "Mom."

"Sorry to interrupt." She gave Fox a sunny smile, then turned it on Layla. "Hi. I'm Joanne Barry. Fox's mother."

Why was there never a handy hole in the floor when you needed one? Layla thought. "It's nice to meet you, Ms. Barry. I'm Layla Darnell."

"I told you Layla's helping me out in the office. We were just . . ."

"Yes, you were."

Still smiling, she left it at that.

She was the kind of woman you'd probably stare at even if you weren't stunned stupid, Layla thought. There was all that rich brown hair waving wild around a strong-boned face with its full, unpainted mouth, and long hazel eyes that managed to look amused, curious, and patient all at once. Joanne had the tall, willowy build that carried the low-slung jeans, boots, and skinny sweater look perfectly.

Since it appeared Fox had been struck dumb, Layla managed to clear her throat. "I, ah, needed a new cartridge. For the printer? It's on the top shelf."

"Right. Right. I was getting that." Fox turned, managed to collide with Layla again. "Sorry." Jesus Christ. He'd no more than pulled the box down when Layla snatched it away, and fled.

"Thanks!"

"Do you have a minute for me?" Jo asked sweetly. "Or do you need to get back to what you were doing when I came in?"

"Cut it out." Fox hunched his shoulders, led the way back to his office.

"She's very pretty. Who could blame you for playing a little boss and secretary?"

"Mom." Now he dragged his hands through his hair. "It wasn't like that. It was . . . Never mind." He dropped into a chair. "What's up?"

"I had some things to do in town. One of which was to drop by your sister's for lunch. Sparrow tells me she hasn't seen you in there for two weeks."

"I've been meaning to."

Jo leaned back against his desk. "Eating something that isn't fried, processed, and full of chemicals once a week won't kill you, Fox. And you should be supporting your sister."

"Okay. I'll go in today."

"Good. Second, I had some pottery to take into Lorrie's. You must've seen what happened to her shop."

"Not specifically." He thought of the smashed windows, the corpses of crows on Main Street. "How bad's the damage?"

"It's bad." Jo lifted a hand to the trio of crystals that hung from a chain around her neck. "Fox, she's talking about closing. Moving away. It breaks my heart. And it scares me. I'm scared for you."

He rose, put his arms around her, rubbed his cheek against hers. "It's going to be okay. We're working on it."

"I want to do something. Your dad and I, all of us, we want to do something."

"You've done something every day of my entire life." He gave her a squeeze. "You've been my mom."

She eased back to take his face in her hands. "You get

that charm from your father. Look right at me and reassure me it's going to be okay."

Without hesitation or guile, his eyes met hers. "It's going to be okay. Trust me."

"I do." She kissed his forehead, his cheek, then the other, then gave him a light peck on the lips. "But you're still my baby. I expect you to take good care of my baby. Now go have lunch at your sister's. Her eggplant salad's on special today."

"Yummy."

Tolerant, she gave him a light poke in the belly. "You ought to close the office for an hour and take that pretty girl to lunch with you."

"The pretty girl works for me."

"How did I manage to raise such a rule follower? It's disheartening." She gave him another poke before starting for the door. "I love you, Fox."

"I love you, Mom. And I'll walk out with you," he added quickly, realizing his mother would have no compunction about stopping by Layla's desk and pumping the pretty girl for information.

"I'll have another chance to get her alone and grill her," Jo said casually.

"Yeah. But not today."

THE SALAD WASN'T BAD, AND SINCE HE'D EATEN at the counter he'd had a little time to hang with his baby sister. Since she never failed to put him in a good mood, he walked back to his office appreciating the sunny, blustery day. He'd have appreciated it more if he hadn't run into Derrick Napper, his childhood nemesis, as the now Deputy Napper came out of the barbershop.

"Well, hell, it's O'Dell." Napper slipped on his dark glasses, looked up, then down the street. "Funny, I don't see any ambulances to chase."

"Did you get that buzz cut on the town nickel? Some-body overpaid."

Napper's smile spread thin on his tough, square face. "I heard you were at the scene yesterday when there was trou-ble at the Square. Didn't stand by and give a statement, or come in to file a witness report. Being the town shyster, you ought to know better."

"You'd be wrong on that, nothing new there. I stopped by and spoke to the chief this morning. I guess he doesn't tell his bootlickers everything."

"You ought to remember how many times my boot kicked your ass in the past, O'Dell."

"I remember a lot of things." Fox walked by. Once a bully, he thought, always an asshole. Before the Seven was over, he imagined he and Napper would tangle again. But for now, he put it out of his mind.

He had work to do, and as he opened the door of his of-fice, admitted he had a road to smooth out. Might as well get it done.

As he came in, Layla walked toward reception holding a vase of the flowers Alice Hawbaker liked having in the of-fices. Layla stopped dead.

"I was just giving these fresh water. There weren't any calls while you were gone, but I finished the trust and printed it out. It's on your desk."

"Good. Listen, Layla—"

"I wasn't sure if there was anything to type up regarding Mr. Edwards, or—"

"Okay, okay, put those down." He settled it by taking the vase out of her hands and setting it on a table.

"They actually go over—"

"Stop. I was out of line, and I apologize."

"You already did."

"I'm apologizing again. I don't want you to feel weirded out because in the office we've got the employer-employee

thing going on, and I made a move on you. I didn't intend . . .
Your mouth was just there."

"My mouth was just there?" Her tone changed from
flustered to dangerously sweet. "As in on my face, under
my nose, and above my chin?"

"No." He rubbed his fingers in the center of his forehead. "Yes, but no. Your mouth was . . . I forgot not to do
what I did, which was completely inappropriate under the
circumstances. And I'm going to start pleading the Fifth in
a minute, or maybe just temporary insanity."

"You can plead whatever you want, but you may want to
consider that my mouth, which was just there, wasn't forming words like *no*, or *stop*, or *get the hell away from me*.
Which it's perfectly capable of doing."

"Okay." He said nothing for a moment. "This is very
awkward."

"Before or after we add your mother into it?"

"That moves it from awkward to farce." He slipped his
hands into his pockets. "Should I assume you're not going
to engage counsel and sue me for sexual harassment?"

She angled her head. "Should I assume you're not going
to fire me?"

"I'm voting yes to both questions. So we're good here?"

"Dandy."

She picked up the vase and carried it to the right table.
"By the way, I ordered another replacement cartridge for
the printer." She slid a glance his way, lips just curved.

"Good thinking. I'll be—" He gestured toward his office.

"And I'll be—" She pointed to her desk.

"Okay." He started back. "Okay," he repeated, then
looked at the supply closet. "Oh boy."

Four

꧁

AT FOUR FORTY-FIVE, FOX WALKED HIS LAST client of the day to the door. Outside, March was kicking thin brown leaves along the sidewalk, and a couple of kids in hoodies walked straight into the whooshing wind. Probably going up to the arcade at the bowling center, he mused. Squeeze in a couple of games before dinner.

There'd been a day he'd have walked through the wind for a couple of games of Galaxia. In fact, he thought, he'd done that last week. If that made him twelve on some level, he could live with it. Some things shouldn't change.

He heard Layla speaking on the phone, telling the caller that Mr. O'Dell was in court tomorrow, but she could make an appointment for later in the week.

When he turned she was keying it into the computer, into the calendar, he supposed, in her efficient way. From his angle he could see her legs in the opening of the desk, the way she tapped a foot as she worked. The silver she wore at her ears glinted as she swiveled to hang up the

phone, then her gaze shifted to meet his. And the muscles of his belly quivered.

He definitely wasn't twelve on this particular level. Thank God some things did change.

It must've been the goofy smile on his face that had her cocking her head at him. "What?"

"Nothing. Just a little internal philosophy. Anything important on that call?"

"Not urgent. It was only regarding a partnership agreement—a couple of women writing a series of cookbooks they believe are going to be bestsellers. Rachael Ray, step back, I'm told. They want to formalize their collaboration before they hit the big time. You have a busy schedule this week."

"Then I should be able to afford Chinese for dinner, if you're still up for it."

"I just need to shut down for the day."

"Go ahead. I'll do the same. We can go up through the kitchen."

In his office, Fox shut down his computer, shouldered his briefcase, then tried to remember exactly what state his apartment might be in.

Uh-oh. He realized he'd just hit another area at which he remained twelve.

Best not to think about it, he decided, since it was too late to do anything about it. Anyway, how bad could it be?

He walked into the kitchen where Mrs. Hawbaker kept the coffeemaker, the microwave, the dishes she'd deemed appropriate for serving clients. He knew she kept cookies in there, because he raided them routinely. And her vases, boxes of fancy teas.

Who'd stock cookies when Mrs. H deserted him? Wistfully, he turned when Layla came in.

"She buys the supplies with the proceeds from the F-word jar in my office. I tend to keep that pretty well funded. I guess she's told you."

"A dollar for every F-word, honor system. Since I've seen your jar, I'd say you're pretty free with the F-word, and honorable about it." He's so sad, she thought, and it made her want to cuddle him, to stroke the messy, waving hair. "I know you're going to miss her."

"Maybe she'll come back. Either way, life moves." He opened the door to the stairway. "I might as well tell you since Mrs. H doesn't deal with my apartment, and in fact, refuses to go up here since an unfortunate incident involving oversleeping and neglected laundry, it's probably a mess."

"I've seen messes before."

But when she stepped up from the tidy office kitchen into Fox's personal one, Layla understood she'd underestimated the definition of mess.

There were dishes in the sink, on the counter, and on the small table that was also covered with what appeared to be several days of newspapers. A couple boxes of cereal (did grown men actually eat Cocoa Puffs?), bags of chips, a bottle of red wine, some bottles of condiments, and an empty jug of Gatorade fought for position on the short counter beside a refrigerator all but wallpapered with sticky notes and snapshots.

There were three pairs of shoes on the floor, a battered jacket slung over one of the two kitchen chairs, and a stack of magazines towered on the other.

"Maybe you want to go away for an hour, or possibly a week, while I deal with this."

"No. No. Is the rest this bad?"

"I don't remember. I can go check before—"

But she was already stepping over shoes and into the living room.

It wasn't as bad, he thought. Not really. Deciding to be proactive, he moved by her and began to grab up the debris. "I live like a pig, I know, I know. I've heard it all before." He stuffed an armload of discarded clothes into the neglected hall closet.

Sheer bafflement covered her face, coated her voice. "Why don't you hire a housekeeper, someone to come in once a week and deal with this?"

"Because they run away and never come back. Look, we'll go out." It wasn't embarrassment—hey, his place—as much as fear of a lecture that had him snatching up an empty beer bottle and a nearly empty bowl of popcorn from the coffee table. "We'll find a nice, sanitary restaurant."

"I roomed with two girls in college. I had to call in the Hazmat team at the end of the semester." She picked up a pair of socks from a chair before he could get there, then handed them to him. "But if there's a clean glass I could use some of that wine."

"I'll put one in an autoclave."

He grabbed more on his way back to the kitchen. Curious, Layla looked around the room, tried to see beyond the disarray. The walls were actually a very nice sagey shade of green, a warm tone that set off the wide oak trim around the windows. A gorgeous woven rug that might have been vacuumed sometime in the last decade spread across a wide-planked floor of deep, dark wood. The art on the walls was lovely—watercolors, pen-and-ink sketches, photographs. The room might've been dominated by a big, flat-screen TV, and a flurry of components, but there was some beautiful pottery.

His brother's, she imagined, or his mother's. He'd shown her his younger brother's pottery business from the road once. She turned when she sensed Fox come in again.

"I love the art, and the pottery. This piece." She trailed a finger along a long, slender bottle in dreamy shades of blue. "It's so fluid."

"My mother's work. My brother, Ridge, did that bowl on the table under the window."

She walked to it. "It's gorgeous." She traced the gentle curve of its lip. "And the colors, the shapes of them. It's like a forest in a wide cup."

She turned back to take the glass of wine. "How about the art?"

"My mother, my brother, my sister-in-law. The photographs are Sparrow's, my younger sister."

"A lot of talent in one family."

"Then there are the lawyers, my older sister and me."

"Practicing law doesn't take talent?"

"It takes something."

She sipped her wine. "Your father's a carpenter, isn't he?"

"Carpentry, cabinetmaking. He made the table Ridge's bowl's on."

"Made the table." Now she crouched to get a closer look. "Imagine that."

"No nails, no screws. Tongue and groove. He's got magic hands."

She swiped a finger over the surface, through the dust. "The finish is like satin. Beautiful things." Eyebrows lifted, she rubbed her finger clean on the sleeve of Fox's shirt. "I'm forced to say you should take better care of them, and their environment."

"You wouldn't be the first. Why don't I distract you with food?" He held out a paper menu. "Han Lee's China Kitchen."

"It's a little early for dinner."

"I'll call ahead, tell them to deliver at seven. That way we can get some work done."

"Sweet and sour pork," she decided after a glance at the menu.

"That's it?" he asked when she handed it back to him. "Pitiful. Sweet and sour pork. I'll take care of the rest."

He left her again to make the call. A few minutes later she heard the sound of water running, dishes clinking. Rolling her eyes, she walked into the kitchen where he was attacking the dishes.

"Okay." Layla took off her jacket.

"No. Really."

"Yes." Rolled up her sleeves. "Really. One-time deal, since you're buying dinner."

"Should I apologize again?"

"Not this time." Her eyebrows lifted. "No dishwasher?"

"See, that's the problem. I keep thinking I should take out that bottom cabinet there, have one installed, but then I think, hey, it's just me, and I use paper plates a lot."

"Not often enough. Is there a clean dish towel somewhere?"

"Oh. Well." He gave her a befuddled frown. "Be right back."

Shaking her head, Layla stepped up to the sink he'd deserted and took over. She didn't mind. It was a mindless chore, oddly relaxing and satisfying. Plus there was a nice view from the window over the sink, one that stretched out to the mountains where the sunlight sprinkled over the steely peaks.

The wind was still kicking at the trees, and it billowed the white sheets hanging on a line in the yard below. She imagined the sheets would smell like the wind and the mountains when they were tucked onto their bed.

A little boy and a big black dog ran around a fenced yard with such joy and energy in the gallop she could almost feel the wind on her own cheeks, rushing through her hair. When the boy in his bright blue coat leaped up to stand on his swing, his fingers tight on the chains, the thrill of height and speed pitched into Layla's belly.

Is his mother in the kitchen making dinner? she wondered dreamily. Or maybe it's the dad's turn to cook. Better, they're cooking together, stirring, chopping, talking about their day while the little boy lifts his face to the wind and flies.

"Who knew washing dishes could be so sexy?"

She laughed, glanced over her shoulder at Fox. "Don't think that's going to convince me to repeat the favor."

He stood where he was, a badly wrinkled dishcloth in his hand. "What?"

"Washing dishes is only sexy when you're not the one with your hands in the soapy water."

He came forward, put a hand on her arm. His eyes locked on hers. "I didn't say that out loud."

"I heard you."

"Apparently, but I was thinking, not talking. I was distracted," he continued when she took a step away from him, "by the way you looked, the way the light hit your hair, the line of your back, the curve of your arms. I was distracted," he repeated. "And open. What were you, Layla? Don't think, don't analyze. Just tell me what you were feeling when you 'heard' me."

"Relaxed. I was watching the little boy on the swing in the yard. I was relaxed."

"Now you're not." He picked up a plate, began to dry it. "So we'll wait until you are."

"You can do that, with me? Hear what I'm thinking?"

"Emotions come easier than words. But I wouldn't, unless you let me."

"You can do it with anyone."

He looked into her eyes. "But I wouldn't."

"Because you're the kind of man who puts a dollar in a jar, even if no one's around to hear you swear."

"If I give my word, I keep my word."

She washed another dish. The charm of sheets flapping in the wind, of a little boy and his big dog dissolved. "Did you always control it? Resist the temptation?"

"No. I was ten when I started tapping in. During the first Seven, it was scary, and I could barely keep a handle on it. But it helped. When it was over, that first time, I figured it would be gone."

"It wasn't."

"No. It was very cool to be ten and be able to sense what people were thinking, or feeling. It was big, and not just in the wow, I've got a superpower kind of thing. It was big because maybe I wanted to ace a history test, and the smartest

kid in history was right there in the next row. Why not reach in, get the answers?"

Since he was drying dishes, he decided to take the extra step and actually put them away. She'd be calmer if they continued with the chore, if all hands were busy. "After a few times, a few aces, I started feeling guilty about it. And weird because I might take a peek into a random teacher's head to see what they were planning to toss at us. And I'd get stuff I shouldn't have known about. Problems at home, that kind of thing. I was raised to respect privacy, and I was invading it right and left. So I stopped." He smiled a little. "Mostly."

"It helps that you're not perfect."

"It took time to figure out how to deal. Sometimes if I wasn't paying enough attention, things would slip through—sometimes if I was paying too much attention, ditto. And sometimes it was deliberate. There were a couple of events with this asshole who liked to razz me. And . . . when I got a little older, there was the girl thing. Take a quick sweep through and maybe I'd see if I had a shot at getting her shirt off."

"Did it work?"

He only smiled, and slid a plate into its cabinet. "Then a couple weeks before we turned seventeen, things started happening again. I knew—we knew—it wasn't finished after all. It came home to me that what I had wasn't something to play around with. I stopped."

"Mostly?"

"Almost entirely. It's there, Layla, it's part of us. I can't control the fact that I might get a sense from someone. I can control pushing in, pulling out more."

"That's what I have to learn."

"And you may have to learn to push. If it comes down to someone's privacy or their life, or the lives of others, you have to push in."

"But how do you know when—when, if, who?"

"We'll work on it."

"I'm not relaxed around you, most of the time."

"I've noticed. Why is that?"

She turned away to get more dishes, then slid a bowl into the sink. The little boy had gone inside, she noted. In to eat dinner. His dog curled on the porch by the back door and slept off playtime.

"Because I'm aware you can, or could, sense what I think or feel. Or I worry that you can, so it makes me nervous. But you don't, because you hold back, or because I'm nervous enough to stop you. Maybe both. You didn't know what I was thinking, or feeling earlier today when you kissed me."

"My circuits were crossed at the time."

"We're attracted to each other. Would that be an accurate reading?"

"It's dead-on from my end."

"And that makes me nervous. It's also confusing, because I don't know how much we're picking up from each other, how much is just basic chemistry." Layla rinsed the bowl, passed it to Fox. "I don't know if this is something we should be dealing with, with everything else we have to worry about."

"Let's back up, just a little. Are you nervous because I'm attracted to you, or because we're attracted to each other?"

"Door number two, and I don't have to see inside your head when I can see by your face you like that idea."

"Best damn idea I've heard in weeks. Possibly years."

She planted a wet, soapy hand on his shirt as he started to lean in. "I can't relax if I'm thinking about going to bed with you. The idea of sex generally stirs me up."

"We could relax later. In fact, I can guarantee we'll be a lot more relaxed later if we finish the stirring-up part first."

She not only left her hand planted, but nudged him a full step back with it. "No doubt. But I compartmentalize things. It's how I'm built, it's how I work. This, between

us, I have to put it in another compartment for a while. I have to think about it, worry about it, wonder about it. If I'm going to learn from you, if I'm going to help end what wants to end us, I need to focus on that."

His expression sober and attentive, he nodded. "I like to juggle."

"I know."

"And I like to negotiate. And." He dried her hand, then brought it to his lips. "I know when to let the opposing party consider all the options. I want you. Naked. In bed, in a room filled with shadows and quiet music. I want to feel your heart pound against my hand while I do things to you. So put that in your compartment, Layla."

He tossed aside his dishcloth as she stared at him. "I'm going to go get your wine. It should help you relax some before we get to work."

She was still staring when he strolled out. She managed to press a hand to her heart, and yes, it was pounding.

Obviously, she had a lot to learn if he'd had that in him and she hadn't sensed it.

It was going to take more than a glass of red wine to help her relax now.

SHE DRANK THE WINE; HE CLEARED OFF THE kitchen table. Then he poured her another glass. She didn't say a word, and he gave her room for silence, room for her thoughts until he sat.

"Okay, do you know how to meditate?"

"I know the concept." There was a thin edge of irritation in her tone. He didn't mind it.

"You ought to sit down so we can get started. The thing about meditating," he began when she joined him, "is most people can't really reach that level where they turn their minds off, where there's not something in there about work or their dentist appointment, the ache in their lower back.

Whatever. But we can get close. Yoga breathing, using the breath. Closing your eyes, picturing a blank white wall—"

"And chanting 'ummm.' How is that going to help me tap in to this thing? I can't walk around in a meditative state."

"It's to help clear yourself out after. To help you—I sound like my mother—cleanse your mind, your aura, balance your chi."

"Please."

"It's a process, Layla. So far, you've only skimmed the surface of it, or dipped your toe in. The deeper you go, the more it takes out of you."

"Such as?"

"Too deep for too long? Headaches, nausea, nosebleeds. It can hurt. It can drain you."

She frowned, then ran her finger down the bowl of her glass. "When we were in the attic of the old library, Quinn had a flashback to Ann Hawkins. And she came out of it pretty shaken up. Severe headache, queasy, clammy." Layla puffed out her cheeks. "All right. I'm crappy at meditating. When we end with the corpse position in yoga class, I'm relaxed, but I'm going to be thinking of what I'm doing next, or if I should buy this great leather jacket that came in. I'll practice. I can practice with Cybil."

Because she's safer than I am, Fox thought, and let that go. "All right, let's just skim along the surface for right now. Relax, clear the clutter out of the front of your mind. Like when you were doing the dishes."

"It's harder when it's deliberate. Things want to pop in."

"That's right. So compartmentalize," he suggested with an easy smile. "Put them in their slot. Tuck them away. Look at me." His hand moved to rest on hers. "Just look at me. Focus on me. You know me."

She felt a little strange, as if the wine had gone straight to her head. "I don't understand you."

"That'll come. Look at me. It's like opening a door.

Turn the knob, Layla. Put your hand on the knob and turn it, ease the door open, just a couple inches. Look at me. What am I thinking?"

"You hope I don't eat all the pot stickers." She *felt* his humor, like a warm blue light. "You did that."

"We did that. Stay at the door. Stay focused. Open it just a little wider and tell me what I'm feeling."

"I . . . calm. You're so calm. I don't know how you manage it. I don't think I'm ever that calm, and now, with what's happened, what's happening, I don't know if I'll ever be really calm again. And . . . You're a little hungry."

"I pretended to eat most of an eggplant salad at lunch. Which is why I ordered . . ."

"Kung Pao beef, snow peas, cold noodles, a dozen egg rolls, pot stickers. A *dozen* egg rolls?"

"If there are any leftovers, they're good for breakfast."

"That's disgusting. And now you're thinking I'd be good for breakfast," she added and drew her hand from under his.

"Sorry, that slipped through. Doing okay?"

"A little light-headed, a lot dazed, but yeah, okay. It's going to be easier with you though, isn't it? Because you know how to work it. Work me."

Picking up his neglected beer, he tipped back in his chair. "A woman comes into the shop you managed in New York. She's just browsing around. How do you know where to direct her, how to work her?"

"Satisfy her," Layla corrected, "not work her. Some of it would be the way she looks—her age, how she's dressed, what kind of bag, what kind of shoes. Those are surface things, and can lead in the wrong direction, but they're a start. And I grew up in the business, so I have a sense of customer types."

"But I'm betting nine times out of ten you knew when to get the flashy leather purse out of the stockroom or steer her toward the conservative black one. If she said she wanted a

business suit, but really had a yen for a sexy little dress and fuck-me shoes."

"I had a lot of experience reading . . . Yes." She let out a hiss of breath, the annoyance self-directed. "I don't know why I keep resisting it. Yes, I'd often tune in. The owner called it my magic touch. I guess she wasn't far off."

"How did you do it?"

"If I'm assisting a customer, I'm, well, I'm focused on them, on what they want, what they like—and yeah, what I can sell them. You have to listen to what they say, and there's body language, and also my own sense of what would look great on them. And sometimes, I always thought it was instinct, I'd get a picture in my head of the dress or the shoes. I'd think it was reading between the lines of what they said when I chatted them up, but I might hear this little voice. Maybe it was their thoughts. I'm not sure."

She was easing into it, he thought, into acceptance of what she held inside her. "You were confident in what you were doing, sure of your ground, which is another kind of relaxation. And you cared. You wanted to get them what they really wanted or would work for them, make them happy. And make a sale. Right?"

"I guess so."

"Same program, different channel." He dug into his pocket, pulled out change. Cupping his palm away from her, he counted it out. "How much am I holding?"

"I—"

"The amount's in my head. Open the door."

"God. Wait." She took another sip of wine first. Too much running through her own head, Layla realized. Put it away. "Don't help me!" she snapped when he reached for her hand. "Just . . . don't."

Put it away, she repeated to herself. Clean it out. Relax. Focus. Why did he think she could do this? Why was he so sure? Why did so many men have such wonderful eye-

lashes? Oops. No side trips. She closed her eyes, visualized the door. "A dollar thirty-eight." Her eyes popped open. "Wow."

"Good job."

She jolted at the knock on the door.

"Delivery guy. Do him."

"What?"

"While I'm talking to him, paying him, read him."

"But that's—"

"Rude and intrusive, sure. We're going to sacrifice courtesy in the name of progress. Read him," Fox commanded as he rose and walked to the door. "Hey, Kaz, how's it going?"

The kid was about sixteen, Layla estimated. Jeans, sweatshirt, high-top Nikes that looked fairly new. Shaggy brown hair, small silver hoop in his right ear. His eyes were brown, and passed over her—lingered briefly—as bags and money changed hands.

She took a deep breath, nudged at the door.

Fox heard her make a sound behind him, something between a gasp and a snort. He kept on talking as he added the tip, made a comment about basketball.

After he closed the door, Fox set the bags on the table. "Well?"

"He thinks you're chill."

"I am."

"He thinks I'm hot."

"You are."

"He wondered if you're going to be getting any of that tonight and he wouldn't mind getting some of that himself. He didn't mean the egg rolls."

Fox opened the bags. "Kaz is seventeen. A guy that age is pretty much always thinking about getting some. Any headache?"

"No. He was easy. Easier than you."

He smiled at her. "Guys my age think about getting

some, too. But we usually know when it's just going to be egg rolls. Let's eat."

HE DIDN'T TRY TO KISS HER AGAIN, NOT EVEN when he drove her home. Layla couldn't tell if he thought about it, and decided that was for the best. Her own thoughts and feelings were a tangle of frayed knots, which told her she'd need to take Fox's advice and go for the meditation.

She found Cybil on the living room sofa with a book and a cup of tea.

"Hi. How'd it go?"

"It went well." Layla dropped into a chair. "Surprisingly well. I'm feeling a little buzzed, actually. Like I knocked back a couple of scotches."

"Want tea? There's more in the pot."

"Maybe."

"I'll get you a cup," Cybil said when Layla started to rise. "You look beat."

"Thanks." Closing her eyes, Layla tried the yoga breathing, tried to envision relaxing from the toes up. She made it to her ankles when she gave it up. "Fox says I should meditate," she told Cybil when Cybil came back with a fancy cup and saucer. "Meditation bores me."

"Then you're not doing it right. Try the tea first," she said as she poured some out. "And say what's on your mind, it's the best way to get it out of your mind so you can meditate."

"He kissed me."

"I'm shocked and amazed." Cybil handed Layla the cup, returned to the couch to curl her legs up. She gave a careless laugh when Layla frowned at her. "Sweetie, the guy's got those foxy Fox eyes on you all the time. He watches you leave the room, watches you come back in. Boy's got it bad."

"He said— Where's Quinn?"

"With Cal. Maverick found himself a card game, so Cal's house is empty for a change. They're taking advantage."

"Oh. Good for them. They're great together, aren't they? Just click, click."

"He's the one for her, no question. All the others she tried out were like O'Doul's."

"O'Doul's?"

"Near-love. Cal's the real deal. Easier to talk about them than you?"

Layla sighed. "It's confusing to feel this way. To feel him feeling this way, and to try not to feel him feeling it. Because that's only more confusing. Add in we're working together on multiple levels, and that creates a kind of intimacy, and that intimacy has to be respected, even protected because the stakes are so damn high. If you mix it up with the separate physical or emotional intimacy of personal relationship and sex, how do you maintain the basic order needed to do what we're all here to do?"

"Wow." Lips curved, Cybil sipped her tea. "That's a lot of thinking."

"I know."

"Try this. Simple and direct. Are you hot for him?"

"Oh God, yes. But—"

"No, no qualifiers. Don't analyze. Lust is an elemental thing, potent, energizing. Enjoy it. Whether you act on it or not, it gets the blood moving. You'll layer the rest onto it eventually. You'll have to. You're human and you're female. We have to layer on emotions and concerns, consequences. But take the opportunity to appreciate the right now." Cybil's dark eyes sparkled with humor. "Enjoy the lust."

Layla considered as she sampled her tea. "When you put it that way. It feels pretty good."

"When you finish your tea, we'll use your lust as your focus point to move into a meditation exercise." Cybil smiled over the rim of her cup. "I don't think you'll be bored."

Five

~~

CYBIL'S LUST-AS-SPRINGBOARD MEDITATION MIGHT'VE given Layla a fit of giggles initially, but then she thought she'd done pretty well. Better, certainly, than her usual faking-it method at yoga class. She'd breathed in the lust, as instructed—navel to spine—breathed out the tension, the stress. Focused on that "tickle in the belly" as Cybil had described it. Owned it.

Somewhere around the laughter, the breathing, and the tickle, she'd relaxed so fully she'd heard her own pulse beating. And that was a first.

She slept deep and dreamless, and woke refreshed. And, Layla had to admit, energized. Apparently, meditation didn't have to bore her senseless.

With Fox in court and Alice at the helm, there was no reason to go into the office until the afternoon. Time, she thought as she showered, to dive into research mode with Cybil and Quinn. To put her energy into finding more answers. She still hadn't added the incident at the Square to

her chart, or catalogued the dream both she and Fox had shared.

She dressed for the morning in jeans and a sweater before earmarking the afternoon wardrobe change for Secretary Layla. And that, she had to admit, was fun. It felt good to need to dress for work, to plan and consider the outfit, the accessories. In the weeks between leaving New York and starting at Fox's office, she'd been busy, certainly. She'd had enormous adjustments to make, monumental obstacles to face. But she'd missed working, missed knowing someone expected her to be in a certain place at a certain time to do specific tasks.

And, shallow or not, she'd missed having a reason to wear a great pair of boots.

As she headed out, intending to hit the kitchen for coffee, she heard the clacking of the keyboard from the office they'd set up in the fourth bedroom.

Quinn sat cross-legged in the chair, typing away. Her long blond hair swayed in its sleek tail as she bopped her head to some internal music.

"I didn't know you were back."

"Back." Quinn hammered a few more keys, then paused to look over. "Swung by the gym, worked off a few hundred calories, screwed that with an enormous blueberry muffin from the bakery, but I figure I'm still ahead considering the stupendous and energetic sex I enjoyed last night. Got coffee, got showered, and am now typing up Cybil's notes on your dream." Quinn stretched up her arms. "And I still feel like I could run the Boston Marathon."

"That must've been some sex."

"Oh boy, oh boy." Wiggling her butt in the chair, Quinn let out her big, bawdy laugh. "I always thought it was romance novel hype that sex was better when you're in love. But I'm living, and extraordinarily satisfied, proof. But that's nearly enough about me. How are you?"

If she hadn't woken feeling energized, Layla mused,

two minutes around Quinn would have perked her right up. "While not extraordinarily satisfied, I'm feeling pretty peppy myself. Is Cybil up?"

"In the kitchen, doing her morning coffee and newspaper thing. We passed briefly, and she grunted something along the lines that you made progress with Fox yesterday."

"Did she mention that we happened to find our lips colliding in the storage closet at his office when his mother came in?"

Quinn's bright blue eyes popped wide. "She wasn't coherent enough. You tell me."

"I just did."

"I require details."

"I require coffee. I'll be back."

Another thing she'd been missing, Layla realized. Having fun and personal details to share with girlfriends.

In the kitchen Cybil nibbled on half a bagel as she read the newspaper spread over the table. "Not a single mention of the crows in today's paper," she announced when Layla walked in. "It's extraordinary, really. Yesterday, a brief article, stingy on the details, and no follow-up."

"It's typical, isn't it?" Thoughtful, Layla poured coffee. "Nobody pays a lot of attention to what happens here. And when there are reports or questions, interest, it doesn't stick, or it comes across as lore."

"Even the people who've lived through it, who live here, gloss it over. Or it glosses over on them."

"Some that remember it too well leave." Layla decided on yogurt, took out a carton. "Like Alice Hawbaker."

"It's fascinating. Still, there aren't any other reports on animal attacks, or unexplained occurrences. Not today, anyway. Well." With a lazy shrug, Cybil started to fold the paper. "I'm going to go tug on a couple of very thin threads toward finding where Ann Hawkins lived for our missing two years. It's damned irritating," Cybil added as she rose.

"There weren't that many people around here in sixteen fifty-two. Why the hell can't I find the right ones?"

BY NOON, LAYLA HAD DONE ALL SHE COULD DO with her housemates. She changed into gray trousers and heeled boots for her afternoon in the office.

On her walk she noticed that the windows on the gift shop had been replaced. Cal's father was a conscientious landlord, one she knew had a lot of pride in his town. And she noticed the large, hand-printed Going Out of Business Sale sign that hung in the display window.

That was a damn shame, she thought as she walked on. The lives people built, or tried to build, tumbling down around them, through no fault of their own. Some let it lie in ruins, unable to find the hope and the will to rebuild, and others shoved up their sleeves and put it back together.

There was new glass at Ma's Pantry, too, and on other shops and houses. People, jackets buttoned or zipped against the chill, came and went, in and out. People stayed. She saw a man in a faded denim jacket, a tool belt slung at his hips, replacing a door on the bookstore. Yesterday, she thought, that door had been scarred, its windows broken. Now it would be fresh and new.

People stayed, she thought again, and others strapped on their tool belts and helped them rebuild.

When the man turned, caught her gaze, he smiled. Layla's heart took a jump, a little bump that was both pleasure and surprise. It was Fox's smile. For a moment she thought she was hallucinating, then she remembered. His father was a carpenter. Fox's father was replacing the door of the bookstore, and smiling at her across Main Street.

She lifted her hand in a wave and continued to walk. Wasn't it interesting to get a glimpse of what Fox B. O'Dell might look like in twenty years?

Pretty damn good.

She was still laughing to herself when she went inside Fox's office and relieved Alice for the day.

Since she had the offices to herself, she slid in a CD and started the work Alice had left her to Michelle Grant on low volume, muting it whenever the phone rang.

Within an hour, she'd cleared the desk, updated Fox's calendar. Since she still considered it Alice's domain, she resisted killing another hour reorganizing the storage room and the desk drawers to her personal specifications.

Instead, she pulled out one of the books in her satchel that covered a local's version of the legend of the Pagan Stone.

She could see it in her mind's eye, ruling the clearing in Hawkins Wood. Rising altarlike out of the scorched ground, somber and gray. Solid, she thought now as she paged through the book. Sturdy and ancient. Small wonder how it had come by its name, she decided, as it had struck her as something forged by gods for whatever, whomever, they might worship.

A center of power, she supposed, not on some soaring mountaintop, but in the quiet, sleepy woods.

There was nothing new in the book she scanned—the small Puritan settlement rocked by accusations of witchcraft, a tragic fire, a sudden storm. She wished she'd brought one of Ann Hawkins's journals instead, but she didn't feel comfortable taking them out of the house.

She put the book away and tried the Internet. But that, too, was old news. She'd read and searched and read again, and there was no question both Quinn and Cybil were better at this end than she was. Her strength was in organizing, in connecting the dots in a logical manner. At the moment, there were simply no new dots to connect.

Restless, she rose to walk to the front windows. She needed something to do, a defined task, something to keep her hands and her mind busy. She needed to do something. Now.

She turned back with the intention of calling Quinn and begging for an assignment, no matter how menial.

The woman stood in front of the desk, her hands folded at her waist. Her dress was a quiet gray, long skirt, long sleeves, high at the neck. She wore her sunny blond hair in a simple roll at the nape.

"I know what it is to be impatient, to be restless," she said. "I could never sit long without an occupation. He would tell me there was purpose in rest, but I found it so hard to wait."

Ghosts, Layla thought. Why should a ghost trip her heartbeat when only moments ago she'd been thinking of gods? "Are you Ann?"

"You know. You are still learning to trust yourself, and what was given to you. But you know."

"Tell me what to do, tell *us* what to do to stop it. To destroy it."

"It is beyond my power. It is even beyond his, my beloved's. It is for you to discover, you who are part of it, you who are part of me and mine."

"Is it evil in me?" Oh, how the possibility of that burned in Layla's belly. "Can you tell me that?"

"It is what you make of it. Do you know the beauty of now? Of holding it?" Both grief and joy radiated in Ann's face, in her voice. "Moment to moment, it moves and it changes. So must you. If you can see into others, into heart and mind, if you can look and know what is real and what is false, can you not look into yourself for the answers?"

"This is now, but you're only giving me more questions. Tell me where you went before the night of the fire at the Pagan Stone."

"To live, as he asked of me. To give life that was precious. They were my faith, my hope, my truth, and it was love that conceived them. Now you are my hope. You must not lose yours. He never has."

"Who? Giles Dent? Fox," Layla realized. "You mean Fox."

"He believes in the justice of things, in the right of them." She smiled now, with absolute love. "This is his great strength, and his vulnerability. Remember, it seeks weakness."

"What can I— Damn it!" Ann was gone, and the phone was ringing.

She'd write it down, Layla thought as she hurried back to the desk. Every word, every detail. She damn well had something to do now.

She reached for the phone. And picked up a hissing snake.

The scream tore out of her as she flung the writhing black mass away. Stumbling back, more screams bubbling up in her throat, she watched it coil like a cobra with its long, slanted eyes latched on hers. Then it lowered its head and began to slither across the floor toward her. Prayers and pleas jostled in her head as she backed toward the door. Its eyes glowed red as it surged, lightning fast, to coil again between her and the exit.

She heard her breath, coming too fast, in quick pants now that hitched and clogged in her throat. She wanted to turn and run, but the fear of turning her back on it was too great. It began to uncoil, inch by sinuous inch, began to wind toward her.

Was it longer now? Oh God, dear God. Its skin glistened an oily black, and it undulated as it slunk its way across the floor. Its hissing intensified when her back hit the wall. When there was nowhere left to run.

"You're not real." But the doubt in her voice was clear even to her, and it continued to come. "Not real," she repeated, struggling to draw in her breath. Look at it! she ordered herself. Look at it and see. Know. "You're not real. Not yet, you bastard."

Gritting her teeth, she shoved away from the wall. "Go

ahead. Slither, strike, you're not *real*." On the last word she
slammed her foot down, stabbing the heel of her boot
through the oily black body. For an instant, she felt substance, she saw blood ooze out of the wound and was both
horrified and revolted. As she ground down with all of her
might, she *felt* its fury and, more satisfying, its pain.

"Yeah, that's right, that's right. We hurt you before, and
we'll hurt you again. Go to hell, you—"

It struck. For an instant, one blinding instant, the pain
was her own. It sent her pitching forward. Before she could
scramble up to fight, to defend, it was gone.

Frantic, she yanked up her pants leg, searching for a
wound. Her skin was unbroken, unmarred. The pain, she
thought as she crawled toward her purse, was an illusion. It
made her feel pain, it had that much in it. But not enough to
wound. Her hands shook as she fumbled her phone out of
her bag.

In court, she remembered, Fox was in court. Can't
come, can't help. She hit speed dial for Quinn. "Come,"
she managed when Quinn answered. "You have to come.
Quick."

"WE WERE ON OUR WAY OUT THE DOOR WHEN
you called," Quinn told her. "You didn't answer the phone,
your cell or the office number."

"It rang." Layla sat on the sofa in reception. She'd gotten her breath back, and had nearly stopped shaking. "It
rang, but when I picked it up . . ." She took the bottle of
water Cybil brought her from the kitchen. "I threw it over
there."

When she gestured, Cybil walked over to the desk. "It's
still here." She lifted the phone off its charger.

"Because I never picked it up," Layla said slowly. "I
never picked anything up. It just made me think I did."

"But you felt it."

"I don't know. I heard it. I saw it. I thought I felt it." She looked down at her hand, and couldn't quite suppress a shudder.

"Cal's here," Cybil said with a glance out the window.

"We called him." Quinn rubbed Layla's arm. "We figured we might as well bring in the whole cavalry."

"Fox is in court."

"Okay." Quinn rose from her crouch in front of Layla when Cal came in.

"Is everyone all right? Nobody's hurt?"

"Nobody's hurt." With her eyes on Cal, Quinn laid a hand on Layla's shoulder. "Just freaked."

"What happened?"

"We were just getting to that. Fox is in court."

"I tried to reach him, got his voice mail. I didn't leave a message. I figured if he was out he didn't need to hear something was wrong when he'd be driving. Gage is on the way." Cal walked over, running a hand down Quinn's arm before he sat down beside Layla.

"What happened here? What happened to you?"

"I had visitors from both teams."

She told them about Ann Hawkins, pausing first when Quinn pulled out her recorder, then again when Gage came in.

"You said you heard her speak?" Cal asked.

"We had a conversation right here. Just me and a woman who's been dead for three hundred years."

"But did she actually speak?"

"I just said . . . Oh. Oh. How stupid am I?" Layla set the water aside, pressed her fingers to her eyes. "I'm supposed to stay in the moment, pay attention to the now, and I didn't. I wasn't."

"It was probably a fairly big surprise to turn around and see a dead woman standing at your desk," Cybil pointed out.

"I was wishing I had something to do, something to

keep me busy, and, well, be careful what you wish for. Let me think." She closed her eyes now, tried to picture the episode. "In my head," she murmured. "I heard her in my head, I'm almost sure. So I had, what, a telepathic conversation with a dead woman. It gets better and better."

"Sounds more like a pep talk from her end," Gage pointed out. "No real information, just get out there and give your all for the team."

"Maybe it's what I needed to hear. Because I can tell you the pep talk might have turned the tide when the other visitor showed up. The phone rang. It was probably you," she said to Quinn. "Then—"

She broke off when the door opened. Fox breezed in. "Somebody's having a party and didn't . . . Layla." He rushed across the room so quickly Quinn had to jump back or be bowled over. "What happened?" He gripped both her hands. "Snake? For fuck's sake. You're not hurt." He yanked up her trouser leg before she could answer.

"Stop. Don't do that. I'm not hurt. Let me tell it. Don't read me that way."

"Sorry, it didn't feel like the moment for protocol. You were alone. You could've—"

"Stop," she commanded, and deliberately pulled her hands from his, just as she deliberately tried to block him out of her mind. "Stop. I can't trust you if you push into my head that way. I won't trust you."

He drew back, on every level. "Fine. Fine. Let's hear it."

"Ann Hawkins came first," Quinn began, "but we'll go back to that if it's okay with you. She's just run that one."

"Then keep going."

"The phone rang," Layla said again, and told them.

"You hurt it," Quinn said. "On your own, by yourself. This is good news. And I like the boots."

"They've recently become my favorite footwear."

"But you felt pain." Cal gestured to her calf. "And that's not good."

"It was only for a second, and I don't know—honestly don't—how much of it was panic or the expectation of pain. I was so scared, for obvious reasons, then add in the snake. I was hyperventilating, and couldn't stop at first. I'd have passed out, I think, if I hadn't been more afraid of having a snake slithering all over me while I was unconscious. I have a thing."

Cybil cocked her head. "A snake thing? You have ophidiophobia? Snake phobia," she explained when Layla simply looked blank.

"She knows all kinds of stuff like that," Quinn said proudly.

"I don't know if it's an actual phobia. I just don't like—okay, I'm afraid of snakes. Things that slither."

Cybil looked at Quinn. "The giant slug you and Layla saw in the hotel dining room the day she checked in."

"Tapping in to her fears. Good one, Cyb."

"It was spiders when the four of you were together at the Sweetheart dance." Cybil cocked her eyebrow. "You've got a spider thing, Q."

"Yeah, but it's an ick rather than an eek."

"Which is why I didn't say you have arachnophobia."

"That would be Fox," Cal volunteered.

"No. I don't like spiders, but—"

"Who wouldn't go see *Arachnophobia*? The movie? Who screamed like a girl when a wolf spider crawled over his sleeping bag when we—"

"I was twelve, for Christ's sake." With the appearance of a man stuck between embarrassment and impatience, Fox jammed his hands in his pockets. "I don't like spiders, which is different from being phobic. They have too many legs, as opposed to snakes, who don't have any, and which I find kind of cool. I'm only somewhat freaked by spiders that are bigger than my goddamn hand."

"They were," Layla agreed.

Fox blew out a breath. "Yeah, I guess they were."

"She said, Ann said that it seeks out our weaknesses."

"Spiders and snakes," Cal offered.

"That ain't what it takes," Gage finished and got a ghost of a smile from Cybil.

"What scares you?" she asked him.

"The IRS, and women who can rattle off words like *ophidiophobia*."

"Everyone has fears, weak spots." Wearily, Layla rubbed the back of her neck. "It'll use them against us."

"We should take a break, get you home." Fox studied Layla's face. "You've got a headache. I see it in your eyes," he said stiffly when her back went rigid. "I'll close up for the day."

"Good idea." Quinn spoke up before Layla could object. "We'll go back to our place. Layla can take some aspirin, maybe a hot bath. Cyb'll cook."

"Will she?" Cybil said dryly, then rolled her eyes as Quinn smiled. "All right, all right, I'll cook."

When the women left, Fox stood in the center of the room, scanning it.

"Nothing here, son," Gage pointed out.

"But there was. We all felt it." Fox looked at Cal, got a nod.

"Yeah. But then none of us thought she imagined it."

"She didn't imagine it," Gage agreed, "and she handled it. There's not a weak spine among the three of them. That's an advantage."

"She was alone." Fox swung back. "She had to *handle* it alone."

"There are six of us, Fox." Cal's voice was calm, reasoned. "We can't be together or even buddied up twenty-four hours out of the day. We have to work, sleep, live, that's just the way it is. The way it's always been."

"She knows the score." Gage spread his hands. "Just like the rest of us."

"It's not a fucking hockey game."

"And she's not Carly."

At Cal's statement, the room went silent.

"She's not Carly," he repeated, quietly now. "What happened here today isn't your fault any more than what happened seven years ago was your fault. If you drag that around with you, you're not doing yourself, or Layla, any favors."

"Neither of you ever lost anyone you loved in this," Fox shot back. "So you don't know."

"We were there," Gage corrected. "So we damn well know. We know." He slid up his sleeve and held out the wrist scored with a thin white scar. "Because we've always been there."

Because it was pure truth, Fox let out a breath. And let go of the anger. "We need to come up with a system, a contact system. So if any of us are threatened while we're alone, all of us get the signal."

"We'll have to come up with something," Fox added. "But right now I need to close up, and get out of this suit. Then I want a beer."

BY THE TIME THEY ARRIVED AT THE RENTAL house, dinner preparations were already under way, with Quinn dragooned into serving as Cybil's line chef.

"What's cooking?" Cal leaned down, tipped Quinn's chin up, and kissed her mouth.

"All I know is I'm ordered to peel these carrots and potatoes."

"It was your idea to have dinner for six," Cybil reminded her, but smiled at Cal. "What's cooking is delicious. You'll like it. Now go away."

"He can peel carrots," Quinn objected.

"Fox can peel carrots," Cal volunteered. "He can handle vegetables because that's about all they ate at his house."

"Which is why you should practice," Fox shot back. "I want to talk to Layla. Where is she?"

"Upstairs. She . . . hmm," Quinn finished when Fox simply turned and walked out. "This ought to be interesting. Sorry I'm missing it."

He headed straight up. Fox knew the layout of the second floor, as he'd been drafted into carting up bits and pieces of furniture when the women were settling in. He turned straight into her bedroom, through the open door, where she was wearing nothing but a bra and a pair of low-cut briefs.

"I need to talk to you."

"Out. Get out. Jesus." She grabbed a shirt from the bed, whipped it in front of her.

"It won't take that long."

"I don't care how long it takes, I'm not dressed."

"For Christ's sake, I've seen women in their underwear before." But since she merely lifted her arm, pointed at the door, he compromised by turning around. "If you've got modesty issues, you should close your door."

"This is a houseful of women, and I . . . never mind."

He heard the rustling of clothes, slamming of drawers. "How's the headache?"

"It's fine—gone, I mean. I'm fine, so if that's all—"

"You might as well dismount."

"Excuse me?"

"From your high horse. And you can toss out the idea of me apologizing for reading you before. You were pumping off fear, and it rammed right into me. What happened after was instinctive, and doesn't make me a psychic Peeping Tom."

"You can curb your instincts, and do it all the time. You told me."

"It's a little tougher when it's someone I care about in crisis. So deal. Meanwhile you might want to start thinking about another job."

"You're *firing* me?"

He figured she'd had enough time to pull something on, so he turned around. He still had a crystal-clear picture of her wearing only bra and panties in his head, but had to admit she made an equally impressive picture wearing jeans, a sweater, and outrage.

"I'm suggesting you think about finding a job where you work around people, so you're not left alone. I'm in and out of the office, and once Mrs. H—"

"You're suggesting I need a babysitter?"

"No, and right now I'm saying you have a big overreact button, and your finger's stuck on it. I'm suggesting you shouldn't feel obligated to come back to the office, that if it makes you uneasy, I get it, and I'll make other arrangements."

"I'm living and working in a town where a demon comes to play every seven years. I have a lot more to be uneasy about than doing your damn filing."

"There are other jobs where you wouldn't be doing anyone's damn filing alone in an office on a regular basis. Alone in an office where you were singled out and attacked."

"In an office where I fought back and did some damage."

"I'm not discounting that, Layla."

"Sounds like it to me."

"I don't want to feel responsible for something happening to you. Don't say it." He held up a hand. "My office, my schedule, my feelings."

She angled her head, the gesture both acknowledgment and challenge. "Then you'll have to fire me or, to toss back your own advice, deal."

"Then I will—deal. We're going to try to come up with some sort of alarm or signal that can reach everyone at the same time. No more phone trees."

"What, like the Bat Signal?"

He had to smile. "That'd be cool. We'll talk about it."

When they walked out together, he asked, "Are we smooth now?"

"Smooth enough."

Despite Cybil's edict, the rest gathered in the kitchen. Whatever was on the menu already scented the air. Cal's dog, Lump, sprawled under the little cafe table, snoring.

"There's a perfectly good living room in the house," Cybil pointed out. "Well-suited for men and dogs, considering its current decor."

"Cyb still objects to the flea-market-special ambiance." Quinn grinned and crunched into a stalk of celery. "Feeling better, Layla?"

"Much. I'm just going to grab a glass of wine then go up and chart this latest business. By the way, why were you calling me? You said you'd tried to call me on the office phone and my cell."

"Oh God, with all the excitement, we forgot." Quinn looked over at Cybil. "Our top researcher's come up with another lead to where Ann Hawkins might have lived after the night at the Pagan Stone."

"A family by the name of Ellsworth, a few miles outside of the settlement here in sixteen fifty-two. They arrived shortly after Hawkins, about three months after from what I've dug up."

"Is there a connection?" Cal asked.

"They both came over from England. Fletcher Ellsworth. Ann named one of her sons Fletcher. And Ellsworth's wife, Honor, was third cousin to Hawkins's wife."

"I define that as connection," Quinn stated.

"Have you pinpointed the location?"

"Working on it," Cybil told Cal. "I got as much as I got because one of Ellsworth's descendents was at Valley Forge with George, and one of *his* descendents wrote a book about the family. I got in touch—chatty guy."

"They always talk to Cyb." Quinn took another bite of celery.

"Yes, they do. He was able to verify that the Ellsworths we're interested in had a farm west of town, in a place that was called Hollow Creek."

"So we just have to—" Quinn broke off, catching Cal's expression. "What?" Because he was staring at Fox, she turned, repeated. "What?"

"Some of the locals still call it that," Fox explained. "Or did, when my parents bought the land thirty-three years ago. That's my family's farm."

Six

~⌘~

IT WAS FULL DARK BY THE TIME FOX PULLED UP
behind his father's truck. The lateness of the hour had been
one of the reasons his parents weren't going to be invaded
by six people on a kind of scavenger hunt.

They'd have handled it, he knew. The house had always
been open to anyone, anytime. Relatives, old friends, new
friends, the occasional stranger could count on a bed, a
meal, a refuge at the Barry-O'Dells. Payment for the hospitality might be feeding chickens, milking goats, weeding a
garden, splitting wood.

Throughout his childhood the house had been noisy,
busy, and often still was. It was a house where those who
lived in it were encouraged to pursue and explore their own
paths, where the rules were flexible and individualized, and
where everyone had been expected to contribute to the
whole.

It was still home, he thought, the rambling house of stone

and wood with its wide front porch, its interesting juts and painted shutters (currently a sassy red). He supposed even if he ever got the chance to make his own, to build his own family, this farm, this house, this place would always be home.

There was music when he stepped into the big living room with its eccentric mix of art, its bold use of color and texture. Every piece of furniture was handcrafted, most by his father. Lamps, paintings, vases, bowls, throws, pillows, candles, all original work—family or friends.

Had he appreciated that as a child? he wondered. Probably not. It was just home.

A pair of dogs rushed from the rear of the house to greet him with welcoming barks and swinging tails. There'd always been dogs here. These, Mick and Dylan, were mutts—as they always were—rescued from the pound. Fox crouched to give them both a rub when his father followed them out.

"Hey." Brian's grin flashed, that instant sign of pleasure. "How's it going? You eat?"

"Yeah."

"Come on back. We're still at it, and there's a rumor about apple cobbler." Brian swung an arm over Fox's shoulders as they walked back to the kitchen.

"I was going to drop by today while I was working in town," Brian continued, "but I got hung up. Look what I found," he said to Jo. "He must've heard about the cobbler."

"It's all over town." Fox went around the big butcher-block table to kiss his mother. The kitchen smelled of his mother's herbs and candles, and the thick soup from the pot on the stove. "And before you ask, I've had dinner."

He sat in a chair he helped make when he'd been thirteen. "I came by to talk to you guys about the house—the farm."

"Moving back in?" Brian asked and picked up his spoon to dig back into what Fox recognized as his mother's lentil and brown rice soup.

"No." Though that door would always be open, he knew. "The main part of the house is pre–Civil War, right?"

"Eighteen fifties," Jo confirmed. "You know that."

"Yeah, but I wondered if you knew if it was built on any earlier structure."

"Possible," his father answered. "The stone shed out back's earlier. It stands to reason there was more here at one time."

"Right. You looked into the history. I remember."

"That's right." Jo studied his face. "There were people farming here before the white man came over to run them out."

"I'm not talking about the indigenous, or their exploitation by invaders." He did *not* want to get her started on that one. "I'm more interested in what you might know about after the settlers came here."

"When the Hollow was settled," Jo said. "When Lazarus Twisse arrived."

"Yeah."

"I know the land was farmed then, that the area was known as Hollow Creek. I have some paperwork on it. Why, Fox? We're not close to the Pagan Stone, we're outside of town."

"We think Ann Hawkins might have stayed here, had her sons here."

"On this farm?" Brian mused. "How about that?"

"She wrote journals, I told you about that, and how there are gaps in them. We haven't found any from the time she left—or supposedly left—the Hollow until she came back a couple years later. If we could find them. . . ."

"That was three hundred years ago," Jo pointed out.

"I know, but we have to try. If we could come by in the morning, first thing in the morning before I have any clients coming in—"

"You know you don't have to ask," Brian said. "We'll be here."

Jo said nothing for a moment. "I'll get the famous cobbler." She rose, stroking a hand over her son's shoulder on her way to the cupboard.

HE'D WANTED TO KEEP ALL OF IT AWAY FROM HIS family, away from home. When he drove the familiar roads back to the farm at the first break of dawn, Fox told himself this search didn't, wouldn't, pull his family in any further. Even if they proved Ann had stayed there on their land, even if they found her journals, it didn't change the fact the farm was one of the safe zones.

None of their families had ever been infected, none of them had ever been threatened. That wasn't going to change. He simply wouldn't allow it to change. The threat was coming sooner, and harder, that was fact. But his family remained safe.

He pulled in front of the farmhouse just ahead of Cal and Gage.

"I've got two hours," he told them as they got out. "If we need more, I can try to shuffle some stuff. Otherwise, it has to wait until tomorrow. Saturday's clear."

"We'll work it out." Cal stepped aside so that Lump and the two host dogs could sniff each other and get reacquainted.

"Here comes the estrogen." Gage lifted his chin toward the road. "Is your lady ready to ante up, Hawkins?"

"She said she is, so she is." But Cal walked to the car, drew Quinn aside when the women piled out. "I don't know if I can help you with this."

"Cal—"

"I know we went over this last night, but I'm allowed to be obsessive about the woman I love."

"Absolutely." She linked her hands around his neck so that her bright blue eyes smiled into his. "Obsess me."

He took the offered mouth, let himself sink in. "I'll do

what I can, you know that. But the fact is, I've been coming here all my life, slept in this house, ate in it, played in it, ran the fields, helped with chores. It was my second home, and I never got a single flash of the past, of Ann, of anything."

"Giles Dent wasn't here, neither were the ones—the guardians that came before him. Not so far as we know. If Ann came here to stay, she came here without him, and stayed on after Dent was already gone. This one's on me, Cal."

"I know." He touched her lips with his again. "Just take it easy on yourself, Blondie."

"It's a wonderful house," Layla said to Fox. "Just a wonderful spot. Isn't it, Cybil?"

"Like a Pissarro painting. What kind of farming, Fox?"

"Organic family farming, you could say. They'll be around back this time of morning, dealing with the animals."

"Cows?" Layla fell into step behind him.

"No. Goats, for the milk. Chickens, for the eggs. Bees for the honey. Vegetables, herbs, flowers. Everything gets used, and what's surplus we—they—sell or barter."

The scent of animals wound through the morning air, exotic to her city-girl senses. She spotted a tire swing hanging from the thick, gnarled branch of what she thought might be a sycamore. "It must've been great growing up here."

"It was. I might not have thought so when I was shoveling chicken manure or hacking at bindweed, but it was great."

Chickens clucked in their busy and urgent voices. As they rounded the house Fox saw his mother casting feed for them. She wore jeans, her ancient Wellingtons, a frayed plaid shirt over a thermal pullover. Her hair was down her back, a long, thick braid.

Now it was his turn for a flash from the past. He saw her in his mind, doing the same chore on a bright summer morning, but she'd worn a long blue dress, with a sling around her, and his baby sister tucked into it.

Singing, he remembered. She so often sang while she worked. He heard her now, as he'd heard her then.

"I'll fly away, O glory, I'll fly away—in the morning."

In the near paddock, his father milked one of the nannies, and sang with her.

And Fox's love for them was almost impossible to hold.

She saw him, smiled at him. "Timed it to miss the chores, I see."

"I was always good at it."

She cast the rest of the seed before setting her bucket down to come to him. She kissed him—forehead, one cheek, the other, the lips. "Morning." Then turned to Cal and did exactly the same. "Caleb. I heard you had news."

"I do. Here she is. Quinn, this is Joanne Barry, my childhood sweetheart."

"Apparently I have quite an act to follow. It's nice to meet you."

"Nice meeting you." She gave Quinn's arm a pat, then turned to Gage. "Where have you been, and why haven't you come to see me?"

She kissed him, then wrapped her arms around him in a hard hug.

He hugged back—that's what Cybil noted. He held on, closed his eyes and held tight. "Missed you," he murmured.

"Then don't stay away so long." She eased back. "Hello, Layla, it's good to see you again. And this must be Cybil."

"It must be. You have a very handsome farm, Ms. Barry."

"Thanks. Here comes my man."

"LaMancha goats?" Cybil commented and had Jo giving her another, longer look.

"That's right. You don't look like a goatherd."

"I saw some a couple of years ago in Oregon. The way the tips of the ears turn up is distinctive. High butterfat content in the milk, isn't that right?"

"It is. Would you like to try some?"

"I have. It's excellent, and fabulous for baking."

"It certainly is. Bri, Cybil, Quinn, and Layla."

"Nice to—hey, we've met." He grinned at Layla. "Sort of. I saw you yesterday, walking down Main."

"You were replacing a door at the bookstore. I thought how comforting it was that there are people who know how to fix what's broken."

"Our specialty. Nice job with the blonde, Cal," he added, giving Cal a one-armed hug and a wink. "About damn time," he said to Gage, and hugged him in turn. "You guys want breakfast?"

"We don't have a lot of time," Fox told him. "Sorry."

"No problem. I'll take the milk in, Jo."

"I'll get the eggs. Go ahead and put tea on, Bri. It's cold this morning." She turned back to Fox. "Let us know if you need anything, or if we can help."

"Thanks." Fox gestured the group aside while his mother began gathering eggs into a basket. "How do you want to start? Inside?"

"We know the house wasn't here then?" Quinn looked at Fox for confirmation.

"About a hundred years later, but it could have been built on another's foundation. I just don't know. That shed? Well, what's left of that shed, the one covered with vines? That was here."

"It's too small." Layla studied the remaining walls. "Would be, even for the time period for a house. If we're talking about a small family taking in a woman and her three babies, that couldn't have been big enough."

"A smokehouse maybe," Cybil mused. "Or an animal shelter. But it's interesting that most of it's still here. There could be a reason for that."

"Let me try the house first." Quinn studied the shed, the land, the big stone house. "Maybe walking around the house out here. I might get something. If not, we'll do a

walk-through, since it's okay with Fox's parents. If nothing then . . . there's the land, that grove of trees, the fields, certainly the little ruin there. Fingers crossed, okay?"

She crossed the fingers of her left hand, held the right out for Cal. "The clearing in the woods, that's sacred ground—magic spot. And the stone, it pushed those flashes right in. The attic in the library, that grabbed hold, too. I didn't have to do anything. I'm not sure what I should do."

"Think about Ann," Cal told her. "You've seen her, you've heard her. Think about her."

Quinn pictured Ann Hawkins as she'd seen her the first time, with her hair loose, carrying pails of water from the stream, her belly huge with her sons, and her face alight with love for the man who waited for her. She pictured her as she'd seen her the second time, slim again, dressed demurely. Older, sadder.

She walked over the tough winter grass, the thick gravel, over stepping stones. The air was cool and brisk on her cheeks, and was tinged with the scent of animal and earth. She held firm to Cal's hand, knowing—feeling—he gave her whatever he had so that their abilities linked as their fingers did.

"I'm just not going there. I'm getting glimpses of you," she said to Cal with a quick laugh. "A little guy, when you still needed your glasses. Fairly adorable. I can get zips of the three of you running around, and a younger boy, a girl. A toddler—another girl. She's so cute."

"You have to go deeper." Cal squeezed her hand. "I'm right with you."

"That might be the problem. I think I may be picking up on things you remember, your pictures." She squeezed his hand in turn, then drew hers free. "I think I have to try it alone. Give me a little space. Okay, everybody? A little room."

She turned, reached the corner of the house, then followed its line. It was so sturdy, she thought, and as Cybil

had said, so handsome. The stone, the wood, the glass. There were flower beds sleeping, and in others sweet and hopeful shoots that must have been daffodils and tulips, hyacinths, and the summer lilies that would follow the spring.

Strong old trees offered shade, so she imagined—or maybe she saw—the flowers that shied from sunlight blooming there.

She smelled smoke, she realized. There must be wood fireplaces inside. Of course there would be. What wonderful old farmhouse didn't have fireplaces? Somewhere to curl up on a cold evening. Flames sending dancing shadow and light, and the warmth so welcome.

She sat in a room lit by firelight and the glow of a single tallow candle. She did not weep though her heart was flooded with tears. With quill and ink, Ann wrote in her careful hand in the pages of her journal.

Our sons are eight months old. They are beautiful, and they are healthy. I see you in them, beloved. I see you in their eyes and it both comforts and grieves me. I am well. The kindness of my cousin and her husband are beyond measure. Surely we are a burden on them, but we are never treated as such. In the weeks before, and some weeks after the birth of our sons there was little I could do to help my cousin. Yet she never complained. Even now with the boys to look after, I cannot do as much as I wish to repay her and cousin Fletcher.

Mending I do. Honor and I made soap and candles, enough for Fletcher to barter.

This is not what I wish to write, but I find it so hard to subscribe these words to this paper. My cousin has told me that young Hester Deale was drowned in the pool of Hawkins Wood, and leaves her infant daughter orphaned. She condemned you that night, as you had foreseen. She condemned me. We know it was not by her

will she did so, as it was not by her will the motherless child was conceived.

The beast is in the child, Giles. You told me again and again that what you would do would change the order, clean the blood. This sacrifice you made, and I and our children with you was necessary. On nights like this, when I am so alone, when I find my heart full of sorrow for a girl I knew who is lost, I fear what was done, what will be done so long from this night will not be enough. I mourn that you gave yourself for nothing, and our children will never see their father's face, or feel his kiss.

I will pray for the strength and the courage you believed lived inside me. I will pray to find them again when the sun rises. Tonight, with the darkness so close, I can only be a woman who longs for her love.

She closed the book as one of the babies began to cry, and his brothers woke to join him. Rising, she went to the pallet beside her own to soothe, to sing, to offer her breast.

You are my hope, she whispered, offering one a sugar teat for comfort while his brothers suckled.

WHEN QUINN'S EYES ROLLED BACK, CAL LIFTED her off her feet. "We need to get her inside." His long, fast strides carried her to the steps leading to the side porch. Fox rushed ahead, getting the door, then going straight into the family's music room.

"I'll get some water."

"She'll need more." Cybil hurried after him. "Which way's the kitchen?"

He pointed, turned in the opposite direction.

Because Quinn was shivering, Layla whipped a throw from the back of a small couch as Cal laid Quinn down.

"My head," Quinn managed. "God, my head. It's off the

Richter scale. I may be sick. I need to . . ." She swung her legs over, dropped her head between her knees. "Okay." She breathed in, breathed out as Cal massaged her shoulders. "Okay."

"Here, try some water. Fox got you some water." Layla took the glass he'd brought back, knelt to urge it on Quinn.

"Take it easy," Cal advised. "Don't sit up until you're ready. Slow breaths."

"Believe me." She eyed the brass bucket Gage set next to her, then shifted her gaze to the kindling now scattered over the hearth. "Good thinking, but I'm pretty sure I'm not going to need that."

She eased up until she could rest her throbbing head on Cal's shoulder. "Intense."

"I know." He pressed his lips lightly to the side of her head.

"Did I say anything? It was Ann. She was writing in her journal."

"You said plenty," Cal told her.

"Why didn't I think to turn on my recorder?"

"Got that." Gage held up her minirecorder. "I pulled it out of your purse when the show started."

She took a slow sip of water, glanced at Fox out of eyes still blurry in a pale, pale face. "Your parents wouldn't happen to have any morphine around here?"

"Sorry."

"It'll pass." Cal kissed her again, rubbed gently at the back of her neck. "Promise."

"How long was I gone?"

"Nearly twenty minutes." Cal glanced over when Cybil came back in carrying a tall pottery mug.

"Here." Cybil stroked Quinn's cheek. "This'll help."

"What is it?"

"Tea. That's all you have to know. Come on, be a good girl." She held the mug to Quinn's lips. "Your mother has an amazing collection of homemade teas, Fox."

"Maybe, but this tastes like—" Quinn broke off when Joanne walked in. "Ms. Barry."

"That blend tastes pretty crappy, but it'll help. Let me have her, Cal." Brushing Cal aside, Joanne took his place, then pressed and rubbed at two points at the base of Quinn's neck. "Try not to tense. That's better. Breathe through it. Breathe the oxygen in, exhale the tension and discomfort. That's good. Are you pregnant?"

"What? No. Um, no."

"There's a point here." She took Quinn's left hand, pressed on the webbing between her thumb and forefinger. "It's effective, but traditionally forbidden for pregnant women."

"The Adjoining Valley," Cybil said.

"You know acupressure?"

"She knows everything," Quinn claimed, and took her first easy breath. "It's better. It's a lot better. Down from blinding to annoying. Thank you."

"You should rest awhile. Cal can take you upstairs if you want."

"Thanks, but—"

"Cal, you ought to take her home." Layla stepped forward to pat a hand on Cal's arm. "I can ride into the office with Fox. Cybil, you can get Gage back to Cal's, right?"

"I could do that."

"We haven't finished," Quinn objected. "We need to move on to part two and find out where she put the journal."

"Not today."

"She's right, Blondie. You haven't got another round in you." To settle the matter, Cal picked her up off the couch.

"Well, hard to argue. I guess I'm going. Thanks, Ms. Barry."

"Jo."

"Thanks, Jo, for letting us screw up your morning."

"Anytime. Fox, give Cal a hand with the door. Gage,

why don't you take Cybil back, let Brian know everything's all right? Layla." Jo put a hand on Layla's arm,
holding her in place while the others left the room. "That
was smoothly done."

"I'm sorry?"

"You maneuvered that so Quinn and Cal would have
time alone, which is exactly what they both need. I'm going to ask you a favor."

"Of course."

"If there's anything we can or should do, will you tell
me? Fox may not. He's protective of those he loves. Sometimes too protective."

"I'll do what I can."

"Can't ask for more than that."

Fox waited for Layla to join him outside. "You don't
have to go into the office."

"Cal and Quinn need some space, and I'd just as soon be
busy."

"Borrow Quinn's car, or Cybil's. Go shopping. Do
something normal."

"Work is normal. Are you trying to get rid of me?"

"I'm trying to give you a break."

"I don't need a break. Quinn does." She turned as Cybil
and Gage came out. "I'm going to go into the office for the
day, unless you need me back at home."

"I've got it covered," Cybil told her. "Other than logging in this morning's fun and games, there isn't much else
to do until we find the journal."

"We're putting a lot of stock in a diary," Gage commented.

"It's the next step." Cybil shrugged.

"I can't find it." Fox spread his hands. "Maybe she
wrote them, maybe she wrote them here—it seems clear
she did. But I lived in this house and never got a glimmer. I
went through it again last night, wide open. Walked around
inside, out, the old shed, the woods. I got nothing."

"Maybe you need me."

His eyes latched on to Layla.

"Maybe it's something we need to do together. We could try that. We've still got a little time now. We could—"

"Not now. Now while my parents are here in case . . . of anything. They'll both be away tomorrow, all morning." Out of harm's way, if there was any harm to be had. "At the pottery, at the stand. We'll come back tomorrow."

"Fine with me. Well, cowboy." Cybil gestured to Quinn's car. "Let's ride." She said nothing else until she and Gage were inside, pulling out ahead of Fox's truck. "What does he think might happen that he doesn't want his parents exposed to?"

"Nothing's ever happened here, or at Cal's parents' place. But, as far as we know, they've never been connected before. So who the hell knows?"

She considered as she drove. "They're nice people."

"About the best."

"You spent a lot of time here as a boy."

"Yeah."

"God, do you ever shut up?" she demanded after a moment. "It's all talk, talk, talk with you."

"I love the sound of my own voice."

She gave it another ten seconds of silence. "Let's try another avenue. How'd you do in the poker game?"

"Did okay. You play?"

"I've been known to."

"Are you any good?"

"I make it a policy to be good, or learn to be good, at everything I do. In fact—"

As she rounded the curve, she saw the huge black dog hunched in the middle of the road a few yards ahead. Meeting its eyes, Cybil checked the instinct to slam the brakes. "Better hang on," she said coolly, then punched the gas instead.

It leaped. A mass of black, the glint of fang and claw. The car shuddered at impact, and she fought to control it with her heart slammed in her throat. The windshield exploded; the hood erupted in flame. Again, she fought the instinct to hit the brakes, spun the car hard into a tight one-eighty. She prepared to ram the dog again, but it was gone.

The windshield was intact; the hood unmarred.

"Son of a bitch, son of a bitch," she said, over and over.

"Turn around, and keep going, Cybil." Gage closed a hand over the one that clamped the steering wheel. It was cold, he noted, but rock steady. "Turn the car around, and drive."

"Yeah, okay." She shuddered once, hard, then turned the car around. "So . . . What was I saying before we were interrupted?"

Sheer admiration for her chutzpah had a laugh rolling out of him. "You got nerve, sister. You got nerves of fucking steel."

"I don't know. I wanted to kill it. I just wanted to kill it. And, well, it's not my car, so if I wrecked it running over a damn devil dog, it's Q's problem." And at the moment, her stomach was a quivering mess. "It was probably stupid. I couldn't see anything for a minute, when the windshield . . . I could've run us into a tree, or off the road into the creek."

"People who are afraid to try something stupid never get anywhere."

"I wanted to pay it back, for what it did to Layla yesterday. And that's not the sort of thing that's going to work."

"It didn't suck," Gage said after a minute.

She laughed a little, then shot him a glance and laughed some more. "No, now that you mention it, it really didn't."

Seven

~✥~

FOX'S FRIDAY SCHEDULE DIDN'T GIVE HIM MUCH time to think, or to brood. He went from appointment to meeting, back to appointment and into phone conference. At midafternoon, he saw a clear hour and decided to use it to take a walk around town to give his brain a rest.

Better yet, he thought, he'd walk up to the Bowl-a-Rama, grab a few minutes with Cal. He'd get a better sense of how Quinn was doing, how they were all doing if he talked with Cal.

When he stepped into reception to tell Layla, he found her talking with Cal's great-grandmother Estelle Hawkins.

"I thought we were meeting at our usual clandestine rendezvous." He walked over to kiss her soft, thin-skinned cheek. "How are we going to keep our secret affair secret?"

"It's all over town." Essie's eyes twinkled through the thick lenses of her glasses. "We might as well start living in sin openly."

"I'll go up and pack."

She laughed, swatted at him. "Before you do, I was hoping you'd have a few minutes for me. Professionally."

"I've always got time for you, in any way. Come on back. Layla's going to hold my calls." He winked at her as he took Essie's arm. "In case our passions overwhelm us."

"Should I just lock the outside door?" Layla called out as he led Essie away.

"It's a wonder you can keep your mind on your work," Essie told him as they moved into his office, "with a pretty girl like that around."

"I have Herculean power of will. Want a Coke?"

"You know, I believe I would."

"Two seconds."

He got a glass, ice, poured. She was one of Fox's favorite people, and he made sure she was comfortable before he sat with her in the sitting area of his office. "Where's Ginger?" he asked, referring to Cal's cousin who lived with Essie.

"She went on to the bank before it closes. She'll be coming back for me. This won't take long."

"What can I do for you? Want to sue somebody?"

She smiled at him. "Can't think of anything I'd like less. I wonder why people are forever suing each other."

"Blame the lawyers. Still, it's a better alternative than beating the hell out of each other. Mostly."

"People do that, too. But I'm not here for either. It's about my will, Fox."

It gave him a little pang. She was ninety-three, and he certainly understood and appreciated the value of having your affairs well in order long before you approached Essie's age. But it still gave him a little pang to think of his world without her in it.

"I updated your will and your trust a few years ago. Do you want changes?"

"Nothing big. I have a couple pieces of jewelry I wanted to earmark for Quinn. Right now, my pearls and my aquamarine earrings are going to Frannie. She understands I want to leave them to her future daughter-in-law. I've talked to her about it. And I know I can leave it like that, I can trust her to give them to Quinn. But, as I recall, you told me it's easier on those left behind if everything's spelled out."

"It generally is. I can take care of that for you." Though he trusted his memory when it came to Essie's business, Fox rose to get a legal pad and note it all down. "It won't take long to draft the change. I can bring it by for your signature on Monday if that works for you."

"That's just fine, but I don't mind coming in."

He knew she continued to go into the library nearly every day, but if he could save her a trip he'd rather. "Tell you what, when it's ready, I'll give you a call. Then we'll see which way it works best. Is there anything else you want to change, add, take out?"

"No, just those two pieces. You have everything spelled out so clearly. It gives me peace of mind, Fox."

"And if any of my grandchildren turn out to be lawyers, they can handle it for you."

Her lips curved, but her eyes stayed somber as she reached out to pat his hand. "I'd like to live to see Cal married next fall. I'd like to live through this next Seven and dance with my boy at his wedding."

"Miss Essie—"

"Wouldn't mind dancing with you at yours. And I can be greedy and say I'd like to hold Cal's firstborn in my arms. But I know that may not be. What's coming this time is worse than all the rest."

"We won't let anything happen to you."

She let out a sigh that was full of affection. "You've seen to this town since you were ten years old. You and Cal and Gage. I'd like to live to see the day you didn't have to see to it. I'm holding out for that." She gave his hand an-

other pat. "Now I expect Ginger will be coming along to fetch me."

He rose to help her to her feet. "I'll walk you out, wait for her."

"You just go about your business. I hope you've got something fun planned for the weekend."

"I would if you'd go out with me."

She laughed, leaning on his arm as he walked her out. "There was a day."

He stood at the window, watching as Ginger eased Essie into the car.

"She's a remarkable woman," Layla commented.

"Yeah, she's something. I need you to pull her estate file. She wants a couple of changes."

"All right."

"Do you ever think we'll lose this? That we'll lose the town, ourselves, the whole damn ball?"

She hesitated. "Don't you?"

"No." He glanced back at her. "No, I know we'll win this. But we won't all make it. Not everyone who's out there going about their business today is going to come through it."

Instead of taking his walk, Fox went back into his office. He took a copy of his own will out of the desk drawer to review it.

JUST AFTER FIVE HE WALKED HIS LAST CLIENT TO the door, then turned to Layla. "We're out of here. Grab your things. We're going bowling."

"I really don't think so, but that's a nice thought. I want to check in with Quinn."

"She's meeting us there. The whole gang's hitting the Bowl-a-Rama. It's Friday night. Pizza, beer, and duckpins."

She thought of the quiet meal of soup she'd planned, a glass of wine and a book. "You like to bowl."

"I hate it, which is problematic seeing as one of my closest friends owns a bowling alley." He got her coat as he spoke. "But the pizza's good, and there are pinball machines. I love me some pinball. Regardless, we earned a break. From everything."

"I guess we did."

He held out her coat. "Friday night in the Hollow? The Bowl-a-Rama's the place to be."

She smiled. "Then I guess we'd better get there. Can we walk?"

"Read my mind. Figuratively speaking. I've been antsy all day." He paused after they'd stepped outside. "Pansies in the tub outside the Flower Pot and see there? That's Eric Moore, clean-shaven. He shaves off his winter beard every March. Spring's coming."

He took her hand as they hit the sidewalk. "Do you know what I love as much as pinball and pizza?"

"What?"

"Taking a walk with a pretty girl."

She aimed a look at him. "Your mood's improved."

"Anticipation of pizza does that for me."

"No, I mean it."

He shot a wave at someone across the street. "I wallowed some. I need a good wallow once in a while, then I scrape it off."

"How?"

"By remembering we all do what we do. By reminding myself I believe good mostly wins out in the long run. Sometimes the long run's a bitch, but good mostly wins out."

"You're cheering me up."

"Good. That was the plan."

"I wasn't exactly wallowing. I think I got jammed up at worrying. Pansies in the tub, that's a good sign, but I hate that it's offset by ones like this." She gestured toward the gift shop. "I want to believe good mostly wins out, too, but

it's hard knowing it costs so much, that some people have to lose."

"Maybe it's not a loss. Maybe they'll relocate to Iowa and hit the lottery, or double their business. Or they'll just be happier there, for whatever reason. The wheel's got to turn before you get anywhere."

"So says the man practicing law in the town where he was born."

"I turned the wheel." They crossed at the Square. "It brought me right back here. Brought you here, too."

He pulled open the door, and led her into the noise of the Bowl-a-Rama.

"To pizza and pinball."

"And pansies, to continue the alliteration. Then there's bowling and bonhomie."

"Bonhomie. Triple word score."

"Play your cards right." He turned her and, letting the mood carry him, laid his lips on hers before she could prepare herself. "There could be sex and satisfaction."

"I'm not playing cards just yet."

"So we settle for friends and frivolity. And boy, am I done with that." He led her to lane six, where Cal sat along with Quinn and Cybil, changing shoes. "Where's Turner?"

"Deserted us for the arcade," Cybil told him.

"And the pinball rivalry continues. Catch you later."

"No problem. I'll have three beautiful women to myself." Cal held out a pair of bowling shoes. "Size seven?"

"That would be me." Layla slid into the booth as Fox gestured Cal a few steps away.

"How'd you get Gage to come in?"

"It's his father's night off. Bill's not around, so . . ."

"Got it. I'm going to go whip his ass at Tomcat. He'll be buying the beer."

"Tomcat?" Cybil's eyebrows rose dramatically. "Isn't that a war game?"

"Maybe." Fox eyed her narrowly. "What are you, my

mother? And you don't have to mention me whipping Gage's ass at a war game to my mother if you should happen to run into her."

An hour with the lights, the bells, the patter of antiaircraft cut away even the fading edges of Fox's pensive mood. It didn't hurt to stand and watch a trio of attractive women bend and stretch while he drank a victory beer. Gage had *never* been able to beat him at Tomcat.

"Best view in the house," Gage commented as they stood back, studying Quinn's posterior as she approached the line.

"Hard to beat. Friday night leagues are coming in." Fox glanced over where men and women in bowling shirts passed by the front desk. "Cal's going to have a full house tonight."

"There's Napper." Gage sipped his beer while he studied the man in the maroon and cream team shirt. "Is he still—"

"Yeah. Had some words with him just a couple days ago. He's just an older asshole now, with a badge."

"A fifty-eight." Layla plopped down to change her shoes after her last frame. "I don't think I've discovered my newest passion."

"I like it," Cybil said as she sat beside her. "I'd vote for more attractive footwear, but I like the game, the destruct, reconstruct of it."

"Meaning?"

"Deliver the ball, destroy the pins. Hit them right, you can make them destroy each other. Then, wait a minute, they're all back again, like ten soldiers. After all those war games," she said with a teasing smile for Fox, "I'm starving." She tipped her head back, looked at Gage. "How'd your battle fare?"

"I do better with cards and women."

"I kicked his ass, as promised. Beer's on Gage."

They didn't discuss the morning as they sat around a table with pizza and beer. They didn't talk about their plans for the next day. For the moment, they were simply a group

of friends enjoying one another and the entertainment offered in a small, rural town.

"My game next time," Gage announced. "A nice friendly game of poker." He sneered at Fox. "We'll see who's buying the beer then."

"Anytime, anywhere." Fox grinned as he grabbed a slice of pizza. "I've been practicing."

"Strip poker doesn't count."

"Does if you win," he said with his mouth full.

"Look who's back!" Shelley Kholer wiggled her way over in jeans designed to bruise internal organs and a shirt sized for an undeveloped twelve-year-old. She grabbed Gage's face with both hands and gave him a long, greedy and slightly drunken kiss.

"Hey, Shell," he said when he had his tongue back.

"I heard you were back, but haven't seen hide or hair. Aren't you just as yummy as ever? Why don't we—"

"What's new?" he interrupted, and picked up a beer to shield his mouth from another assault.

"I'm getting a divorce."

"Sorry to hear it."

"I'm not. Block's a worthless, two-timing bastard with a dick the size of a pickle. One of those little ones, you know?"

"I didn't know that."

"Shoulda run away with you," she said and sent everyone at the table a blurry smile. "Hi, y'all. Hey, Fox! I want to talk to you about my divorce."

She wanted to talk about her divorce twenty hours out of every twenty-four, Fox thought. The other four were reserved for talking about her sister who'd gotten a little too friendly with Shelley's husband. "Why don't you come into the office next week?"

"I can talk freely here. I got no secrets. I got no secrets in the whole damn town. Every sumbitch in it knows my husband got caught with his hand on my sister's tit. I wanna

add that thing, that loss of consortium—that loss of nookie thing to the complaint."

"We'll talk about that. Why don't I buy you a cup of coffee up at the counter, and we can—"

"Don't want coffee. I got a nice buzz on to celebrate my upcoming divorce. I want another beer, and I want to make out with Gage. Like the old days."

"Why don't we have one anyway?"

"I could make out with you," she said to Fox as he rose to lead her away. "Did we ever make out?"

"I was fifteen in the old days," Gage announced when Fox steered Shelley to the counter. "I just want that on record."

"She's so unhappy. Sorry," Layla murmured. "It's one of those things I can't help but pick up on. She's so miserable."

"Fox'll help her through it. It's what he does." Cal nodded toward the counter where Shelley sat, listening to Fox, her head resting on his shoulder. "He's the sort of lawyer who takes the term *counselor* to heart."

"If my sister played squeeze the melons with my husband, I'd want to skin him in a divorce, too." Cybil broke off a tiny corner of a nacho. "That's if I were married. And after I'd beaten them both to bloody pulps. Is her husband really named Block?"

"Unfortunately," Cal confirmed.

At the counter, Shelley ignored the coffee, but she listened.

"It'd be better if you didn't badmouth Block in public. Say whatever you want about him to me, okay? But it's not good for you to go off on him, especially the size of his dick, in public."

"He doesn't really have a little pickle dick," Shelley muttered. "But he should. He shouldn't have any dick at all."

"I know. Are you here by yourself?"

"No." She sighed now. "I came with my girlfriends. We're in the arcade. We're having a Fuck Men night. In the bad way."

"That's fine. You're not driving, are you, Shelley?"

"No, we walked from Arlene's. We're going back there after. She's pissed at her boyfriend."

"If you're ready to go while I'm still here, and you want someone to drive you, or walk you, come and get me."

"You're the sweetest damn thing in the whole world."

"Do you want to go back to the arcade?"

"Yeah. We're going home soon anyway to make apple martinis and watch *Thelma and Louise*."

"Sounds great." He took her arm, steered her clear of Gage and the table, and walked her to the arcade.

Deciding he'd earned another beer, he swung back by the counter, ordered one on Gage's tab.

"So, you're sticking it to Shelley in more ways than one."

Fox didn't turn at Napper's voice. "Slow night for crime, Deputy Take-a-Nap?"

"People with real jobs take nights off. What's your excuse?"

"I like watching people without balls throw them."

"I wonder what'll happen to yours when Block finds out you're doing his wife."

"Here you go, Fox." Behind the counter, Holly set down Fox's drink, gave him a quick, understanding look. She'd worked the counter for enough years to know when trouble was brewing. "Get you something, Deputy?"

"Pitcher of Bud. I bet Block's going to kick your pansy ass into next week."

"You're going to want to stay out of that." Fox turned now, faced Napper. "Block and Shelley have enough problems without you screwing with them."

"You telling me what to do?" He jabbed a finger into Fox's chest, bared his teeth in a fierce "dare you" grin.

"I'm telling you Block and Shelley are going through a tough time and don't need you making it worse because you want to fuck with me." Fox picked up his beer. "You need to move."

"I don't need to do a goddamn thing. It's my night off."

"Yeah? Mine, too." Fox, who'd never been able to walk away from a dare, tipped the beer down Napper's shirt. "Oops. Butterfingers."

"You stupid fuck." He shoved, and the force of it would've knocked Fox on his ass, if he hadn't anticipated it.

He danced lightly to the side, so that Napper's forward motion sent the deputy careening into one of the counter stools. When he righted himself, spun to retaliate, he wasn't just facing Fox, but Gage and Cal as well.

"That's a damn shame," Gage drawled. "All that beer wasted. Looks good on you though, Napper."

"We run your kind out of town these days, Turner."

Gage spread his arms in invitation. "Run me."

"None of us are looking for trouble here, Derrick." Cal took a step forward, his eyes hard on Napper's. "This is a family place. Lots of kids in here. Lots of witnesses. I'll take you over to our gift shop, get you a new shirt. No charge."

"I don't want a damn thing from you." He sneered at Fox. "Your friends won't always be around to protect you, O'Dell."

"You keep forgetting the rules." Now Gage stepped forward, effectively blocking Fox before his friend rose to the bait. "You mess with one of us, you mess with all of us. But Cal and I? We'll be happy to hold Fox's coat while he kicks the shit out of you. Wouldn't be the first time."

"Times change." Napper shoved his way past them.

"Not so much," Gage murmured. "He's as big a dick as ever."

"Told you." With apparent ease, Fox stepped back up to the counter. "I'm going to need another beer, Holly."

When he walked back to the table, Quinn gave him a sunny smile. "Dinner and a show. This place has it all."

"That show's been running about twenty-five years."

"He hates you," Layla said quietly. "He doesn't even know why."

"There doesn't have to be a why for some people." Fox laid a hand over hers. "Forget him. How about a round of pinball—any machine. And you get a thousand-point handicap."

"I think that may be an insult, but . . . Don't! Don't drink that. God. Look."

The beer glass in Fox's hand foamed with blood. He set it down slowly. "Two wasted beers in one night. I guess the party's over."

WHEN QUINN OPTED TO STAY AT THE BOWLING center with Cal until closing, Fox walked Layla and Cybil home. It was only a couple of blocks, and he knew they were far from defenseless. But he didn't like the idea of them being out at night on their own.

"What's the back story on the jerk currently wearing your beer?" Cybil asked him.

"Just a bully who's needled me since we were kids. Deputy Bully now."

"No particular reason?"

"I was skinny, smaller than him—smarter, too—and came from tree-hugger stock."

"More than enough. Well . . ." Her fingers gave his biceps a testing pinch. "You're not skinny now. And you're still smarter than him." She sent Fox an approving smirk. "Quicker, too."

"He wants to hurt you. It's on his top ten list of things to accomplish." Layla studied Fox's profile as they crossed the street. "He won't stop. His kind doesn't."

"Napper's top ten list isn't my biggest concern. He has to get in line."

"Ah, home again." Cybil climbed the first step, turned, looked around the quiet street. "We managed bowling, dinner, a minor brawl, and a memo from evil, and it's still shy of eleven. The fun never ends in Hawkins Hollow." She laid her hands on Fox's shoulders. "Thanks for walking us home, cutie." She gave him a light kiss. "See you in the morning. Layla, why don't you work out the logistics—timing, transportation—with Fox and let me know. I'll be upstairs."

"My parents should be out of the house by eight," he told Layla when Cybil strolled away. "I can come by and pick you all up if you need."

"That's all right. We'll take Quinn's car, I imagine. Who's going to walk you home, Fox?"

"I remember the way."

"You know what I mean. You should come in, stay here."

He smiled, eased in a little closer. "Where here?"

"On the couch, for now anyway." She put a fingertip to his chest, eased him right back.

"Your couch is lumpy, and you only have basic cable. You need to work on your strategy. If you'd asked me to stay because you were worried about it just being you and Cybil in the house, I'd be trying to sleep on your couch with a rerun of *Law and Order* while I was thinking about you upstairs in bed. Kiss me good night, Layla."

"Maybe I am worried about being in the house, just me and Cybil."

"No, you're not. Kiss me good night."

She sighed. She really was going to have to work on her strategy. Deliberately, she tipped her face up, and gave him the light, friendly kiss Cybil had. "Good night. Be careful."

"Careful doesn't always get the job done. Case in point."

He caught her face in his hands, lowered his lips to hers.

Though the kiss was soft, though it was slow, she felt the impact from the top of her head to the soles of her feet. The glide of his tongue, the brush of his thumbs at her temples, the solid line of his body dissolved her bones.

He held her face even as he lifted his head, looked into her eyes. "That was a kiss good night."

"It was. No question about it."

He kissed her again with the same silky confidence until she had to grip his forearms for balance.

"Now neither one of us will get any sleep." He stepped back. "So my work here is done. Unfortunately. I'll see you tomorrow."

"Okay." She made it to the door before she turned, looked back at him from what she considered a safe distance. "I have a careful nature, especially when it's important. I think sex is important, or should be."

"It's on my top ten list of personal priorities."

She laughed, opened the door. "Good night, Fox."

Inside, Layla went straight upstairs where Cybil came out of the office, eyebrow lifted. "Alone?"

"Yeah."

"Can I ask why you're not about to get a good taste of adorable lawyer?"

"I think he might matter too much."

"Ah." With a knowing nod, Cybil leaned on the doorjamb. "That always tangles things up. Want to work off some sexual frustration with research and logs?"

"I'm not sure charts and graphs have that kind of power, but I'll give it a shot." She shrugged out of her jacket as she stepped into the office. "What do you do when they might matter too much?"

"Generally, I run—either straight into it or away. It's had mixed results." Cybil walked over to study the map of the town Layla had generated and pinned to the wall.

"I tend to circle around and around, weigh and think entirely too much. I'm wondering now if it was because I

tuned in." She tapped her head. "Without really knowing I was tuning in."

"That may be." Cybil picked up a red pushpin—representing blood—stuck it into the bowling center on the map to signal another incident. "But Fox would be a lot to think about under normal circumstances. Add in the abnormal, and it's a lot to consider. Take your time if time's what you need."

"Under normal circumstances that would be reasonable." At the desk, Layla chose a red index card, wrote: *Bloody Beer, Fox, Bowl-a-Rama*, and the time and date. "But time is one of the issues, isn't it? And how much we may actually have."

"You sound like Gage. It's a good thing you two didn't hook up or you'd never look beyond the dark side."

"That may be, but . . ." Frowning, Layla studied the map. "There's another pin, a black pin on the road between Fox's house and Cal's."

"Standing for the big, ugly dog. Didn't I tell you? No, that's right, you went straight from work to the center. Sorry."

"Tell me now."

Once she had, Layla selected a dark blue card, the color she'd chosen for any demon-in-animal-form sighting, filled it in.

"I hate to say this, but while my mind is now occupied and my hands busy, I'm still sexually frustrated."

"There, there." Cybil patted Layla's shoulder. "I'm going to go make some tea. We'll add some chocolate. That always helps."

Layla doubted if candy was going to satisfy her appetite for adorable lawyer, but she'd take what she could get.

Eight

~◊~

A CHILLY TRICKLE OF RAIN DAMPENED THE morning. It was the sort, Fox knew, that tended to hang around all day like a sick headache. Nothing to do but tolerate it.

He dug out a hooded sweatshirt from a basket of laundry he'd managed to wash, but hadn't yet put away. At least he was ninety percent sure he'd washed it. Maybe seventy-five. So he sniffed it, then bumped that up to a hundred percent.

He found jeans, underwear, socks—though the socks took longer as he actually wanted them to match. As he dressed, glanced around his bedroom, he vowed he'd find the time and the willpower to put the stupid laundry away, even though it would eventually be in need of washing and putting away again. He'd make the bed sometime in this decade, and shovel out the rest of the junk.

If he could get it to that point, maybe he could find a cleaning lady who'd stick it out. Maybe a cleaning guy, he

considered over his first Coke of the day. A guy would get it better, probably.

He'd look into it.

He laced on his old workboots, and because house-keeping was on his mind, tossed discarded shoes in the closet and, inspired, shoved the laundry basket in after them.

He grabbed his keys, another Coke and a Devil Dog that would serve as his while-driving breakfast. Halfway down the outside steps, he spotted Layla standing at the base.

"Hey."

"I was just coming up. We saw your truck was still here, so I had Quinn drop me off. I thought I'd ride with you."

"Great." He held up the snack cake. "Devil Dog?"

"Actually, I've had enough of devil dogs on four legs."

"Oh yeah." He ripped the wrapper as he joined her. "Strangely, that's never put me off the joy of the Devil Dog."

"That is not your breakfast," she said as he bit in. He only smiled, kept walking.

"My stomach stopped maturing at twelve." He pulled open the passenger door of his truck. "How'd you sleep?"

She shot a look at him over her shoulder as she climbed in. "Well enough." She waited until he'd rounded the hood and slid behind the wheel. "Even after Cybil told me about her and Gage's run-in—literally—with a devil dog. It happened when they were driving to Cal's from your place."

"Yeah, Gage filled me in while I was skinning him at pinball." He set his Coke in the drink holder, took another bite of the cake. After a quick check, he pulled away from the curb.

"I wanted to ride with you because I had some ideas on how to approach this thing today."

"And I thought it was because you can't keep away from me."

"I'm trying not to react with my hormones."

"Damn shame."

"That may be, but . . . It took so much out of Quinn yesterday. I'm hoping we could try, you and me, and take her out of the mix. The whole point is to find the journals, if they're there. If they are, they're in the now. If not, then we'd have to fall back to Quinn. But—"

"You'd like to spare her the migraine. We can try it. I'm also assuming you didn't mention this idea to her."

"I figured, if you agreed, we could bring it up as something we came up with on the drive over." She smiled over at him. "There, I'm working on my strategy. Did you dream last night?"

"Only about you. We were in my office, and you were wearing this really, really little red dress and those high heels with the ankle straps? Those kill me. You sat on my desk, facing me. I was in the chair. And you said, after you'd licked your lips: 'I'm ready to take dictation, Mr. O'Dell.' "

She listened, head cocked. "You just made that up."

He shot her a quick and charming grin. "Maybe, but I guarantee I'll have that dream tonight. Maybe we should go out. There's this bar over the river? A nice bar. They have live music on Saturday nights. They get some pretty decent musicians in."

"It sounds so normal. I keep trying to keep a grip on normal with one hand while I'm digging into the impossible with the other. It's . . ."

"Surreal. I forget about it—between the Sevens, I can forget about it for weeks, even months sometimes. Then something reminds me. That's surreal, too. Going along, doing the work, having fun, whatever and *zap*, it's right back in my head. The closer it gets, the more it's in my head." His fingers danced against the steering wheel to the beat of Snow Patrol. "So a nice bar with good music is a way to remember it's a lot, but it's not everything."

"That's a smart way to look at it. I'm not sure I can get

to that point, but I'd like to listen to some music across the river. What time?"

"Ah . . . nine? Is nine good for you?"

"All right." She drew in a breath when he turned in the lane to the farmhouse. She was making a date with a man she was about to link with psychically. Surreal didn't quite cover it.

It also felt rude, she discovered, to go inside the house without invitation. It was Fox's childhood home, true enough, but he no longer lived there. She thought about going into her parents' condo when they weren't there, deliberately choosing a time they weren't there, and simply couldn't.

"This feels wrong," she said as they stood in the living room. "It feels wrong and intrusive. I understand why we want to do this while they're not home, but it feels . . ." At a loss, she settled for the standby. "Rude."

"My parents don't mind people coming in. Otherwise, they'd lock the doors."

"Still—"

"We have to prioritize, Layla." Quinn spread her hands. "The reason we're here is more important than standard guidelines of courtesy. I got so much outside the house yesterday. I'm bound to get more inside."

"About that. I had this idea, talked it over with Layla on the drive. If you don't mind us cutting in line, Quinn, I'd like to try something with Layla first. We may be able to visualize where the journals are, if they're here. Or at least get a sense of them."

"That's good thinking. And not just because I'd rather you didn't go through it again," Cal added when Quinn narrowed her eyes at him. "It could work, and better yet, with Fox and Layla linked, it downscales the side effects."

"And if it doesn't work," Fox added, "back to you."

"All right, that makes sense. Believe me, it's not as if I look forward to having my head explode."

"Okay, then we're up. This is the oldest part of the house. Actually, this room and the ones directly above *were* the house as far as anyone can tell. So, logically, if there was a cabin or a house here before this one was built, it could be over the same spot. Maybe, especially given Quinn's trip yesterday, they used some of the same materials."

"Like the fireplace." Quinn crossed to it, stepped over Lump, who'd already stretched out in front of the low fire, to run her hand over the stones. "I'm big on the idea of hiding stuff behind bricks and stones."

"And if we hack at that mortar, start pulling out stones without being a hundred percent, my father will kill me. Ready?" Fox asked Layla.

"As I'll ever be."

"Look at me." He took her hands. "Just look at me. Don't think. Imagine. A small book, the writing inside. The ink's faded. Imagine her handwriting. You've seen it in her other journals."

His eyes were so rich. That old gold color so fascinating. His hands weren't lawyer-smooth. Not like the hands of a man who carried a briefcase, who worked at a desk. There was labor on them, strength and capability in them. He smelled of the rain, just a little of rain.

He would taste like cake.

He wanted her. Imagined touching her, gliding his hands over bare skin, sliding them over her breasts, her belly. Laying his lips there, his tongue, tasting the heat, the flesh . . .

In bed, when there's only us.

She gasped, jerked back. His voice had been clear inside her head.

"What did you see?" Cal demanded. "Did you see it?"

With his eyes still locked on Layla's, Fox shook his head. "We had to get something out of the way first. One more time?" he said to Layla. "Use your compartments."

Her skin felt hot, inside and out, but she nodded. And she did her best to set her own desires, and his, aside.

Everything drew together into a narrow point. In it she heard the jumbled thoughts of her companions, like background chatter at a cocktail party. There was concern, doubt, anticipation, a mix of feelings. These, too, she set aside.

The book was in her head. Brown leather cover, dried from age. Yellowed pages and faded ink.

With the dark so close outside, I long for my love.

"It's not here." Fox spoke first as he carefully let the connection between him and Layla fade. "It's not in this room."

"No."

"Then I need to try again." Quinn squared her shoulders. "I can try to home in on her, on the journal. See when she packed it away, maybe to take back to her father's house in town. The old library."

"No, they're not in the old library," Layla said slowly. "They're not in this room."

"But they're here," Fox finished. "It was too clear. They have to be here."

Gage tapped a foot on the floor. "Could be under. She might have hidden them under floorboards, if there were floorboards."

"Or buried them," Cybil continued.

"If they're under the house, we're pretty well screwed," Gage pointed out. "If Brian would be unhappy with us taking some stones out of the fireplace, he'd be pretty well crazed if we suggested razing the damn house to get under it for some diaries."

"You don't have enough respect for diaries," Cybil commented. "But you're right about the first part."

"We need to try again. We can go room to room," Layla suggested. "The basement? Is there a basement? If she did bury them, we might get a better signal from there. Be-

cause I can't believe they're inaccessible. Giles told her what would happen, told her about us—about you."

"She may have hidden them to keep them from being lost or destroyed." Cal paced as he tried to think it through. "From being found too soon, or by the wrong people. But she'd want us to find them, she'd have wanted that. Even if just for sentiment."

"I agree with that. I know what I felt from her. She loved Giles. She loved her sons. And everything in her hoped for what those who came after her would do. We're her chance to be with Giles again, to free him."

"Let's take it outside. Yeah, there's a basement," Fox told Layla. "But we could focus on the whole house from outside. And the shed. The shed was here, most likely, when Ann was here. We should try the shed."

As Fox had expected, the rain continued, slow and thin. He put his parents' dogs in the house with Lump to keep them out of the way. And with the others, stepped out in the stubborn drizzle.

"Before we do this, I had an idea—came to me in there—about the Bat Signal?"

"The what?" Quinn interrupted.

"Alarm system," Fox explained. "I can get it, the way I could get all the mental chatter in there. It's just like tuning a radio, really. If you push toward me, I should pick it up. If I push toward any of you, same goes. We'll want to run it a few times, but it should work faster than phone tag."

"Psychic team alert." Cybil adjusted her black bucket hat. "Unlimited minutes, and fewer dropped calls. I like it."

"What if you're the one in trouble?" Under her light jacket, Layla wore a hoodie in what he supposed should be called an orchid color. She drew the hood up and over her hair as they crossed the yard.

"Then I push to Cal or Gage. We've done that during the Seven before. Or to you," he added, "once you've gotten a

better handle on it. We used to play in there. Remember?" Fox called out to Cal and Gage. "We used it for a fort for a while, only we didn't call it a fort—too warlike for the Barry-O'Dells. So we said it was our clubhouse."

"We murdered thousands from in there." Gage stopped, hands tucked in his pockets. "Died a million deaths."

"We made our plans for the birthday hike to the Pagan Stone while we were in there." Cal stopped. "Do you remember? I'd forgotten that. A couple weeks before our birthday, we got the idea."

"Gage's idea."

"Yeah, blame me."

"We were—what the hell, let me think. School was out. Just out. It was the first full day of freedom, and my mom let me come over and hang all day."

"No chores," Fox continued. "I remember now. I got a pass on chores, one-day pass. First day after school let out. We were playing in there."

"Vice cops against drug lords," Gage put in.

"A change from cowboys and Indians," Cybil commented.

"Hippie boy wouldn't play greedy invaders against indigenous peoples. And if you'd ever gotten one of Joanne Barry's lectures on same, you wouldn't either." The memory had a smile ghosting around Gage's mouth. "We were so juiced up, September was a lifetime off. Everything was hot and bright, green and blue. I didn't want that to end, I remember that, too. Yeah, it was my idea. Major adventure, total freedom."

"We all jumped on it," Cal reminded him. "Plotted the whole thing out right in there." He gestured toward the vine-wrapped stones. "I'm damned if that's a coincidence."

They stood there a moment, side by side. Remembering, Layla supposed. Three men of the same age, who'd come from the same place. Gage in his black leather jacket, Cal in his flannel overshirt and watch cap, Fox in

his hooded sweatshirt. Odd, she thought, how something as basic as their choice in outerwear spoke to their individuality even while their stance spoke of their absolute unity.

"Layla." Fox reached out. Her hands were wet and cool. Rain sparkled on her lashes. Even without the psychic link, her anxiety and eagerness flowed toward him.

"Just let it come," he told her. "Don't push, don't even reach for it. Relax, look at me."

"I have a hard time doing both of those things at the same time."

His grin was pure male pleasure. "We'll see what we can do about that later. For right now, bring the book into your head. Just the book. Here we go."

He was both bridge and anchor. She would realize that later, that he had the skill, had the understanding to offer her both. As she crossed the bridge, he was with her. She felt the rain on her face, the ground under her feet. She smelled the earth, the wet grass, even the wet stone. There was a hum, low and steady. She understood with a stab of awe that it was the growing. Grass, leaves, flowers. All humming toward spring and sunlight. Toward the green.

She heard the faint whoosh of air that was a bird winging by, and the scrape that was a squirrel scampering across a branch.

Amazing, she thought, to understand that she was a part of it, and always had been. Always would be. What grew, what breathed, what slept. What lived and died.

There was the smell of earth, of smoke, of wet, of skin. She heard the sigh of rain leaving a cloud, and the murmur of the clouds drifting.

So she drifted, across the bridge.

The pain was sudden and shocking, like a vicious and violent rip inside her. Head, belly, heart. Even as she cried out, she saw the book—just a flash. Then the flash was gone, and so was the pain, leaving her weak and dizzy.

"Sorry. I lost it."

Gage's hands hooked under her armpits as she toppled. "Steady, baby. Easy does it. Cybil."

"Yes, I've got her. Lean on me a minute. You had quite a ride."

"I could hear the clouds moving, and the garden grow. It hums. The flowers hum under the ground. God, I feel . . ."

"Stoned?" Quinn suggested. "You look stoned."

"That's about right. Wow. Fox, did you—" She broke off when she managed to focus. He was on his knees on the wet gravel, his friends crouched on either side of him. And there was blood on his shirt.

"Oh my God, what happened?" She pushed instinctively with her mind, but rammed into a wall. She stumbled, went down on her hands and knees in front of him. "You're hurt. Your nose is bleeding."

"Wouldn't be the first time. Damn it, I just washed this stupid sweatshirt. Just give me some room. Give me room." He dragged a bandanna out of his pocket, pressing it to his nose as he sat back on his heels.

"Let's get him inside," Quinn began, but Fox shook his head, then pressed his free hand to it as if the movement threatened to break it away from his shoulders. "Need a minute."

"Cal, go get him some water. Let's try your mother's trick, Fox." Cybil moved behind him. "Just breathe." She found the points, pressed. "Should I ask if you're pregnant?"

"Not a good time to make me laugh. Little sick here."

"Why was it worse for him than for Quinn?" Layla demanded. "It was supposed to be less, because we were linked. But it's worse. You know." She aimed a fierce look at Gage. "Why?"

"Being O'Dell, he stepped in front of you and took the full punch. That'd be my guess. And because of the link, it was a hell of a punch."

"Is that it?" Furious, Layla turned on Fox. "I'm listening to clouds and you're getting kicked in the face."

"Your face is prettier than mine. Marginally. Quiet a minute, okay? Have a little pity for the wounded."

"Don't ever do it again. You look at me, you listen to me. Don't ever do it again. You promise that, or I'm done with this."

"I don't like ultimatums." Even through the glaze of pain in his eyes, the temper sparked. "In fact, they piss me off."

"You know what pisses me off? You didn't trust me to carry my share."

"It has nothing to do with trust or shares. Thanks, Cybil, it's better." He got carefully to his feet, took the water Cal offered and drank it straight down. "They're wrapped in oilcloth, behind the south wall. I couldn't tell how many. Two, maybe three. You know where the tools are, Cal. I'll be back out to help in a minute."

He made it into the house, into the bathroom off the kitchen before he was as sick as a man after a two-day drunk. With his stomach raw and his head a misery, he rinsed his face, his mouth. Then just leaned on the sink until he had his breath back.

When he came out, Layla stood in the kitchen. "We're not finished."

"You want to fight? We'll fight later. Right now we've got a job to do."

"I'm not doing anything until you give me your word you won't shield me again."

"Can't do it. I only give my word when I'm sure I can keep it." He turned, started rooting through cupboards. "Nothing but holistic shit in this house. Why is there never any damn Excedrin?"

"You had no right—"

"Sue me. I know some good lawyers. We do what we do, Layla. That's the way it is. That's the way I am. I took

a shot because I knew it was a good one. I got there because of you, because of us. I wasn't going to let you get hurt if I could stop it, and I'm not going to promise not to do what I can to stop you from being hurt down the road."

"If you think because I'm a woman I'm weaker, less capable, less—"

His face was sheet pale as he rounded on her. Even temper couldn't push the color back into his face. "Christ, don't start waving the feminist flag. Did you meet my mother? Your sex has nothing to do with it—other than the fact that I'm gone on you, which, being straight, I wouldn't be if you were a guy. I survived. I got a headache, a nosebleed, and I lost my breakfast—and dinner, and possibly a couple of internal organs. But other than wishing to goddamn hell and back there was some aspirin and a can of Coke around this house, I'm fine. You want to be pissed, be pissed. But be pissed correctly."

As he drilled his fingers into his forehead, she opened the purse she'd left on the kitchen table. From it she took a little box with a crescent moon on the top.

"Here." She handed him two pills. "It's Advil."

"Praise the lord. Don't be stingy. Give me a couple more."

"I'm still pissed, correctly or incorrectly." She handed him two more pills, inwardly wincing when he dry-swallowed the lot. "But I'm going out to help do the job because I'm part of this team. Let me say this first, if you're so gone over me, consider how I feel seeing you on the ground, bleeding and in pain. There are lots of ways to be hurt. Think about that."

When she stalked out he stayed where he was. She might've had a point, but he was too worn out to think about it. Instead, he got the pitcher of his mother's cold tea out of the fridge and downed a glass to wash the dregs of annoyance and sickness from his throat.

Because he still felt shaky, he left the chiseling to Gage

and Cal. Eventually, he'd have to tell his parents, he thought. Especially if they weren't able to replace the stone in such a way the removal didn't show.

No, he thought, he'd have to tell them either way or he'd feel guilty.

In any case, they'd understand—a lot better than a certain brunette—why he'd wanted to try this when they were away from home. They may not like it, but they wouldn't start shoveling the you-don't-trust-me crap over his head. Not their style.

"Try not to chip it."

"It's a fucking stone, O'Dell." Gage slammed the hammer on the knob of the chisel. "Not a damn diamond."

"Tell that to my parents," he muttered, then jammed his hands in his pockets.

"You'd better be sure this is the one." Cal struck from the other side. "Or else we're going to be doing a lot more than chipping one rock."

"That's the one. The wall's four deep, one of the reasons it's still standing. That one was probably loose or she worked it loose. The past shit's your milieu."

"Milieu, my ass." Wet, his knuckles scraped, Cal struck again. By the next strike, the knuckles had already healed, but he was still soaked to the skin. "It's coming."

He and Gage worked it loose by hand as Fox fought the image of the whole wall crumbling like a game of Jenga.

"Sucker weighs a ton," Gage complained. "More like a damn boulder. Watch the fingers." He cursed as the movement pinched his fingers between rocks, then let the weight of the stone carry it to the ground. Sitting back on his heels, he sucked at his bleeding hand as Cal reached into the opening.

"Son of a bitch. I've got it." Cal drew out a package wrapped in oilcloth. "Score one for O'Dell." Carefully, hunching over to protect the contents from the rain, he unwrapped the cloth.

"Don't open them," Quinn warned from behind them. "It's too wet out here. The ink might run. Ann Hawkins's journals. We found them."

"We'll take them back to my place. Get out of these wet clothes, then—"

The blast shook the ground. It knocked Fox off his feet, smashing him into the stone wall with his hip and shoulder taking the brunt. Head ringing, he turned to see the house burning. Flames shot through the roof, clawed through broken windows with the roaring belch of black smoke behind them. He ran toward home, through a blistering wall of heat.

When Gage tackled him, he slammed hard into the ground and swung out with blind fury. "The dogs are inside. Goddamn it."

"Pull yourself together." Gage shouted over the bellow of fire. "Is it real? Pull it together, Fox. Is it real?"

He could feel the burn. He swore he could feel it, and the smoke stinging his eyes, scoring his throat as he choked in air. He had to fight back the image of his home going up in flames, of three helpless dogs trapped and panicked.

He gripped Gage's shoulder as an anchor, then Cal's forearm as his friends pulled him to his feet. They stood linked for a moment, and a moment was all he needed.

"It's a lie. Damn. Just another lie." He heard Cal's breath shudder out. "Lump's fine. The dogs are fine. It's just more bullshit."

The fire wavered, spurted, died, so the old stone house stood whole under the thin and steady rain.

Fox let out a breath of his own. "Sorry about the fist in the face," he said to Gage.

"You hit like a girl."

"Your mouth's bleeding."

Gage swiped at it, grinned. "Not for long."

Cal strode to the house, threw open the door to let the

dogs out. Then simply sat on the floor of the back porch with his arms full of Lump.

"It's not supposed to come here." Fox walked forward, too, set a hand on the porch rail he'd helped build. "It's never been able to come here. Not to our families."

"Things are different now." Cybil crouched down and rubbed the other two dogs as they wagged tails. "These dogs aren't scared. It didn't happen for them. Just us."

"And if my parents had been in there?"

"It wouldn't have happened for them either." Quinn dropped down beside Cal. "How many times have the three of you seen things no one else has?"

"Sometimes they're real," Fox pointed out.

"This wasn't. It just wanted to shake us up, scare us. It—Oh God, the journals."

"I have them."

Fox turned, saw Layla standing in the rain, clutching the wrapped package against her breasts. "It wanted to hurt you. Couldn't you feel it? Because you found them. Couldn't you feel the hate?"

He'd felt nothing, Fox realized, but panic—and that was a mistake. "So he scored one, too." He crossed to Layla, drew up the hood that had fallen away. "But we're still ahead."

Nine

~⌒~

THERE WAS COFFEE FOR THOSE WHO WANTED IT, and a fire burning bright in Cal's living room to warm chilled bones. There were enough dry clothes to go around, though Layla wasn't sure what sort of a fashion statement she made in a pair of Cal's jogging shorts bagging well past her knees and a shirt several sizes too big. But Cybil had snagged the spare jeans Quinn had left at Cal's, and beggars couldn't be choosers.

While the washer and dryer churned away, she topped off her coffee. Her feet swished over the kitchen floor in enormous wool socks.

"Nice outfit," Fox said from the doorway.

"Could start a trend." She turned to face him. Cal's clothes fit him a great deal better than they did her. "Are you all right now?"

"Yeah." He got a Coke out of the fridge. "I'm going to ask you to put whatever mad you've still got on aside for a while. We'll deal with them later, if we have to."

"That's the problem, isn't it? Personal feelings, reactions, relationships. They get in the way, knot things up."

"Maybe. Can't do much about it as *person*'s the root of personal. We can't stop being people, or it wins."

"What would have happened if Gage hadn't stopped you, if you'd gotten inside the house?"

"I don't know."

"You do, or you can speculate. Here's what I speculate. At that moment, the fire was real to you, you believed it, so it was real. You felt the heat, the smoke. And if you'd gotten in, despite how quickly you heal, you could've died because you believed."

"I let the son of a bitch scam me. My mistake."

"Not the point. It could kill you. I never really considered that before. It could use your mind to end your life."

"So we have to be smarter." He shrugged, but the gesture was an irritable jerk that told her temper was still lurking inside him. "It got one over on me today because nothing's ever happened at the farm, or at Cal's parents' house. They've always been out-of-bounds. Safe zones. So I didn't think, I just reacted. That's never smart."

"If it had been real, you'd have gone in. You'd have risked your life to save three dogs. I don't know what to think of you," she said after a moment. "I don't know what to feel. So I guess, like my mad, I need to put that aside and deal with it later."

"Sorry." Quinn stood in the doorway of the adjoining dining room. "We're ready in here."

"Just coming." Layla walked out. A few seconds later, Fox followed.

"I guess we should just dive in." Quinn took a seat beside Cal at the table. She glanced over to where Cybil sat with a notepad, ready to write down thoughts, impressions. "So, who wants to do the honors?"

Six people studied the wrapped package on the table. Six people said nothing.

"Oh, hell, this is silly." Quinn picked up the books, carefully unwrapped them. "Even considering they were protected, they're awfully well preserved."

"We can assume, under the circumstances, she had some power, some knowledge of magicks," Cybil pointed out. "Pick one, read an entry aloud."

"Okay, here goes." There were three, so she took the top one, opened it to the first entry. The ink was faded, but legible, the handwriting—familiar now—careful and clear.

" 'There must be a record, I think, of what was, what is, what will be. I am Ann. My father, Jonathan Hawkins, brought my mother, my sister, brother, and me to this place we call the Hollow. It is a new world where he believes we will be happy. So we have been. It is a green place, a rough place, a quiet place. He and my uncle cleared land for shelter, for crops. The water is cold and clear in the spring. More came, and the Hollow became Hawkins Hollow. My father has built a small and pretty stone house, and we have been comfortable there.

" 'There is work, as there should be work, to keep the mind and hands busy, to provide and to build. Those who settle here have built a stone chapel for worship. I have attended the services, as is expected. But I do not find God there. I have found him in the wood. It is there I feel at peace. It is there I first met Giles.

" 'Perhaps love does not come in an instant, but takes lifetimes. Is this how I knew, in that instant, such love? Is this how I felt, even saw in my mind's eye lifetime by lifetime with this man who lived alone in a stone cabin in the green shadowed wood that held the altar stone?

" 'He waited for me. This I knew as well. He waited for me to come to him, to see him, to know him. When we met we spoke of simple things, as is proper. We spoke of the sun and the wild berries I picked, of my father, of the hide Giles tanned.

" 'We did not speak of gods and demons, of magic and destiny, not then. That would come.

" 'I walked the wood, wandered my way to the stone cabin and the altar at every opportunity. He was always waiting for me. So the love of lifetimes bloomed again, in the green wood, in secret. I was his again, as I ever was, as I ever will be.' "

Quinn paused, sighed. "That's the first entry. It's lovely."

"Pretty words don't make much of a weapon," Gage commented. "They don't provide answers."

"I disagree with that," Cybil said. "And I think she deserves to have those words read as she wrote them. Lifetimes," she continued, tapping her notes. "That indicates her understanding that she and Dent were reincarnations of the guardian and his mate. Time and again. And he waited for her to accept it. He didn't launch right into, 'Hey, guess what, you and I are going to get cozy. You'll get knocked up with triplets, we'll hassle with some Big Evil Bastard, and a few hundred years from now our ancestors are going to fight the fight.' "

"Boy, a guy hits me with a line like that, I'm naked in a heartbeat." Quinn traced a finger down the page. "I'm with Cyb on this. There's value in every word because she wrote it. It's hard not to be impatient, just skim over looking for some magic formula for destroying demons."

Layla shook her head. "It won't be like that anyway."

"No, I don't think so either. Should I read on, in order?"

"I think we should see how it evolved, from her eyes." Fox glanced at Gage, at Cal. "Keep going, Quinn."

She read of love, of changes of seasons, of chores and quiet moments. Ann wrote of death, of life, of new faces. She wrote of the people who came to the stone cabin for healing. She wrote of her first kiss beside a stream where the water sparkled in the sun. She wrote of sitting with Giles in the stone cabin, in front of a fire that flamed red and gold as he told her of what had come before.

" 'He said to me that the world is old, older than any man can know. It is not as we have been taught, nor what we are told to believe in the faith of my father and my mother. Or that is not all of it. For, he said, in this old, old time before man came to be, there were others. Of the others there were the dark and the light. This was their choice, for there is always the freedom to choose. Those who chose the light were called gods, and the dark ones demons.

" 'There was death and blood, battles and war. Many of both were destroyed as man came to be. It was man who would spread over the world, who would rule it and be ruled by it. It was coming to, he said, the time of man, as was right. Demons hated man even more than they hated gods. They despised and envied their minds and hearts, their vulnerable bodies, their needs and weaknesses. Man became prey for the demons who survived. It came to be that those gods who survived as well became guardians. Battle after battle raged until there were only two, one light, one dark. One demon, one guardian. The light pursued the dark over the world, but the demon was clever and cunning. In this last battle, the guardian was wounded mortally, and left to die. There came upon this dying god a young boy, innocent and pure of heart. Dying, the god passed his power and his burden to the boy. So the boy, a mortal with the power of gods, became guardian. The boy became a man, hunting the dark. The boy became a man who loved a woman with the power of magic, and they had a son. At his death, the guardian passed his power and his burden to his son, and so it was done over all the years. Lifetime by lifetime, until this time, until this place. Now, he said, it is for us.

" 'I knew he spoke truth, for I saw it in the fire as he spoke. I understood the dreams I have had all of my life that I never dared speak of to any living soul. There, in the firelight, I pledged myself to him. There, in the firelight, I gave myself to him. I would not go back to the house of my

father but live with my beloved in the wood, in the stone cabin near the altar Giles called the Pagan Stone.'"

Quinn leaned back. "Sorry, my eyes are blurring."

"It's enough for now." Cal handed her the glass of water he'd poured. "It's a lot for now."

"It jibes with some versions of the lore that trickled down." Shifting, Cybil studied her notes. "The battles, the passing of power. The way I'm reading this is there's only this single demon left. I'm not sure if I buy that, I'm a little too superstitious. But it could be interpreted that this is the only demon known to walk the world freely, at least every seven years. Why didn't he mate before Hester Deale? That's curious, isn't it?"

"Maybe he couldn't get it up." Gage smiled thinly.

"I don't think that's far off. I think, however sarcastic, it's a viable theory." Cybil held up a finger. "Maybe they couldn't mate with humans, it couldn't. But as Giles apparently discovered a way to imprison the thing, at least for a time, it discovered a way to procreate. Each side evolving, so to speak. Every living thing evolves."

"Good thought," Fox agreed. "Or it might be that up until Hester, it was shooting blanks, so to speak. Or the women it violated never came to term for one reason or another. We should take a break. Quinn's been at it a couple hours now, and I don't know about anyone else, but I could use some fuel."

"Don't look at me," Cybil said firmly. "I cooked last time."

"I'll do it." Layla pushed to her feet. "Can I root around in the kitchen, Cal, until I come up with something?"

"Have at it."

She was bent over, head in the refrigerator, when Fox walked in. When a man thought how good a woman's ass looked in baggy, drooping shorts, he decided, that man had it bad.

"Thought I could give you a hand."

She straightened, turned with her hands full of a pack of American cheese slices, a pound of bacon, and a couple of hothouse tomatoes. "I thought grilled cheese, bacon, and tomato sandwiches. Maybe a quick pasta salad on the side if he's got something I can throw together for that. I can handle it."

"Because you want me out of here."

"No." She dumped the armload on the counter. "I'm not mad. It's too much trouble to stay mad. You could see if the clothes are dry so I could get out of these shorts and into my own clothes."

"Sure. But you look kind of cute."

"No, I don't."

"You're not looking at you." Gauging her mood, he stepped forward. "I can slice tomatoes. In fact, it's one of my more amazing skills. Plus." He kept moving in until she was backed against the counter with his hands planted on either side of her. "I know where Cal keeps the pasta."

"Making you invaluable in the kitchen?"

"I hope not. Layla." His eyes roamed her face. "I'm not going to tell you what to think or how to feel, or when to take those thoughts and feelings out of whatever box you need to keep them in. But I think about you. I feel for you. Unlike slicing tomatoes, packing away thoughts and feelings isn't one of my finer skills."

"I'm afraid of you."

Instant and complete shock ran over his face. "What? Of me? Nobody's afraid of me."

"That's absolutely not true. Deputy Napper is afraid of you. It's part of the reason he keeps after you. But that's a different kind of thing anyway. I'm afraid because you make me feel things I'm not sure I'm ready to feel, want things I'm not sure I'm ready to want. It would probably be easier if you rushed me, just did the sweep-off-the-feet routine because then I wouldn't have to feel responsible for my own choices."

"I could try that."

"No." She shook her head. "You won't. You're not built that way. Relationships are partnerships, sex is a mutual act and decision. That's how you were raised from the ground up, that's who you are. And it's part of what attracts me and makes it harder at the same time."

She put a hand on his chest, nudged slightly. When he eased back, she smiled as the basic action and reaction proved her point.

"I'm afraid of you," she continued, "because you'd run into a burning building to save a dog. Because you'd take what was my share of pain and trauma. You were right before. It's your nature. It wasn't just because it was me. You'd have done the same if it had been Cal or Gage, Quinn or Cybil. A complete stranger. I'm afraid of what you are because I've never known anyone like you. And I'm afraid that I'll take the chance, I'll reach out and take hold, then I'll lose you because, exactly because of who you are."

"All this time, I never knew I was such a scary guy."

She turned away, took a knife from the block, set it on the cutting board. "Slice the tomatoes."

She opened a cupboard, found the pasta herself. As she hunted up pan and skillet, his phone rang. She glanced over as he read the caller ID. "Hey, Mom and/or Dad. Yeah. Really?" He set the knife down again, leaned on the counter. "When? No kidding. Sure, sure." He tipped the phone away, murmured to Layla. "My sister and her partner are flying in. What?" he said into the phone. "No, not a problem. Ah, listen, while I've got you . . . We were out at the farm today, me and the rest. Early this morning. The thing is . . ." He trailed off, walked away into the adjoining laundry room.

Layla smiled as she heard the murmur of his voice. Yes, it was his nature, she thought as she put on water for the pasta. To save dogs, to be honest. And to explain to Mom and/or Dad just why he'd chiseled a stone out of their old shed.

It was hardly a wonder she was half in love with him.

The rain continued into the damp and dreary afternoon. They ate before moving into the living room by mutual consent where Quinn continued to read by the fire.

It was almost dreamy now, Layla thought. The patter of rain, the crackle of flame and wood, the sound of Quinn's voice speaking Ann's words. She curled in her chair, cozy again in her own warm clothes, drinking tea while Fox and Lump stretched out on the floor nearby.

If she were to take a picture, it would look like a group of friends, gathered together on a rainy day, in that chilly window between winter and spring. Quinn with her book, Cal beside her on the couch. Cybil curled like a lazy cat on the other end, and Gage sprawled in a chair drinking yet another cup of coffee.

But she had only to listen to the words for the picture to change. She had only to listen to see a young woman building another fire in a hearth, her bright hair sweeping down her back. To feel the ache in the heart that had stopped beating so long ago.

I am with child. There is such joy in me, and there is such grief.

Joy for the lives inside her, Layla thought. Grief as those lives signaled the beginning of the end of Ann's time with Giles. She imagined Ann preparing meals, fetching water from the stream, writing in the first journal with the cover Giles had made her from the leather he'd tanned himself. She wrote of ordinary things, of ordinary days. Pages and pages of the simple and the human.

"I'm tapped," Quinn said at length. "Somebody else can take over, but the fact is, my brain's just plain tired. I don't think I can take any more in right now even if someone else reads."

Cal shifted her to rub at her shoulders, while Quinn stretched in obvious relief. "If we try to take in too much at once, we'll probably miss something anyway."

"Lots of daily minutiae in that section." Cybil flexed her

writing hand. "He's tutoring her, showing her simple mag-icks. Herbs, candles, drawing out what she already had. She's very open to it. It seems obvious he didn't want to leave her without weapons, tools, defenses."

"Pioneer days," Fox commented. "Hard life."

"I think life was part of the point," Layla added. "The ordinary. We've all felt that, mentioned it at one time or an-other through this. The ordinary matters, it's very much what we're fighting for. I think she wrote about it, often, because she understood that. Or maybe because she needed to remind herself of it so she could face whatever was coming."

"We're more than halfway through the first journal." Quinn marked the page before setting the book down. "She still hasn't mentioned specifics on what's coming. Either he hasn't told her yet, specifically, or she hasn't wanted to write of it." She yawned hugely. "I vote we get out of here awhile or take a nap."

"They can all get out of here." Cal lowered his head to nip at her neck. "We'll take a nap."

"That's a lame euphemism for rainy-day sex, and you guys already get enough sex." Cybil uncurled a leg to give Cal a light kick. "Option two, another form of entertain-ment. That isn't poker," she added before Gage could speak.

"Sex and poker are the top two forms of entertainment," he told her.

"While I have no objection to either, there must be something a group of young, attractive people can find to do around here. No offense to the Bowl-a-Rama, Cal, but there must be somewhere we can get adult beverages, noise, maybe music, bad bar food."

"Actually— Ow!" Layla glared down at Fox when he pinched her foot. "Actually," she began again, "Fox men-tioned a place that seemed to fit that bill. A bar across the river with live music on Saturday nights."

"We're so going there." Cybil pushed to her feet. "Who's

stuck being designated drivers? I nominate Quinn from our side."

"Seconded," Layla called out.

"Aw."

"You're getting sex," Cybil reminded her. "No complaints will be registered."

"Gage." Fox mimed a gun with his thumb and forefinger.

"Always is," Gage said.

Even with the agreement it took thirty minutes for such vital matters as redoing makeup, dealing with hair. Then there was the debate over who was riding with whom, complicated by the fact that Cal remained adamant over not leaving Lump unattended.

"That thing came after my dog once, it could come after him again. Where I go, so goes the Lump. Plus, I ride with my woman."

Which left Fox squeezing into Cal's truck with Gage behind the wheel and Lump riding shotgun.

"Why can't he ride in the middle?" Fox demanded.

"Because he'll slobber on me, shed on me, and I'll smell like dog."

"I'm going to."

"Your problem, son." Gage slid a glance over. "And I guess it might be as the pretty brunette may object to being slobbered on by you scented with eau de Lump."

"She hasn't complained yet." Fox reached over to let the window down a few inches for Lump's sniffing nose.

"I can't blame you for moving in that direction. She's got that classy waif with brains and an underlayment of valor you'd go for."

"Is that what I go for?" Amused, Fox leaned against the bulk of Lump to study Gage's profile.

"She's right up your alley, with the unexpected addition of urban polish. Just don't let it screw you up."

"Why would it?"

When Gage didn't answer, Fox shifted. "That was seven years ago, and Carly didn't screw me up. What happened did, for a while. Layla's part of this, Carly wasn't. Or shouldn't have been."

"Does the fact that she's part of this worry you at all? You two have the connection, like Cal and Quinn. Now Cal's picking out china patterns."

"Is he?"

"Metaphorically speaking. Now here you are moving on Layla, and getting that cocker spaniel look in your eye when she's within sniffing distance."

"If I have to be a dog I want a Great Dane. They have dignity. And no, it doesn't worry me. I feel what I feel." He caught a glimmer. He couldn't help it; it was just there. And it made him smile as only brothers smile at each other. "But it worries you. Cal and Quinn, me and Layla. That leaves you and Cybil. You afraid fate's going to take a hand? Destiny's about to kick your ass? Should I order the monogrammed towels?"

"I'm not worried. I factor the odds in any game I play, make the players."

"The third female player is extremely hot."

"I've had hotter."

Fox snorted, turned to Lump. "He's had hotter."

"Plus, she's not my type."

"I didn't know there was any woman who wasn't your type."

"Complicated women aren't my type. You tangle in the sheets with a complicated woman, you're going to pay a price for it in the morning. I like them simple." He grinned over at Fox. "And plenty of them."

"A complicated woman will give you more play. And you like play."

"Not that kind. Simple gets you through. And plenty of simple gets you through a lot. I figure going for quantity, seeing as we might not live past our next birthday."

Reaching over, Fox gave Gage a friendly punch on the arm. "You always cheer me up with that sunny, optimistic nature of yours."

"What are you bitching about? You're going to eat, drink, and possibly make Layla, while I settle for club soda and bad music in a crowded West Virginia bar."

"You could get lucky. I bet there's at least one simple woman inside."

Gage considered as he pulled to the curb near the bar. "There is that."

IT WASN'T WHAT HE'D PLANNED, FOX THOUGHT. He'd had the idea of sitting with Layla at a corner table, well in the back where the music wasn't loud enough to hamper conversation. A little get-to-know-each-other-better-as-regular-people interlude, maybe followed by a little low-key necking. Which, if done right, might have led to some fooling around in his truck, and ended with her in his bed.

He'd considered it a pretty damn good plan, with room for flexible options.

He'd ended up crammed with five other people at a table for four, drinking beer and eating nachos while the juke blasted out twangy country.

And laughing, a lot.

The live music wasn't bad when it started. The five guys stuffed in the stage corner managed to pump it out pretty well. He knew them and, feeling generous, bought them a round on their break.

"Whose idea was this?" Quinn demanded. "This was a *great* idea. And I'm not even drinking."

"Mine, technically." Fox clinked his beer to her glass of diet something. "I routinely have great ideas."

"It was your general concept," Layla corrected. "My execution. But you were right. It's a nice bar."

"I particularly like the Bettie Page wall clock." Cybil gestured toward it.

"You know Bettie Page?" Gage wanted to know.

"Know of, certainly. The fifties pinup sensation who became a cult icon, partially due to being the target of a Senate investigation—read witch hunt in my opinion—on porn."

"Cybil met her." Quinn lifted her soda, sipped.

Gage peered over his drink. "Get out."

"I helped research the script for the biopic that came out a couple of years ago. She was lovely, inside and out. Are you a fan, Mr. Turner?"

"Yeah, actually, I am." He took a sip of club soda as he studied Cybil. "You've got a lot of unusual avenues in there."

She smiled her slow, feline smile. "I love to travel."

When the band came back, two of its members stopped by the table. "Want to jam one, O'Dell?"

"You guys are doing fine without me."

"You play?" Cybil poked him in the shoulder.

"Family requirement."

"Then go jam one, O'Dell." Now she gave him a push. "We insist."

"I'm drinking here."

"Don't make us cause a scene. We're capable. Q?"

"Oh yeah. Fox," she said. "Fox. Fox. Fox." Letting her voice rise a bit on each repetition.

"Okay. Okay."

When he rose, Quinn put her fingers between her lips and whistled.

"Control your girl."

"Can't." Cal only grinned. "I like 'em wild."

Shaking his head, Fox lifted a guitar from its stand, held a brief conference with the band as he slung the strap over his shoulder.

Cybil leaned over to Layla. "Why are guitar players so sexy?"

"I think it's the hands."

His certainly seemed to know what they were doing as he turned, tapped out the time, then led with a complex riff.

"Show-off," Gage muttered, and made Cybil laugh.

He went with "Lay Down Sally," an obvious crowd pleaser. Layla had to admit it had a tingle working in her when he leaned into the mike and added vocals.

He looked the part, didn't he? she thought. Faded jeans over narrow hips, feet planted in run-down work boots, shaggy hair around a handsome face. And when those tiger eyes, full of fun, latched on hers, the tingle went right up to the top of the scale.

Cybil scooted over until her lips were a half inch from Layla's ear. "He's really good."

"Yeah, damn it. I think I'm in trouble."

"Right this minute? I wish I was." With another laugh, she leaned back while the song ended, and the bar erupted with applause.

Fox was already shaking his head, taking off the strap.

"Come on," Cybil called out. "Encore."

He kept shaking his head as he came back to the table. "I do more than one in a row, they have to pry the guitar out of my greedy hands."

"Why aren't you a rock star instead of a lawyer?" Layla asked him.

"Rock starring's too much work." The music pumped out again as he leaned close to her. "I resisted the more obvious Clapton. How many guys have hit you with 'Layla' over the years?"

"Pretty much all of them."

"That's what I figured. I've got this individualist streak. Never go for the obvious."

Oh yeah, she thought when he grinned at her. She was definitely in trouble.

Ten

THE RAIN HUNG AROUND, IRRITATINGLY, INTO the kind of gloomy, windswept morning where sleeping in was mandatory. Or would've been, Fox thought as he shut his apartment door behind him, if a guy didn't have demon research on his Sunday morning schedule.

Despite the damp, he opted to walk the handful of blocks to Layla's. Like juggling, walking was thinking time. Apparently the other residents of the Hollow didn't share his view or had nothing much to think about. Cars crammed nose to ass at the curb outside Ma's Pantry and Coffee Talk, windshields running, bumpers dripping. And inside, he mused, people would be tucking into the breakfast special, getting their coffee topped off, complaining about the windy rain.

From across the street, he eyeballed the new door on the bookstore and thought, Nice job, Dad. As Layla had done, he studied the Going Out of Business sign on the gift shop. Nothing to be done about that. Another business would

move in. Jim Hawkins would find another tenant who'd slap fresh paint on the walls and fill the place with whatevers. A Grand Opening sign would go up; customers would wander in to check it all out. Through the transition, people would still be eating the breakfast special, sleeping in on a rainy Sunday morning, or nagging their kids to get dressed for church.

But things would change. This time, when the Seven came around, they'd be more than ready for the Big Evil Bastard. They'd do more than mop up the blood, put out the fires, lock up the deranged until the madness passed.

They had to do more.

Meanwhile, they'd do the work, look for answers. They'd had fun the night before, he mused. Hanging out, letting music and conversation wash away a long, hard day. Progress had been made during that day. He could feel all of them taking a step toward something.

So while he might not be sleeping in or tucking into the breakfast special at Ma's, he'd spend the day with friends, and the woman he wanted for his lover, working toward making sure others in the Hollow could keep right on doing the everyday, even during the week of July seventh, every seventh year.

He made the turn at the Square, hands in the kangaroo pockets of his hooded sweatshirt, head ducked down in the rain.

He glanced up idly as he heard the squeal of brakes on wet pavement. Fox recognized Block Kholer's truck, and thought, Shit, even before Block slammed out of it.

"You little son of a bitch."

Now, as Block strode forward, ham-sized hands fisted, size fourteen Wolverines slapping the pavement, Fox thought: Shit.

"You're going to want to step back, Block, and calm down." They'd known each other since high school, so Fox's hopes of Block doing either were slim. As tempers

went, Block's was fairly mild—but once Block worked up a head of steam, somebody was going to get pounded.

Since he sincerely didn't want it to be him, Fox tuned in and managed to evade the first swing.

"Cut it out, Block. I'm Shelley's lawyer, that's reality. If I wasn't, somebody else would be."

"I heard that's not all you are." He swung again, missed again when Fox ducked. "How long you been doing my wife, you cocksucker?"

"I've never been with Shelley that way. You know me, goddamn it. If you got that tune from Napper, consider who was whistling it."

"I got kicked out of my own goddamn house." Block's blue eyes were bright with rage in a wide face stained red with more. "I gotta go into Ma's to get a decent breakfast because of you."

"I wasn't the one with my hand down my sister-in-law's shirt." Talk was his business, Fox reminded himself. Talk him down. So he kept his voice cool and even as he danced back from another punch. "Don't hang this on me, Block, and don't do something now you're going to have to pay for."

"You're going to fucking pay."

Fox was fast, but Block hadn't lost all the skill he'd owned on the football field back in his day. He didn't punch Fox as much as mow him down. Fox hit the ivy-covered slope of a lawn—and the rocks underneath the drenched ivy—and slid painfully down to the sidewalk with the enraged former defensive tackle on top of him.

Block outweighed him by a good fifty pounds, and most of that was muscle. Pinned, he couldn't avoid the short-armed, bare-knuckled punch to the face, or the punishing rabbit jabs in his kidneys. Through the vicious pain, the blurred vision, he could see a kind of madness on Block's face that had panic snaking in.

And the thoughts sparking out were every bit as mad and murderous.

Fox did the only thing left to him. He fought dirty. He clawed, going for those mad eyes. At Block's howl, he rammed his fist into the exposed throat. Block gagged, choked, and Fox had room to maneuver, to jam his knee between Block's legs. He got in a few punches, aiming for the face and throat.

Run. That single thought bloomed like blood in Fox's mind. But when he tried to roll, crawl, fight his way clear and gain his feet, Block slammed Fox's head against the sidewalk. He felt something inside him break as the steel-toed boot kicked viciously at his side. Then he fought for air as meaty hands closed around his throat.

Die here.

He didn't know if it was Block's thoughts or his own circling in his screaming head. But he knew he was slipping away. His burning lungs couldn't draw air, and his vision was dimmed and doubled. He struggled to push what he had into this man he knew, a man who loved the Redskins and NASCAR, who was always good for a bad, dirty joke and was a genius with engines. A man stupid enough to cheat on his wife with her sister.

But he couldn't find it. He couldn't find himself or the man who was killing him on the sidewalk a few steps from the Town Square on a rainy Sunday morning.

Then all he could see was red, like a field of blood. All he could see was his own death.

The pressure on his throat released, and the horrible weight on his chest lifted. As he rolled, retching, he thought he heard shouting. But his ears rang like Klaxons, and he spat blood.

"Fox! Fox! O'Dell!"

A face swam in front of his. Fox lay across the sidewalk, the rain blessedly cool on his battered face. He saw a blurred triple image of Chief of Police Wayne Hawbaker.

"Better not move," Wayne told him. "I'll call an ambulance."

Not dead, Fox thought, though the red still swam at the edges of his vision. "No, wait." It croaked out of him, but he managed to sit up. "No ambulance."

"You're hurt pretty bad."

He knew his one eye was swollen shut, but he managed to focus the other on Wayne. "I'll be okay. Where the fuck is Block?"

"Cuffed and locked in the back of my car. Christ, Fox, I had to damn near knock him cold to get him off you. What the hell was going on here?"

Fox wiped blood from his mouth. "Ask Napper."

"What does he have to do with it?"

"He'd be the one who got Block worked up, making him think I'd been screwing around with Shelley." Fox wheezed in another breath that felt like broken glass inside his throat. "Never mind, doesn't matter. No law against lying to an idiot, is there?"

Wayne said nothing for a moment. "I'll call down to the firehouse, get the paramedics here to look you over at least."

"I don't need them." As helpless anger, helpless pain churned inside him, Fox braced a bleeding hand on the sidewalk. "I don't want them."

"I'll be taking Block in. I'll need you to come in when you're able, file formal assault charges."

Fox nodded. Attempted murder was closer to the mark, but assault would do.

"Let me help you into the front of the car. I'll take you where you want to go."

"Just go on. I can get where I'm going."

Wayne dragged a hand through his wet, graying hair. "Chrissakes, Fox, you want me to leave you on the sidewalk, bleeding?"

Once again, Fox focused his good eye. "You know me, Chief. I heal quick."

Acknowledgment and worry clouded Wayne's eyes. "Let

me see you get to your feet. I'm not driving off until I know you can stand and walk."

He managed it, every inch of him screaming. Three broken ribs, Fox thought. He could already feel them trying to heal, and the pain was hideous. "Lock him up. I'll be in when I can."

He limped off, didn't stop until he heard Hawbaker drive away. Then he turned, and stared at the grinning boy standing across the street.

"I'll heal, you fucker, and when the time comes, I'll do a lot worse to you."

The demon in a child's form laughed. Then it opened its mouth, wide as a cave, and swallowed itself.

By the time Fox made it to the rental house, one of his ribs had healed, and the second was working on it. His loosened teeth were solid again; the most minor of the scrapes and cuts had closed.

Should've gone home to finish this up, he realized. But the beating and the agony of the healing left him exhausted and fuzzy-headed. The women would just have to deal with it, he told himself. They'd probably have to deal with worse before it was over.

"We're up here!" Quinn called down at the sound of the door opening, closing again. "Be down in a minute. Coffee's on the stove, Coke's in the fridge, depending on who you are."

The bruising on his windpipe was still too severe. He didn't have it in him to call back, so he made his way painfully to the kitchen.

He started to reach for the refrigerator, frowned at his broken wrist. "Come on, you bastard, finish it up." While the bones knit, he used his left hand to get out a Coke, then fought bitterly with the tab of the can.

"We're getting a late start. I guess we were— Oh my God." Layla rushed forward. "Fox! God. Quinn, Cybil, Cal! Get down here. Fox is hurt!"

She tried to get an arm around him, take his weight. "Just open this, will you? Open the stupid can."

"Sit down. You need to sit down. Your face. Your poor face. Here, sit down here."

"Just open the goddamn can." He snapped it out, but she only pulled out a chair. The fact that she could ease him down on it with little effort told him he was still in bad shape.

She opened the can, started to cup his hands around it. Her voice was thin, but steady when she spoke. "Your wrist is broken."

"Not for long."

He took his first long, desperate sip as Cal ran in. One look had Cal cursing. "Layla, get some water, some towels to clean him up some." He crouched, put a hand on Fox's thigh. "How bad?"

"Worst in a long time."

"Napper?"

"Indirectly."

"Quinn," Cal said with his eyes still on Fox. "Call Gage. If he isn't on his way, tell him to get here."

"I'm getting ice." She dragged the ice bin out of the freezer. "Cybil."

"I'll call." But first she bent over, laid her lips gently on Fox's bloody cheek. "We'll take care of you, baby."

Layla brought a basin and cloth. "It hurts. Can we give him anything for the pain?"

"You have to go through it, even use it. It helps if the three of us are together." Cal's eyes never left Fox's face. "Give me something."

"Ribs, left side. He got three, one's finished, one's working."

"Okay."

"They should go." He hissed on a fresh flood of pain. "Tell them to go."

"We're not going anywhere." Gently, efficiently, Layla began to stroke the cold damp cloth over Fox's face.

"Here, honey." Quinn held the ice bag to Fox's swollen eye.

"I got him on his cell." Cybil hurried back in. "He was already in town. He'll be here any second." She stopped, and despite her horror at Fox's condition, watched in fascination as the raw bruises on his throat began to fade.

"He messed me up inside," Fox managed. "Can't focus, can't find it, but something's bleeding. Concussion. Can't think clear through it."

Cal kept his gaze steady on Fox's face. "Focus on that first, the concussion. You have to push the rest of it back."

"Trying."

"Let me." Layla shoved the bloodied cloths at Cybil before kneeling at Fox's feet. "I can see if you let me in. But I need you to let me. Let me see the pain, Fox, so I can help you focus on it, heal it. We're connected. I can help."

"You can't help if you freak. Remember that." He closed his eyes, and opened for her. "Just the head. I can handle the rest once I clear that."

He felt her shock, her horror, then her compassion. That was warm, soft. She guided him to where he needed to go just as she'd guided him to the chair.

And there, the pain was fierce and full, a monster with jagged teeth and stiletto claws. They bit, and mauled. They tore. For an instant he shied from it, started to struggle back. But she nudged him on.

A hand gripped his sweaty fist, and he knew it was Gage.

So he opened to himself, to them, rode on the pain, on the hot, bucking back of it, as he knew he must. When it ebbed enough for him to speak again, perspiration soaked him.

"Ease back now," he said to Layla. "Ease back. It's a little too much, a little too fast."

He kept riding the pain. Bones, muscles, organs. And clung unashamed to Gage's hand, to Cal's. When the worst

had passed, and he could take his first easy breath, he stopped. His own nature would do the rest.

"Okay. It's okay."

"You don't look okay."

He looked at Cybil, saw there were tears running down her cheeks. "The rest is just surface. It'll take care of itself."

When she nodded, turned away, he looked down at Layla. Her eyes were swimming, but to his relief, no tears fell. "Thanks."

"Who did this to you?"

"That's the question." His voice raw, Gage straightened, then walked to the stove for coffee. "The second being, and when are we going to go kick the shit out of him?"

"I'd like to help with that." Cybil got a mug for Gage herself, then laid a hand over his, squeezed hard.

"It was Block," Fox told them as Quinn brought fresh water to clean the healing cuts and scrapes on his face.

"Block Kholer?" Gage tore his gaze from his hand, still warm from Cybil's though she now stood two feet away. "What the hell for?"

"Napper convinced him I'd screwed his wife."

Cal shook his head. "Block might be stupid enough to believe that asshole, which makes him monumentally stupid. And if he did, I could see him looking for some pushy-shovey, maybe even taking a swing at you. But, bro, he damn near killed you. That's just not . . ."

Fox managed a small, slow sip of the Coke when he saw Cal understood. "It was there. The little fucker. Across the street. I had my attention on Block, since I sensed he wanted to pound me to pulp, so I missed it. I saw it in Block's face though, in his eyes. The infection. If Wayne Hawbaker hadn't come by, he wouldn't have damn near killed me. I'd be dead."

"It's stronger." Quinn gripped Cal's shoulder. "It's gotten stronger."

"We had to figure it would. Everything's accelerated this time. You said Wayne came by. What did he do?"

"I was out of it at first. When I got it together, he had Block cuffed, locked in the car. He said he had to just about knock him cold to get him there. He was fine—Wayne—he was fine. Himself. Concerned, a little pissed, a lot confused. It didn't affect him."

"Maybe it couldn't." Layla pushed to her feet. She took the bloodied water to dump because if her hands were in the sink, no one could see them shake. "I think if it could have, it would have. You said Block meant to kill you. It wouldn't want the police, wouldn't want anyone to stop that from happening."

"One at a time." Composed again, Cybil pursed her lips. "Not good news, but not all bad." She brushed at Fox's wet, tangled hair. "Your eye's healing. You're almost back to full handsome again."

"What are you going to do about Block?" Quinn asked.

"I'll go over and talk to him, and Wayne later. Right now, I could really use a shower, if you ladies don't mind."

"I'll take you up." Layla held out a hand.

"You need to sleep," Cal said.

"A shower's probably enough."

"That kind of healing empties you out. You know that."

"I'll start with the shower." He walked out with Layla. The pain still nipped, but its teeth were dull, its claws stunted.

"I'll wash your clothes while you're in there," she told him. "There are a few things of Cal's around here you can use. Those jeans are toast now anyway."

He glanced down at his torn, ripped, and bloody Levi's. "Toast? They're just broken in."

She tried for a smile as they climbed the stairs, but couldn't quite pull it off. "Does it still hurt?"

"Mostly just sore now."

"Then . . ." She turned at the top of the stairs, put her arms around him and held close.

"It's all right now."

"Of course it's not all right now. None of it's all right. So I'm just going to hold on to you until I can handle it again."

"You handled it just fine." He lifted a hand, stroked it down her hair. "Right down the line."

Needing to be steady for him, Layla eased back to take his face carefully in her hands. His left eye looked red and painful, but the swelling was nearly gone. She kissed it, then his cheeks, his temples. "I was scared to death."

"I know. That's what heroism is, isn't it? Doing what has to be done when you're scared to death."

"Fox." She kissed his lips now, gently. "Take off your clothes."

"I've been waiting to hear you say that for weeks."

Now she was able to smile. "And get in the shower."

"Better and better."

"If you need someone to wash your back . . . I'll send Cal."

"And my dreams are crushed."

In the end, she untied his shoes while he sat on the side of the tub. She helped him out of his shirt and jeans with a depressingly sisterly affection. When he stood in his boxers, and she said, "Oh, Fox," he knew by the tone it wasn't due to delight in his manly physique, but to the bruises that covered it.

"When so much is internal, it just takes longer for the outside to heal."

She only nodded, and carrying his clothes, left him to shower.

It felt like glory—the hot water, the soft spray. It felt like glory to be alive. He stayed under the water, his hands braced on the shower wall, until it ran cool, until the pain circled the drain and slid away like the water. Jeans and a sweatshirt sat neatly folded on the counter when he stepped out. He managed to get them on, forced to pause several times to rest, to wait until nasty little bouts of dizziness

passed. Once he'd wiped the steam from the mirror over the sink and taken stock of his face, the still-fading bruises, the raw look of his eye, the cuts not quite healed, he had to admit Cal was right, as usual.

He needed to sleep.

So he walked—felt like floating—into Layla's room. He crawled onto her bed and fell asleep with the comforting scent of her all around him.

When he woke, there was a throw tucked around him, the shades were drawn and the door shut. He sat up carefully to take fresh stock. No pain, he thought, no aches. Not even when he poked his fingers around his left eye. The dragging fatigue no longer weighed on him. And he was starving. All good signs.

He stepped out, found Layla in the office with Quinn. "I dropped out awhile."

"Five hours." Layla moved to him immediately, searched his face. "You look perfect. The sleep did you good."

"*Five* hours?"

"And change," Quinn added. "It's good to have you back."

"Somebody should've shoved me out of bed. We were supposed to go through the rest of the first journal, at least."

"We did. And we're putting the notes together." Layla gestured to Quinn's laptop. "We'll have the CliffsNotes version for you later. It's enough for now, Fox."

"I guess it has to be."

"Give yourself a break. Isn't that what you tell me? Cybil made some amazing leek and potato soup."

"Please tell me there's some left."

"Plenty, even for you. Come on, I'll fix you a bowl."

Downstairs, Gage stood at the living room window. He glanced over. "Rain stopped. I see you're back to your ugly self."

"Still prettier than you. Where's Cal?"

"He headed over to the bowling alley a few minutes ago. He wants us to let him know when you decide to join the living again."

"I'll get the soup."

Gage waited until he was alone with Fox. "Fuel up, then we'll call Cal. He'll meet us at the police station. Quinn's putting the main points of today's reading session down for you."

"Anything major?"

"It didn't answer anything for me, but you need to read it for yourself."

He wolfed down two bowls of soup and a hunk of olive bread. By the time he finished, Quinn came down with a folder, and the journal. "I think you'll get the gist from the synopsis, but since the rest of us have read this one, you should take it for tonight. In case you want to look anything over."

"Thanks, for the notes, the soup, the TLC." He cupped Layla's chin, pressed his lips firmly to hers. "Thanks for the bed. I'll see you tomorrow."

When the men left, Cybil cocked her head. "He's got very nice lips."

"He does," Layla agreed.

"And I think what I saw in the kitchen, when I watched him fight to heal, suffer to heal . . . I think it was the bravest thing I've ever witnessed. You're a very lucky woman. And . . ." She drew a piece of paper out of her pocket. "You're also the lucky winner of today's whose turn is it to go to the market sweepstakes."

Layla took the list and sighed. "Woo hoo."

CHIEF HAWBAKER STARED AT FOX'S UNMARRED face when the three of them walked into the station house. Wayne had seen that sort of thing before, Fox thought. But he supposed it wasn't something most people got used to.

The fact was, in the Hollow, most people just didn't notice, or pretended not to.

"I guess you're doing all right. I came by the house Ms. Black rented, seeing as you were hobbling off in that direction. A certain Ms. Kinski answered the door. Gave me quite a piece of her mind. But she said you were taken care of."

"That's right. How's Block?"

"Had the paramedics come clean him up some." Wayne scratched at his jaw. "Even so, he looks a lot worse than you. In fact, if I hadn't seen what went down, I'd tend to think you went after him instead of the other way around. I think he must have hit his head." Hawbaker kept his eyes steady, and his voice just casual enough to let them know he was going to let Fox decide how to handle it. "He doesn't remember it all very clearly. He did admit he went for you, went hard for you, but he's a little confused as to why."

"I'd like to talk to him."

"I can arrange that. Should I be talking to Derrick?"

"He's your deputy. But I'd advise you to keep him clear of me. To keep him way clear."

Wayne said nothing, only got the keys and led Fox through the offices, and into the detention area. "He hasn't asked for a lawyer, hasn't asked to make a phone call. Block? Fox wants a word with you."

Block sat on the cot in one of the three cells, with his head in his big, raw-knuckled hands. He sat up quickly, shoved to his feet. As Block strode to the bars, Fox saw the nasty cuts where he'd clawed him. He didn't consider it petty to feel satisfaction over Block's two black eyes and split lip.

"Jesus, Fox." Block's black-and-blue eyes were as wide and pitiful as a kid's on time-out. "I mean, Jesus H. Christ."

"Can we have a minute, Chief?"

"That all right with you, Block?"

"Sure, yeah, sure. Jesus H. Christ, Fox, I thought I beat the hell out of you. You're not hurt."

"You hurt me, Block. You damn near killed me, and that's what you were trying to do."

"But—"

"You remember when I was playing second base back in our junior year, and the ball took a bad hop? It smashed right into my face. Bottom of the third, two out, runner on first. They thought maybe it broke my cheekbone. You remember how I was back on second in the bottom of the fourth?"

As both a little fear and a lot of confusion ran over his battered face, Block licked his swollen lip. "I guess I sort of do. I was thinking maybe this was a dream. I was sitting here thinking that, and that it never really happened. But I guess it did. I swear to God Almighty, Fox, I don't know what came over me. I never went at anybody like that before."

"Did Napper tell you I'd been at Shelley?"

"Yeah." In obvious disgust, Block kicked lightly at the bottom of the bars. "Asshole. I didn't believe him. He hates your ever-fucking guts, and always has. 'Sides, I knew Shelley hadn't been running around. But . . ."

"The idea of it gnawed at you."

"It did. I mean, shit, Fox, she kicked me out, and she's done served me with papers, and she won't talk to me." His fingers clamped around the bars as he hung his head. "I got to thinking that, well, maybe it was because she had you on the side. Just maybe."

"And not because she caught you with Sami's tit in your hand?"

"I screwed up. I screwed up bad. Shelley and me, we'd been fighting some, and Sami—" He broke off, shrugged. "She'd been coming on to me awhile, and that day, she says how I should come on into the back and help her with

something. Then she's rubbing against me, and she's got a lot to rub against a man. She's got her shirt undone. Hell, Fox, her tit was right *there*. I screwed up bad."

"Yeah, you did."

"I don't want a divorce. I wanna go home, Fox, you know?" Misery coated the man-to-man appeal. "Shelley won't even talk to me. I just wanna fix it, and she's talking around town about how you're going to skin my ass for her in court, and shit like that."

"Pissed you off," Fox prompted as Block frowned down at his boots.

"Jesus, Fox, it steamed me up, sure, then Napper's trash talk on top. But I've never gone after somebody like that. I've never beat on a man when he's done that way." Block's head lifted, and the confusion covered his face again. "It was like being crazy or something. I couldn't stop. I thought maybe I'd killed you. I don't know how I'd live with that."

"Lucky for both of us you won't have to."

"Damn, Fox. I mean *damn*. You're a friend of mine. We go back. I don't know what . . . I guess I went crazy or something."

Fox thought of the boy laughing, swallowing itself. "I'm not going to press charges, Block. We never had any problems, you and me."

"We get along okay."

"As far as I'm concerned, we don't have any problems now. As for Shelley, I'm her lawyer, and that's it. I can't tell you what to do about the state of your marriage. If you were to tell me that you want to try marriage counseling, I could pass that on to my client. I might be able to give her my opinion, as her lawyer and her friend, that she try that route before going any further with the divorce proceedings."

"I'll do anything she wants." Block's Adam's apple rippled as he took a hard swallow. "I owe you, Fox."

"No, you don't. I'm Shelley's lawyer, not yours. I want you to promise me that when Chief Hawbaker lets you out, you go home. Watch some NASCAR. Gotta be a race on today."

"Staying at my ma's. Yeah, I'll go on home. You got my word."

Fox went back out to Wayne. "I'm not filing charges." He ignored Gage's muttered curse. "Obviously I'm not hurt. We had an altercation that looked more serious than it was, and is now resolved to the satisfaction of both parties."

"If that's the way you want it, Fox."

"That's the way it is. I'm grateful you came along when you did." Fox held out a hand.

Outside, Gage cursed again. "For a lawyer, you've sure got a bleeding heart."

"You'd have done the same. Exactly the same," he said before Gage could object. "He wasn't responsible."

"We'd have done the same," Cal affirmed. "And have. Why don't you come up to the center and watch the game?"

"Tempting, but I'll pass. I've got a lot of reading to do."

"I'll drive you home," Gage told him.

But for a few moments the three of them stood, just stood outside the station house looking over the town that was already under a cloud.

Eleven

~⌐∿

Fox spent a long time reading, making his own notes, checking back over specific passages Quinn had marked in the journal.

He juggled and mulled, and read more.

No guardian ever had succeeded in destroying the Dark. Some gave their lives in the attempt. Giles prepared to give his, as no other had before him.

No precedent for whatever mumbo-jumbo Dent had used that night in the woods, Fox considered. Which meant he couldn't have been sure it would work. But he was willing to risk his life, his existence. Hell of a gamble, even considering he'd sent Ann, and the lives in her, to safety first.

He has gone beyond what has been done, what was deemed could be done. The blood of the innocent is shed, and so it will be, my love believes, dark against dark. And it will be my love who pays the price for this sin. It will be blood and fire, and it will be sacrifice and loss. Death on death before there is life, before there is hope.

Ritual magic, Fox decided, and used laundry and house-keeping chores as he had juggling. Blood magic. He glanced at the scar on his wrist. Then, and three hundred years later. Blood and fire at the Pagan Stone in Dent's time, and blood, in a boyhood ritual in theirs. A campfire, the words he and Cal and Gage had written down to say together when Cal made the cuts.

Young boys—the blood of the innocent.

He toyed with various ideas and strategies as he thought of them. He climbed into bed late, on righteously clean sheets, to let himself sleep on it.

It came to him in the morning, while he was shaving. He hated shaving, and as he did many mornings, considered growing a beard. But every time he attempted one, it itched, and it looked stupid. Talk about pagan rituals, he mused as he drew blade through lather and over skin. Every freaking morning unless a guy wanted the hairy face, he had to scrape some sharp implement over his throat until—shit.

He nicked himself, as he nearly always did, pressed a finger to the wound that would close again almost before it bled. The sting came and went, and still he scowled in disgust at his blood-smeared fingertip.

Then stared.

Life and death, he thought. Blood was life, blood was death.

Dull horror embedded in his brain, in his heart. Had to be wrong, he told himself. Yet it made terrible sense. It was a hell of a strategy, if you're willing to shed innocent blood.

What did it mean? he asked himself. What did it make Dent, if this had been his sacrifice?

What did it make all of them?

He twisted and turned it in his head as he made himself finish shaving, as he dressed and readied for the workday. He had the Town Council breakfast meeting, and as town

lawyer, he couldn't get out of it. Probably for the best, he decided as he grabbed his jacket, his briefcase. It was probably best to let this stew. Probably best to wait, think, before he broached the idea to the others. Even to Cal and Gage.

He ordered himself to put his head into the meeting, and though painting Town Hall and new plantings at the Square weren't high on his current list of priorities, he thought he'd done a good job of it.

But Cal was on him the minute they walked out of Ma's.

"What's going on?"

"I think Town Hall needs a new coat of paint, and damn the expense."

"Cut it out. You left half your breakfast on your plate. When you don't eat, something's up."

"I'm working on something, but I need to fine-tune it, to look at it some more before I talk about it. Plus, Sage is in town. I'm meeting her and the family for lunch at Sparrow's, ergo, my appetite's already dead."

"Walk up to the center with me, run it by me."

"Not now. I've got stuff anyway. I've got to digest this, which is an easier proposition than the lentils I'll probably get stuck with at lunch. We'll roll it over tonight."

"All right. You know where I am if you want to roll it sooner."

They separated. Fox pulled out his cell phone to contact Shelley. There, at least, he'd worked out his approach. As he talked to her about coming into the office, listened to her latest idea of retribution on Block, Derrick Napper passed by in his cruiser. Napper slowed, grinned, and lifted his middle finger from the steering wheel.

Fox thought, Asshole, and kept walking. He closed the phone as he reached his office door.

"Morning, Mrs. H."

"Good morning. How was the meeting?"

"I suggested the image of a naked Jessica Simpson as the new town symbol. It's currently under consideration."

"That ought to get the Hollow some attention. I'm only in for an hour this morning. I called Layla, and she's fine coming in early."

"Oh."

"I have an appointment with our real estate agent. We sold the house."

"You—when?"

"Saturday. A lot to do," she said briskly. "You'll handle the settlement for us, won't you?"

"Sure, of course." Too fast, he thought. This was happening too fast.

"Fox, I won't be coming in after today. Layla can handle everything now."

"But—" But what, he thought. He'd known this was coming.

"We've decided to drive out to Minneapolis, and take our time. We've got most everything packed up, and ready to ship out. Our girl's found a condo she thinks we'll like, only a few miles from her. I've drawn up a limited power of attorney for you, so you can handle the settlement. We won't be here for it."

"I'll look it over. I have to run upstairs. I'll be back in a minute."

"Your first appointment's in fifteen minutes," she called after him.

"I'll be back in one."

He was true to his word, and walked straight to her desk. He put a wrapped box in front of her. "It's not a going-away present. I'm too mad at you for leaving me to give you a present for that. It's for everything else."

"Well." She sniffled a little as she unwrapped the box, and made him smile at the way she preserved the paper, folded it neatly before opening the lid.

They were pearls, as dignified and traditional as she was. The clasp was fashioned as a jeweled bouquet of roses. "I know how you are about flowers," he began when she said nothing. "So these caught my eye."

"They're absolutely beautiful. Absolutely—" Her voice cracked. "They're too expensive."

"I'm still the boss around here." He took them out, put them around her neck himself. "And you're part of the reason I can afford them." His credit card had let out a single short scream on being swiped, but the look on her face made it all worthwhile. "They look nice on you, Mrs. H."

She brushed her fingertips over the strand. "I'm so proud of you." Rising, she put her arms around him. "You're such a good boy. I'll think of you. I'll pray for you." She sighed, stepped back. "And I'll miss you. Thank you, Fox."

"Go ahead. You know you want to."

She managed a watery laugh and rushed to a decorative wall mirror. "Oh my goodness! I feel like a queen." In the glass her eyes met his. "Thank you, Fox, for everything."

When the door opened, she bustled back to her desk to log in his first appointment. By the time he escorted the client out again, she was gone.

"Alice said you and she had said your good-byes." Understanding shone in Layla's eyes. "And she showed off her pearls. You did good there. They couldn't have been more perfect."

"Stick around a few years, you may cop some." He rolled his shoulders. "Gotta shake it off, I know. Listen, Shelley's coming in—a quick squeeze-in."

"Are you going to tell her about what happened with Block?"

"Why would I?"

"Why would you?" Layla murmured. "I'll pull her file."

"No, I'm hoping we won't need it. Let me ask you something. If you loved a guy enough to marry him, and he

screwed up big time, would that just be it? Say you still love him. One of the reasons you fell in the first place was because he wasn't altogether bright, but pretty affable, and he loved you back. Or would you give him another chance?"

"You want Shelley to give him another chance."

"I'm Shelley's lawyer, so I want what she wants, within reason. Maybe what she wants is marriage counseling."

"You asked her to come in so you can *suggest* she might want to try counseling." Studying him, Layla nodded slowly. "After he beat the crap out of you?"

"Extenuating circumstances there. She doesn't want the divorce, Layla. She just wants him to feel as crappy as she does and more so. I'm just going to give her another option. The rest is up to her. So, would you give him another chance?"

"I believe in second chances, but it would depend. How much did I love him, how much did I make him pay before giving him that second chance. Both would have to be a lot."

"That's what I figured. Just send her back when she gets here."

Layla sat where she was. She thought of Alice's damp eyes and beautiful pearls. She thought of Fox bleeding in the kitchen, and the pain that leeched every drop of color from his face. She thought of him playing guitar in a noisy bar, and running toward a burning house to save the dogs.

When Shelley came in, eyes glittering with fury and misery, Layla sent her back. She thought a great deal more as she answered the phone, as she finished the Monday morning business Alice had begun.

When Shelley came out again, she was weeping a little, but there was something in her eyes that hadn't been in them when she'd come in. And that was hope.

"I want to ask you something."

Here, Layla thought, we go again. "What is it?"

"Would I be a complete fool if I called this number?" She held out a business card. "If I made an appointment

with this marriage counselor Fox said is really good? If I gave that idiot Block a chance and saw if maybe we could fix things between us?"

"I think you'd be a complete fool if you didn't do whatever it takes to get what you want most."

"I don't know why I want that man." Shelley looked down at the card in her hand. "But I guess maybe this could help me find out. Thanks, Layla."

"Good luck, Shelley."

What was the point in being a complete fool? Layla asked herself. Before she bogged down in what-ifs and maybes, she pushed back from her desk and marched straight back to Fox's office.

He hammered at the keyboard, brows knitted. He barely gave her a grunt as she stepped to his desk.

"All right," she said. "I'll sleep with you."

His fingers paused. He cocked his head up, aimed his eyes to hers. "This is excellent news." Swiveling, he faced her more fully. "Right now?"

"This is so easy for you, isn't it?"

"Actually—"

"Just 'sure, let's go.'"

"I feel, under the circumstances, I shouldn't have to point out that yes, I am a guy."

"It's not just that." She threw out her arms as she whirled into a pace. "I bet you were raised to think of sex as a natural act, as a basic form of human expression, even a physical celebration between two consenting adults."

He waited a beat. "Isn't it?"

Stopping, facing him, she made a helpless gesture with her hands. "I was raised to think of it as an enormous and weighty step. One that carries responsibility, that has repercussions. That because sex and intimacy are synonymous, you don't just go around jumping into bed because you want an itch scratched."

"But you're going to sleep with me anyway."

"I said I was, didn't I?"

"Why?"

"Because Shelley's calling a marriage counselor." And now, Layla sighed. "Because you play the damn guitar, and I know without counting that there's another dollar in that stupid jar even though Alice is gone, because you said fuck. Because Cal told Quinn you wouldn't press charges against Block."

"All of those sound like fairly good reasons to be pals," Fox considered. "They don't sound like reasons to have sex."

"I can have any reasons I like to have sex with you," she said, just prissily enough to make him fight off a grin. "Including the fact that you've got a great ass, that you can look at me and make me feel like you've already got your hands on me. And just because I want to. So I'm going to have sex with you."

"As I said, this is excellent news. Hey, Sage, how's it going?"

"Really good. Sorry to interrupt."

With her stomach already sinking to her knees, Layla turned. The woman who stood in the doorway had a big O'Dell grin on her face. Her hair was a short sweep of fiery red around a pretty face made compelling by a pair of golden brown eyes.

"Layla, this is my sister Sage. Sage, Layla."

"Nice to meet you." In snug jeans tucked into stylish boots, Sage stepped forward to offer a hand.

"Yes. Well. I'm just going to go out to reception and beat my head against the wall for a few minutes. Excuse me."

Sage watched her walk away, then turned back to her brother. "Very nice package."

"Cut it out. It's too weird to have you checking out the same woman I am. Besides, you're married."

"Marriage doesn't pluck out the eyes. Hey." She spread her arms.

He rose, walked into them, and banding her with his, lifted her off her feet for a quick swing. "I thought I was meeting you at Sparrow's."

"You are, but I wanted to drop by."

"Where's Paula?"

"She's taking the meeting that gave us the excuse to come East. In D.C. She'll be up later. Let me look at you, Foxy Loxy."

"Looking back at you, Parsley Sage."

"Still enjoying small-town law?"

"Still a lesbian?"

She laughed. "Okay, enough of that. I guess I should come back later, when you're not having sex with your office manager."

"I think that's been postponed due to acute embarrassment."

"I hope I didn't screw it up."

"I'll fix it. Mom said you weren't clear about how long you're staying."

"I guess we weren't. It sort of depends." She blew out a breath. "It sort of depends on you."

"You and Paula want to practice small-town lesbian law, and want to go into partnership with me in the Hollow." He got them a couple of Cokes.

"No. Partnership might be a factor, depending on your definition."

He handed her the Coke. "What's up, Sage?"

"If you're busy, we can talk about this tonight. Maybe have a drink."

She was nervous, Fox noted, and Sage was rarely nervous. "I've got time."

"Well, the thing is, Fox." She tapped her fingers on the can as she wandered around the room. "The thing is, Paula and I have decided to have a baby."

"That's great. That's terrific. How do you guys do that? Do you call Rent-a-Penis? Sperm R Us?"

"Don't be an ass."

"Sorry, there are jokes here waiting to happen."

"Ha ha. We've thought about it a lot, talked it through. We actually think we'll want a couple of kids. And we decided, for the first one, Paula will get pregnant. I'll, you know, take round two."

"You'll be great parents." Reaching out, he gave her hair a quick tug. "The kids'll be lucky to have both of you."

"We want to be. We're sure as hell going to try to be. To take the first step, we need a donor." She turned back, faced him. "We want it to be you."

"Sorry, what? What?" The Coke, fortunately not yet opened, slipped right out of his hands.

"I know it's big, and strange." Smoothly, she bent to retrieve his Coke and hand it to him while he simply goggled at her. "And we won't hold it against you if you say no."

"Why? I mean, lame jokes aside, there are, like banks for this kind of thing. You can make a withdrawal."

"And there are very good places, where donors are very well screened, and you can select specific qualities. That's an option, but far from our first. You and I are the same blood, Fox, the same gene pool. The baby, the baby would be more ours because of that."

"Um, Ridge? He's already proven himself in this department."

"Which is one of the reasons I don't feel right asking him. And, while I love him like crazy, both Paula and I zeroed in on you. Our Ridge is a dreamer, an artist, a beautiful soul. You're a doer, Fox. You're always going to try to do the right thing, but you get things done. And you and I are closer personality-wise, physically, too. Same coloring." She tugged on her hair herself now. "I went red, but under the dye, my hair's the same color as yours."

He was, he realized, still stuck back on the term *donor*. "I'm a little weirded out here, Sage."

"I bet. I'm going to ask you to think about it. Don't say

yes or no yet because it's a lot to think about. After you do, if it's no, we'll understand. I haven't said anything to anyone else in the family, so there's no pressure there."

"Appreciate it. Listen, I'm oddly flattered that you and Paula would, ah . . . want me to sub for you. I'll think about it."

"Thanks." She pressed her cheek to his. "I'll see you at lunch."

When she left he stared down at the Coke in his hand, then crossed over and put it back in his little fridge. He didn't think he needed any more stimulation. One thing at a time, he decided, and went out to Layla.

"Okay," he said.

"Your sister was very friendly, positively breezy. She behaved as if she hadn't heard me announce I was going to have sex with her brother."

"It's probably that natural act, celebration of human expression thing. And she had stuff on her mind."

"I'm a grown woman. I'm a single, healthy adult." In a gesture that smacked of defiance, she shook back her hair. "So I'm telling myself there's absolutely no cause for me to be embarrassed because . . . Is something wrong?"

"No. I don't know. It's been a really strange morning. It turns out . . ." How did he put this? "I told you my sister's gay, right?"

"It was mentioned."

"She and Paula, they've been together some years now. They're good together, really good together. And . . ." He paced to the window, back. "They want a baby."

"That's nice."

"They want me to provide the Y chromosome."

"Oh. *Oh*." Layla pursed her lips. "I guess you have had a strange morning. What did you say?"

"I don't remember, exactly, with all the going blind and deaf. I'm supposed to think about it. Which, of course, I'd have a hard time not."

"They both must think a great deal of you. Since you didn't say no, straight off, you must think a great deal of them."

"Right this minute, I can't think at all. Can we close the office and go have sex?"

"No."

"I was afraid of that."

"Your last appointment is at four thirty. We can go have sex after that."

He stared at her. "It continues to be a really strange day."

"Your schedule on this strange day says that I'm to make a conference call for you on the Benedict case. Here's the file."

"Go ahead on that. Do you want to come to lunch with me, over to Sparrow's with the family?"

"Not for a million dollars."

He couldn't blame her, all things considered. Still it was an easy hour for him with his brother and Ridge's wife and little boy, with his sisters, his parents, filling Sparrow's little restaurant.

Layla went to lunch when he returned, and that gave him room to think. He tried not to watch the clock while he worked, but he'd never, at any time in his life, wished quite so much for time to fly.

Naturally, his last client of the day was chatty, and didn't seem the least bit concerned about billable hours, or the fact that it was now ten minutes after five. The price of small-town law, Fox thought as he fought the urge to check his watch, again. People wanted to shoot the breeze, before, during, and after business. Any other time, he'd have been perfectly happy to kick back and talk about preseason baseball, the O's chances this year, and the rookie infielder who showed such potential.

But he had a woman waiting, and his own engine was revving.

He didn't precisely drag his client to the door and give him a boot to the sidewalk for good measure. But he didn't linger.

"I thought he'd never shut up," Fox said as he locked the door behind him. "We're closed. Shut down, don't answer the phone. And come with me."

"Actually, I was thinking maybe we should consider."

"No, no thinking, no considering. Don't make me beg." He solved the matter by grabbing her hand and pulling her toward the stairs. "Marriage counseling, burning buildings, nice ass—in no particular order—just to refresh your memory."

"I haven't forgotten, I just—when did you clean?" she asked when he drew her into the apartment.

"Yesterday. It was an ugly business, but fortuitous."

"In that case I have the name of a cleaning woman, Marcia Biggons."

"I went to school with her sister."

"So I'm told. She'll give you a chance. Call her."

"First thing tomorrow. Now." He leaned in, took her mouth while his hands skimmed down from her shoulders to her wrist. "We're going to have some wine."

Her eyes blinked open. "Wine?"

"I'm going to put on some music, we're going to have some wine. We're going to sit down in my fairly clean living room and relax."

She let out a breathless laugh. "You've just added one to the list of why I'm here. I'd love some wine, thanks."

He opened the bottle of Shiraz a client had given him at Christmas, put on Clapton—it just seemed right—and poured two glasses.

"Your artwork shows off better without the mountain of clutter. Mmm, this is nice," she said after the first sip when he joined her on the couch. "I wasn't sure what I'd get, seeing as you're more of a beer guy."

"I have deep wells."

"Yes, you do." And gorgeous, thick brown hair, wonderful tiger's eyes. "I didn't get a chance to ask if you'd read our notes, or the marked—" She swallowed the rest of the words when his mouth met hers again.

"Here's what we're not going to talk about. Office work and missions from gods. Tell me what you did in New York for fun."

Okay, she thought, small talk would be good. She could talk small with the best of them. "Clubs, because I like music. Galleries because I like art. But my job was fun, too. I guess it's always fun to do what you're good at."

"Your parents owned a dress shop."

"I loved working there, too. Well, playing there when I was a kid. All the colors and textures. I liked putting things together. This jacket with this skirt, this coat with this bag. We thought I'd take over one day, but it just got to be too much for them."

"So you went to New York, left Philly behind."

"I thought I'd go where fashion rules, on this side of the Atlantic anyway." The wine was lovely, just slid over her tongue. "I'd get some polish, some more experience in a more specialized arena, then open my own place."

"In New York?"

"I flirted with that for about five minutes. I was never going to be able to afford the rent in the city. I thought maybe the suburbs, maybe one day. Then one day became next year, and so on. Plus I liked managing the boutique, and there wasn't any risk. I stopped taking risks."

"Until recently."

She met his eyes. "Apparently."

He smiled, topped off their wine. "The Hollow doesn't have a dress shop, or fashion boutique, or whatever you'd call that kind of thing."

"At the moment, I'm gainfully employed and no longer thinking about opening a boutique. My risk quota's been reached."

"What kind of music? Do you like to listen to?" he added when she frowned at him.

"Oh, I'm pretty open there."

He reached down, slipped off her shoes, then brought her feet up into his lap. "How about art?"

"There, too. I think . . ." Her whole body sighed when he began rubbing the balls of her feet. "Any art, or music, that gives you pleasure, or makes you think—or better makes you wonder; it's—it's what makes us human. The need to create it, to have it."

"I grew up soaked in it, various forms. Nothing was out-of-bounds." His thumb, just rough enough to thrill, ran down her arch, back again. "Anything out-of-bounds for you?"

He wasn't talking about art or music now. Her stomach jittered with lust, fear, anticipation. "I don't know."

"You can tell me if I hit any boundaries." His hand went to work on her calf muscles. "Tell me what you like."

Flustered, she stared.

"That's okay. I'll figure it out. I like the shape of you. The high arch of your feet, the muscles in your calves. They draw my eye especially when you're wearing heels."

"That's the point of heels." Her throat was dry; her pulses skipping.

"I like the line of your neck and shoulders. I'm planning on spending some time on those later. I like your knees, your thighs." His hand slid up slowly, barely touching, then again, just a little higher until he found the lacy top of her stocking. "I like this," he murmured, "this little surprise under a black skirt." He hooked a finger under the top, eased it down.

"Oh, God."

"I plan on going slow." He watched her as he worked the stocking down her leg. "But if you want me to stop—I hope you won't—just say so."

His fingers skimmed over the back of her knee, down her calf, her ankle, until her leg was bare, and her skin humming. "I don't want you to stop."

"Have some more wine," he suggested. "This is going to take a while."

Twelve

~⌇~

SHE ALREADY FELT DRUNK, AND THOUGH SHE considered herself fairly adept, Layla didn't think she was quite adept enough to casually sip wine while he undressed her. By the time he slipped off the second stocking it was all she could do to set the glass aside without spilling it.

He smiled, and pressed his lips to the arch of her foot. Excitement shot straight up to her belly, and pulsed there like a second agitated heart. He took his time, stirring and seducing, kindling little fires under her skin, exploiting odd and wondrous points of pleasure. When he gripped her ankles, slid her toward him in one smooth motion, she let out a sound of surprise and gratitude.

Now their faces were close, so close the rich, golden brown of his irises mesmerized her. His hand—callused fingertips—glided up her legs, under her rucked-up skirt. Slowly, slowly. And down again while his mouth toyed with hers. A brush, a taste, a bare whisper of torturous contact

even when her arms locked around his neck, even when her needy body pressed to his. Once again, the easy touch, the easy taste, left her drained and dazzled.

His hands cupped her hips, lifted her. The quick shock had her gasping, instinct had her wrapping her legs around his waist as he rose with her. This time the kiss was deep and seeking as he stood with her eagerly twined around him.

"My head's actually spinning," she managed as he began to walk.

"I plan on keeping it that way awhile." In the bedroom, he sat on the side of the bed with her straddling him. "I figured candlelight for the first time, but we'll have to save that."

He trailed his fingers over her shoulders, over the soft wool of the pretty blue sweater, along the tiny pearl buttons down the front. "You always look just right." He drew it down her arms to her elbows, left it there. "You've got a knack for it."

With her arms roped in cashmere, he pressed his lips, just a light hint of teeth, to the side of her neck, down her skin to the edge of the little sweater she wore beneath.

He loved the light tremor that ran through her, the sound of her breath quickening, thickening. And the look of her, flushed, just a little anxious. He ran his hands down her arms until both his fingers and the cashmere cuffed her wrists. Then he took her mouth, ravishing it, saturating himself with the taste of her, devouring the quick, helpless sounds she made while her pulse thundered under his hands.

He eased back, a whisper back, and smiled into her dazed eyes. "We'll save this one for later, too," he said and released her hands.

He watched her face as he drew the little sweater up and away; he watched her face as he played his fingertips over her warm, bare skin. Then he pleased himself, looked down at breasts clothed in a fancy bra of blue lace. "Yeah, you always look just right."

Reaching behind her, he eased down the zipper of her skirt.

She felt as if she moved through water, warm, softened with fragrance. Her heart thudded, slow and hard as she unbuttoned his shirt, as she found the hard muscles of his shoulders, his chest, his back. When he kissed her again, when he lowered her to her back, she was the water. Warm, soft, and fluid. His hands, his lips played over her, tirelessly, relentlessly. She had no defense against them, against her own need, and wanted none. When he freed her breasts, she arched to him. Thrilled to the steady greed of his lips, of his tongue.

He worked down her, coating her with pleasure until he drew the matching lace away and exposed her.

Then came the whirlpool. She was caught in it, a mad spin that dragged her under to where the water whirled hot and fast. She cried out, shocked, her hands fisting in the sheets for purchase as the orgasm ripped through her. Even when she sobbed out his name, he didn't stop. When she came again, it was like going mad.

Her body quivered and writhed under him, clawing at what was left of his control. She sprawled over the tangled sheets in absolute surrender while the dim light of the dying evening spilled over her and sheened her in gold. Once more he cupped her hips, lifted them. Once more his eyes met hers, held hers as he filled her. As he trapped himself inside her. He watched her eyes as he thrust deep. Watched them as he took her, and as she wrapped tight to take him.

Watched until they closed on the peak of her pleasure, and until his own needs swallowed him whole.

SHE WASN'T SURE SHE COULD MOVE, OR THAT THE bones in her body would ever solidify again and hold her upright.

She wasn't sure she cared.

He sprawled on top of her, dead weight, and that didn't seem to matter either. She liked his weight, his warmth, liked feeling the thunder of his heartbeat so she knew she hadn't been the only one to fly.

She'd known he'd be gentle, and that he'd be fun. But she hadn't known he'd be . . . astonishing.

"Want me to move?" His voice was thick, just a little sleepy.

"Not especially."

"Good, 'cause I like it here. I'll get the wine and maybe order us some dinner at some point."

"No hurry."

"Got a question." He brushed his lips over her cheek as he lifted his head. "Do you always match your underwear to your clothes?"

"Not always. But often. I'm a little obsessive."

"Really worked for me." He toyed with the glittery chain she wore around her neck. "So does this, or the fact that this and earrings are all you're wearing." He lowered his head again to kiss her, and while he lingered over it, released the chain to rub his thumbs over her nipples. His lips curved to hers when she let out a little moan.

"I was hoping you'd say that," he murmured and slipped inside her again, hard as steel.

Her eyes went wide. "How can you—don't you have to . . . Oh God. Oh God."

"You're all soft now. Wet and soft and even more sensitive than the first time." He moved in her, long, long, slow thrusts, leaving her shuddering on each stroke. "I'll take you deeper this time. Close your eyes, Layla. Let yourself take what I'm giving you."

She had no choice; she was beyond will. Her body was so heavy, while inside it a thousand small eruptions burst. He touched her, his hands alighting needs she thought had gone quiet.

So she went deeper, into pleasure both intense and foreign.

"Don't stop. Don't."

"Not until you get there."

When she did, it was like plummeting out of the sky, a tumbling free fall that stole the breath.

SHE WAS STILL LIMP WHEN HE BROUGHT HER A glass of wine. "I ordered pizza. That okay?"

She managed a nod. "How do you . . . Can you always recover that quickly?"

"One of the perks." He sat cross-legged on the bed with his own glass of wine, and cocked his head. "Hasn't Quinn mentioned it? Come on, I know your breed talks about sex."

"Mentioned . . . Well, she said it's the best sex of her life, if that's what you mean. And that he's . . ." She felt very strange, talking about their friends this way. "Well, he's got amazing staying power."

"You know how we heal fast, since that night? Sort of the same thing here."

"Oh." She drew the word out, and slaked her thirst with wine. "That is a very fine perk."

"It's a particular favorite of mine." He rose, walked around the room lighting candles.

Yes, yes, she thought, that was a *very* nice ass. His hair tumbled messily around that sharp-featured face. Those gilded eyes were satisfied, and just a little sleepy.

She wanted to lap him up like melted chocolate.

"What's your record?"

He glanced back and grinned. "What time frame? An evening, an overnight, a lost weekend?"

Over the rim of her glass her eyes challenged him. "We'll start with an evening, and I bet we can beat it."

They ate pizza in bed. The pie was cold by the time they got to it, but they were both too ravenous to care. The music changed to B. B. King, and the candles wafted out lovely light and fragrance.

"My mother makes them," he told her when she commented.

"Your mother makes candles—gorgeous, fragrant candles—throws pots, and does watercolors."

"And weaves. Does other needlework when the mood strikes." He licked sauce off his thumb. "Now if only she'd cook real food, she'd be perfect."

"Are you the only carnivore in the family?"

"My father sneaks a Big Mac now and then, and Sage fell off the veggie wagon, too." He contemplated another slice of pizza. "I decided to do it."

"To do what?"

"To, ah, give Sage—or I guess it would be give Paula—the magic elixir."

"The . . . Oh." She angled her head. "What made you decide?"

"I just figured I'm not doing anything with it, right at the moment. And they're family. If I can help make them happy, help give them a family, why wouldn't I?"

"Why wouldn't you?" she repeated quietly, then took his face in her hands to kiss him. "You're one in a million."

"Let's hope I've got one or two in a million that'll get the job done for them. I know it's a strange thing to bring up under the current conditions, but I thought you should know. Some women might find it a little weird, or offputting. I'm not getting that you do."

"I think it's loving, and lovely." She kissed him again, just before the phone rang.

"Hold that thought." He scooted back to answer the bedside phone. "Hey. Oh yeah." He tipped the phone to address

Layla. "It's Cal. No, we'll get to that tomorrow. It can wait until tomorrow. Because I'm with Layla," he said. He hung up the phone, looked at her. "I'm with Layla."

SHE HADN'T MEANT TO SPEND THE NIGHT, AND was vaguely surprised by the sun streaming through the windows. "Oh my God. What time is it?"

She started to roll out of bed, was rolled right back and under Fox. "It's morning, it's early. What's the rush?"

"I have to get home, change. Fox!" Amusement, arousal, and sheer bafflement warred inside her as his hands got busy under the covers. "Stop."

"That's not what you said last night. How many times was that?" He laughed as his mouth covered hers. "Relax. So you'll be a little late. I can guarantee your boss won't mind."

Later, a great deal later while she hunted up her second stocking, he offered her a can of Coke. "Sorry, it's the only caffeine on the premises."

She winced at it, then shrugged. "It'll have to do. It's a good thing you don't have an appointment until ten thirty, because I'm barely going to make it into the office by ten."

He watched her slip her foot into the hose. "Maybe I should help you with that."

"Stay away from me." She laughed, but pointed a finger at him. "I mean it. It's almost business hours." She drew up the stocking, slipped on her shoes. "I'll be in the office as soon as I can manage it."

"I'll drive you home."

"Thanks, but I'll walk. I think I need some air." She stood, pointed at him again. "Hands up." When he grinned, held up his hands, she leaned in to kiss him.

Then she escaped before she could change her mind.

Her hopes to dash straight upstairs when she got home

were scotched as Cybil stood on the bottom landing, leaning on the banister. "Ah, look who's doing the Walk of Shame. Hey, Q, baby sister's home."

"I've got to change and get to work. Talk later."

She made the dash, but Cybil was right behind her. "Oh no, you don't. Talk while you change."

Since Quinn swung out of the office and into Layla's bedroom with Cybil, Layla gave up.

"Obviously, I spent the night with Fox."

"Playing chess?" Quinn grinned as Layla stripped on her way to the shower. "Isn't that his game?"

"We never got to that. Maybe next time."

"From the smile on your face, it's obvious he has a few other games," Cybil commented.

"I feel . . ." She jumped into the shower. "Used and energized, amazed and stupefied." She whipped the shower curtain back an inch. "Why didn't you tell me about the perk?" she demanded. "About how they recover, sexually, the same way they heal?"

"Didn't I mention that?"

"No." It was Cybil who answered, giving Quinn a hard poke.

"Speaking of energy, the Energizer Bunny is a worn-out, sluggish rabbit comparatively." Quinn gave Cybil a sympathetic hug. "I didn't want to make you feel sad and deprived, Cyb."

Cybil just narrowed her eyes. "How many times? And don't try to tell me you didn't count," she added as she pulled the shower curtain open.

Layla pulled it back, then stuck out a hand, five fingers spread.

"Five?"

Then put the tips of her pinky and thumb together to add another three.

"*Eight?* Holy Mother of God."

Layla switched off the shower, grabbed a towel. "That's not counting twice this morning. I have to admit, I'm a little tired, and I'm starving. And I'd *kill* for coffee."

"You know what?" Cybil said after a moment. "I'm going to go down and scramble you some eggs, pour you a giant cup of coffee. Because right at the moment, you're my hero."

Quinn stayed behind as Layla, wrapped in the towel, rubbed lotion on her arms and legs. "He's a sweetie."

"I know he is."

"Are you going to be able to work together, sleep together, and fight the forces of evil together?"

"You're managing it with Cal."

"Which is why I ask, because the combination can have its moments. I guess I wanted to say that if you run into one of those moments, you can talk to me."

"I've been able to talk to you from the first. I guess that's one of our perks." Because it was true, Layla considered as she drew on her robe. "My feelings for him, for just about everything right now, are tangled and confused. And for just about the first time in my life, confusion isn't such a bad thing."

"Good enough. Well, try not to work too hard today because we're having a summit meeting tonight. Cal wants to know what Fox came up with."

"About what?"

"I don't know." Quinn pursed her lips. "He didn't mention anything to you? A theory."

"No. No, he didn't."

"Maybe he's still working it out. In any case, we'll talk about whatever we talk about tonight."

By the time Layla got to the office, Fox was already in and on the phone. With his next client due in shortly after, it wasn't the time, in her opinion, to pin him down about their other collaboration and theories.

She checked his schedule, hunting for a reasonable span

of free time, then stewed while she worried about why he hadn't mentioned anything about it to her.

When Sage came in just as Layla was about to take advantage of a lull, Layla decided she was outnumbered for the workday.

"Fox gave me a call, asked me to come by. Is he free now?"

"As a bird."

"I'll just go on back."

Thirty minutes passed before Sage came out again. It was obvious she'd been crying even when she sent Layla a brilliant smile. "Just in case you're not aware, you're working for the most amazing, most beautiful, most incredible man in the entire universe. Just in case you didn't know," she added, and ran out.

With a sigh, Layla tried to bury her own questions—and the annoyance that had been working up through them—and went back to see how Fox had weathered what must have been an emotional half hour.

He sat at his desk with the look of a man who was seriously worn at the edges. "She cried," he said immediately. "Sage, she's not much of a crier, but she sure cut loose. Then she called Paula, and Paula cried. I'm feeling a little overwhelmed, so if crying's on your agenda, could we get a continuance?"

Saying nothing, Layla walked to his fridge, got him a Coke.

"Thanks. I've got an appointment to . . . Since I just had a physical a few months ago, they're sending my records to the place where they do it. Sage, she's got a friend in Hagerstown who's her doctor. So I've got—we've got—an appointment day after tomorrow, and the day after, since Paula's going to be . . ."

"Ovulating?"

He winced. "Even with my upbringing, I'm not completely at ease with all this. So day after tomorrow. Eight.

I've got court, so I'll just go there after." He rose, put a dollar in the jar. "This is fucking bizarre. There, that's better. So what's up next?"

"I am. Quinn told me you were supposed to meet with Cal and Gage last night, and that you wanted to meet with them to tell them about a theory you have."

"Yeah, then I got a better offer, so . . ." He trailed off. He knew that look in her eyes. "That pisses you off?"

"I don't know. It depends. But it certainly baffles me that you have an idea you think worth discussing with your *men* friends, and not with me."

"I would have discussed it with you, but I was busy enjoying mutual multiple orgasms."

True, she had to admit. But not altogether the point. "I was with you all day in this office, all night in bed. I think there was time in that frame to bring this up."

"Sure. But I didn't want to bring it up."

"Because you wanted to talk to Cal and Gage first."

"Partly, because I've always talked to Cal and Gage first. A thirty-year habit doesn't change overnight." The first hint of annoyance danced around the edges of his voice. "And mostly because I wasn't thinking about anything but you. I didn't want to think about anything but you. And I'm damn well entitled to take time for that. I didn't consider my idea about Giles Dent as foreplay, and I sure as hell didn't consider talk about human sacrifice as postcoital conversation. Hang me."

"You should've . . . Human sacrifice? What are you talking about? What do you mean?"

The phone rang, and cursing, Layla reached across his desk to answer. "Good afternoon, Fox B. O'Dell's office. I'm sorry, Mr. O'Dell's with a client. May I take a message?" She scribbled a name and number on Fox's memo pad. "Yes, of course, I'll see he gets it. Thank you."

She hung up. "You can call them back when we're done here. I need to know what you're talking about."

"A possibility. Ann wrote that Dent intended to do something no guardian had done, and that there'd be a price. The guardians are the good guys, right? That's how we've always looked at them, at Dent. The white hats. But even white hats can step into the gray. Or past the gray. I see it all the time in my line of work. What people do if they're desperate enough, if they feel justified, if they stop believing they have another choice. Blood sacrifice. That's the province of the other side. Usually."

"The deer, the one Quinn saw in her dream last winter, lying across the path in the woods with its throat slit. The blood of the innocent. It's in the notes. We speculated that Dent did that, that he sacrificed the fawn. But you said human."

"Do you think that sacrificing Bambi could have given Dent the power he needed to hold Twisse for three hundred years? The power to pass what he did to me, Cal, and Gage when the time came? That's what I asked myself, Layla. And I don't think it could've been enough."

He paused, because even now it left him slightly ill to consider it. "He told Hester to run. On the night of July seventh, sixteen fifty-two, after she'd condemned him as a witch, he told her to run. That came from you."

"Yes, he told her to run."

"He knew what was about to happen. Not just that he'd pull Twisse into some other dimension for a few centuries, but what it would cost to do it."

She put a fist to her heart, rubbed it there as she stared at Fox. "The people who were at the Pagan Stone."

"About a dozen of them, as far as we can tell. That's a lot of blood. That's a major sacrifice."

"You think he used them." Slowly, carefully, she lowered to a chair. "You think he killed them. Not Twisse, but Dent."

"I think he let them die, which being a lawyer I could argue isn't the same by law. Depraved indifference we could call it, except for the little matter of intent. He used their

deaths." Fox's voice was heavy on the words. "I think he used the fire—the torches they carried, and the fire he made, to engulf them, to scorch the ground, to draw from that act—one no guardian had ever committed, the power to do what he'd decided had to be done."

The color died out of her face, leaving her eyes eerily green. "If it's true, what does that make him? What does that make any of us?"

"I don't know. Damned maybe, if you subscribe to damnation. I've been a subscriber for nearly twenty-one years now."

"We thought, we assumed, it was Twisse who caused the deaths of all those people that night."

"Maybe it was. In part, even if my idea's crap, it was. How many of them would have gone to the Pagan Stone, looking to kill Giles Dent and Ann Hawkins if they hadn't been under Twisse's influence? But if we tip that to the side, and we look at the grays, isn't it possible Dent used Twisse? He knew what was coming, according to the journals, he knew. He sent Ann away to protect her and his sons. He gave his life—white hat time. But if he took the others, that put a lot of bloodstains on the white."

"It makes horrible sense. It makes sickening sense."

"We need to look at it, and maybe when we do, we'll know better what has to be done." He studied her face, the shock that covered it. "Pack it in, go on home."

"It's barely two. I have work."

"I can handle the phones for the next couple of hours. Take a walk, get some air. Take a nap, a bubble bath, whatever."

Bracing a hand on the arm of the chair, she got slowly to her feet. "Is that what you think of me? That I crumble at the first ugly slap? That I can't or won't stand up to it? It took me a while to get my feet when I came to the Hollow—hang *me*—but I've got them now. I don't need a goddamn bubble bath to soothe my sensibilities."

"My mistake."

"Don't underestimate me, Fox. However diluted, I have that bastard's blood in me. It could be, in the long run, I can handle the dark better than you."

"Maybe. But don't expect me to want that for you, or you overestimate me. Now you might have a better idea why I didn't bring this up yesterday, or you might just want to stay pissed about it."

She closed her eyes and steadied herself. "No, I don't want to be mad about it, and yes, I have a better idea." She also had a much better idea what Quinn had meant by her warning. Working, sleeping with, fighting beside. It was a lot to ask of a relationship.

"It's hard to separate the different things we are to each other," she said carefully. "And when the lines get blurred, it's harder yet. You said, when I came in, you were feeling overwhelmed. You overwhelm me, Fox, on a lot of levels. So I keep losing my balance."

"I haven't had mine since I met you. I'll try to catch you when you stumble if you do the same for me."

And didn't that say it all. She glanced at her watch. "Oh, look at that. I nearly missed my afternoon break. Only a couple minutes left. Well, I'd better put them to good use."

She walked around the desk, leaned down. "You're on break, too, by the way, so this office is closed for the next thirty seconds." She laid her lips on his, brushing her fingertips over his face, back into his hair.

And there, she thought, as strange as it was, she found her balance again.

Straightening, she took his hand between both of hers for the last few seconds, then letting it go, stepped back. "Mrs. Mullendore would like to speak with you. Her number's on your desk."

"Layla," he said when she reached the doorway. "I'm going to have to give you longer breaks."

She smiled over her shoulder as she continued out. Alone, Fox sat quietly at his desk another moment, and thought of what a good man, even the best of men might do if all he loved was threatened.

WHEN THE SIX OF THEM WERE TOGETHER THAT evening in the sparsely furnished living room of the rental house, Fox read the passages from Ann's journal that had flicked the switch for him. He laid out his theory, as he had for Layla.

"Jesus, Fox. Guardian." Cal's resistance to the idea was palpable. "It means he protected. He'd dedicated his life to that purpose, and all the lives he remembered before the last. I've felt some of what he felt, I've seen some of what he saw."

"But not all." Gage paced in front of the window as he often did during discussions. "Bits and pieces, Cal, and that's it. If it went down this way, I'd say that these particular bits and pieces would be ones Dent would do his best to keep hidden, for as long as he could."

"Then why let Hester go?" Cal demanded. "Wasn't she both the most innocent there, and the most dangerous to him?"

"Because we had to be." Cybil looked at Quinn, at Layla. "We three had to become, and Hester's child had to survive for that to happen. It's a matter of power. The guardian, lifetime after lifetime, played by the rules—as far as we know—and could never win. He could never completely stop his foe."

"And becoming more human," Layla added. "I was thinking that through today. Every generation, wouldn't he have become more human, with all the frailties? But Twisse remained as ever. How much longer could Dent have fought? How many more lifetimes did he have?"

"So he made a choice." Fox nodded. "And used the kind of weaponry Twisse had always used."

"And killed innocent people so he could buy time? So he could wait for us?"

"It's horrible." Quinn reached for Cal's hand. "It's horrible to think about it, to consider it. But I guess we have to."

"So if we go with this, you're descendents of a demon, and we're descendents of a mass murderer." Cal shook his head. "That's a hell of a mix."

"We are what we make ourselves." There was a whiff of heat in Cybil's words. "We use what we have and we decide what we are. Was what he did right, was it justified? I don't know. I'm not going to judge him."

Gage turned from the window. "And what do we have?"

"We have words on a page, a stone broken in three equal parts, a place of power in the woods. We have brains and guts," Cybil continued. "And a hell of a lot of work to do, I'd say, before we put everything together and kill the bastard."

Thirteen

~⌘~

THERE WERE TIMES, TO FOX'S WAY OF THINKING, when a man just needed to be around guys. Things had been quiet since Block had pounded him into the sidewalk, and that gave him thinking time. Of course, one of his thoughts had been Giles Dent killing a dozen people in a fiery blaze, and that one wasn't sitting well with anyone.

They were in the process of reading the second journal now. Though there'd been no stunning revelations so far, he kept his own notes. He knew it wasn't always what a person said, or wrote, but what they were thinking when they said or wrote it.

It was telling to him that while she wrote about the kindness of her cousin, the movements in her womb, even the weather, the daily chores, Ann Hawkins wrote nothing of Giles or the night at the Pagan Stone for weeks after the events.

So he spent some time turning over in his mind what she hadn't written.

He sat with his feet on Cal's coffee table, a Coke in his hand, and chips within easy reach. The basketball game was on TV, but he couldn't concentrate on it. He had a big day tomorrow, he mused, and a lot on his mind. The trip to the doctor's office would be pretty quick, all in all. There wasn't that much for him to do, really. And it wasn't anything he hadn't done before. A man of thirty knew how to—ha—handle the job.

He was prepared for court. The docket gave them two days, but he thought they'd wrap it up in one. After that, they'd all meet. They'd read, they'd discuss. And they'd wait.

What he should do was go home, get out Cybil's notes, his own, Quinn's transcriptions. He should take a harder, closer look at Layla's charts and graphs. Somewhere in there was another piece of the whole. It needed to be shaken out and studied.

Instead he sat where he was, took another swallow of Coke. And said what was on his mind.

"I'm going into the doctor's tomorrow with Sage and Paula to donate sperm so they can have a kid."

There was a very long stretch of silence into which Cal finally said, "Huh."

"Sage asked me, and I thought about it, and I figured sure, why not? They're good together, Sage and Paula. It's just strange to know that I'm going to try to get somebody pregnant tomorrow, by remote."

"You're giving your sister a shot at a family," Cal pointed out. "Not so strange."

Just that one remark made Fox feel considerably better. "I'm going to bunk here tonight. If I go home, I'm going to be tempted to go by and see Layla. If I see Layla, I'm going to want to get her naked."

"And you want to go in tomorrow fully loaded," Gage concluded.

"Yeah. Stupid and superstitious probably, but yeah."

"You've got the couch," Cal told him. "Especially since I know you won't be jacking off on it."

Yes, Fox thought, there were times a man just needed to be around other guys.

THE LATE MARCH SNOWSTORM WAS ANNOYING. IT would've been less so if he'd bothered to listen to the weather before leaving the house that morning. Then he'd have had his winter coat, since winter decided to make the return trip. A thin, chilly white coated the early yellow haze of forsythia. Wouldn't hurt them, Fox thought as he drove back toward the Hollow. Those heralding spring bloomers were hardy, and used to the caprices, even the downright nastiness, of nature.

He was sick of winter. Even though spring was the gateway to summer, and this summer the portal to the Seven, he wished the door would hit winter in the ass on its way out. The problem was there'd been a couple of nice days before this season-straddling storm blew in. Nature held those warm, sunny days like a bright carrot on a frozen stick, teasing.

The snow would melt, he reminded himself. It was better to remember he'd had a pretty good day. He'd done his duty by his sister, and by his client. Now he was going home, getting out of the suit, having a nice cold beer. He was going to see Layla. And after tonight's session, he would do his best to talk himself into her bed, or talk her into his.

As he turned onto Main, Fox spotted Jim Hawkins outside the gift shop. He stood, hands on his hips, studying the building. Fox pulled over to the curb, hit the button to lower the window. "Hey!"

Jim turned. He was a tall man with thoughtful eyes, a steady hand. He walked to the truck, leaned on the open window. "How you doing, Fox?"

"Doing good. It's cold out there. Do you want a ride?"

"No, just taking a walk around." He looked back toward the shop. "I'm sorry Lorrie and John are closing down, leaving town." When he looked back at Fox, his eyes were somber, and another layer of worry weighed in his voice. "I'm sorry the town has to lose anyone."

"I know. They took a hard hit."

"I heard you did, too. I heard what happened with Block."

"I'm all right."

"At times like this, when I see the signs. All the signs, Fox, I wish there was more I could do than call your father and have him fix broken windows."

"We're going to do more than get through this time, Mr. Hawkins. We're going to stop it this time."

"Cal believes that, too. I'm trying to believe it. Well." He let out a sigh. "I'll be calling your father shortly, have him take a look at this place. He'll fix it up, spruce it here and there. And I'll look for somebody who wants to start a business on Main Street."

Fox frowned at the building. "I might have an idea on that."

"Oh?"

"I have to think about it, see if . . . See. Maybe you could let me know before you start looking, or before you decide on a new tenant."

"I'm happy to do that. The Hollow needs ideas. It needs businesses on Main Street."

"And people who care enough to fix what's broken," Fox said, thinking of Layla's words. "I'll get back to you on it."

Fox drove on. He had something new to turn over in his mind now, something interesting. And something, for him, that symbolized hope.

He parked in front of his office, stepped out into the cold, wet snow, and noticed his office lights glinting against

the windows. When he walked in, Layla glanced up from her keyboard.

"I told you that you didn't have to come in today."

"I had busywork." She stopped typing to swivel toward him. "I rearranged the storage closet so it works better for me. And the kitchen, and some of the files. Then . . . Is it still snowing?"

"Yeah." He shrugged out of his light jacket. "It's after five, Layla." And he didn't like the idea of her being alone in the building for hours at a time.

"I got caught up. We've been so focused on the journal entries, we've let some of the other areas go. Cybil's hunted up all the newspaper reports on anything related to the Seven, the anecdotal evidence, specifics we've gleaned from you guys, coordinating passages from some of the books on the Hollow. I've been putting them together in various files. Chronologically, geographically, type of incident, and so on."

"Twenty years of that. It'll take a while."

"I do better when I have a system, have order. Plus, we all know that considering the amount of time, the amount of damage, the actual reports are scarce." She brushed back her hair, cocked her head. "How did it go in court?"

"Good."

"Should I ask how things went before court?"

"I did my part. They said I could just, ah, pass off the . . . second round to Sage for transport in the morning. Then I guess we wait and see if any soldier makes a landing."

"You don't have to wait long these days."

He shrugged, slipped his hands into his pockets. "I didn't think of you."

"Sorry?"

"I mean, you know, when I . . . donated. I didn't think of you because it seemed rude."

Layla's lips twitched. "I see. Who did you think of?"

"They provide visual stimulation in the form of skin mags. I didn't actually catch her name."

"Men."

"I'm thinking of you now."

Her brows lifted when he walked back, locked the door. "Are you?"

"And I'm thinking I need you to come back to my office." He came over, took her hand. "And put in a little overtime."

"Why, Mr. O'Dell. If only I'd put my hair in a bun and worn glasses."

He grinned as he drew her across the room, down the hall. "If only. But . . ." He let go of her hands to unbutton her crisp white shirt. "Let's see what's under here today."

"I thought you wanted me to take a letter."

"To whom it may concern, frilly white bras with—oh yeah—front hooks are now standard office attire."

"I don't think this one will fit you," she said, then surprised him by tugging on his tie. "Let's see what's under here. I've thought about you, Mr. O'Dell." She slid the tie off, tossed it aside. "About your hands, your mouth, about how many ways you used them on me." She unhooked his belt as she backed him into his office. "About how many ways you might use them on me again."

Like the tie, she whipped off the belt, let it fall. She shoved his suit jacket off his shoulders, tugged it away. "Start now."

"You're pretty bossy for a secretary."

"Office manager."

"Either way." He bit her bottom lip. "I like it."

"Then you're going to love this." She pushed him down into his desk chair, pointed a finger to keep him in place. Then with her eyes on his, wiggled out of her panties.

"Oh. Boy."

After tossing them aside, she straddled him.

He'd been thinking couch, maybe the floor, but at the moment, with her mouth like a fever on his, the chair seemed perfect. He yanked at her shirt, closed his mouth

over her lace-covered breast. This wasn't a woman looking for slow seduction, but for fire and speed. So he used his hands, his mouth, and let her set the pace.

"As soon as you walked in, I wanted this." She fumbled between them, dragged down the zipper of his trousers. "As soon as you walked in, Fox."

She closed around him the moment he was inside her. Tightened as her head fell back, as she gasped. Then her lips were on his throat, on his face, were clashing against his in desperation as her hips pumped.

She took him over with her urgency, her sudden, fierce greed. He let himself be taken, be ruled. Unable to resist, he let himself be filled, and let himself empty. When he came, when his mind was still dazzled by his body's race, she caught his face in her hands and rode him ruthlessly to her own end.

He continued to sit, bemused, after they'd gotten their breath back, even after she rose and started to step back into her panties.

"Wait. I think those are mine now."

When she laughed, he solved the matter by getting up and snatching them out of her hand.

"Give me those. I can't walk around without—"

"You and I will be the only ones who know. It's already driving me crazy. I need to go up, change out of this suit. Come on up, then I'll drive you home."

"I'll wait here, because if I go up there, you'll get me into bed. Fox, I need those panties. They match the bra."

He only smiled as he strolled out. He intended to get the bra later. And was considering having them preserved in Lucite, along with his desk chair.

ALL GOOD THINGS MUST COME TO AN END, FOX thought, as they spent the next few hours picking through the second journal, turning Ann's ordinary words to every

possible angle looking for hidden meanings. Once again, Gage's demand to skip the hell ahead was outvoted.

"Same reasons against apply," Cybil pointed out, taking advantage of the break to roll tension out of her neck and shoulders. "We have to consider the fact that she's lost the man she loved, a traumatic event. That she's about to give birth to triplets. And if that isn't a traumatic event I don't know what would be. This is her lull. She needs to steady herself and gear up at the same time. I think we have to respect that."

"I think it's more." Layla reached out to touch the book Quinn had set down. "I think she's writing about sewing, about cooking, about the heat because she needs some distance. She doesn't write about Giles, about the deaths, what was done. She doesn't write about what she thinks or fears about what's going to happen. It's all the moment."

She looked at Fox, and he nodded.

"I've been leaning that way. It's what she's not writing about. Every day she gets through is an effort. She fills them with routines. But I can't believe that she's not thinking about before and after. Not feeling all of that. It's not a lull so much as . . . She wanted us to find the journals, even this one that seems to be so full of daily debris. To me it says—she's saying—that after great loss, personal sacrifice, horror, put a name on it. After that, before and after a new beginning, the births, there's still life. That it's still important to live, to go about your business. Isn't that what we do, seven years at a time? We live, and that's important."

"And what the hell does that tell us?" Gage demanded.

"That part of the process is just living. That's giving Twisse the finger, every day. Does it know? In whatever hellhole Dent took it to, does it know? I think it does, and I think it burns its ass that we get up every morning and do what we do."

"I like it." Quinn tapped a finger on her lips. "Maybe it

even sucks on its power. It thrives on violent emotions, violent acts. When it's able, it feeds on them, creates them and feeds. Wouldn't the opposite be true? That ordinary emotions and acts, or loving ones starve it?"

"Sweetheart dance." Layla straightened in her chair. "Ordinary, fun, happy. It came there to ruin that."

"And before, in the dining room of the hotel. Sure it wanted to scare us off," Quinn said to Layla. "But its choice of time and place may be a factor. There was a couple celebrating, flirting over candlelight and wine."

"What do you do when a bee stings you?" Cybil asked. "You swat at it. Maybe we're giving him a few stings. We'll take a closer look at the known incidents, known sightings. And this idea rolls into another for me. Writing something down gives it power, especially names. It's possible she wanted to wait, or needed to wait until some time had passed. Until she felt more secure."

"We wrote down the words," Cal murmured. "We wrote down the words we said that night at the stone, for the blood brothers ritual."

"Adding to their power," Quinn agreed. "Writing, it's another answer. We're writing everything down. While that may be giving him more power—bringing him earlier— it's giving him more stings."

"When we know what we have to do, when we think we know what it's going to take," Fox continued, "we have to write it down. Like Ann did, like we did that night."

"Signed in blood at the dark of the moon."

Amused, Cybil glanced over at Gage. "I wouldn't discount that."

Gage rose to go to the kitchen. He wanted more coffee. He wanted, more than the coffee, a few minutes without the chatter. At this point, and as far as he could see for the next several points, it was all talk, no action. He was a patient man, had to be, but he was starting to itch for action.

When Cybil came in he ignored her. It took some doing. She wasn't a woman fashioned to be ignored, but he'd been working on it.

"Being irritable and negative doesn't add much."

He leaned back against the counter with his coffee. "That's why I left."

After a moment's consideration, she opted for wine over tea. "You're a little bored, too. But your way hasn't finished the job. New days, new ways." She mirrored his pose, leaning against the other counter with her wine. "It's harder for people like you and me."

"You and me?"

"We're plagued with glimpses of what might come, and sometimes does. How do we know what to do, or if we should do anything, to stop it, or change it? If we do, will it be worse?"

"Everything's a risk. That doesn't worry me."

"Annoys you though." She sipped. "You're annoyed right now because of the way things are shaping up."

"How are things shaping up?"

"Our little group's paired off. Q and Cal, Layla and Fox. That leaves you and me, big guy. So you're annoyed, and I can't blame you. Just FYI, I'm no happier than you are with the idea that some hand of fate might be moving you and me together like chess pieces."

"Chess is Fox's game."

She drew in a breath. "Dealing us into the same hand then."

His brows rose in acknowledgment. "That's why there's a discard pile. No offense."

"None taken."

"You're just not my type."

When she smiled, just that way, a man heard siren songs. "Believe me, if I aimed at you, you wouldn't have any other type. But that's neither here nor there. I came in

to propose a kind of alliance, a bargain, a deal. However it suits you."

"What's the deal?"

"That you and I will work together, we'll fight together if it comes to it. We'll join our particular talents when and if necessary. And I won't seduce you or pretend to let you seduce me."

"You wouldn't be pretending."

"There, we've each gotten a shot in. Score's even. You're here because you love your friends, however else you feel about this place, about some of the people in it, you love your friends and are absolutely loyal to them. I respect that, Gage, and I understand it. I love my friends, and I'm loyal to them. That's why I'm here."

Glancing toward the doorway, she took a slow sip of wine. "This town isn't mine, but those people in the other room are. I'll do whatever I need to do for them. So will you.

"So, do we have a deal?"

He pushed away from the counter, crossed to her. He stood close, his eyes on hers. She smelled, he thought, of mysteries that were exclusively female. "Tell me something. Do you believe we're going to come out on the other side of this, throwing the confetti and popping the champagne?"

"They do. That's almost enough for me. The rest is possibility."

"I like probabilities better. But . . ." He held out a hand, taking hers when she offered it. "Deal."

"Good. Then—" She started to step away, but he held her hand firm in his.

"What if I'd said no?"

"Then, I suppose I'd have been forced to seduce you and make you my love puppy to keep you in line."

His grin spread, full of appreciation. "Love puppy my ass."

"You'd be surprised. Or would if we didn't have a deal." She put down her wine to pat his hand before pulling hers free. Picking up her wine again, she started to walk out, then stopped, turned back. The amusement was gone. "He's in love with her."

Fox, Gage realized. Cal was already a given. "Yeah, I know."

"I don't know if he does, certainly Layla doesn't. Yet. It makes them stronger, and it makes it all more difficult for them."

"Fox especially. That's his story," Gage said, with finality, when her eyes asked how.

"All right. They're going to need more of us soon, more from us. You're not going to have the luxury of being bored much longer."

"Did you see something?"

"I dreamed they were all dead, piled like offerings on the Pagan Stone. And my hands were red with their blood. Fire crawled up the stone, over the stone, and consumed them while I watched. While I did nothing. When it came out of the dark, it smiled at me. It called me daughter, and it embraced me. Then you leaped out of the shadows and killed us both."

"That's a nightmare, not a vision."

"I hope to God you're right. Either way, it tells me you and I have to start to work together soon. I won't have their blood on my hands." Her fingers tightened on the stem of her glass. "Whatever has to be done, I won't have that."

When she left, he stayed, and he wondered how much she would be willing to do to save the people they both loved.

NO TRACE OF SNOW REMAINED WHEN FOX LEFT his office in the morning. The sun beamed out of a rich blue sky that seemed to laugh at the mere idea of winter.

On the trees the leaves of summer were in tight buds of anticipation. Pansies rioted in the tub in front of the flower shop.

He peeled off his coat—really had to start listening to the weather—and strolled as others did along the wide bricked sidewalks. He smelled spring, the freshness of it, felt it in the balm of the air on his face. It was too nice a day to huddle inside an office. It was a day for the park, or porch sitting.

He should take Layla to the park, hold her hand and stroll over the bridge, talk her into letting him push her on one of the swings. Push her high, hear her laugh.

He should buy her flowers. Something simple and springlike. The idea had him backtracking, checking traffic, then dashing across the street. Daffodils, he thought as he pulled open the door of the shop.

"Hi, Fox." Amy sent him a cheery wave as she came in from the back. She'd run the Flower Pot for years, and to Fox's mind never tired of flowers. "Terrific day, huh?"

"And then some. That's what I'm after." He gestured to the daffodils, bright as butter in the glass refrigerated display.

"Pretty as a picture." She turned, and in the glass, the dim reflection of her face grinned back at his with sharply pointed teeth in a face that ran with blood. Even as he took a step back, she turned around, smiling her familiar and pretty smile. "Who doesn't love daffodils?" she said cheerfully as she wrapped them. "Are they for your girl?"

"Yeah." *I'm jumpy*, he realized. *Just jumpy. Too much in my head.* As he got out his wallet to pay, he caught a scent under the sweet fragrance of blooms. A swampy odor, as if some of the flowers had rotted in water.

"Here you go! She's going to love them."

"Thanks, Amy." He paid, took the flowers.

"See you later. Tell Carly I said hi."

He stopped dead, spun around. "What? What did you say?"

"I said tell Layla I said hi." Her eyes shone with puzzled concern. "Are you all right, Fox?"

"Yeah. Yeah." He pushed through the door, grateful to be back outside.

As traffic was light, he walked across the street in the middle of the block. The light changed as a cloud rolled over the sun, and he felt a prickle of cold against his skin— the breath of winter out of a springtime sky. His hand tightened on the stems of the flowers as he whirled around, expected to see it, in whatever form it chose to take. But there was nothing, no boy, no dog, no man or dark shadow.

Then he heard her call his name. This time the cold washed over him, into him, through his bones, at the fear in her voice. She called out again as he ran, as he followed her terror to the old library. He rushed through the open door that slammed like death behind him.

Where there should have been empty space, some tables, folding chairs for what was now the community center, the room was as it had been years before. Books in stacks, the scent of them, the desks, the carts.

He ordered himself to steady. It wasn't real. It was making him see what was not. But she screamed, and Fox ran for the steps, taking them two and three at a time. He ran on legs that trembled, that remembered running this way before. Up the stairs, up past the attic, to heave himself against the door leading out to the roof. When his body hurtled through, the early spring day had died into a hot summer night.

Sweat ran down his skin like water, and fear twisted tearing claws in his belly.

She stood on the ledge of the turret above his head. Even in the dark he could see the blood on her hands, on the stone that had torn at them when she climbed.

Carly. Her name pounded in his head. Carly, don't. Don't move. I'm coming up to get you.

But it was Layla who looked down at him. Layla's tears spilling onto pale cheeks. It was Layla who said his name once, desperately. Layla who looked into his eyes and said, "Help me. Please help me."

And Layla who dived off the ledge to die on the street below.

Fourteen

~◊~

HE WOKE IN A COLD SWEAT WITH LAYLA SAYING his name over and over. The urgency in her voice, the solid grip of her hands on his shoulders pulled him out of the dream and back to the now.

But the terror came with him, riding on the raw and wrenching grief. He locked himself around her, the shape of her, the scent, the rapid beat of her heart. Alive. He hadn't been too late, not for her. She was alive. She was here.

"Just hold on." A shudder ripped through him, an echo of that stupefying fear. "Just hold on."

"I am. I will. You had a nightmare." While she murmured to him, her hands soothed at the knotted muscles of his back. "You're awake now. It's all right."

Was it? he wondered. Would it ever be?

"You're so cold. Fox, you're so cold. Let me get the blanket. I'm right here, just let me get the blanket. You're shaking."

She pulled back, yanked up the blanket, then positioned

herself so she could rub the warmth back into his arms. In the dim light, her eyes never left his face. "Better? Is that better? I'm going to get you some water."

"Yeah, okay. Yeah, thanks."

She scrambled out of bed, darted out of the room. And Fox put his head in his hands. He needed a minute to pull himself together, to push the rest away. The dream had him twisted up, mixing his memories, tying in his fears, his loss.

He'd been too late on that ugly summer night, too busy being the hero. He'd screwed it up, and Carly died. He should have kept her safe. He should've made sure of it, should have protected her, above all else. She'd been his, and he hadn't helped her.

Layla hurried back, knelt on the bed as she pressed the water into his hand. "Are you warm enough now? Do you want another blanket?"

"No. No, I'm good. Sorry about that."

"You were like ice, and you were calling out." Gently, she brushed the hair back from his face. "I couldn't wake you up, not at first. What was it, Fox? What did you dream?"

"I don't—" He started to tell her he didn't remember, but the lie stuck bitterly in the back of his throat. He'd lied to Carly, and Carly was dead. "I can't talk about it." That wasn't quite the truth either. "I don't want to talk about it now."

He felt her hesitation, her *need* to press. And ignored it.

Saying nothing, she took the empty glass from him, set it on the nightstand. Then she drew him back, cradling his head on her breast. "It's all right now." Her murmur was as soft as the hand that stroked his hair. "It's all right. Sleep awhile longer."

And her comfort chased his demons away so he could.

IN THE MORNING, SHE EASED OUT OF BED LIKE A thief out of a second-story window. He looked exhausted,

she thought, and still very pale. All she could hope was some of the sorrow she'd felt from him in the night had softened with sleep. She could find its source; he couldn't block her now. If she knew the root, she might help him dig it out, help heal whatever hurt his heart.

And while that was true enough, it was only part of what tempted her. The rest was selfish, even petty. He'd called out her name in the grip of the nightmare, called in terror and despair. But not only hers, Layla remembered. He'd called out another's.

Carly.

No, looking into his mind and heart while he slept, whether the motive was selfless or selfish, was a violation. The worst kind. A breach of trust and intimacy.

She'd let him sleep, and if she had to breach something, she'd breach his kitchen and find something reasonably sane to fix him for breakfast.

She slipped on his discarded shirt and out of the room.

In the kitchen, she got a quick jolt. Not from piles of dirty dishes and scattered newspaper. The room was what she thought of as man-clean. A few dishes in the sink, some unopened mail on the table, counters hastily wiped around countertop appliances.

The jolt came from the addition of a shiny new countertop coffeemaker.

Everything in her went soft toward the point of gooey. He never drank coffee, but he'd gone out and bought a coffeemaker for her—one that had a fresh bean grinder. And when she opened the cupboard overhead, she found the bag of beans.

Could he *be* sweeter?

She was holding the brown bag, smiling at the appliance when Fox walked in. "You bought a coffeemaker."

"Yeah. I figured you ought to be able to get your morning fix."

When she turned, his head was already in the fridge. "Thank you. And just for that I'm going to cook you breakfast. You must have something in here I can morph into actual food."

She came around the refrigerator door to poke her own head in. When he straightened, stepped back, she saw his face.

"Oh, Fox." Instinctively she lifted a hand to his cheek. "You don't look well. You should go back to bed. You've got a light schedule today anyway. I can cancel—"

"I'm fine. We don't get sick, remember?"

Not in body, she thought, but heart and mind were different matters. "You get tired. You're tired now, and you need a day off."

"What I need is a shower. Look, I appreciate the breakfast offer, but I don't have much of an appetite this morning. Go ahead and make your coffee, if you can figure that thing out."

Whose voice was that? Layla asked herself as he walked away. That cool and distant voice? With careful movements, she put the beans away, quietly closed the cupboard door. Walking back to the bedroom, she began to dress while the sound of the water striking tile in the bathroom drummed in her ears.

A woman knew when a man wanted her gone, and a woman with any pride obliged him. She'd shower at home, dress for the workday at home, have her coffee at home. The man wanted space, she'd damn well give him space.

When the phone rang, she ignored it. Then, cursing, gave in. It could be important, she thought, an emergency. Then she winced when Fox's mother gave her a cheery good morning and addressed her by name.

In the shower, Fox let the hot water pound over him while he gulped down his cold caffeine. The combination dulled some of the sharp edges, but there were plenty more where they came from. He felt hungover, headachy, queasy.

It would pass. It always passed. But a nightmare could give him a rougher morning-after than any drunken spree.

He'd probably chased Layla off, snapping at her that way. Which, he admitted, had been the purpose. He didn't want her hovering, stroking, and soothing, watching him with that worry in her eyes. He wanted to be alone so he could wallow and brood.

As was his damn right.

He turned off the shower, whipped a towel around his waist. When he walked into the bedroom, trailing drips, there she was.

"I was just leaving," she began in the frosty tone that told him he'd done his job very well. "But your mother called."

"Oh. Okay, I'll get back to her."

"Actually, I'm to tell you that since Sage and Paula have to be in D.C. on Monday, and may have to head back to Seattle from there, she's having everyone over for dinner tomorrow."

He pressed his fingers to his eyes. Probably no way out of that one. "Okay."

"She expects me to come. Me—all of us. I'm supposed to help you spread the word. You probably know she's impossible to say no to, but you can make excuses for me tomorrow."

"Why would I do that? Why wouldn't you go? Why should you get out of eating stuffed artichokes?" Since she didn't smile, he shoved at his dripping hair. "Look, I'm feeling a little rugged this morning. Maybe you could cut me a very narrow break."

"Believe me, I already have. I'm trying to cut it even wider by convincing myself you're being moody and secretive because you're an ass, not because you don't trust me. But it's tricky because while you may be an ass, you're not a big enough one to hold back the details of a major trauma like the one you went through last night just to be stupid. So

I circle right back to the matter of trust. I let you inside me, I took you inside me in that bed, but you won't let me inside you. You won't tell me what hurt and scared you."

"You need to back off, Layla. This just isn't the time."

"You get to choose the time? Well, that's fine. Just let me know when it's convenient for you, and I'll pencil me in."

She started out, and he did nothing to stop her. Then she stopped, looked dead into his eyes. "Who's Carly?"

When he said nothing, when his eyes went blank, she walked away and left him alone.

HE DIDN'T EXPECT HER TO COME INTO THE OF-fice, actively hoped she wouldn't. But while he was in his law library trying to concentrate on research, he heard her come in. There was no mistaking it for anyone else. Fox knew the way she moved, even her morning routine.

Open the door of the foyer closet, hang up coat, close the door. Cross to the desk, open the bottom right-hand drawer, stow purse. Boot up the computer.

He heard all the busy little sounds. They made him feel guilty, and the guilt annoyed him. They'd ignore each other for a few hours, he decided. Until she calmed down and he settled down.

Then, they'd just move past it.

Ignoring and avoidance worked well enough for most of the morning. Every time the phone rang, he braced for her voice to come snipping over the intercom. But she never buzzed him.

He told himself he didn't sneak from the library to his office. He simply walked very, very quietly.

When he heard her go out to lunch, he strolled out to reception, took a casual scan of her desk. He noted the short stack of while-you-were-outs for him. So she wasn't passing the calls through, he mused. No problem, that worked.

He'd do the callbacks later, he decided. Because if he took the messages into his office, it would become obvious he'd been out there poking around her desk.

Now he felt stupid. Stupid, tired, beleaguered, and a little pissed off. Stuffing his hands in his pockets, he started back to his office and jolted when the door opened. Relief came when he saw Shelley walk in rather than Layla.

"Hi. I was hoping I could talk to you for a minute. I just saw Layla outside, and she said you were in, probably not real busy."

"Sure. You want to come back?"

"No." She walked to him, and just put her arms around him. "Thanks. I just wanted to say thanks."

"You're welcome. What for?"

"Block and I had our first counseling session last night." She gave a sigh, stepped back. "It was kind of intense and it got pretty emotional, I guess. I don't know how it's all going to end up, but I think it helped. I think it's better to try, to talk, even if we're yelling, than to just say screw you, you bastard. If I end up saying that, at least I'll know I gave it a good shot first. I don't know if I would have if you hadn't been looking out for me."

"I want you to get what you want, whatever that is. And to be happy when you get it."

She nodded, dabbed at her eyes with a tissue. "I know Block went after you, and you didn't press charges. He's feeling, I guess the word's *chastised*. I wanted to thank you for that, too, for not pressing charges."

"It wasn't all his fault."

"Oh, it was, too." But she laughed a little. "He's got some making up to do, but he knows it. He's got a black eye. I don't give a rat's ass if it's small of me, but I appreciate that, too."

"No charge."

She laughed a little. "Anyway. We're going to keep going, see what happens. I get to go alone next, and I am *so*

unloading." Now she grinned. "Already feels good. I gotta get back to work."

He went back to his office, worked and brooded. He heard Layla come back in. Closet, coat, desk, drawer, purse. He went out the kitchen door, making just enough noise to let her know he'd headed out.

The sun was brilliant in a ripe blue sky. Though the air was warm enough to keep him comfortable in his light jacket, the chill shot up his spine.

The afternoon mirrored his dream.

He forced himself to round the building to Main. Pansies rioted in the tub in front of the flower shop. People strolled, some in shirtsleeves, as if sucking down this taste of spring after the last gulp of winter. He curled his hands into fists, and followed the steps.

He waited for a break in traffic, crossed the street.

Amy came out of the back of the flower shop. "Hey, Fox. How you doing? Fabulous day, isn't it? About time, too."

Close enough, he thought, keeping his eyes on her face. "Yeah. How've you been?"

"No complaints. Are you looking for something for the office? Mrs. Hawbaker usually picked out an arrangement on Mondays. You don't want to buy office flowers on a Friday, Fox."

"No." Though some of the knots in his belly loosened—not the same—they tightened again when he glanced over and saw the daffodils. "It's personal. Those are what I'm after."

"Aren't they sweet? All cheerful and hopeful." She turned, and he stared at the faint reflection of her face in the glass. She smiled, but it was Amy's smile, as cheerful as the flowers.

She chattered as she prepared them, wrapped them, but the words slipped in and out of his mind as he searched the air for the scent of something rotting. And found nothing but fresh and floral.

"Are they for your girl?"

He gave her a quick, sharp look. "Yeah. Yeah, they're for my girl."

Her smile only went brighter as they exchanged money for blooms. "She'll love them. If you want something for the office, I'll have a nice arrangement for you Monday."

"Okay, thanks." He turned to go.

"Say hi to Layla for me."

He closed his eyes, relief, guilt, gratitude rushing through him. "I will. See you later."

Maybe he was a little dizzy when he stepped outside, a little shaky in the knees, but when he made himself look, the door of the old library was closed. His gaze traveled up, up, but no one he loved stood poised for death on the narrow ledge of the turret.

He crossed the street again. She was at her desk when he came in the front door. She flicked him a glance, then looked deliberately away.

"There are messages on your desk. Your two o'clock called to reschedule for next week."

He walked to her, held out the flowers. "I'm sorry."

"They're very nice. I'll go put them in water."

"I'm sorry," he repeated when she rose and made to brush by him.

She paused, just two beats. "All right." And taking the flowers, walked away.

He wanted to let it go. What was the point in dredging it all up? What could possibly be the point? It wasn't about trust, it was about pain. Wasn't he entitled to his own pain? Hurting, he strode back to the kitchen where she filled a vase with water.

"Listen, are we supposed to turn ourselves inside out, show off our guts? Is that what it takes?"

"No."

"We don't have to know every damn detail about each other."

"No, we don't." She began to slip the tender green stems into the water, one by one.

"I had a nightmare. I've had nightmares almost as long as I can remember. We've all had them now."

"I know."

"Is that your way of dragging it out of me? To agree with everything I say?"

"It's my way of controlling myself so I don't kick your ass and step over it on my way out."

"I don't want to fight."

"Yes, you do. That's exactly what you want, and I'm not going to give you what you want. You don't deserve it."

"Jesus Christ." He stormed around the little room and in a rare show of violence kicked at the cabinets. "She's dead. Carly's dead. I didn't save her, and she died."

Layla turned away from the sunbeams in the bright blue vase. "I'm so sorry, Fox."

"Don't." He pressed his fingers to his eyes. "Just don't."

"Don't be sorry because you lost someone who must have mattered a great deal to you? Don't be sorry because you're hurting? What do you expect from me?"

"Right now, I don't have the first clue." He dropped his hands. "We met the spring before my twenty-third birthday, when I was in New York, in law school. She was a medical student. She wanted to work in emergency medicine. We met at a party. We started seeing each other. Casually. Casually at first, for a while. We were both studying, crazy schedules. She stayed in New York during the summer break, and I came home. But I went up a few times because things were getting more serious."

When he sat at the kitchen table, Layla opened the refrigerator. Instead of his usual Coke, she brought him a bottle of water, and one for herself.

"We moved in together that fall. Crappy place, the kind of crappy place you expect a couple of students to be able to afford in New York. We loved it. She loved it," he cor-

rected. "I was always a little out of step in New York, a little on edge. But she loved it, so I did because I loved her. I loved her, Layla."

"I know. I can hear it in your voice."

"We made plans. Long-range, colorful plans, the way you do. I never told her about the Hollow, not what was under it. I told myself we'd stopped it, during the last Seven. We'd ended it, so I didn't need to tell her. I knew it was a lie. I was sure it was a lie when the dreams came back. Cal called. I still had weeks to go in the semester, my job as a law clerk. I had Carly. But I had to come back. So I lied to her, made excuses that were lies. Family emergency."

Not really a lie, he told himself now, as he'd told himself then. The Hollow was his family.

"I went back and forth, back and forth, for those weeks between New York and the Hollow. And I piled lie on top of lie. And I used my *gift* to read her so I could tell what sort of lie would work best."

"Why didn't you tell her, Fox?"

"She'd never have believed me. There wasn't a fanciful bone in her body. Carly was all about science. Maybe that was part of the attraction. None of this would or could be real for her, I told myself. But that was only part of the reason, maybe that was just another lie."

He paused, pinching the bridge of his nose to relieve tension. "I wanted something that wasn't part of this. I wanted the reality of her, of what we had away from here. So when summer came and I knew I had to be here, I made more excuses, told more lies. I picked fights with her. It was better if she was pissed at me than that any part of this touch her. I told her we needed to take a break, that I was going home for a few weeks. Needed some space. I hurt her, and justified it as protecting her."

He took a long, slow drink of water. "Things got ugly before the seventh day of the seventh month. Fights and fires, vandalism. We were busy, me and Cal and Gage. I

called her. I shouldn't have called her, but I did, to tell her I missed her, that I'd be back in a couple of weeks. If I hadn't wanted to hear her voice . . ."

"She came," Layla said. "She came to Hawkins Hollow."

"The day before our birthday, she drove down from New York. She got directions to the farm, and showed up on the doorstep. I wasn't there. Cal had an apartment in town back then, and we were staying there. Carly called from the kitchen of the farmhouse. Didn't think she'd miss my birthday, did I?

"I was terrified. She didn't belong here, wasn't supposed to come here. When I got to the farm, nothing I said would budge her. We were going to have this out, that was her stand. Whatever was wrong, we were going to have it out. What could I tell her?"

"What did you tell her?"

"Too much, not enough. She didn't believe me. Why would she? She thought I was overstressed. She wanted me to come back to New York for tests. I walked over, turned on the burner on the stove, and stuck my hand on it."

He did the same now, in the little office kitchen, but stopped short of holding his hand to the burner. What would be the point now? "She had the expected reaction, human and medical," he added, switching the burner off. "Then she saw my hand healing. She was full of questions then, more insistent that I go in for tests. I agreed to everything, anything, on the condition that she go back to New York. She wouldn't, not unless I went with her, so we compromised. She promised she'd stay at the farm, day and night, until I could go with her.

"She stayed that night, the next day, the next night. But the night after . . ."

He walked to the sink, leaned against it as he looked out the window to the neighboring houses and lawns beyond. "Things were insane in town, and in the middle of it, my mother called. She woke up when a car started outside, and

she'd gone running. Carly was gone. She'd driven off in the car she'd borrowed from a friend to drive down from New York. I was frantic, more frantic when Mom told me she'd been gone twenty minutes, maybe a little more. She hadn't been able to reach me, just got static when she tried."

When he broke off, when he came back to sit, Layla simply reached across the table to take his hand.

"There was a house on fire over on Mill. Cal got burned pretty bad when we got the kids out. Three kids. Jack Proctor, he ran the hardware store, had a shotgun. He was just walking along, shooting at anything that moved. One barrel, second barrel, reload. A couple of teenagers were raping a woman right on Main Street, right in front of the Methodist Church. There was more. No point going into it. I couldn't find her. I tried to find her thoughts, but there was so much interference. Like the static on the line. Then I heard her calling for me."

He didn't see the houses and lawns now. He saw the fire and the blood. "I ran, and Napper was there, blocking the sidewalk. He had his car pulled across it. Had a ball bat, and came at me with it, swinging. I wouldn't have gotten past him if Gage hadn't taken him down, and Cal right behind with his burns still healing. I climbed over the car and kept running, because I heard her calling me. The door to the library, the old library, was open. I could feel her now, how afraid she was. I went up the steps, yelling for her, so she'd know I was coming. Carts hurtling at me, books flying."

Because it was as real as yesterday, he squeezed his eyes shut, scrubbed his hands over his face. "I went down a couple of times, maybe more. I don't know, it's a blur. I got out on the roof. It was like a hurricane out there. Carly was on the ledge above, standing on that spit of stone. Her hands were bleeding; the stone was stained with it. I told her not to move. Don't move. Oh God, don't move. I'm coming up to get you. She looked at me, and she was in there, for an instant it let her come all the way out so she could look at

me with all that fear. She said, 'Help me. Please, God, help me.' Then she went off."

Layla moved her chair beside his, and as she had the night before, drew his head down to her breast.

"I didn't get there in time."

"Not your fault."

"Every choice I made with her was the wrong one. All those wrong choices killed her."

"No. It killed her."

"She wasn't part of this. She'd never have been part of this except for me." He drew back, drew away so he could finish. "Last night, I dreamed," he began, and told her.

"I don't know what to say to you," Layla told him. "I don't know what I should say to you. But . . ." She took his hand, pressed it between her breasts. "My heart aches. I can't imagine what you feel if my heart aches. Others who know what happened, who know you, have told you it wasn't your fault. You'll accept that or you won't. If Carly loved you, she'd want you to accept it. I don't know if you were wrong to lie to her. And I don't know if I could accept as truth everything I know if I hadn't seen and experienced it myself. You wanted to keep her separate from this, to keep what you had, who you were, who she was apart from what you have, who you are here. I know what that's like, the wanting to keep everything in its proper place. But your worlds collided, Fox, and it was out of your control."

"If I'd made different choices."

"You might have changed it," she agreed. "Or it all would have taken a different route to the same end. How can you know? I'm not Carly, Fox. And like it or not, we share what's happening in the Hollow. They aren't all your choices now."

"I've seen too much death, Layla. Too much blood and pain. I know more's coming, and I know we'll all do whatever we can, whatever we have to do. But I don't know if I can survive if I lose you."

It was his sadness that lay on her heart now. The unbearable weight of his sorrow. "We'll find a way. You've always believed that. You've made me believe it. Come on.
You're going upstairs to lie down. No arguments."

She cajoled, bullied, and nagged him upstairs. By the
time she got him into bed, he was too exhausted to argue,
or make suggestive jokes when she undressed him and
tucked him in. When she was sure he was asleep, she ran
down to close the office, then back up again to call Cal and
ask him to come.

Layla put her finger to her lips when he came in the
back way. "He's sleeping. He had a rough night, and a
rough day. A nightmare," she added, gesturing him into the
kitchen. "One that blurred me and Carly together."

"Oh. Shit."

She poured coffee without asking if he wanted it. "He
told me about her, not without considerable struggle, and
considerable pain. He's worn out now."

"Better he told you though. Fox doesn't do well holding
stuff in." He started to drink, lowered the mug and
frowned. "How did coffee get in here?"

"He bought me a coffeemaker."

Cal let out a half laugh. "He'll be all right, Layla. It hits
him sometimes. Not often, but when it does, it hits hard."

"He blames himself, and that's stupid," she said so
briskly, Cal lifted his brows. "But he loved her so he can't do
anything else. He told me as soon as he knew she'd left the
farm, he tried to find her. You were burned getting people out
of a house—kids out—some guy was shooting up the town,
that son of a bitch Napper came at him with a baseball bat,
and he's sick because he couldn't stop her from jumping."

"Here's what he probably didn't tell you, stop me if I'm
wrong. He was burned, too, not as bad as I was, that time,
but bad enough. When the call came through, he took off
ahead of me and Gage. On the way he kicked Proctor—
that was the guy with the shotgun—square in the nuts,

tossed Gage the gun, and kept going. He punched out one of two boys tearing into a woman on the sidewalk. I got the other one, but it slowed me down. And there was Napper. He got a good swing in with that bat. Broke Fox's arm."

"My God."

"Gage went in like a battering ram, and Fox took off again. It took both of us to take Napper out. Fox was already running up the stairs when we got inside the old library. And it was hell in there. We were too late, too. She was jumping, hell, she was diving off that ledge when we ran out on the roof. I thought he was going to go over after her. He was bloody from fights, from being rammed by books that flew around like missiles, and God knew what else. There was nothing he could do. He knows it. But once in a while it takes ahold of him and gives him a good, hard squeeze."

"If she'd believed him, believed in him and done what he asked—what she promised him—she'd be alive."

Cal kept his calm gray eyes even with hers. "That's right. Exactly right."

"But he won't blame her."

"It's harder to blame the dead."

"Not for me, not at the moment. If she'd loved him enough, believed in him enough to keep her promise— only that, to keep her promise—he wouldn't have had to risk his life to try to save her. I didn't say that to him, and I'm going to try very hard not to. But I feel better now that I've said it out loud."

"I've said it out loud, and to his face. I felt better, too, but it didn't seem to do the same for him."

Layla nodded. "There's something else. Why Carly? She wasn't part of the town, but she was infected, apparently, in minutes. So strongly that she committed suicide."

"It's happened before. It's mostly people who live in the Hollow, but outsiders can get caught up."

"I bet most of them get caught up as victims of someone who's infected. But here she is, the woman one of you

loves, and she's *caught up* immediately. I wonder about that, Cal, and I wonder how it was he heard her calling, that she was able to call him, that she was able to wait until he ran out on the roof so he had to watch her jump."

"Where are you going with this?"

"I'm not sure. But it might be worthwhile to have Cybil do a search on her, a genealogy. What if she's connected? What if Carly was on one of our twisted family trees?"

"And Fox just happened to fall in love with her?"

"That's the point. I don't think any of this just happened. Cal, have you ever been in love—really in love—with anyone before Quinn?"

"No." He answered without hesitation, then took another contemplative sip of coffee. "I can tell you Gage hasn't either."

"It uses emotions," she pointed out. "What better way to cause pain than to use love against one of you? To twist it like a knife in the heart? I don't think she was just infected, Cal. I think she was chosen."

Fifteen

~

THAT NIGHT, THEY READ, AND FOR THE FIRST time in many pages, the first in the many months that had passed for Ann, she wrote of Giles and Twisse.

It is a new year. What was has passed into what is, and what may be. Giles asked that I wait until the new to make record of what came to be in the old. Do such turnings of time truly form shields to block the dark?

He sent me away before I ever had birth pangs. He could not do what he had determined to do with me beside him. It shames me that I wept, even begged, that I would hurt him with my tears and my pleas. He would not be swayed, nor would he send me from him weeping. He dried my tears with his fingers, and pledged that if the gods were willing, we would find each other again.

At that moment, what did I care for gods, with their demands, their fickle natures and cold hearts? Yet

*my beloved had pledged to them before ever to me,
and so I was no match for gods. He had his work, his
war, he told me, and I—and he put his hands on my
belly and the lives growing in them—had mine. Without
me, his work would be nothing, and his war would be
lost.*

*I did not leave him weeping, but with a kiss as our
sons squirmed between us. I went with the husband of
my cousin, away from my love, the cabin, the stone. I
went away on a soft night in June, and as I did, he
called these words to me.*

It is not death.

*There was kindness in my cousin's house, such kind-
ness I have written on other pages. They took me in, kept
my secret even when it came. Bestia, the Dark. Twisse. I
lay in fear and in pain on the cot in the small loft of
their little house. It came in the lie of a man while my
sons began their struggle toward life.*

*I felt its weight on my heart. I felt its fingers gliding
through the air, seeking me, like the hawk seeks the rabbit. But it did not find me. When my cousin's husband
would not go with him, would not join him with torch
and hate on the journey to my love, to the cabin, to the
stone, I felt its fury. I think I felt its confusion. It had no
power here.*

*And Fletcher, dear Fletcher, would be spared what
would come to the Pagan Stone.*

*It would be tonight. I knew it at the first pain. An end
that was not an end, and this beginning. These tied together as Giles wished it, as he willed it. Let the demon
believe it was his work, his will, but it was Giles who
turned the key. Giles who would pay for opening the
lock.*

*My sweet cousin bathed my face. We could not call
for the midwife, or for my mother, whom I longed for. It
was not my beloved who paced the room below, but*

Fletcher, so steady, so true. As the pain built until I could no longer hold back my cries, I saw my love standing by the stone. I saw the torches lighting the dark. I saw all that happened there.

Was this the delirium of birthing, or my small power? I think it was both, the first strengthening the other. He knew I was there. I pray this is not merely the wish of an aching heart, but truth. He knew I was with him, for I heard his thoughts reach for mine, and meet for one blessed moment.

Love, be safe, be strong.

He wore the bloodstone amulet, and those red drops gleamed in his fire, and in the torches they carried toward him.

I remembered his words to me when he spelled the stone.

Our blood, its blood, their blood. One for three. Three into one.

Now I pushed, pushed, through the pain, through the blood, fighting my war for life. I saw the faces of those who'd come for him. And grieved for what had been done to them, what would be done to them. I heard young Hester Deale condemn him, and me. And still I pushed, and pushed. Sweat and blood and half mad from it all. I watched her run as Giles freed her.

I saw the demon in the eyes of a man, and the hate in the men and the women who carried its curse like a plague.

It came in fire, my beloved's power. His sacrifice came in fire and in light, and in the blood that boiled around the stone. Our first son was born while that light blinded me. While my screams rose with the screams of the damned.

As the fire blazed, as it scorched the earth, my son loosed his first cry. In it, and in the cries of his brothers as they left my womb, I heard hope. I heard love.

"It confirms a lot of what we knew," Cal said when Quinn closed the book. "Adds more questions. It can't be a coincidence that Ann gave birth as Dent confronted Twisse."

"The power of life. Innocent life." Cybil ticked points off on her fingers. "Mystical life. Pain and blood—Ann's, Dent's, the demon's—the people Twisse brought with him. Interesting, too, that Twisse came to the house where Ann was hidden, and got nothing. Even then, he couldn't infect the people in that house, or on that land."

"Dent would have made sure of it, wouldn't he?" Layla suggested. "He wouldn't have sent Ann away without knowing she was safe. Ann, and their sons." She glanced at Fox. "And those who came after."

"She knew what was coming." As he had no taste for beer or wine, even Coke, Fox drank water. "She knew anyone there when Dent made his move was dead. Sacrificed."

"Who gets the blame?" Gage demanded. "They wouldn't have been there if Twisse hadn't brought them. And if Dent hadn't made his move, they'd have torched him."

"They were still human, still innocent. But," Cybil continued before he could argue. "I agree with you, for the most part. We can add that if Giles had done nothing, or whatever he'd done hadn't worked, the infection would only have grown until they ended up killing each other and feeding the beast. Ann accepted that. Apparently, I do, too."

"She mentioned the bloodstone." Quinn picked up her neglected wine. "Three into one, one into three, all that's easy enough to get. Three pieces of the stone, to each of you. The trick is making one again out of three."

"Blood." Cybil scanned the faces of the three men. "He told her blood. Have you tried using your blood? Your mixed blood?"

"We're not stupid." Gage slumped in his chair. "We've tried that more than once."

"We haven't." Layla raised her shoulders. "Its, ours, theirs. We—Quinn, Cybil, and I—have its blood. Fox, Cal,

Gage, that's the 'our blood' portion. It seems if you add them all, you get the theirs."

"Logical, smart, a little disgusting," Quinn decided. "Let's try it."

"Not tonight." Cybil waved Quinn back to her chair. "You don't just jump into bloodletting. Even at ten, these three knew such things required ritual. Let me do a little research. If I'm going to bleed, I don't want to waste it—or worse, call up the wrong side."

"Good point." Quinn settled back. "Pretty good point. But Jesus, it's hard not to just *do* something. It's been five days since the Big Evil Bastard has come out to play."

"Not so long," Gage said dryly, "when you've done a couple seven-year waits."

"It used a lot of juice—the fire at the farm, infecting Block." Cal glanced toward the front window, and the dark beyond it. "So it's juicing back up. The longer it takes, the harder it's going to come back at us."

"On that happy note, I'm heading out." Gage pushed to his feet. "Somebody let me know when I need to slash my wrist again."

"I'll send you a memo." Cybil rose as well. "Research time. I'll see all you handsome men at the O'Dells' tomorrow. I'm looking forward to it," she added, and gave Fox a brush on the shoulder as she passed.

"Cal, I need you to look at the toaster."

Cal's brows drew together as he glanced at Quinn. "The toaster? Why?"

"There's this thing." She wondered how an intelligent man could be so dense. Didn't he see it was time to clear the room and give Layla and Fox a minute alone? She grabbed his hand, tugged, rolled her eyes. "Come take a look at the thing."

"I guess I'd better get going, too," Fox said when they were alone.

"Why don't you stay? We don't have to . . . We can just sleep."

"Do I look that bad?"

"You look a little tired yet."

"Too much sleep does that, too."

And sad, she thought. Even when he smiled, she could see the shadow in his eyes. "We could go out. I know this nice little bar across the river."

He framed her face, touched his lips to hers. "I'm lousy company tonight, Layla, even for myself. I'm going to go home, and do some research. Of the kind that pays the bills. But I appreciate the offer. I'll come by, pick you up tomorrow."

"If you change your mind, just call."

But he didn't call, and she spent a restless night worrying about him, second-guessing herself. What if he had another nightmare and she wasn't there to help him through it?

And somehow he'd managed to get through much worse than nightmares for the last twenty years without her.

But he wasn't himself. She rolled in bed to stare at the ceiling. He wasn't Fox. The dream, the memories, the telling her about Carly—all of that had just snuffed out the light inside him. Comfort, anger, understanding, rest. None of those had brought the light back. When it came back, because she had to believe it would, would she put it out again if she told him her thoughts about Carly's connection? If her thoughts proved to be fact, would it be worse for him?

Because the thoughts and worries wouldn't stop circling, she got out of bed. Downstairs, she brewed herself a cup of Cybil's tea, carried it up to the office. While the house slept, she selected the correct color index cards to note down the key words and phrases she remembered from the reading. She studied the charts, the graphs, the map, willing for something new and illuminating to jump out at her.

She frowned over Cybil's notepads, but even after the

weeks of working together she couldn't decipher the odd shorthand Quinn often called Cybilquick. Though she'd already told both her friends the details, she sat now and typed up a report on Fox's dream, another, longer one of Carly's death.

For a time, she simply watched out the window, but the night was empty. When she returned to bed, when she finally slept, so were her dreams.

FOX KNEW HOW TO FEEL ONE THING AND PROject another. His profession, after all, wasn't so different from Gage's. Law and gambling had a lot in common. Many times he had to show a certain face to a judge, a jury, a client, opposing counsel that might not reflect what he had in his heart, his head, his gut.

When he arrived with Layla, his brother, Ridge, and his family were already there, as was Sparrow and her guy. With so many people in the house, it was easy to deflect attention.

So he introduced Layla around, tickled his nephew. He teased Sparrow and hunkered down with her live-in, who was a vegan, played the concertina, and had a passion for baseball.

Because Layla seemed occupied, and he could *feel* her trying to scope out his mood, Fox slipped off to the kitchen. "Mmm, smell that tofu." He came up behind his mother at the stove, gave her a hug. "What else is on the menu?"

"All your favorites."

"Don't be a smart-ass."

"If I wasn't, how could I have passed the quality on to you?" She turned, started to give him her ritual four kisses, then frowned into his eyes. "What's wrong?"

"Nothing. Worked late, that's all."

Someone had talked Sparrow into picking up the fiddle

from the music room, so Fox used the music as an excuse to dance his mother around the room. He wouldn't fool her, he knew, but she'd leave it alone. "Where's Dad?"

"In the wine cellar." It was a highfalutin name for the section in the basement where they stored homemade wine. "I made deviled eggs."

"All is not lost."

He lowered his mother into a dip as Layla came in. "I thought I'd see if there was something I could do to help."

"Absolutely." Jo straightened, patted Fox's cheek. "What do you know about artichokes?" she asked Layla.

"They're a vegetable."

Jo smiled slyly, crooked her finger. "Come into my parlor."

Layla did better when put to work, and felt very at home when Brian O'Dell handed her a glass of apple wine, and added a kiss on the cheek.

People came in and out of the room. Cybil arrived with a miniature shamrock plant, Cal with a six-pack of Brian's favored beer. There was a lot of conversation in the kitchen, a lot of music outside of it. She saw Sparrow, who lived up to her name with her sweet, airy looks, walking her nephew outside so he could chase the chickens. And there was Ridge with his dreamy eyes and big hands tossing the boy in the air.

It was a happy house, Layla thought as she heard the boy's laughs and shouts through the windows. Even Ann had found some happiness here.

"Do you know what's wrong with Fox?" Jo kept her voice quiet as she and Layla worked side by side.

"Yes."

"Can you tell me?"

Layla glanced around. Fox had gone out again. He wasn't able to settle, she thought. Just wasn't able to settle quite yet. "He told me about Carly. Something happened to remind him and upset him, so he told me."

Saying nothing, Jo nodded and continued to prepare her vegetables. "He loved her very much."

"Yes. I know."

"It's good that you do, that you understand that. It's good that he told you, that he could tell you. She made him happy, then she broke his heart. If she'd lived, she'd have broken his heart in a different way."

"I don't know what you mean."

Jo looked at her. "She would never, never have seen him, not the whole of him, not everything he is. She would never have accepted the whole of him. Can you?"

Before Layla could answer, Fox shoved in the kitchen door with his nephew clinging like a monkey to his back. "Somebody get this thing off me!"

More bodies pressed into the kitchen, more drinks were poured. Hands grabbed at the finger food spread on platters on the sturdy kitchen table. Into the noise, Sage walked, holding the hand of a pretty brunette with clear hazel eyes who could only be Paula.

"I'll have some of that." Sage picked up the wine bottle and poured a large glass. "Paula won't." Sage let out a breathless, giddy laugh. "We're having a baby."

She was still laughing as she turned to Paula, as Paula touched her face. They kissed in the old farmhouse kitchen while shouts of congratulations rang around them.

"We're having a baby," Sage said again, then turned to Fox. "Good job." And threw herself into his arms. "Mom." She swung from Fox to her mother, to her father, her siblings while Fox stood, a dazed expression on his face.

What Layla saw was Paula stepping through the excitement. As she had with Sage, Paula touched Fox's face. "Thank you." And she pressed her cheek to his. "Thank you, Fox."

What Layla saw was the light come back into his eyes. She saw the sadness drop away, and the joy leap into its place. Her own eyes went damp as she watched him kiss

Paula, and wrap his arm around his sister so that the three of them stood for a moment as a unit.

Then Jo moved into her vision, stopped in front of her. She kissed Layla on the forehead, on one cheek, the other, then lightly on the lips. "You've just answered my question."

THE WEEKEND SLID INTO THE WORKWEEK, AND still the Hollow stayed quiet. Rain dogged the sky, keeping the temperatures lower than most hoped for in April. But farmers tilled their fields, and bulbs burst into bloom. Pink cups covered the tulip magnolia behind Fox's offices, and spears that would open into tulips of butter yellow and scarlet waved in the easy breeze. Along High Street, the Bradford pears gleamed with bud and bloom. Windows gleamed as well as merchants and homeowners scrubbed away the winter dull. When the rains passed, the town Fox loved shone like a jewel beneath the mountains.

He'd wanted a sunny day for it. Taking advantage of it, he pulled Layla up from her desk. "We're going out."

"I was just—"

"You can just when we get back. I checked the calendar, and we're clear. Do you see that out there? The strange, unfamiliar light? It's called the sun. Let's go get us a little."

He solved the matter by pulling her to the door, outside, then locking up himself.

"What's gotten into you?"

"Sex and baseball. The young man's fancies of spring."

The ends of her hair danced in the breeze as she narrowed her eyes at him. "We're not having sex and/or playing baseball at noon on a Wednesday."

"Then I guess I have to settle for a walk. We'll be able to do some real gardening in a couple more weeks."

"You garden?"

"You can take the boy off the farm. I do some containers

for the front of the office. I'd plant and Mrs. H would kibitz."

"I'm sure I can kibitz."

"Counting on it. You girls could put in a nice little vegetable and herb patch in back of your house, some flower beds street side."

"Could we?"

He took her hand, swung it lightly as they walked. "Don't like to get your hands dirty?"

"I might. I don't have any real gardening experience. My mother puttered around a little, and I had a couple of houseplants in my apartment."

"You'd be good at it. Color, shapes, tones, textures. You like doing what you're good at." He turned off the sidewalk toward the building that had housed the gift shop. Its display window was empty now. Depressingly so.

"It looks forlorn," Layla decided.

"Yeah, it does. But it doesn't have to stay that way."

Her eyes widened when he pulled out keys and unlocked the front door. "What are you doing?"

"Showing you possibilities." He stepped in, flipped on the lights.

Like many of the businesses on Main, it had been a home first. The entrance was wide, the old wood floors clean and bare. On the side, a stairway curved up with its sturdy banister smooth from the slide of generations of hands. Straight back an open doorway led to three more rooms, stacked side by side. The middle one held the back entrance, and its tidy covered porch that opened to its narrow strip of yard where a lilac waited to bloom.

"You would hardly know it was ever here." Layla brushed her fingertips over the stair rail. "The gift shop. Nothing left of it but some shelves, some marks on the wall where things were hung."

"I like empty buildings, for their potential. This one has plenty. Solid foundation, good plumbing—both that and

the electric are up to code—location, light, conscientious landlord. Roomy, too. The gift shop used the second floor for storage and office space. Probably a good plan. If you have customers going up and down steps, you're just asking one to trip and sue you."

"So speaks the lawyer."

"It needs the nail holes plugged, fresh paint. The woodwork's nice." He skimmed a hand over some trim. "Original. Somebody made this a couple hundred years ago. Adds character, respects the history. What do you think of it?"

"The woodwork? It's gorgeous."

"The whole place."

"Well." She wandered, walking slowly as people did in empty buildings. "It's bright, spacious, well kept, with just enough creaky in the floors to add to that character you spoke of."

"You could do a lot with this place."

She swung back to him. "I could?"

"The rent's reasonable. The location's prime. Plenty of space. Enough to curtain off an area in the back for a couple of dressing rooms. You'd need shelves, displays, racks, I guess, to hang clothes." As he looked around, he hooked his thumbs in his front pockets. "I happen to know a couple of guys very handy with tools."

"You're suggesting I open a shop here?"

"Doing what you're good at. There's nothing like that in town. Nothing like it for miles. You could make something here, Layla."

"Fox, that's just . . . out of the question."

"Why?"

"Because I . . ." Let me count the ways, she thought. "I could never afford it, even if—"

"That's why they have business loans."

"I haven't given any serious thought to opening my own place in, well, in years, really. I don't know where I'd begin even if I was sure I wanted to open my own place. For God's

sake, Fox, I don't know what's going to happen tomorrow much less a month from now. Six months from now."

"But what do you want today?" He moved toward her. "I know what I want. I want you. I want you to be happy. I want you to be happy here, with me. Jim Hawkins will rent it to you, and you won't have any trouble getting a start-up loan. I talked to Joe at the bank—"

"You talked to them, about this? About me?"

"Not specifics. Just general information. Ballparking what you'd need to start up, what you'd need to qualify, the cost of licensing. I've got a file. You like files, so I put together a file."

"Without consulting me."

"I put together the file so I could consult you and you'd have something tangible to look over when you thought about it."

She walked away from him. "You shouldn't have done all that."

"It's the sort of thing I do. This"—he swept his arm in the air—"is the sort of thing you do. You're not going to tell me you're going to be happy doing office work the rest of your life."

"No, I'm not going to tell you that." She turned back. "I'm not going to tell you I'm going to dive headfirst into starting a business that I'm not sure I want in the first place, in a town that may not exist in a few months. And if I want my own business, I haven't thought about having it here. If I want my own, how can I *think* about all the details involved when all this madness is going on?"

He was silent a moment, so silent she swore she heard the old house breathing.

"It seems to me it's most important to go after what you want when there's madness going on. I'm asking you to think about it. More, I guess I'm asking you to think about something you haven't yet. Staying. Open the shop, manage my office, found a nudist colony, or take up macrame,

I don't care as long as it makes you happy. But I want you to think about staying, Layla, not just to destroy ancient fucking evil, but to live. To have a life, with me."

As she stared at him, he stepped closer. "Put this in one of your slots. I'm in love with you. Completely, absolutely, no-turning-back in love with you. We could build something good, and solid, and real. Something that makes every day count. That's what I want. So you think about it, and when you know, you tell me what you want."

He walked back to the door, opened it, and waited for her.

"Fox—"

"I don't want to hear you don't know. I've already got that. Let me know when you do. You're upset and a little ticked off, I get that, too," he said as he locked up. "Take the rest of the day off."

She started to object, he saw it on her face. Then she changed her mind. "All right. There are some things I need to do."

"I'll see you later then." He stepped back, stopped. "The building's not the only thing with potential," he told her. And he turned, walked away down the bricked sidewalk in the April sunshine.

Sixteen

〜

HE THOUGHT ABOUT GETTING DRUNK. HE COULD call Gage, who'd sit and drink coffee or club soda, bitching only for form, and spend the evening in some bar getting steadily shit-faced. Cal would go, too; he had only to ask. That's what friends were for, being the company misery loved.

Or he could just pick up the beer—maybe a bottle of Jack for a change of pace—take it to Cal's and get his drunk on there.

But he knew he wouldn't do either of those things. Planning to get drunk took all the fun out of it. He preferred it to be a happy accident. Work, Fox decided, was a better option than getting deliberately trashed.

He had enough to keep him occupied for the rest of the day, particularly at the easy pace he liked to work. Handling the office on his own for an afternoon added the perk of giving him time and space to brood. Fox considered

brooding an inalienable human right, unless it dragged out more than three hours, at which point it became childish indulgence.

Did she really think he'd crossed some line and gone behind her back? That he tried to manipulate, bully, or pressure? Manipulation wasn't beyond him, he admitted, but that just hadn't been the case with this. Knowing her, he'd believed she'd appreciate having some facts, projected figures, the steps, stages compiled in an orderly fashion. He'd equated handing them to her on the same level as handing her a bouquet of daffodils.

Just a little something he'd picked up because he was thinking about her.

He stood in the center of his office, juggling the three balls as he walked back over it all in his mind. He'd wanted to show her the building, the space, the possibilities. And yeah, he'd wanted to see her eyes light up as she saw them, as she opened herself to them. That had been strategy, not manipulation. Jesus, it wasn't like he'd signed a lease for her, or applied for a loan, a business license. He'd just taken the time to find out what it would take for her to do those things.

But there was one thing he hadn't factored into that strategy. He'd never considered that *she* wasn't considering staying in the Hollow. Staying with him.

He dropped one of the balls, managed to snag it on the bounce. Setting himself, he started the circle again.

If he'd made a mistake it was in assuming she loved him, that she intended to stay. He'd never questioned, not seriously—her conviction matched his—that there would be something to stay for, something to build on, after the week of July seventh. He believed he'd felt those things from her, but he had to accept now those feelings and needs were just a reflection of his own.

That wasn't just a bitter pill to swallow, but the kind that caught in your throat and choked you for a while before

you managed to work it down. But like it or not, he thought, a guy had to take his medicine.

She wasn't required to feel what he felt or want what he wanted. God knew he'd been raised to respect, even require, individuality. It was better to know if she didn't share his feelings, his wants, better to deal with the reality rather than the fantasy. That was another nasty pill, as he'd had a beauty of a fantasy going.

Her smart, fashionable shop a couple blocks up from his office, Fox mused as he dropped the balls back in his drawer. Maybe grabbing lunch together a couple times a week. Scouting for a house in town, like that old place on the corner of Main and Redbud. Or a place a little ways out, if she liked that better. But an old house they could put their mark on together. Something with a yard for kids and dogs and a garden.

Something in a town that was safe and whole, and no longer threatened. A porch swing—he had a fondness for them.

And that was the problem, wasn't it? he admitted, walking to the window to study the distant roll of the mountains. All that was what he wanted, what he hoped for. All that couldn't be if it didn't mesh with her wants and hopes and visions.

So he'd swallow that, too. They had today to get through, and all the others until Hawkins Hollow was clean. Futures were just that—the tomorrow. Maybe the foundation for them couldn't and shouldn't be built when the ground was still unsettled.

Priorities, O'Dell, he reminded himself, and sat back at his desk. He pulled up his own files on the journals to begin picking through his notes.

And the first spider crawled out of his keyboard.

It bit the back of his hand, striking quickly before he could jerk back. The pain was instant and amazing, a vicious ice-pick jab that dug fire under the skin. As he shoved away,

they poured out like black water, from the keys, from the drawers.

And they grew.

LAYLA WALKED INTO THE HOUSE WITH HER SYStem still reeling. Escape, that's what she'd done. Fox had given her the out, and she leaped at it. Walk away, don't deal with this now.

He loved her. Had she known it? Had she slipped that knowledge into a neat file, tucked it away until it was more convenient or more sensible to examine it?

He loved her. He wanted her to stay. More, he wanted her to commit to him, to the town. To herself, Layla admitted. In his Fox-like way, he'd laid it all out for her, presented it to her in a way he'd believed she'd appreciate.

What he'd done, Layla thought, was scare her to death.

Her own shop? That was just one of the airy little dreams she'd enjoyed playing with years before. One she'd let go—almost. Hawkins Hollow? Her commitment there was to save it, and to—even though it sounded pretentious—fulfill her destiny. Anything beyond that was too hard to see. And Fox?

He was the most beautiful man she'd ever known.

Hardly a wonder she was reeling.

She stepped into the office where Quinn and Cybil worked on dueling keyboards.

"Fox is in love with me."

Her fingers still flying, Quinn didn't bother to look up. "Bulletin!"

"If you knew, why didn't I?" Layla demanded.

"Because you've been too worried about being in love with him." Cybil's fingers paused after another click of the mouse. "But the rest of us have been watching the little hearts circling over your heads for weeks. Aren't you home early?"

"Yeah. I think we had a fight." Layla leaned against the doorjamb, rubbed her shoulder as if it ached.

Something ached, she realized, but it was too deep to reach.

"It didn't seem like a fight, except I was annoyed, among other things. He took me up to the building where the gift shop used to be. It's cleared out now. Then he started talking about potential, how I should open a boutique there, and—"

"What a great idea." Quinn stopped now, beamed enthusiasm over Layla like sunbeams over a meadow. "Speaking as someone who's going to be living here, I'll be your best customer. Urban fashion in small-town America. I'm already there."

"I can't open a shop here."

"Why?"

"Because . . . Do you have any idea what's involved in starting up a business, opening a retail store, even a small one?"

"No." Quinn replied. "You would, and I imagine Fox does, on the legal front. I'd help. I love a project. Would there be buying trips? Can you get it for me wholesale?"

"Q, take a breath," Cybil advised. "The big hurdle isn't the logistics, is it, Layla?"

"They're a hurdle, a big one. But . . . God, can we be realistic, just the three of us, right now? There might not be a town after July. Or there might be a town that, after a week of violence and destruction and death, settles down for the next seven years. If I could even think about starting my own business with everything else we have to think about, I'd have to be out of my mind to consider having one here at Demon Central."

"Cal has one. He's not out of his mind."

"I'm sorry, Quinn, I didn't mean—"

"No, that's okay. I'm pointing that out because people do have businesses here, and homes here. Otherwise, there's

no real point to any of what we're doing. But if it's not right for you, then it's not."

Layla threw out her arms. "How can I know? Oh, he apparently thinks he knows. He's already talked to Jim Hawkins about renting me the building, talked to the bank about a start-up loan."

"Oops," Cybil murmured.

"He has a *file* for me on it. And okay, okay, to be fair, he didn't go to Mr. Hawkins or the bank about me, specifically. He just got basic information and figures. Projections."

"I take back the oops. Sorry, sweetie, that sounds like a man who just wanted to give you the answers to questions you'd have if this was appealing to you." Considering, Cybil tucked her legs up in the lotus position. "I'll happily reinstate the oops, even add a 'screw him' if you tell me he tried to shove it down your throat and got pissy about it."

"No." Trapped by logic, Layla let out a huge sigh. "I guess I was the one who got pissy, but it all just blindsided me. He said he was in love with me, and he wanted me to be happy, to have what I wanted. He thought my own place was something I wanted. That he was, that a life with him was."

"If it's not, if he's not, you have to tell him straight," Quinn said after a long moment. "Or I'll be forced to aim Cybil's 'screw you' in your direction. He doesn't deserve to be left dangling."

"How can I tell him what I don't know?" Layla stepped out, walked to her own room and closed the door.

"Tougher for her than you," Cybil commented. "You always made up your heart in a snap, Q. Or your mind. Sometimes both agreed. If not, you bounced. That's your way. With you and Cal, it all clicked. The idea of marrying the guy, staying here, it's a pretty easy slide for you."

"I love the guy. Where we live isn't as important to me as living together."

"And your keyboard fits anywhere. If you need to pop off somewhere for a story, Cal's going to be easy with that. The

big change here for you, Quinn, is being in love and settling down. Those aren't the only big changes for Layla."

"Yeah, yeah, yeah. I'd like—and it's not just because I've got stars in my eyes—I'd like to see the two of them work it out. And for purely selfish reasons, I'd love to have Layla stay. But if she decided it's not for her, then it's not. I should go get ice cream."

"Of course you should."

"No, seriously. She's bummed out. She needs girl-friends and ice cream. As soon as I finish this up, I'm going to walk over and buy some. No, I'll go now, and walk around the block a few times first so I can eat my share without guilt."

"Get some pistachio," Cybil called out as Quinn left the room.

Quinn stopped by Layla's room, tapped on the door, eased it open. "Sorry if I was harsh."

"You weren't. You gave me more to think about."

"While you're thinking, I'm going out for some exer-cise. On the way back, I'm picking up ice cream. Cybil wants pistachio. What's your poison?"

"Cookie dough."

"Got you covered."

When the door closed, Layla pushed at her hair. A little caloric bliss was just the ticket. Ice cream and friends. She might as well complete the trio of comfort with a hot shower and cozy clothes.

She undressed, then chose cotton pants and her softest sweatshirt. In her robe, she decided what the hell, and opted to give herself a facial before the shower.

How many women in town would actually shop in a place stocked as she'd want to stock a boutique? How many, she thought as she cleansed, exfoliated, would really support that sort of business, instead of heading straight out to the mall? Even if the Hollow was just a normal small town, how could she afford to invest so much—time, money,

emotion, hope—into something logic told her would prob-ably fail within two years?

Applying the masque, she toyed with the idea of colors, layout. Curtained off dressing rooms? Absolutely not. It was just like a man to suggest that women felt comfortable stripping down behind a sheet of fabric in a public place.

Walls and doors. Had to be secure, private, and some-thing the customer could lock from the inside.

And damn him for making her speculate about dressing rooms.

I'm completely in love with you.

Layla closed her eyes. Even now, hearing him say those words in her head made her heart do a long, slow roll.

But she hadn't been able to say the words back to him, hadn't been able to respond. Because they hadn't been standing in an old building full of character in a normal small town. They'd been standing in one that had been bat-tered and bruised, in a town that was cursed. Wasn't that the word for it? And at any time, it all could go up in flames.

Better to take one cautious step at a time, to tell him it would be best for both of them—for all of them—to go on just as they were. It was, most essentially, a matter of get-ting through.

In the shower, she let the water soothe. She'd make it up to him. Maybe she wasn't sure what she wanted, or what she dared to wish for. But she knew she loved him. Maybe that could be enough to get them through.

As she lifted her face to the spray, the snake began its silent slither out of the drain.

QUINN STARTED OFF WITH A POWER WALK BE-cause it made her feel righteous. It wasn't a hardship to do the extra stint of exercise—not with ice cream at the end of it, and with spring stirring all around. Daffodils and hy-

acinths, she thought, swinging her arms to kick up her
heart rate. Blooming trees and grass starting to green up.

It was a damn pretty town, and Cybil was right. It had
been easy for her to slide into the idea of living there. She
liked the old houses, the covered porches, the sloping
lawns as the ground rose. She liked, being a sociable sort,
coming to know so many people by name.

She turned at a corner, kept up the steady pace. Pistachio and cookie dough, she thought. And she might go for
the fudge ripple, and screw the healthy, balanced dinner
idea. Her friend needed ice cream and girl vibes. Who was
she to count the calories?

She paused a moment, frowned at the houses on the corners. Hadn't she already passed this corner? She could've
sworn . . . shaking her head, she picked up her pace again,
turned, and in moments found herself back at the exact
same spot.

A trickle of fear worked down her spine. Deliberately,
she turned the opposite way, kicked up to a jog. There was
the same corner, the same houses. She ran straight, only to
arrive at the same spot, as if the street itself shifted its position to taunt her. Even when she tried to run to one of the
houses, call for help, her feet were somehow back on the
sidewalk again, back on that same corner.

When the dark dropped on her, she ran full out, chased
by her own panic.

IN THE BOWLING CENTER, CAL STOOD BESIDE HIS
father, hands on hips as they watched the new (reconditioned) automatic scoring systems being installed.

"It's going to be great."

"Hope you're right." Jim puffed out his cheeks. "Big expense."

"Gotta spend it to make it."

They'd had to close the lanes for the day, but the arcade

and the grill were both open. Cal's idea there had been to have anyone who came in get a look at the process—the progress.

"Computers run everything. I know how that sounds," Jim muttered before Cal could speak. "It sounds like my old man crabbing when I finally talked him into going with automatic pin setters instead of having a couple guys back there putting it up by hand."

"You were right."

"Yeah, I was right. I couldn't help but be right." Jim tucked his hands into the pockets of his traditional khakis. "I guess you're feeling the same way about this."

"It's going to streamline the business, and increase it. It's going to pay for itself in the long run."

"Well, we're in it now, so we'll see how it goes. And damn it, that sounds like my old man, too."

With a laugh, Cal patted Jim's shoulder. "I've got to take Lump out for a walk, Grandpa. You want to come along?"

"No. I'll stay here, scowl some and complain about newfangled ways."

"I'll be back in a few minutes."

Amused, Cal went up to get Lump. The dog enjoyed going out when they were in town, but was filled with sorrow at the sight of the leash. It gleamed out of his eyes as Cal clipped it to his collar.

"Don't be such a baby. It's the law, pal. I know and you know you're not going to do anything stupid, but the law's the law. Or do you want me to have to come up to the pen and bail you out?"

Lump walked, head lowered like a prisoner of war, as they went down the back stairs, and out. Since they'd had this routine for a while, Cal knew the dog would perk up, as much as Lump ever perked, after the first few minutes.

He kept his eyes on the dog, waiting for the moment of acceptance as they started around the building. Unless they were walking to Quinn's, Lump preferred his leg-stretching

along Main Street, where Larry at the barbershop would wander out as they passed, and give Lump a biscuit and a rub.

Cal waited patiently while Lump lifted his leg and peed lavishly on the trunk of the big oak between the buildings, then let the dog lead him out to the sidewalk on Main.

There, Cal's heart slammed into his throat.

Scarred and broken asphalt marred the street; charred bricks heaved out of the sidewalk. The rest of the town was gone, leveled into rubble. And the rubble still smoked. Blackened, splintered trees lay like maimed soldiers on jagged shards of glass and blood-smeared stone. Scorched to ruin, the grass of the Square and its cheerful spring plantings steamed. Bodies, or the horrible remnants of them, scattered over the ground, hung obscenely from the torn trees.

Beside him, Lump quivered, then sat on his haunches, lifted his head, and howled. Still holding the leash, Cal ran to the entrance of the bowling center, yanked at the door. But the door refused him. There was no sound, within or without, but his pounding fists and frantic calls.

When his hands were bloody from the beating, he ran, the dog galloping beside him. He had to get to Quinn.

GAGE WASN'T SURE WHY HE'D COME BY. HE'D BEEN itchy at home—well, at Cal's. Home was wherever he stayed long enough to bother to unpack his bag. He started to knock, then shrugging, just opened the unlocked door of the rental house. His concession to the inhabitants was to call out.

"Anybody home?"

He heard the footsteps, knew they were Cybil's before she appeared at the top of the stairs. "I'm anybody." She started down. "What brings you by before happy hour?"

She had her hair scooped back at the nape—all that thick, curling black—as she was prone to do when work-ing. Her feet were bare. Even wearing faded jeans and a sweater, she managed to look like stylish royalty.

It was a hell of a knack, in Gage's opinion. "I had a conversation with Professor Litz, the demon expert in Europe. I told him about the idea of a blood ritual. He's against it."

"Sounds like a sensible man." She angled her head. "Come on back. You can have what's probably your tenth cup of coffee of the day, and I'll have some tea while you tell me his very sensible reasons."

"His first, and most emphatic echoed something you said." Gage followed her into the kitchen. "We could let something out we aren't prepared for. Something worse, or stronger, simply because of the ritual."

"I agree." She put the kettle on, and while it heated, started to measure for a fresh pot of coffee. "Which makes it essential not to rush into it. To gather all information possible first, and to proceed with great care."

"So you're voting to do it."

"I am, or I'm leaning that way, once we're as protected as possible. Aren't you?"

"I figure the odds at fifty-fifty, and that's good enough."

"Maybe, but I'm hoping to weigh them a little heavier in our favor first." She lifted a hand, pressed it against her eye. "I've been . . ."

"What is it?"

"Maybe I've been at the monitor too long today. My eyes are tired." She reached up to open the cupboard for cups, missed the handle by inches. "My eyes are . . . Oh God. I can't see. I can't see."

"Hold on. Here, let me look." When he took her shoulders to turn her, she gripped his arm.

"I can't see anything. It's all gray. Everything's gray."

He turned her around, bit off his own sharp intake of breath. Her eyes, those exotic gypsy eyes, were filmed over white.

"Let's sit you down. It's a trick. It's just another trick. It's not real, Cybil."

But as she clung to him, shuddering, he felt himself fade away.

He stood in the dull and dingy apartment he'd once shared with his father over the bowling alley. The smells struck him with violent memory. Whiskey, tobacco, sweat, unwashed sheets and dishes.

There was the old couch with the frayed arms, and the folding chair with the duct-taped X over the torn seat. The lamp was on, the pole lamp beside the couch. But that had been broken, Gage thought. Years ago, that had been broken when he'd shoved his father back. When he'd finally been big enough, strong enough to use his fists.

No, Gage thought. No, I won't be here again. He walked to the door, grabbed the knob. It wouldn't budge, no matter how he turned, how he pulled. And in shock he looked at the hand on the knob, and saw the hand of a child.

Out the window then, he told himself as sweat slid down his back. It wouldn't be the first time he'd escaped that way. Fighting the urge to run, he went into his old room—unmade bed, a scatter of school books, single dresser, single lamp. Nothing showing. Any treasures—comics, candy, toys—he'd hid away, out of sight.

The window refused to open. When he was desperate enough to try, the glass in it wouldn't break. Whirling around, he looked for escape, and saw himself in the mirror over the dresser. Small, dark, thin as a rail. And terrified.

A lie. Another lie. He wasn't that boy now, he told himself. Wasn't that helpless boy of seven or eight. He was a man, full grown.

But when he heard the door slam open, when he heard the stumbling tread of his drunken father, it was the boy who trembled.

FOX BEAT AND KICKED AT THE SPIDERS. THEY covered his desk now, spilled in a waterfall from the edge

to the floor. They leaped on him, hungrily bit. Where they bit, their poison burned, and the flesh swelled and broke like rotted fruit.

His mind couldn't cool, couldn't steady, not with dozens of them crawling up his legs, down his shirt. He stomped them into the floor, into the rug, while his breath whistled out between gritted teeth. The pocket doors he'd left open slammed shut. As he backed against them, the windows ran black with spiders.

He shook like a man in a fever, but he shut his eyes, ordered himself to control his breathing. As they crawled and clawed and bit, as they covered him he wanted to give in and scream.

I've seen worse than this, he told himself. His heart pounded, hammer to anvil, as he struggled for some level of calm. Sure, I've seen worse. I've had worse, you fucker. Just a bunch of spiders. I'd call the exterminator tomorrow except *they're not real*, you asshole. I can wait you out. I can wait till you run out of juice.

The sheer rage inside him won over the fear and disgust until he could bring his heart rate down. "Play all the games you want, you bastard. We won't be playing when we come for you. This time, we'll *end* you."

He felt the rush of cold that burned as bright as the bites.
You will die screaming.

Don't count on it, Fox thought, gathering himself. Don't you fucking count on it. He grabbed one of the spiders on his arm, crushed it in his fist. Let the blood and pus run like fire through his fingers.

They dropped from him, first one, then another. It was they who screamed as they died. With his swollen hands, Fox pushed open the doors. And now he ran. Not for himself, but for Layla. One of the screams inside his head was hers.

As he ran, he bled; as he bled, he healed.

He cut through buildings, leaped fences, sprinted across

yards. He saw Quinn standing in the middle of the street, shaking.

"I'm lost. I'm lost. I don't know what to do. I can't get home."

He grabbed her hand, dragged her with him.

"It's the same place. It's always the same place. I can't—"

"Shut it down," he snapped at her. "Shut everything down."

"I don't know how long. I don't even know how long I've been . . . Cal!"

She jerked away from Fox, and whatever she had left, she pulled into her, and ran to where Cal stood with his howling dog.

"It's gone, it's all gone." He caught Quinn in his arms, pressed his face to her neck. "I thought you were gone. I couldn't find you."

"It's lies." Fox shoved Cal back. "It's lies. My God, can't you hear her screaming?"

He hurtled across the street, up it, then burst into the rental house. Charging up the stairs he felt his fear tearing at him as the spiders had torn at his flesh. Her screaming stopped. But its echo led him to her, had him shoving open the bathroom door where she lay naked and unconscious on the floor.

In the kitchen, Cybil cried out when she heard the front door slam open. She threw her arms up, took a blind step forward. The gray wavered, thinned. And she sobbed as her vision cleared. She saw Gage, only Gage, pale as a sheet, staring back at her. When she threw herself into his arms, he caught her, and held her as much for himself as for her.

Seventeen

〜

SHE WAS WET AND COLD, SO FOX CARRIED LAYLA to the bed, wrapped the blanket around her. A bruising scrape marred her temple, and would undoubtedly ache when she came to. No blood, no breaks as far as he could see on a quick and cursory look. Getting her warm and dry were priorities, he thought. Then he'd make certain, then he'd look closer, look deeper. He'd barely had time to check her pulse before Quinn and Cal rushed in.

"Is Layla— Oh, God."

"Fainted, I think. I think she just fainted," Fox told Quinn when she dropped down beside him. "Maybe hit her head. Something happened when she was in the shower. I don't think there's anything there now, but Cal—"

"I'll check."

"You said . . . Sorry." Quinn mopped at her own tears. "Really bad day. You said you heard her screaming."

"Yeah, I heard her." Her terror had been so huge, he thought as he pushed her wet hair away from her face. It

had reached out and gripped him by the throat, had filled his head with her screams. "I heard all of you."

"What?"

"I guess our Bat Signal worked. It was jumbled, but I heard all of you. She needs a towel. Her hair's wet."

"Here." Cal handed him one. "Bathroom's clear."

"Cybil, Gage?"

Cal squeezed the hand Quinn held out to him. "I'll go check on them. Stay here."

"What happened to you?"

Fox shook his head. "Later." He lifted Layla's head to spread the towel under her hair. "She's coming around. Layla." Relief gushed through him when her eyelids fluttered. "Come on back, Layla. It's all right. It's over."

She surfaced with a wheezing gasp, with her hands slapping wildly, her eyes wide with horror.

"Stop. Stop." He did all he could think to do. He wrapped himself around her, pushed calm into her mind. "It's over. I've got you."

"In the shower."

"Gone. They're gone." But he could see in her mind how they'd come out of the drain, slid across the tiles.

"I couldn't get out. The door wouldn't open. They were everywhere, they were all over me." Shuddering, shuddering, she burrowed against him. "They're gone? You're sure?"

"I'm sure. Are you hurt? Let me see."

"No, I don't think . . . My head a little. And—" She focused on him. "Your face! Oh God, your hand. It's swollen."

"It's healing. It's okay." And the healing pain was nothing against the overwhelming relief. "It looks like Twisse took a shot at all of us at once."

Quinn nodded. "He hit me and Cal. Grand slam."

"More a clean sweep," Cybil said from the doorway. "He hit me and Gage, too. Six for six. Fox, why don't you

go on downstairs? Your pals are still pretty shaken. We'll help Layla get dressed, then we'll be down in a few."

She was ice pale, he noted. It was the first time he'd seen Cybil that far off her stride in the months he'd known her. Quinn was already rising, going to her. Because the room became essentially and completely female again, Fox decided it was probably best for each sector to retreat to its particular corner, take a deep breath before mixing again.

"All right." But he touched Layla's face, kissed her gently. "I'll be right downstairs."

TIMES LIKE THESE, FOX THOUGHT, CALLED FOR whiskey. He found the single, unopened bottle of Jameson among the wine, and figured it had been Cal's contribution to the liquor supply. He got glasses, ice, and poured a generous two fingers in each.

"Good thinking." Cal downed half of his in one swallow, and still his eyes remained haunted. "You healed up. You looked bad when I saw you outside."

"Spiders. Lots of them. Big bastards."

"Where?"

"My office."

"The town was gone for me." Cal studied the whiskey, swirled it. "I came out of the center with Lump, and it was gone. Like a bomb had gone off. Buildings leveled, fire and smoke. Bodies. Jesus, pieces of them everywhere." He took another, slower sip. "We'll need to write this down, get everybody's deal."

"Oh yeah, that'll help." Gage downed a single, bitter swallow. "It got us, big-time. Now we're going to take minutes of the meeting."

"You got better?" Cal shot back. "You got the final solution, bro? Because if you do, don't hold back."

"I know we're not going to talk it to death. And sitting

around taking notes doesn't mean dick unless you're writing a book. That's your lady's business, not mine."

"So what are you going to do? Take a walk? You're good at that. Are you just going to catch a plane to wherever the hell and come back for the finale? Or do you want to just skip that part this year?"

"I come back to this hellhole because I swore on it." Rage whirling around him like wind, Gage moved in on Cal. "If I hadn't, it could blow to hell as far as I'm concerned. It doesn't mean a damn to me."

"Not much does."

"Stop!" Fox's voice snapped out as he wedged between them. "It doesn't do any good to start swiping at each other."

"Maybe we should make peace signs and daisy chains."

"Look, Gage. If you want out, there's the goddamn door. And if all you can do is kick him while he's down," Fox added, swinging around to Cal, "don't let the same goddamn door hit you on the ass on your way out."

"I'm not kicking anyone, and who the hell asked you?"

Raised voices had Cybil quickening her steps. She took stock of the scene in the kitchen quickly, and stepped into it before someone threw a punch. "Well, this is productive."

She walked right in the middle of three furious men, snatched the glass out of Gage's hand, drank. And her voice held the faintest edge of boredom. "At least someone had the good sense to get out the whiskey before the testosterone attack. If you boys want to fight, go outside and beat on each other. You'll heal quickly enough, but the furniture in here won't."

Fox settled down first. He set the whiskey he no longer wanted aside, gave a sheepish shrug. "They started it."

Appreciating him, Cybil cocked a brow. "And do you do everything they do? Jump off bridges, play with matches? Let's try this instead. I'm going to put food and drink to-

gether to address that basic human need. The comfort it brings should help us get through telling each other what happened."

"Gage doesn't want to talk," Cal said.

"Neither do I." She looked at Gage as she spoke. "But I'm going to. It's another basic human need, and shows us we've got that all over the Big Evil Bastard." Smiling with lips she'd painted a defiant coral before coming down, she shook back her hair. "Why doesn't somebody order pizza?"

IT LACKED EFFICIENCY, BUT THERE WAS SOME-thing more comforting about gathering in the living room rather than sitting at the dining room table like sensible adults. Cybil set out a platter of antipasto while they waited for pizza.

Fox sat on the floor at Layla's feet. "Ladies first," he suggested. "Quinn?"

"I went out for ice cream, and since I was going to eat ice cream, I went for the power walk first." Her fingers twisted the chunky silver chain around her neck. "But I kept ending up in the same place, on the same corner. It didn't matter which direction I took. I couldn't find my way, couldn't get home." She gripped Cal's hand, pressed her forehead to his shoulder. "I couldn't find you. It went pitch dark. There was no one, and I couldn't get back."

"Everything was gone for me." Sliding an arm around her shoulders, Cal gathered her close. "The town was destroyed, everyone dead, blown to pieces. I ran here, but there was nothing. Just a smoking hole in the ground. I don't know where I was going. Looking for you. Because I couldn't, I wouldn't believe . . . Then I saw you, and Fox."

"I saw you first," Quinn said to Fox. "It was like you came through a wall of water. You were blurred at first, and your footsteps—you were running—but the sound was

smothered. Then it all cleared. You grabbed my hand, and it all cleared.

"That has to mean something, don't you think?" She glanced around as she asked. "I was heading for hysterical. I think I'd been there and back at least once already, and was making the return trip. Then I saw Fox, and when he took my hand everything went back the way it's meant to be. Then Cal was coming."

"You weren't there, either of you. Nothing was. Then you were." Cal shook his head. "It was almost like switching a channel. Like a click. You were bleeding," he said to Fox.

"Spiders," Fox said and told them. "I didn't notice anything off about the town when I got out. I saw you on the corner, Quinn. Looking lost, I guess. I'd heard you—sensed you, and the others. Like a bad connection, fuzzy and weak. But I could hear Layla screaming. I heard that loud and clear."

"You were two blocks away," Quinn pointed out.

"I could hear her screaming," he repeated. "Right up until I got into the house. Then it stopped. It must've been when you passed out."

"It was after Quinn went out. She went for ice cream because I was upset." Her gaze flicked to Fox, then back to the fingers linked in her lap. "I decided to take a shower while she was gone. I felt it first, sliding over my foot. They were coming out of the drain. Snakes. With the screams I let out, I'm surprised they didn't hear me in the next county."

"I didn't hear you," Cybil told her. "I was right downstairs and I didn't hear a thing."

"They kept coming." When her breath wanted to snag, Layla eased it out slowly, deliberately. "I got out of the shower, but they were on the floor, too. Coming up out of the sink. Not real, that's what I kept trying to tell myself, but I couldn't—I didn't keep my head. When the door

wouldn't open, I went a little crazy, beating at them with a towel, with my hands. The window was too small, and it wouldn't open anyway. I must've fainted, because I don't remember anything else until Fox was there. I was in bed, and Fox and Quinn were there."

"Your passing out might be part of the reason it stopped," Cybil speculated. "There's no maintaining an illusion when you're unconscious."

"What happened to you?" Layla asked her.

"I couldn't see. Gage and I were in the kitchen, and my eyes stung for a minute, then went blurry. Then everything went gray. I went blind."

"Oh, Cyb."

She smiled at Quinn. "Q knows that's a small, personal terror of mine. My father lost his sight in an accident. He was never able to adjust, accept. Two years later he killed himself. So blindness holds a particular terror for me. You were there," she said to Gage, "then you weren't. I couldn't hear you, and I asked you to help me, but you didn't. I guess you couldn't."

She paused, but he said nothing. "I heard the front door slam open. I heard Fox. My vision started to clear, and then . . . you were there again." He'd held her, she thought. They'd held each other. "Where did you go, Gage? We need to know what happened to each one of us."

"I didn't go far. Back to the apartment where I used to live. Above the bowling alley."

At the knock on the door, Cal rose, but he kept his eyes on Gage's face. "I'll get that."

"There was a physical thing with you," Gage went on. "With your eyes. The irises, the pupils were covered, the whole of your eyes were white. And no, I couldn't help. I stepped toward you, and right into the apartment."

Cal came back, set the pizza boxes on the table. "Were you alone?"

"At first. I couldn't get the door open, the windows. That seems to be a recurring theme."

"Trapped," Layla murmured. "Everyone's afraid of being trapped, being locked in."

"I heard him coming. I knew—I know the sound of his feet on the stairs, when he's drunk, when he's not. He was, and he was coming. Then I was back in the kitchen."

"There's more. Why are you holding back?" Cybil demanded. "We all went through something."

"When I reached for the doorknob, it wasn't my hand. Not this hand." Gage held his up, turned it, studied it. "I saw myself in the mirror. I was about seven, maybe eight. Before that night at the Pagan Stone, younger than that. Before things changed. Before we changed. And he was drunk, and he was coming. Clear enough?"

In the silence, Quinn reached down for her tape recorder, ejected the tape, put in a fresh one. "This hasn't happened before, am I right on that? That all of you were affected at the same time, that so many were affected?"

"Dreams," Cal said. "The three of us have dreams, usually on the same night, not always about the same thing. That can happen weeks, even months before the Seven. But something like this, no. Not outside of those seven days."

"It went to a lot of trouble to get to us," Fox commented, "to cherry-pick our particular and specific fears."

"Why were you the only one who was hurt?" Layla demanded. "I felt them bite me, but I didn't have any bites when I came out of it. But you did. They're healed now, but you did."

"Maybe I let it in too far, and my own ability worked against me. Made my fear more real, more tangible. I don't know."

"It's possible." Quinn considered. "Could it have started with you? Given the timing, it could have started with you first. Used more, well, juice. Fed off that for the rest. Not just your fear, but your pain, too. It used the connections.

You to Cal or me—one of us was probably next. Then Layla, then Cybil, and rounding it up with Gage."

"Like a current. The energy." Layla nodded. "Moving from one to the other. Fox weakened the current when he broke free. And back down the line. If that's the way it happened, it could be a kind of defense, couldn't it? Something we could use."

"Our energy against its energy." Quinn gave in and flipped open the pizza box. "Positive against negative."

"I think we'll need to do more than think of raindrops on roses." Cybil slid a slice out for herself. "And whiskers on kittens."

"While I doubt we're going to hear the guys do a chorus of 'Do-Re-Mi,' even if lives depend on it, roses and kittens are a springboard." Considering big trauma, Quinn treated herself to an entire slice. "If each of us has personal fears, don't we all have personal joys? Yes, yes, hokey, but not really over the top. Oh God, this is good. See, personal joy. Pepperoni pizza."

"That's not how Fox broke its hold," Layla pointed out. "I don't think he mentioned focusing on pizza or rainbows."

"Not entirely true." Because Lump's eyes filled with love, Fox peeled a piece of pepperoni off his slice, fed it to the dog. "I thought about how what was happening was bullshit. Not easy when hungry mutant spiders are crawling all over you."

"Eating here," Cal reminded him.

"But I thought more about how we were going to kick the Big Evil Bastard's ass. How we were going to end him. I kept thinking that, like I was telling him. Trash talking, lots of very foul language. That's a personal pleasure, on a very real level. And when those things started falling off me, thumping on the ground, I started feeling fairly perky. Not, the hills are alive, spinning around like a lunatic perky. But not half bad, considering."

"It's always worked that way for you. Once you figured it out," Cal added. "And it's worked for me, for Gage. We've been able to break down the illusions—when they are illusions. But I tried, and I couldn't this time."

"So you bought it."

"I—"

"You bought it, at least for a few minutes. Because it was too much, Cal. Everything that matters to you gone. Quinn, your family, us, the town. And just you left. You didn't stop it, so everyone and everything was gone, killed, destroyed. But you. It was too damn much," Fox repeated. "Those spiders weren't real, not all the way real. But I saw my hand after they had at me, and it was swollen to the size of a cantaloupe, and bleeding. The wounds were real, so I'm saying Twisse put a hell of a lot into this one."

"It's been over a week since the last incident. Also starting with you, Fox." Cybil laid a slice on a plate, walked it over to Gage. "It used Block's jealousy, his anger, maybe his guilt, fed off that, used that to infect him enough to have him attack you."

"So where did it get the extra amps for this?" Gage shrugged. "If that's the question, there are plenty of negative emotions running around this town, just like any place else."

"It's specific," Cal disagreed. "It was specific to Block. This was specific to us."

Cybil slid a glance toward Layla, but said nothing as she took her seat again.

"I was upset, and angry. So were you," Layla said to Fox. "We had . . . a disagreement."

"If it can cook up something like that every time one of us gets pissed off, we're toast," Gage decided.

"They were both upset." Quinn considered how best to phrase it. "With each other. That could factor. And it may be that when the emotions involved are particularly intense, when there's sexuality involved, it's more potent."

Gage lifted his beer. "Again. Toast."

"I happen to think intense human emotion, emotion that draws from a well of affection," Cybil added, "and good healthy sex, is a hell of a lot more potent than anything the son of a bitch can throw at us. That's not spinning in circles on a mountaintop naïveté. It comes from studying human relationships and their power, and this particular situation specifically—and how it's come to us. How many times have the three of you had a scene like you did before in the kitchen?"

"What scene?" Quinn wanted to know.

"It was nothing," Cal muttered.

"You were in each other's faces, shouting obscenities, and about to come to blows. It was . . ." Cybil's smile was sly and just a little feline. "Stimulating. Countless times, I wager—want to take the bet?" she asked Gage. "Countless times, and I up my bet to wager several of them have resulted in fists in faces. But here you are. Here you are because at the core, you love each other. That's the base, and nothing changes it. It can't shake that base. It must beat its fists—if fists it has—at the barrier it can't pass. We're going to need that base, and we're going to need all those intense human emotions, especially if we're going to do the incredibly foolish and attempt a blood ritual."

"You've got something," Quinn stated.

"I think I do. I want to wait to hear back from a couple more sources. But yeah, I think I do."

"Spill!"

"For one thing, it means all six of us, and we'll have to go back to the source."

"The Pagan Stone," Fox said.

"Where else?"

LATER, CAL GRABBED A MOMENT ALONE WITH Quinn. He drew her into her bedroom, and with his arms

around her, just breathed her in. "It was worse," he said quietly, "worse than it's ever been because for a while I thought I might have lost you."

"It was worse, because I couldn't find you." She tipped her head back, sank into the kiss with him. "It's harder when you love someone. It's better and it's harder, and it's pretty much everything."

"I want to ask you a favor. I want you to go away, just for a few days," he continued, talking fast. "A week, maybe two. I know you've got other writing projects you're squeezing in. Take a break, maybe go back home to—"

"This is my home now."

"You know what I mean, Quinn."

"Sure. And no problem." Her smile was sunny as June. "As long as you come with me. We'll have ourselves a little holiday. How's that?"

"I'm serious."

"So am I. I'll go if you go. Otherwise, you're going to want to drop this. Don't even think about picking a fight," she warned him. "I can practically see you trying it out in your head, calculating if you got me mad enough I'd walk. You can't. I won't." For emphasis, she put her hands on his cheeks, squeezed. "You're scared for me. So am I, just like I'm scared for you. It's all part of the package now."

"You could go buy a wedding dress."

"Now that's fighting dirty." But she laughed, kissed him hard. "I've already got some lines on that, thank you very much. Your mother and mine are bonding like Super Glue and . . . more Super Glue over wedding plans. Everything's under control. We had a bad day, Cal, but we came through it."

He drew her back, breathed her in once more. "I need to take a walk around town. I need to . . . I need to see it."

"Okay."

"I need to take a walk with Gage and Fox."

"I get it. Go on. Just come back to me."

"Every day," he told her.

WHEN HE GOT THEM OUTSIDE, CAL WALKED THE neighborhood first. The light was soft, easing in on evening. There were the houses he knew, the yards, the sidewalks. He walked by his great-grandmother's house, where his cousin's car sat in the drive, and flowers budded and bloomed along the walk.

There was the house of the girl he'd been crazy about when he'd been sixteen. Where was she now? Columbus? Cleveland? He couldn't quite remember where she'd gone, only that she'd moved away with her family in the fall of the year he'd turned seventeen.

After that Seven, when her father had tried to hang himself from the black walnut tree in their backyard. Cal remembered cutting the man down himself, and having no time for more, tying him to the tree with the hanging rope to hold him until the rage passed.

"You never did score with Melissa Eggart, did you, hotshot?"

How like Gage to remember and to turn the memory into something normal. "I doubled. Was working my way up to stealing third. Then things got busy."

"Yeah." Gage slid his hands into his pockets. "Things got busy."

"I'm sorry about before. And you were right," he added to Fox. "It's stupid to swipe at each other."

"Forget it," Gage told him. "I've thought about walking plenty of times."

"Thinking and doing got miles between them." They turned, headed toward Main. "I wanted to punch something, and you were handy."

"O'Dell's handier, and he's used to getting punched."

When there was no sarcastic rejoinder from Fox, Gage eyed him. He thought of the ways he could handle Fox's mood, and opted for what he did best. Needling him. "Are you having intense human emotions?"

"Oh, suck off."

"There he is." Gage swung an arm over Fox's shoulders.

"Punching you still isn't out of the question."

"If she was pissed at you," Cal said helpfully, "she's not now. Not after your white-charger routine."

"It's not about that. About being pissed, about saving the girl. It's about wanting and needing different things. Look, I'm heading home from here. I didn't shut anything down, lock anything up."

"We'll go with you, check it out."

"No, I got it. I've got some actual work to do. If anything else needs going over tonight, I'll crib off your notes. See you later."

"He's got it bad," Gage commented as they watched Fox head down Main. "Real bad."

"Maybe we should go with him anyway."

"No. We're not what he wants right now."

They turned, walking the opposite way as night crept closer.

Eighteen

COUNTING ON PAPERWORK TO KEEP HIM BUSY
and distracted, Fox settled down in his home office. Flipping his CD player to shuffle for the variety and surprise
factors, he prepared to make up for the fractured workday
with a couple of hours at his desk.

He drafted some court petitions on an estate case he
hoped to wrap up within another ninety days, shifted to
fine-tune a letter of response to opposing counsel on a personal injury matter, then moved on to adjusting the language in a partnership agreement.

He loved the law, the curves and angles of it, its flour-
ishes and hard lines. But at the moment, he was forced to
admit, the work couldn't light a spark in him. He'd be better off cruising ESPN.

The file he'd put together for Layla still sat on his desk.
Because it annoyed him, Fox dropped it in a drawer. Stupid, he thought. Stupid to think he understood her simply

because he usually understood people. Stupid to think he knew what she wanted because it was what *he* wanted.

Love, he had good reason to know, didn't always do the job.

Better to stay in the moment, he reminded himself. He was good at that, had always been good at that. Much better to focus on the now than to push himself, and Layla, toward some blurry and nebulous tomorrow. She had a point about there being no clear future for the town. Who the hell wanted to set up shop in a place that might not exist in a few months? Why should anyone invest the time and the energy, plant the roots, sweat it out, and hope the good guys won in the end? They'd all gotten today's ugly memo that the clock was ticking down for the Hollow, and for the six of them.

And that was bullshit. Annoyed, he shoved away from the desk. That was absolute bullshit. If people thought that way why did they bother to get the hell out of bed in the morning? Why did most of them at least try to do the right thing, or at least their version of it? Why buy a house or have kids, or hell, buy season tickets if tomorrow was so damn uncertain?

Maybe he'd been stupid to assume where Layla was concerned—he'd cop to that. But she was just as stupid to back away from what they could make together because tomorrow wasn't lined up in neat columns. What he needed was a different approach, he realized. For Christ's sake, he was a lawyer, he knew how to change angles, detour around obstacles and reroute to the goal. He knew about compromise and negotiation and finding that middle ground.

So what was the goal? he asked himself as he wandered to the window.

Saving the town and the people in it, destroying the evil that wanted to suck it dry. Those were the big ones, but if he set those life-and-death matters aside, what was Fox B. O'Dell's goal?

Layla. A life with Layla. Everything else was just details. He'd fumbled the ball on the way to the goal because
he'd gotten bogged down with details. The first thing to do
was carve them away. Once he did, what was left was a guy
and a girl. It was as simple and as complex as that.

He turned back to his desk. He'd toss the file, it was
just a symbol of those details. As he reached for the
drawer, the knock at the door had him frowning. It had to
be Gage or Cal, he thought as he walked out of the office
to answer. He didn't have time to hang out. He needed to
work on his more simplified, whittled-down approach
to winning the woman he loved.

When he opened the door, the woman he loved stood on
the other side.

"Hey, I was just . . . Are you alone?" His tone changed
from flustered surprise to irritation as he grabbed her hand
and pulled her inside. "What are you thinking, wandering
around town at night alone?"

"Don't start on me. Twisse will go under after a day like
this, and I wasn't wandering. I came straight here. You
didn't come back."

"We don't know what the hell Twisse might be able to
do after a day like this. And I didn't come back because I
figured you'd want to get some sleep. Besides, before this
afternoon's performance, you weren't real happy with me."

"Which is exactly why I thought you'd come back, so
we could talk about it." She poked a finger at his chest.
"You don't get to be mad at me over this."

"Excuse me?"

"You heard me. You don't get to be mad because I
didn't jump headfirst into plans you made without consulting me."

"Wait a damn minute."

"No, I will not wait a damn minute. You decided what I
should do for the rest of my life, where I should live, how I
should make my living. You made a *file*." Indignation flashed

from her eyes, her voice. From where he was standing, it all but flashed out of her fingertips. "I wouldn't be surprised if it includes paint chips and possible names for this imaginary boutique."

"I was thinking puce, color-wise. I don't think puce gets enough play. As for names, topping my list right now is Get a Fucking Grip—but it probably needs work."

"Don't curse at me, or try to make this a joke."

"If those are your two requirements, you're in the wrong place with the wrong guy. I'll drive you home."

"You will not." Feet planted, she folded her arms. "I'll walk when I'm ready to go, and I'm not ready. Don't even think about kicking me out or I'll—"

"What?" How could he help but make it a joke? It was ludicrous. He lifted his fists in a boxing pose. "Think you can take me?"

The temper that gushed out of her was hot enough to boil the air. "Don't tempt me. You sprang this on me. Out of the blue, then when I don't do a happy dance and fling myself into the program, you walk away. You tell me you love me, and you walk away."

"Sorry, I guess I needed a little alone time after realizing the woman I'm in love with isn't interested in building a life with me."

"I didn't say—I never meant . . . Hell." Layla covered her face with her hands, took several deep breaths. The anger evaporated as she lowered her hands. "I told you once you scare me. You don't understand that. You're not easily scared."

"That's not true."

"Oh, yes, yes, it is. You've lived with this threat too long to be easily scared. You face things. Some of it's circumstance, some of it's just your nature, but you face what comes at you. I haven't had to do a lot of that. Things were pretty ordinary for me, right up until February. No big bumps in my road, no particularly big moments. All in all,

I think I'm doing reasonably well. All in all," she repeated on a sigh as she began to wander the room.

"You're doing fine."

"I'm scared of what's here, of what's coming, what may happen. I don't have Quinn's energy or Cybil's . . . savoir faire," she decided. "I do have persistence, once I commit to something I do my best to see it through, and I have a way of putting the big picture into components that I can reason out. So that's something. It's not as overwhelming, not as frightening when you have those smaller pieces to work with. But I can't seem to reason things out with you and me, Fox. And that scares me."

She turned back to him. "It scares me that I've never felt for anyone what I feel for you. And I told myself it was okay, it was all right to have all these feelings rush in and grab me. Because everything's crazy. But the fact is, it's all crazy, but it's all real. What's happening around us, what's happening inside me, it's all real. I just don't know what to do about it."

"And I added to the mix with the idea of starting a business here, making it more complicated and scary. Understood. We'll take it off the table. I didn't look into it to put pressure on you. We've all got enough of that as it is."

"I wanted to be mad, because it's easier to be mad than scared. I don't want to be at odds with you, Fox. Everything that happened today . . . you were there. I woke up from that nightmare, and you were right there. Then you didn't come back." She closed her eyes. "You didn't come back."

"I didn't go far."

Emotion swam into her eyes when she opened them. "I thought you might have. And that scared me more than anything else."

"I love you," he said simply. "Where would I go?"

She launched herself into his arms. "Don't go far." Her mouth found his. "Don't kick me out. Let me be with you."

"Layla." He took her face in his hands, easing her back until their eyes met. "All I want at the end of the day is for you to be with me."

"I'm here. It's the end of the day, and I'm here. That's where I want to be."

Her lips were so soft, so giving. Her sigh, as her body molded to his, like music. Her hands brushed his face, through his hair as he circled her toward the bedroom. And in the dark, they lowered to the bed. She reached out, their legs tangling as they lay facing each other. As they stirred each other with long, lingering kisses, he could see the gleam of her eyes in the dark, the curve of her cheek, feel the shape of her lips and the beat of her heart against his.

She shifted, kneeling to unbutton his shirt. Then her body bowed down as she pressed her lips to his heart. Lightly, her fingertips grazed down his sides as her mouth brushed, her tongue slicked along his skin. She felt his muscles quiver as she trailed those slow openmouthed kisses over his belly, as she flipped open the button of his jeans.

She wanted him to quiver.

She eased the zipper down, a slick hiss of sound in the dark, and drew denim down those narrow hips where the skin was warm. He groaned as she pleasured him.

She ruled his body. Her mouth and hands guided him slowly, inexorably into the rocking sea of heat until he was drenched in it. And when the blood began to burn under his skin, she shifted again. He heard the soft rustle as she undressed.

"I want to ask you for something." She came toward him across the bed on her hands and knees and his mouth went dry as dust.

"If you want a favor, this is probably a good time to ask for it."

Teasing, she lowered her lips to his, brushed, retreated. When he cupped the back of her head to bring her mouth to his again, she took it, brought it to her breast.

"When you touch me, when you make love with me, when you're inside me, can you feel what I feel? Can I feel what you feel? I want that with you. I want to know what it's like to be together that way, when we're like this."

A gift, he thought, of complete trust, on both sides. He sat up, looked into her eyes. "Open," he murmured, and rubbed his lips to hers. "Just open."

He felt her nerves, her needs, and the thoughts that came and went in her head like soft shimmers. To be wanted, to be touched. By him. When her hands ran up his back, he knew both her pleasure and her approval. He knew the press of their bodies, the beats of their hearts.

Then easing her down, he deepened the kiss. And opened himself to her.

At first it was like a sigh, through her body, through her mind. She thought: Lovely. It's lovely. Anticipation built. She turned her head to give him the pulse in her throat when she felt his need to taste there.

Her breath caught, a quick little shock when his mouth took her breast. So much to feel, to know, she trembled with each new sensation that slipped and slid inside her, around her. His hands, her skin, his lips, her taste. Her needs tied, tangled with his on a free-falling leap.

Greed—was it hers or his that had her rolling over the bed with him, desperate for more, and the more only unleashed new, wild cravings. His hands used her, rougher than before, answering her unspoken demands. Take, take, take. Pleasure swelled, unfurled, then burst with shock after radiant shock.

Her nails bit, his teeth nipped. And when he drove into her she thought she'd go mad from the force of mingled power.

"Stay with me, stay with me." Desperate, delirious, she wrapped her legs around him like chains when she sensed him start to close off. Pleasure, a two-edged sword, was brutally keen. She gripped it with him.

She held his body, his thoughts, his heart, until neither could hold any longer.

He sprawled facedown on the bed, head swimming, lungs laboring. He didn't have the strength, as yet, to ask her if she was all right, much less to try to link to make sure for himself.

She'd taken him apart, and he wasn't quite capable of putting himself back together. None of his thoughts would coalesce. He wasn't quite sure if there weren't still echoes of hers inside him.

Still, after a few minutes, he realized he might die of thirst if he didn't crawl off for water.

"Water." He croaked it out.

"God. Please."

He started to roll, bumped her where she'd flung herself crossways on the bed. "Sorry."

He only grunted as he got his feet on the floor, then stumbled his way to the kitchen. The light in the refrigerator branded his eyes like the blaze of the sun. With one hand pressed over them, Fox felt his way over the shelves for a bottle of water.

He drank half of it where he stood, naked in front of the open refrigerator, his eyes slammed shut against any source of light. Steadier, he opened his eyes to slits, grabbed a second bottle and took it into the bedroom.

She hadn't moved a muscle.

"Are you all right? Did I—"

"Water." Her hand flayed in the air. "Water."

He opened the bottle, then slid an arm under her to prop her up. Leaning back against his arm she drank with the same urgent gusto as he had.

"Are your ears ringing?" she asked him. "My ears are ringing. And I think I may be blind."

He hauled her around so she was propped against the pillows instead of his arm, then he switched on the bedside light.

She screamed and slapped a hand over her eyes. "Okay, I wasn't blind, but now I may be." Cautiously she peeked out between two spread fingers. "Have you ever . . ."

"No. That was the first." Because his legs were still a little weak, he sat down beside her. Which was too bad, he mused, because he'd liked the full-length view. "Intense."

"*Intense* is too mild a word. There isn't a word. They need to invent one. I guess that's not something we could handle every time."

"Save it for special occasions."

She smiled and stirred up the energy to sit up, rest her head on his shoulder. "Arbor Day's coming up, I think. That's pretty special."

He laughed, turned his head to rub his cheek against her hair. I love you, he thought, but kept the words to himself this time.

SINCE FOX HAD OUTSIDE MEETINGS, LAYLA TOOK advantage of a slow afternoon to read over portions of Ann Hawkins's third journal. There was not, as they'd hoped, a spell, a formula, step-by-step directions on how to kill a centuries-old demon. It led Layla to believe Giles Dent hadn't told his lover the answers. Cybil's take was more mystical, Layla supposed. If Ann knew, she also knew that whatever needed to be done to end Twisse would be diluted, even invalidated if the answers were simply handed over.

That seemed too cryptic and irritating to Layla, so she spent considerable time trying to read between the lines. And came away from it frustrated and headachy. Why couldn't people just be straightforward. She *liked* step-by-step directions. And she was sure as hell going to record them, if they ever found them, used them, and were successful, on the off-chance some future generation had a similar problem.

"Why don't you come back here?" Layla muttered. "Come on back and talk to me, Ann. Just spell it out. Then we'll all go about our normal lives."

Even as she said it, Layla heard the front door creak open. She bulleted to her feet. Brian O'Dell sauntered in.

"Hey, Layla. Sorry, did I startle you?"

"No. A little. I wasn't expecting anyone. Fox is out of the office this afternoon."

"Oh. Well." Brian dipped his hands in his pockets, rocked back on his heels. "I was in town, thought I'd drop in."

"He probably won't be back until after six. If you want to leave a message—"

"No. No big. You know, since I'm here, maybe I'll just go back." He pulled a hand free to gesture with his thumb. "Fox is talking about new flooring in the kitchen, and a couple of things. I'll just go measure. Want any coffee or anything?"

Layla tilted her head. "How are you going to measure without a measuring tape?"

"Right. Right. I'll get one out of the truck."

"Mr. O'Dell, did Fox ask you to come in this afternoon?"

"Ah. He's not here."

"Exactly." Like the son, Layla thought, the father was a poor liar. "So he asked if you'd come in, check on me. Which I might not have copped to except that your wife dropped in about an hour ago, with a dozen eggs. Putting that together with this, I smell babysitters."

Brian grinned, scratched his head. "Busted. He doesn't like you being here alone. I can't say I blame him." He strolled over, dropped into one of the visitors' chairs. "I hope you're not going to give him a hard time about it."

"No." She sighed, sat herself. "I guess, one way or another, we all worry about each other. But I've got my cell

in my pocket, and everyone I know on speed dial. Mr. O'Dell—"

"Brian."

"Brian. How do you handle it? Knowing what's happening, what may happen to Fox?"

"You know, I was nineteen when Sage was born." In the language of a man settling in for a spell, he propped one work-booted foot on his knee. "Jo was eighteen. Couple of kids who thought we knew it all, had it all covered. Then, you have a kid of your own, and the whole world shifts. There's a part of me that's been worried for thirty-three years now." He smiled as he said it. "I guess there's just more parts of me worried when it comes to Fox. And truth? It pisses me off that he had his childhood, his innocence stolen from him. He came home that day, his tenth birthday, and he was never a little boy, not in the same way, again."

"Did he tell you what happened? The morning he came back from the Pagan Stone?"

"I like to think we got a lot right with our kids, but one thing I know we got right. They know they can tell us anything. He'd spun that one about camping out in Cal's backyard, but Jo and I saw through that."

"You knew he was going to spend the night in the woods?"

"We knew he was taking an adventure, and we gave him the room. If we hadn't, he'd've found a way around it. Birds have to fledge. You can't stop it, no matter how much you want to keep them safe in the nest."

He paused a moment, and Layla could see him looking back, wondered what it was like to look back over the course of another's lifetime. Someone you loved.

"He had Gage with him when he came home," Brian continued. "You could see, in both of them, something had changed. Then they told us, and everything changed. We

talked about leaving. Jo and I talked about selling the farm and moving on. But he needed to be here. After the week was up, we all thought it was over. But more than that, we knew Fox needed to be here, with Cal and Gage."

"You've seen him face this three times before, and now he's facing it again. I think it must take tremendous courage to accept what he's doing. Not to try to stop him."

The smile was easy, the smile clear. "It's not courage, it's faith. I have complete faith in Fox. He's the best man I know."

Brian stayed until she closed the office, then insisted on driving her home. The best man I know, she mused as she walked in the house. Was there a higher tribute from father to son? She walked upstairs to take the journal back to the home office.

Quinn sat at her desk, scowling at her monitor.

"How's it going?"

"Crappy. I'm on deadline with the article, and I can't keep my head in the game."

"Sorry. I'll go down, give you the room."

"No. Shit." She shoved away. "I shouldn't have said I'd write the stupid article except, hello, money. But we've been pushing on this idea of the blood ritual, and clever words to go with it, and Cybil's snarly."

"Where is she?"

"Working in her room because apparently I think too loud." Quinn waved it away. "We get like this with each other if we work on a project for any serious length of time. Only *she* gets like this more. I wish I had a cookie." Quinn propped her chin on her hand. "I wish I had a bag of Milanos. Crap." She picked up the apple from the desk, bit in. "What are you smiling at, size freaking two?"

"Four, and I'm smiling because it's reassuring to come home and find you in this lousy mood wishing for cookies, and Cybil holed up in her room. It's so normal."

With something between a grunt and a snort, Quinn

took another bite of apple. "My mother sent a swatch for bridesmaids' gowns. It's fuchsia. How's that for normal, Sunny Jane?"

"I could wear fuchsia if I had to. Please don't make me."

Blue eyes wickedly amused, Quinn chewed and smiled. "Cyb would look horrible in fuchsia. If she keeps crabbing at me, I'll make her wear it. You know what? We need to get out of here for a while. All work, no play. We're taking tomorrow off and shopping for my wedding dress."

"Seriously?"

"Seriously."

"I thought you'd never ask. I've been *dying* to do this. Where—"

Layla turned as Cybil's door opened. "We're going shopping. For Quinn's wedding gown."

"Good, that's good." At the doorway, Cybil leaned on the jamb, studied both her friends. "That's what we could call a ritual—a white one, a female one. Unless we want to take a closer look at the symbolism. White equals virginal, veil equals submission—"

"We don't," Quinn interrupted. "I will, without shame, toss my feminist principles to the wind for the perfect wedding dress. I'll live with it."

"Right. Well, anyway . . ." Absently, Cybil shoved back her mass of hair. "It's still a female ritual. Maybe it'll balance out what we'll be doing in another two weeks. Blood magic."

FOX DROVE STRAIGHT TO LAYLA'S AFTER HIS AP-pointments. She opened the door as he started up the walk, her hair swinging, her lips curved in a welcoming smile. Could he help it if that was exactly what he hoped to come home to every night?

"Hey." He leaned down to kiss her, leaned up and cocked

his head at the absent response. "Why don't we try that again?"

"Sorry. I'm distracted." She took the lapels of his jacket in her hands, and put herself into the kiss.

"That's what I'm talking about." But he saw now there was no reflection of that smile of greeting in her eyes. "What's the matter?"

"Did you get my voice mail?"

"Meeting here, as soon as I could make it. I made it."

"We're in the living room. It's—Cybil thinks she's nailed down the blood ritual."

"Fun and games for all." Concerned, he brushed his thumb over her cheekbone. "What's the problem?"

"She— She's waiting until you get here to explain it to the three of you."

"Whatever she explained to you didn't put roses in your cheeks."

"Some of the variables on the potential outcome aren't rosy." She took his hand. "You'd better hear it for yourself. But before . . . I have to tell you something else."

"Okay."

"Fox . . ." Her fingers tightened on his, as if in comfort. "Can we just sit here a minute?"

They sat on the porch steps, looking out at the quiet street. Her hands clasped on her knee, one of her signs— Gage would call it a tell—of nerves. "How bad is it?" Fox asked her.

"I don't know. I don't know how you'll feel about it." She pressed her lips together once, hard. "I'm going to say it straight out, then you can take whatever time you need to, well, absorb it. Carly was connected. To this. She was a descendent of Hester Deale's."

It hit him, a hard, fast punch to the solar plexus. His thoughts spun, so he asked the first question that popped. "How do you know?"

"I asked Cybil—" She broke off, shifted to face him,

started again. "It seemed that there had to be a reason for what happened, Fox, a reason she was infected so quickly, so . . . fatally. So I asked Cybil to look into it, and she has been."

"Why didn't you say anything to me?"

"I wasn't sure, and if I'd been wrong, I'd have upset you for nothing. And . . . I should've told you," she amended. "I'm sorry."

"No." The spinning stopped; the ache just under his heart eased. She'd wanted to shield him until supposition became fact and he'd have done exactly the same. "No, I get it. Cybil climbed Carly's family tree?"

"Yes. Tonight she told me she'd found the connection. She has the details of the genealogy if you want to see them."

When he only shook his head, she went on. "I don't know if this makes it better for you, or worse, or if it changes nothing. But I thought you should know."

"She was part of it," he said quietly. "All along."

"Twisse used that, and you, and her. I'm sorry. I'm so sorry, but nothing you did, nothing you didn't do would have changed that."

"I don't know if that's true, but there's nothing I can do now to change it. Maybe we found each other, Carly and me, because of this. But then we made choices, both of us, that led to the end of it. Different choices, maybe a different result. No way to know."

After a moment, he laid his hand over hers. "There's always going to be guilt, and grief, when I think of her. But now, I know at least part of the why. I never understood why, Layla, and that twisted me up."

"Twisse took her to hurt you. And was able to take her, the way he did, because she was of his bloodline. And because . . ."

"Keep going," he told her when she trailed off.

"I think because she didn't believe, not really. She didn't

believe enough to be afraid, or to fight, even to run. That's just speculation, and I might be overstepping, but—"

"No." He said it quietly. "No, you're exactly right. She didn't believe, even when she saw with her own eyes." He lifted his free hand, studied the unmarred palm. "She told me what she thought I wanted to hear, promised to stay at the farm that night without ever intending to keep the promise. She was built skeptical, she couldn't help it."

He closed his hand into a loose fist, lowered it. And for the first time in nearly seven years, he let it go. "I never thought of a connection. That was smart. And you were right to tell me." He lifted their hands, slid his fingers between hers. "Being up-front with each other, even when it's hard, that's the best choice for us."

"I want to say this one thing more before we go in. If I promise you something—if you ask me to do something, or not to, and I give you my promise, I'll keep it."

Understanding, he brought their joined hands to his lips. "And I'll believe what you tell me. Let's go inside."

He couldn't change the past, Fox thought. He could only prepare for the future. But he could prize and hold the now. Layla was his now. The people in this house were his as well. They needed him, and he needed them. That was enough for any man.

He settled into his usual spot on the floor with Lump. Whatever was in the air, Fox thought, was something between nerves and fear. That was from the women. From Cal and Gage he sensed both interest and impatience.

"What's going on? And whatever it is, let's get on with it."

Cybil took the stage.

"I've talked with a number of people I know and, for the most part, trust, regarding performing a blood ritual, the object being to re-form the three pieces of Dent's bloodstone into one. We're assuming that's something we need to do. There are a lot of assumptions here based on bits and pieces of information, on speculation."

"The three separate pieces haven't done us much good up till now," Gage pointed out.

"Well, you don't know that, do you?" Cybil tossed back. "It's very possible that those individual pieces are what's given you your gifts—your sight, your healing. Once whole, you might lose that. And without those gifts in your arsenal, you'll be all the more vulnerable to Twisse."

"If you don't put them back together," Cal pointed out, "they're just three pieces of stone we don't understand. We agreed to try. We *have* tried. If you've found another way, that's what we'll try next."

"Blood rites are powerful and dangerous magicks. We're dealing with a powerful and dangerous force already. You need to know all the possible consequences. All of us need to know. And all of us have to agree because all of us need to be part of it for the ritual to have any chance of working. I'm not going to agree until everyone understands."

"We get it." Gage shrugged. "Cal may need to dig out his glasses, and the three of us will be susceptible to the common cold."

"Don't make light of this." Cybil turned to him. "You could lose what you have, and more. It could all blow up in our faces. You've seen that possibility. The mix of blood and fire, the stone on the stone. Every living thing consumed. It was your blood that let the demon out. We need to consider that performing this rite could loose something worse."

"You have to play to win."

"He's right." Fox nodded at Gage. "We risk it, or we do nothing. We believe Ann Hawkins or we don't. This was the time, that's what she told Cal. This Seven is the all or nothing, and the stone—whole—is a potential weapon. I believe her. She sacrificed her life with Dent, and that sacrifice led to us. One into three, three into one. If there's a way, we go."

"There's another three. Q, Layla, and me. Our blood, tainted if you will, with that of the demon."

"And carrying that of the innocent." Layla sat with her

hands folded, as if she held something delicate inside them. "Hester Deale wasn't evil. Innocent blood, you said, Cybil, innocent blood is a powerful element in ritual."

"So I'm told." Cybil let out a sigh. "I was also warned that the innocent can be used to give the demon strain more power. That a ritual such as we're suggesting could be an invitation. Three young boys were changed by a blood rite on that ground. It could happen again, with us." She looked at Layla, at Quinn. "And what's diluted, or dormant, or just outweighed in us by who we are, could rise."

"Not going to happen." Quinn spoke briskly. "Not only because I don't consider horns and cloven feet a fashion statement but"—she ignored Cybil's annoyed oath—"because we won't let it. Cyb, you're too goddamn hard-headed to let a little demon DNA run your show. And you're not responsible. Don't even," Quinn ordered when Cybil started to speak. "Nobody knows you like I do. If we vote go, we're all in it, we're all making the choice. And whatever happens, thumbs-up or -down, it's not on you. You're just the messenger."

"Understand if it goes wrong, it could go seriously and violently wrong."

"If it goes right," Fox reminded Cybil, "it's a step toward saving lives. Toward ending this."

"More likely we'll lose a little blood and not a damn thing will change. Any way you look at it, it's a long shot," Gage added. "I like a long shot. I'm in."

"Anyone not?" Quinn scanned the room. "That's a big go."

"Let's get started."

"Not so fast, big guy," Cybil said to Gage. "While the ritual's pretty straightforward, there are details and procedure. It requires the six of us—boy-girl, boy-girl—like any good dinner party, in the standard ritual circle. On the ritual ground at the Pagan Stone. Cal, I don't suppose you have the knife you used before?"

"My Boy Scout knife? Sure I do."

"Sure he does." Charmed, Quinn leaned over to kiss his cheek.

"We'll need that. I have a list of what we'll need. And we'll work out the wording of the incantation. We have to wait for the night of the full moon, and begin in the half hour before midnight, finish before the half hour after."

"Oh, for Christ's sake."

"Ritual requires ritual," she snapped at Gage. "And respect, and a hell of a lot of faith. The full moon gives us light, literally and magickally. The half hour before midnight is the time of good, and the half hour after, evil. That's the time, that's the place, and that's our best shot of making it work. Think of it as stacking the odds in our favor. We've got two weeks to fine-tune it, work out the kinks—or to call off the whole deal and go to St. Barts. Meanwhile . . ." She looked into her empty glass. "I'm out of wine."

As the discussion started immediately, Gage slipped off to follow Cybil into the kitchen. "What's got you spooked?"

"Oh, I don't know." She poured herself a generous glass of cabernet. "Must be the death and damnation."

"You don't spook easy, so spill."

She took a small sip as she turned to him. "You're not the only one who gets previews of coming attractions."

"What did you see this time?"

"I saw my best friend die, and the death of the woman I've come to love and respect. I saw the men who love them die trying to save them. I saw your death in blood and fire. And I lived. Why is that worse? That I saw everyone die, and I lived."

"Sounds more like nerves and guilt than a premonition."

"I don't do guilty, as a rule. On the plus side, in my dream it worked. I saw the bloodstone whole, resting on

the Pagan Stone under the light of the full moon. And for a moment, it was brighter than the sun."

She took a long, quiet breath. "I don't want to walk out of the clearing alone, so do me a favor. Don't die."

"I'll see what I can do."

Nineteen

~⌐~

OUTSIDE, UNDER THE DIM LIGHT OF THE WAXING
moon, Layla kissed Fox good night. And that brush of lips
slid into a second, soft and seductive as the night air. "I just
think I need to stay here tonight." But she melted into him
for another. "Cybil's edgy, Quinn's distracted. And they've
been poking at each other. They need a referee."

"I could stay." Gently, he grazed his teeth over her bottom lip. "Back you up."

"Then I'd be distracted. I'm already distracted." With a
little groan, she eased away. "Besides, I have a feeling you'll
be going to Cal's. The three of you are going to want to talk
this over."

"It's a lot." He ran his hands down her arms. "You're up
for it."

"That wasn't a question."

"No. I could see it. I can see it now."

Very little could have pleased her more than that single,

almost casual, vote of confidence. "Time to take the next step. And by the way, I need tomorrow off."

"Okay."

"Just okay?" She shook her head. "No what for, or who the hell's going to run the office?"

"Three or four times a year—that was the limit—we could take a day off school. We just said, I don't want to go to school tomorrow, and that was okay. Never had to fake sick or sneak a hook day in. I figure the same applies to work."

She leaned into him, arms around his waist, hands linked together. "I've got a terrific boss. He even sends his parents in to check on me when he's out of the office."

Fox winced. "I may have mentioned that—"

"It's all right. In fact, it's better than all right. I had a nice chat with your mother, then one with your dad—who dazzles me a little because you look so much like him when you smile."

"Number One O'Dell Charm Tool. Never fails."

She laughed, leaned back. "There's something I should tell you before you go. I've been working it out in my head for a while now, then today, when I was talking to your father, something occurred to me. Why was I working on it so much? Why couldn't it just be? Because, well, it is."

"What is?"

"I'm in love with you." She let out a half laugh. "I love you, Fox. You're the best man I know."

He couldn't find words, not with so much blowing through him. I love you, she said, with a smile that made the words sparkle in the dark. So he lowered his brow to hers, closed his eyes, and gave himself to the moment. Here she was, he thought. Everything else was details.

Then tipping her head back, he kissed her brow, her cheeks before laying his lips on hers. "You're telling me this, then sending me home?"

She laughed again. "Afraid so."

"Maybe you could just come over for an hour. Make it

two." He kissed her again, deeper, and deeper. "Let's go for three."

"I want to, but . . ."

Even as she started to yield—what was an hour or two when you were in love—Gage came out of the front door. "Sorry." He glanced at Fox, cocked his head. Fox nodded.

"How do the two of you manage to have a conversation without speaking?" Layla wondered as Gage strode down to his car.

"Probably has something to do with knowing each other since birth. I'm going to ride with him." Fox caught her face in his hands. "Tomorrow night."

"Yes. Tomorrow night."

"I love you." He kissed her again. "Damn it, I've gotta go." And again. "Tomorrow."

When he walked to the car, his mind was too full of her for him to notice the dark cloud that smothered the moon.

LEAVE IT TO QUINN, LAYLA THOUGHT, TO FIND the perfect bridal boutique. Every minute of the two-and-a-half-hour drive had been worth it once they'd arrived at the charming three-story Victorian house with its stunning gardens. Layla's retailer's eye noted the details—the color schemes, the decor, the fussily female sitting areas, the oh-so-flattering lighting.

And the stock. Displays of gowns, shoes, headdresses, underpinnings, all so creatively contrived, made Layla feel as if she wandered along a wedding cake, with all its froth and elegance.

"Too many choices. Too many. I'm going to choke." Quinn gripped Cybil's arm.

"You're not. We've got all day. God, have you ever seen so much white? It's a blizzard of tulle, a winter forest of shantung."

"Well, there's white, and ivory, cream, champagne, ecru,"

Layla began. "I'd go for the white with your coloring, Quinn. You can pull it off."

"You pick one. That's what you do—did—right?" Quinn rubbed a hand over her throat. "Why am I so nervous?"

"Because you only get married the first time once."

Quinn poked at Cybil and laughed. "Shut up. Okay." She took a steadying breath. "Natalie's setting up the dressing room," she said, referring to the shop's manager. "I'll try on what she's picked out. But we're all going to pick at least one gown each. And we have to vow to be honest. If the gown sucks on me, we say so. Everybody, spread out. Dressing room, twenty minutes."

"You'll know yours when you see yourself in it. That's the way it works." But Layla wandered off.

She looked at lace, silk, satin, beads. She studied lines and trains and necklines. As she stood, eyeing a gown, visualizing Quinn in it, Natalie bustled over.

Her cap of salt-and-pepper hair suited her gamine face. Small, black-framed glasses set it off. She was tiny and trim in a dark suit Layla imagined she chose to contrast rather than blend with the gowns.

"Quinn's ready, but doesn't want to start without you. We've got six gowns to start."

"I wonder if we can add this one."

"Of course, I'll take care of it."

"How long have you been in business?"

"My partner and I opened four years ago. I managed a bridal boutique in New York for several years before relocating."

"Really? Where?"

"I Do, Upper East Side."

"Terrific place. A friend of mine bought her gown there just a few years ago. I live—lived—" Which was it? Layla wondered. "Um, in New York. I managed a boutique downtown. Urbania."

"I know that store." Natalie beamed. "Small world."

"It is. Can I ask what made you leave I Do and New York, open here?"

"Oh, Julie and I talked about it endlessly over the years. We've been friends since our college days. She found this place, called me and said, 'Nat, this is it.' She was right. I thought she was crazy. I thought *I* was crazy, but she was right." Natalie angled her head. "Do you know what it's like when you find the customer exactly what she wants— exactly what's right. The look on her face, the tone in her voice?"

"Yes, I do."

"Triple it when it's your own place. Should I take you to the dressing room?"

"Yes, thanks."

There was tea in delicate china cups in a spacious room with a tall triple mirror and chairs with needlepoint cushions. Paper-thin cookies waited on a silver tray while blush pink lilies and white roses scented the air.

Layla sat, sipped, while Quinn worked her way through the selections.

"It doesn't suck." Cybil pursed her lips as Quinn turned in front of the mirror. "But it's too fussy for you. Too much . . ." She circled her hand. "Poof," she decided.

"I like the beadwork. It's all sparkly."

"No," was all Layla said, and Quinn sighed.

"Next."

"Better," Cybil decided. "And I'm not just saying that because it's the one I picked out. But if we're considering this the most important dress of your life, it's still not ringing the bell. I think it's too dignified—not quite enough fun."

"But I look so elegant." Quinn turned, her eyes shining as she watched herself in the triple glass. "Almost, I don't know, regal. Layla?"

"You can carry it with your height and build, and the lines are classic. No."

"But—" Quinn blew out a breath that vibrated her lips.

After two more tries and rejections, Quinn took a tea break in her bra and panties. "Maybe we should elope. We could go to Vegas, have an Elvis impersonator marry us. That could be fun."

"Your mother would kill you," Cybil reminded her as she broke one of the delicate cookies in two and offered Quinn half. "So would Frannie," she added, referring to Cal's mother.

"Maybe I'm just not built for the gown kind of thing. Maybe a cocktail dress is a better idea. We don't have to go so formal and fussy," she said as she set down the tea and picked another gown at random. "This skirt is probably going to make my ass look ten feet square." Her glance at Layla was apologetic. "Sorry, this one's your pick."

"It's your pick that counts. It's ruching—called a pickup skirt," Layla explained.

"Or we could just go for completely casual, a backyard wedding and reception. All this is just trappings." She spoke to Cybil as Layla helped her into the dress. "I love Cal. I want to marry Cal. I want the day to be a celebration of that, of what we are to each other, and to what the six of us have accomplished. I want it to symbolize our commitment, and our happiness, with a kick-ass party. I mean, for God's sake, with all we've faced, and are going to face, one stupid dress doesn't mean a thing."

As Layla stepped back, she turned around. "Oh my God." Breathless, she stared at herself. The heart-shaped bodice of the strapless gown showed off strong, toned shoulders and arms, and glittered with a sprinkle of cut-glass beads. The skirt fell from a trim waist in soft ruches of taffeta accented with pearls.

With her fingertips, Quinn touched the skirt very lightly "Cyb?"

"Well, God." Cybil knuckled a tear away. "I didn't expect to react this way. Jesus, Q, it's perfect. You're perfect."

"Please tell me it doesn't make my ass look ten feet square. Lie if you must."

"Your ass looks great. Damn, I need a tissue."

"Remember everything I just said about the dress and the trappings not being important? Now forget I said any of that. Layla." Quinn closed her eyes, crossed her fingers. "What do you think?"

"I don't have to tell you. You know it's yours."

SPRING BROUGHT COLOR TO THE HOLLOW WITH greening willows reflected in the pond at the park, with the redbuds and wild dogwoods blooming in the woods, along the roadsides. The days lengthened and warmed in a teasing preview of the summer to come.

With spring, porches gleamed with fresh paint and gardens shot out a riot of blooms. Lawnmowers hummed and buzzed until the smell of freshly cut grass sweetened the air. Kids played baseball, and men cleaned their barbecue grills.

And with spring, the dreams came harder.

Fox woke in a cold sweat. He could still smell the blood, the hellsmoke, the charred bodies of the doomed and damned. His throat throbbed from the shouts that had ripped out of him in dreams. Running, he thought, he'd been running. His lungs still burned from the effort, and his heart still drummed. He'd been running through the deserted streets of the Hollow, flaming buildings around him, as he tried to reach Layla before she . . .

He reached over; found her gone.

He leaped out of bed, snagging a pair of boxers on the run. He called out for her, but he knew—before he saw the door standing open, he knew where her own dream lured her.

He was out the door, into the cool spring night, and running, just as he'd run in the dream. Bare feet slapping in a wild tattoo on brick, asphalt, grass. Fetid smoke hazed the

deserted streets, stinging his eyes, scoring his throat. All
around him, buildings roared with flame. Not real, he told
himself. The fires were lies, but the danger was real. Even
as the heat scorched his skin, as it seemed to burn up
through the bricks to sear his feet, he ran.

His heart hammered even when he saw her, walking
through the false flames. She glided through the smoke, like
a wraith, the mad lights from the fires rippling over her body.
He called, but she didn't turn, didn't stop. When he caught
her, yanked her around to face him, her eyes were blind.

"Layla." He shook her. "Wake up. What are you doing?"

"I am damned." She almost sang it, and her smile was
tortured. "We are all of us damned."

"Come on. Come home."

"No. No. I am the Mother of Death."

"Layla. You're Layla." He tried to push himself into the
haze of her mind, and found only Hester's madness. "Come
back." Chaining down his own panic, he tightened his grip.
"Layla, come back." As she fought to break free, he simply
locked his arms around her. "I love you. Layla, I love you."
Holding tight, he drowned everything else, fear, rage, pain,
with love.

In his arms, she went limp, then began to shudder.
"Fox."

"It's okay. It's not real. I've got you. I'm real. Do you
understand?"

"Yes. I can't think. Are we dreaming?"

"Not anymore. We're going to go back. We're going to
get inside." He kept an arm firmly around her waist as he
turned.

The boy skimmed along the fire. He rode it as a human
child might a skateboard, with glee and delight while his
dark hair flew in the wild wind. As the rage rolled into Fox,
he poised to spring.

"Don't." Her voice was thick with exhaustion as Layla

leaned her weight against Fox. "It wants you to, it wants to separate us. I think we're stronger together, holding on to each other."

Death for one, life for the other. I'll drink your blood, boy, then plant my young in your human bitch.

"Don't!" This time Layla had to lock her arms around Fox's neck to keep him from rushing forward. She pushed her thoughts into his head. *We can't win here. Stay with me. You have to stay with me.* "Don't leave me," she said aloud.

It was brutal, walking away, struggling to ignore the filth the thing hurled at them. To continue to walk as the boy whipped around them in circles, taunting, howling as it flew on its skate of flame. But as they walked, the fires sputtered. By the time they climbed the steps to his apartment, the night was clear and cool again, and carried only the dying hint of brimstone.

"You're cold. Let's get back in bed."

"I just need to sit." She lowered to a chair, and helpless to do otherwise, let the trembling take her. "How did you find me?"

"I dreamed it. Running across town, the fire, all of it." To warm her, he grabbed the throw his mother had made him off the couch, spread it over Layla's bare legs. "To the park, to the pond. But in the dream, I was too late. You were dead when I pulled you out of the water."

She reached for his hands, found them as icy as hers. "I need to tell you. It was like back in New York, when I dreamed it raped me. When I dreamed I was Hester, and how it raped me. I wanted it to stop, to end. I was going to kill myself, drown myself. She was. I couldn't stop her. It had my mind."

"It doesn't have it now."

"It's stronger. You felt that. You know that. Fox, it nearly made me kill myself. If it's strong enough to do that, if we're not immune—Quinn, Cybil, and I—it could make us hurt you. It could make me kill you."

"No."

"Damn it, what if he had made me go into the kitchen, get a knife, and stab it into your heart? If it can take us over when we sleep then—"

"If it could have infected you that way, to kill me, it would have. Offing me or Cal or Gage, that's its number one. You come from it and Hester, so it used Hester against you. Otherwise, I'd be dead with a knife in my heart, and you'd be going under for the third time in the pond. You've got a logical mind, Layla. That's logical."

She nodded, and though she struggled, the first tears escaped. "It raped me. I know it wasn't me, I know it wasn't real, but I *felt* it. Clawing at me. Ramming inside me. Fox."

As she broke, he gathered her in, gathered her up. There was no hell dark enough, he thought, cradling her in his lap, rocking her as she sobbed.

"I couldn't scream," she managed, and pressed her face to the plane of his shoulder. "I couldn't stop it. Then I didn't care, or couldn't. It was Hester. She just wanted to end it."

"Do you want me to call Quinn and Cybil? Would you rather—"

"No. No."

"It used that. The shock, the trauma, to push your will down." He brushed at her hair. "We won't let it happen again. I won't let him touch you again." He lifted her face, brushed at her tears with his thumbs. "I swear to you, Layla, whatever has to be done, he won't touch you again."

"You found me, before I found myself." She laid her head on his shoulder, closed her eyes. "We won't let it happen again."

"In a few days, we'll take the next step. We're not going through this to lose. And when we end this thing, you'll be part of that. You'll be part of what ends it."

"I want it to hurt." On that realization, her voice strengthened. "I want it to scream, the way I was screaming in my head." When she opened her eyes again, they were clear. "I

wish there was a way we could lock him out of our heads. Like garlic with vampires. That sounds stupid."

"It sounds good to me. Maybe our research ace can come up with something."

"Maybe. I need to take a shower. That sounds stupid, too, but—"

"No, it doesn't."

"Will you talk to me while I do? Just talk?"

"Sure."

She left the door open, and he stood leaning against the jamb. "Pretty close to morning," he commented. "I've got some farm fresh eggs, courtesy of my mother." Switch to normal, he told himself. That's what they both needed. "I can scramble some up. I haven't cooked for you yet."

"I think you opened a couple of soup cans during the blizzard when we stayed at Cal's."

"Oh, well, then I have cooked. I'll still scramble some eggs. Bonus feature."

"When we went to the Pagan Stone before, it wasn't as strong as it is now."

"No."

"It'll get stronger."

"So will we. I can't love you this much—scrambling eggs much—and not get stronger than I was before you."

Under the hot spray, she closed her eyes. It wasn't the soap and water making her feel clean. It was Fox. "No one's ever loved me scrambling eggs much. I like it."

"Play your cards right, and that might bump up one day to my regionally famous BLT."

She turned off the water, stepped out for a towel. "I'm not sure I'm worthy."

"Oh." He grinned as he trailed his gaze over her. "Believe me. I can also toast a bagel, if I have the incentive."

She stopped in the doorway. "Got a bagel?"

"Not at the moment, but the bakery'll be open in about an hour."

She laughed—God what a relief to laugh—and moved by him to get the robe she stashed in his closet.

"Lots of excellent bakeries in New York," he commented. "The city of bagels. So, I've been thinking, as I like a good bakery, and a good bagel, after this summer I could look into taking the bar up there."

She turned back as she belted the robe. "The bar?"

"Most law firms are fussy about hiring on associates unless they pass their particular bar. The sublet on your apartment runs through August. Maybe you'd want to hang here until after Cal and Quinn get married in September anyway. Or you might want to find a new place up there. Plenty of time to decide."

She stood where she was, studying his face. "You're talking about moving to New York."

"I'm talking about being with you. It doesn't matter where."

"This is your home. Your practice is here."

"I love you. We covered that, didn't we?" He stepped to her. "We covered the part about you loving me back, right?"

"Yes."

"People in love generally want to be together. You want to be with me, Layla?"

"Yes. Yes, I want to be with you."

"Okay then." He kissed her lightly. "I'll go break some eggs."

LATER THAT MORNING, FOX SAT IN CAL'S OFFICE, rubbing a foot over Lump's hindquarters. Gage paced. He hated being here, Fox knew, but it couldn't be helped. It was private, and it was convenient. Most of all, Fox had taken a personal vow to stay within hailing distance of Layla until the full moon.

"There has to be a reason it targets her, specifically, for this. Fucking rapist."

"And if we knew the reason, we could stop it." Cal nodded. "It could be that she's the loosest link. Meaning, the three of us go back all the way. Quinn and Cybil since college. None of us knew Layla until February."

"Or the evil bastard could've just rolled the dice." Gage stopped by the window, saw nothing of interest, moved on. "None of the others have shown any signs of infection."

"It's different. It's not like what happens to people during the Seven. It's only happened, the rape, when she's asleep. And it was a kind of sleepwalking after. Following the same pattern as Hester Deale. Lots of ways to kill yourself, and we've seen plenty. But it was going to be drowning, in an outdoor body of water. Same as Hester. Maybe it had to be."

"One of us stays at the house at night until this is over," Cal decided. "Even if Layla's at your place, Fox, none of them are left alone at night from here on."

"That's where I was heading. Once we've done our full-moon dance, we should look into this angle more. We need to find a way to stop this, to protect her—all of them."

"Day after tomorrow," Gage muttered. "Thank Christ. Has anybody been able to squeeze more details out of Madam Voltar?"

Cal's lips twitched. "Not really. If Quinn knows, she's got it zipped, too. All she'll say is Cybil's fine-tuning. Then, she distracts me with her body, which isn't hard to do."

"She writes the script." Fox lifted his hands at Gage's snort. "Look, we tried it our way, various ways, and managed dick. Let the lady have a shot at it."

"The lady's worried we're all going to die. Or five out of six of us."

"Better worried than too cocky," Fox decided. "She'll

cross all her t's. That's one smart skirt. Added to, she loves
Quinn. Layla, too, but she and Quinn are as tight as it
gets."

Fox pushed to his feet. "I've got to get back to the office. Speaking of which, I'm thinking I'll probably be
moving to New York after you and Quinn get married."

"God, another with a hook in his mouth." Gage shook
his head. "Or maybe it's a ring through the nose."

"Bite me. I haven't said anything to my family yet. I'm
going to ease into that by degrees." Fox studied Cal's face
as he spoke. "But I thought I'd give you a heads-up. I'm
figuring I'll wait until after the Seven to put the building on
the market. I've got some decent equity in it, and the market's pretty stable, so—"

"Eternally the optimist. Brother, for all you know that
place'll be rubble come July fourteenth."

This time Fox simply shot Gage his middle finger.
"Anyway. I thought you or your father might be interested
in it. If you are, we'll kick around some figures at some
point."

"It's a big step, Fox," Cal said slowly. "You're established here, not just personally, but with your practice."

"Not everybody can stay. You won't," Fox said to Gage.

"No, I won't."

"But you come back, and you'll keep coming back. So
will I." Fox turned his wrist up, and that scar that ran
across it. "Nothing erases this. Nothing can. And hell, New
York's only a few hours away. I zipped up and down
Ninety-five the whole time I was in law school. It's . . ."

"When you were with Carly."

"Yeah." He nodded at Cal. "It's different now. I've still
got a few lines up there, so I'll put some feelers out, see
what comes. But right now I've got some town lawyer business to take care of. I can take a shift at the house tonight,"
he added as he started for the door. "But I still say those
women *have* to get ESPN."

Gage sat on the corner of Cal's desk when Fox left. "He'll hate it."

"Yeah, he will."

"He'll do it anyway, and he'll find a way to make it work. Because that's what O'Dell's about. Making it work."

"He'd have tried with Carly. I don't know if he could've pulled it off, but he'd have tried. But he's right. It's different with Layla. He'll make it work, and I'm the one who's going to hate it. Not being able to see his stupid face every damn day."

"Cheer up. Five out of six of us could be dead in a couple days."

"Thanks. That helps."

"Anything I can do." Gage straightened. "I've got some business of my own. Catch you later."

He was nearly to the door when his father stepped up to it. They both stopped as if they'd walked into a wall. Helplessly, Cal got to his feet.

"Ah . . . Bill, why don't you check the exhaust fan on the grill? I'll be down in a minute. I'm nearly done here."

As the pink the climb up had put in his cheeks faded, Bill stared at his son. "Gage—"

"No." It was an empty word in an empty voice as Gage walked out. "We are done."

At his desk, Cal rubbed at the fresh tension in his neck as Bill turned shamed eyes on him. "Um . . . What'd you want me to check?"

"The grill exhaust. It's running a little rough. Take your time."

Alone, Cal lowered to his chair, pressed his fingers to his eyes. His friends, his brothers, he thought, had both chosen rocky roads. There was nothing he could do but go with them, as far as it took.

Twenty

SOME PEOPLE MIGHT THINK IT WAS A LITTLE ODD to get up in the morning, go to work as usual when the evening plans included blood rituals. But Fox figured it was pretty much standard operating procedure for him and his friends.

Layla, who in straight managerial areas could make the beloved Alice Hawbaker look like a slacker, had squeezed and manipulated his schedule to ensure the office closed promptly at three on the big day. He'd already packed his kit. Most might not know what to take along on an early evening hike through the woods by a haunted pool toward a mystical clearing ruled by an ancient altar stone, but Fox had that down. For once, he'd even remembered to check the forecast.

Clear skies—that was a plus—with temps sliding from a balmy seventy to the cool but pleasant midfifties.

Layers were the key to comfort.

In his pocket was his third of the bloodstone. He hoped it would prove to be another key.

While Layla changed, he added some essentials to his cooler. He glanced around when she came in, and he broke into a smile. "You look like the cover for *Hiking Style*—if there is such a thing."

"I actually debated with myself over earrings." She surveyed his cooler and open pack. Coke, Little Debbies, Nutter Butters. "I guess it's like you say, we all do what we do."

"These particular provisions are a time-honored tradition."

"At least the sugar rush is guaranteed. God, Fox, are we crazy?"

"It's the times that are crazy. We're just in them."

"Is that a knife?" She gaped at the sheath on his belt. "You're taking a knife? I didn't know you had a knife."

"It's actually a gardening saw. Japanese sickle knife. It's a nice one."

"And what?" She put a hand to the side of her head as if the pressure would help her mind make sense of it all. "You're planning on doing a little pruning while we're there?"

"You never know, do you?"

She put a hand on his arm as he closed his pack. "Fox."

"Odds are Twisse is going to take an interest in what we're doing tonight. It can be hurt. Cal did some damage with his handy Boy Scout knife the last time we were there. You can bet Gage is bringing that damn gun. I'm not going in there with just my Nutter Butters."

She started to argue—he saw it in her eyes—then something else came into them. "Have you got a spare?"

Saying nothing, he went to the utility closet, rooted around. "It's called a froe." He showed her the long, flat blade. "It's good for splitting wooden pins in joinery work.

Or taking a slice out of a demon. Keep it in the scabbard," he added, sliding it into the leather. "It's sharp."

"Okay."

"Don't take this the wrong way." He laid his hands on her shoulders. "Remember I'm a strong proponent of equality, of women's rights. I'm going to protect you, Layla."

"Don't take this the wrong way. I'm going to protect you, too."

He brushed his lips to hers. "I guess we're set then."

THEY MET AT CAL'S TO BEGIN THE HIKE ON THE path near his home. The woods had changed, Layla thought, since her previous trip. There had been snow then, pooled in pockets of shade, and the trail had been slick with mud, the trees barren and stark. Now, leaves were tender on the branches, and the soft white of the wild dogwoods shimmered in the slanting sun.

Now, she had a knife in a leather scabbard bumping against her hip.

She'd walked here before, toward the unknown, with five other people and Cal's affable dog. This time, she knew what might be waiting, and she went toward it as part of a team. She went toward it beside the man she loved. Because of that, this time she had more to lose.

Quinn slowed, pointed at the scabbard. "Is that a knife?"

"Actually, it's a froe."

"What the hell's a froe?"

"It's a tool." Cybil reached out from behind Layla to test the weight of the scabbard. "Used for cutting wood by splitting it along the grain. Safer than an ax. This one, by its size and shape, is probably a bamboo froe, and it's used for splitting out the bamboo pins used in Japanese joinery."

"What she said," Layla agreed.

"Well, I want a froe, or something. I want a sheath. No," Quinn decided. "I want a machete. Nice long handle, wicked curved blade. I need to buy a machete."

"You can use mine next time," Cal told her.

"You have a machete? Gosh, my man is full of hidden pockets. Why do you have a machete?"

"For whacking at weeds and brush. Maybe it's more of a scythe."

"What's the difference? No." Quinn held up her hand before Cybil could speak. "Never mind."

"Then I'll just say you probably want the scythe, as, traditionally, it has a long handle. However . . ." Cybil trailed off. "The trees are bleeding."

"It happens," Gage told her. "Puts off the tourists."

The thick red ran in rivulets down bark to spread over the carpeting leaves. The air stank of burnt copper as they followed the path to Hester's Pool.

There they stopped beside the brown water, and there the brown water began to bubble and redden.

"Does it know we're here?" Layla spoke quietly. "Or is this the demon version of a security system? Can it think this kind of thing scares us at this point, or is it what Gage said? A show for the tourists?"

"Maybe it's some of both." Fox offered her a Coke, but she shook her head. "Security systems send out an alert. So if the Big Evil Bastard doesn't know when we head in, it knows when we reach certain points."

"And this is a cold spot—in paranormal speak," Quinn explained. "A place of import and power. When we . . . Oh, Jesus."

She wrinkled her nose as something bobbed to the surface.

"Dead rabbit." Cal put a hand on her shoulder, then tightened his grip when other corpses rose to the bubbling surface.

Birds, squirrels, foxes. Quinn made a sound of distress,

but she lifted her camera and began to document. Death smeared its stench on the air.

"It's been busy in here," Gage mumbled.

As he spoke, the bloated body of a doe floated up.

"That's enough, Quinn," Cal murmured.

"It's not." But she lowered the camera. Her voice was raw, her eyes fierce. "It's not enough. They were harmless, and this is *their* world. And I know, I know it's stupid to get so upset about . . . fauna when human lives are at stake, but—"

"Come on, Q." Cybil draped an arm around her, turned Quinn away. "There's nothing to be done."

"We need to get them out." Fox stared at the obscenity, made himself see it, made himself harden. "Not now, but we'll have to come back, get them out. Burn the corpses. It's not just their world, it's ours, too. We can't leave it like this."

With a sick rage lodged in his gut, he turned away. "It's here." He said it almost casually. "It's watching." And it's waiting, he thought, as he moved up to take point on the path to the Pagan Stone.

The cold rolled in. It didn't matter that the cold was a lie, it still chilled the bones. Fox zipped up his hooded jacket, and kept the pace steady. He took Layla's hand to warm it in his.

"It just wants to give us grief."

"I know."

His mind tracked toward the sounds of rustling, of growling. Keeping pace, he thought. Knows where we're going, but not what we plan to do when we get there.

Thunder rumbled across a clear sky, and the rain pelted down from it to stab and pinch the skin like needles. Fox flipped up his hood as Layla did the same. Next roared the wind in frigid, sweeping gusts that bent trees and tore new leaves from their branches. He wrapped an arm around her waist for support, hunched his shoulders, and plowed through it.

Raindrops on roses, my ass, he thought, but kept his mind calm.

"All right back there?" He'd already looked with his mind, but was reassured by the affirming shouts. "We're going to do a chain," he told Layla. "Get behind me, get a good hold on my belt. Cal knows what to do. He'll hook to you, pass it back."

"Sing something," she shouted.

"What?"

"Sing, something we all know the words to. Make a goddamn joyful noise."

He grinned through the teeth of the storm. "I'm in love with a brilliant woman." Songs everyone knew, he thought as Layla got behind him, gripped his belt. That was easy.

He launched with Nirvana, calculating that none of the six could've gotten through high school without picking up the lyrics from "Smells Like Teen Spirit." The chorus of *Hello!* rang out defiantly while the diamond-sharp rain slashed. He tossed in some Smashing Pumpkins, a little Springsteen (he was the Boss for a reason), swung into Pearl Jam, sweetened it up with Sheryl Crow.

For the next twenty minutes, they trudged, one combative step at a time through the lashing storm, singing Fox's version of Demon Rock.

It eased by degrees until it was no more than a chilly breeze stirring a weak drizzle. As one, they dropped onto the sodden ground to catch their breath and rest aching muscles.

"Is that the best it's got?" Quinn's hands trembled as she passed around a thermos of coffee. "Because—"

"It's not," Fox interrupted. "It's just playing with us. But damned if we didn't play right back. Wood's going to be wet. We may have some trouble starting a fire." He met Cal's eyes as Cal unhooked Lump's leash from his belt.

"I got that handled. We'd better get moving. I'll take point for a while."

The dog leaped onto the path. Huge and black, fangs gleaming, it snarled out threats. Even as Fox reached for his sheath, Cybil pushed to her feet. She drew a revolver from under her jacket, and coolly fired six shots.

The dog howled in pain and in fury; its blood smoked and sizzled on the ground. With one wild leap, it vanished into the swirling air.

"That's for ruining my hair." Cybil shook back the curling mess of it as she unzipped a pocket in her jacket for a box of ammo.

"Nice." On his feet as well, Gage held out a hand. He examined the revolver—a trim .22 with a polished pearl handle. Ordinarily, he'd have smirked at that sort of weapon, but she'd handled it like a pro.

"Just something I picked up, through *legal* channels." She took the gun back, competently reloaded.

"Wow." Fox hated guns—it was knee-jerk. But he had to admire the . . . pizzazz. "That's given the Big Evil Bastard something to think about."

She slid it into the holster under her jacket. "Well, it's no froe, but it has its merits."

The air warmed again, and the evening sun sparkled on young leaves as they hiked the rest of the way to the Pagan Stone.

It rose from the burned ground in a clearing that formed a near-perfect circle. What every test had deemed ordinary limestone speared up, then spread altarlike in the quieting light of the spring evening.

"Fire first," Cal decided, dragging off his pack. "Before we lose the light." Opening the pack, he pulled out two Dura-Logs.

After the miserable journey there, Fox's laughter was like a balm. "Only you, Hawkins."

"Be prepared. We start one of these, tent wood around it, the flames should dry out the wet wood. Should do the job."

"Isn't he cute?" Quinn demanded, wrapping her arms around Cal for a cheerful snuggle. "Seriously."

They gathered stones and branches, stripped off wet jackets to hang on the poles Fox fashioned in hopes the fire would dry them. They roasted Quinn's contribution of turkey dogs on sharpened sticks, passed out Cybil's brie and Layla's sliced apples and ate like the starving.

As darkness settled, Fox broke out the Little Debbies while Cal checked the flashlights. "Go ahead," he told Quinn as she gave the snack cakes a wistful look. "Indulge."

"They go straight to my ass. If we live, I have to fit into my absolutely spectacular wedding dress." She took one, broke it prudently in half. "I think we're going to live, and half a Little Debbie doesn't count."

"You're going to look amazing." Layla smiled at her. "And the shoes we found? So exactly right. Plus, Cybil and I aren't going to look shabby. I love the dresses we found. The idea of the plum with the orchid's just—"

"I feel an irresistible urge to talk about baseball," Fox said, and got an elbow jab from Layla.

Conversation trailed off until there was only the crackle of wood, the lonely hoot of an owl. So they sat in silence as the fat moon glowed like a white torch in a star-struck sky. Fox pushed to his feet to gather trash. Busy hands packed away food or added wood to the fire.

At a signal from Cybil, the women unpacked what Layla thought of as the ritual bag. A small copper bowl, a bag of sea salt, fresh herbs, candles, springwater.

As instructed, Fox poured the salt in a wide circle around the Pagan Stone.

"Well." Cybil stepped back, studied the arrangement of supplies on the stone. "I don't know how much of this is visual aids, but all my research recommended these elements. The salt's for protection against evil, a kind of barrier. We're to stand inside the circle Fox made. There

are six white candles. Each of us lights one, in turn. But first, the springwater goes into the bowl, then the herbs, then the three pieces of stone—in turn. Q?"

"I printed out six copies of the words we need to say." Quinn took the file out of her pack. "We do that one at a time, around the circle, as each one of us draws his or her own blood with Cal's knife."

"Over the bowl," Cybil reminded her.

"Yeah, over the bowl. When the last one's done that, we join hands, and repeat the words together six times."

"It should be seven," Layla said. "I know there are six of us, but seven is the key number. Maybe the seventh is for the guardian, or symbolizes the innocent, the sacrifice. I don't know, but it should be seven times."

"And seven candles," Fox realized. "A seventh candle we all light. Shit, why didn't we think of this?"

"A little late now." Gage shrugged. "We got six, we go with six."

"We can do seven." Cal held out a hand to Layla. "Can I borrow your froe?"

"Wait. I got you." Fox pulled out his knife. "This'll work better. Let me see." He picked up one of the thick, white columns. "Beeswax—good. I spent a lot of time working with beeswax and wicks growing up." After he'd laid it on its side, he glanced at Cybil. "Any reason for the dimensions of these? The height?"

"No, but my sources said six." She looked at Layla, nodded. "Screw the sources. Make us another candle."

He set to work. The wax was going to do a number on his blade, he thought, but all things being right in the world, he'd be able to clean and sharpen it when he got home. It took time, enough that he wondered why the hell Cybil hadn't picked up a half dozen tapers. But he cut off three inches, then took Layla's tool to dig a well for the wick.

"Not my best work," he decided, "but it'll burn."

"We light it last." Layla scanned the other faces. "Light it together." She had to take a breath to keep her voice steady. "It's almost time."

"We need the stones," Cybil began, "and the ritual Boy Scout knife," she added with a faint smile.

The boy came out of the woods, executing cheerful handsprings. The claws on his hands, his feet, dug grooves in the ground, and the grooves welled with blood.

"You should know we've used salt before." Gage drew his Luger from the small of his back. "Didn't do squat." His brows lifted as the boy's hand brushed the salt. It squealed in pain, leaped back. "Must be a different brand." Even as Gage aimed, the boy hissed and vanished.

"We need to start." With a steady hand, Cybil poured the water into the bowl, then sprinkled the herbs. "Now the stones. Cal, Fox, Gage."

Thunder boomed, and with a flash of lightning, bloody rain gushed from the sky. The burned ground drank it, and steamed.

"It's holding." Layla looked up. "It's not coming inside the circle."

Fox held the stone inside his fist. He'd carried it with him like hope for nearly twenty-one years. And with that hope, he slipped it into the water after Cal's. Outside the circle, the world went mad. The ground shook, and blood swam across it to lap and burn at the barrier of salt.

It's eating it away, Fox thought, burning and eating away the barrier. He set his candle to flame, passed the lighter to Layla.

In the light of six candles, they laid hand over hand, fired the seventh.

"Hurry," Fox ordered. "It's coming back, and it's pissed."

Cal held his hand over the bowl, drew the knife across his palm as he read the words. As did Quinn, then Fox.

"My blood, their blood. Our blood, its blood. One into

three, three into one. Dark with the light. We make this sacrifice, we take this oath."

Screams, ululations neither human nor animal rolled
through the dark. Tethered to the base of the stone, Lump
lifted his big head to howl.

Layla took the knife, hissing against the quick pain as
she read the words. Then her mind flew to Fox's while
Gage took his turn. *The cold! It's nearly through!*

As the ground quivered underfoot, he clasped her
bloodied hand with his.

The wind tore in. He couldn't hear the others, not with
his ears or his mind, but shouted the words, prayed they
were with him. On the Pagan Stone, the seven candles
burned with unwavering flame, and in the bowl, reddened
water bubbled. The ground heaved, ramming him into the
table of the stone with enough force to knock his breath
away. Something like claws raked at his back. He felt himself spinning, impossibly. In desperation, his mind reached
out for Layla's. Then the blast of light and heat flung him
blindly into the black.

He crawled, dragging himself over the ground toward
the faint echo of her. He yanked his knife free, pulled himself over the bucking ground.

She crawled toward him, and the worst of his fears
broke away when he found her hand. When their fingers
linked, the light burst again with a sound terrible as a
scream. Fire engulfed the Pagan Stone, sheathed it as
leather sheathed a blade. In a deafening roar the flame gey-
sered up toward the cold, watching moon. And it *flew* to
ring the clearing in a writhing curtain of fire. In its savage
light, Fox saw the others, sprawled on, kneeling on the
ground.

All of them, all of them trapped inside a circling wall of
flame while in its center, the Pagan Stone spewed more.

Together, he thought as the vicious heat slicked his skin
with sweat. Live or die, it would be together. With his hand

locked on Layla's, he pulled them both across the clearing. Then her arm was around him, and they were pulling each other. Cal gripped his forearm, dragged him forward. He met Gage's eyes. With the air burning, they once again clasped hands.

Together, Fox thought, as the deadly walls of fire edged closer. "For the innocent," Fox gasped out against the smoke coating his throat. The fire, blinding bright, ate across the ground. There was nowhere to go and, he knew, only moments left. He pressed his cheek to Layla's. "What we did, we did for the innocent, for each other, and fucking A, we'd do it again."

Cal managed an exhausted laugh, brought Quinn's hand to his lips. "Fucking A."

"Fucking A," Gage agreed. "Might as well go out with a bang." He jerked Cybil against him, covered her mouth with his.

"Well, hell, we might as well try to get through it." Fox blinked his stinging eyes. "No point in just sitting here getting toasted when we could . . . It's dying back."

"Busy here." Gage lifted his head, scanned the clearing. His smile was both grim and satisfied. "I'm a hell of a good kisser."

"Idiot." Cybil shoved him back, pushed up to her knees. Flames retreated toward the stone, began to slide up it. "It didn't kill us."

"Whatever we did must've been right." With dazzled eyes, Layla stared as the fire poured itself back into the bowl, shimmered gold. "I think what we did here, especially, finding each other, staying together."

"We didn't run." Quinn rubbed her filthy cheek against Cal's shoulder. "Any sensible person would have, but we didn't run. I'm not sure we could have."

"I heard you," Layla said to Fox. "Live or die, it was going to be together."

"We swore an oath. Me, Cal, Gage when we were ten. The

six of us tonight. We swore an oath. The fire's out." He managed to gain his feet. "I guess we'd better go take a look."
When he turned to the stone, he was struck speechless.

The candles were gone, as was the bowl. The Pagan
Stone stood in the moonlight, unmarred. In its center the
bloodstone lay, whole.

"Jesus Christ." Cybil choked the words out. "It worked.
I can't believe it worked."

"Your eyes." Fox whipped around to Cal, waved a hand
in front of his face. "How's the vision?"

"Cut it out." Cal slapped the hand aside. "It's fine. It's
just fine, good enough to see three's back into one. Nice
job, Cybil."

They walked toward it, and much as they had during the
ritual, formed a circle around the stone on the stone.

"Okay, well." Quinn moistened her lips. "Somebody's
got to pick it up—meaning one of the guys because it's
theirs."

Before he could lift his hand to point at Cal, both Cal
and Gage pointed at Fox. "Damn it." He rubbed his hands
on his jeans, rolled his shoulders, reached out.

His head fell back, his body convulsed. And as Layla
grabbed him, he laughed like a loon. "Just kidding."

"God*damn* it, Fox!"

"A little levity, that's all." He scooped the stone into his
hand. "It's warm. Maybe from the scary magic fire, or
maybe it just is. Is it glowing? Are the red splotches glowing?"

"They are now," Layla murmured.

"It . . . it doesn't understand this. It doesn't know this. I
can't see . . ." Fox swayed, the world rocked around him.
Then Layla gripped his hand, and it steadied again. "I'm
holding its death."

Nudging by Gage, Cybil edged closer. "How, Fox? How
is that stone its death?"

"I don't know. It holds all of us now. You know, from

what we did. Our blood is what fused it. And this is part of what can—will—end it. We have the power to do that. We had it all along."

"But it was in pieces," Layla finished. "Until now. Until us—all of us."

"We did what we came to do." Reaching out, Quinn brushed her fingertips over the stone. "And we lived. Now we have a new weapon."

"Which we don't know how to use," Gage pointed out.

"Let's just get it home, find the safest place to keep it." Cal looked around the clearing. "I hope nobody had anything important in their pack, because they're incinerated. Coolers, too."

"There go my Nutter Butters." Fox took Layla's hand, kissed the wounded palm. "Wanna take a walk in the moonlight?"

"I'd love to." Could there be a better time, she thought. Could there be a more perfect time? "Good thing I left my purse at Cal's. Which reminds me. Cal, I've got the keys in there, but I'd like to hang on to them if it's okay with you and your father."

"No problem."

"What keys?" Fox asked as he rubbed some soot off her face.

"To the shop on Main Street. I needed them so Quinn and Cybil could look it over with me. It's all fine for you to look at the space with carpenter eyes, or lawyer eyes, whichever, but if I'm going to open a boutique for women, I wanted women's eyes."

"You're—what?"

"But I am going to need you, and hopefully your father, to go through it with me. And I'm going to charm your father into an I'm-in-love-with-your-son discount. Hopefully a deep discount because of deep love." Fussily, she brushed at the dirt coating his shirt. "And the fact that even with the loan—and I'm counting on you to put in a really

good word for me at the bank—I'm going to be on a very tight budget."

"You said you didn't want it."

"I said I didn't know what I wanted. Now I do." Clear, green, amused, her eyes met his. "Did I forget to mention it?"

"Yeah, pretty much altogether."

"Well." She gave him a shoulder bump. "I've had a lot on my mind lately."

"Layla."

"I want my own." She tipped her head to his shoulder as they walked. "I'm ready to go after what I want. After all, *Jesus*, if not now, when? By the way, consider this my two-weeks' notice."

He stopped, took her face in his hands as the others trudged and limped by them. "Are you sure?"

"I'm going to be too busy supervising the remodeling, buying stock, fighting demons to manage your office. You'll just have to deal with it."

He touched his lips to her forehead, her cheeks, her mouth, then grinned at her. "Okay."

Exhausted, content, he walked with her behind the others on a path spattered with moonlight. They'd made magic tonight, he thought. They'd chosen their path, and found their way.

The rest was just details.

Turn the page for a look at

THE PAGAN STONE

the final book in the
Sign of Seven Trilogy

Available now from Jove Books.

April 2001
Mazatlán, Mexico

SUN STREAKED PEARLY PINK ACROSS THE SKY, splashed onto blue, blue water that rolled against white sand as Gage Turner walked the beach. He carried his shoes—the tattered laces of the ancient Nikes tied to hang on his shoulder. The hems of his jeans were frayed, and the jeans themselves had long since faded to white at the stress points. The tropical breeze tugged at hair that hadn't seen a barber in more than three months.

At the moment, he supposed he looked no more kempt than the scattering of beach bums still snoring away on the sand. He'd bunked on beaches a time or two when his luck was down, and knew someone would come along soon to shoo them off before the paying tourists woke for their room-service coffee.

At the moment, despite the need for a shower and a shave, his luck was up. Nicely up. With his night's winnings hot in his pocket, he considered upgrading his ocean-view room for a suite.

Grab it while you can, he thought, because tomorrow could suck you dry.

Time was already running out; it spilled like that white, sun-kissed sand held in a closed fist. His twenty-fourth birthday was less than three months away, and the dreams crawled back into his head. Blood and death, fire and madness. All of that and Hawkins Hollow seemed a world away from this soft tropical dawn.

But it lived in him.

He unlocked the wide glass door of his room, stepped in, tossed aside his shoes. After flipping on the lights, closing the drapes, he took his winnings from his pocket, gave the bills a careless flip. With the current rate of exchange, he was up about six thousand USD. Not a bad night, not bad at all. In the bathroom, he popped off the bottom of a can of shaving cream, tucked the bills inside the hollow tube.

He protected what was his. He'd learned to do so from childhood, secreting small treasures away so his father couldn't find and destroy them on a drunken whim. He might've flipped off any notion of a college education, but Gage figured he'd learned quite a bit in his not-quite twenty-four years.

He'd left Hawkins Hollow the summer he'd graduated from high school. Just packed up what was his, stuck out his thumb, and booked.

Escaped, Gage thought as he stripped for a shower. There'd been plenty of work—he'd been young, strong, healthy, and not particular. But he'd learned a vital lesson while digging ditches, hauling lumber, and most especially during the months he'd sweated on an offshore rig. He could make more money at cards than he could with his back.

And a gambler didn't need a home. All he needed was a game.

He stepped into the shower, turned the water hot. It sluiced over tanned skin, lean muscles, through thick black hair in need of a trim. He thought idly about ordering some

coffee, some food, then decided he'd catch a few hours' sleep first. Another advantage of his profession, in Gage's mind. He came and went as he pleased, ate when he was hungry, slept when he was tired. He set his own rules, broke them whenever it suited him.

Nobody had any hold over him.

Not true, Gage admitted as he studied the white scar across his wrist. Not altogether true. A man's friends, his true friends, always had a hold over him. There were no truer friends than Caleb Hawkins and Fox O'Dell.

Blood brothers.

They'd been born the same day, the same year, even—as far as anyone could tell—at the same moment. He couldn't remember a time when the three of them hadn't been . . . a unit, he supposed. The middle-class boy, the hippie kid, and the son of an abusive drunk. Probably shouldn't have had a thing in common, Gage mused as a smile curved his mouth, warmed the green of his eyes. But they'd been family, they'd been brothers long before Cal had cut their wrists with his Boy Scout knife to ritualize the pact.

And that had changed everything. Or had it? Gage wondered. Had it just opened what was always there, waiting?

He could remember it all vividly, every step, every detail. It had started as an adventure—three boys on the eve of their tenth birthday hiking through the woods. Loaded down with skin mags, beer, smokes—his contribution—with junk food and Cokes from Fox, and the picnic basket of sandwiches and lemonade Cal's mother had packed. Not that Frannie Hawkins would've packed a picnic if she'd known her son planned to camp the night at the Pagan Stone in Hawkins Wood.

All that wet heat, Gage remembered, and the music on the boom box, and the complete innocence they'd carried along with the Little Debbies and Nutter Butters they would lose before they hiked out in the morning.

Gage stepped out, rubbed his dripping hair with a towel.

His back had ached from the beating his father had given him the night before. As they'd sat around the campfire in the clearing those welts had throbbed. He remembered that, as he remembered how the light had flickered and floated over the gray table of the Pagan Stone.

He remembered the words they'd written down, the words they'd spoken as Cal made them blood brothers. He remembered the quick pain of the knife across his flesh, the feel of Cal's wrist, of Fox's as they'd mixed their blood.

And the explosion, the heat and cold, the force and fear when that mixed blood hit the scarred ground of the clearing.

He remembered what came out of the ground, the black mass of it, and the blinding light that followed. The pure evil of the black, the stunning brilliance of the white.

When it was over, there'd been no welts on his back, no pain, and in his hand lay one third of a bloodstone. He carried it still, as he knew Cal and Fox carried theirs. Three pieces of one whole. He supposed they were the same.

Madness came to the Hollow that week, and raged through it like a plague, infecting, driving good and ordinary people to do the horrible. And for seven days every seven years, it came back.

So did he, Gage thought. What choice did he have?

Naked, still damp from the shower, he stretched out on the bed. There was time yet, still some time for a few more games, for hot beaches and swaying palms. The green woods and blue mountains of Hawkins Hollow were thousands of miles away, until July.

He closed his eyes, and as he'd trained himself, dropped almost instantly into sleep.

In sleep came the screams, and the weeping, and the fire that ate so joyfully at wood and cloth and flesh. Blood ran warm over his hands as he dragged wounded to safety. For how long? he wondered. Where was safe? And who could

say when and if the victim would turn and become the attacker?

Madness ruled the streets of the Hollow.

In the dream he stood with his friends on the south end of Main Street, across from the Qwik Mart and its four gas pumps. Coach Moser, who'd guided the Hawkins Hollow Bucks to a championship football season Gage's senior year, gibbered with laughter as he soaked himself, the ground, the buildings with the flood of gas from the pumps.

They ran toward him, the three of them, even as Moser held up his lighter like a trophy, as he splashed in the pools of gas like a boy in rain puddles. They ran even as he flicked the lighter.

It was flash and boom, searing the eyes, bursting the ears. The force of heat and air flung him back so he landed in a bone-shattering heap. Fire, blinding clouds of it, spewed skyward as hunks of wood and concrete, shards of glass, burning twists of metal flew.

Gage felt his broken arm try to knit, his shattered knee struggle to heal with pain worse than the wound itself. Gritting his teeth, he rolled, and what he saw stopped his heart in his chest.

Cal lay in the street, burning like a torch.

No, no, no, no! He crawled, shouting, gasping for oxygen in the tainted air. There was Fox, facedown in a widening pool of blood.

It came, a black smear on that burning air that formed into a man. The demon smiled. *You don't heal from death, do you, boy?*

Gage woke, sheathed in sweat and shaking. He woke with the stench of burning gas scoring his throat.

Time's up, he thought.

He got up, got dressed. Once dressed, he began to pack for the trip back to Hawkins Hollow.

Series

Irish Born Trilogy
BORN IN FIRE
BORN IN ICE
BORN IN SHAME

Dream Trilogy
DARING TO DREAM
HOLDING THE DREAM
FINDING THE DREAM

Chesapeake Bay Saga
SEA SWEPT
RISING TIDES
INNER HARBOR
CHESAPEAKE BLUE

Gallaghers of Ardmore Trilogy
JEWELS OF THE SUN
TEARS OF THE MOON
HEART OF THE SEA

Three Sisters Island Trilogy
DANCE UPON THE AIR
HEAVEN AND EARTH
FACE THE FIRE

Key Trilogy
KEY OF LIGHT
KEY OF KNOWLEDGE
KEY OF VALOR

In the Garden Trilogy
BLUE DAHLIA
BLACK ROSE
RED LILY

Circle Trilogy
MORRIGAN'S CROSS
DANCE OF THE GODS
VALLEY OF SILENCE

Sign of Seven Trilogy
BLOOD BROTHERS
THE HOLLOW
THE PAGAN STONE

Bride Quartet
VISION IN WHITE
BED OF ROSES
SAVOR THE MOMENT
HAPPY EVER AFTER

The Inn BoonsBoro Trilogy
THE NEXT ALWAYS
THE LAST BOYFRIEND
THE PERFECT HOPE

The Cousins O'Dwyer Trilogy
DARK WITCH
SHADOW SPELL
BLOOD MAGICK

The Guardians Trilogy
STARS OF FORTUNE
BAY OF SIGHS
ISLAND OF GLASS

For Fox, Caleb, Gage, and the other residents of Hawkins Hollow, the number seven portends doom—ever since, as boys, they freed a demon trapped for centuries when their blood spilled upon the Pagan Stone . . .

Their innocent bonding ritual led to seven days of madness, every seven years. And now, as the dreaded seventh month looms before them, the men can feel the storm brewing. Already they are plagued by visions of death and destruction. But this year they are better prepared, joined in their battle by three women who have come to the Hollow. Layla, Quinn, and Cybil are somehow connected to the demon, just as the men are connected to the force that trapped it.

Since that fateful day at the Pagan Stone, town lawyer Fox has been able to see into others' minds, a talent he shares with Layla. He must earn her trust, because their link will help fight the darkness that threatens to engulf the town. But Layla is having trouble coming to terms with her newfound ability—and with this intimate connection to Fox. She knows that once she opens her mind, she'll have no defense against the desire that threatens to consume them both . . .

**Turn the page for a complete list of titles by
Nora Roberts and J. D. Robb
from The Berkley Publishing Group . . .**

It had been the Pagan Stone for hundreds of years, long before three boys stood around it and spilled their blood in a bond of brotherhood, unwittingly releasing a force bent on destruction . . .

Every seven years, there comes a week in July when the locals do unspeakable things—and then don't seem to remember them. The collective madness has made itself known beyond the town borders and has given Hawkins Hollow the reputation of a village possessed.

This modern-day legend draws reporter and author Quinn Black to Hawkins Hollow with the hope of making the eerie happening the subject of her new book. It is only February, but Caleb Hawkins, descendent of the town founders, has already seen and felt the stirrings of evil. Though he can never forget the beginning of the terror in the woods twenty-one years ago, the signs have never been this strong before. Cal will need the help of his best friends, Fox and Gage, but surprisingly he must rely on Quinn as well. She, too, can see the evil that the locals cannot, somehow connecting her to the town— and to Cal. As winter turns to spring, Cal and Quinn will shed their inhibitions, surrendering to a growing desire. They will form the cornerstone of a group of men and women bound by fate, passion, and the fight against what is to come from out of the darkness . . .

Turn the page for a complete list of titles by Nora Roberts and J. D. Robb from Berkley . . .

Nora Roberts

Series

Irish Born Trilogy
BORN IN FIRE
BORN IN ICE
BORN IN SHAME

Dream Trilogy
DARING TO DREAM
HOLDING THE DREAM
FINDING THE DREAM

Chesapeake Bay Saga
SEA SWEPT
RISING TIDES
INNER HARBOR
CHESAPEAKE BLUE

Gallaghers of Ardmore Trilogy
JEWELS OF THE SUN
TEARS OF THE MOON
HEART OF THE SEA

Three Sisters Island Trilogy
DANCE UPON THE AIR
HEAVEN AND EARTH
FACE THE FIRE

Key Trilogy
KEY OF LIGHT
KEY OF KNOWLEDGE
KEY OF VALOR

In the Garden Trilogy
BLUE DAHLIA
BLACK ROSE
RED LILY

Circle Trilogy
MORRIGAN'S CROSS
DANCE OF THE GODS
VALLEY OF SILENCE

Sign of Seven Trilogy
BLOOD BROTHERS
THE HOLLOW
THE PAGAN STONE

Bride Quartet
VISION IN WHITE
BED OF ROSES
SAVOR THE MOMENT
HAPPY EVER AFTER

The Inn BoonsBoro Trilogy
THE NEXT ALWAYS
THE LAST BOYFRIEND
THE PERFECT HOPE

The Cousins O'Dwyer Trilogy
DARK WITCH
SHADOW SPELL
BLOOD MAGICK

The Guardians Trilogy
STARS OF FORTUNE
BAY OF SIGHS
ISLAND OF GLASS

Ebooks by Nora Roberts

Cordina's Royal Family
AFFAIRE ROYALE
COMMAND PERFORMANCE
THE PLAYBOY PRINCE
CORDINA'S CROWN JEWEL

The Donovan Legacy
CAPTIVATED
ENTRANCED
CHARMED
ENCHANTED

The O'Hurleys
THE LAST HONEST WOMAN
DANCE TO THE PIPER
SKIN DEEP
WITHOUT A TRACE

Night Tales
NIGHT SHIFT
NIGHT SHADOW
NIGHTSHADE
NIGHT SMOKE
NIGHT SHIELD

The MacGregors
PLAYING THE ODDS
TEMPTING FATE
ALL THE POSSIBILITIES
ONE MAN'S ART
FOR NOW, FOREVER
REBELLION/IN FROM THE COLD
THE MACGREGOR BRIDES
THE WINNING HAND
THE MACGREGOR GROOMS
THE PERFECT NEIGHBOR

The Calhouns
COURTING CATHERINE
A MAN FOR AMANDA
FOR THE LOVE OF LILAH
SUZANNA'S SURRENDER
MEGAN'S MATE

Irish Legacy
IRISH THOROUGHBRED
IRISH ROSE
IRISH REBEL

LOVING JACK
BEST LAID PLANS
LAWLESS

BLITHE IMAGES
SONG OF THE WEST
SEARCH FOR LOVE
ISLAND OF FLOWERS
THE HEART'S VICTORY
FROM THIS DAY
HER MOTHER'S KEEPER
ONCE MORE WITH FEELING
REFLECTIONS
DANCE OF DREAMS
UNTAMED
THIS MAGIC MOMENT
ENDINGS AND BEGINNINGS
STORM WARNING
SULLIVAN'S WOMAN
FIRST IMPRESSIONS
A MATTER OF CHOICE

LESS OF A STRANGER
THE LAW IS A LADY
RULES OF THE GAME
OPPOSITES ATTRACT
THE RIGHT PATH
PARTNERS
BOUNDARY LINES
DUAL IMAGE
TEMPTATION
LOCAL HERO
THE NAME OF THE GAME
GABRIEL'S ANGEL
THE WELCOMING
TIME WAS
TIMES CHANGE
SUMMER LOVE
HOLIDAY WISHES

Anthologies

FROM THE HEART
A LITTLE MAGIC
A LITTLE FATE

MOON SHADOWS
(with Jill Gregory, Ruth Ryan Langan, and Marianne Willman)

The Once Upon Series
(with Jill Gregory, Ruth Ryan Langan, and Marianne Willman)

ONCE UPON A CASTLE   ONCE UPON A ROSE
ONCE UPON A STAR   ONCE UPON A KISS
ONCE UPON A DREAM   ONCE UPON A MIDNIGHT

SILENT NIGHT
(with Susan Plunkett, Dee Holmes, and Claire Cross)

OUT OF THIS WORLD
(with Laurell K. Hamilton, Susan Krinard, and Maggie Shayne)

BUMP IN THE NIGHT
(with Mary Blayney, Ruth Ryan Langan, and Mary Kay McComas)

DEAD OF NIGHT
(with Mary Blayney, Ruth Ryan Langan, and Mary Kay McComas)

THREE IN DEATH

SUITE 606
(with Mary Blayney, Ruth Ryan Langan, and Mary Kay McComas)

IN DEATH

THE LOST
(with Patricia Gaffney, Mary Blayney, and Ruth Ryan Langan)

THE OTHER SIDE
(with Mary Blayney, Patricia Gaffney, Ruth Ryan Langan, and Mary Kay McComas)

TIME OF DEATH

THE UNQUIET
(with Mary Blayney, Patricia Gaffney, Ruth Ryan Langan, and Mary Kay McComas)

MIRROR, MIRROR
(with Mary Blayney, Elaine Fox, Mary Kay McComas, and R. C. Ryan)

DOWN THE RABBIT HOLE
(with Mary Blayney, Elaine Fox, Mary Kay McComas, and R. C. Ryan)

Also available . . .

THE OFFICIAL NORA ROBERTS COMPANION
(edited by Denise Little and Laura Hayden)

NORA ROBERTS

BLOOD BROTHERS

JOVE
New York

A JOVE BOOK
Published by Berkley
An imprint of Penguin Random House LLC
375 Hudson Street, New York, New York 10014

Copyright © 2007 by Nora Roberts
Excerpt from *The Hollow* copyright © 2007 by Nora Roberts

ISBN: 9780515143805

First Edition: December 2007

Printed in the United States of America
21 23 24 22

Cover photo of *Lightning* © Thomas Allen/Getty Images
Cover design by Rich Hasselberger
Text design by Kristin del Rosario

To my boys,
who roamed the woods,
even when they weren't supposed to.

Where God hath a temple,
the Devil will have a chapel.

—ROBERT BURTON

The childhood shows the man
As morning shows the day.

—JOHN MILTON

Prologue

❧

Hawkins Hollow
Maryland Province
1652

IT CRAWLED ALONG THE AIR THAT HUNG HEAVY
as wet wool over the glade. Through the snakes of fog that
slid silent over the ground, its hate crept. It came for him
through the heat-smothered night.

It wanted his death.

So he waited as it pushed its way through the woods, its
torch raised toward the empty sky, as it waded across the
streams, around the thickets where small animals huddled
in fear of the scent it bore with it.

Hellsmoke.

He had sent Ann and the lives she carried in her womb
away, to safety. She had not wept, he thought now as he
sprinkled the herbs he'd selected over water. Not his Ann.
But he had seen the grief on her face, in the deep, dark eyes
he had loved through this lifetime, and all the others before.

The three would be born from her, raised by her, and
taught by her. And from them, when the time came, there
would be three more.

What power he had would be theirs, these sons, who

would loose their first cries long, long after this night's work was done. To leave them what tools they would need, the weapons they would wield, he risked all he had, all he was.

His legacy to them was in blood, in heart, in vision.

In this last hour he would do all he could to provide them with what was needed to carry the burden, to remain true, to see their destiny.

His voice was strong and clear as he called to wind and water, to earth and fire. In the hearth the flames snapped. In the bowl the water trembled.

He laid the bloodstone on the cloth. Its deep green was generously spotted with red. He had treasured this stone, as had those who'd come before him. He had honored it. And now he poured power into it as one would pour water into a cup.

So his body shook and sweat and weakened as light hovered in a halo around the stone.

"For you now," he murmured, "sons of sons. Three parts of one. In faith, in hope, in truth. One light, united, to strike back dark. And here, my vow. I will not rest until destiny is met."

With the athame, he scored his palm so his blood fell onto the stone, into the water, and into the flame.

"Blood of my blood. Here I will hold until you come for me, until you loose what must be loosed again on the world. May the gods keep you."

For a moment there was grief. Even through his purpose, there was grief. Not for his life, as the sands of it were dripping down the glass. He had no fear of death. No fear of what he would soon embrace that was not death. But he grieved that he would never lay his lips on Ann's again in this life. He would not see his children born, nor the children of his children. He grieved that he would not be able to stop the suffering to come, as he had been unable to stop the suffering that had come before, in so many other lifetimes.

He understood that he was not the instrument, but only the vessel to be filled and emptied at the needs of the gods.

So, weary from the work, saddened by the loss, he stood outside the little hut, beside the great stone, to meet his fate.

It came in the body of a man, but that was a shell. As his own body was a shell. It called itself Lazarus Twisse, an elder of "the godly." He and those who followed had settled in the wilderness of this province when they broke with the Puritans of New England.

He studied them now in their torchlight, these men and the one who was not a man. These, he thought, who had come to the New World for religious freedom, and then persecuted and destroyed any who did not follow their single, narrow path.

"You are Giles Dent."

"I am," he said, "in this time and this place."

Lazarus Twisse stepped forward. He wore the unrelieved formal black of an elder. His high-crowned, wide-brimmed hat shadowed his face. But Giles could see his eyes, and in his eyes, he saw the demon.

"Giles Dent, you and the female known as Ann Hawkins have been accused and found guilty of witchcraft and demonic practices."

"Who accuses?"

"Bring the girl forward!" Lazarus ordered.

They pulled her, a man on each arm. She was a slight girl, barely six and ten by Giles's calculation. Her face was wax white with fear, her eyes drenched with it. Her hair had been shorn.

"Hester Deale, is this the witch who seduced you?"

"He and the one he calls wife laid hands on me." She spoke as if in a trance. "They performed ungodly acts upon my body. They came to my window as ravens, flew into my room in the night. They stilled my throat so I could not speak or call for help."

"Child," Giles said gently, "what has been done to you?"

Those fear-swamped eyes stared through him. "They called to Satan as their god, and cut the throat of a cock in sacrifice. And drank its blood. They forced its blood on me. I could not stop them."

"Hester Deale, do you renounce Satan?"

"I do renounce him."

"Hester Deale, do you renounce Giles Dent and the woman Ann Hawkins as witches and heretics?"

"I do." Tears spilled down her cheeks. "I do renounce them, and pray to God to save me. Pray to God to forgive me."

"He will," Giles whispered. "You are not to blame."

"Where is the woman Ann Hawkins?" Lazarus demanded, and Giles turned his clear gray eyes to him.

"You will not find her."

"Stand aside. I will enter this house of the devil."

"You will not find her," Giles repeated. For a moment he looked beyond Lazarus to the men and the handful of women who stood in his glade.

He saw death in their eyes, and more, the hunger for it. This was the demon's power, and his work.

Only in Hester's did Giles see fear or sorrow. So he used what he had to give, pushed his mind toward hers. *Run!*

He saw her jolt, stumble back, then he turned to Lazarus.

"We know each other, you and I. Dispatch them, release them, and it will be between us alone."

For an instant he saw the gleam of red in Lazarus's eyes. "You are done. Burn the witch!" he shouted. "Burn the devil house and all within it!"

They came with torches, and with clubs. Giles felt the blows rain on him, and the fury of the hate that was the demon's sharpest weapon.

They drove him to his knees, and the wood of the hut began to flame and smoke. Screams rang in his head, the madness of them.

With the last of his power he reached out toward the demon inside the man, with red rimming its dark eyes as it fed on the hate, the fear, the violence. He felt it gloat, he felt it *rising*, so sure of its victory, and the feast to follow.

And he ripped it to him, through the smoking air. He heard it scream in fury and pain as the flames bit into flesh. And he held it to him, close as a lover as the fire consumed them.

And with that union the fire burst, spread, destroyed every living thing in the glade.

It burned for a day and a night, like the belly of hell.

One

〜⌇〜

Hawkins Hollow
Maryland
July 6, 1987

INSIDE THE PRETTY KITCHEN OF THE PRETTY house on Pleasant Avenue, Caleb Hawkins struggled not to squirm as his mother packed her version of campout provisions.

In his mother's world, ten-year-old boys required fresh fruit, homemade oatmeal cookies (they weren't so bad), half a dozen hard-boiled eggs, a bag of Ritz crackers made into sandwiches with Jif peanut butter for filling, some celery and carrot sticks (yuck!), and hearty ham-and-cheese sandwiches.

Then there was the thermos of lemonade, the stack of paper napkins, and the two boxes of Pop-Tarts she wedged into the basket for breakfast.

"Mom, we're not going to *starve* to death," he complained as she stood deliberating in front of an open cupboard. "We're going to be right in Fox's backyard."

Which was a lie, and kinda hurt his tongue. But she'd never let him go if he told her the truth. And, sheesh, he was ten. Or would be the very next day.

Frannie Hawkins put her hands on her hips. She was a pert, attractive blonde with summer blue eyes and a stylish curly perm. She was the mother of three, and Cal was her baby and only boy. "Now, let me check that backpack."

"Mom!"

"Honey, I just want to be sure you didn't forget anything." Ruthless in her own sunny way, Frannie unzipped Cal's navy blue pack. "Change of underwear, clean shirt, socks, good, good, shorts, toothbrush. Cal, where are the Band-Aids I told you to put in, and the Bactine, the bug repellant."

"Sheesh, we're not going to Africa."

"All the same," Frannie said, and did her signature finger wave to send him along to gather up the supplies. While he did, she slipped a card out of her pocket and tucked it into the pack.

He'd been born—after eight hours and twelve minutes of vicious labor—at one minute past midnight. Every year she stepped up to his bed at twelve, watched him sleep for that minute, then kissed him on the cheek.

Now he'd be ten, and she wouldn't be able to perform the ritual. Because it made her eyes sting, she turned away to wipe at her spotless counter as she heard his tromping footsteps.

"I got it all, okay?"

Smiling brightly, she turned back. "Okay." She stepped over to rub a hand over his short, soft hair. He'd been her towheaded baby boy, she mused, but his hair was darkening, and she suspected it would be a light brown eventually.

Just as hers would be without the aid of Born Blonde.

In a habitual gesture, Frannie tapped his dark-framed glasses back up his nose. "You make sure you thank Miss Barry and Mr. O'Dell when you get there."

"I will."

"*And* when you leave to come home tomorrow."

"Yes, ma'am."

She took his face in her hands, looked through the thick lenses into eyes the same color as his father's calm gray ones. "Behave," she said and kissed his cheek. "Have fun." Then the other. "Happy birthday, my baby."

Usually it mortified him to be called her *baby*, but for some reason, just then, it made him feel sort of gooey and good.

"Thanks, Mom."

He shrugged on the backpack, then hefted the loaded picnic basket. How the hell was he going to ride all the way out to Hawkins Wood with half the darn grocery store on his bike?

The guys were going to razz him something fierce.

Since he was stuck, he carted it into the garage where his bike hung tidily—by Mom decree—on a rack on the wall. Thinking it through, he borrowed two of his father's bungee cords and secured the picnic basket to the wire basket of his bike.

Then he hopped on his bike and pedaled down the short drive.

FOX FINISHED WEEDING HIS SECTION OF THE vegetable garden before hefting the spray his mother mixed up weekly to discourage the deer and rabbits from invading for an all-you-can-eat buffet. The garlic, raw egg, and cayenne pepper combination stank so bad he held his breath as he squirted it on the rows of snap beans and limas, the potato greens, the carrot and radish tops.

He stepped back, took a clear breath, and studied his work. His mother was pretty damn strict about the gardening. It was all about respecting the earth, harmonizing with Nature, and that stuff.

It was also, Fox knew, about eating, and making enough food and money to feed a family of six—and whoever dropped by. Which was why his dad and his older sister, Sage, were down at their stand selling fresh eggs, goat's milk, honey, and his mother's homemade jams.

He glanced over to where his younger brother, Ridge,

was stretched out between the rows playing with the weeds instead of yanking them. And because his mother was inside putting their baby sister, Sparrow, down for her nap, he was on Ridge duty.

"Come on, Ridge, pull the stupid things. I wanna go."

Ridge lifted his face, turned his I'm-dreaming eyes on his brother. "Why can't I go with you?"

"Because you're eight and you can't even weed the dumb tomatoes." Annoyed, Fox stepped over the rows to Ridge's section and, crouching, began to yank.

"Can, too."

As Fox hoped, the insult had Ridge weeding with a vengeance. Fox straightened, rubbed his hands on his jeans. He was a tall boy with a skinny build, a mass of bark brown hair worn in a waving tangle around a sharp-boned face. His eyes were tawny and reflected his satisfaction now as he trooped over for the sprayer.

He dumped it beside Ridge. "Don't forget to spray this shit."

He crossed the yard, circling what was left—three short walls and part of a chimney—of the old stone hut on the edge of the vegetable garden. It was buried, as his mother liked it best, in honeysuckle and wild morning glory.

He skirted past the chicken coop and the cluckers that were pecking around, by the goat yard where the two nannies stood slack-hipped and bored, edged around his mother's herb garden. He headed toward the kitchen door of the house his parents had mostly built. The kitchen was big, and the counters loaded with projects—canning jars, lids, tubs of candle wax, bowls of wicks.

He knew most of the people in and around the Hollow thought of his family as the weird hippies. It didn't bother him. For the most part they got along, and people were happy to buy their eggs and produce, his mother's needlework and handmade candles and crafts, or hire his dad to build stuff.

Fox washed up at the sink before rooting through the

cupboards, poking in the big pantry searching for *some-thing* that wasn't health food.

Fat chance.

He'd bike over to the market—the one right outside of town just in case—and use some of his savings to buy Little Debbies and Nutter Butters.

His mother came in, tossing her long brown braid off the shoulder bared by her cotton sundress. "Finished?"

"I am. Ridge is almost."

Joanne walked to the window, her hand automatically lifting to brush down Fox's hair, staying to rest on his neck as she studied her young son.

"There's some carob brownies and some veggie dogs, if you want to take any."

"Ah." Barf. "No, thanks. I'm good."

He knew that she knew he'd be chowing down on meat products and refined sugar. And he knew she knew he knew. But she wouldn't rag him about it. Choices were big with Mom.

"Have a good time."

"I will."

"Fox?" She stood where she was, by the sink with the light coming in the window and haloing her hair. "Happy birthday."

"Thanks, Mom." And with Little Debbies on his mind, he bolted out to grab his bike and start the adventure.

THE OLD MAN WAS STILL SLEEPING WHEN GAGE shoved some supplies into his pack. Gage could hear the snoring through the thin, crappy walls of the cramped, crappy apartment over the Bowl-a-Rama. The old man worked there cleaning the floors, the johns, and whatever else Cal's father found for him to do.

He might've been a day shy of his tenth birthday, but Gage knew why Mr. Hawkins kept the old man on, why they had the apartment rent-free with the old man supposedly being the maintenance guy for the building. Mr. Hawkins felt sorry for them—and mostly sorry for Gage because he was stuck as the motherless son of a mean drunk.

Other people felt sorry for him, too, and that put Gage's back up. Not Mr. Hawkins though. He never let the pity show. And whenever Gage did any chores for the bowling alley, Mr. Hawkins paid him in cash, on the side. And with a conspirator's wink.

He knew, hell, everybody knew, that Bill Turner knocked his kid around from time to time. But Mr. Hawkins was the *only* one who'd ever sat down with Gage and asked *him* what he wanted. Did he want the cops, Social Services, did he want to come stay with him and his family for a while?

He hadn't wanted the cops or the do-gooders. They only made it worse. And though he'd have given anything to live in that nice house with people who lived decent lives, he'd only asked if Mr. Hawkins would please, please, not fire his old man.

He got knocked around less whenever Mr. Hawkins kept his father busy and employed. Unless, of course, good old Bill went on a toot and decided to whale in.

If Mr. Hawkins knew how bad it could get during those times, he would call the cops.

So he didn't tell, and he learned to be very good at hiding beatings like the one he'd taken the night before.

Gage moved carefully as he snagged three cold ones out of his father's beer supply. The welts on his back and butt were still raw and angry and they stung like fire. He'd expected the beating. He always got one around his birthday. He always got another one around the date of his mother's death.

Those were the big, traditional two. Other times, the whippings came as a surprise. But mostly, when the old man was working steady, the hits were just a careless cuff or shove.

He didn't bother to be quiet when he turned toward his

father's bedroom. Nothing short of a raid by the A-Team would wake Bill Turner when he was in a drunken sleep.

The room stank of beer sweat and stale smoke, causing Gage to wrinkle his handsome face. He took the half pack of Marlboros off the dresser. The old man wouldn't remember if he'd had any, so no problem there.

Without a qualm, he opened his father's wallet and helped himself to three singles and a five.

He looked at his father as he stuffed the bills in his pocket. Bill sprawled on the bed, stripped down to his boxers, his mouth open as the snores pumped out.

The belt he'd used on his son the night before lay on the floor along with dirty shirts, socks, jeans.

For a moment, just a moment, it rippled through Gage with a kind of mad glee—the image of himself picking up that belt, swinging it high, laying it snapping hard over his father's bare, sagging belly.

See how you like it.

But there on the table with its overflowing ashtray, the empty bottle, was the picture of Gage's mother, smiling out.

People said he looked like her—the dark hair, the hazy green eyes, the strong mouth. It had embarrassed him once, being compared to a woman. But lately, since everything but that one photograph was so faded in his head, when he couldn't hear her voice in his head or remember how she'd smelled, it steadied him.

He looked like his mother.

Sometimes he imagined the man who drank himself into a stupor most nights wasn't his father.

His father was smart and brave and sort of reckless.

And then he'd look at the old man and know that was all bullshit.

He shot the old bastard the finger as he left the room. He had to carry his backpack. No way he could put it on with the welts riding his back.

He took the outside steps down, went around the back where he chained up his thirdhand bike.

Despite the pain, he grinned as he got on.
For the next twenty-four hours, he was free.

THEY'D AGREED TO MEET ON THE WEST EDGE OF town where the woods crept toward the curve of the road. The middle-class boy, the hippie kid, and the drunk's son.

They shared the same birthday, July seventh. Cal had let out his first shocked cry in the delivery room of Washington County Hospital while his mother panted and his father wept. Fox had shoved his way into the world and into his laughing father's waiting hands in the bedroom of the odd little farmhouse while Bob Dylan sang "Lay, Lady, Lay" on the record player, and lavender-scented candles burned. And Gage had struggled out of his terrified mother in an ambulance racing up Maryland Route 65.

Now, Gage arrived first, sliding off his bike to walk it into the trees where nobody cruising the road could spot it, or him.

Then he sat on the ground and lit his first cigarette of the afternoon. They always made him a little sick to his stomach, but the defiant act of lighting up made up for the queasiness.

He sat and smoked in the shady woods, and imagined himself on a mountain path in Colorado or in a steamy South American jungle.

Anywhere but here.

He'd taken his third puff, and his first cautious inhale, when he heard the bumps of tires over dirt and rock.

Fox pushed through the trees on Lightning, his bike so named because Fox's father had painted lightning bolts on the bars.

His dad was cool that way.

"Hey, Turner."

"O'Dell." Gage held out the cigarette.

They both knew Fox took it only because to do otherwise made him a dweeb. So he took a quick drag, passed it

back. Gage nodded to the bag tied to Lightning's handle-
bars. "What'd you get?"

"Little Debbies, Nutter Butters, some TastyKake pies.
Apple and cherry."

"Righteous. I got three cans of Bud for tonight."

Fox's eyes didn't pop out of his head, but they were
close. "No shit?"

"No shit. Old man was trashed. He'll never know the
difference. I got something else, too. Last month's *Penthouse* magazine."

"No way."

"He keeps them buried under a bunch of crap in the
bathroom."

"Lemme see."

"Later. With the beer."

They both looked over as Cal dragged his bike down the
rough path. "Hey, jerkwad," Fox greeted him.

"Hey, dickheads."

That said with the affection of brothers, they walked
their bikes deeper into the trees, then off the narrow path.

Once the bikes were deemed secure, supplies were untied and divvied up.

"Jesus, Hawkins, what'd your mom put in here?"

"You won't complain when you're eating it." Cal's arms
were already protesting the weight as he scowled at Gage.
"Why don't you put your pack on, and give me a hand?"

"Because I'm carrying it." But he flipped the top on the
basket and after hooting at the Tupperware, shoved a couple of the containers into his pack. "Put something in
yours, O'Dell, or it'll take us all day just to get to Hester's
Pool."

"Shit." Fox pulled out a thermos, wedged it in his pack.
"Light enough now, Sally?"

"Screw you. I got the basket and my pack."

"I got the supplies from the market and my pack." Fox
pulled his prized possession from his bike. "You carry the
boom box, Turner."

Gage shrugged, took the radio. "Then I pick the tunes."

"No rap," Cal and Fox said together, but Gage only grinned as he walked and tuned until he found some Run-DMC.

With a lot of bitching and moaning, they started the hike.

The leaves, thick and green, cut the sun's glare and summer heat. Through the thick poplars and towering oaks, slices and dabs of milky blue sky peeked. They aimed for the wind of the creek while the rapper and Aerosmith urged them to walk this way.

"Gage has a *Penthouse*," Fox announced. "The skin magazine, numbnut," he said at Cal's blank stare.

"Uh-uh."

"Uh-huh. Come on, Turner, break it out."

"Not until we're camped and pop the beer."

"Beer!" Instinctively, Cal sent a look over his shoulder, just in case his mother had magically appeared. "You got beer?"

"Three cans of suds," Gage confirmed, strutting. "Smokes, too."

"Is this far-out or what?" Fox gave Cal a punch in the arm. "It's the best birthday ever."

"Ever," Cal agreed, secretly terrified. Beer, cigarettes, and pictures of naked women. If his mother ever found out, he'd be grounded until he was thirty. That didn't even count the fact he'd lied. Or that he was hiking his way through Hawkins Wood to camp out at the expressly forbidden Pagan Stone.

He'd be grounded until he died of old age.

"Stop worrying." Gage shifted his pack from one arm to the other, with a wicked glint of what-the-hell in his eyes. "It's all cool."

"I'm not worried." Still, Cal jolted when a fat jay zoomed out of the trees and let out an irritated call.

Two

HESTER'S POOL WAS ALSO FORBIDDEN IN CAL'S world, which was only one of the reasons it was irresistible.

The scoop of brown water, fed by the winding Antietam Creek and hidden in the thick woods, was supposed to be haunted by some weird Pilgrim girl who'd drowned in it way back whenever.

He'd heard his mother talk about a boy who'd drowned there when she'd been a kid, which in Mom Logic was the number one reason Cal was *never allowed* to swim there. The kid's ghost was supposed to be there, too, lurking under the water, just waiting to grab another kid's ankle and drag him down to the bottom so he'd have somebody to hang out with.

Cal had swum there twice that summer, giddy with fear and excitement. And both times he'd *sworn* he'd felt bony fingers brush over his ankle.

A dense army of cattails trooped along the edges, and around the slippery bank grew bunches of the wild orange lilies his mother liked. Fans of ferns climbed up the rocky slope, along with brambles of wild berries, which when ripe would stain the fingers a kind of reddish purple that looked a little like blood.

The last time they'd come, he'd seen a black snake slither its way up the slope, barely stirring the ferns.

Fox let out a shout, dumped his pack. In seconds he'd dragged off his shoes, his shirt, his jeans and was sailing over the water in a cannonball without a thought for snakes or ghosts or whatever else might be under that murky brown surface.

"Come on, you pussies!" After a slick surface dive, Fox bobbed around the pool like a seal.

Cal sat, untied his Converse All Stars, carefully tucked his socks inside them. While Fox continued to whoop and splash, he glanced over where Gage simply stood looking out over the water.

"You going in?"

"I dunno."

Cal pulled off his shirt, folded it out of habit. "It's on the agenda. We can't cross it off unless we all do it."

"Yeah, yeah." But Gage only stood as Cal stripped down to his Fruit of the Looms.

"We have to all go in, dare the gods and stuff."

With a shrug, Gage toed off his shoes. "Go on, what are you, a homo? Want to watch me take my clothes off?"

"Gross." And slipping his glasses inside his left shoe, Cal sucked in breath, gave thanks his vision blurred, and jumped.

The water was a quick, cold shock.

Fox immediately spewed water in his face, fully blinding him, then stroked off toward the cattails before retaliation. Just when he'd managed to clear his myopic eyes, Gage jumped in and blinded him all over again.

"Sheesh, you guys!"

Gage's choppy dog paddle worked up the water, so Cal swam clear of the storm. Of the three, he was the best swimmer. Fox was fast, but he ran out of steam. And Gage, well, Gage sort of attacked the water like he was in a fight with it.

Cal worried—even as part of him thrilled at the idea—that he'd one day have to use the lifesaving techniques his dad had taught him in their aboveground pool to save Gage from drowning.

He was picturing it, and how Gage and Fox would stare at him with gratitude and admiration, when a hand grabbed his ankle and yanked him underwater.

Even though he *knew* it was Fox who pulled him down, Cal's heart slammed into his throat as the water closed over his head. He floundered, forgetting all his training in that first instant of panic. Even as he managed to kick off the hold on his ankle and gather himself to push to the surface, he saw a movement to the left.

It—she—seemed to glide through the water toward him. Her hair streamed back from her white face, and her eyes were cave black. As her hand reached out, Cal opened his mouth to scream. Gulping in water, he clawed his way to the surface.

He could hear laughter all around him, tinny and echoing like the music out of the old transistor radio his father sometimes used. With terror biting inside his throat, he slapped and clawed his way to the edge of the pool.

"I saw her, I saw her, in the water, I saw her." He choked out the words while fighting to climb out.

She was coming for him, fast as a shark in his mind, and in his mind he saw her mouth open, and the teeth gleam sharp as knives.

"Get out! Get out of the water!" Panting, he crawled through the slippery weeds and rolling, saw his friends treading water. "She's in the water." He almost sobbed it, bellying over to fumble his glasses out of his shoe. "I *saw* her. Get out. Hurry up!"

"Oooh, the ghost! Help me, help me!" With a mock gurgle, Fox sank underwater.

Cal lurched to his feet, balled his hands into fists at his

sides. Fury tangled with terror to have his voice lashing through the still summer air. "Get the fuck out."

The grin on Gage's face faded. Eyes narrowed on Cal, he gripped Fox by the arm when Fox surfaced laughing.

"We're getting out."

"Come *on*. He's just being spaz because I dunked him."

"He's not bullshitting."

The tone got through, or when he bothered to look, the expression on Cal's face tripped a chord. Fox shot off toward the edge, spooked enough to send a couple of wary looks over his shoulder.

Gage followed, a careless dog paddle that made Cal think he was daring something to happen.

When his friends hauled themselves out, Cal sank back down to the ground. Drawing his knees up, he pressed his forehead to them and began to shake.

"Man." Dripping in his underwear, Fox shifted from foot to foot. "I just gave you a tug, and you freak out. We were just fooling around."

"I saw her."

Crouching, Fox shoved his sopping hair back from his face. "Dude, you can't see squat without those Coke bottles."

"Shut up, O'Dell." Gage squatted down. "What did you see, Cal?"

"*Her*. She had all this hair swimming around her, and her eyes, oh man, her eyes were black like the shark in *Jaws*. She had this long dress on, long sleeves and all, and she reached out like she was going to grab me—"

"With her bony fingers," Fox put in, falling well short of his target of disdain.

"They weren't bony." Cal lifted his head now, and behind the lenses his eyes were fierce and frightened. "I thought they would be, but she looked, all of her, looked just . . . real. Not like a ghost or a skeleton. Oh man, oh God, I saw her. I'm not making it up."

"Well Jee-sus." Fox crab-walked another foot away

from the pond, then cursed breathlessly when he tore his forearm on berry thorns. "Shit, now I'm bleeding." Fox yanked a handful of weedy grass, swiped at the blood seeping from the scratches.

"Don't even think about it." Cal saw the way Gage was studying the water—that thoughtful, wonder-what'll-happen gleam in his eye. "Nobody's going in there. You don't swim well enough to try it anyway."

"How come you're the only one who saw her?"

"I don't know and I don't care. I just want to get away from here."

Cal leaped up, grabbed his pants. Before he could wiggle into them, he saw Gage from behind. "Holy cow. Your back is messed up bad."

"The old man got wasted last night. It's no big deal."

"Dude." Fox walked around to get a look. "That's gotta hurt."

"The water cooled it off."

"I've got my first aid kit—" Cal began, but Gage cut him off.

"I said no big deal." He grabbed his shirt, pulled it on. "If you two don't have the balls to go back in and see what happens, we might as well move on."

"I don't have the balls," Cal said in such a deadpan, Gage snorted out a laugh.

"Then put your pants on so I don't have to wonder what that is hanging between your legs."

Fox broke out the Little Debbies, and one of the six-pack of Coke he'd bought at the market. Because the incident in the pond and the welts on Gage's back were too important, they didn't speak of them. Instead, hair still dripping, they resumed the hike, gobbling snack cakes and sharing a can of warm soda.

But with Bon Jovi claiming they were halfway there, Cal thought of what he'd seen. Why had he been the only one? How had her face been so clear in the murky water, and with his glasses tucked in his shoe? How could he have seen her? With every step he took away from the pond, it was easier to convince himself he'd just imagined it.

Not that he'd ever, *ever* admit that maybe he'd just freaked out.

The heat dried his damp skin and brought on the sweat. It made him wonder how Gage could stand having his shirt clinging to his sore back. Because, man, those marks were all red and bumpy, and really had to hurt. He'd seen Gage after Old Man Turner had gone after him before, and it hadn't ever, ever been as bad as this. He wished Gage had let him put some salve on his back.

What if it got infected? What if he got blood poisoning, got all delirious or something when they were all the way to the Pagan Stone?

He'd have to send Fox for help, yeah, that's what he'd do—send Fox for help while he stayed with Gage and treated the wounds, got him to drink something so he didn't—what was it?—dehydrate.

Of course, all their butts would be in the sling when his dad had to come get them, but Gage would get better.

Maybe they'd put Gage's father in jail. Then what would happen? Would Gage have to go to an orphanage?

It was almost as scary to think about as the woman in the pond.

They stopped to rest, then sat in the shade to share one of Gage's stolen Marlboros. They always made Cal dizzy, but it was kind of nice to sit there in the trees with the water sliding over rocks behind them and a bunch of crazy birds calling out to each other.

"We could camp right here," Cal said half to himself.

"No way." Fox punched his shoulder. "We're turning ten at the Pagan Stone. No changing the plan. We'll be there in under an hour. Right, Gage?"

Gage stared up through the trees. "Yeah. We'd be moving faster if you guys hadn't brought so much shit with you."

"Didn't see you turn down a Little Debbie," Fox reminded him.

"Nobody turns down Little Debbies. Well . . ." He crushed out the cigarette, then planted a rock over the butt. "Saddle up, troops."

Nobody came here. Cal knew it wasn't true, knew when deer was in season these woods were hunted.

But it *felt* like nobody came here. The two other times he'd been talked into hiking all the way to the Pagan Stone he'd felt exactly the same. And both those times they'd started out early in the morning instead of afternoon. They'd been back out before two.

Now, according to his Timex, it was nearly four. Despite the snack cake, his stomach wanted to rumble. He wanted to stop again, to dig into what his mother had packed in the stupid basket.

But Gage was pushing on, anxious to get to the Pagan Stone.

The earth in the clearing had a scorched look about it, as if a fire had blown through the trees there and turned them all to ash. It was almost a perfect circle, ringed by oaks and locus and the bramble of wild berries. In its center was a single rock that jutted two feet out of the burned earth and flattened at the top like a small table.

Some said altar.

People, when they spoke of it at all, said the Pagan Stone was just a big rock that pushed out of the ground. Ground so colored because of minerals, or an underground stream, or maybe caves.

But others, who were usually more happy to talk about it, pointed to the original settlement of Hawkins Hollow and the night thirteen people met their doom, burned alive in that very clearing.

Witchcraft, some said, and others devil worship.

Another theory was that an inhospitable band of Indians had killed them, then burned the bodies.

But whatever the theory, the pale gray stone rose out of the soot-colored earth like a monument.

"We made it!" Fox dumped his pack and his bag to dash forward and do a dancing run around the rock. "Is this cool? Is this cool? Nobody knows where we are. And we've got *all* night to do anything we want."

"Anything we want in the middle of the woods," Cal added. Without a TV, or a refrigerator.

Fox threw back his head and let out a shout that echoed away. "See that? Nobody can hear us. We could be attacked by mutants or ninjas or space aliens, and nobody would hear us."

That, Cal realized, didn't make his stomach feel any steadier. "We need to get wood for a campfire."

"The Boy Scout's right," Gage decided. "You guys find some wood. I'll go put the beer and the Coke in the stream. Cool off the cans."

In his tidy way, Cal organized the campsite first. Food in one area, clothes in another, tools in another still. With his Scout knife and compass in his pocket, he set off to gather twigs and small branches. The brambles nipped and scratched as he picked his way through them. With his arms loaded, he didn't notice a few drops of his blood drip onto the ground at the edge of the circle.

Or the way the blood sizzled, smoked, then was sucked into that scarred earth.

Fox set the boom box on the rock, so they set up camp with Madonna and U2 and the Boss. Following Cal's advice, they built the fire, but didn't set it to light while they had the sun.

Sweaty and filthy, they sat on the ground and tore into the picnic basket with grubby hands and huge appetites. As the food, the familiar flavors filled his belly and soothed his system, Cal decided it had been worth hauling the basket for a couple of hours.

Replete, they stretched out on their backs, faces to the sky.

"Do you really think all those people died right here?" Gage wondered.

"There are books about it in the library," Cal told him. "About a fire of, like, 'unknown origin' breaking out and these people burned up."

"Kind of a weird place for them to be."

"We're here."

Gage only grunted at that.

"My mom said how the first white people to settle here were Puritans." Fox blew a huge pink bubble with the Bazooka he'd bought at the market. "A sort of radical Puritan or something. How they came over here looking for religious freedom, but really only meant it was free if it was, you know, their way. Mom says lots of people are like that about religion. I don't get it."

Gage thought he knew, or knew part. "A lot of people are mean, and even if they're not, a lot more people think they're better than you." He saw it all the time, in the way people looked at him.

"But do you think they were witches, and the people from the Hollow back then burned them at the stake or something?" Fox rolled over on his belly. "My mom says that being a witch is like a religion, too."

"Your mom's whacked."

Because it was Gage, and because it was said jokingly, Fox grinned. "We're all whacked."

"I say this calls for a beer." Gage pushed up. "We'll share one, let the others get colder." As Gage walked off to the stream, Cal and Fox exchanged looks.

"You ever had beer before?" Cal wanted to know.

"No. You?"

"Are you kidding? I can only have Coke on special occasions. What if we get drunk and pass out or something?"

"My dad drinks beer sometimes. He doesn't, I don't think."

They went quiet when Gage walked back with the dripping can. "Okay. This is to, you know, celebrate that we're going to stop being kids at midnight."

"Maybe we shouldn't drink it until midnight," Cal supposed.

"We'll have the second one after. It's like . . . it's like a ritual."

The sound of the top popping was loud in the quiet

woods, a quick *crack*, almost as shocking to Cal as a gun-shot might have been. He smelled the beer immediately, and it struck him as a sour smell. He wondered if it tasted the same.

Gage held the beer up in one hand, high, as if he gripped the hilt of a sword. Then he lowered it, took a long, deep gulp from the can.

He didn't quite mask the reaction, a closing in of his face as if he'd swallowed something strange and unpleasant. His cheeks flushed as he let out a short, gasping breath.

"It's still pretty warm but it . . ." He coughed once. "It hits the spot. Now you."

He passed the can to Fox. With a shrug, Fox took the can, mirrored Gage's move. Everyone knew if there was anything close to a dare, Fox would jump at it. "Ugh. It tastes like piss."

"You been drinking piss lately?"

Fox snorted at Gage's question and passed the can to Cal. "Your turn."

Cal studied the can. It wasn't like a sip of beer would kill him or anything. So he sucked in a breath and swallowed some down.

It made his stomach curl and his eyes water. He shoved the can back at Gage. "It does taste like piss."

"I guess people don't drink it for how it tastes. It's how it makes you feel." Gage took another sip, because he wanted to know how it made him feel.

They sat cross-legged in the circular clearing, knees bumping, passing the can from hand to hand.

Cal's stomach pitched, but it didn't feel sick, not exactly. His head pitched, too, but it felt sort of goofy and fun. And the beer made his bladder full. When he stood, the whole world pitched and made him laugh helplessly as he staggered toward a tree.

He unzipped, aimed toward the tree but the tree kept moving.

Fox was struggling to light one of the cigarettes when

Cal stumbled back. They passed that around the circle as well until Cal's almost ten-year-old stomach revolted. He crawled off to sick it all up, crawled back, and just lay flat, closing his eyes and willing the world to go still again.

He felt as if he were once again swimming in the pond, and being slowly pulled under.

When he surfaced again it was nearly dusk.

He eased up, hoping he wouldn't be sick again. He felt a little hollow inside—belly and head—but not like he was going to puke. He saw Fox curled against the stone, sleeping. He crawled over on all fours for the thermos and as he washed the sick and beer out of his throat, he was never so grateful for his mother and her lemonade.

Steadier, he rubbed his fingers on his eyes under his glasses, then spotted Gage sitting, staring at the tented wood of the campfire they'd yet to light.

"'Morning, Sally."

With a wan smile, Cal scooted over.

"I don't know how to light this thing. I figured it was about time to, but I needed a Boy Scout."

Cal took the book of matches Gage handed him, and set fire to several spots on the pile of dried leaves he'd arranged under the wood. "That should do it. Wind's pretty still, and there's nothing to catch in the clearing. We can keep feeding it when we need to, and just make sure we bury it before we go tomorrow."

"Smokey the Bear. You all right?"

"Yeah. I guess I threw most everything up."

"I shouldn't have brought the beer."

Cal lifted a shoulder, glanced toward Fox. "We're okay, and now we won't have to wonder what it tastes like. We know it tastes like piss."

Gage laughed a little. "It didn't make me feel mean." He picked up a stick, poked at the little flames. "I wanted to know if it would, and I figured I could try it with you and Fox. You're my best friends, so I could try it with you and see if it made me feel mean."

"How did it make you feel?"

"It made my head hurt. It still does a little. I didn't get sick like you, but I sorta wanted to. I went and got one of the Cokes and drank that. It felt better then. Why does he drink so goddamn much if it makes him feel like that?"

"I don't know."

Gage dropped his head on his knees. "He was crying when he went after me last night. Blubbering and crying the whole time he used the belt on me. Why would anybody want to feel like that?"

Careful to avoid the welts on Gage's back, Cal draped an arm over his shoulders. He wished he knew what to say.

"Soon as I'm old enough I'm getting out. Join the army maybe, or get a job on a freighter, maybe an oil rig."

Gage's eyes gleamed when he lifted his head, and Cal looked away because he knew the shine was tears. "You can come stay with us when you need to."

"It'd just be worse when I went back. But I'm going to be ten in a few hours. And in a few years I'll be as big as he is. Bigger maybe. I won't let him come after me then. I won't let him hit me. Screw it." Gage rubbed his face. "Let's wake Fox up. Nobody sleeps tonight."

Fox moaned and grumbled, and he got himself up to pee and fetch a cool Coke from the stream. They shared it with another round of Little Debbies. And, at last, the copy of *Penthouse*.

Cal had seen naked breasts before. You could see them in the *National Geographic* in the library, if you knew where to look.

But these were different.

"Hey guys, did you ever think about doing it?" Cal asked.

"Who doesn't?" they both replied.

"Whoever does it first has to tell the other two everything. All about how it feels," Cal continued. "And how you did it, and what she does. Everything. I call for an oath."

A call for an oath was sacred. Gage spat on the back of his hand, held it out. Fox slapped his palm on, spat on the back of his hand, and Cal completed the contact.

"And so we swear," they said together.

They sat around the fire as the stars came out, and deep in the woods an owl hooted its night call.

The long, sweaty hike, ghostly apparitions, and beer puke were forgotten.

"We should do this every year on our birthday," Cal decided. "Even when we're old. Like thirty or something. The three of us should come here."

"Drink beer and look at pictures of naked girls," Fox added. "I call for—"

"Don't." Gage spoke sharply. "I can't swear. I don't know where I'm going to go, but it'll be somewhere else. I don't know if I'll ever come back."

"Then we'll go where you are, when we can. We're always going to be best friends." Nothing would change that, Cal thought, and took his own, personal oath on it. Nothing ever could. He looked at his watch. "It's going to be midnight soon. I have an idea."

He took out his Boy Scout knife and, opening the blade, held it in the fire.

"What's up?" Fox demanded.

"I'm sterilizing it. Like, ah, purifying it." It got so hot he had to pull back, blow on his fingers. "It's like Gage said about ritual and stuff. Ten years is a decade. We've known each other almost the whole time. We were born on the same day. It makes us . . . different," he said, searching for words he wasn't quite sure of. "Like special, I guess. We're best friends. We're like brothers."

Gage looked at the knife, then into Cal's face. "Blood brothers."

"Yeah."

"Cool." Already committed, Fox held out his hand.

"At midnight," Cal said. "We should do it at midnight, and we should have some words to say."

"We'll swear an oath," Gage said. "That we mix our blood, um, three into one? Something like that. In loyalty."

"That's good. Write it down, Cal."

Cal dug pencil and paper out of his pack. "We'll write

words down, and say them together. Then we'll do the cut and put our wrists together. I've got Band-Aids for after if we need them."

Cal wrote the words with his Number Two pencil on the blue lined paper, crossing out when they changed their minds.

Fox added more wood to the fire so that the flames crackled as they stood by the Pagan Stone.

At moments to midnight, they stood, three young boys with faces lit by fire and starlight. At Gage's nod, they spoke together in voices solemn and achingly young.

"We were born ten years ago, on the same night, at the same time, in the same year. We are brothers. At the Pagan Stone we swear an oath of loyalty and truth and brotherhood. We mix our blood."

Cal sucked in a breath and geared up the courage to run the knife across his wrist first. "Ouch."

"We mix our blood." Fox gritted his teeth as Cal cut his wrist.

"We mix our blood." And Gage stood unflinching as the knife drew over his flesh.

"Three into one, and one for the three."

Cal held his arm out. Fox, then Gage pressed their scored wrists down to his. "Brothers in spirit, in mind. Brothers in blood for all time."

As they stood, clouds shivered over the fat moon, misted over the bright stars. Their mixed blood dripped and fell onto the burnt ground.

The wind exploded with a voice like a raging scream. The little campfire spewed up flame in a spearing tower. The three of them were lifted off their feet as if a hand gripped them, tossed them. Light burst as if the stars had shattered.

As he opened his mouth to shout, Cal felt something shove inside him, hot and strong, to smother his lungs, to squeeze his heart in a stunning agony of pain.

The light shut off. In the thick dark blew an icy cold that numbed his skin. The sound the wind made now was like an animal, like a monster that only lived inside books. Beneath him the ground shook, heaving him back as he tried to crawl away.

And something came out of that icy dark, out of that quaking ground. Something huge and horrible.

Eyes bloodred and full of . . . hunger. It looked at him. And when it smiled, its teeth glittered like silver swords.

He thought he died, and that it took him in, in one gulp.

But when he came to himself again, he could hear his own heart. He could hear the shouts and calls of his friends.

Blood brothers.

"Jesus, Jesus, what was that? Did you see?" Fox called out in a voice thin as a reed. "Gage, God, your nose is bleeding."

"So's yours. Something . . . Cal. God, Cal."

Cal lay where he was, flat on his back. He felt the wet warmth of blood on his face. He was too numb to be frightened by it. "I can't see." He croaked out a weak whisper. "I can't see."

"Your glasses are broken." Face filthy with soot and blood, Fox crawled to him. "One of the lenses is cracked. Dude, your mom's going to kill you."

"Broken." Shaking, Cal reached up to pull off his glasses.

"Something. Something was here." Gage gripped Cal's shoulder. "I felt something happen, after everything went crazy, I felt something happen inside me. Then . . . did you see it? Did you see that thing?"

"I saw its eyes," Fox said, and his teeth chattered. "We need to get out of here. We need to get out."

"Where?" Gage demanded. Though his breath still wheezed, he grabbed Cal's knife from the ground, gripped it. "We don't know where it went. Was it some kind of bear? Was it—"

"It wasn't a bear." Cal spoke calmly now. "It was what's been here, in this place, a long time. I can see . . . I can see it. It looked like a man once, when it wanted. But it wasn't."

"Man, you hit your head."

Cal turned his eyes on Fox, and the irises were nearly black. "I can see it, and the other." He opened the hand of the wrist he'd cut. In the palm was a chunk of a green stone spotted with red. "His."

Fox opened his hand, and Gage his. In each was an identical third of the stone. "What is it?" Gage whispered. "Where the hell did it come from?"

"I don't know, but it's ours now. Uh, one into three, three into one. I think we let something out. And something came with it. Something bad. I can see."

He closed his eyes a moment, then opened them to look at his friends. "I can see, but not with my glasses. I can see without them. It's not blurry. I can see without my glasses."

"Wait." Trembling, Gage pulled up his shirt, turned his back.

"Man, they're gone." Fox reached out to touch his fingers to Gage's unmarred back. "The welts. They're gone. And . . ." He held out his wrist where the shallow cut was already healing. "Holy cow, are we like superheroes now?"

"It's a demon," Cal said. "And we let it out."

"Shit." Gage stared off into the dark woods. "Happy goddamn birthday to us."

Three

~~

IT WAS COLDER IN HAWKINS HOLLOW, MARYLAND, than it was in Juneau, Alaska. Cal liked to know little bits like that, even though at the moment he was in the Hollow where the damp, cold wind blew like a mother and froze his eyeballs.

His eyeballs were about the only things exposed as he zipped across Main Street from Coffee Talk, with a to-go cup of mochaccino in one gloved hand, to the Bowl-a-Rama.

Three days a week, he tried for a counter breakfast at Ma's Pantry a couple doors down, and at least once a week he hit Gino's for dinner.

His father believed in supporting the community, the other merchants. Now that his dad was semiretired and Cal oversaw most of the businesses, he tried to follow that Hawkins tradition.

He shopped the local market even though the chain supermarket a couple miles outside town was cheaper. If he wanted to send a woman flowers, he resisted doing so with a couple of clicks on his computer and hauled himself down to the Flower Pot.

He had relationships with the local plumber, electrician, painter, the area craftsmen. Whenever possible, he hired for the town from the town.

Except for his years away at college, he'd always lived in the Hollow. It was his place.

Every seven years since his tenth birthday, he lived through the nightmare that visited his place. And every seven years, he helped clean up the aftermath.

He unlocked the front door of the Bowl-a-Rama, re-locked it behind him. People tended to walk right in, whatever the posted hours, if the door wasn't locked.

He'd once been a little more casual about that, until one fine night while he'd been enjoying some after-hours Strip Bowling with Allysa Kramer, three teenage boys had wandered in, hoping the video arcade was still open.

Lesson learned.

He walked by the front desk, the six lanes and ball returns, the shoe rental counter and the grill, turned and jogged up the stairs to the squat second floor that held his (or his father's if his father was in the mood) office, a closet-sized john, and a mammoth storage area.

He set the coffee on the desk, stripped off gloves, scarf, watch cap, coat, insulated vest.

He booted up his computer, put on the satellite radio, then sat down to fuel up on caffeine and get to work.

The bowling center Cal's grandfather had opened in the postwar forties had been a tiny, three-lane gathering spot with a couple of pinball machines and counter Cokes. It expanded in the sixties, and again, when Cal's father took the reins, in the early eighties.

Now, with its six lanes, its video arcade, and its private party room, it was *the* place to gather in the Hollow.

Credit to Grandpa, Cal thought as he looked over the party reservations for the next month. But the biggest chunk of credit went to Cal's father, who'd morphed the lanes into a family center, and had used its success to dip into other areas of business.

The town bears our name, Jim Hawkins liked to say. *Respect the name, respect the town.*

Cal did both. He'd have left long ago otherwise.

An hour into the work, Cal glanced up at the rap on his doorjamb.

"Sorry, Cal. Just wanted you to know I was here. Thought I'd go ahead and get that painting done in the rest rooms since you're not open this morning."

"Okay, Bill. Got everything you need?"

"Sure do." Bill Turner, five years, two months, and six days sober, cleared his throat. "Wonder if maybe you'd heard anything from Gage."

"Not in a couple months now."

Tender area, Cal thought when Bill just nodded. Boggy ground.

"I'll just get started then."

Cal watched as Bill moved away from the doorway. Nothing he could do about it, he told himself. Nothing he was sure he should do.

Did five years clean and sober make up for all those whacks with a belt, for all those shoves and slaps, all those curses? It wasn't for him to judge.

He glanced down at the thin scar that ran diagonally across his wrist. Odd how quickly that small wound had healed, and yet the mark of it remained—the only scar he carried. Odd how so small a thing had catapulted the town and people he knew into seven days of hell every seven years.

Would Gage come back this summer, as he had every seventh year? Cal couldn't see ahead, that wasn't his gift or his burden. But he knew when he, Gage, and Fox turned thirty-one, they would all be together in the Hollow.

They'd sworn an oath.

He finished up the morning's work, and because he couldn't get his mind off it, composed a quick e-mail to Gage.

Hey. Where the hell are you? Vegas? Mozambique?
Duluth? Heading out to see Fox. There's a writer
coming into the Hollow to do research on the history,
the legend, and what they're calling the anomalies.
Probably got it handled, but thought you should
know.

    It's twenty-two degrees with a windchill factor of fif-
teen. Wish you were here and I wasn't.

Cal

He'd answer eventually, Cal thought as he sent the
e-mail, then shut down the computer. Could be in five minutes or in five weeks, but Gage would answer.

He began to layer on the outer gear again over a long
and lanky frame passed down by his father. He'd gotten his
outsized feet from dear old Dad, too.

The dark blond hair that tended to go as it chose was
from his mother. He knew that only due to early photos of
her, as she'd been a soft, sunny blonde, perfectly groomed,
throughout his memory.

His eyes, a sharp, occasionally stormy gray, had been
twenty-twenty since his tenth birthday.

Even as he zipped up his parka to head outside, he
thought that the coat was for comfort only. He hadn't had
so much as a sniffle in over twenty years. No flu, no virus,
no hay fever.

He'd fallen out of an apple tree when he'd been twelve.
He'd heard the bone in his arm snap, had felt the breathless
pain.

And he'd felt it knit together again—with more pain—
before he'd made it across the lawn to the house to tell his
mother.

So he'd never told her, he thought as he stepped outside
into the ugly slap of cold. Why upset her?

He covered the three blocks to Fox's office quickly,
shooting out waves or calling back greetings to neighbors
and friends. But he didn't stop for conversation. He might

not get pneumonia or postnasal drip, but he was *freaking* tired of winter.

Gray, ice-crusted snow lay in a dirty ribbon along the curbs, and above, the sky mirrored the brooding color. Some of the houses or businesses had hearts and Valentine wreaths on doors and windows, but they didn't add a lot of cheer with the bare trees and winter-stripped gardens.

The Hollow didn't show to advantage, to Cal's way of thinking, in February.

He walked up the short steps to the little covered porch of the old stone townhouse. The plaque beside the door read: FOX B. O'DELL, ATTORNEY AT LAW.

It was something that always gave Cal a quick jolt and a quick flash of amusement. Even after nearly six years, he couldn't quite get used to it.

The long-haired hippie freak was a goddamn lawyer.

He stepped into the tidy reception area, and there was Alice Hawbaker at the desk. Trim, tidy in her navy suit with its bowed white blouse, her snowcap of hair and no-nonsense bifocals, Mrs. Hawbaker ran the office like a Border collie ran a herd.

She looked sweet and pretty, and she'd bite your ankle if you didn't fall in line.

"Hey, Mrs. Hawbaker. Boy, it is *cold* out there. Looks like we might get some more snow." He unwrapped his scarf. "Hope you and Mr. Hawbaker are keeping warm."

"Warm enough."

He heard something in her voice that had him looking more closely as he pulled off his gloves. When he realized she'd been crying he instinctively stepped to the desk. "Is everything okay? Is—"

"Everything's fine. Just fine. Fox is between appointments. He's in there sulking, so you go right on back."

"Yes, ma'am. Mrs. Hawbaker, if there's anything—"

"Just go right on back," she repeated, then made herself busy with her keyboard.

Beyond the reception area a hallway held a powder room on one side and a library on the other. Straight back,

Fox's office was closed off by a pair of pocket doors. Cal didn't bother to knock.

Fox looked up when the doors slid open. He did appear to be sulking as his gilded eyes were broody and his mouth was in full scowl.

He sat behind his desk, his feet, clad in hiking boots, propped on it. He wore jeans and a flannel shirt open over a white insulated tee. His hair, densely brown, waved around his sharp-featured face.

"What's going on?"

"I'll tell you what's going on. My administrative assistant just gave me her notice."

"What did you do?"

"Me?" Fox shoved back from the desk and opened the minifridge for a can of Coke. He'd never developed a taste for coffee. "Try *we*, brother. We camped out at the Pagan Stone one fateful night, and screwed the monkey."

Cal dropped into a chair. "She's quitting because—"

"Not just quitting. They're leaving the Hollow, she and Mr. Hawbaker. And yeah, because." He took a long, greedy drink the way some men might take a pull on a bottle of whiskey. "That's not the reason she gave me, but that's the reason. She said they decided to move to Minneapolis to be close to their daughter and grandchildren, and that's bogus. Why does a woman heading toward seventy, married to a guy older than dirt, pick up and move north? They've got another kid lives outside of D.C., and they've got strong ties here. I could tell it was bull."

"Because of what she said, or because you took a cruise through her head?"

"First the one, then the other. Don't start on me." Fox gestured with the Coke, then slammed it down on his desk. "I don't poke around for the fun of it. Son of a bitch."

"Maybe they'll change their minds."

"They don't want to go, but they're afraid to stay. They're afraid it'll happen again—which I could tell her it will—and they just don't want to go through it again. I offered her a raise—like I could afford it—offered her the whole month of July off, letting her know that I knew what was at the bottom of it. But they're going. She'll give me until April first. April frickin' Fools," he ranted. "To find somebody else, for her to show them the ropes. I don't know where the damn ropes are, Cal. I don't know half the stuff she does. She just does it. Anyway."

"You've got until April, maybe we'll think of something."

"We haven't thought of the solution to this in twenty years plus."

"I meant your office problem. But yeah, I've been thinking a lot about the other." Rising, he walked to Fox's window, looked out on the quiet side street. "We've got to end it. This time we've got to end it. Maybe talking to this writer will help. Laying it out to someone objective, someone not involved."

"Asking for trouble."

"Maybe it is, but trouble's coming anyway. Five months to go. We're supposed to meet her at the house." Cal glanced at his watch. "Forty minutes."

"We?" Fox looked blank for a moment. "That's today? See, see, I didn't tell Mrs. H, so it didn't get written down somewhere. I've got a deposition in an hour."

"Why don't you use your damn BlackBerry?"

"Because it doesn't follow my simple Earth logic. Reschedule the writer. I'm clear after four."

"It's okay, I can handle it. If she wants more, I'll see about setting up a dinner, so keep tonight open."

"Be careful what you say."

"Yeah, yeah, I'm going to. But I've been thinking. We've been careful about that for a long time. Maybe it's time to be a little reckless."

"You sound like Gage."

"Fox . . . I've already started having the dreams again."

Fox blew out a breath. "I was hoping that was just me."

"When we were seventeen they started about a week before our birthday, then when we were twenty-four, over a month. Now, five months out. Every time it gets stronger.

I'm afraid if we don't find the way, this time could be the last for us, and the town."

"Have you talked to Gage?"

"I just e-mailed him. I didn't tell him about the dreams. You do it. Find out if he's having them, too, wherever the hell he is. Get him home, Fox. I think we need him back. I don't think we can wait until summer this time. I gotta go."

"Watch your step with the writer," Fox called out as Cal started for the door. "Get more than you give."

"I can handle it," Cal repeated.

QUINN BLACK EASED HER MINI COOPER OFF THE exit ramp and hit the usual barrage at the interchange. Pancake House, Wendy's, McDonald's, KFC.

With great affection, she thought of a Quarter Pounder, with a side of really salty fries, and—natch—a Diet Coke to ease the guilt. But since that would be breaking her vow to eat fast food no more than once a month, she wasn't going to indulge.

"There now, don't you feel righteous?" she asked herself with only one wistful glance in the rearview at the lovely Golden Arches.

Her love of the quick and the greasy had sent her on an odyssey of fad diets, unsatisfying supplements, and miracle workout tapes through her late teens and early twenties. Until she'd finally slapped herself silly, tossed out all her diet books, her diet articles, her I LOST TWENTY POUNDS IN TWO WEEKS—AND YOU CAN, TOO! ads, and put herself on the path to sensible eating and exercising.

Lifestyle change, she reminded herself. She'd made a lifestyle change.

But boy, she missed those Quarter Pounders more than she missed her ex-fiancé.

Then again, who wouldn't?

She glanced at the GPS hooked to her dashboard, then

over at the directions she'd printed out from Caleb Hawkins's e-mail. So far, they were in tandem.

She reached down for the apple serving as her mid-morning snack. Apples were filling, Quinn thought as she bit in. They were good for you, and they were tasty.

And they were no Quarter Pounder.

In order to keep her mind off the devil, she considered what she hoped to accomplish on this first face-to-face interview with one of the main players in the odd little town of Hawkins Hollow.

No, not fair to call it odd, she reminded herself. Objectivity first. Maybe her research leaned her toward the odd label, but there would be no making up her mind until she'd seen for herself, done her interviews, taken her notes, scoped out the local library. And, maybe most important, seen the Pagan Stone in person.

She loved poking at all the corners and cobwebs of small towns, digging down under the floorboards for secrets and surprises, listening to the gossip, the local lore and legend.

She'd made a tiny name for herself doing a series of articles on quirky, off-the-mainstream towns for a small press magazine called *Detours*. And since her professional appetite was as well-developed as her bodily one, she'd taken a risky leap and written a book, following the same theme, but focusing on a single town in Maine reputed to be haunted by the ghosts of twin sisters who'd been murdered in a boardinghouse in 1843.

The critics had called the result "engaging" and "good, spooky fun," except for the ones who'd deemed it "preposterous" and "convoluted."

She'd followed it up with a book highlighting a small town in Louisiana where the descendent of a voodoo priestess served as mayor and faith healer. And, Quinn had discovered, had been running a very successful prostitution ring.

But Hawkins Hollow—she could just feel it—was going to be bigger, better, meatier.

She couldn't wait to sink her teeth in.

The fast-food joints, the businesses, the ass-to-elbow houses gave way to bigger lawns, bigger homes, and to fields sleeping under the dreary sky.

The road wound, dipped and lifted, then veered straight again. She saw a sign for the Antietam Battlefield, something else she meant to investigate and research firsthand. She'd found little snippets about incidents during the Civil War in and around Hawkins Hollow.

She wanted to know more.

When her GPS and Caleb's directions told her to turn, she turned, following the next road past a grove of naked trees, a scatter of houses, and the farms that always made her smile with their barns and silos and fenced paddocks.

She'd have to find a small town to explore in the Midwest next time. A haunted farm, or the weeping spirit of a milkmaid.

She nearly ignored the directions to turn when she saw the sign for Hawkins Hollow (est. 1648). As with the Quarter Pounder, her heart longed to indulge, to drive into town rather than turn off toward Caleb Hawkins's place. But she hated to be late, and if she got caught up exploring the streets, the corners, the *look* of the town, she certainly would be late for her first appointment.

"Soon," she promised, and turned to take the road winding by the woods she knew held the Pagan Stone at their heart.

It gave her a quick shiver, and that was strange. Strange to realize that shiver had been fear and not the anticipation she always felt with a new project.

As she followed the twists of the road, she glanced with some unease toward the dark and denuded trees. And hit the brakes hard when she shifted her eyes back to the road and saw something rush out in front of her.

She thought she saw a child—oh God, oh God—then thought it was a dog. And then . . . it was nothing. Nothing at all on the road, nothing rushing to the field beyond. Nothing there but herself and her wildly beating heart in the little red car.

"Trick of the eye," she told herself, and didn't believe it. "Just one of those things."

But she restarted the car that had stalled when she'd slammed the brakes, then eased to the strip of dirt that served as the shoulder of the road. She pulled out her notebook, noted the time, and wrote down exactly what she thought she'd seen.

Young boy, abt ten. Lng blck hair, red eyes. He LOOKED right at me. Did I blink? Shut my eyes? Opened, & saw lrg blck dog, not boy. Then poof. Nothing there.

Cars passed her without incident as she sat a few moments more, waited for the trembling to stop.

Intrepid writer balks at first possible phenom, she thought, turns around, and drives her adorable red car to the nearest Mickey D's for a fat-filled antidote to nerves.

She could do that, she considered. Nobody could charge her with a felony and throw her into prison. And if she did that, she wouldn't have her next book, or any self-respect.

"Man up, Quinn," she ordered. "You've seen spooks before."

Steadier, she swung back out on the road, and made the next turn. The road was narrow and twisty with trees looming on both sides. She imagined it would be lovely in the spring and summer, with the green dappling, or after a snowfall with all those trees ermine drenched. But under a dull gray sky the woods seemed to crowd the road, bare branches just waiting to reach out and strike, as if they and only they were allowed to live there.

As if to enforce the sensation, no other car passed, and when she turned off her radio as the music seemed too loud, the only sound was the keening curse of the wind.

Should've called it Spooky Hollow, she decided, and nearly missed the turn into the gravel lane.

Why, she wondered, would anyone *choose* to live here? Amid all those dense, thrusting trees where bleak pools of snow huddled to hide from the sun? Where the only sound was the warning growl of Nature. Everything was brown and gray and moody.

She bumped over a little bridge spanning a curve of a creek, followed the slight rise of the stingy lane.

There was the house, exactly as advertised.

It sat on what she would have termed a knoll rather than a hill, with the front slope tamed into step-down terraces decked with shrubs she imagined put on a hell of a show in the spring and summer.

There wasn't a lawn, so to speak, and she thought Hawkins had been smart to go with the thick mulch and shrubs and trees skirting the front instead of the traditional grass that would probably be a pain in the ass to mow and keep clear of weeds.

She approved of the deck that wrapped around the front and sides, and she'd bet the rear as well. She liked the earthy tones of the stone and the generous windows.

It sat like it belonged there, content and well-settled in the woods.

She pulled up beside an aging Chevy pickup, got out of her car to stand and take a long view.

And understood why someone would choose this spot. There was, unquestionably, an aura of spookiness, especially for one who was inclined to see and feel such things. But there was considerable charm as well, and a sense of solitude that was far from lonely. She could imagine very well sitting on that front deck some summer evening, drinking a cold one, and wallowing in the silence.

Before she could move toward the house, the front door opened.

The sense of déjà vu was vivid, almost dizzying. He stood there at the door of the cabin, the blood like red flowers on his shirt.

We can stay no longer.

The words sounded in her head, clear, and in a voice she somehow knew.

"Miss Black?"

She snapped back. There was no cabin, and the man standing on the lovely deck of his charming house had no blood blooming on him. There was no force of great love and great grief shining in his eyes.

And still, she had to lean back against her car for a minute and catch her breath. "Yeah, hi. I was just . . . admiring the house. Great spot."

"Thanks. Any trouble finding it?"

"No, no. Your directions were perfect." And, of course, it was ridiculous to be having this conversation outside in the freezing wind. From the quizzical look on his face, he obviously felt the same.

She pushed off the car, worked up what she hoped was a sane and pleasant expression as she walked to the trio of wooden steps.

And wasn't he a serious cutie? she realized as she finally focused on the reality. All that windblown hair and those strong gray eyes. Add the crooked smile, the long, lean body in jeans and flannel, and a woman might be tempted to hang a SOLD! sign around his neck.

She stepped up, held out a hand. "Quinn Black, thanks for meeting with me, Mr. Hawkins."

"Cal." He took her hand, shook it, then held it as he gestured to the door. "Let's get you out of the wind."

They stepped directly into a living room that managed to be cozy and male at the same time. The generous sofa faced the big front windows, and the chairs looked as though they'd allow an ass to sink right in. Tables and lamps probably weren't antiques, but looked to be something a grandmother might have passed down when she got the urge to redecorate her own place.

There was even a little stone fireplace with the requisite large mutt sprawled sleeping in front of it.

"Let me take your coat."

"Is your dog in a coma?" Quinn asked when the dog didn't move a muscle.

"No. Lump leads an active and demanding internal life that requires long periods of rest."

"I see."

"Want some coffee?"

"That'd be great. So would the bathroom. Long drive."

"First right."

"Thanks."

She closed herself into a small, spotlessly clean powder room as much to pull herself back together from a couple of psychic shocks as to pee.

"Okay, Quinn," she whispered. "Here we go."

Four

~᷍~

HE'D READ HER WORK; HE'D STUDIED HER AU-
thor photos and used Google to get some background, to
read her interviews. Cal wasn't one to agree to talk to any
sort of writer, journalist, reporter, Internet blogger about
the Hollow, himself, or much of anything else without doing a thorough check.

He'd found her books and articles entertaining. He'd
enjoyed her obvious affection for small towns, had been intrigued by her interest and treatment of lore, legend, and
things that went bump in the night.

He liked the fact that she still wrote the occasional article for the magazine that had given her a break when she'd
still been in college. It spoke of loyalty.

He hadn't been disappointed that her author photo had
shown her to be a looker, with a sexy tumble of honey blond
hair, bright blue eyes, and the hint of a fairly adorable over-
bite.

The photo hadn't come close.

She probably wasn't beautiful, he thought as he poured coffee. He'd have to get another look when, hopefully, his brain wouldn't go to fuzz, then decide about that.

What he did know, unquestionably, was she just plain radiated energy and—to his fuzzed brain—sex.

But maybe that was because she was built, another thing the photo hadn't gotten across. The lady had some truly excellent curves.

And it wasn't as if he hadn't seen curves on a woman before or, in fact, seen his share of naked female curves alive and in person. So why was he standing in his own kitchen frazzled because an attractive, fully dressed woman was in his house? For professional purposes.

"Jesus, grow up, Hawkins."

"Sorry?"

He actually jumped. She was in the kitchen, a few steps behind him, smiling that million-watt smile.

"Were you talking to yourself? I do that, too. Why do people think we're crazy?"

"Because they want to suck us into talking to them."

"You're probably right." Quinn shoved back that long spill of blond.

Cal saw he was right. She wasn't beautiful. The top-heavy mouth, the slightly crooked nose, the oversized eyes weren't elements of traditional beauty. He couldn't label her pretty, either. It was too simple and sweet a word. Cute didn't do it.

All he could think of was *hot*, but that might have been his brain blurring again.

"I didn't ask how you take your coffee."

"Oh. I don't suppose you have two percent milk."

"I often wonder why anybody does."

With an easy laugh that shot straight to his bloodstream, she wandered over to study the view outside the glass doors that led—as she'd suspected—to the rear portion of the circling deck. "Which also means you probably don't have any fake sugar. Those little pink, blue, or yellow packets?"

"Fresh out. I could offer you actual milk and actual sugar."

"You could." And hadn't she eaten an apple like a good girl? "And I could accept. Let me ask you something else, just to satisfy my curiosity. Is your house always so clean and tidy, or did you do all this just for me?"

He got out the milk. "*Tidy*'s a girlie word. I prefer the term *organized*. I like organization. Besides." He offered her a spoon for the sugar bowl. "My mother could—and does—drop by unexpectedly. If my house wasn't clean, she'd ground me."

"If I don't call my mother once a week, she assumes I've been hacked to death by an ax murderer." Quinn held herself to one scant spoon of sugar. "It's nice, isn't it? Those long and elastic family ties."

"I like them. Why don't we go sit in the living room by the fire?"

"Perfect. So, how long have you lived here? In this particular house," she added as they carried their mugs out of the kitchen.

"A couple of years."

"Not much for neighbors?"

"Neighbors are fine, and I spend a lot of time in town. I like the quiet now and then."

"People do. I do myself, now and again." She took one of the living room chairs, settled back. "I guess I'm surprised other people haven't had the same idea as you, and plugged in a few more houses around here."

"There was talk of it a couple of times. Never panned out."

He's being cagey, Quinn decided. "Because?"

"Didn't turn out to be financially attractive, I guess."

"Yet here you are."

"My grandfather owned the property, some acres of Hawkins Wood. He left it to me."

"So you had this house built."

"More or less. I'd liked the spot." Private when he needed to be private. Close to the woods where everything had changed. "I know some people in the trade, and we put the house up. How's the coffee?"

"It's terrific. You cook, too?"

"Coffee's my specialty. I read your books."

"How were they?"

"I liked them. You probably know you wouldn't be here if I hadn't."

"Which would've made it a lot tougher to write the book I want to write. You're a Hawkins, a descendent of the founder of the settlement that became the village that became the town. And one of the main players in the more recent unexplained incidents related to the town. I've done a lot of research on the history, the lore, the legends, and the various explanations," she said, and reached in the bag that served as her purse and her briefcase. Taking out a minirecorder, she switched it on, set it on the table between them.

Her smile was full of energy and interest when she set her notebook on her lap, flipped pages to a clear one. "So, tell me, Cal, about what happened the week of July seventh, nineteen eighty-seven, ninety-four, and two thousand one."

The tape recorder made him . . . itchy. "Dive right in, don't you?"

"I love knowing things. July seventh is your birthday. It's also the birthday of Fox O'Dell and Gage Turner—born the same year as you, who grew up in Hawkins Hollow with you. I read articles that reported you, O'Dell, and Turner were responsible for alerting the fire department on July eleventh, nineteen eighty-seven, when the elementary school was set on fire, and also responsible for saving the life of one Marian Lister who was inside the school at the time."

She continued to look straight into his eyes as she spoke. He found it interesting she didn't need to refer to notes, and that she didn't appear to need the little breaks from direct eye contact.

"Initial reports indicated the three of you were originally suspected of starting the fire, but it was proven Miss

Lister herself was responsible. She suffered second-degree burns on nearly thirty percent of her body as well as a concussion. You and your friends, three ten-year-old boys, dragged her out and called the fire department. Miss Lister was, at that time, a twenty-five-year-old fourth-grade teacher with no history of criminal behavior or mental illness. Is that all correct information?"

She got her facts in order, Cal noted. Such as the facts were known. They fell far short of the abject terror of entering that burning school, of finding the pretty Miss Lister cackling madly as she ran through the flames. Of how it felt to chase her through those hallways as her clothes burned.

"She had a breakdown."

"Obviously." Smile in place, Quinn lifted her eyebrows. "There were also over a dozen nine-one-one calls on domestic abuse during that single week, more than previously had been reported in Hawkins Hollow in the six preceding months. There were two suicides and four attempted suicides, numerous accounts of assault, three reported rapes, and a hit-and-run. Several homes and businesses were vandalized. None—virtually none—of the people involved in any of the reported crimes or incidents has a clear memory of the events. Some speculate the town suffered from mass hysteria or hallucinations or an unknown infection taken through food or water. What do you think?"

"I think I was ten years old and pretty much scared shitless."

She offered that brief, sunny smile. "I bet." Then it was gone. "You were seventeen in nineteen ninety-four when during the week of July seventh another—let's say outbreak—occurred. Three people were murdered, one of them apparently hanged in the town park, but no one came forward as a witness or to admit participation. There were more rapes, more beatings, more suicides, two houses burned to the ground. There were reports that you, O'Dell, and Turner were able to get some of the wounded and traumatized onto a school bus and transport them to the hospital. Is that accurate?"

"As far as it goes."

"I'm looking to go further. In two thousand one—"

"I know the pattern," Cal interrupted.

"Every seven years," Quinn said with a nod. "For seven nights. Days—according again to what I can ascertain—little happens. But from sundown to sunset, all hell breaks loose. It's hard to believe that it's a coincidence this anomaly happens every seven years, with its start on your birthday. Seven's considered a magickal number by those who profess to magicks, black and white. You were born on the seventh day of the seventh month of nineteen seventy-seven."

"If I knew the answers, I'd stop it from happening. If I knew the answers, I wouldn't be talking to you. I'm talking to you because maybe, just maybe, you'll find them, or help find them."

"Then tell me what happened, tell me what you *do* know, even what you think or sense."

Cal set his coffee aside, leaned forward to look deep into her eyes. "Not on a first date."

Smart-ass, she thought with considerable approval. "Fine. Next time I'll buy you dinner first. But now, how about playing guide and taking me to the Pagan Stone."

"It's too late in the day. It's a two-hour hike from here. We wouldn't make it there and back before dark."

"I'm not afraid of the dark."

His eyes went very cool. "You would be. I'll tell you this, there are places in these woods no one goes after dark, not any time of the year."

She felt the prick of ice at the base of her spine. "Have you ever seen a boy, about the age you'd have been in eighty-seven. A boy with dark hair. And red eyes." She saw by the way Cal paled she'd flicked a switch. "You have seen him."

"Why do you ask about that?"

"Because I saw him."

Now Cal pushed to his feet, paced to the window, stared

out at the woods. The light was dimmer, duller already than it had been an hour before.

They'd never told anyone about the boy—or the man—whatever form the thing chose to take. Yes, he'd seen him, and not only during that one hellish week every seven years.

He'd seen it in dreams. He'd seen it out of the corner of his eye, or loping through the woods. Or with its face pressed to the dark glass of his bedroom window . . . and its mouth grinning.

But no one, no one but he, Fox, and Gage had ever seen it in the between times.

Why had she?

"When and where did you see him?"

"Today, just before I turned off onto Pagan Road. He ran in front of my car. Came out of nowhere. That's what people always say, but this time it's true. A boy, then it wasn't a boy but a dog. Then it wasn't anything. There was nothing there."

He heard her rise, and when he turned was simply stunned to see that brilliant smile on her face. "And this kind of thing makes you happy?"

"It makes me thrilled. Excited. I'm saying wow! I had myself what we could call a close encounter with an unspecified phenomenon. Scary, I grant you, but again, wow. This sort of thing completely winds me up."

"I can see that."

"I knew there was something here, and I thought it was big. But to have it confirmed, the first day out, that's hitting the mother lode with the first whack of the pick."

"I haven't confirmed anything."

"Your face did." She picked up her recorder, turned it off. He wasn't going to tell her anything today. Cautious man, Caleb Hawkins. "I need to get into town, check into the hotel, get a lay of the land. Why don't I buy you that dinner tonight?"

She moved fast, and he made a habit of taking his time. "Why don't you take some time to settle in? We can talk about dinner and so on in a couple days."

"I love a man who's hard to get." She slipped her recorder, her notepad back in her bag. "I guess I'll need my coat."

After he'd brought it to her, she studied him as she shrugged it on. "You know, when you first came outside, I had the strangest sensation. I thought I recognized you, that I'd known you before. That you'd waited for me before. It was very strong. Did you feel anything like that?"

"No. But maybe I was too busy thinking, she looks better than her picture."

"Really? Nice, because I looked terrific in that picture. Thanks for the coffee." She glanced back to the dog who'd snored lightly the entire time they'd talked. "See you later, Lump. Don't work so hard."

He walked her out. "Quinn," he said as she started down the stairs. "Don't get any ideas about Lois Laning it and trying to find the Pagan Stone on your own. You don't know the woods. I'll take you there myself, sometime this week."

"Tomorrow?"

"I can't, I've got a full plate. Day after if you're in a hurry."

"I almost always am." She walked backward toward her car so she could keep him in view. "What time?"

"Let's say we'll meet here at nine, weather permitting."

"That's a date." She opened her car door. "The house suits you, by the way. Country boy with more style than pretention. I like it."

He watched her drive off—strange and sexy Quinn Black.

And he stood for a long time watching the light go dimmer in the woods where he'd made his home.

CAL HEADED FOX OFF WITH A PHONE CALL AND arranged to meet him at the bowling alley. Since the Pin Boys and the Alley Cats were having a league game on lanes one and two, he and Fox could have dinner and a show at the grill.

Added to it, there was little as noisy as a bowling alley, so their conversation would be covered by the crash of balls against pins, the hoots and hollers.

"First, let's backtrack into the land of logic for a minute." Fox took a swig of his beer. "She could've made it up to get a reaction."

"How did she know what to make up?"

"During the Seven, there are people who see it—who've said they did before it starts to fade on them. She got wind."

"I don't think so, Fox. Some talked about seeing something—boy, man, woman, dog, wolf—"

"The rat the size of a Doberman," Fox remembered.

"Thanks for bringing that one back. But no one ever claimed they'd seen it before or after the Seven. No one but us, and we've never told anyone." Cal arched his brow in question.

"No. You think I'm going to spread it around that I see red-eyed demons? I'd just rake in the clients that way."

"She's smart. I don't see why she'd claim to have seen it, outside the norm—ha-ha—if she hadn't. Plus she was psyched about it. Juiced up. So, let's accept she did and continue to dwell in the land of logic. One logical assumption is that the bastard's stronger, we know he will be. But strong enough to push out of the Seven into the between time."

Fox brooded over his beer. "I don't like that logic."

"Second option could be she's somehow connected. To one of us, the town, the incident at the Pagan Stone."

"I like that better. Everyone's connected. It's not just Kevin Bacon. If you work at it, you can put a handful of degrees between almost any two people." Thoughtful, Fox picked up his second slice of pizza. "Maybe she's a distant cousin. I've got cousins up the wazoo and so do you. Gage, not so much, but there's some out there."

"Possible. But why would a distant cousin see something none of our immediate family has? They'd tell us, Fox. They all know what's coming better and clearer than anyone else."

"Reincarnation. That's not off the Planet Logic, considering. Besides, reincarnation's big in the family O'Dell. Maybe she was there when it all happened. Another life."

"I don't discount anything. But more to the point, why is she here now? And will it help us put a goddamn end to this?"

"It's going to take more than an hour's chat in front of the fire to figure that out. I don't guess you heard from Gage."

"Not yet. He'll be in touch. I'm going to take her out to the stone day after tomorrow."

"Leaping forward fast, Cal."

Cal shook his head. "If I don't take her soon enough, she'll try it on her own. If something happened . . . We can't be responsible for that."

"We are responsible—isn't that the point? On some level it's on us." Frowning now, he watched Don Myers, of Myers Plumbing, make a seven-ten split to appropriate hoots and shouts. All three hundred twenty pounds of Myers did a flab-wriggling victory dance that was not a pretty sight.

"You go on," Fox said quietly, "day after day, doing what you do, living your life, making your life. Eating pizza, scratching your ass, getting laid if you're lucky. But you know, on some level you try to keep buried just to get through, that it's coming back. That some of the people you see on the street every day, maybe they won't make it through the next round. Maybe we won't. What the hell." He rapped his beer against Cal's. "We've got the now, plus five months to figure this out."

"I can try to go back again."

"Not unless Gage is here. We can't risk it unless we're together. It's not worth it, Cal. The other times you only got bits and pieces, and took a hell of a beating for it."

"Older and wiser now. And I'm thinking, if it's showing itself now—our dreams, what happened to Quinn—it's expending energy. I might get more than I have before."

"Not without Gage. That's . . . Hmm," he said as his attention wandered over his friend's shoulder. "Fresh flowers."

Glancing back, Cal saw Quinn standing behind lane one, her coat open and a bemused expression on her face as she watched Myers, graceful as a hippo in toe shoes, make his approach and release his lucky red ball.

"That's Quinn."

"Yeah, I recognized her. I read the books, too. She's hotter than her picture, and that was pretty hot."

"I saw her first."

Fox snorted, shifted his eyes to sneer at Cal. "Dude, it's not about who saw her first, it's who *she* sees. I pull out the full power of my sexual charm, and you'll be the Invisible Man."

"Shit. The full power of your sexual charm wouldn't light up a forty-watt bulb."

Cal pushed off the stool when Quinn walked toward him.

"So this is why I got the brush-off tonight," she said. "Pizza, beer, and bowling."

"The Hawkins Hollow hat trick. I'm on manager duty tonight. Quinn, this is Fox O'Dell."

"The second part of the triad." She shook Fox's hand. "Now I'm doubly glad I decided to check out what seems to be the town's hot spot. Mind if I join you?"

"Wouldn't have it any other way. Buy you a beer?" Fox asked.

"Boy, could you, but . . . make it a light one."

Cal stepped back to swing around the counter. "I'll take care of it. Anything to go with it? Pizza?"

"Oh." She looked at the pizza on the counter with eyes that went suddenly dewy. "Um, I don't suppose you have any with whole-wheat crust and low-fat mozzarella?"

"Health nut?" Fox asked.

"Just the opposite." Quinn bit her bottom lip. "I'm in a lifestyle change. Damn it, that really looks good. How about if we cut one of those slices in half." She sawed the side of her hand over the plate.

"No problem."

Cal got a pizza cutter and slid it down a slice.

"I love fat and sugar like a mother loves her child," Quinn told Fox. "I'm trying to eat more sensibly."

"My parents are vegetarians," Fox said as they each picked up a half slice. "I grew up on tofu and alfalfa."

"God. That's so sad."

"Which is why he ate at my house whenever he could manage it, and spent all his money on Little Debbies and Slim Jims."

"Little Debbies are food for the gods." She smiled at Cal when he set her beer on the counter. "I like your town. I took a walk up and down several blocks of Main Street. And since I was freezing my ass off, went back to the really charming Hotel Hollow, sat on my windowsill, and watched the world go by."

"Nice world," Cal said, "that moves a little slow this time of year."

"Umm," was her agreement as she took a minute bite of the point of her narrow triangle of pizza. She closed her eyes on a sigh. "It *is* good. I was hoping, being bowling-alley pizza, it wouldn't be."

"We do okay. Gino's across the street is better, and has more selections."

She opened her eyes to find him smiling at her. "That's a lousy thing to tell a woman in the middle of a lifestyle change."

Cal leaned on the counter, bringing that smile a little closer, and Quinn found herself losing her train of thought. He had the best quick and crooked grin, the kind a woman wanted to take a testing nibble of.

Before he could speak, someone hailed him, and those eyes of quiet gray glanced away from hers toward the end of the counter. "Be right back."

"Well." Jeez, her pulse had actually tripped. "Alone at last," she said to Fox. "So you and Cal and the as-yet-absent Gage Turner have been friends since you were kids."

"Babies, actually. In utero, technically. Cal's and Gage's mother got together with mine when my mother was teaching a Lamaze class. They had a kind of roundup with the

class a couple months after everyone delivered the packages, and the deal about the three of us being born on the
same day, same time came out."

"Instant mommy bonding."

"I don't know. They always got along, even though you
could say they all came from different planets. They were
friendly without being friends. My parents and Cal's still
get along fine, and Cal's dad kept Gage's employed when
nobody else in town would've hired him."

"Why wouldn't anyone have hired him?"

Fox debated for a minute, drank some of his beer. "It's
no secret," he decided. "He drank. He's been sober for a
while now. About five years, I guess. I always figured Mr.
Hawkins gave him work because that's just the way he is,
and, in a big part, he did it for Gage. Anyway, I don't remember the three of us not being friends."

"No 'you like him better than me,' major falling-outs or
your basic and usual drifting apart?"

"We fought—fight still—now and then." Didn't all
brothers? Fox thought. "Had your expected pissy periods,
but no. We're connected. Nothing can snap that connection.
And the 'you like him better than me'? Mostly a girl thing."

"But Gage doesn't live here anymore."

"Gage doesn't live anywhere, really. He's the original
footloose guy."

"And you? The hometown boy."

"I thought about the bright lights, big city routine, even
gave it a short try." He glanced over in the direction of the
moans coming from one of the Alley Cats who had failed
to pick up a spare. "I like the Hollow. I even like my family, most of the time. And I like, as it turns out, practicing
small-town law."

Truth, Quinn decided, but not the whole truth of it.
"Have you seen the kid with the red eyes?"

Off balance, Fox set down the beer he'd lifted to drink.
"That's a hell of a segue."

"Maybe. But that wasn't an answer."

"I'm going to postpone my answer until further deliberation. Cal's taking point on this."

"And you're not sure you like the idea of him, or anyone, talking to me about what may or may not go on here."

"I'm not sure what purpose it serves. So I'm weighing the information as it comes in."

"Fair enough." She glanced over as Cal came back. "Well, boys, thanks for the beer and the slice. I should get back to my adorable room."

"You bowl?" Cal asked her, and she laughed.

"Absolutely not."

"Oh-oh," Fox said under his breath.

Cal walked around the counter, blocking Quinn before she could slide off the stool. He took a long, considering look at her boots. "Seven and a half, right?"

"Ah . . ." She looked down at her boots herself. "On the money. Good eye."

"Stay." He tapped her on the shoulder. "I'll be right back."

Quinn frowned after him, then looked at Fox. "He is *not* going to get me a pair of bowling shoes."

"Oh yeah, he is. You mocked the tradition, which—if you give him any tiny opening—he'll tell you started five thousand years ago. Then he'll explain its evolution and so on and so on."

"Well, Christ," was all Quinn could think to say.

Cal brought back a pair of maroon and cream bowling shoes, and another, larger pair of dark brown ones, which were obviously his. "Lane five's open. You want in, Fox?"

"Sadly, I have a brief to finish writing. I'll rain-check it. See you later, Quinn."

Cal tucked the shoes under his arm, then, taking Quinn's hand, pulled her off the stool. "When's the last time you bowled?" he asked as he led her across the alley to an open lane.

"I think I was fourteen. Group date, which didn't go well, as the object of my affection, Nathan Hobbs, only had eyes for the incessantly giggly and already well-developed Missy Dover."

"You can't let previous heartbreak spoil your enjoyment."

"But I didn't like the bowling part either."

"That was then." Cal sat her down on the smooth wooden bench, slid on beside her. "You'll have a better time with it tonight. Ever make a strike?"

"Still talking bowling? No."

"You will, and there's nothing much that beats the feeling of that first strike."

"How about sex with Hugh Jackman?"

He stopped tying his bowling shoe to stare over at her. "You had sex with Hugh Jackman?"

"No, but I'm willing to bet any amount of money that having sex with Hugh Jackman would, for me, beat out the feeling of knocking down ten pins with one ball."

"Okay. But I'm willing to bet—let's make it ten bucks—that when you throw a strike, you'll admit it's up there on the Thrill-O-Meter."

"First, it's highly unlikely I'll throw anything resembling a strike. Second, I could lie."

"You will. And you won't. Change your shoes, Blondie."

Five

~

IT WASN'T AS RIDICULOUS AS SHE'D ASSUMED IT
would be. Silly, yes, but she had plenty of room for silly.

The balls were mottled black—the small ones without
the three holes. The job was to heave it down the long polished alley toward the red-necked pins he called Duck
Pins.

He watched as she walked up to the foul line, swung
back, and did the heave.

The ball bounced a couple of times before it toppled
into the gutter.

"Okay." She turned, tossed back her hair. "Your turn."

"You get two more balls per frame."

"Woo-hoo."

He shot her the quick grin. "Let's work on your delivery
and follow-through, then we'll tackle approach." He
walked toward her with another ball as he spoke. He
handed her the ball. "Hold it with both hands," he instructed as he turned her around to face the pins. "Now you
want to take a step forward with your left foot, bend your

knees like you were doing a squat, but bend over from the waist."

He was snuggled up right behind her now, his front sort of bowing over her back. She tipped her face around to meet his eyes.

"You use this routine to hit on women, right?"

"Absolutely. Eighty-five percent success ratio. You're going to want to aim for the front pin. You can worry about the pockets and the sweet spot later. Now you're just going to bring your right arm back, then sweep it forward with your fingers aimed at the front pin. Let the ball go, following your fingers."

"Hmm." But she tried it. This time the ball didn't bounce straight into the gutter, but actually stayed on the lane long enough to bump down the two pins on the far right.

Since the woman in the next lane, who *had* to be sixty if she was a day, slid gracefully to the foul line, released, and knocked down seven pins, Quinn didn't feel like celebrating.

"Better."

"Two balls, two pins. I don't think that earns my bootie dance."

"Since I'm looking forward to your bootie dance, I'll help you do better yet. More from your shoulder down this time. Nice perfume," he added before he walked back to get her another ball.

"Thanks." Stride, bend, swing, release, she thought. And actually managed to knock down the end pin on the other side of the alley.

"Overcompensated." He hit the reset button. The grate came down, pins were swept off with a lot of clattering, and another full triangle thudded into place.

"She knocked them all down." Quinn gave a head nod toward the woman in the next lane who'd taken her seat. "She didn't seem all that excited."

"Mrs. Keefafer? Bowls twice a week, and has become

jaded. On the outside. Inside, believe me, she's doing her bootie dance."

"If you say so."

He adjusted Quinn's shoulders, shifted her hips. And yeah, she could see why he had such a high success rate with this routine. Eventually, after countless attempts, she was able to take down multiple pins that took odd bites out of the triangle.

There was a wall of noise, the low thunder of balls rolling, the sharp clatter of pins, hoots and cheers from bowlers and onlookers, the bright bells of a pinball machine.

She smelled beer and wax, and the gooey orange cheese—a personal favorite—from the nachos someone munched on in the next lane.

Timeless, all-American, she mused, absently drafting an article on the experience. Centuries-old sport—she'd need to research that part—to good, clean, family fun.

She thought she had the hang of it, more or less, though she was shallow enough to throw a deliberate gutter ball here and there so Cal would adjust her stance.

As he did, she considered changing the angle of the article from family fun to the sexiness of bowling. The idea made her grin as she took her position.

Then it happened. She released the ball and it rolled down the center of the alley. Surprised, she took a step back. Then another with her arms going up to clamp on the sides of her head.

Something tingled in her belly as her heartbeat sped up.

"Oh. Oh. Look! It's going to—"

There was a satisfying *crack* and *crash* as ball slapped pins and pins tumbled in all directions. Bumping into each other, rolling, spinning, until the last fell with a slow, drunken sway.

"Well, my *God!*" She actually bounced on the toes of her rented shoes. "Did you see that? Did you—" And when she spun around, a look of stunned delight on her face, he was grinning at her.

"Son of a bitch," she muttered. "I owe you ten bucks."

"You learn fast. Want to try an approach?"

She wandered back toward him. "I believe I'm . . . spent. But I may come by some evening for lesson number two."

"Happy to oblige." Sitting hip-to-hip, they changed shoes. "I'll walk you back to the hotel."

"All right."

He got his coat, and on the way out shot a wave at the skinny young guy behind the shoe rental counter. "Back in ten."

"Quiet," she said the minute they stepped outside. "Just listen to all that quiet."

"The noise is part of the fun and the quiet after part of the reward."

"Did you ever want to do anything else, or did you grow up with a burning desire to manage a bowling alley?"

"Family fun center," he corrected. "We have an arcade—pinball, skee-ball, video games, and a section for kids under six. We do private parties—birthday parties, bachelor parties, wedding receptions—"

"Wedding receptions?"

"Sure. Bar mitzvahs, bat mitzvahs, anniversaries, corporate parties."

Definitely meat for an article, she realized. "A lot of arms on one body."

"You could say that."

"So why aren't you married and raising the next generation of Bowl-a-Rama kingpins, pun intended."

"Love has eluded me."

"Aw."

Despite the biting cold, it was pleasant to walk beside a man who naturally fit his stride to hers, to watch the clouds of their breath puff out, then merge together before the wind tore them to nothing.

He had an easy way about him and killer eyes, so there were worse things than feeling her toes go numb with cold in boots she knew were more stylish than practical.

"Are you going to be around if I think of some pertinent question to ask you tomorrow?"

"'Round and about," he told her. "I can give you my cell phone number if—"

"Wait." She dug into her bag and came out with her own phone. Still walking, she punched a few keys. "Shoot."

He rattled it off. "I'm aroused by a woman who not only immediately finds what she's looking for in the mysterious depths of her purse, but who can skillfully operate electronic devices."

"Is that a sexist remark?"

"No. My mother always knows where everything is, but is still defeated by the universal remote. My sister Jen can operate anything from a six-speed to a wireless mouse, but can never find anything without a twenty-minute hunt, and my other sister, Marly, can't find anything, ever, and gets intimidated by her electric can opener. And here you are, stirring me up by being able to do both."

"I've always been a siren." She tucked her phone back in her bag as they turned to the steps leading to the long front porch of the hotel. "Thanks for the escort."

"No problem."

There was one of those beats; she recognized it. Both of them wondering, did they shake hands, just turn and go, or give in to curiosity and lean into a kiss.

"Let's stay to the safe road for now," she decided. "I admit, I like the look of your mouth, but moving on that's bound to tangle things up before I really get started on what brought me here."

"It's a damn shame you're right about that." He dipped his hands into his pockets. "So I'll just say good night. I'll wait, make sure you get inside."

"Good night." She walked up the steps to the door, eased it open. Then glanced back to see him standing, hands still in his pockets, with the old-fashioned streetlight spotlighting him.

Oh, yeah, she thought, it was a damn shame.

"See you soon."

He waited until the door shut behind her, then taking a couple of steps, studied the windows of the second and third floor. She'd said her window faced Main Street, but he wasn't sure what level she was on.

After a few moments, a light flashed on in a second-floor window, telling him Quinn was safe in her room.

He turned and had taken two steps when he saw the boy. He stood on the sidewalk half a block down. He wore no coat, no hat, no protection against the bite of wind. The long stream of his hair didn't stir in it.

His eyes gleamed, eerily red, as his lips peeled back in a snarl.

Cal heard the sound inside his head while ice balled in his belly.

Not real, he told himself. Not yet. A projection only, like in the dreams. But even in the dreams, it could hurt you or make you think you were hurt.

"Go back where you came from, you bastard." Cal spoke clearly, and as calmly as his shaken nerves would allow. "It's not your time yet."

When it is, I'll devour you, all of you, and everything you hold precious.

The lips didn't move with the words, but stayed frozen in that feral snarl.

"We'll see who feels the bite this round." Cal took another step forward.

And the fire erupted. It spewed out of the wide brick sidewalk, fumed across the street in a wall of wild red. Before he could register that there was no heat, no burn, Cal had already stumbled back, thrown up his hands.

The laughter rang in his head, as wild as the flames. Then both snapped off.

The street was quiet, the brick and buildings unmarred.

Tricks up his sleeve, Cal reminded himself. Lots of tricks up his sleeve.

He made himself stride forward, through where the false fire had run. There was a strong acrid odor that puffed then vanished like the vapor of his own breath. In that instant he recognized it.

Brimstone.

UPSTAIRS IN THE ROOM THAT MADE HER BLISS-fully happy with its four-poster bed and fluffy white duvet, Quinn sat at the pretty desk with its curved legs and polished surface writing up the day's notes, data, and impressions on her laptop.

She loved that there were fresh flowers in the room, and a little blue bowl of artfully arranged fresh fruit. The bath held a deep and delightful claw-foot tub and a snowy white pedestal sink. There were thick, generous towels, two bars of soap, and rather stylish minibottles of shampoo, body cream, and bath gel.

Instead of boring, mass-produced posters, the art on the walls were original paintings and photos, which the discreet note on the desk identified as works by local artists available at Artful, a shop on South Main.

The room was full of homey welcoming touches, *and* provided high-speed Internet access. She made a note to reserve the same room after her initial week was up, for the return trips she planned in April, then again in July.

She'd accomplished quite a bit on her first day, which was a travel day on top of it. She'd met two of the three focal players, had an appointment to hike to the Pagan Stone. She'd gotten a feel for the town, on the surface in any case. And had, she believed, a personal experience with the manifestation of an unidentified (as yet) force.

And she had the bare bones for a bowling article that should work for her friends at *Detour*.

Not bad, especially when you added in she'd dined

sensibly on the grilled chicken salad in the hotel dining room, had *not* given in to temptation and inhaled an entire pizza but had limited herself to half a slice. And she'd bowled a strike.

On the personal downside, she supposed, as she shut down to prepare for bed, she'd also resisted the temptation to lock lips with the very appealing Caleb Hawkins.

Wasn't she all professional and unsatisfied?

Once she'd changed into her bedtime flannel pants and T-shirt, she nagged herself into doing fifteen minutes of pilates (okay, ten), then fifteen of yoga, before burrowing under the fabulous duvet with her small forest of down pillows.

She took her current book off the nightstand, burrowed into that as well until her eyes began to droop.

Just past midnight, she marked the novel, switched off the lamp, and snuggled into her happy nest.

As was her habit, she was asleep in a finger snap.

Quinn recognized the dream as a dream. Always, she enjoyed the sensation of the disjointed, carnival world of dreamscapes. It was, for her, like having some crazy adventure without any physical exertion. So when she found herself on a crooked path through a thick wood where the moonshine silvered the leaves and the curling fog rippled along the ground, a part of her mind thought: Oh boy! Here we go.

She thought she heard chanting, a kind of hoarse and desperate whisper, but the words themselves were indiscernible.

The air felt like silk, so soft, as she waded through the pools of fog. The chanting continued, drawing her toward it. A single word seemed to fly out of that moonstruck night, and the word was *bestia*.

She heard it over and over as she followed the crooked path through the silken air and the silver-laced trees. She felt a sexual pull, a heat and reaching in the belly toward whatever, whoever called out in the night.

Twice, then three times, the air seemed to whisper.

Beatus. The murmur of that warmed her skin. In the dream, she quickened her steps.

Out of the moon-drenched trees swam a black owl, its great wings stirring a storm in that soft air, chilling it until she shivered. And was, even in the dream, afraid.

With that cold wind stirring, she saw, stretched across the path, a golden fawn. The blood from its slit throat drenched the ground so it gleamed wet and black in the night.

Her heart squeezed with pity. So young, so sweet, she thought as she made herself approach it. Who could have done such a thing?

For a moment, the dead, staring eyes of the fawn cleared, shone as gold as its hind. It looked at her with such sorrow, such wisdom, tears gathered in her throat.

The voice came now, not through the whipped air, but in her mind. The single word: *devoveo.*

Then the trees were bare but for the ice that sheathed trunk and branch, and the silver moonlight turned gray. The path had turned, or she had, so now she faced a small pond. The water was black as ink, as if any light the sky pushed down was sucked into its depths and smothered there.

Beside the pond was a young woman in a long brown dress. Her hair was chopped short, with the strings and tufts of it sticking out wildly. Beside the black pond she bent to fill the pockets of her brown dress with stones.

Hello! Quinn called out. *What are you doing?*

The girl only continued to fill her pockets. As Quinn walked closer, she saw the girl's eyes were full of tears, and of madness.

Crap. You don't want to do that. You don't want to go Virginia Woolf. Wait. Just wait. Talk to me.

The girl turned her head, and for one shocked moment, Quinn saw the face as her own. *He doesn't know everything,* the mad girl said. *He didn't know you.*

She threw out her arms, and her slight body, weighed heavy with her cache of stones, tipped, tipped, tipped until it met the black water. The pond swallowed it like a waiting mouth.

Quinn leaped—what else could she do? Her body braced for the shock of cold as she filled her lungs with air.

There was a flash of light, a roar that might have been thunder or something alive and hungry. She was on her knees in a clearing where a stone rose out of the earth like an altar. Fire spewed around her, above her, through her, but she felt none of its heat.

Through the flames she saw two shapes, one black, one white, grappling like mad animals. With a terrible rending sound, the earth opened up, and like the waiting mouth of the pond, swallowed everything.

The scream ripped from her throat as that maw widened to take her. Clawing, she dragged herself toward the stone, fought to wrap her arms around it.

It broke into three equal parts, sending her tumbling, tumbling into that open, avid mouth.

She woke, huddled on the lovely bed, the linens tangled around her legs as she gripped one of the bedposts as if her life depended on it.

Her breath was an asthmatic's wheeze, and her heart beat so fast and hard it had her head spinning.

A dream, just a dream, she reminded herself, but couldn't force herself—not quite yet—to release her hold on the bedpost.

Clinging to it, she let her cheek rest on the wood, closed her eyes until the shaking had lessened to an occasional quiver.

"Hell of a ride," she mumbled.

The Pagan Stone. That's where she'd been at the end of the dream, she was certain of it. She recognized it from pictures she'd seen. Small wonder she'd have a scary dream about it, about the woods. And the pond . . . Wasn't there something in her research about a woman drowning in the pond? They'd named it after her. Hester's Pond. No, pool. Hester's Pool.

It all made sense, in dream logic.

Yeah, a hell of a ride, and she'd die happy if she never took another like it.

She glanced at her travel alarm, and saw by its luminous dial it was twenty after three. Three in the morning, she thought, was the dead time, the worst time to be wakeful. So she'd go back to sleep, like a sensible woman. She'd straighten the bed, get herself a nice cool drink of water, then tune out.

She'd had enough jolts and jumps for her first day.

She slid out of bed to tug the sheets and duvet back into some semblance of order, then turned, intending to go to the adjoining bath for a glass of water.

The scream wouldn't sound. It tore through her head like scrabbling claws, but nothing could tear its way out of the hot lock of her throat.

The boy grinned obscenely through the dark window. His face, his hands pressed against the glass bare inches away from her own. She saw its tongue flick out to roll across those sharp, white teeth, and those eyes, gleaming red, seemed as bottomless and hungry as the mouth of earth that had tried to swallow her in her dream.

Her knees wanted to buckle, but she feared if she dropped to the ground it would come crashing through the glass to latch those teeth on her throat like a wild dog.

Instead, she lifted her hand in the ancient sign against evil. "Get away from here," she whispered. "Stay away from me."

It laughed. She heard the horrible, giddy sound of it, saw its shoulders shake with mirth. Then it pushed off the glass into a slow, sinuous somersault. It hung suspended for a moment above the sleeping street. Then it . . . condensed, was all she could think. It shrank into itself, into a pinpoint of black, and vanished.

Quinn launched herself at the window, yanked the shade down to cover every inch of glass. And lowering to the floor at last, she leaned back against the wall, trembling.

When she thought she could stand, she used the wall as

a brace, quick-stepping to the other windows. She was out of breath again by the time all the shades were pulled, and tried to tell herself the room didn't feel like a closed box.

She got the water—she needed it—and gulped down two full glasses. Steadier, she stared at the covered windows.

"Okay, screw you, you little bastard."

Picking up her laptop, she went back to her position on the floor—it just felt safer under the line of the windowsills—and began to type up every detail she remembered from the dream, and from the thing that pressed itself to the night glass.

WHEN SHE WOKE, THE LIGHT WAS A HARD YEL-low line around the cream linen of the shades. And the battery of her laptop was stone dead. Congratulating herself on remembering to back up before she'd curled onto the floor to sleep, she got her creaky self up.

Stupid, of course, she told herself as she tried to stretch out the worst of the stiffness. Stupid not to turn off her machine, then crawl back into that big, cozy bed. But she'd forgotten the first and hadn't even considered the second.

Now, she put the computer back on the pretty desk, plugged it in to recharge the batteries. With some caution—after all, it had been broad daylight when she'd seen the boy the first time—she approached the first window. Eased up the shade.

The sun was lancing down out of a boiled blue sky. On the pavement, on awnings and roofs, a fresh white carpet of snow shimmered.

She spotted a few merchants or their employees busily shoveling sidewalks or porches and steps. Cars putted along the plowed street. She wondered if school had been called or delayed due to the snow.

She wondered if the boy had demon classes that day.

For herself, Quinn decided she was going to treat her abused body to a long soak in the charming tub. Then she'd try Ma's Pantry for breakfast, and see who she could get to talk to her over her fruit and granola about the legends of Hawkins Hollow.

Six

CAL SAW HER COME IN WHILE HE CUT INTO HIS short stack at the counter. She had on those high, sharp-heeled boots, faded jeans, and a watch cap, bright as a cardinal, pulled over her hair.

She'd wound on a scarf that made him think of Joseph's coat of many colors, which added a jauntiness with her coat opened. Under it was a sweater the color of ripe blueberries.

There was something about her, he mused, that would have been bright and eye-catching even in mud brown.

He watched her eyes track around the diner area, and decided she was weighing where to sit, whom to approach. Already working, he concluded. Maybe she always was. He was damn sure, even on short acquaintance, that her mind was always working.

She spotted him. She aimed that sunbeam smile of hers, started over. He felt a little like the kid in the pickup game of ball, who got plucked from all the others waving their arms and shouting: Me! Me! Pick me!

"Morning, Caleb."

"Morning, Quinn. Buy you breakfast?"

"Absolutely." She leaned over his plate, took a long, dramatic sniff of his butter-and-syrup-loaded pancakes. "I bet those are fabulous."

"Best in town." He stabbed a thick bite with his fork, held it out. "Want a sample?"

"I can never stop at a taste. It's a sickness." She slid onto the stool, swiveled around to beam at the waitress as she unwound her scarf. "Morning. I'd love some coffee, and do you have any granola-type substance that could possibly be topped with any sort of fruit?"

"Well, we got Special K, and I could slice you up some bananas with it."

"Perfect." She reached over the counter. "I'm Quinn."

"The writer from up in PA." The waitress nodded, took Quinn's hand in a firm grip. "Meg Stanley. You watch this one here, Quinn," Meg said with a poke at Cal. "Some of those quiet types are sneaky."

"Some of us mouthy types are fast."

That got a laugh out of Meg as she poured Quinn's coffee. "Being quick on your feet's a strong advantage. I'll get that cereal for you."

"Why," Cal wondered aloud as he forked up another dripping bite of pancake, "would anyone willingly choose to eat trail mix for breakfast?"

"It's an acquired taste. I'm still acquiring it. But knowing myself, and I do, if I keep coming in here for breakfast, I'll eventually succumb to the allure of the pancake. Does the town have a gym, a health club, a burly guy who rents out his Bowflex?"

"There's a little gym down in the basement of the community center. You need a membership, but I can get you a pass on that."

"Really? You're a handy guy to know, Cal."

"I am. You want to change your order? Go for the gold, then the treadmill?"

"Not today, but thanks. So." After she'd doctored her

coffee, she picked up the cup with both hands, sipping as she studied him through the faint rise of steam. "Now that we're having our second date—"

"How'd I miss the first one?"

"You bought me pizza and a beer and took me bowling. In my dictionary, that falls under the definition of date. Now you're buying me breakfast."

"Cereal and bananas. I do appreciate a cheap date."

"Who doesn't? But since we're dating and all . . ." She took another sip as he laughed. "I'd like to share an experience with you."

She glanced over as Meg brought her a white stoneware bowl heaped with cereal and sliced bananas. "Figured you'd be going for the two percent milk with this."

"Perceptive and correct, thanks."

"Get you anything else?"

"We're good for now, Meg," Cal told her. "Thanks."

"Just give a holler."

"An experience," Cal prompted, as Meg moved down the counter.

"I had a dream."

His insides tensed even before she began to tell him, in a quiet voice and in careful detail of the dream she'd had during the night.

"I knew it was a dream," she concluded. "I always do, even during them. Usually I get a kick out of them, even the spooky ones. Because, you know, not really happening. I haven't actually grown a second head so I can argue with myself, nor am I jumping out of a plane with a handful of red balloons. But this . . . I can't say I got a charge out of it. I didn't just think I felt cold, for instance. I *was* cold. I didn't just think I felt myself hit and roll on the ground. I found bruises this morning that weren't there when I went to bed. Fresh bruises on my hip. How do you get hurt in a dream, if it's just a dream?"

You could, he thought, in Hawkins Hollow. "Did you fall out of bed, Quinn?"

"No, I didn't fall out of bed." For the first time, there

was a whiff of irritation in her voice. "I woke up with my arms locked around the bedpost like it was my long-lost lover. And all this was before I saw that red-eyed little bastard again."

"Where?"

She paused long enough to spoon up some cereal. He wasn't sure if the expression of displeasure that crossed her face was due to the taste, or her thoughts. "Did you ever read King's *Salem's Lot*?"

"Sure. Small town, vampires. Great stuff."

"Remember that scene? The little boys, brothers. One's been changed after they snatched him off the path in the woods. He comes to visit his brother one night."

"Nothing scarier than kiddie vampires."

"Not much, anyway. And the vampire kid's just *hanging* outside the window. Just floating out there, scratching on the glass. It was like that. He was pressed to the glass, and I'll point out I'm on the second floor. Then he did a stylish back flip in the air, and poofed."

He laid a hand over hers, found it cold, rubbed some warmth into it. "You have my home and cell numbers, Quinn. Why didn't you call me?"

She ate a little more, then, smiling at Meg, held up her cup for a top-off. "I realize we're dating, Cal, but I don't call all the guys I go bowling with at three thirty in the morning to go: eek! I slogged through swamps in Louisiana on the trail of the ghost of a voodoo queen—and don't think I don't know how that sounds. I spent the night, alone, in a reputedly haunted house on the coast of Maine, and interviewed a guy who was reported to be possessed by no less than thirteen demons. Then there was the family of werewolves in Tallahassee. But this kid . . ."

"You don't believe in werewolves and vampires, Quinn."

She turned on the stool to face him directly. "My mind's as open as a twenty-four-hour deli, and considering the circumstances, yours should be, too. But no, I don't think this thing is a vampire. I saw him in broad daylight, after all.

But he's not human, and just because he's not human doesn't make him less than real. He's part of the Pagan Stone. He's part of what happens here every seven years. And he's early, isn't he?"

Yeah, he thought, her mind was always working and it was sharp as a switchblade. "This isn't the best place to go into this any deeper."

"Say where."

"I said I'd take you to the stone tomorrow, and I will. We'll get into more detail then. Can't do it today," he said, anticipating her. "I've got a full plate, and tomorrow's better anyway. They're calling for sun and forties today and tomorrow." He hitched up a hip to take out his wallet. "Most of this last snow'll be melted." He glanced down at her boots as he laid bills on the counter to cover both their tabs. "If you don't have anything more suitable to hike in than those, you'd better buy something. You won't last a half mile otherwise."

"You'd be surprised how long I can last."

"Don't know as I would. I'll see you tomorrow if not before."

Quinn frowned at him as he walked out, then turned back as Meg slid her rag down the counter. "Sneaky. You were right about that."

"Known the boy since before he was born, haven't I?"

Amused, Quinn propped an elbow back on the bar as she toyed with the rest of her cereal. Apparently a serious scare in the night and mild irritation with a man in the morning was a more effective diet aid than any bathroom scale. Meg struck her as a comfortable woman, wide-hipped in her brown cords and flannel shirt, sleeves rolled up at the elbows. Her hair curled tight as a poodle's fur in a brown ball around a soft and lined face. And there was a quick spark in her hazel eyes that told Quinn she'd be inclined to talk.

"So, Meg, what else do you know? Say about the Pagan Stone."

"Buncha nonsense, you ask me."

"Really?"

"People just get a little"—she circled her finger at her ear—"now and again. Tip too much at the bottle, get all het up. One thing leads to another. Good for business though, the speculation, if you follow me. Get plenty of flatlanders in here wondering about it, asking about it, taking pictures, buying souvenirs."

"You never had any experiences?"

"Saw some people usually have good sense acting like fools, and some who got a mean streak in them acting meaner for a spell of time." She shrugged. "People are what people are, and sometimes they're more so."

"I guess that's true."

"If you want more about it, you should go on out to the library. There's some books there written about the town, the history and whatnot. And Sally Keefafer—"

"Bowling Sally?"

Meg snorted a laugh. "She does like to bowl. Library director. She'll bend your ear plenty if you ask her questions. She loves to talk, and never found a subject she couldn't expound on till you wanted to slap some duct tape over her mouth."

"I'll do that. You sell duct tape here?"

Meg hooted out another laugh, shook her head. "If you really want to talk, and get some sense out of it, you want Mrs. Abbott. She ran the old library, and she's at the new one for a spell most every day."

Then scooping up the bills Cal left, she went to refill waiting cups at the other end of the counter.

CAL HEADED STRAIGHT TO HIS OFFICE. HE HAD the usual morning's paperwork, phone calls, e-mails. And he had a morning meeting scheduled with his father and the arcade guy before the center opened for the afternoon leagues.

He thought of the wall of fire across Main Street the night before. Add that to two sightings by Quinn—an outsider—and it sure as hell seemed the *entity* that plagued the town was starting its jollies early.

Her dream troubled him as well. The details—he'd recognized where she'd been, what she'd seen. For her to have dreamed so lucidly about the pond, about the clearing, to have bruises from it, meant, in his opinion, she had to be connected in some way.

A distant relation wasn't out of the question, and there should be a way to do a search. But he had other relations, and none but his immediate family had ever spoken of any effects, even during the Seven.

As he passed through the bowling center, he sent a wave toward Bill Turner, who was buffing the lanes. The big, burly machine's throaty hum echoed through the empty building.

The first thing he checked in his office was his e-mail, and he let out a breath of relief when he saw one from Gage.

Prague. Got some business to clear up. Should be back in the U.S. of A. inside a couple weeks. Don't do anything stupider than usual without me.

No salutation, no signature. Very Gage, Cal thought. And it would have to do, for now.

Contact me as soon as you're Stateside, Cal wrote back. *Things are already rumbling. Will always wait for you to do the stupid, because you're better at it.*

After clicking Send, he dashed another off to Fox.

Need to talk. My place, six o'clock. Got beer. Bring food that's not pizza.

Best he could do, for now, Cal thought. Because life just had to keep rolling on.

QUINN WALKED BACK TO THE HOTEL TO REtrieve her laptop. If she was going to the library, she might as well use it for a couple hours' work. And while she expected she had most, if not all, of the books tucked into the town's library already, maybe this Mrs. Abbott would prove to be a valuable source.

Caleb Hawkins, it appeared, was going to be a clam until the following day.

As she stepped into the hotel lobby she saw the pert blond clerk behind the desk—Mandy, Quinn thought after a quick scroll through her mental PDA—and a brunette in the curvy chair being checked in.

Quinn's quick once-over registered the brunette with the short, sassy do as mid to late twenties, with a travel-weary look about her that didn't do anything much to diminish the seriously pretty face. Jeans and a black sweater fit well over an athletic build. Pooled at her feet were a suitcase, a laptop case, a smaller bag probably for cosmetics and other female necessities, and an excellent and roomy hobo in slick red leather.

Quinn had a moment of purse envy as she aimed a smile.

"Welcome back, Miss Black. If you need anything, I'll be with you in just a minute."

"I'm fine, thanks."

Quinn turned to the stairs and, starting up, heard Mandy's cheerful, "You're all checked in, Miss Darnell. I'm just going to call Harry to help with your bags."

As was her way, Quinn speculated on Miss Gorgeous Red Bag Darnell as she climbed up to her room. Passing through on her way to New York. No, too odd a place to stop over, and too early in the day to stop a road trip.

Visiting relatives or friends, but why wouldn't she just bunk with said relatives or friends? Then again, she had some of both she'd rather not bunk with.

Maybe a business trip, Quinn mused as she let herself into her room.

Well, if Red Bag I Want for My Very Own stayed more than a few hours, Quinn would find out just who and what and why. It was, after all, what she was best at.

Quinn packed up her laptop, added a spare notebook and extra pencils in case she got lucky. Digging out her phone, she set it on vibrate. Little was more annoying, to her mind, than ringing cell phones in libraries and theaters.

She slipped a county map into her case in the event she decided to explore.

Armed, she headed down for the drive to the other end of town and the Hawkins Hollow Library.

From her own research, Quinn knew that the original stone building tucked on Main Street now housed the community center, and the gym she intended to make use of. At the turn of the current century the new library had been built on a pretty rise of land on the south end of town. It, too, was stone, though Quinn was pretty sure it was the facing used on concrete and such rather than quarried. It was two levels with short wings on either side and a portico-style entrance. The style, she thought, was attractively old-fashioned. One, she guessed, the local historic society had likely fought a war to win.

She admired the benches, and the trees she imagined made shady reading nooks in season as she pulled up to park in the side lot.

It smelled like a library, she thought. Of books and a little dust, of silence.

She saw a brightly lettered sign announcing a Story Hour in the Children's section at ten thirty.

She wound her way through. Computers, long tables, carts, a few people wandering the stacks, a couple of old men paging through newspapers. She heard the soft *hum-chuck* of a copier and the muted ringing of a phone from the Information Desk.

Reminding herself to focus because if she wandered she'd be entranced by the spell she believed all libraries wove, she aimed straight for Information. And in the hushed tone reserved for libraries and churches, addressed the stringy man on duty. "Good morning, I'm looking for books on local history."

"That would be on the second floor, west wing. Steps over to the left, elevator straight back. Anything in particular you're after?"

"Thanks, but I'm just going to poke. Is Mrs. Abbott in today?"

"Mrs. Abbott is retired, but she's in most every day by eleven. In a volunteer capacity."

"Thanks again."

Quinn used the stairs. They had a nice curve to them, she thought, almost a *Gone With the Wind* sort of swish. She put on mental blinders so as not to be tempted by stacks and reading areas until she found herself in Local Interest.

It was more a room—a mini-library—than a section. Nice cozy chairs, tables, amber-shaded lamps, even footrests. And it was larger than she'd expected.

Then again, she should have accounted for the fact that there had been battles fought in and around the Hollow in both the Revolutionary and Civil Wars.

Books pertaining to those were arranged in separate areas, as were books on the county, the state, and the town.

In addition there was a very healthy section for local authors.

She tried that section first and saw she'd hit a treasure trove. There had to be more than a dozen she hadn't come across on her own hunt before coming to town. They were self-published, vanity-pressed, small local publishers.

Titles like *Nightmare Hollow* and *The Hollow, The Truth* had her giddy with anticipation. She set up her laptop, her notebook, her recorder, then pulled out five books. It was then she noticed the discreet bronze plaque.

The Hawkins Hollow Library
gratefully acknowledges the generosity of
the Franklin and Maybelle Hawkins Family

Franklin and Maybelle. Very probably Cal's ancestors. It struck Quinn as both suitable and generous that they would have donated the funds to sponsor this room. This particular room.

She settled at the table, chose one of the books at random, then began to read.

She'd covered pages of her notebook with names, locations, dates, reputed incidents, and any number of theories
when she scented lavender and baby powder.

Surfacing, she saw a trim and tidy old woman standing
in black, sensible shoes with her hands folded neatly at the
waist of her purple suit.

Her hair was a thinning snowball; her clear framed
glasses so thickly lensed Quinn wondered how the tiny
nose and ears supported their weight.

She wore pearls around her neck, a gold wedding band
on her finger, and a leather-banded watch with a huge face
that looked to be as practical as her thick-soled shoes.

"I'm Estelle Abbott," she said in her creaky voice.
"Young Dennis said you asked after me."

As Quinn had gauged Dennis at Information as tumbling down the back end of his sixties, she imagined the
woman who termed him young must have him by a good
two decades.

"Yes." Quinn got to her feet, crossed over to offer her
hand. "I'm Quinn Black, Mrs. Abbott. I'm—"

"Yes, I know. The writer. I've enjoyed your books."

"Thank you very much."

"No need. If I hadn't liked them I'd've told you straight-
out. You're researching for a book on the Hollow."

"Yes, ma'am, I am."

"You'll find quite a bit of information here. Some of it
useful." She peered at the books on the table. "Some of
it nonsense."

"Then in the interest of separating the wheat from the
chaff, maybe you could find some time to talk to me at
some point. I'd be happy to take you to lunch or dinner
whenever you—"

"That's very nice of you, but unnecessary. Why don't
we sit down for a while, and we'll see how things go?"

"That would be great."

Estelle crossed to a chair, sat, then with her back ruler-
straight and her knees glued together, folded her hands in

her lap. "I was born in the Hollow," she began, "lived here all of my ninety-seven years."

"Ninety-seven?" Quinn didn't have to feign the surprise. "I'm usually pretty good at gauging age, and I'd put you a solid decade under that."

"Good bones," Estelle said with an easy smile. "I lost my husband, John, also born and raised here, eight years back come the fifth of next month. We were married seventy-one years."

"What was your secret?"

That brought on another smile. "Learn to laugh, otherwise, you'll beat them to death with a hammer first chance."

"Just let me write that down."

"We had six children—four boys, two girls—and all of them living still and not in jail, thank the Lord. Out of them, we had ourselves nineteen grandchildren, and out of them got ourselves twenty-eight greats—last count, and five of the next generation with two on the way."

Quinn simply goggled. "Christmas must be insane in a good way."

"We're scattered all over, but we've managed to get most everybody in one place at one time a few times."

"Dennis said you were retired. You were a librarian?"

"I started working in the library when my youngest started school. That would be the old library on Main Street. I worked there more than fifty years. Went back to school myself and got my degree. Johnnie and I traveled, saw a lot of the world together. For a time we thought about moving on down to Florida. But our roots here were too deep for that. I went to part-time work, then I retired when my Johnnie got sick. When he passed, I came back—still the old one while this was being built—as a volunteer or as an artifact, however you look at it. I tell you this so you'll have some idea about me."

"You love your husband and your children, and the children who've come from them. You love books, and you're proud of the work you've done. You love this town, and respect the life you've lived here."

Estelle gave her a look of approval. "You have an efficient and insightful way of summing up. You didn't say I loved my husband, but used the present tense. That tells me you're an observant and sensitive young woman. I sensed from your books that you have an open and seeking mind. Tell me, Miss Black, do you also have courage?"

Quinn thought of the thing outside the window, the way its tongue had flicked over its teeth. She'd been afraid, but she hadn't run. "I like to think so. Please call me Quinn."

"Quinn. A family name."

"Yes, my mother's maiden."

"Irish Gaelic. I believe it means 'counselor.' "

"It does, yes."

"I have a well of trivial information," Estelle said with a tap of her finger to her temple. "But I wonder if your name isn't relevant. You'll need to have the objectivity, and the sensitivity of a counselor to write the book that should be written on Hawkins Hollow."

"Why haven't you written it?"

"Not everyone who loves music can play the tune. Let me tell you a few things, some of which you may already know. There is a place in the woods that borders the west of this town, and that place was sacred ground, sacred and volatile ground long before Lazarus Twisse sought it out."

"Lazarus Twisse, the leader of the Puritan sect—the radical sect—which broke off or, more accurately, was cut off, from the godly in Massachusetts."

"According to the history of the time, yes. The Native Americans held that ground as sacred. And before them, it's said, powers battled for that circle of ground, both—the dark and the light, good and evil, whatever terms you prefer—left some seeds of that power there. They lay dormant, century by century, with only the stone to mark what had passed there. Over time the memories of the battle were forgotten or bastardized in folklore, and only the

sense many felt that this ground and its stone were not ordinary dirt and rock remained."

Estelle paused, fell into silence so that Quinn heard the
click and hum of the heater, and the light slap of leather
shoes on the floor as someone passed by the room toward
other business.

"Twisse came to the Hollow, already named for Richard
Hawkins, who, with his wife and children, had carved a
small settlement in 1648. You should remark that Richard's
eldest daughter was Ann. When Twisse came, Hawkins, his
family, and a handful of others—some who'd fled Europe
as criminals, political or otherwise—had made their life
here. As had a man calling himself Giles Dent. And Dent
built a cabin in the woods where the stone rose out of the
ground."

"What's called the Pagan Stone."

"Yes. He troubled no one, and as he had some skill and
knowledge of healing, was often sought out for sickness or
injury. There are some accounts that claim he was known
as the Pagan, and that this was the basis of the name the Pagan Stone."

"You're not convinced those accounts are accurate."

"It may be that the term stuck, entered the language and
the lexicon at that time. But it was the Pagan Stone long before the arrival of Giles Dent or Lazarus Twisse. There are
other accounts that claim Dent dabbled in witchcraft, that
he enspelled Ann Hawkins, seduced and impregnated her.
Others state that Ann and Dent were indeed lovers, but that
she went to his bed of her own free will, and left her family
home to live with him in the little cabin with the Pagan
Stone."

"It would've been difficult for her—for Ann Hawkins—
either way," Quinn speculated. "Enspelled or free will, to
live with a man, unmarried. If it was free will, if it was
love, she must have been very strong."

"The Hawkinses have always been strong. Ann had to
be strong to go to Dent, to stay with him. Then she had
to be strong enough to leave him."

"There are a lot of conflicting stories," Quinn began. "Why do you believe Ann Hawkins left Giles Dent?"

"I believe she left to protect the lives growing inside her."

"From?"

"Lazarus Twisse. Twisse and those who followed him came to Hawkins Hollow in sixteen fifty-one. He was a powerful force, and soon the settlement was under his rule. His rule decreed there would be no dancing, no singing, no music, no books but the Bible. No church but his church, no god but his god."

"So much for freedom of religion."

"Freedom was never Twisse's goal. In the way of those thirsty for power above all else, he intimidated, terrorized, punished, banished, and used as his visible weapon, the wrath of his chosen god. As Twisse's power grew, so did his punishments and penalties. Stocks, lashings, the shearing of a woman's hair if she was deemed ungodly, the branding of a man should he be accused of a crime. And finally, the burning of those he judged to be witches. On the night of July the seventh, sixteen fifty-two, on the accusation of a young woman, Hester Deale, Twisse led a mob from the settlement to the Pagan Stone, and to Giles Dent. What happened there . . ."

Quinn leaned forward. But Estelle sighed and shook her head. "Well, there are many accounts. As there were many deaths. Seeds planted long before stirred in the ground. Some may have sprouted, only to die in the blaze that scorched the clearing.

"There are . . . fewer reports of what immediately followed, or followed over the next days and weeks. But in time, Ann Hawkins returned to the settlement with her three sons. And Hester Deale gave birth to a daughter eight months after the killing blaze at the Pagan Stone. Shortly, very shortly after her child, whom she claimed was sired by the devil, was born, Hester drowned herself in a small pond in Hawkins Wood."

Loading her pockets with stones, Quinn thought with a

suppressed shudder. "Do you know what happened to her child? Or the children of Ann Hawkins?"

"There are some letters, some journals, family Bibles. But most concrete information has been lost, or has never come to light. It will take considerable time and effort to dig out the truth. I can tell you this, those seeds stayed dormant until a night twenty-one years ago this July. They were awakened, and what sowed them awakened. They bloom for seven nights every seven years, and they strangle Hawkins Hollow. I'm sorry, I tire so quickly these days. It's irritating."

"Can I get you something? Or drive you home?"

"You're a good girl. My grandson will be coming along to pick me up. You'll have spoken, I imagine, to his son by now. To Caleb."

Something in the smile turned a switch in Quinn's brain. "Caleb would be your—"

"Great-grandson. Honorary, you could say. My brother Franklin and his wife, my dearest friend, Maybelle, were killed in an accident just before Jim—Caleb's father was born. My Johnnie and I stood as grandparents to my brother's grandchildren. I'd have counted them and theirs in that long list of progeny before."

"You're a Hawkins by birth then."

"I am, and our line goes back, in the Hollow, to Richard Hawkins, the founder—and through him to Ann." She paused a moment as if to let Quinn absorb, analyze. "He's a good boy, my Caleb, and he carries more than his share of weight on his shoulders."

"From what I've seen, he carries it well."

"He's a good boy," Estelle repeated, then rose. "We'll talk again, soon."

"I'll walk you downstairs."

"Don't trouble. They'll have tea and cookies for me in the staff lounge. I'm a pet here—in the nicest sense of the word. Tell Caleb we spoke, and that I'd like to speak with you again. Don't spend all this pretty day inside a book. As much as I love them, there's life to be lived."

"Mrs. Abbott?"

"Yes?"

"Who do you think planted the seeds at the Pagan Stone?"

"Gods and demons." Estelle's eyes were tired, but clear. "Gods and demons, and there's such a thin line between the two, isn't there?"

Alone, Quinn sat again. Gods and demons. Those were a big, giant step up from ghosts and spirits, and other bump-in-the-night residents. But didn't it fit, didn't it click right together with the words she remembered from her dreams?

Words she'd looked up that morning.

Bestia, Latin for beast.

Beatus, Latin for blessed.

Devoveo, Latin for sacrifice.

Okay, okay, she thought, if we're heading down that track, it might be a good time to call in the reserves.

She pulled out her phone. When she was greeted by voice mail, Quinn pushed down impatience and waited for her cue to leave a message.

"Cyb, it's Q. I'm in Hawkins Hollow, Maryland. And, wow, I've hooked a big one. Can you come? Let me know if you can come. Let me know if you can't come so I can talk you into it."

She closed the phone, and for the moment she ignored the stack of books she'd selected. Instead, she began to busily type up notes from Estelle Hawkins Abbott's recitation.

Seven

~⌇~

CAL DID WHAT HE THOUGHT OF AS THE PASS-OFF
to his father. Since the meetings and the morning and afternoon league games were over and there was no party or
event scheduled, the lanes were empty but for a couple of
old-timers having a practice game on lane one.

The arcade was buzzing, as it tended to between the last
school bell and the dinner hour. But Cy Hudson was running herd there, and Holly Lappins manned the front desk.
Jake and Sara worked the grill and fountain, which would
start hopping in another hour.

Everything, everyone was in its place, so Cal could sit
with his father at the end of the counter over a cup of coffee before he headed for home, and his dad took over the
center for the night.

They could sit quietly for a while, too. Quiet was his father's way. Not that Jim Hawkins didn't like to socialize.
He seemed to like crowds as much as his alone time, remembered names, faces, and could and would converse on
any subject, including politics and religion. The fact that he

could do so without pissing anyone off was, in Cal's opinion, one of his finest skills.

His sandy-colored hair had gone a pure and bright silver over the last few years, and was trimmed every two weeks at the local barbershop. He rarely altered his uniform of khakis, Rockports, and oxford shirts on workdays.

Some would have called Jim Hawkins habitual, even boring. Cal called him reliable.

"Having a good month so far," Jim said in his take-your-time drawl. He took his coffee sweet and light, and by his wife's decree, cut off the caffeine at six p.m. sharp. "Kind of weather we've been having, you never know if people are going to burrow in, or get cabin fever so bad they want to be anywhere but home."

"It was a good idea, running the three-game special for February."

"I get one now and again." Jim smiled, lines fanning out and deepening around his eyes. "So do you. Your mom's wishing you'd come by, have dinner some night soon."

"Sure. I'll give her a call."

"Heard from Jen yesterday."

"How's she doing?"

"Fine enough to flaunt that it was seventy-four in San Diego. Rosie's learning to write her letters, and the baby's getting another tooth. Jen said she'd send us pictures."

Cal heard the wistfulness. "You and Mom should take another trip out there."

"Maybe, maybe in a month or two. We're heading to Baltimore on Sunday to see Marly and her brood. I saw your great-gran today. She told me she had a nice chat with that writer who's in town."

"Gran talked with Quinn?"

"In the library. She liked the girl. Likes the idea of this book, too."

"And how about you?"

Jim shook his head, contemplated as Sara drew off Cokes for a couple of teenagers taking a break from the arcade. "I don't know what I think, Cal, that's the plain truth.

I ask myself what good's it going to do to have somebody—and an outsider at that—write all this down so people can read about it. I tell myself that what happened before won't happen again—"

"Dad."

"I know that's not true, or most likely not true."

For a moment Jim just listened to the voices from the boys at the other end of the counter, the way they joked and poked at each other. He knew those boys, he thought. He knew their parents. If life worked as it ought to work, he'd know their wives and kids one day.

Hadn't he joked and poked at his own friends here once upon a time, over fountain Cokes and fries? Hadn't his own children run tame through this place? Now his girls were married and gone, with families of their own. And his boy was a man, sitting with worry in his eyes over problems too big to be understood.

"You have to prepare for it to happen again," Jim continued. "But for most of us, it all hazes up, it just hazes up so you can barely remember what did happen. Not you, I know. It's clear for you, and I wish that wasn't so. I guess if you believe this writer can help find the answers, I'm behind you on that."

"I don't know what I believe. I haven't worked it out yet."

"You will. Well. I'm going to go check on Cy. Some of the evening rollers'll be coming in before long, wanting a bite before they suit up."

He pushed away from the counter, took a long look around. He heard the echoes of his boyhood, and the shouts of his children. He saw his son, gangly with youth, sitting at the counter with the two boys Jim knew were the same as brothers to him.

"We've got a good place here, Cal. It's worth working for. Worth fighting to hold it steady."

Jim gave Cal a pat on the shoulder, then strolled away.

Not just the center, Cal thought. His father had meant the town. And Cal was afraid that holding it steady this time was going to be one hell of a battle.

He went straight home where most of the snow had melted off the shrubs and stones. Part of him had wanted to hunt Quinn down, pump out of her what she and his great-grandmother had talked about. Better to wait, he thought as he jingled his keys, better to wait then ease it out of her the next day. When they went to the Pagan Stone.

He glanced toward the woods where trees and shadows held pockets and rivers of snow, where he knew the path would be muddy from the melt.

Was it in there now, gathering itself? Had it somehow found a way to strike outside the Seven? Maybe, maybe, but not tonight. He didn't feel it tonight. And he always did.

Still, he couldn't deny he felt less exposed when he was inside the house, after he'd put on lights to push away the gloom.

He went through to the back door, opened it, and gave a whistle.

Lump took his time as Lump was wont to do. But the dog eased his way out of the doghouse and even stirred up the energy for a couple of tail wags before he moseyed across the backyard to the bottom of the deck stairs.

He gave a doggie sigh before clumping up the short flight. Then he leaned his whole body against Cal.

And that, Cal thought, was love. That was welcome home, how ya doing, in Lump's world.

He crouched down to stroke and ruffle the fur, to scratch between the floppy ears while Lump gazed at him soulfully. "How's it going? Get all your work done? What do you say we have a beer?"

They went inside together. Cal filled the dog bowl from the bin of chow while Lump sat politely, though Cal assumed a large portion of his dog's manners was sheer laziness. When the bowl was set in front of him, Lump ate slowly, and with absolute focus on the task at hand.

Cal pulled a beer out of the fridge and popped the top. Leaning back on the counter he took that first long swallow that signaled the end of the workday.

"Got some serious shit on my mind, Lump. Don't know what to do about it, think about it. Should I have found a way to stop Quinn from coming here? Not sure that would've worked since she seems to go where the hell she wants, but I could've played it different. Laughed it off, or pushed it higher, so the whole thing came off as bogus. Played it straight, so far, and I don't know where that's going to lead."

He heard the front door open, then Fox shouted, "Yo!" Fox came in carrying a bucket of chicken and a large white takeout bag. "Got tub-o-cluck, got fries. Want beer."

After dumping the food on the table, Fox pulled out a beer. "Your summons was pretty abrupt, son. I might've had a hot date tonight."

"You haven't had a hot date in two months."

"I'm storing it up." After the first swig, Fox shrugged off his coat, tossed it over a chair. "What's the deal?"

"Tell you while we eat."

As he'd been too brainwashed by his mother to fall back on the single-man's friend of paper plates, Cal set out two of stoneware in dull blue. They sat down to fried chicken and potatoes with Lump—as the only thing that lured the dog from food was more food—caging fries by leaning against Cal's knee or Fox's.

He told Fox everything, from the wall of fire, through Quinn's dream, and up to the conversation she'd had with his great-grandmother.

"Seeing an awful lot of the fucker for February," Fox mused. "That's never happened before. Did you dream last night?"

"Yeah."

"Me, too. Mine was a replay of the first time, the first summer. Only we didn't get to the school in time, and it wasn't just Miss Lister inside. It was everybody." He scrubbed a hand over his face before taking a long pull of beer. "Everybody in town, my family, yours, all inside. Trapped, beating on the windows, screaming, their faces at the windows while the place burned." He offered Lump another fry, and his eyes were as dark and soulful as the dog's. "Didn't happen that way, thank Christ. But it felt like it did. You know how that goes."

"Yeah." Cal let out a breath. "Yeah, I know how that goes. Mine was from that same summer, and we were all riding our bikes through town the way we did. Buildings were burned out, windows broken, cars wrecked and smoking. Bodies everywhere."

"It didn't happen that way," Fox repeated. "We're not ten anymore, and we're not going to let it happen that way."

"I've been asking myself how long we can do this, Fox. How long can we hold it back as much as we do? This time, the next. Three more times? How many more times are we going to watch people we know, people we see most every day turn? Go crazy, go mean. Hurt each other, hurt themselves?"

"As long as it takes."

Cal shoved his plate aside. "Not good enough."

"It's all we've got, for now."

"It's like a virus, an infection, passing from one person to another. Where's the goddamn antidote?"

"Not everyone's affected," Fox reminded him. "There has to be a reason for that."

"We've never found it."

"No, so maybe you were right. Maybe we do need fresh eyes, an outsider, objectivity we just don't have. Are you still planning to take Quinn to the stone tomorrow?"

"If I don't, she'll go anyway. So yeah, it's better I'm there."

"You want me? I can cancel some stuff."

"I can handle it." Had to handle it.

QUINN STUDIED THE MENU IN THE HOTEL'S ALmost empty dining room. She'd considered getting some takeout and eating in her room over her laptop, but she fell too easily into that habit, she knew. And to write about a town, she had to experience the town, and couldn't do that closed up in her pretty room eating a cold-cut sub.

She wanted a glass of wine, something chilly with a subtle zip. The hotel's cellar was more extensive than she'd expected, but she didn't want a whole bottle. She was frowning over the selections offered by the glass when Miss Fabulous Red Bag stepped in.

She'd changed into black pants, Quinn noted, and a cashmere sweater in two tissue-thin layers of deep blue under pale. The hair was great, she decided, pin straight with those jagged ends just past chin length. What Quinn knew would look messy on her came off fresh and stylish on the brunette.

Quinn debated catching her eye, trying a wave. She could ask Red Purse to join her for dinner. After all, who didn't hate to eat alone? Then she could pump her dinner companion for the really important details. Like where she got that bag.

Even as she charged up her smile, Quinn saw it.

It *slithered* across the glossy planks of the oak floor, leaving a hideous trail of bloody ooze behind it. At first she thought snake, then slug, then could barely think at all as she watched it slide up the legs of a table where an attractive young couple were enjoying cocktails by candlelight.

Its body, thick as a truck tire, mottled red over black, wound its way over the table, leaving that ugly smear on the snowy linen while the couple laughed and flirted.

A waitress walked briskly in, stepped in and through the sludge on the floor, to serve the couple their appetizers.

Quinn swore she could hear the table creak under its weight.

And its eyes when they met hers were the eyes of the boy, the red gleam in them bright and somehow *amused*. Then it began to wiggle wetly down the skirt of the table-cloth, and toward the brunette.

The woman stood frozen in place, her face bone white. Quinn pushed to her feet and, ignoring the surprised look from the waitress, leaped over the ugly path. She gripped the brunette's arm, pulled her out of the dining room.

"You saw it, too," Quinn said in a whisper. "You saw that thing. Let's get out of here."

"What? What?" The brunette cast shocked glances over her shoulder as she and Quinn stumbled for the door. "You saw it?"

"Sluggy, red-eyed, very nasty wake. Jesus. Jesus." She gulped in the raw February air on the hotel's porch. "They didn't see it, but you did. I did. Why is that? Fuck if I know, but I have an idea who might. That's my car right there. Let's go. Let's just go."

The brunette didn't say another word until they were in the car and Quinn was squealing away from the curb. "Who the hell are you?"

"Quinn. Quinn Black. I'm a writer, mostly on the spooky. Of which there is a surplus in this town. Who are you?"

"Layla Darnell. What *is* this place?"

"That's what I want to find out. I don't know if it's nice to meet you or not, Layla, under the circumstances."

"Same here. Where are we going?"

"To the source, or one of them." Quinn glanced over, saw Layla was still pale, still shaky. Who could blame her? "What are you doing in Hawkins Hollow?"

"I'm damned if I know, but I think I've decided to cut my visit short."

"Understandable. Nice bag, by the way."

Layla worked up a wan smile. "Thanks."

"Nearly there. Okay, you don't know why you're here, so where did you come from?"

"New York."

"I knew it. It's the polish. Do you love it?"

"Ah." Layla combed her fingers through her hair as she swiveled to look back. "Most of the time. I manage a boutique in SoHo. Did. Do. I don't know that anymore either."

Nearly there, Quinn thought again. *Let's keep calm.* "I bet you get great discounts."

"Yeah, part of the perks. Have you seen anything like that before. Like that *thing*?"

"Yeah. Have you?"

"Not when I was awake. I'm not crazy," Layla stated. "Or I am, and so are you."

"We're not crazy, which is what crazy people tend to say, so you'll just have to take my word." She swung onto Cal's lane, and aimed the car over the little bridge toward the house where lights—thank God—glowed in the windows.

"Whose house is this?" Layla gripped the front edge of her seat. "Who lives here?"

"Caleb Hawkins. His ancestors founded the town. He's okay. He knows about what we saw."

"How?"

"It's a long story, with a lot of holes in it. And now you're thinking, what am I doing in this car with a complete stranger who's telling me to go into this house pretty much in the middle of nowhere."

Layla took firm hold on the short strap of her bag, as if she might use it as a weapon. "The thought's crossed."

"Your instinct put you in the car with me, Layla. Maybe you could follow along with that for the next step. Plus, it's cold. We didn't bring our coats."

"All right. Yes, all right." With a bracing breath, Layla opened the door, and with Quinn walked toward the house. "Nice place. If you like isolated houses in the woods."

"Culture shock for the New Yorker."

"I grew up in Altoona, Pennsylvania."

"No kidding. Philadelphia. We're practically neighbors." Quinn knocked briskly on the door, then just opened the door and called in, "Cal!"

She was halfway across the living room when he hurried in. "Quinn? What?" Spotted Layla. "Hello. What?"

"Who's here?" Quinn demanded. "I saw another car in the drive."

"Fox. What's going on?"

"The bonus-round question." She sniffed. "Do I smell

fried chicken? Is there food? Layla—this is Layla Darnell; Layla, Cal Hawkins—Layla and I haven't had dinner."

She moved right by him, and walked toward the kitchen.

"I'm sorry, I think, to bust in on you," Layla began. It passed through her mind that he didn't look like a serial killer. But then again, how would she know? "I don't know what's happening, or why I'm here. I've had a confusing few days."

"Okay. Well, come on back."

Quinn already had a drumstick in her hand, and was taking a swig of Cal's beer. "Layla Darnell, Fox O'Dell. I'm not really in the mood for beer," she said to Cal. "I was about to order some wine when Layla and I were disgustingly interrupted. Got any?"

"Yeah. Yeah."

"Is it decent? If you run to jug or twist caps, I'll stick with beer."

"I've got some damn decent wine." He yanked a plate out, pushed it at her. "Use a plate."

"He's completely Sally about things like that," Fox told her. He'd risen, and pulled out a chair. "You look a little shaken up—Layla, right? Why don't you sit down?"

She just couldn't believe psycho killers sat around a pretty kitchen eating bucket chicken and debating wine over beer. "Why don't I? I'm probably not really here." She sat, dropped her head in her hands. "I'm probably in some padded room imagining all this."

"Imagining all what?" Fox asked.

"Why don't I take it?" Quinn glanced at Layla as Cal got out wineglasses. "Then you can fill in as much of your own backstory as you want."

"Fine. That's fine."

"Layla checked into the hotel this morning. She's from New York. Just a bit ago, I was in the hotel dining room, considering ordering the green salad and the haddock, along with a nice glass of white. Layla was just coming in, I assume, to have her own dinner. I was going to ask you to join me, by the way."

"Oh. Ah, that's nice."

"Before I could issue the invite, what I'd describe as a sluglike creature thicker than my aunt Christine's thigh and about four feet in length oozed its way across the dining room, up over the table where a couple happily continued their dining foreplay, then oozed down again, leaving a revolting smear of God-knows-what behind it. She saw it."

"It looked at me. It looked right at me," Layla whispered.

"Don't be stingy with the wine, Cal." Quinn stepped over to rub a hand on Layla's shoulder. "We were the only ones who saw it, and no longer wishing to dine at the hotel, and believing Layla felt the same, we booked. And I'm now screwing my caloric intake for the day with this drumstick."

"You're awfully . . . blithe. Thanks." Layla accepted the wineglass Cal offered, then drank half the contents at one go.

"Not really. Defense mechanism. So here we are, and I want to know if either of you have ever seen anything like I just described."

There was a moment of silence, then Cal picked up his beer, drank. "We've seen a lot of things. The bigger question for me is, why are you seeing them, and part two, why are you seeing them now?"

"Got a theory."

Cal turned to Fox. "Such as?"

"Connections. You said yourself there had to be some connection for Quinn to see it, to have the dream—"

"Dreams." Layla's head came up. "You've had dreams?"

"And so, apparently, have you," Fox continued. "So we'll connect Layla. Figuring out how they're connected may take a while, but let's just go with the hypothesis that they are, and say, what if. What if, due to this connection, due to Quinn, then Layla being in the Hollow, particularly during the seventh year, gives it some kind of psychic boost? Gives it the juice to manifest?"

"That's not bad," Cal replied.

"I'd say it's damn good." Quinn cocked her head as she considered. "Energy. Most paranormal activity stems from energy. The energy the . . . well, entity or entities, the actions, the emotions thereof, leave behind, and the energy of the people within its sphere, let's say. And we could speculate that this psychic energy has built over time, strengthened, so that now, with the addition of other connected energies, it's able to push out into our reality, to some extent, outside of its traditional time frame."

"What in God's name are you people talking about?" Layla demanded.

"We'll get to that, I promise." Quinn offered her a bolstering smile. "Why don't you eat something, settle the nerves?"

"I think it's going to be a while before food holds any appeal for me."

"Mr. Slug slimed right over the bread bowl," Quinn explained. "It was pretty damn gross. Sadly, nothing puts me off food." She snagged a couple of cold fries. "So, if we run with Fox's theory, where is its counterpoint? The good to its bad, the white to its dark. All my research on this points to both sides."

"Maybe it can't pull out yet, or it's hanging back."

"Or the two of you connect to the dark, and not the light," Cal added.

Quinn narrowed her eyes at him, with something glinting between her lashes. Then she shrugged. "Insulting, but unarguable at this time. Except for the fact that, logically, if we were more a weight on the bad side, why is said bad side trying to scare the living daylights out of us?"

"Good point," Cal conceded.

"I want some answers."

Quinn nodded at Layla. "I bet you do."

"I want some serious, sensible answers."

"Thumbnail: The town includes an area in the woods known as the Pagan Stone. Bad stuff happened there. Gods, demons, blood, death, fire. I'm going to lend you a couple of books on the subject. Centuries pass, then something opened it up again. Since nineteen eighty-seven, for seven nights in July, every seventh year, it comes out to play. It's mean, it's ugly, and it's powerful. We're getting a preview."

Gratefully, Layla held out her glass for more wine as she studied Quinn. "Why haven't I ever heard of this? Or this place?"

"There have been some books, some articles, some reports—but most of them hit somewhere between alien abductions and sightings of Bigfoot," Quinn explained. "There's never been a serious, thorough, fully researched account published. That's going to be my job."

"All right. Say I believe all this, and I'm not sure I'm not just having the mother of all hallucinations, why you, and you?" she said to Fox and Cal. "Where do you come in?"

"Because we're the ones who opened it," Fox told her. "Cal, me, and a friend who's currently absent. Twenty-one years ago this July."

"But you'd have been kids. You'd have had to have been—"

"Ten," Cal confirmed. "We share a birthday. It was our tenth birthday. Now, we showed some of ours. How about seeing some of yours. Why did you come here?"

"Fair enough." Layla took another slow sip of her wine. Whether it was that or the brightly lit kitchen with a dog snoring under the table or just having a group of strangers who were likely to believe what she was about to tell them, her nerves were steadier.

"I've been having dreams for the last several nights. Nightmares or night terrors. Sometimes I'd wake up in my bed, sometimes I'd wake up trying to get out the door of my apartment. You said blood and fire. There was both in the dreams, and a kind of altar in a clearing in the woods. I think it was stone. And there was water, too. Black water. I was drowning in it. I was captain of the swim team in high school, and I was drowning."

She shuddered, took another breath. "I was afraid to sleep. I thought I heard voices even when I wasn't asleep. I couldn't understand them, but I'd be at work, doing my

job, or stopping by the dry cleaners on the way home, and
these voices would just *fill* my head. I thought I was having
a breakdown. But why? Then I thought maybe I had a brain
tumor. I even thought about making an appointment with a
neurologist. Then last night, I took a sleeping pill. Maybe I
could just drug my way out of it. But it came, and in the
dream something was in bed with me."

Her breath trembled out this time. "Not my bed, but
somewhere else. A small room, a small hot room with a
tiny window. I was someone else. I can't explain it, really."

"You're doing fine," Quinn assured her.

"It was happening to me, but I wasn't me. I had long
hair, and the shape of my body, it was different. I was
wearing a long nightgown. I know because it . . . it pulled it
up. It was touching me. It was cold, it was so cold. I
couldn't scream, I couldn't fight, even when it raped me. It
was inside me, but I couldn't see, I couldn't move. I felt it,
all of it, as if it were happening, but I couldn't stop it."

She wasn't aware of the tears until Fox pressed a napkin
into her hand. "Thanks. When it was over, when it was
gone, there was a voice in my head. Just one voice this
time, and it calmed me, it made me warm again and took
away the pain. It said: 'Hawkins Hollow.'"

"Layla, were you raped?" Fox spoke very quietly. "When
you came out of the dream, was there any sign you'd been
raped?"

"No." She pressed her lips together, kept her gaze on his
face. His eyes were golden brown, and full of compassion.
"I woke up in my own bed, and I made myself go . . .
check. There was nothing. It hurt me, so there would've
been bruises, there would've been marks, but there was
nothing. It was early in the morning, not quite four in the
morning, and I kept thinking Hawkins Hollow. So I
packed, and I took a cab out to the airport to rent a car.
Then I drove here. I've never been here."

She paused to look at Quinn now, at Cal. "I've never
heard of Hawkins Hollow that I can remember, but I *knew*
what roads to take. I knew how to get here, and how to get

to the hotel. I checked in this morning, went up to the room they gave me, and I slept like the dead until nearly six. When I walked into the dining room and saw that thing, I thought I was still asleep. Dreaming again."

"It's a wonder you didn't bolt," Quinn commented.

Layla sent her an exhausted look. "To where?"

"There's that." Quinn put a hand on Layla's shoulder, rubbing gently as she spoke. "I think we all need as much information as there is to be had, from every source there is. I think, from this point, it's share and share alike, one for goddamn all and all for goddamn one. You don't like that," she said with a nod toward Cal, "but I think you're going to have to get used to it."

"You've been in this for days. Fox and I have lived with it for years. Lived *in* it. So, don't put on your badge and call yourself captain yet, Blondie."

"Living in it for twenty-one years gives you certain advantages. But you haven't figured it out, you haven't stopped it or even identified it, as far as I can tell, in your twenty-one-year experience. So loosen up."

"You poked at my ninety-seven-year-old great-grandmother today."

"Oh, bull. Your remarkable and fascinating ninety-seven-year-old great-grandmother came up to where I was researching in the library, sat down, and had a conversation with me of her own free will. There was no poking. My keen observation skills tell me you didn't inherit your tight-ass tendencies from her."

"Kids, kids." Fox held up a hand. "Tense situation, agreed, but we're all on the same side, or are on the same side potentially. So chill. Cal, Quinn makes a good point, and it bears consideration. At the same time, Quinn, you've been in the Hollow a couple of days, and Layla less than that. You're going to have to be patient, and accept the fact that some areas of information are more sensitive than others, and may take time to be offered. Even if we start with what can and has been corroborated or documented—"

"What are you, a lawyer?" Layla asked.

"Yeah."

"Figures," she said under her breath.

"Let's just table this," Cal suggested. "Let's let it sit, so we can all think about it for the night. I said I'd take you to the Pagan Stone tomorrow, and I will. Let's see how it goes."

"Accepted."

"Are you two all right at the hotel? You can stay here if you're not easy about going back."

The fact that he'd offered had Quinn's hackles smoothing down again. "We're not wimps, are we, Layla?"

"I wouldn't have said I was a few days ago. Now, I'm not so sure. But I'll be all right at the hotel." In fact, she wanted to go back, crawl into that big, soft bed and pull the covers over her head. "I slept better there than I have all week, so that's something."

Quinn decided she'd wait until they were back before she advised Layla to lower all the shades, and maybe leave a light burning.

Eight

~⌒~

IN THE MORNING, QUINN PRESSED AN EAR AGAINST
the door to Layla's room. Since she heard the muted sounds
of the *Today* show, she gave the door a knuckle rap. "It's
Quinn," she added, in case Layla was still jumpy.

Layla opened the door in a pretty damn cute pair of
purple-and-white-striped pajama pants and a purple sleep
tank. There was color in her cheeks, and her quiet green eyes
had the clarity that told Quinn she'd been awake awhile.

"I'm about to head out to Cal's. Mind if I come in a
minute?"

"No." She stepped back. "I was trying to figure out what
I'm supposed to do with myself today."

"You can come with me if you want."

"Into the woods? Not quite ready for that, thanks. You
know . . ." Layla switched off the TV before dropping into a
chair. "I was thinking about the wimp statement you made
last night. I've never been a wimp, but it occurred to me as I
was huddled in bed with the shades drawn and this stupid

chair under the doorknob that I've never had anything happen that tested that before. My life's been pretty normal."

"You came here, and you're still here. So I'm thinking that puts you pretty low on the wimp scale. How'd you sleep?"

"Good. Once I got there, good. No dreams, no visitations, no bumps in the night. So, of course, now I'm wondering why."

"No dreams for me either." Quinn glanced around the room. Layla's bed was a sleigh style and the color scheme was muted greens and creams. "We could theorize that your room here's a safe zone, but that's off because mine isn't, and it's two doors down. It could be that whatever it is just took the night off. Maybe needed to recharge some expended energy."

"Happy thought."

"You've got my cell number, Cal's, Fox's. We've got yours. We're—connected. I wanted to let you know that the diner across the street, figuring you're not going to try the dining room here again, has a nice breakfast."

"I'm thinking I might try room service, and start on the books that you gave me last night. I didn't want to try them for bedtime reading."

"Wise. Okay. If you head out, it's a nice town. Some cute little shops, a little museum I haven't had time to explore so can't give you a rating, and there's always the Bowl-a-Rama."

A hint of a smile appeared around Layla's mouth. "Is there?"

"It's Cal's family's place. Interesting, and it feels like the hub of the town. So, I'll look you up when I get back?"

"Okay. Quinn?" Layla added as Quinn reached for the door. "Wimp scale or not, I'm not sure I'd still be here if I hadn't run into you."

"I know how you feel. I'll see you later."

CAL WAS WAITING FOR HER WHEN SHE DROVE UP. He stepped out, started down the steps, the dog wandering behind him, as she got out of the car. He took a scan, starting with her feet. Good, sturdy hiking boots that showed some scars and wear, faded jeans, tough jacket in I'm-Not-a-Deer red, and a multistriped scarf that matched the cloche-style cap on her head. Silly hat, he mused, that was unaccountably appealing on her.

In any case, he decided she knew what to wear on a hike through the winter woods.

"Do I pass muster, Sergeant?"

"Yeah." He came down the rest of the steps. "Let's start this off with me saying I was off base by a couple inches last night. I haven't completely resolved dealing with you, and now there's another person in the mix, another unknown. When you live with this as long as I have, part of you gets used to it, and other parts just get edgier. Especially when you're into the seventh year. So, I'll apologize, if you need it."

"Well. Wind, sails sucked out. Okay, I can't be pissed off after that or it's just bitchy instead of righteous. So let me say this. Before I came here, this was an idea for a book, a job I enjoy on a level some might consider twisted, and that I consider vastly fascinating. Now, it's more personal. While I can appreciate you being somewhat edgy, and somewhat proprietary, I'm bringing something important to the table. Experience and objectivity. And guts. I've got some impressive guts."

"I've noticed."

"So, we're going to do this thing?"

"Yeah, we're going to do it."

She gave the dog who came over to lean on her a rub. "Is Lump seeing us off on our adventure?"

"He's coming. He likes to walk in the woods when the mood strikes. And if he's had enough, he'll just lie down and sleep until he's in the mood to walk back home again."

"Strikes me as a sensible attitude." She picked up a small pack, hitched it on, then drew her tape recorder out of her pocket. It was attached to the pocket with a small clamp. "I'm going to want to record observations, and whatever you tell me. Okay with that?"

"Yeah." He'd given it a lot of thought overnight. "I'm okay with that."

"Then I'm ready when you are, Tonto."

"Trail's going to be sloppy," he said as they started toward the woods. "Given that, from this point it'll take about two hours—a little more depending—to reach the clearing."

"I'm in no hurry."

Cal glanced up at the sky. "You will be if the weather turns, or anything holds us up after sundown."

She clicked on her recorder, and hoped she'd been generous enough with her cache of extra tapes and batteries. "Why?"

"Years back people hiked or hunted in this section of the woods routinely. Now they don't. People got lost, turned around, spooked. Some reported hearing what they thought were bear or wolves. We don't have wolves and it's rare for bear to come this far down the mountains. Kids, teens mostly, used to sneak in to swim in Hester's Pool in the summer, or to screw around. Now they don't. People used to say the pool was haunted, it was kind of a local legend. Now, people don't like to talk about it."

"Do you think it's haunted?"

"I know there's something in it. I saw it myself. We'll talk about that once we get to the pool. No point in going into it now."

"All right. Is this the way the three of you came in on your birthday twenty-one years ago?"

"We came in from the east." He gestured. "Track closest to town. This way's shorter, but it would've been a longer ride around for us from town. There wasn't anything . . . off about it, until we got to the pool."

"Have the three of you been back together since that night?"

"Yeah, we went back. More than once." He glanced toward her. "I can tell you that going back anytime near the Seven isn't an experience I look forward to repeating."

"The Seven?"

"That's what we call the week in July."

"Tell me more about what happens during the Seven."

It was time to do just that, he thought. To say it straight-out to someone who wanted to know. To someone, maybe, who was part of the answer.

"People in the Hollow get mean, violent, even murder-ous. They do things they'd never do at any other time. De-stroy property, beat the hell out of each other, start fires. Worse."

"Murders, suicides."

"Yeah. After the week's up, they don't remember clearly. It's like watching someone come out of a trance, or a long illness. Some of them are never the same. Some of them leave town. And some fix up their shop or their house, and just go on. It doesn't hit everyone, and it doesn't hit those it does all in the same way. The best I can explain is it's like a mass psychotic episode, and it gets stronger each time."

"What about the police?"

Out of habit, Cal reached down, picked up a stick. There was no point in tossing it for Lump, that would only em-barrass them both. So he held it down so Lump could take it into his mouth and plod contentedly along.

"Chief Larson was in charge last time. He was a good man, went to school with my father. They were friends. The third night, he locked himself in his office. I think he, some part of him anyway, knew what was happening to him, and didn't want to risk going home to his wife and kids. One of the deputies, guy named Wayne Hawbaker, nephew to Fox's secretary, came in looking for him, needed help. He heard Larson crying in the office. Couldn't get him to come out. By the time Wayne knocked down the door, Larson had shot himself. Wayne's chief of police now. He's a good man, too."

How much loss had he seen? Quinn wondered. How many losses had he suffered since his tenth birthday? And yet he was walking back into these woods, back where it all began for him. She didn't think she'd ever known a braver stand.

"What about the county cops, the state cops?"

"It's like we're cut off for that week." A cardinal winged by, boldly red, carelessly free. "Sometimes people get out, sometimes they get in, but by and large, we're on our own. It's like . . ." He groped for words. "It's like this veil comes down, and nobody sees, not clearly. Help doesn't come, and after, nobody questions it too closely. Nobody looks straight on at what happened, or why. So it ends up being lore, or *Blair Witch* stuff. Then it fades off until it happens again."

"You stay, and you look at it straight on."

"It's my town," he said simply.

No, Quinn thought, *that* was the bravest stand she'd ever known.

"How'd you sleep last night?" he asked her.

"Dreamlessly. So did Layla. You?"

"The same. Always before, once it started, it didn't stop. But then, things are different this time around."

"Because I saw something, and so did Layla."

"That's the big one. And it's never started this early, or this strong." As they walked, he studied her face. "Have you ever had a genealogy done?"

"No. You think we're related back when, or I'm related to someone who was involved in whatever happened at the Pagan Stone way back when?"

"I think, we've always thought, this was about blood." Absently, he glanced at the scar on his wrist. "So far, knowing or sensing that hasn't done any good. Where are your ancestors from?"

"England primarily, some Irish tossed in."

"Mine, too. But then a lot of Americans have English ancestry."

"Maybe I should start researching and find out if there are any Dents or Twisses in my lineage?" She shrugged when he frowned at her. "Your great-grandmother sent me down that path. Have you tried to trace them? Giles Dent and Lazarus Twisse?"

"Yeah. Dent may be an ancestor, if he did indeed father the three sons of Ann Hawkins. There's no record of him. And other than accounts from the time, some old family letters and diaries, no Giles Dent on anything we've dug up. No record of birth, death. Same for Twisse. They could've dropped down from Pluto as far as we've been able to prove."

"I have a friend who's a whiz on research. I sent her a heads-up. And don't get that look on your face again. I've known her for years, and we've worked together on other projects. I don't know as yet if she can or will come in on this, but trust me, if she does, you'll be grateful. She's brilliant."

Rather than respond, he chewed on it. How much of his resistance was due to this feeling of losing control over the situation? And had he ever had any control to begin with? Some, he knew, was due to the fact that the more people who became involved, the more people he felt responsible for.

And maybe most of all, how much was all this exposure going to affect the town?

"The Hollow's gotten some publicity over the years, focused on this whole thing. That's how you found out about us to begin with. But it's been mild, and for the most part, hasn't done much more than bring interested tourists through. With your involvement, and now potentially two others, it could turn the Hollow into some sort of lurid or ridiculous caption in the tourist guides."

"You knew that was a risk when you agreed to talk to me."

She was keeping pace with him, stride-by-stride on the sloppy ground. And, she was striding into the unknown without a quake or a quiver. "You'd have come whether or not I agreed."

"So part of your cooperation is damage control." She nodded. "Can't blame you. But maybe you should be thinking bigger picture, Cal. More people invested means more brains and more chance of figuring out how to stop what's been happening. Do you want to stop it?"

"More than I can possibly tell you."

"I want a story. There's no point in bullshitting you about that. But I want to stop it, too. Because despite my famous guts, this thing scares me. Better shot at that, it seems to me, if we work together and utilize all our resources. Cybil's one of mine, and she's a damn good one."

"I'll think about it." For now, he thought, he'd given her enough. "Why don't you tell me what made you head down the woo-woo trail, writing-wise."

"That's easy. I always liked spooky stuff. When I was a kid and had a choice between, say, *Sweet Valley High* or Stephen King, King was always going to win. I used to write my own horror stories and give my friends nightmares. Good times," she said and made him laugh. "Then, the turning point, I suppose, was when I went into this reputed haunted house with a group of friends. Halloween. I was twelve. Big dare. Place was falling down and due to be demolished. We were probably lucky we didn't fall through floorboards. So we poked around, squealed, scared ourselves, and had some laughs. Then I saw her."

"Who?"

"The ghost, of course." She gave him a friendly elbow poke. "Keep up. None of the others did. But I saw her, walking down the stairs. There was blood all over her. She looked at me," Quinn said quietly now. "It seemed like she looked right at me, and walked right by. I felt the cold she carried with her."

"What did you do? And if I get a guess, I'm guessing you followed her."

"Of course, I followed her. My friends were running around, making spooky noises, but I followed her into the falling-down kitchen, down the broken steps to the basement by the beam of my Princess Leia flashlight. No cracks."

"How can I crack when I had a Luke Skywalker flash-light?"

"Good. What I found were a lot of spiderwebs, mouse droppings, dead bugs, and a filthy floor of concrete. Then the concrete was gone and it was just a dirt floor with a hole—a grave—dug in it. A black-handled shovel beside it. She went to it, looked at me again, then slid down, hell, like a woman might slide into a nice bubble bath. Then I was standing on the concrete floor again."

"What did you do?"

"Your guess?"

"I'd guess you and Leia got the hell out of there."

"Right again. I came out of the basement like a rocket. I told my friends, who didn't believe me. Just trying to spook them out as usual. I didn't tell anyone else, because if I had, our parents would have known we were in the house and we'd have been grounded till our Social Security kicked in. But when they demolished the house, started jackhammering the concrete floor, they found her. She'd been in there since the thirties. The wife of the guy who'd owned the house had claimed she'd run off. He was dead by then, so nobody could ask him how or why he'd done it. But I knew. From the time I saw her until they found her bones, I dreamed about her murder, I saw it happen.

"I didn't tell anyone. I was too afraid. Ever since, I've told what I find, confirming or debunking. Maybe partly to make it up to Mary Bines—that was her name. And partly because I'm not twelve anymore, and nobody's going to ground me."

He said nothing for a long time. "Do you always see what happened?"

"I don't know if it's seeing or just intuiting, or just my imagination, which is even more far-famed than my guts. But I've learned to trust what I feel, and go with it."

He stopped, gestured. "This is where the tracks cross.

We came in from that direction, picked up the cross trail here. We were loaded down. My mother had packed a picnic basket, thinking we were camping out on Fox's family farm. We had his boom box, his load from the market, our backpacks full of the stuff we figured we couldn't live without. We were still nine years old. Kids, pretty much fearless. That all changed before we came out of the woods again."

When he started to walk once more, she put a hand on his arm, squeezed. "Is that tree bleeding, or do you just have really strange sap in this part of the world?"

He turned, looked. Blood seeped from the bark of the old oak, and seeped into the soggy ground at its trunk.

"That kind of thing happens now and again. It puts off the hikers."

"I bet." She watched Lump plod by the tree after only a cursory sniff. "Why doesn't he care?"

"Old hat to him."

She started to give the tree a wide berth, then stopped. "Wait, wait. This is the spot. This is the spot where I saw the deer across the path. I'm sure of it."

"He called it, with magick. The innocent and pure."

She started to speak, then looking at Cal's face, held her tongue. His eyes had darkened; his cheeks had paled.

"Its blood for the binding. Its blood, his blood, the blood of the dark thing. He grieved when he drew the blade across its neck, and its life poured onto his hands and into the cup."

As his head swam, Cal bent over from the waist. Prayed he wouldn't be sick. "Need a second to get my breath."

"Take it easy." Quickly, Quinn pulled off her pack and pulled out her water bottle. "Drink a little."

Most of the queasiness passed when she took his hand, pressed the bottle into it. "I could see it, *feel* it. I've gone by this tree before, even when it's bled, and I never saw that. Or felt that."

"Two of us this time. Maybe that's what opened it up."

He drank slowly. Not just two, he thought. He'd walked this path with Fox and Gage. We two, he decided. Something about being here with her. "The deer was a sacrifice."

"I get that. *Devoveo*. He said it in Latin. Blood sacrifice. White witchery doesn't ascribe to that. He had to cross over the line, smear on some of the black to do what he felt he needed to do. Was it Dent? Or someone who came long before him?"

"I don't know."

Because she could see his color was eking back, her own heart rate settled. "Do you see what came before?"

"Bits, pieces, flashes. Not all of it. I generally come back a little sick. If I push for more, it's a hell of a lot worse."

"Let's not push then. Are you okay to go on?"

"Yeah. Yeah." His stomach was still mildly uneasy, but the light-headedness had passed. "We'll be coming to Hester's Pool soon."

"I know. I'm going to tell you what it looks like before we get there. I'm telling you I've never been there before, not in reality, but I've seen it, and I stood there night before last. There are cattails and wild grass. It's off the path, through some brush and thorny stuff. It was night, so the water looked black. Opaque. Its shape isn't quite round, not really oval. It's more of a fat crescent. There were a lot of rocks. Some more like boulders, some no more than pebbles. She filled her pockets with them— they looked to be about hand-sized or smaller—until her pockets were sagging with the weight. Her hair was cut short, like it'd been hacked at, and her eyes looked mad."

"Her body didn't stay down, not according to reports."

"I've read them," Quinn acknowledged. "She was found floating in the pool, which came to bear her name, and because it was suicide, they buried her in unconsecrated ground. Records I've dug up so far don't indicate what happened to the infant daughter she left behind."

Before replacing the pack, she took out a bag of trail mix. Opened it, offered. Cal shook his head. "There's plenty of bark and twigs around if I get that desperate."

"This isn't bad. What did your mother pack for you that day?"

"Ham-and-cheese sandwiches, hard-boiled eggs, apple slices, celery and carrot sticks, oatmeal cookies, lemonade." Remembering made him smile. "Pop-Tarts, snack pack cereal for breakfast."

"Uppercase *M* Mom."

"Yeah, always has been."

"How long do we date before I meet the parents?"

He considered. "They want me to come for dinner some night soon if you want in."

"A home-cooked meal by Mom? I'm there. How does she feel about all this?"

"It's hard for them, all of this is hard. And they've never let me down in my life."

"You're a lucky man, Cal."

He broke trail, skirting the tangles of blackberry bushes, and following the more narrow and less-trod path. Lump moved on ahead, as if he understood where they were headed. The first glint of the pool brought a chill down his spine. But then, it always did.

Birds still called, and Lump—more by accident than design, flushed a rabbit that ran across the path and into another thicket. Sunlight streamed through the empty branches onto the leaf-carpeted ground. And glinted dully on the brown water of Hester's Pool.

"It looks different during the day," Quinn noted. "Not nearly as ominous. But I'd have to be very young and very hot to want to go splashing around in that."

"We were both. Fox went in first. We'd snuck out here before to swim, but I'd never much liked it. Who knew what was swimming under there? I always thought Hester's bony hand was going to grab my ankle and pull me under. Then it did."

Quinn's eyebrows shot up, and when he didn't continue, she sat on one of the rocks. "I'm listening."

"Fox was messing with me. I was a better swimmer, but he was sneaky. Gage couldn't swim for crap, but he was game. I thought it was Fox again, dunking me, but it was her. I saw her when I went under. Her hair wasn't short the way you saw her. I remember how her hair streamed out. She didn't look like a ghost. She looked like a woman. Girl," he corrected. "I realized when I got older she was just a girl. I couldn't get out fast enough, and I made Fox and Gage get out. They hadn't seen anything."

"But they believed you."

"That's what friends do."

"Did you ever go back in?"

"Twice. But I never saw her again."

Quinn gave Lump, who wasn't as particular as his master, a handful of trail mix. "It's too damn cold to try now, but come June, I'd like to take a dip and see what happens." She munched some mix as she looked around. "It's a nice spot, considering. Primitive, but still picturesque. Seems like a great place for three boys to run a little wild."

She cocked her head. "So do you usually bring your women here on dates?"

"You'd be the first."

"Really? Is that because they haven't been interested, or you haven't wanted to answer questions pertaining."

"Both."

"So I'm breaking molds here, which is one of my favorite hobbies." Quinn stared out over the water. "She must've been so sad, so horribly sad to believe there was no other way for her. Crazy's a factor, too, but I think she must've been weighed down by sadness and despair before she weighed herself down with rocks. That's what I felt in the dream, and it's what I feel now, sitting here. Her horrible, heavy sadness. Even more than the fear when it raped her."

She shuddered, rose. "Can we move on? It's too much, sitting here. It's too much."

It would be worse, he thought. If she felt already, sensed or understood this already, it would be worse. He took her hand to lead her back to the path. Since, at least for the moment, it was wide enough to walk abreast, he kept ahold of her hand. It almost seemed as if they were taking a simple walk in the winter woods.

"Tell me something surprising about you. Something I'd never guess."

He cocked his head. "Why would I tell you something about me you'd never guess?"

"It doesn't have to be some dark secret." She bumped her hip against his. "Just something unexpected."

"I lettered in track and field."

Quinn shook her head. "Impressive, but not surprising. I might've guessed that. You've got a yard or so of leg."

"All right, all right." He thought it over. "I grew a pumpkin that broke the county record for weight."

"The fattest pumpkin in the history of the county?"

"It missed the state record by ounces. It got written up in the paper."

"Well, that is surprising. I was hoping for something a bit more salacious, but am forced to admit, I'd never have guessed you held the county record for fattest pumpkin."

"How about you?"

"I'm afraid I've never grown a pumpkin of any size or weight."

"Surprise me."

"I can walk on my hands. I'd demonstrate, but the ground's not conducive to hand-walking. Come on. You wouldn't have guessed that."

"You're right. I will, however, insist on a demo later. I, after all, have documentation of the pumpkin."

"Fair enough."

She kept up the chatter, light and silly enough to make him laugh. He wasn't sure he'd laughed along this path since that fateful hike with his friends. But it seemed natural enough now, with the sun beaming down through the trees, the birds singing.

Until he heard the growl.

She'd heard it, too. He couldn't think of another reason her voice would have stopped so short, or her hand would have gripped his arm like a vise. "Cal—"

"Yeah, I hear it. We're nearly there. Sometimes it makes noise, sometimes it makes an appearance." Never this time of year, he thought, as he hitched up the back of his jacket. But these, apparently, were different times. "Just stay close."

"Believe me, I . . ." Her voice trailed off this time as he drew the large, jagged-edged hunting knife. "Okay. Okay. Now *that* would have been one of those unexpected things about you. That you, ah, carry a Crocodile Dundee around."

"I don't come here unarmed."

She moistened her lips. "And you probably know how to use it, if necessary."

He shot her a look. "I probably do. Do you want to keep going, or do you want to turn around and go back?"

"I'm not turning tail."

He could hear it rustling in the brush, could hear the slide of mud underfoot. Stalking them, he thought. He imagined the knife was as useless as a few harsh words if the thing meant business, but he felt better with it in his hand.

"Lump doesn't hear it," Quinn murmured, lifting her chin to where the dog slopped along the path a few feet ahead. "Even he can't be that lazy. If he heard it, scented it, he'd show some concern. So it's not real." She took a slow breath. "It's just show."

"Not real to him, anyway."

When the thing howled, Cal took her firmly by the arm and pulled her through the edge of the trees into the clearing where the Pagan Stone speared up out of the muddy earth.

"I guess, all things considered, I was half expecting something along the lines of the king stone from Stonehenge." Quinn stepped away from Cal to circle the stone.

"It's amazing enough though, when you take a good look, the way it forms a table, or altar. How flat and smooth the top is." She laid her hand on it. "It's warm," she added. "Warmer than stone should be in a February wood."

He put his hand beside hers. "Sometimes it's cold." He fit the knife back into its sheath. "Nothing to worry about when it's warm. So far." He shoved his sleeve back, examined the scar on his wrist. "So far," he repeated.

Without thinking, he laid his hand over hers. "As long as—"

"It's heating up! Feel that? Do you feel that?"

She shifted, started to place her other hand on the stone. He moved, felt himself move as he might have through that wall of fire. Madly.

He gripped her shoulders, spinning her around until her back was pressed to the stone. Then sated the sudden, desperate appetite by taking her mouth.

For an instant, he was someone else, as was she, and the moment was full of grieving desperation. Her taste, her skin, the beat of her heart.

Then he was himself, feeling Quinn's lips heat under his as the stone had heated under their hands. It was her body quivering against his, and her fingers digging into his hips.

He wanted more, wanted to shove her onto the table of rock, to cover her with his body, to surround himself with all she was.

Not him, he thought dimly, or not entirely him. And so he made himself pull back, forced himself to break that connection.

The air wavered a moment. "Sorry," he managed. "Not altogether sorry, but—"

"Surprised." Her voice was hoarse. "Me, too. That was definitely unexpected. Made me dizzy," she whispered. "That's not a complaint. It wasn't us, then it was." She took another steadying breath. "Call me a slut, but I liked it both ways." With her eyes on his, she placed her hand on the stone again. "Want to try it again?"

"I think I'm still a man, so damn right I do. But I don't think it'd be smart, or particularly safe. Plus, I don't care for someone—something—else yanking on my hormones. Next time I kiss you, it's just you and me."

"All right. Connections." She nodded. "I'm more in favor than ever about the theory regarding connections. Could be blood, could be a reincarnation thing. It's worth exploring."

She sidestepped away from the stone, and him. "So, no more contact with each other and that thing for the time being. And let's take it back to the purpose at hand."

"Are you okay?"

"Stirred me up, I'll admit. But no harm, no foul." She took out her water bottle, and this time drank deep.

"I wanted you. Both ways."

Lowering the bottle, she met those calm gray eyes. She'd just gulped down water, she thought, but now her throat was dry again. "I know. What I don't know is if that's going to be a problem."

"It's going to be a problem. I'm not going to care about that."

Her pulse gave a couple of quick jumps. "Ah . . . This probably isn't the place to—"

"No, it's not." He took a step forward, but didn't touch her. And still her skin went hot. "There's going to be another place."

"Okay." She cleared her throat. "All right. To work."

She did another circle while he watched her. He'd made her a little jumpy. He didn't mind that. In fact, he considered it a point for his side. Something might have pushed him to kiss her that way, but he knew what he'd felt as that *something* released its grip. He knew what he'd been feeling since she'd stepped out of her car at the top of his lane.

Plain and simple lust. Caleb Hawkins for Quinn Black.

"You camped here, the three of you, that night." Apparently taking Cal at his word about the safety of the area,

Quinn moved easily around the clearing. "You—if I have any understanding of young boys—ate junk food, ragged on each other, maybe told ghost stories."

"Some. We also drank the beer Gage stole from his father, and looked at the skin mags he'd swiped."

"Of course, though I'd have pegged those activities for more like twelve-year-olds."

"Precocious." He ordered himself to stop thinking about her, to take himself back. "We built a fire. We had the boom box on. It was a pretty night, still hot, but not oppressive. And it was our night. It was, we thought, our place. Sacred ground."

"So your great-grandmother said."

"It called for ritual." He waited for her to turn to him. "We wrote down words. Words we made. We swore an oath, and at midnight, I used my Boy Scout knife to cut our wrists. We said the words we'd made and pressed our wrists together to mix the blood. To make us blood brothers. And hell opened up."

"What happened?"

"I don't know, not exactly. None of us do, not that we can remember. There was a kind of explosion. It seemed like one. The light was blinding, and the force of it knocked me back. Lifted me right off my feet. Screams, but I've never known if they were mine, Fox's, Gage's, or something else. The fire shot straight up, there seemed to be fire everywhere, but we weren't burned. Something *pushed* out, pushed into me. Pain, I remember pain. Then I saw some kind of dark mass rising out, and felt the cold it brought with it. Then it was over, and we were alone, scared, and the ground was scorched black."

Ten years old, she thought. Just a little boy. "How did you get out?"

"We hiked out the next morning pretty much as we'd hiked in. Except for a few changes. I came into this clearing when I was nine. I was wearing glasses. I was nearsighted."

Her brows rose. "Was?"

"Twenty–one hundred in my left eye, twenty-ninety in my right. I walked out ten, and twenty-twenty. None of us had a mark on him when we left, though Gage especially had some wounds he brought in with him. Not one of us has been sick a day since that night. If we're injured, it heals on its own."

There was no doubt on her face, only interest with a touch, he thought, of fascination. It struck him that other than his family she was the only one who knew. Who believed.

"You were given some sort of immunity."

"You could call it that."

"Do you feel pain?"

"Damn right. I came out with perfect vision, not X-ray. And the healing can hurt like a mother, but it's pretty quick. I can see things that happened before, like out on the trail. Not all the time, not every time, but I can see events of the past."

"A reverse clairvoyance."

"When it's on. I've seen what happened here on July seventh, sixteen fifty-two."

"What happened here, Cal?"

"The demon was bound under the stone. And Fox, Gage, and I, we cut the bastard loose."

She moved to him. She wanted to touch him, to soothe that worry from his face, but was afraid to. "If you did, you weren't to blame."

"Blame and responsibility aren't much different."

The hell with it. She laid her hands on his cheeks even when he flinched. Then touched her lips gently to his. "That was normal. You're responsible because, to my mind, you're willing to take responsibility. You've stayed when a lot of other men would've walked, if not run, away from here. So I say there's a way to beat it back where it belongs. And I'm going to do whatever I can to help you do just that."

She opened her pack. "I'm going to take photos, some measurements, some notes, and ask a lot of annoying questions."

She'd shaken him. The touch, the words, the faith. He wanted to draw her in, hold on to her. Just hold on. Normal, she'd said, and looking at her now, he craved the bliss of normality.

Not the place, he reminded himself, and stepped back. "You've got an hour. We start back in an hour. We're going to be well out of the woods before twilight."

"No argument." This time, she thought, and went to work.

Nine

～✦～

SHE SPENT A LOT OF TIME, TO CAL'S MIND, WAN-
dering around, taking what appeared to be copious notes
and a mammoth number of photographs with her tiny little
digital, and muttering to herself.

He didn't see how any of that was particularly helpful,
but since she seemed to be absorbed in it all, he sat under a
tree with the snoring Lump and let her work.

There was no more howling, no more sense of anything
stalking the clearing, or them. Maybe the demon had
something else to do, Cal thought. Or maybe it was just
hanging back, watching. Waiting.

Well, he was doing the same, he supposed. He didn't
mind waiting, especially when the view was good.

It was interesting to watch her, to watch the way she
moved. Brisk and direct one minute, slow and wandering
the next. As if she couldn't quite make up her mind which
approach to take.

"Have you ever had this analyzed?" she called out. "The
stone itself? A scientific analysis?"

"Yeah. We took scrapings when we were teenagers, and took them to the geology teacher at the high school. It's limestone. Common limestone. And," he continued, anticipating her, "we took another sample a few years later, that Gage took to a lab in New York. Same results."

"Okay. Any objection if I take a sample, send it to a lab I've used, just for one more confirmation?"

"Help yourself." He started to hitch up a hip for his knife, but she was already taking a Swiss Army out of her pocket. He should've figured her for it. Still, it made him smile.

Most of the women he knew might have lipstick in their pocket, but wouldn't consider a Swiss Army. He was betting Quinn had both.

He watched her hands as she scraped stone dust into a Baggie she pulled out of her pack. A trio of rings circled two fingers and the thumb of her right hand to catch quick glints of the sun with the movement.

The glints brightened, beamed into his eyes.

The light changed, softened like a summer morning even as the air warmed and took on a weight of humidity. Leaves budded, unfurled, then burst into thick green on the trees, casting shade and light in patterns on the ground, on the stone.

On the woman.

Her hair was long and loose, the color of raw honey. Her face was sharp-featured with eyes long and tipped up slightly. She wore a long dress of dusky blue under a white apron. She moved with care, and still with grace, though her body was heavily pregnant. And she carried two pails across the clearing toward a little shed behind the stone.

As she walked she sang in a voice clear and bright as the summer morning.

All in a garden green where late I laid me down upon a bank of chamomile where I saw upon a style sitting, a country clown . . .

Hearing her, seeing her, Cal was filled with love so urgent, so ripe, he thought his heart might burst from it.

The man stepped through the door of the shed, and that love was illuminated on his face. The woman stopped, gave a knowing, flirtatious toss of her head, and sang as the man walked toward her.

. . . holding in his arms a comely country maid. Courting her with all his skill, working her unto his will. Thus to her he said, Kiss me in kindness, sweetheart.

She lifted her face, offered her lips. The man brushed them with his, and as her laugh burst like a shooting star, he took the pails from her, setting them on the ground before wrapping her in an embrace.

Have I not told you, you are not to carry water or wood? You carry enough.

His hands stroked over the mound of her belly, held there when hers covered them. *Our sons are strong and well. I will give you sons, my love, as bright and brave as their father. My love, my heart.* Now Cal saw the tears glimmer in those almond-shaped eyes. *Must I leave you?*

You will never leave me, not truly, nor I you. No tears. He kissed them away, and Cal felt the wrench of his own heart. *No tears.*

No. I swore an oath against them. So she smiled. *There is time yet. Soft mornings and long summer days. It is not death. You swear to me?*

It is not death. Come now. I will carry the water.

When they faded, he saw Quinn crouched in front of him, heard her saying his name sharply, repeatedly.

"You're back. You went somewhere. Your eyes . . . Your eyes go black and . . . *deep* is the only word I can think of when you go somewhere else. Where did you go, Cal?"

"She's not you."

"Okay." She'd been afraid to touch him before, afraid if she did she'd push them both into that somewhere else, or yank him back before he was done. Now she reached out to rest her hand on his knee. "I'm not who?"

"Whoever I was kissing. Started to, then it was you, but before, at first . . . Jesus." He clamped the heels of his hands at his temple. "Headache. Bitch of a headache."

"Lean back, close your eyes. I'll—"

"It'll pass in a minute. They always do. We're not them. It's not a reincarnation deal. It doesn't feel right. Sporadic possession maybe, which is bad enough."

"Who?"

"How the hell do I know?" His head screamed until he had to lower his head between his knees to fight off the sudden, acute nausea. "I'd draw you a damn picture if I could draw. Give me a minute."

Rising, Quinn went behind him and, kneeling, began to massage his neck, his shoulders.

"Okay, all right. Sorry. Christ. It's like having an electric drill inside my head, biting its way out through my temples. It's better. I don't know who they were. They didn't call each other by name. But best guess is Giles Dent and Ann Hawkins. They were obviously living here, and she was really, really pregnant. She was singing," he said and told her what he'd seen.

Quinn continued to rub his shoulders while she listened. "So they knew it was coming, and from what you say, he was sending her away before it did. 'Not death.' That's interesting, and something to look into. But for now, I think you've had enough of this place. And so have I."

She sat on the ground then, hissed a breath out, sucked one in. "While you were out, let's say, it came back."

"Jesus Christ." He started to spring up, but she gripped his arm.

"It's gone. Let's just sit here until we both get our legs back under us. I heard it growling, and I spun around. You were taking a trip, and I quashed my first instinct to grab you, shake you out of it, in case doing that pulled me in with you."

"And we'd both be defenseless," he said in disgust.

"And now Mr. Responsibility is beating himself up because he didn't somehow see this coming, fight off the magickal forces so he could stay in the here and now and protect the girl."

Even with the headache, he could manage a cool, steely stare. "Something like that."

"Something like that is appreciated, even if it is annoying. I had my handy Swiss Army knife, which, while it isn't up to Jim Bowie standards, does include a nice corkscrew and tweezers, both of which you never know when you may need."

"Is that spunk? Are you being spunky?"

"I'm babbling until I level out and I'm nearly there. The thing is, it just circled, making its nasty 'I'll eat you, my pretty and your big, lazy dog, too.' Rustling, growling, snarling. But it didn't show itself. Then it stopped, and you came back."

"How long?"

"I don't know. I think just a couple minutes, though it seemed longer at the time. However long, I'm so ready to get gone. I hope to hell you can walk back, Cal, because strong and resilient as I am, there's no way I can carry you piggyback."

"I can walk."

"Good, then let's get the hell out of here, and when we get to civilization, Hawkins, you're buying me a really big drink."

They gathered their packs; Cal whistled Lump awake. As they started back he wondered why he hadn't told her of the bloodstone—the three pieces he, Fox, and Gage held. The three pieces that he now knew formed the stone in the amulet Giles Dent had worn when he'd lived at the Pagan Stone.

WHILE CAL AND QUINN WERE HIKING OUT OF Hawkins Wood, Layla was taking herself out for an aimless walk around town. It was odd to just let her feet choose any direction. During her years in New York she'd always had a specific destination, always had a specific task, or several specific tasks to accomplish within a particular time frame.

Now, she'd let the morning stretch out, and had accomplished no more than reading sections of a few of the odd books Quinn had left with her. She might have stayed right there, inside her lovely room, inside that safe zone as Quinn had termed it.

But she'd needed to get away from the books. In any case, it gave the housekeeper an opportunity to set the room to rights, she supposed. And gave herself an opportunity to take a real look at the town she'd been compelled to visit.

She didn't have the urge to wander into any of the shops, though she thought Quinn's assessment was on the mark. There were some very interesting possibilities.

But even window shopping made her feel guilty for leaving the staff of the boutique in the lurch. Taking off the way she had, barely taking the time to call in from the road to tell the owner she'd had a personal emergency and wouldn't be in for the next several days.

Personal emergency covered it, Layla decided.

And it could very well get her fired. Still, even knowing that, she couldn't go back, pick things up, forget what had happened.

She'd get another job if she had to. When and if, she'd find another. She had some savings, she had a cushion. If her boss couldn't cut her some slack, she didn't want that stupid job anyway.

And, oh God, she was already justifying being unemployed.

Don't think about it, she ordered herself. Don't think about that right this minute.

She didn't think about it, and didn't think twice when her feet decided to continue on beyond the shops. She couldn't have said why they wanted to stop at the base of the building. LIBRARY was carved into the stone lintel over the door, but the glossy sign read HAWKINS HOLLOW COM-MUNITY CENTER.

Innocuous enough, she told herself. But when a chill danced over her skin she ordered her feet to keep traveling.

She considered going into the museum, but couldn't work up the interest. She thought about crossing the street to Salon A and whiling away some time with a manicure, but simply didn't care about the state of her nails.

Tired and annoyed with herself, she nearly turned around and headed back. But the sign that caught her eye this time drew her forward.

FOX O'DELL, ATTORNEY AT LAW.

At least he was someone she knew—more or less. The hot lawyer with the compassionate eyes. He was probably busy with a client or out of the office, but she didn't care. Going in was something to do other than wander around feeling sorry for herself.

She stepped into the attractive, homespun reception area. The woman behind the gorgeous old desk offered a polite smile.

"Good morning—well, afternoon now. Can I help you?"

"I'm actually . . ." What? Layla wondered. What exactly was she? "I was hoping to speak to Mr. O'Dell for a minute if he's free."

"Actually, he's with a client, but they shouldn't be much longer if you'd like to . . ."

A woman in tight jeans, a snug pink sweater, and an explosion of hair in an improbable shade of red marched out on heeled boots. She dragged on a short leather jacket. "I want him skinned, Fox, you hear? I gave that son of a bitch the best two years and three months of my life, and I want him skinned like a rabbit."

"So noted, Shelley."

"How could he do that to me?" On a wail she collapsed into Fox's arms.

He wore jeans as well, and an untucked pinstriped shirt, along with an expression of resignation as he glanced over at Layla. "There, there," he said, patting the sobbing Shelley's back. "There, there."

"I just bought him new tires for his truck! I'm going to go slash every one of them."

"Don't." Fox took a good hold of her before Shelley, tears streaming away in fresh rage, started to yank back. "I don't want you to do that. You don't go near his truck, and for now, honey, try to stay away from him, too. And Sami."

"That turncoat slut of a bitch."

"That's the one. Leave this to me for now, okay? You go on back to work and let me handle this. That's why you hired me, right?"

"I guess. But you skin him raw, Fox. You crack that bastard's nuts like pecans."

"I'm going to get right on that," he assured her as he led her to the door. "You just stay above it all, that's the way. I'll be in touch."

After he'd closed the door, leaned back on it, he heaved out a breath. "Holy Mother of God."

"You should've referred that one," Alice told him.

"You can't refer off the first girl you got to second base with when she's filing for divorce. It's against the laws of God and Man. Hello, Layla, need a lawyer?"

"I hope not." He was better looking than she remembered, which just went to show the shape she'd been in the night before. Plus he didn't look anything like a lawyer. "No offense."

"None taken. Layla . . . It's Darnell, right?"

"Yes."

"Layla Darnell, Alice Hawbaker. Mrs. H, I'm clear for a while?"

"You are."

"Come on back, Layla." He gestured. "We don't usually put a show on this early in the day, but my old pal Shelley walked into the back room over at the diner to visit her twin sister, Sami, and found her husband—that would be Shelley's husband, Block—holding Sami's tip money."

"I'm sorry, she's filing for divorce because her husband was holding her sister's tip money?"

"It was in Sami's Victoria's Secret Miracle Bra at the time."

"Oh. Well."

"That's not privileged information as Shelley chased them both out of the back room and straight out onto Main

Street—with Sami's miraculous bra in full view—with a rag mop. Want a Coke?"

"No, I really don't. I don't think I need anything to give me an edge."

Since she looked inclined to pace, he didn't offer her a chair. Instead, he leaned back against his desk. "Rough night?"

"No, the opposite. I just can't figure out what I'm doing here. I don't understand any of this, and I certainly don't understand my place in it. A couple hours ago I told myself I was going to pack and drive back to New York like a sane person. But I didn't." She turned to him. "I couldn't. And I don't understand that either."

"You're where you're supposed to be. That's the simplest answer."

"Are you afraid?"

"A lot of the time."

"I don't think I've ever been really afraid. I wonder if I'd be so damned edgy if I had something to *do*. An assignment, a task."

"Listen, I've got to drive to a client a few miles out of town, take her some papers."

"Oh, sorry. I'm in the way."

"No, and when I start thinking beautiful women are in my way, please notify my next of kin so they can gather to say their final good-byes before my death. I was going to suggest you ride out with me, which is something to do. And you can have chamomile tea and stale lemon snaps with Mrs. Oldinger, which is a task. She likes company, which is the real reason she had me draw up the fifteenth codicil to her will."

He kept talking, knowing that was one way to help calm someone down when she looked ready to bolt. "By the time that's done, I can swing by another client who's not far out of the way and save him a trip into town. By my way of thinking, Cal and Quinn should be just about back home by the time we're done with all that. We'll go by, see what's what."

"Can you be out of the office all that time?"

"Believe me." He grabbed his coat, his briefcase. "Mrs.
H will holler me back if I'm needed here. But unless
you've got something better to do, I'll have her pull out the
files I need and we'll take a drive."

It was better than brooding, Layla decided. Maybe she
thought it was odd for a lawyer, even a small-town lawyer
to drive an old Dodge pickup with a couple of Ring Ding
wrappers littering the floorboards.

"What are you doing for the second client?"

"That's Charlie Deen. Charlie got clipped by a DUI
when he was driving home from work. Insurance company's trying to dance around some of the medical bills.
Not going to happen."

"Divorce, wills, personal injury. So you don't specialize?"

"All law, all the time," he said and sent her a smile that
was a combination of sweet and cocky. "Well, except for
tax law if I can avoid it. I leave that to my sister. She's tax
and business law."

"But you don't have a practice together."

"That'd be tough. Sage went to Seattle to be a lesbian."

"I beg your pardon?"

"Sorry." He boosted the gas as they passed the town limits. "Family joke. What I mean is my sister Sage is gay, and
she lives in Seattle. She's an activist, and she and her partner of, hmm, I guess about eight years now run a firm they
call Girl on Girl. Seriously," he added when Layla said
nothing. "They specialize in tax and business law for
gays."

"Your family doesn't approve?"

"Are you kidding? My parents eat it up like tofu. When
Sage and Paula—that's her partner—got married. Or had
their life-partner affirmation, whatever—we all went out
there and celebrated like mental patients. She's happy
and that's what counts. The alternate lifestyle choice is just
kind of a bonus for my parents. Speaking of family, that's
my little brother's place."

Layla saw a log house all but buried in the trees, with a sign near the curve of the road reading HAWKINS CREEK POTTERY.

"Your brother's a potter."

"Yeah, a good one. So's my mother when she's in the mood. Want to stop in?"

"Oh, I . . ."

"Better not," he decided. "Ridge'll get going and Mrs. H has called Mrs. Oldinger by now to tell her to expect us. Another time."

"Okay." Conversation, she thought. Small talk. Relative sanity. "So you have a brother and sister."

"Two sisters. My baby sister owns the little vegetarian restaurant in town. It's pretty good, considering. Of the four of us I veered the farthest off the flower-strewn path my counterculture parents forged. But they love me anyway. That's about it for me. How about you?"

"Well . . . I don't have any relatives nearly as interesting as yours sound, but I'm pretty sure my mother has some old Joan Baez albums."

"There, that strange and fateful crossroads again."

She started to laugh, then gasped with pleasure as she spotted the deer. "Look! Oh, look. Aren't they gorgeous, just grazing there along the edge of the trees?"

To accommodate her, Fox pulled over to the narrow shoulder so she could watch. "You're used to seeing deer, I suppose," she said.

"Doesn't mean I don't get a kick out of it. We had to run herds off the farm when I was a kid."

"You grew up on a farm."

There was that urban-dweller wistfulness in her voice. The kind that said she saw the pretty deer, the bunnies, the sunflowers, and happy chickens. And not the plowing, the hoeing, weeding, harvesting. "Small, family farm. We grew our own vegetables, kept chickens and goats, bees. Sold some of the surplus, some of my mother's crafts, my father's woodwork."

"Do they still have it?"

"Yeah."

"My parents owned a little dress shop when I was a kid. They sold out about fifteen years ago. I always wished— Oh God, oh my God!"

Her hand whipped over to clamp on his arm.

The wolf leaped out of the trees, onto the back of a young deer. It bucked, it screamed—she could hear its high-pitched screams of fear and pain—it bled while the others in the small herd continued to crop at grass.

"It's not real."

His voice sounded tinny and distant. In front of her horrified eyes the wolf took the deer down, then began to tear and rip.

"It's not real," he repeated. He put his hands on her shoulders, and she felt something click. Something inside her pushed toward him and away from the horror at the edge of the trees. "Look at it, straight on," he told her. "Look at it and *know* it's not real."

The blood was so red, so wet. It flew in ugly rain, smearing the winter grass of the narrow field. "It's not real."

"Don't just say it. Know it. It lies, Layla. It lives in lies. It's not real."

She breathed in, breathed out. "It's not real. It's a lie. It's an ugly lie. A small, cruel lie. It's not real."

The field was empty; the winter grass ragged and un-stained.

"How do you live with this?" Shoving around in her seat, Layla stared at him. "How do you stand this?"

"By knowing—the way I knew that was a lie—that some day, some way, we're going to kick its ass."

Her throat burned dry. "You did something to me. When you took my shoulders, when you were talking to me, you did something to me."

"No." He denied it without a qualm. He'd done something *for* her, Fox told himself. "I just helped you remember it wasn't real. We're going on to Mrs. Oldinger. I bet you could use that chamomile tea about now."

"Does she have any whiskey to go with it?"

"Wouldn't surprise me."

QUINN COULD SEE CAL'S HOUSE THROUGH THE trees when her phone signaled a waiting text-message. "Crap, why didn't she just call me?"

"Might've tried. There are lots of pockets in the woods where calls drop out."

"Color me virtually unsurprised." She brought up the message, smiling a little as she recognized Cybil's short-hand.

Bzy, but intrig'd. Tell u more when. Cn B there in a wk, 2 latest. Tlk whn cn. Q? B-ware. Serious. C.

"All right." Quinn replaced the phone and made the decision she'd been weighing during the hike back. "I guess we'll call Fox and Layla when I'm having that really big drink by the fire you're going to build."

"I can live with that."

"Then, seeing as you're a town honcho, you'd be the one to ask about finding a nice, attractive, convenient, and somewhat roomy house to rent for the next, oh, six months."

"And the tenant would be?"

"Tenants. They would be me, my delightful friend Cybil, whom I will talk into digging in, and most likely Layla, whom—I believe—will take a bit more convincing. But I'm very persuasive."

"What happened to staying a week for initial research, then coming back in April for a follow-up?"

"Plans change," she said airily, and smiled at him as they stepped onto the gravel of his driveway. "Don't you just love when that happens?"

"Not really." But he walked with her onto the deck and opened the door so she could breeze into his quiet home ahead of him.

Ten

~◆~

THE HOUSE WHERE CAL HAD GROWN UP WAS, IN his opinion, in a constant state of evolution. Every few years his mother would decide the walls needed "freshening," which meant painting—or often in his mother's vocabulary a new "paint treatment."

There was ragging, there was sponging, there was combing, and a variety of other terms he did his best to tune out.

Naturally, new paint led to new upholstery or window treatments, certainly to new bed linens when she worked her way to bedrooms. Which invariably led to new "arrangements."

He couldn't count the number of times he'd hauled furniture around to match the grafts his mother routinely generated.

His father liked to say that as soon as Frannie had the house the way she wanted, it was time for her to shake it all up again.

At one time, Cal had assumed his mother had fiddled, fooled, painted, sewed, arranged, and re-arranged out of boredom. Although she volunteered, served on various committees, or stuck her oar in countless organizations, she'd never worked outside the home. He'd gone through a period in his late teens and early twenties where he'd imagined her (pitied her) as an unfulfilled, semidesperate housewife.

At one point he, in his worldliness of two college semesters, got her alone and explained his understanding of her sense of repression. She'd laughed so hard she'd had to set down her upholstery tacks and wipe her eyes.

"Honey," she'd said, "there's not a single bone of repression in my entire body. I love color and texture and patterns and flavors. And oh, just all sorts of things. I get to use this house as my studio, my science project, my laboratory, and my showroom. I get to be the director, the designer, the set builder, and the star of the whole show. Now, why would I want to go out and get a job or a career—since we don't need the money—and have somebody else tell me what to do and when to do it?"

She'd crooked her finger so he leaned down to her. And she'd laid a hand on his cheek. "You're such a sweetheart, Caleb. You're going to find out that not everybody wants what society—in whatever its current mood or mode might be—tells them they should want. I consider myself lucky, even privileged, that I was able to make the choice to stay home and raise my children. And I'm lucky to be able to be married to a man who doesn't mind if I use my talents— and I'm damned talented—to disrupt his quiet home with paint samples and fabric swatches every time he turns around. I'm happy. And I love knowing you worried I might not be."

He'd come to see she was exactly right. She did just as she liked, and was terrific at what she did. And, he'd come to see that when it came down to the core, she was the power in the house. His father brought in the money, but his mother handled the finances. His father ran his business, his mother ran the home.

And that was exactly the way they liked it.

So he didn't bother telling her not to fuss over Sunday dinner—just as he hadn't attempted to talk her out of extending the invitation to Quinn, Layla, and Fox. She lived to fuss, and enjoyed putting on elaborate meals for people, even if she didn't know them.

Since Fox volunteered to swing into town and pick up the women, Cal went directly to his parents' house, and went early. It seemed wise to give them some sort of groundwork—and hopefully a few basic tips on how to deal with a woman who intended to write a book on the Hollow, since the town included people, and those people included his family.

Frannie stood at the stove, checking the temperature of her pork tenderloin. Obviously satisfied with that, she crossed to the counter to continue the layers of her famous antipasto squares.

"So, Mom," Cal began as he opened the refrigerator.

"I'm serving wine with dinner, so don't go hunting up any beer."

Chastised, he shut the refrigerator door. "Okay. I just wanted to mention that you shouldn't forget that Quinn's writing a book."

"Have you noticed me forgetting things?"

"No." The woman forgot nothing, which could be a little daunting. "What I mean is, we should all be aware that things we say and do may end up in a book."

"Hmm." Frannie layered pepperoni over provolone. "Do you expect me or your father to say or do something embarrassing over appetizers? Or maybe we'll wait until dessert. Which is apple pie, by the way."

"No, I— You made apple pie?"

She spared him a glance, and a knowing smile. "It's your favorite, isn't it, my baby?"

"Yeah, but maybe you've lost your knack. I should sample a piece before company gets here. Save you any embarrassment if it's lousy pie."

"That didn't work when you were twelve."

"I know, but you always pounded the whole if-you-don't-succeed chestnut into my head."

"You just keep trying, sweetie. Now, why are you worried about this girl, who I'm told you've been seen out and about with a few times, coming around for dinner?"

"It's not like that." He wasn't sure what it was like. "It's about why she's here at all. We can't forget that, that's all I'm saying."

"I never forget. How could I? We have to live our lives, peel potatoes, get the mail, sneeze, buy new shoes, in spite of it all, maybe because of it all." There was a hint of fierceness in her voice he recognized as sorrow. "And that living includes being able to have a nice company meal on a Sunday."

"I wish it were different."

"I know you do, but it's not." She kept layering, but her eyes lifted to his. "And, Cal, my handsome boy, you can't do more than you do. If anything, there are times I wish you could do less. But . . . Tell me, do you like this girl? Quinn Black?"

"Sure." Like to get a taste of that top-heavy mouth again, he mused. Then broke off that train of thought quickly since he knew his mother's skill at reading her children's minds.

"Then I intend to give her and the others a comfortable evening and an excellent meal. And, Cal, if you didn't want her here, didn't want her to speak with me or your dad, you wouldn't let her in the door. I wouldn't be able, though my powers are fierce, to shove you aside and open it myself."

He looked at her. Sometimes when he did, it surprised him that this pretty woman with her short, streaked blond hair, her slim build and creative mind could have given birth to him, could have raised him to be a man. He could look and think she was delicate, and then remember she was almost terrifyingly strong.

"I'm not going to let anything hurt you."

"Back at you, doubled. Now get out of my kitchen. I need to finish up the appetizers."

He'd have offered to lend her a hand, but would have earned one of her pitying stares. Not that she didn't allow kitchen help. His father was not only allowed to grill, but encouraged to. And any and all could and were called in as line chefs from time to time.

But when his mother was in full-out company-coming mode, she wanted the kitchen to herself.

He passed through the dining room where, naturally, the table was already set. She'd used festive plates, which meant she wasn't going for elegant or drop-in casual. Tented linen napkins, tea lights in cobalt rounds, inside a centerpiece of winter berries.

Even during the worst time, even during the Seven, he could come here and there would be fresh flowers artfully arranged, furniture free of dust and gleaming with polish, and intriguing little soaps in the dish in the downstairs powder room.

Even hell didn't cause Frannie Hawkins to break stride.

Maybe, Cal thought as he wandered into the living room, that was part of the reason—even the most important reason—he got through it himself. Because whatever else happened, his mother would be maintaining her own brand of order and sanity.

Just as his father would be. They'd given him that, Cal thought. That rock-solid foundation. Nothing, not even a demon from hell had ever shaken it.

He started to go upstairs, hunt down his father who, he suspected, would be in his home office. But saw Fox's truck pull in when he glanced out the window.

He stood where he was, watched Quinn jump out first, cradling a bouquet wrapped in green florist paper. Layla slid out next, holding what looked to be a wine gift bag. His mother, Cal thought, would approve of the offerings. She herself had shelves and bins in her ruthlessly organized workroom that held carefully selected emergency hostess gifts, gift bags, colored tissue paper, and an assortment of bows and ribbons.

When Cal opened the door, Quinn strode straight in. "Hi. I love the house and the yard! Shows where you came by your eye for landscaping. What a great space. Layla, look at these walls. Like an Italian villa."

"It's their latest incarnation," Cal commented.

"It looks like home, but with a kick of style. Like you could curl up on that fabulous sofa and take a snooze, but you'd probably read *Southern Homes* first."

"Thank you." Frannie stepped out. "That's a lovely compliment. Cal, take everyone's coats, will you? I'm Frannie Hawkins."

"It's so nice to meet you. I'm Quinn. Thanks so much for having us. I hope you like mixed bouquets. I have a hard time deciding on one type of mostly anything."

"They're wonderful, thank you." Frannie accepted the flowers, smiled expectantly at Layla.

"I'm Layla Darnell, thank you for having us in your home. I hope the wine's appropriate."

"I'm sure it is." Frannie took a peek inside the gift bag. "Jim's favorite cabernet. Aren't you clever girls? Cal, go up and tell your father we have company. Hello, Fox."

"I brought you something, too." He grabbed her, lowered her into a stylish dip, and kissed both her cheeks. "What's cooking, sweetheart?"

As she had since he'd been a boy, Frannie ruffled his hair. "You won't have long to wait to find out. Quinn and Layla, you make yourselves comfortable. Fox, you come with me. I want to put these flowers in water."

"Is there anything we can do to help?"

"Not a thing."

When Cal came down with his father, Fox was doing his version of snooty French waiter as he served appetizers. The women were laughing, candles were lit, and his

mother carried in her grandmother's best crystal vase with
Quinn's flowers a colorful filling.

Sometimes, Cal mused, all really was right with the
world.

HALFWAY THROUGH THE MEAL, WHERE THE CON-
versation stayed in what Cal considered safe territories,
Quinn set down her fork, shook her head. "Mrs. Hawkins,
this is the most amazing meal, and I have to ask. Did you
study? Did you have a career as a gourmet chef at some
point or did we just hit you on a really lucky day?"

"I took a few classes."

"Frannie's taken a lot of 'a few classes,' " Jim said. "In
all kinds of things. But she's just got a natural talent for
cooking and gardening and decorating. What you see
around here, it's all her doing. Painted the walls, made the
curtains—sorry, window treatments," he corrected with a
twinkle at his wife.

"Get out. You did all the faux and fancy paintwork?
Yourself?"

"I enjoy it."

"Found that sideboard there years back at some flea
market, had me haul it home." Jim gestured toward the
gleaming mahogany sideboard. "A few weeks later, she
has me haul it in here. Thought she was pulling a fast
one, had snuck out and bought something from an antique
store."

"Martha Stewart eats your dust," Quinn decided. "I
mean that as a compliment."

"I'll take it."

"I'm useless at all of that. I can barely paint my own
nails. How about you?" Quinn asked Layla.

"I can't sew, but I like to paint. Walls. I've done some
ragging that turned out pretty well."

"The only ragging I've done successfully was on my ex-
fiancé."

"You were engaged?" Frannie asked.

"I thought I was. But our definition of same differed widely."

"It can be difficult to blend careers and personal lives."

"Oh, I don't know. People do it all the time—with varying degrees of success, sure, but they do. I think it just has to be the right people. The trick, or the first of probably many tricks, is recognizing the right person. Wasn't it like that for you? Didn't you have to recognize each other?"

"I knew the first time I saw Frannie. There she is." Jim beamed down the table at his wife. "Frannie now, she was a little more shortsighted."

"A little more practical," Frannie corrected, "seeing as we were eight and ten at the time. Plus I enjoyed having you moon over and chase after me. Yes, you're right." Frannie looked back at Quinn. "You have to see each other, and see in each other something that makes you want to take the chance, that makes you believe you can dig down for the long haul."

"And sometimes you think you see something," Quinn commented, "but it was just a—let's say—trompe l'oeil."

ONE THING QUINN KNEW HOW TO DO WAS FINA-gle. Frannie Hawkins wasn't an easy mark, but Quinn managed to charm her way into the kitchen to help put together dessert and coffee.

"I love kitchens. I'm kind of a pathetic cook, but I love all the gadgets and tools, all the shiny surfaces."

"I imagine with your work, you eat out a lot."

"Actually, I eat in most of the time or call for takeout. I implemented a lifestyle change—nutrition-wise—a couple of years ago. Determined to eat healthier, depend less on fast or nuke-it-out-of-a-box food. I make a really good salad these days. That's a start. Oh God, oh God, that's apple pie. Homemade apple pie. I'm going to have to do double duty in the gym as penance for the huge piece I'm going to ask for."

Her enjoyment obvious, Frannie shot her a wicked smile. "À la mode, with vanilla bean ice cream?"

"Yes, but only to show my impeccable manners." Quinn hesitated a moment, then jumped in. "I'm going to ask you, and if you want this off-limits while I'm enjoying your hospitality, just tell me to back off. Is it hard for you to nurture this normal life, to hold your family, yourself, your home together when you know all of it will be threatened?"

"It's very hard." Frannie turned to her pies while the coffee brewed. "Just as it's very necessary. I wanted Cal to go, and if he had I would have convinced Jim to leave. I could do that, I could turn my back on it all. But Cal couldn't. And I'm so proud of him for staying, for not giving up."

"Will you tell me what happened when he came home that morning, the morning of his tenth birthday?"

"I was in the yard." Frannie walked over to the window that faced the back. She could see it all, every detail. How green the grass was, how blue the sky. Her hydrangeas were headed up and beginning to pop, her delphiniums towering spears of exotic blue.

Deadheading her roses, and some of the coreopsis that had bloomed off. She could even hear the busy *snip, snip* of her shears, and the hum of the neighbor's—it had been the Petersons, Jack and Lois, then—lawn mower. She remembered, too, she'd been thinking about Cal, and his birthday party. She'd had his cake in the oven.

A double-chocolate sour cream cake, she remembered. She'd intended to do a white frosting to simulate the ice planet from one of the *Star Wars* movies. Cal had loved *Star Wars* for years and years. She'd had the little action figures to arrange on it, the ten candles all ready in the kitchen.

Had she heard him or sensed him—probably some of both—but she'd looked around as he'd come barreling up on his bike, pale, filthy, sweaty. Her first thought had been accident, there'd been an accident. And she'd been on her feet and rushing to him before she'd noticed he wasn't wearing his glasses.

"The part of me that registered that was ready to give him a good tongue-lashing. But the rest of me was still running when he climbed off his bike, and ran to me. He ran to me and he grabbed on so tight. He was shaking—my little boy—shaking like a leaf. I went down on my knees, pulling him back so I could check for blood or broken bones."

What is it, what happened, are you hurt? All of that, Frannie remembered had flooded out of her, so fast it was like one word. *In the woods,* he'd said. *Mom. Mom. In the woods.*

"There was that part of me again, the part that thought what were you doing in the woods, Caleb Hawkins? It all came pouring out of him, how he and Fox and Gage planned this adventure, what they'd done, where they'd gone. And that same part was coldly devising the punishment to fit the crime, even while the rest of me was terrified, and relieved, so pitifully relieved I was holding my dirty, sweaty boy. Then he told me the rest."

"You believed him?"

"I didn't want to. I wanted to believe he'd had a nightmare, which he richly deserved, that he'd stuffed himself on sweets and junk food and had a nightmare. Even, that someone had gone after them in the woods. But I couldn't look at his face and believe that. I couldn't believe the easy that, the fixable that. And then, of course, there were his eyes. He could see a bee hovering over the delphiniums across the yard. And under the dirt and sweat, there wasn't a bruise on him. The nine-year-old I'd sent off the day before had scraped knees and bruised shins. The one who came back to me hadn't a mark on him, but for the thin white scar across his wrist he hadn't had when he left."

"Even with that, a lot of adults, even mothers, wouldn't have believed a kid who came home with a story like that."

"I won't say Cal never lied to me, because obviously he did. He had. But I knew he wasn't lying. I knew he was telling me the truth, all the truth he knew."

"What did you do?"

"I took him inside, told him to clean up, change his clothes. I called his father, and got his sisters home. I burned his birthday cake—completely forgot about it, never heard the timer. Might've burned the house down if Cal himself hadn't smelled the burning. So he never got his ice planet or his ten candles. I hate remembering that. I burned his cake and he never got to blow out his birthday candles. Isn't that silly?"

"No, ma'am. No," Quinn said with feeling when Frannie looked at her, "it's not."

"He was never really, not wholly, a little boy again." Frannie sighed. "We went straight over to the O'Dells, because Fox and Gage were already there. We had what I guess you could call our first summit meeting."

"What did—"

"We need to take in the dessert and coffee. Can you handle that tray?"

Understanding the subject was closed for now, Quinn stepped over. "Sure. It looks terrific, Mrs. Hawkins."

In between moans and tears of joy over the pie, Quinn aimed her charm at Jim Hawkins. Cal, she was sure, had been dodging and weaving, avoiding and evading her since their hike to the Pagan Stone.

"Mr. Hawkins, you've lived in the Hollow all your life."

"Born and raised. Hawkinses have been here since the town was a couple of stone cabins."

"I met your grandmother, and she seems to know town history."

"Nobody knows more."

"People say you're the one who knows real estate, business, local politics."

"I guess I do."

"Then you may be able to point me in the right direction." She slid a look at Cal, then beamed back at his father. "I'm looking to rent a house, something in town or close to it. Nothing fancy, but I'd like room. I have a friend coming in soon, and I've nearly talked Layla into staying longer. I think we'd be more comfortable, and it would be more efficient, for the three of us to have a house instead of using the hotel."

"How long are you looking for?"

"Six months." She saw it register on his face, just as she noticed the frown form on Cal's. "I'm going to stay through July, Mr. Hawkins, and I'm hoping to find a house that would accommodate three women—potentially three—" she said with a glance at Layla.

"I guess you've thought that over."

"I have. I'm going to write this book, and part of the angle I'm after is the fact that the town remains, the people—a lot of them—stay. They stay and they make apple pie and have people over to Sunday dinner. They bowl, and they shop. They fight and they make love. They live. If I'm going to do this right, I want to be here, before, during, and after. So I'd like to rent a house."

Jim scooped up some pie, chased it with coffee. "It happens I know a place on High Street, just a block off Main. It's old, main part went up before the Civil War. It's got four bedrooms, three baths. Nice porches, front and back. Had a new roof on her two years ago. Kitchen's eat-in size, though there's a little dining room off it. Appliances aren't fancy, but they've only got five years on them. Just been painted. Tenants moved out just a month ago."

"It sounds perfect. You seem to know it well."

"Should. We own it. Cal, you should take Quinn by. Maybe run her and Layla over there on the way home. You know where the keys are."

"Yeah," he said when Quinn gave him a big, bright smile. "I know where the keys are."

As it made the most sense, Quinn hitched a ride with Cal, and left Fox and Layla to follow. She stretched out her legs, let out a sigh.

"Let me start off by saying your parents are terrific, and you're lucky to have grown up in such a warm, inviting home."

"I agree."

"Your dad's got that Ward Cleaver meets Jimmy Stewart thing going. I could've eaten him up like your mother's—Martha Stewart meets Grace Kelly by way of Julia Child—apple pie."

His lips twitched. "They'd both like those descriptions."

"You knew about the High Street house."

"Yeah, I did."

"You knew about the High Street house, and avoided telling me about it."

"That's right. You found out about it, too, before dinner, which is why you did the end-run around me to my father."

"Correct." She tapped her finger on his shoulder. "I figured he'd point me there. He likes me. Did you avoid telling me because you're not comfortable with what I might write about Hawkins Hollow?"

"Some of that. More, I was hoping you'd change your mind and leave. Because I like you, too."

"You like me, so you want me gone?"

"I like you, Quinn, so I want you safe." He looked at her again, longer. "But some of the things you said about the Hollow over apple pie echoed pretty closely some of the things my mother said to me today. It all but eliminates any discomfort with what you may decide to write. But it makes me like you more, and that's a problem."

"You had to know, after what happened to us in the woods, I wouldn't be leaving."

"I guess I did." He pulled off into a short, steep driveway.

"Is this the house? It *is* perfect! Look at the stonework, and the big porch, the windows have shutters."

They were painted a deep blue that stood out well against the gray stone. The little front yard was bisected by a trio of concrete steps and the narrow walkway. A trim tree Quinn thought might be a dogwood highlighted the left square of front yard.

As Fox's truck pulled in behind, Quinn popped out to stand, hands on hips. "Pretty damned adorable. Don't you think, Layla?"

"Yes, but—"

"No buts, not yet. Let's take a look inside." She cocked her head at Cal. "Okay, landlord?"

As they trooped up to the porch, Cal took out the keys he'd grabbed off their hook from his father's home office. The ring was clearly labeled with the High Street address.

The fact that the door opened without a creak told Quinn the landlords were vigilant in the maintenance department.

The door opened straight into the living area that stood twice as long as it was wide, with the steps to the second floor a couple of strides in on the left. The wood floors showed wear, but were spotlessly clean. The air was chilly and carried the light sting of fresh paint.

The small brick fireplace delighted her.

"Could use your mother's eye in the paint department," Quinn commented.

"Rental properties get eggshell, through and through. It's the Hawkins's way. Tenants want to play around with that, it's their deal."

"Reasonable. I want to start at the top, work down. Layla, do you want to go up and fight over who gets which bedroom?"

"No." Cal thought there was mutiny, as well as frustration on her face. "I *have* a bedroom. In New York."

"You're not in New York," Quinn said simply, then dashed up the steps.

"She's not listening to me," Layla muttered. "I don't seem to be listening to me either about going back."

"We're here." Fox gave a shrug. "Might as well poke around. I really dig empty houses."

"I'll be up." Cal started up the stairs.

He found her in one of the bedrooms, one that faced the tiny backyard. She stood at the long, narrow window, the fingertips of her right hand pressed to the glass. "I thought I'd go for one of the rooms facing the street, catch the who's going where when and with who. I usually go for that. Just have to know what's going on. But this is the one for me. I bet, in the daylight, you can stand here, see backyards, other houses, and wow, right on to the mountains."

"Do you always make up your mind so fast?"

"Yeah, usually. Even when I surprise myself like now. Bathroom's nice, too." She turned enough to gesture to the door on the side of the room. "And since it's girls, if any of us share that one, it won't be too weird having it link up the two bedrooms on this side."

"You're sure everyone will fall in line."

Now she turned to him, fully. "Confidence is the first step to getting what you want, or need. But we'll say I'm hoping Layla and Cyb will agree it's efficient, practical, and would be more comfortable to share the house for a few months than to bunk at the hotel. Especially considering the fact that both Layla and I are pretty well put off of the dining room there after Slugfest."

"You don't have any furniture."

"Flea markets. We'll pick up the essentials. Cal, I've stayed in less stellar accommodations and done it for one thing. A story. This is more. Somehow or other I'm connected to this story, this place. I can't turn that off and walk away."

He wished she could, and knew if she could his feelings for her wouldn't be as strong or as complex. "Okay, but let's agree, here and now, that if you change your mind and do just that, no explanations needed."

"That's a deal. Now, let's talk rent. What's this place going to run us?"

"You pay the utilities—heat, electric, phone, cable."

"Naturally. And?"

"That's it."

"What do you mean, that's it?"

"I'm not going to charge you rent, not when you're staying here, at least in part, because of me. My family, my friends, my town. We're not going to make a profit off that."

"Straight arrow, aren't you, Caleb?"

"About most."

"I'll make a profit—she says optimistically—from the book I intend to write."

"If we get through July and you write a book, you'll have earned it."

"Well, you drive a hard bargain, but it looks like we have a deal." She stepped forward, offered a hand.

He took it, then cupped his other at the back of her neck. Surprise danced in her eyes, but she didn't resist as he eased her toward him.

He moved slow, the closing together of bodies, the meeting of lips, the testing slide of tongues. There was no explosion of need as there had been in that moment in the clearing. No sudden, almost painful shock of desire. Instead, it was a long and gradual glide from interest to pleasure to ache while her head went light and her blood warmed. It seemed everything inside her went quiet so that she heard, very clearly, the low hum in her own throat as he changed the angle of the kiss.

He felt her give, degree by degree, even as he felt the hand he held in his go lax. The tension that had dogged him throughout the day drained away, so there was only the moment, the quiet, endless moment.

Even when he drew back, that inner stillness held. And she opened her eyes, met his.

"That was just you and me."

"Yeah." He stroked his fingers over the back of her neck. "Just you and me."

"I want to say that I have a policy against becoming romantically, intimately, or sexually—just to cover all my bases—involved with anyone directly associated with a story I'm researching."

"That's probably smart."

"I am smart. I also want to say I'm going to negate that policy in this particular case."

He smiled. "Damn right you are."

"Cocky. Well, mixed with the straight arrow, I have to like it. Unfortunately, I should get back to the hotel. I have a lot of . . . things. Details to see to before I can move in here."

"Sure. I can wait."

He kept her hand in his, switching off the light as he led her out.

Eleven

~~

CAL SENT A DOZEN PINK ROSES TO HIS MOTHER.
She liked the traditional flower for Valentine's Day, and he
knew his father always went for the red. If he hadn't
known, Amy Yost in the flower shop would have reminded
him, as she did every blessed year.

"Your dad ordered a dozen red last week, for delivery
today, potted geranium to his grandma, *and* he sent the
Valentine's Day Sweetheart Special to your sisters."

"That suck-up," Cal said, knowing it would make Amy
gasp and giggle. "How about a dozen yellow for my gran.
In a vase, Amy. I don't want her to have to fool with them."

"Aw, that's sweet. I've got Essie's address on file, you
just fill out the card."

He picked one out of the slot, gave it a minute's thought
before writing: *Hearts are red, these roses are yellow.
Happy Valentine's Day from your best fellow.*

Corny, sure, he decided, but Gran would love it.

He reached for his wallet to pay when he noticed the

red-and-white-striped tulips behind the glass doors of the refrigerated display. "Ah, those tulips are . . . interesting."

"Aren't they pretty? And they just make me feel like spring. It's no problem if you want to change either of the roses for them. I can just—"

"No, no, maybe . . . I'll take a dozen of them, too. Another delivery in a vase, Amy."

"Sure." Her cheerful round face lit up with curiosity and the anticipation of good gossip. "Who's your valentine, Cal?"

"It's more a housewarming kind of thing." He couldn't think of any reason why *not* to send Quinn flowers. Women liked flowers, he thought as he filled out the delivery form. It was Valentine's Day, and she was moving into the High Street house. It wasn't like he was buying her a ring and picking out a band for the wedding.

It was just a nice gesture.

"Quinn Black." Amy wiggled her eyebrows as she read the name on the form. "Meg Stanley ran into her at the flea market yesterday, along with that friend of hers from New York. They bought a bunch of stuff, according to Meg. I heard you were going around with her."

"We're not . . ." Were they? Either way, it was best to leave it alone. "Well, what's the damage, Amy?"

With his credit card still humming, he stepped outside, hunched his shoulders against the cold. There might be candy-striped tulips, but it didn't feel as if Mother Nature was giving so much as a passing thought to spring. The sky spat out a thin and bitter sleet that lay slick as grease on the streets and sidewalks.

He'd walked down from the bowling center as was his habit, timing his arrival at the florist to their ten o'clock opening. It was the best way to avoid the panicked rush of others who had waited until the last minute to do the Valentine's thing.

It didn't appear he'd needed to worry. Not only had no other customers come in while he'd been buying his roses and impulsive tulips, but there was no one on the sidewalks, no cars creeping cautiously toward the curb in front of the Flower Pot.

"Strange." His voice sounded hollow against the sizzle of sleet striking asphalt. Even on the crappiest day, he'd pass any number of people on his walks around town. He shoved his gloveless hands into his pockets and cursed himself for not breaking his routine and driving.

"Creatures of habit freeze their asses off," he muttered. He wanted to be inside in his office, drinking a cup of coffee, even preparing to start the cancellation process on the evening's scheduled Sweetheart Dance if the sleet worsened. If he'd just taken the damn truck, he'd already be there.

So thinking, he looked up toward the center, and saw the stoplight at the Town Square was out.

Power down, Cal thought, and that was a problem. He quickened his steps. He knew Bill Turner would make certain the generator kicked on for the emergency power, but he needed to be there. School was out, and that meant kids were bound to be scattered around in the arcade.

The hissing of the sleet increased until it sounded like the forced march of an army of giant insects. Despite the slick sidewalk, Cal found himself breaking into a jog when it struck him.

Why weren't there any cars at the Square, or parked at the curbs? Why weren't there any cars anywhere?

He stopped, and so did the hiss of the sleet. In the ensuing silence, he heard his own heart thumping like a fist against steel.

She stood so close he might have reached out to touch her, and knew if he tried, his hand would pass through her as it would through water.

Her hair was deep blond, worn long and loose as it had been when she'd carried the pails toward the little cabin in Hawkins Wood. When she'd sung about a garden green. But her body was slim and straight in a long gray dress.

He had the ridiculous thought that if he had to see a ghost, at least it wasn't a pregnant one.

As if she heard his thoughts, she smiled. "I am not your fear, but you are my hope. You and those who make up the whole of you. What makes you, Caleb Hawkins, is of the past, the now, and the yet to come."

"Who are you? Are you Ann?"

"I am what came before you, and you are formed through love. Know that, know that long, long before you came into the world, you were loved."

"Love isn't enough."

"No, but it is the rock on which all else stands. You have to look; you have to see. This is the time, Caleb. This was always to be the time."

"The time for what?"

"The end of it. Seven times three. Death or life. He holds it, prevents it. Without his endless struggle, his sacrifice, his courage, all this . . ." She held out her arms. "All would be destroyed. Now it is for you."

"Just tell me what I need to do. Goddamn it."

"If I could. If I could spare you." She lifted a hand, let it fall again. "There must be struggle, and sacrifice, and great courage. There must be faith. There must be love. It is courage, faith, love that holds it so long, that prevents it from taking all who live and breathe within this place. Now it is for you."

"We don't know *how*. We've tried."

"This is the time," she repeated. "It is stronger, but so are you, and so are we. Use what you were given, take what it sowed but could never own. You cannot fail."

"Easy for you to say. You're dead."

"But you are not. They are not. Remember that."

When she started to fade, he did reach out, uselessly. "Wait, damn it. Wait. Who are you?"

"Yours," she said. "Yours as I am and always will be his."

She was gone, and the sleet sizzled on the pavement again. Cars rumbled by as the traffic light on the Square glowed green.

"Not the spot for daydreaming." Meg Stanley skidded by, giving him a wink as she pulled open the door of Ma's Pantry.

"No," Cal muttered. "It's not."

He started toward the center again, then veered off to take a detour to High Street.

Quinn's car was in the drive, and through the windows he could see the lights she must've turned on to chase back the gloom. He knocked, heard a muffled call to come in.

When he did, he saw Quinn and Layla trying to muscle something that resembled a desk up the stairs.

"What are you doing? Jesus." He stepped over to grip the side of the desk beside Quinn. "You're going to hurt yourselves."

In an annoyed move, she tossed her head to flip the hair away from her face. "We're managing."

"You'll be managing a trip to the ER. Go on up, take that end with Layla."

"Then we'll both be walking backward. Why don't you take that end?"

"Because I'm going to be taking the bulk of the weight this way."

"Oh." She let go, squeezed between the wall and the desk.

He didn't bother to ask why it had to go up. He'd lived with his mother too long to waste his breath. Instead he grunted out orders to prevent the edge of the desk from bashing into the wall as they angled left at the top of the stairs. Then followed Quinn as she directed the process to the window in the smallest bedroom.

"See, we were right." Quinn panted, and tugged down a Penn State sweatshirt. "This is the spot for it."

There was a seventies chair that had seen better days, a pole lamp with a rosy glass shade that dripped long crystals, and a low bookshelf varnished black over decades that wobbled when he set a hand on it.

"I know, I know." Quinn waved away his baleful look.

"But it just needs a little hammering or something, and it's really just to fill things out. We were thinking about making it a little sitting room, then decided it would be better as a little office. Hence the desk we originally thought should be in the dining room."

"Okay."

"The lamp looks like something out of *The Best Little Whorehouse in Texas*." Layla gave one of the crystals a flick with her fingers. "But that's what we like about it. The chair is hideous."

"But comfortable," Quinn inserted.

"But comfortable, and that's what throws are for."

Cal waited a beat as both of them looked at him expectantly. "Okay," he repeated, which was generally how he handled his mother's decorating explanations.

"We've been busy. We turned in Layla's rental car, then hit the flea market just out of town. Bonanza. Plus we agreed no secondhand mattresses. The ones we ordered should be here this afternoon. Anyway, come see what we've got going so far."

Quinn grabbed his hand, pulled him across the hall to the room she'd chosen. There was a long bureau desperately in need of refinishing, topped by a spotted mirror. Across the room was a boxy chest someone had painted a murderous and shiny red. On it stood a Wonder Woman lamp.

"Homey."

"It'll be very livable when we're done."

"Yeah. You know I think that lamp might've been my sister Jen's twenty, twenty-five years ago."

"It's classic," Quinn claimed. "It's kitschy."

He fell back on the standard. "Okay."

"I think I have Danish modern," Layla commented from the doorway. "Or possibly Flemish. It's absolutely horrible. I have no idea why I bought it."

"Did you two haul this stuff up here?"

"Please." Quinn tossed her head.

"We opted for brain over brawn."

"Every time. That and a small investment. Do you know how much a couple of teenage boys will cart and carry for twenty bucks each and the opportunity to ogle a couple of hot chicks such as we?" Quinn fisted a hand on her hip, struck a pose.

"I'd've done it for ten. You could have called."

"Which was our intention, actually. But the boys were handy. Why don't we go down and sit on our new third- or fourthhand sofa?"

"We did splurge," Layla added. "We have an actual new coffeemaker and a very eclectic selection of coffee mugs."

"Coffee'd be good."

"I'll get it started."

Cal glanced after Layla. "She seems to have done a one-eighty on all this."

"I'm persuasive. And you're generous. I think I should plant one on you for that."

"Go ahead. I can take it."

Laughing, she braced her hands on his shoulders, gave him a firm, noisy kiss.

"Does that mean I don't get ten bucks?"

Her smile beamed as she poked him in the belly. "You'll take the kiss and like it. Anyway, part of the reason for Layla hanging back was the money. The idea of staying was—is—difficult for her. But the idea of taking a long leave, unpaid, from her job, coming up with rent money here, keeping her place in New York, that was pretty much off the table."

She stepped up to the bright red chest to turn her Wonder Woman lamp on and off. From the look on her face, Cal could see the act pleased her.

"So, the rent-free aspect checked one problem off her list," Quinn went on. "She hasn't completely committed. Right now, it's a day at a time for her."

"I've got something to tell you, both of you, that may make this her last day."

"Something happened." She dropped her hand, turned. "What happened?"

"I'll tell you both. I want to call Fox first, see if he can swing by. Then I can tell it once."

HE HAD TO DO IT WITHOUT FOX, WHO, ACCORD-ing to Mrs. Hawbaker, was at the courthouse being a lawyer. So he sat in the oddly furnished living room on a couch so soft and saggy he was already wishing for the op-portunity to get Quinn naked on it, and told them about the visitation on Main Street.

"An OOB," Quinn decided.

"An oob?"

"No, no. Initials, like CYA. Out of body—experience. It sounds like that might be what you had, or maybe there was a slight shift in dimensions and you were in an alter-nate Hawkins Hollow."

He might have spent two-thirds of his life caught up in something beyond rational belief, but he'd never heard an-other woman talk like Quinn Black. "I was not in an alternate anything, and I was right inside my body where I belong."

"I've been studying, researching, and writing about the paranormal for some time now." Quinn drank some coffee and brooded over it.

"It could be he was talking to a ghost who caused the il-lusion that they were alone on the street, and caused every-one else out there to—I don't know—blip out for a few minutes." Layla shrugged at Quinn's narrowed look. "I'm new at this, and I'm still working really hard not to hide under the covers until somebody wakes me up and tells me this was all a dream."

"For the new kid, your theory's pretty good," Quinn told her.

"How about mine? Which is what she said is a hell of a lot more important right now than how she said it."

"Point taken." Quinn nodded at Cal. "This is the time, she said. Three times seven. That one's easy enough to figure."

"Twenty-one years." Cal pushed up to pace. "This July makes twenty-one years."

"Three, like seven, is considered a magickal number. It sounds like she was telling you it was always going to come now, this July, this year. It's stronger, you're stronger, they're stronger." Quinn squeezed her eyes shut.

"So, it and this woman—this spirit—have both been able to . . ."

"Manifest." Quinn finished Layla's thought. "That follows the logic."

"Nothing about this is logical."

"It is, really." Opening her eyes again, Quinn gave Layla a sympathetic look. "Inside this sphere, there's logic. It's just not the kind we deal with, or most of us deal with, every day. The past, the now, the yet to be. Things that happened, that are happening, and that will or may are all part of the solution, the way to end it."

"I think there's more to that part." Cal turned back from the window. "After that night in the clearing, the three of us were different."

"You don't get sick, and you heal almost as soon as you're hurt. Quinn told me."

"Yeah. And I could see."

"Without your glasses."

"I could also see before. I started—right there minutes afterward—to have flashes of the past."

"The way you did—both of us did," Quinn corrected, "when we touched the stone together. And later, when we—"

"Like that, not always that clear, not always so intense. Sometimes awake, sometimes like a dream. Sometimes completely irrelevant. And Fox . . . It took him a while to understand. Jesus, we were ten. He can see now." Annoyed with himself, Cal shook his head. "He can see, or sense what you're thinking, or feeling."

"Fox is psychic?" Layla demanded.

"Psychic lawyer. He's so hired."

Despite everything, Quinn's announcement made Cal's lips twitch. "Not like that, not exactly. It's never been something we can completely control. Fox has to deliberately push it, and it doesn't always work then. But since then he has an instinct about people. And Gage—"

"He sees what could happen," Quinn added. "He's the soothsayer."

"It's hardest for him. That's why—one of the reasons why—he doesn't spend much time here. It's harder here. He's had some pretty damn vicious dreams, visions, nightmares, whatever the hell you want to call them."

And it hurts you when he hurts, Quinn thought. "But he hasn't seen what you're meant to do?"

"No. That would be too easy, wouldn't it?" Cal said bitterly. "Has to be more fun to mess up the lives of three kids, to let innocent people die or kill and maim each other. Stretch that out for a couple of decades, then say: Okay, boys, now's the time."

"Maybe there was no choice." Quinn held up a hand when Cal's eyes fired. "I'm not saying it's fair. In fact, it sucks. Inside and out, it sucks. I'm saying maybe it couldn't be another way. Whether it was something Giles Dent did, or something set in motion centuries before that, there may have been no other choice. She said he was holding it, that he was preventing it from destroying the Hollow. If it was Ann, and she meant Giles Dent, does that mean he trapped this thing, this *bestia*, and in some form— *beatus*—has been trapped with it, battling it, all this time? Three hundred and fifty years and change. That sucks, too."

Layla jumped at the brisk knock on the door, then popped up. "I'll get it. Maybe it's the delivery."

"You're not wrong," Cal said quietly. "But it doesn't make it easier to live through it. It doesn't make it easier to know, in my gut, that we're coming up to our last chance."

Quinn got to her feet. "I wish—"

"It's flowers!" Layla's voice was giddy with delight as she came in carrying the vase of tulips. "For you, Quinn."

"Jesus, talk about weird timing," Cal muttered.

"For me? Oh God, they look like lollipop cups. They're gorgeous!" Quinn set them on the ancient coffee table. "Must be a bribe from my editor so I'll finish that article on—" She broke off as she ripped open the card. Her face was blank with shock as she lifted her eyes to Cal. "You sent me flowers?"

"I was in the florist before—"

"You sent me flowers on Valentine's Day."

"I hear my mother calling," Layla announced. "Coming, Mom!" She made a fast exit.

"You sent me tulips that look like blooming candy canes on Valentine's Day."

"They looked like fun."

"That's what you wrote on the card. 'These look like fun.' Wow." She scooped a hand through her hair. "I have to say that I'm a sensible woman, who knows very well Valentine's Day is a commercially generated holiday designed to sell greeting cards, flowers, and candy."

"Yeah, well." He slid his hands into his pockets. "Works."

"And I'm not the type of woman who goes all mushy and gooey over flowers, or sees them as an apology for an argument, a prelude to sex, or any of the other oft-perceived uses."

"I just saw them, thought you'd get a kick out of them. Period. I've got to get to work."

"But," she continued and moved toward him, "strangely, I find none of that applies in the least in this particular case. They are fun." She rose up on her toes, kissed his cheek. "And they're beautiful." Then his other cheek. "And thoughtful." Now his lips. "Thank you."

"You're welcome."

"I'd like to add that . . ." She trailed her hands down his shirt, up again. "If you'll tell me what time you finish up tonight, I'll have a bottle of wine waiting in my bedroom upstairs, where I can promise you, you're going to get really, really lucky."

"Eleven," he said immediately. "I can be here at eleven-oh-five. I— Oh shit. Sweetheart Dance, that's midnight. Special event. No problem. You'll come."

"That's my plan." When he grinned, she rolled her eyes. "You mean to this dance. At the Bowl-a-Rama. A Sweetheart Dance at the Bowl-a-Rama. God, I'd *love* that. But, I can't leave Layla here, not at night. Not alone."

"She can come, too—to the dance."

Now her eyeroll was absolutely sincere. "Cal, no woman wants to tag along with a couple to a dance on Valentine's Day. It paints a big *L* for loser in the middle of her forehead, and they're so damn hard to wash off."

"Fox can take her. Probably. I'll check."

"That's a possibility, especially if we make it all for fun. You check, then I'll check, then we'll see. But either way." She grabbed a fistful of his shirt, and this time brought him to her for a long, long kiss. "My bedroom, twelve-oh-five."

LAYLA SAT ON HER BRAND-NEW DISCOUNT MATtress while Quinn busily checked out the clothes she'd recently hung in her closet.

"Quinn, I appreciate the thought, I really do, but put yourself in my place. The third-wheel position."

"It's perfectly acceptable to be the third wheel when there're four wheels altogether. Fox is going."

"Because Cal asked him to take pity on the poor dateless V-Day loser. Probably told him or bribed him or—"

"You're right. Fox certainly had to have his arm twisted to go out with such an ugly hag like yourself. I admit every time I look at you, I'm tempted to go: woof, woof, what a dog. Besides . . . Oh, I love this jacket! You have the best clothes. But this jacket is seriously awesome. Mmm." Quinn stroked it like a cat. "Cashmere."

"I don't know why I packed it. I don't know why I packed half the stuff I did. I just started grabbing things. And you're trying to distract me."

"Not really, but it's a nice side benefit. What was I saying? Oh, yeah. Besides, it's not a date. It's a gang bang," she said and made Layla laugh. "It's just the four of us going to a bowling alley, for God's sake, to hear some local band play and dance a little."

"Sure. After which, you'll be hanging a scarf over the doorknob of your bedroom. I went to college, Quinn. I had a roommate. Actually, I had a nympho of a roommate who had an endless supply of scarves."

"Is it a problem?" Quinn stopped poking in the closet long enough to look over her shoulder. "Cal and me, across the hall?"

"No. No." And now didn't she feel stupid and petty? "I think it's great. Really, I do. Anybody can tell the two of you rev like engines when you're within three feet of each other."

"They can?" Quinn turned all the way around now. "We do."

"*Vroom, vroom.* He's great, it's great. I just feel . . ." Layla rolled her shoulders broadly. "In the way."

"You're not. I couldn't stay here without you. I'm pretty steady, but I couldn't stay in this house alone. The dance isn't a big deal. We don't have to go, but I think it'd be fun, for all of us. And a chance to do something absolutely normal to take our minds off everything that isn't."

"That's a good point."

"So get dressed. Put on something fun, maybe a little sexy, and let's hit the Bowl-a-Rama."

THE BAND, A LOCAL GROUP NAMED HOLLOWED Out, was into its first set. They were popular at weddings and corporate functions, and regularly booked at the center's events because their playlist ran the gamut from old standards to hip-hop. The something-for-everybody kept the dance floor lively while those sitting one out could chat at one of the tables circling the room, sip drinks, or nibble from the light buffet set up along one of the side walls.

Cal figured it was one of the center's most popular annual events for good reason. His mother headed up the decorating committee, so there were flowers and candles, red and white streamers, glittering red hearts. It gave people a chance to get a little dressed up in the dullness that was

February, get out and socialize, hear some music, show off their moves if they had them. Or like Cy Hudson, even if they didn't.

It was a little bright spot toward the end of a long winter, and they never failed to have a full house.

Cal danced with Essie to "Fly Me to the Moon."

"Your mother was right to make you take those dance lessons."

"I was humiliated among my peers," Cal said. "But light on my feet."

"Women tend to lose their heads over a good dancer."

"A fact I've exploited whenever possible." He smiled down at her. "You look so pretty, Gran."

"I look dignified. Now, there was a day when I turned plenty of heads."

"You still turn mine."

"And you're still the sweetest of my sweethearts. When are you going to bring that pretty writer to see me?"

"Soon, if that's what you want."

"It feels like time. I don't know why. And speaking of—" She nodded toward the open double doors. "Those two turn heads."

He looked. He noticed Layla, in that she was there. But his focus was all for Quinn. She'd wound that mass of blond hair up, a touch of elegance, and wore an open black jacket over some kind of lacey top—camisole, he remembered. They called them camisoles, and God bless whoever invented them.

Things glittered at her ears, at her wrists, but all he could think was she had the sexiest collarbone in the history of collarbones, and he couldn't wait to get his mouth on it.

"You're about to drool, Caleb."

"What?" He blinked his attention back to Essie. "Oh. Jeez."

"She does look a picture. You take me on back to my table now and go get her. Bring her and her friend around to say hello before I leave."

By the time he got to them, Fox had already scooped them up to one of the portable bars and sprung for champagne. Quinn turned to Cal, glass in hand, and pitched her voice over the music. "This is great! The band's hot, the bubbly's cold, and the room looks like a love affair."

"You were expecting a couple of toothless guys with a washboard and a jug, some hard cider, and a few plastic hearts."

"No." She laughed, jabbed him with her finger. "But something between that and this. It's my first bowling alley dance, and I'm impressed. And look! Isn't that His Honor, the mayor, getting down?"

"With his wife's cousin, who is the choir director for the First Methodist Church."

"Isn't that your assistant, Fox?" Layla gestured to a table.

"Yeah. Fortunately, the guy she's kissing is her husband."

"They look completely in love."

"Guess they are. I don't know what I'm going to do without her. They're moving to Minneapolis in a couple months. I wish they'd just take off for a few weeks in July instead of—" He caught himself. "No shop talk tonight. Do you want to scare up a table?"

"Perfect for people-watching," Quinn agreed, then spun toward the band. " 'In the Mood'!"

"Signature piece for them. Do you swing?" Cal asked her.

"Damn right." She glanced at him, considered. "Do you?"

"Let's go see what you've got, Blondie." He grabbed her hand, pulled her out to the dance floor.

Fox watched the spins and footwork. "I absolutely can't do that."

"Neither can I. Wow." Layla's eyes widened. "They're really good."

On the dance floor, Cal set Quinn up for a double spin, whipped her back. "Lessons?"

"Four years. You?"

"Three." When the song ended and bled into a slow number, he fit Quinn's body to his and blessed his mother. "I'm glad you're here."

"Me, too." She nuzzled her cheek to his. "Everything feels good tonight. Sweet and shiny. And mmm," she murmured when he led her into a stylish turn. "Sexy." Tipping back her head, she smiled at him. "I've completely reversed my cynical take on Valentine's Day. I now consider it the perfect holiday."

He brushed his lips over hers. "After this dance, why don't we sneak off to the storeroom upstairs and neck?"

"Why wait?"

With a laugh, he started to bring her close again. And froze.

The hearts bled. The glittery art board dripped, and splattered red on the dance floor, plopped on tables, slid down the hair and faces of people while they laughed, or chatted, strolled or swayed.

"Quinn."

"I see it. Oh God."

The vocalist continued to sing of love and longing as the red and silver balloons overhead popped like gunshots. And from them rained spiders.

Twelve

~~

QUINN BARELY MANAGED TO MUFFLE A SCREAM, and would have danced back as the spiders skittered over the floor if Cal hadn't gripped her.

"Not real." He said it with absolute and icy calm. "It's not real."

Someone laughed, and the sound spiked wildly. There were shouts of approval as the music changed tempo to hip-grinding rock.

"Great party, Cal!" Amy from the flower shop danced by with a wide, blood-splattered grin.

With his arm still tight around Quinn, Cal began to back off the floor. He needed to see his family, needed to see . . . And there was Fox, gripping Layla's hand as he wound his way through the oblivious crowd.

"We need to go," Fox shouted.

"My parents—"

Fox shook his head. "It's only happening because we're here. I think it only can happen because we're here. Let's move out. Let's move."

As they pushed between tables, the tiny tea lights in the centerpieces flashed like torches, belching a volcanic spew of smoke. Cal felt it in his throat, stinging, even as his foot crunched down on a fist-sized spider. On the little stage, the drummer swung into a wild solo with bloodied sticks. When they reached the doors, Cal glanced back.

He saw the boy floating above the dancers. Laughing.

"Straight out." Following Fox's line of thought, Cal pulled Quinn toward the exit. "Straight out of the building. Then we'll see. Then we'll damn well see."

"They didn't see." Out of breath, Layla stumbled outside. "Or feel. It wasn't happening for them."

"It's outside the box, okay, it's pushed outside the lines. But only for us." Fox stripped off his jacket and tossed it over Layla's shaking shoulders. "Giving us a preview of coming attractions. Arrogant bastard."

"Yes." Quinn nodded, even as her stomach rolled. "I think you're right, because every time it puts on a show, it costs energy. So we get that lull between production numbers."

"I have to go back." He'd left his family. Even if retreat was to defend, Cal couldn't stand and do nothing while his family was inside. "I need to be in there, need to close down when the event's over."

"We'll all go back," Quinn linked her cold fingers with Cal's. "These performances are always of pretty short duration. It lost its audience, and unless it's got enough for a second act, it's done for tonight. Let's go back. It's freezing out here."

Inside, the tea lights glimmered softly, and the hearts glittered. The polished dance floor was unstained. Cal saw his parents dancing, his mother's head resting on his father's shoulder. When she caught his eye and smiled at him, Cal felt the fist twisting in his belly relax.

"I don't know about you, but I'd really like another glass of champagne." Quinn blew out a breath, as her eyes went sharp and hard. "Then you know what? Let's dance."

FOX WAS SPRAWLED ON THE COUCH WATCHING some drowsy black-and-white movie on TV when Cal and Quinn came into the rental house after midnight. "Layla went up," he said as he shoved himself to sitting. "She was beat."

The subtext, that she'd wanted to be well tucked away before her housemate and Cal came up, was perfectly clear.

"Is she all right?" Quinn asked.

"Yeah. Yeah, she handles herself. Anything else happen after we left?"

Cal shook his head as his gaze tracked over to the window, and the dark. "Just a big, happy party momentarily interrupted for some of us by supernatural blood and spiders. Everything okay here?"

"Yeah, except for the fact these women buy Diet Pepsi. Classic Coke," he said to Quinn. "A guy has to have some standards."

"We'll look right into that. Thanks, Fox." She stepped up and kissed his cheek. "For hanging out until we got back."

"No big. It got me out of cleanup duty and let me watch . . ." He looked back at the little TV screen. "I have no idea. You ought to think about getting cable. ESPN."

"I don't know how I've lived without it these last few days."

He grinned as he pulled on his coat. "Humankind shouldn't live by network alone. Call me if you need anything," he added as he headed for the door.

"Fox." Cal trailed behind him. After a murmured conversation, Fox sent Quinn a quick wave and left.

"What was that?"

"I asked if he'd bunk at my place tonight, check on Lump. It's no problem. I've got Coke and ESPN."

"You've got worry all over you, Cal."

"I'm having a hard time taking it off."

"It can't hurt us, not yet. It's all head games. Mean, disgusting, but just psychological warfare."

"It means something, Quinn." He gave her arms a quick, almost absent rub before turning to check the dark, again. "That it can do it now, with us. That I had that episode with Ann. It means something."

"And you have to think about it. You think a lot, have all sorts of stores up here." She tapped her temple. "The fact that you do is, well, it's comforting to me and oddly attractive. But you know what? After this really long, strange day, it might be good for us not to think at all."

"That's a good idea." Take a break, he told himself. Take some normal. Walking back to her, he skimmed his fingers over her cheek, then let them trail down her arm until they linked with hers. "Why don't we try that?"

He drew her toward the steps, started up. There were a few homey creaks, the click and hum of the furnace, and nothing else.

"Do you—"

He cut her off by cupping a hand on her cheek, then laying his lips on hers. Soft and easy as a sigh. "No questions either. Then we'd have to think of the answers."

"Good point."

Just the room, the dark, the woman. That was all there would be, all he wanted for the night. Her scent, her skin, the fall of her hair, the sounds two people made when they discovered each other.

It was enough. It was more than enough.

He closed the door behind him.

"I like candles." She drew away to pick up a long, slim lighter to set the candles she'd scattered around the room to flame.

In their light she looked delicate, more delicate than she was. He enjoyed the contrast of reality and illusion. The mattress and box spring sat on the floor, covered by sheets that looked crisp and pearly against a blanket of deep, rich purple. His tulips sat like a cheerful carnival on the scarred wood of her flea market dresser.

She'd hung fabric in a blurry blend of colors over the windows to close out the night. And when she turned from them, she smiled.

It was, for him, perfect.

"Maybe I should tell you—"

He shook his head, stepped toward her.

"Later." He did the first thing that came to mind, lifting his hands to her hair. He drew the pins out, let them fall. When the weight of it tumbled free, over her shoulders, down her back, he combed his fingers through it. With his eyes on hers, he wrapped her hair around his fist like a rope, gave a tug.

"There's still a lot of later," he said, and took her mouth with his.

Her lips, for him, were perfect. Soft and full, warm and generous. He felt a quick tremble from her as her arms wound around him, as she pressed her body to his. She didn't yield, didn't soften—not yet. Instead she met his slow, patient assault with one of her own.

He slid the jacket from her shoulders, let it fall like the pins so his hands, his fingertips could explore silk and lace and flesh. While their lips brushed, rubbed, pressed, her hands came to his shoulders, then shoved at his jacket until it dropped away.

He tasted her throat, heard her purr of approval. As he eased back, he danced his fingers over the alluring line of her collarbone. Her eyes were vivid, alight with anticipation. He wanted to see them heavy. He wanted to see them go blind. Watching them, watching her, he let his fingers trail down to the swell of her breast where the lace flirted. And watching her still, glided them over the lace, over the silk to cup her while his thumb lightly rubbed, rubbed to tease her nipple.

He heard her breath catch, release, felt her shiver even

as she reached to him to unbutton his shirt. Her hands slid up his torso, spread. He knew his heartbeat skipped, but his own hand made the journey almost lazily to the waistband of her pants. The flesh there was warm, and her muscles quivered as his fingers did a testing sweep. Then with a flick and a tug, her pants floated down her legs.

The move was so sudden, so unexpected, she couldn't anticipate or prepare. Everything had been so slow, so dreamy, then his hands hooked under her arms, lifted her straight off her feet. The quick, careless show of strength shocked her system, made her head swim. Even when he set her back down, her knees stayed weak.

His gaze skimmed down, over the camisole, over the frothy underwear she'd donned with the idea of making him crazy. His lips curved as his eyes came back to hers.

"Nice."

It was all he said, and her mouth went dry. It was ridiculous. She'd had other men look at her, touch her, want her. But he did, and her throat went dry. She tried to find something clever and careless to say back, but could barely find the wit to breathe.

Then he hooked his finger in the waist of her panties, gave one easy tug. She stepped toward him like a woman under a spell.

"Let's see what's under here," he murmured, and lifted the camisole over her head. "Very nice," was his comment as he traced his fingertip along the edge of her bra.

She couldn't remember her moves, had to remind herself she was *good* at this—actively good, not just the type who went limp and let a guy do all the work. She reached for the hook of his trousers, fumbled.

"You're shaking."

"Shut up. I feel like an idiot."

He took her hands, brought them both to his lips and she knew she was as sunk as the *Titanic*. "Sexy," he corrected. "What you are is stupendously sexy."

"Cal." She had to concentrate to form the words. "I really need to lie down."

There was that smile again, and though it might have transmitted *self-satisfied male*, she really didn't give a damn.

Then they were on the bed, aroused bodies on cool, crisp sheets, candlelight flickering like magic in the dark. And his hands, his mouth, went to work on her.

He runs a bowling alley, she thought as he simply saturated her with pleasure. How did he get hands like this? Where did he learn to . . . Oh my God.

She came in a long, rolling wave that seemed to curl up from her toes, ride over her legs, burst in her center then wash over heart and mind. She clung to it, greedily wringing every drop of shock and delight until she was both limp and breathless.

Okay, okay, was all her brain could manage. Okay, wow.

Her body was a feast of curves and quivers. He could have lingered over those lovely breasts, the strong line of torso, that feminine flare of hip for days. Then there were her legs, smooth and strong and . . . sensitive. So many places to touch, so much to taste, and all the endless night to savor.

She rose to him, wrapped around him, arched and flowed and answered. He felt her heart thundering under his lips, heard her moan as he used his tongue to torment. Her fingers dug into his shoulders, his hips, her hands squeezing then gliding to fray the taut line of his control.

Kisses became more urgent. The cool air of the room went hot, went thick as smoke. When the need became a blur, he slipped inside her. And yes, watched her eyes go blind.

He gripped her hands to anchor himself, to stop himself from simply plunging, from bulleting by the aching pleasure to release. Her fingers tightened on his, and that pleasure glowed on her face with each long, slow thrust. Stay with me, he thought, and she did, beat for beat. Until it built and built in her ragged breaths, in the shivering of her body. She made a helpless sound as she closed her eyes, turned her head on the pillow. When her body melted under him, he pressed his face to that exposed curve of her neck. And let himself go.

HE LAY QUIET, THINKING SHE MIGHT HAVE FALLEN asleep. She'd rolled so that her head was on his shoulder, her arm tossed across his chest, and her leg hooked around his. It was, he thought, a little like being tied up with a Quinn bow. And he couldn't find anything not to like about it.

"I was going to say something."

Not asleep, he realized, though her words were drunk and slurry.

"About what?"

"Mmm. I was going to say, when we first came into the room. I was going to say something." She curled closer, and he realized the heat sex had generated had ebbed, and she was cold.

"Hold on." He had to unwind her, to which she gave a couple of halfhearted mutters of protest. But when he pulled up the blanket, she snuggled right in. "Better?"

"Couldn't be any. I was going to say that I've been—more or less—thinking about getting you naked since I met you."

"That's funny. I've been more or less thinking the same about you. You've got an amazing body there, Quinn."

"Lifestyle change, for which I could now preach like an evangelist. However." She levered up so she could look down into his face. "Had I known what it would be like, I would've had you naked in five minutes flat."

He grinned. "Once again, our thoughts run on parallel lines. Do that thing again. No," he said with a laugh when her eyebrows wiggled. "This thing."

He tugged her head down again until it rested on his shoulder, then drew her arm over his chest. "And the leg. That's it," he said when she obliged. "That's perfect."

The fact that it was gave her a nice warm glow under her

heart. Quinn closed her eyes, and without a worry in the world, drifted off to sleep.

IN THE DARK, SHE WOKE WHEN SOMETHING FELL on her. She managed a breathless squeal, shoved herself to sitting, balled her hands into fists.

"Sorry, sorry."

She recognized Cal's whisper, but it was too late to stop the punch. Her fist jabbed into something hard enough to sting her knuckles. "Ow! Ow! Shit."

"I'll say," Cal muttered.

"What the hell are you doing?"

"Tripping, falling down, and getting punched in the head."

"Why?"

"Because it's pitch-dark." He shifted, rubbed his sore temple. "And I was trying not to wake you up, and you hit me. In the head."

"Well, I'm sorry," she hissed right back. "For all I knew you could've been a mad rapist, or more likely, given the location, a demon from hell. What are you doing milling around in the dark?"

"Trying to find my shoes, which I think is what I tripped over."

"You're leaving?"

"It's morning, and I've got a breakfast meeting in a couple hours."

"It's dark."

"It's February, and you've got those curtain deals over the windows. It's about six thirty."

"Oh God." She plopped back down. "Six thirty isn't morning, even in February. Or maybe especially."

"Which is why I was trying not to wake you up."

She shifted. She could make him out now, a little, as her eyes adjusted. "Well, I'm awake, so why are you still whispering?"

"I don't know. Maybe I have brain damage from getting punched in the head."

Something about the baffled irritation in his voice stirred her juices. "Aw. Why don't you crawl back in here with me where it's all nice and warm? I'll kiss it and make it better."

"That's a cruel thing to suggest when I have a breakfast meeting with the mayor, the town manager, and the town council."

"Sex and politics go together like peanut butter and jelly."

"That may be, but I've got to go home, feed Lump, drag Fox out of bed as he's in on this meeting. Shower, shave, and change so it doesn't look like I've been having hot sex."

As he dragged on his shoes, she roused herself to push up again, then slither around him. "You could do all that after."

Her breasts, warm and full, pressed against his back as she nibbled on the side of his throat. And her hand snuck down to where he'd already gone rock hard.

"You've got a mean streak, Blondie."

"Maybe you ought to teach me a lesson." She let out a choked laugh when he swiveled and grabbed her.

This time when he fell on her, it was on purpose.

HE WAS LATE FOR THE MEETING, BUT HE WAS feeling too damn good to care. He ordered an enormous breakfast—eggs, bacon, hash browns, two biscuits. He worked his way through it while Fox gulped down Coke as if it were the antidote to some rare and fatal poison in his bloodstream, and the others engaged in small talk.

Small talk edged into town business. It may have been February, but plans for the annual Memorial Day parade had to be finalized. Then there was the debate about installing new benches in the park. Most of it washed over Cal as he ate, as he thought about Quinn.

He tuned back in, primarily because Fox kicked him under the table.

"The Branson place is only a couple doors down from the Bowl-a-Rama," Mayor Watson continued. "Misty said it looked like the house on either side went dark, too, but across the street, the lights were on. Phones went out, too. Spooked her pretty good, she said when Wendy and I picked her up after the dance. Only lasted a few minutes."

"Maybe a breaker," Jim Hawkins suggested, but he looked at his son.

"Maybe, but Misty said it all flickered and snapped for a few seconds. Power surge maybe. But I think I'm going to urge Mike Branson to get his wiring checked out. Could be something's shorting out. We don't want an electrical fire."

How did they manage to forget? Cal wondered. Was it a defense mechanism, amnesia, or simply part of the whole ugly situation?

Not all of them. He could see the question, the concern in his father's eyes, in one or two of the others. But the mayor and most of the council were moving on to a discussion of painting the bleachers in the ballpark before Little League season began.

There had been other odd power surges, other strange power outages. But never until June, never before that final countdown to the Seven.

When the meeting was over, Fox walked to the bowling center with Cal and his father. They didn't speak until they were inside, and the door closed behind them.

"It's too early for this to happen," Jim said immediately. "It's more likely a power surge, or faulty wiring."

"It's not. Things have been happening already," Cal told him. "And it's not just Fox and I who've seen them. Not this time."

"Well." Jim sat down heavily at one of the tables in the grill section. "What can I do?"

Take care of yourself, Cal thought. Take care of Mom. But it would never be enough. "Anything feels off, you tell me. Tell Fox, or Gage when he gets here. There are more of us this time. Quinn and Layla, they're part of it. We need to figure out how and why."

His great-grandmother had known Quinn was connected, Cal thought. She'd sensed something. "I need to talk to Gran."

"Cal, she's ninety-seven. I don't care how spry she is, she's still ninety-seven."

"I'll be careful."

"You know, I'm going to talk to Mrs. H again." Fox shook his head. "She's jumpy, nervous. Making noises about leaving next month instead of April. I figured it was just restlessness now that she's decided to move. Maybe it's more."

"All right." Jim blew out a breath. "You two go do what you need to do. I'll handle things here. I know how to run the center," he said before Cal could protest. "Been doing it awhile now."

"Okay. I'll run Gran to the library if she wants to go today. I'll be back after, and we can switch off. You can pick her up, take her home."

CAL WALKED TO ESSIE'S HOUSE. SHE ONLY LIVED a block away in the pretty little house she shared with his cousin Ginger. Essie's concession to her age was to have Ginger live in, take care of the house, the grocery shopping, most of the cooking, and be her chauffeur for duties like doctor and dentist appointments.

Cal knew Ginger to be a sturdy, practical sort who stayed out of his gran's way—and her business—unless she needed to do otherwise. Ginger preferred TV to books, and lived for a trio of afternoon soaps. Her disastrous and childless marriage had turned her off men, except television beefcake or those within the covers of *People* magazine.

As far as Cal could tell, his gran and his cousin bumped along well enough in the little dollhouse with its trim front yard and cheerful blue porch.

When he arrived he didn't see Ginger's car at the curb, and wondered if his gran had an early medical appointment. His father kept Essie's schedule in his head, as he kept so much else, but he'd been upset that morning.

Still, it was more likely that Ginger had taken a run to the grocery store.

He crossed the porch and knocked. It didn't surprise him when the door opened. Even upset, his father rarely forgot anything.

But it did surprise him to see Quinn at the threshold.

"Hi. Come on in. Essie and I are just having some tea in the parlor."

He gripped her arm. "Why are you here?"

The greeting smile faded at the sharp tone. "I have a job to do. And Essie called me."

"Why?"

"Maybe if you come in instead of scowling at me, we'll both find out."

Seeing no other choice, Cal walked into his great-grandmother's lovely living room where African violets bloomed in purple profusion in the windows, where built-in shelves Fox's father had crafted were filled with books, family pictures, little bits and bobs of memories. Where the company tea set was laid out on the low table in front of the high-backed sofa his mother had reupholstered only the previous spring.

Where his beloved gran sat like a queen in her favored wingback chair. "Cal." She lifted her hand for his, and her cheek for his kiss. "I thought you'd be tied up all morning between the meeting and center business."

"Meeting's over, and Dad's at the center. I didn't see Ginger's car."

"She's off running some errands since I had company. Quinn's just pouring the tea. Go get yourself a cup out of the cupboard."

"No, thanks. I'm fine. Just had breakfast."

"I would've called you, too, if I'd realized you'd have time this morning."

"I've always got time for you, Gran."

"He's my boy," she said to Quinn, squeezing Cal's hand

before she released it to take the tea Quinn offered. "Thank you. Please, sit down, both of you. I might as well get right to it. I need to ask you if there was an incident last night, during the dance. An incident just before ten."

She looked hard at Cal's face as she asked, and what she saw had her closing her eyes. "So there was." Her thin voice quivered. "I don't know whether to be relieved or afraid. Relieved because I thought I might be losing my mind. Afraid because I'm not. It was real then," she said quietly. "What I saw."

"What did you see?"

"It was as if I were behind a curtain. As if a curtain had dropped, or a shroud, and I had to look through it. I thought it was blood, but no one seemed to notice. No one noticed all the blood, or the things that crawled and clattered over the floor, over the tables." Her hand lifted to rub at her throat. "I couldn't see clearly, but I saw a shape, a black shape. It seemed to float in the air on the other side of the curtain. I thought it was death."

She smiled a little as she lifted her tea with a steady hand. "You prepare for death at my age, or you damn well should. But I was afraid of that shape. Then it was gone, the curtain lifted again, and everything was exactly as it should be."

"Gran—"

"Why didn't I tell you last night?" she interrupted. "I can read your face like a book, Caleb. Pride, fear. I simply wanted to get out, to be home, and your father drove me. I needed to sleep, and I did. This morning, I needed to know if it was true."

"Mrs. Hawkins—"

"You'll call me Essie now," she said to Quinn.

"Essie, have you ever had an experience like this before?"

"Yes. I didn't tell you," she said when Cal cursed. "Or anyone. It was the summer you were ten. That first summer. I saw terrible things outside the house, things that couldn't be. That black shape that was sometimes a man, sometimes a dog. Or a hideous combination of both. Your grandfather didn't see, or wouldn't. I always thought he simply wouldn't see. There were horrible things that week."

She closed her eyes a moment, then took another soothing sip of tea. "Neighbors, friends. Things they did to themselves and each other. After the second night, you came to the door. Do you remember, Cal?"

"Yes, ma'am, I remember."

"Ten years old." She smiled at Quinn. "He was only a little boy, with his two young friends. They were so afraid. You could see and feel the fear and the, valor, I want to say, coming off them like light. You told me we had to pack up, your grandfather and I. We had to come stay at your house. That it wasn't safe in town. Didn't you ever wonder why I didn't argue, or pat you on the head and shoo you on home?"

"No. I guess there was too much else going on. I just wanted you and Pop safe."

"And every seven years, I packed for your grandfather and me, then when he died, just for me, now this year it'll be Ginger and me. But it's coming sooner and stronger this time."

"I'll pack for you, Gran, for you and Ginger right now."

"Oh, I think we're safe enough for now," she said to Cal. "When it's time, Ginger and I can put what we'll need together. I want you to take the books. I know I've read them, you've read them. It seems countless times. But we've missed something, somehow. And now, we have fresh eyes."

Quinn turned toward Cal, narrowed her eyes. "Books?"

Thirteen

~J~

FOX MADE A RUN TO THE BANK. IT WAS COM-
pletely unnecessary since the papers in his briefcase could
have been dropped off at any time—or more efficiently,
the client could have come into his office to ink them.

But he'd wanted to get out, get some air, walk off his
frustration.

It was time to admit that he'd still held on to the hope
that Alice Hawbaker would change her mind, or that he
could change it for her. Maybe it was selfish, and so what?
He depended on her, he was used to her. And he loved her.

The love meant he had no choice but to let her go. The
love meant if he could take back the last twenty minutes
he'd spent with her, he would.

She'd nearly broken down, he remembered as he strode
along in his worn-down hiking boots (no court today). She
never broke. She never even cracked, but he'd pushed her
hard enough to cause fissures. He'd always regret it.

If we stay, we'll die. She'd said that with tears in her
voice, with tears glimmering in her eyes.

He'd only wanted to know why she was so set to leave, why she was jumpier every day to the point she wanted to go sooner than originally planned.

So he'd pushed. And finally, she'd told him.

She'd seen their deaths, over and over, every time she closed her eyes. She'd seen herself getting her husband's deer rifle out of the locked case in his basement workroom. Seen herself calmly loading it. She'd watched herself walk upstairs, through the kitchen where the dinner dishes were loaded into the dishwasher, the counters wiped clean. Into the den where the man she'd loved for thirty-six years, had made three children with, was watching the Orioles battle the Red Sox. The O's were up two-zip, but the Sox were at the plate, with a man on second, one out. Top of the sixth. The count was one and two.

When the pitcher wound up, she pumped a bullet through the back of her husband's head as he sat in his favorite recliner.

Then she'd put the barrel under her own chin.

So, yes, he had to let her go, just as he'd had to make an excuse to leave the office because he knew her well enough to understand she didn't want him around until she was composed again.

Knowing he'd given her what she wanted and needed didn't stop him from feeling guilty, frustrated, and inadequate.

He ducked in to buy flowers. She'd accept them as a peace offering, he knew. She liked flowers in the office, and often picked them up herself as he tended to forget.

He came out with an armload of mixed blooms, and nearly ran over Layla.

She stumbled back, even took a couple extra steps in retreat. He saw upset and unhappiness on her face, and wondered if it was his current lot to make women nervous and miserable.

"Sorry. Wasn't looking."

She didn't smile, just started fiddling with the buttons of her coat. "It's okay. Neither was I."

He should just go. He didn't have to tap in to her mind to feel the jangle of nerves and misery surrounding her. It seemed to him she never relaxed around him, was always making that little move away. Or maybe she never relaxed ever. Could be a New York thing, he mused. He sure as hell hadn't been able to relax there.

But there was too much of the how-can-I-fix-this in him. "Problem?"

Now *her* eyes glimmered with tears, and Fox quite simply wanted to step into the street into the path of a passing truck.

"Problem? How could there possibly be a problem? I'm living in a strange house in a strange town, seeing things that aren't there—or worse, *are* there and want me dead. Nearly everything I own is sitting in my apartment in New York. An apartment I have to pay for, and my very understanding and patient boss called this morning to tell me, regretfully, that if I couldn't come back to work next week, she'll have to replace me. So do you know what I did?"

"No."

"I started to pack. Sorry, really, sorry, but I've got a *life* here. I have responsibilities and bills and a goddamn routine." She gripped her elbows in opposite hands as if to hold herself in place. "I need to get back to them. And I couldn't. I just couldn't do it. I don't even know why, not on any reasonable level, but I couldn't. So now I'm going to be out of a job, which means I won't be able to afford my apartment. And I'm probably going to end up dead or institutionalized, and that's after my landlord sues me for back rent. So problems? No, not me."

He listened all the way through without interruption, then just nodded. "Stupid question. Here." He shoved the flowers at her.

"What?"

"You look like you could use them."

Flummoxed, she stared at him, stared at the colorful blooms in her arms. And felt the sharpest edge of what might have been hysteria dulling into perplexity. "But . . . you bought them for someone."

"I can buy more." He waved a thumb at the door of the flower shop. "And I can help with the landlord if you get me the information. The rest, well, we're working on it. Maybe something pushed you to come here, and maybe something's pushing you to stay, but at the bottom of it, Layla, it's your choice. If you decide you have to leave . . ." He thought of Alice again, and some of his own frustration ebbed. "Nobody's going to blame you for it. But if you stay, you need to commit."

"I've—"

"No, you haven't." Absently, he reached out to secure the strap of her bag, which had slipped down to the crook of her elbow, back on her shoulder. "You're still looking for the way out, the loophole in the deal that means you can pack your bags and go without consequences. Just go back to the way things were. Can't blame you for it. But choose, then stick. That's all. I've got to finish up and get back. Talk to you later."

He stepped back into the florist and left her standing speechless on the sidewalk.

QUINN SHOUTED DOWN FROM THE SECOND FLOOR when Layla came in.

"It's me," Layla called up, and still conflicted, walked back to the kitchen with the flowers and the bottles and pots she'd bought in a gift shop on the walk home.

"Coffee." Quinn bustled in a few moments later. "Going to need lots and lots of . . . Hey, pretty," she said when she saw the flowers Layla was clipping to size and arranging in various bottles.

"They really are. Quinn, I need to talk to you."

"Need to talk to you, too. You go first."

"I was going to leave this morning."

Quinn stopped on the way to fill the coffeepot. "Oh."

"And I was going to do my best to get out before you came back, and talked me out of it. I'm sorry."

"Okay. It's okay." Quinn busied herself making the coffee. "I'd avoid me, too, if I wanted to do something I didn't want me to do. If you get me."

"Oddly enough, I do."

"Why aren't you gone?"

"Let me backtrack." While she finished fussing with the flowers, Layla related the telephone conversation she'd had with her boss.

"I'm sorry. It's so unfair. I don't mean your boss is unfair. She's got a business to run. But that this whole thing is unfair." Quinn watched Layla arrange multicolored daisies in an oversized teacup. "On a practical level I'm okay, because this is my job, or the job I picked. I can afford to take the time to be here and supplement that with articles. I could help—"

"That's not what I'm looking for. I don't want you to loan me money, or to carry my share of the expenses. If I stay, it's because I've chosen to stay." Layla looked at the flowers, thought of what Fox had said. "I think, until today, I didn't accept that, or want to accept it. Easier to think I'd been driven to come here, and that I was being pressured to stay. I wanted to go because I didn't want any of this to be happening. But it is. So I'm staying because I've decided to stay. I'll just have to figure out the practicalities."

"I've got a couple of ideas on that, maybe just a thumb in the dike. Let me think about them. The flowers were a nice idea. Cheer up a bad news day."

"Not my idea. Fox gave them to me when I ran into him outside the florist. I cut loose on him." Layla shrugged, then gathered up the bits of stems she'd cut off, the florist wrappings. "He's basically, 'How are you doing,' and I'm 'How am I doing? I'll tell you how I'm doing.'" She tossed the leavings in the trash, then leaned back and laughed. "God, I just blasted him. So he gives me the flowers he'd just bought, thrust them at me, really, and gave me a short, pithy lecture. I guess I deserved it."

"Hmm." Quinn added the information to the think-pot she was stirring. "And you feel better?"

"Better?" Layla walked into the little dining room to arrange a trio of flowers on the old, drop-leaf table they'd picked up at the flea market. "I feel more resolved. I don't know if that's better."

"I've got something to keep you busy."

"Thank God. I'm used to working, and all this time on my hands makes me bitchy."

"Come with me. Don't leave all the flowers; you should have some of them in your room."

"I thought they'd be for the house. He didn't buy them for me or—"

"He gave them to you. Take some of them up. You made me take the tulips up to mine." To solve the matter, Quinn picked up one of the little pots and a slender bottle herself. "Oh, coffee."

"I'll get it." Layla poured one of the mugs for Quinn, doctored it, then got a bottle of water for herself. "What's the project that's going to keep me busy?"

"Books."

"We already have the books from the library."

"Now we have some from Estelle Hawkins's personal store. Some of them are journals. I haven't really scratched the surface yet," Quinn explained as they headed up. "I'd barely gotten home ahead of you. But there are three of them written by Ann Hawkins. After her children were born. Her children with Giles Dent."

"But Mrs. Hawkins must have read them before, shown them to Cal."

"Right, and right. They've all been read, studied, pondered over. But not by us, Layla. Fresh eyes, different angle." She detoured to Layla's room to set the flowers down, then took the coffee mug on her way to the office. "And I've already got the first question on my notes: Where are the others?"

"Other journals?"

"Ann's other journals, because I'm betting there are

more, or were. Where's the journal she kept when she lived with Dent, when she was carrying her triplets? That's one of the new angles I hope our fresh eyes can find. Where would they be, and why aren't they with the others?"

"If she did write others, they might have been lost or destroyed."

"Let's hope not." Quinn's eyes were sharp as she sat, lifted a small book bound in brown leather. "Because I think she had some of the answers we need."

CAL COULDN'T REASONABLY BREAK AWAY FROM the center until after seven. Even then he felt guilty leaving his father to handle the rest of the night. He'd called Quinn in the late afternoon to let her know he'd be by when he could. And her absent response had been for him to bring food with him.

She'd have to settle for pizza, he thought as he carried the takeout boxes up the steps. He hadn't had the time or inclination to figure out what her lifestyle-change option might be.

As he knocked, the wind whistled across the back of his neck, had him glancing uneasily behind him. Something coming, he thought. Something's in the wind.

Fox answered the door. "Thank God, pizza and a testosterone carrier. I'm outnumbered here, buddy."

"Where's the estrogen?"

"Up. Buried in books and notes. Charts. Layla makes charts. I made the mistake of telling them I had a dry-wipe board down at the office. They made me go get it, haul it in here, haul it upstairs." The minute Cal set the pizza down on the kitchen counter, Fox shoved up the lid and took out a slice. "There's been talk of index cards. Colored index cards. Don't leave me here alone again."

Cal grunted, opened the fridge, and found, as he'd hoped and dreamed, Fox had stocked beer. "Maybe we were never organized enough, so we missed some detail. Maybe—"

He broke off as Quinn rushed in. "Hi! Pizza. Oh-oh. Well, I'll work it off with the power of my mind and with a session in the gym tomorrow morning."

She got down plates, passed one to Fox, who was already halfway through with his first slice. Then she smiled that smile at Cal. "Got anything else for me?"

He leaned right in, laid his mouth on hers. "Got that."

"Coincidentally, exactly what I wanted. So how about some more." She got a fistful of his shirt and tugged him down for another, longer kiss.

"You guys want me to leave? Can I take the pizza with me?"

"As a matter of fact," Cal began.

"Now, now." Quinn patted Cal's chest to ease him back. "Mommy and Daddy were just saying hello," she told Fox. "Why don't we eat in the dining room like the civilized. Layla's coming right down."

"How come I can't say hello to Mommy?" Fox complained as Quinn sailed off with the plates.

"Because then I'd have to beat you unconscious."

"As if." Amused, Fox grabbed the pizza boxes and started after Quinn. "Beverages on you, bro."

Shortly after they were seated, drinks, plates, napkins, pizza passed around, Layla came in with a large bowl and a stack of smaller ones. "I put this together earlier. I wasn't sure what you might bring," she said to Cal.

"You made salad?" Quinn asked.

"My specialty. Chop, shred, mix. No cooking."

"Now, I'm forced to be good." Quinn gave up the dream of two slices of pizza, settled on one and a bowl of Layla's salad. "We made progress," she began as she forked up the first bite.

"Yeah, ask the ladies here how to make tallow candles or black raspberry preserves," Fox suggested. "They've got it down."

"So, some of the information contained in the books we're going through may not currently apply to our situation." Quinn raised her eyebrows at Fox. "But one day I may be called on in some blackout emergency to make a tallow candle. By progress, however, I mean that there's a lot of interesting information in Ann's journals."

"We've read them," Cal pointed out. "Multiple times."

"You're not women." She held up a finger. "And, yes, Essie is. But Essie's a woman who's a descendent, who's part of this town and its history. And however objective she might try to be, she may have missed some nuances. First question, where are the others?"

"There aren't any others."

"I disagree. There aren't any others that were found. Essie said these books were passed to her by her father, because she loved books. I called her to be sure, but he never said if there were more."

"If there'd been more," Cal insisted, "he'd have given them to her."

"If he had them. There's a long span between the sixteen hundreds and the nineteen hundreds," Quinn pointed out. "Things get misplaced, lost, tossed out. According to the records and your own family's oral history, Ann Hawkins lived most of her life in what's now the community center on Main Street, which was previously the library. Books, library. Interesting."

"A library Gran knew inside and out," Cal returned. "There couldn't have been a book in there she didn't know about. And something like this?" He shook his head. "She'd have it if it was to be had."

"Unless she never saw it. Maybe it was hidden, or maybe, for the sake of argument, she wasn't *meant* to find it. It wasn't meant to be found, not by her, not then."

"Debatable," Fox commented.

"And something to look into. Meanwhile, she didn't date her journals, so Layla and I are dating them, more or less, by how she writes about her sons. In what we're judging to be the first, her sons are about two to three. In the next they're five because she writes about their fifth birthday very specifically, and about seven, we think, when that one ends. The third it seems that they're young men. We think about sixteen."

"A lot of years between," Layla said.

"Maybe she didn't have anything worth writing about during those years."

"Could be," Quinn said to Cal. "But I'm betting she did, even if it was just about blackberry jam and a trio of active sons. More important now, at least I think so, is where is the journal or journals that cover her time with Dent, to the birth of her sons through to the first two years of their lives? Because you can just bet your ass those were interesting times."

"She writes of him," Layla said quietly. "Of Giles Dent. Again and again, in all the journals we have. She writes about him, of her feelings for him, her dreams about him."

"And always in the present tense," Quinn added.

"It's hard to lose someone you love." Fox turned his beer bottle in his hand.

"It is, but she writes of him, consistently, as if he were alive." Quinn looked at Cal. "It is not death. We talked about this, how Dent found the way to exist, with this thing. To hold it down or through or inside. Whatever the term. Obviously he couldn't—or didn't—kill or destroy it, but neither could it kill or destroy him. He found a way to keep it under, and to continue to exist. Maybe only for that single purpose. She knew it. Ann knew what he did, and I'm betting she knew how he did it."

"You're not taking into account love and grief," Cal pointed out.

"I'm not discounting them, but when I read her journals, I get the sense of a strong-minded woman. And one who shared a very deep love with a strong-minded man. She defied convention for him, risked shunning and censure. Shared his bed, but I believe, shared his obligations, too. Whatever he planned to do, attempted to do, felt bound to do, he would have shared it with her. They were a unit.

Isn't that what you felt, what we both felt, when we were in the clearing?"

"Yeah." He couldn't deny it, Cal thought. "That's what I felt."

"Going off that, Ann knew, and while she may have told her sons when they were old enough, that part of the Hawkins's oral history could have been lost or bastardized. It happens. I think she would have written it out, too. And put the record somewhere she believed would be safe and protected, until it was needed."

"It's been needed for twenty-one years."

"Cal, that's your responsibility talking, not logic. At least not the line of logic that follows this route. She told you this was the time. That it was always to be this time. Nothing you had, nothing you could have done would have stopped it before this time."

"We let it out," Fox said. "Nothing would have been needed if we hadn't let it out."

"I don't think that's true." Layla shifted toward him, just a little. "And maybe, if we find the other journals, we'll understand. But, we noticed something else."

"Layla caught it right off the bat," Quinn put in.

"Because it was in front of me first. But in any case, it's the names. The names of Ann's sons. Caleb, Fletcher, and Gideon."

"Pretty common for back then." Cal gave a shrug as he pushed his plate away. "Caleb stuck in the Hawkins line more than the other two did. But I've got a cousin Fletch and an uncle Gideon."

"No, first initials," Quinn said impatiently. "I told you they'd missed it," she added to Layla. "C, F, G. Caleb, Fox, Gage."

"Reaching," Fox decided. "Especially when you consider I'm Fox because my mother saw a pack of red foxes running across the field and into the woods about the time she was going into labor with me. My sister Sage? Mom smelled the sage from her herb garden right after Sage was born. It was like that with all four of us."

"You were named after an actual fox? Like a . . . release-the-hounds fox?" Layla wanted to know.

"Well, not a specific one. It was more a . . . You have to meet my mother."

"However Fox got his famous name, I don't think we discount coincidences." Quinn studied Cal's face, saw he was considering it. "And I think there's more than one of Ann Hawkins's descendents at this table."

"Quinn, my father's people came over from Ireland, four generations back," Fox told her. "They weren't here in Ann Hawkins's time because they were plowing fields in Kerry."

"What about your mother's?" Layla asked.

"Wider mix. English, Irish. I think some French. No-body ever bothered with a genealogy, but I've never heard of any Hawkins on the family tree."

"You may want to take a closer look. How about Gage?" Quinn wondered.

"No idea." And Cal was more than considering it now. "I doubt he does either. I can ask Bill, Gage's father. If it's true, if we're direct descendents, it could explain one of the things we've never understood."

"Why it was you," Quinn said quietly. "You three, the mix of blood from you, Fox, and Gage that opened the door."

"I ALWAYS THOUGHT IT WAS ME."

With the house quiet, and night deep, Cal lay on Quinn's bed with her body curled warm to his. "Just you?"

"They helped trigger it maybe, but yes, me. Because it was my blood—not just that night, but my heritage, you could say. I was the Hawkins. They weren't from here, not the same way I was. Not forever, like I was. Generations back. But if this is true . . . I still don't know how to feel about it."

"You could give yourself a tiny break." She stroked her hand over his heart. "I wish you would."

"Why did he let it happen? Dent? If he'd found a way to stop it, why did he let it come to this?"

"Another question." She pushed herself up until they were eye-to-eye. "We'll figure it out, Cal. We're supposed to. I believe that."

"I'm closer to believing it, with you." He touched her cheek. "Quinn, I can't stay again tonight. Lump may be lazy, but he depends on me."

"Got another hour to spare?"

"Yeah." He smiled as she lowered to him. "I think he'll hold out another hour."

LATER, WHEN HE WALKED OUT TO HIS CAR, THE air shivered so that the trees rattled their empty branches. Cal searched the street for any sign, anything he needed to defend against. But there was nothing but empty road.

Something's in the wind, he thought again, and got in his car to drive home.

IT WAS AFTER MIDNIGHT WHEN THE LOW-GRADE urge for a cigarette buzzed through Gage's brain. He'd given them up two years, three months, and one week before, a fact that could still piss him off.

He turned up the radio to take his mind off it, but the urge was working its way up to craving. He could ignore that, too; he did so all the time. To do otherwise was to believe there was solid truth in the old adage: like father, like son.

He was nothing like his father.

He drank when he wanted a drink, but he never got drunk. Or hadn't since he'd been seventeen, and then the drunkenness had been with absolute purpose. He didn't blame others for his shortcomings, or lash out with his fists on something smaller and weaker so he could feel bigger and stronger.

He didn't even blame the old man, not particularly. You

played the cards you were dealt, to Gage's mind. Or you folded and walked away with your pockets empty.

Luck of the draw.

So he was fully prepared to ignore this sudden, and surprisingly intense desire for a cigarette. But when he considered he was within miles of Hawkins Hollow, a place where he was very likely to die an ugly and painful death, the surgeon general's warnings seemed pretty goddamn puny, and his own self-denial absolutely useless.

When he saw the sign for the Sheetz, he decided what the hell. He didn't want to live forever. He swung into the twenty-four-hour mart, picked up coffee, black, and a pack of Marlboros.

He strode back to the car he'd bought that very evening in D.C. after his plane had landed, and before he'd paid off a small debt. The wind whipped through his hair. The hair was dark as the night, a little longer than he usually wore it, a little shaggy, as he hadn't trusted the barbers in Prague.

There was stubble on his face since he hadn't bothered to shave. It added to the dark, dangerous look that had had the young female clerk who rung up the coffee and cigarettes shivering inwardly with lust.

He'd topped off at six feet, and the skinny build of his youth had filled out. Since his profession was usually sedentary, he kept his muscles toned and his build rangy with regular, often punishing workouts.

He didn't pick fights, but he rarely walked away from one. And he liked to win. His body, his face, his mind, were all tools of his trade. As were his eyes, his voice, and the control he rarely let off the leash.

He was a gambler, and a smart gambler kept all of his tools well honed.

Swinging back onto the road, Gage let the Ferrari rip. Maybe it had been foolish to toss so much of his winnings into a car, but Jesus, it *moved*. And fucking A, he'd ridden his thumb out of the Hollow all those years ago. It felt damn good to ride back in in style.

Funny, now that he'd bought the damn cigarettes, the urge for one had passed. He didn't even want the coffee, the speed was kick enough.

He flew down the last miles of the interstate, whipped onto the exit that would take him to the Hollow. The dark rural road was empty—no surprise to him, not this time of night. There were shadows and shapes—houses, hills, fields, trees. There was a twisting in his gut that he was heading back instead of away, and yet that pull—it never quite left him—that pull toward home was strong.

He reached toward his coffee more out of habit than desire, then was forced to whip the wheel, slam the brakes as headlights cut across the road directly into his path. He blasted the horn, saw the other car swerve.

He thought: Fuck, fuck, *fuck!* I just bought this sucker.

When he caught his breath, and the Ferrari sat sideways in the middle of the road, he thought it was a miracle the crash hadn't come. Inches, he realized. Less than inches.

His lucky goddamn day.

He reversed, pulled to the shoulder, then got out to check on the other driver he assumed was stinking drunk.

She wasn't. What she was, was hopping mad.

"Where the hell did you come from?" she demanded. She slammed out of her car, currently tipped into the shallow ditch along the shoulder, in a blur of motion. He saw a mass of dark gypsy curls wild around a face pale with shock.

Great face, he decided in one corner of his brain. Huge eyes that looked black against her white skin, a sharp nose, a wide mouth, sexily full that may have owned its sensuality to collagen injections.

She wasn't shaking, and he didn't sense any fear along with the fury as she stood on a dark road facing down a complete stranger.

"Lady," he said with what he felt was admirable calm, "where the hell did *you* come from?"

"From that stupid road that looks like all the other stupid roads around here. I looked both damn ways, and you weren't there. Then. How did you . . . Oh never mind. We didn't die."

"Yay."

With her hands on her hips she turned around to study her car. "I can get out of there, right?"

"Yeah. Then there's the flat tire."

"What flat . . . Oh for God's sake! You have to change it." She gave the flat tire on the rear of her car an annoyed kick. "It's the least you can do."

Actually, it wasn't. The least he could do was stroll back to his car and wave good-bye. But he appreciated her bitchiness, and preferred it over quivering. "Pop the trunk. I need the spare and the jack."

When she had, and he'd lifted a suitcase out, set it on the ground, he took one look at her spare. And shook his head. "Not your day. Your spare's toast."

"It can't be. What the hell are you talking about?" She shoved him aside, peered in herself by the glow of the trunk light. "Damn her, damn her, damn her. My sister." She whirled away, paced down the shoulder a few feet, then back. "I loaned her my car for a couple of weeks. This is so typical. She ruins a tire, but does she get it fixed, does she even bother to mention it? No."

She pushed her hair back from her face. "I'm not calling a tow truck at this time of night, then sitting in the middle of nowhere. You're just going to have to give me a ride."

"Am I?"

"It's your fault. At least part of it is."

"Which part?"

"I don't know, and I'm too tired, I'm too mad, I'm too lost in this foreign wilderness to give a damn. I need a ride."

"At your service. Where to?"

"Hawkins Hollow."

He smiled, and there was something dark in it. "Handy. I'm heading there myself." He gestured toward his car. "Gage Turner," he added.

She gestured in turn, rather regally, toward her suitcase. "Cybil Kinski." She lifted her eyebrows when she got her first good look at his car. "You have very nice wheels, Mr. Turner."

"Yeah, and they all work."

Fourteen

〜✦〜

CAL WASN'T PARTICULARLY SURPRISED TO SEE Fox's truck in his driveway, despite the hour. Nor was he particularly surprised when he walked in to see Fox blinking sleepily on the couch in front of the TV, with Lump stretched out and snoring beside him.

On the coffee table were a can of Coke, the last of Cal's barbecue potato chips, and a box of Milk Bones. The remains, he assumed, of a guy-dog party.

"Whatcha doing here?" Fox asked groggily.

"I live here."

"She kick you out?"

"No, she didn't kick me out. I came home." Because they were there, Cal dug into the bag of chips and managed to pull out a handful of crumbs. "How many of those did you give him?"

Fox glanced at the box of dog biscuits. "A couple. Maybe five. What're you so edgy about?"

Cal picked up the Coke and gulped down the couple of

warm, flat swallows that were left. "I got a feeling, a . . . thing. You haven't felt anything tonight?"

"I've had feelings and things pretty much steady the last couple weeks." Fox scrubbed his hands over his face, back into his hair. "But yeah, I got something just before you drove up. I was half asleep, maybe all the way. It was like the wind whooshing down the flue."

"Yeah." Cal walked over to stare out the window. "Have you checked in with your parents lately?"

"I talked to my father today. It's all good with them. Why?"

"If all three of us are direct descendents, then one of your parents is in the line," Cal pointed out.

"I figured that out on my own."

"None of our family was ever affected during the Seven. We were always relieved by that." He turned back. "Maybe relieved enough we didn't really ask why."

"Because we figured it, at least partly, was because they lived outside of town. Except for Bill Turner, and who the hell could tell what was going on with him?"

"My parents and yours, they came into town during the Seven. And there were people, you remember what happened out at the Poffenberger place last time?"

"Yeah. Yeah, I remember." Fox rubbed at his eyes. "Being five miles out of town didn't stop Poffenberger from strangling his wife while she hacked at him with a butcher knife."

"Now we know Gran felt things, saw things that first summer, and she saw things the other night. Why is that?"

"Maybe it picks and chooses, Cal." Rising, Fox walked over to toss another log on the fire. "There have always been people who weren't affected, and there have always been degrees with those who were."

"Quinn and Layla are the first outsiders. We figured a connection, but what if that connection is as simple as blood ties?"

Fox sat again, leaned back, stroked a hand over Lump's head as the dog twitched in his sleep. "Good theory. It shouldn't weird you out if you happen to be rolling naked with your cousin a couple hundred times removed."

"Huh." That was a thought. "If they're descendents, the next point to figure is if having them here gives us more muscle, or makes us more vulnerable. Because it's pretty clear this one's it. This one's going to be the all or nothing. So . . . Someone's coming."

Fox pushed off the couch, strode quickly over to stand by Cal. "I don't think the Big Evil's going to drive up to your house, and in a . . ." He peered closer as the car set off Cal's motion lights. "Holy Jesus, is that a Ferrari?" He shot a grin at Cal.

"Gage," they said together.

They went on the front porch, in shirtsleeves, leaving the door open behind them. Gage climbed out of the car, his eyes skimming over them both as he walked back to get his bag out of the trunk. He slung its strap over his shoulder, started up the steps. "You girls having a slumber party?"

"Strippers just left," Fox told him. "Sorry you missed them." Then he rushed forward, flung his arms around Gage in a hard hug. "Man, it's good to see you. When can I drive your car?"

"I was thinking never. Cal."

"Took your goddamn time." The relief, the love, the sheer pleasure pushed him forward to grip Gage just as Fox had.

"Had some business here and there. Want a drink. Need a room."

"Come on in."

In the kitchen, Cal poured whiskey. All of them understood it was a welcome-home toast for Gage, and very likely a drink before war.

"So," Cal began, "I take it you came back flush."

"Oh yeah."

"How much you up?"

Gage turned the glass around in his hand. "Considering expenses, and my new toy out there, about fifty."

"Nice work if you can get it," Fox commented.

"And I can."

"Look a little worn there, brother."

Gage shrugged at Cal. "Long couple of days. Which nearly ended with me in a fiery crash right out on Sixty-seven."

"Toy get away from you?" Fox asked.

"Please." Gage smirked at the idea. "Some ditz, of the female and very hot variety, pulled out in front of me. Not another car on the road, and she pulls out in this ancient Karmann Ghia—nice wheels, actually—then she jumps out and goes at me like it was my fault."

"Women," Fox said, "are an endless source of every damn thing."

"And then some. So she's tipped down in the little runoff," Gage went on, gesturing with his free hand. "No big deal, but she's popped a flat. No big deal either, except her spare's a pancake. Turns out she's heading into the Hollow, so I manage to load her two-ton suitcase into my car. Then she's rattling off an address and asking me, like I'm MapQuest, how long it'll take to get there."

He took a slow sip of whiskey. "Lucky for her I grew up here and could tell her I'd have her there in five. She snaps out her phone, calls somebody she calls Q, like James freaking Bond, tells her, as it turns out from the look I got of Q in the doorway—very nice, by the way—to wake up, she'll be there in five minutes. Then—"

Cal rattled off an address. "That the one?"

Gage lowered his glass. "As a matter of fact."

"Something in the wind," Cal murmured. "I guess it was you, and Quinn's Cybil."

"Cybil Kinski," Gage confirmed. "Looks like a gypsy by way of Park Avenue. Well, well." He downed the rest of the whiskey in his glass. "Isn't this a kick in the ass?"

"HE CAME OUT OF NOWHERE." THERE WAS A glass of red wine on the dresser Quinn had picked up in anticipation of Cybil's arrival.

As that arrival had woken Layla, Quinn sat beside her on what would be Cybil's bed while the woman in question swirled around the room, hanging clothes, tucking them in drawers, taking the occasional sip of wine.

"I thought that was it, just it, even though I've never seen any death by car in my future. I swear, I don't know how we missed being bloody pulps tangled in burning metal. I'm a good driver," Cybil said to Quinn.

"You are."

"But I must be better than I thought, and so—fortunately—was he. I know I'm lucky all I got was a scare and a flat tire out of it, but damn Rissa for, well, being Rissa."

"Rissa?" Layla looked blank.

"Cyb's sister, Marissa," Quinn explained. "You loaned her your car again."

"I know, I know. I *know*," she said, puffing out a breath that blew curls off her forehead. "I don't know how she manages to talk me into these things. My spare was flat, thanks to Rissa."

"Which explains why you were dropped off from a really sexy sports car."

"He could hardly leave me there, though he looked like the type who'd consider it. All scruffy, gorgeous, and dangerous looking."

"Last time I had a flat," Quinn remembered, "the very nice guy who stopped to help had a paunch over his belt the size of a sack of cement, and ass crack reveal."

"No paunch on this one, and though his coat prevented me from a good look, I'm betting Gage Turner has a superior ass."

"Gage Turner." Layla put a hand on Quinn's thigh. "Quinn."

"Yeah." Quinn let out a breath. "Okay, I guess it's hail, hail, the gang's all here."

IN THE MORNING, QUINN LEFT HER HOUSEMATES sleeping while she jogged over to the community center.

She already knew she'd regret jogging over, because that meant she'd have to jog back—after her workout. But it seemed a cheat on the lifestyle change to drive three blocks to the gym.

And she wanted the thinking time.

There was no buying, for any price, Cybil and Gage Turner had run into each other—almost literally—in the middle of the night just outside of town as a coincidence.

One more thing to add to the list of oddities, Quinn thought as she puffed out air in frosty vapors.

Another addition would be the fact that Cybil had a very sharp sense of direction, but had apparently made wrong turn after wrong turn to end up on that side road at the exact moment Gage was coming up the main.

One more, Quinn decided as she approached the back entrance of the community center, would be Cybil saying "he came out of nowhere." Quinn was willing to take that literally. If Cybil didn't see him, then maybe—in her reality, for just those vital moments—he *hadn't* been there.

So why had it been important for them to meet separately, outside the group? Wasn't it strange enough that they'd both arrived on the same night, at the same time?

She dug out her membership key—thanks, Cal—to open the door to the fitness area, pressed her guest pass number on the keypad.

The lights were still off, which was a surprise. Normally when she arrived, they were already on, and at least one of the trio of swivel TVs was tuned to CNN or ESPN or one of the morning talk shows. Very often there was somebody on one of the treadmills or bikes, or pumping weights.

She flipped on the lights, called out. And her voice echoed hollowly. Curious, she walked through, pushed open the door, and saw the lights were also off in the tiny attendant's office, and in the locker room.

Maybe somebody had a late date the night before, she decided. She helped herself to a locker key, stripped down to her workout gear, then grabbed a towel. Opting to start her session with cardio, she switched on the *Today* show before climbing onto the single elliptical trainer the club boasted.

She programmed it, resisting the urge to cheat a few pounds off her weight. As if it mattered, Quinn reminded herself. (Of course, it mattered.)

She started her warm-up pleased with her discipline, and her solitude. Still, she expected the door to slam open any minute, for Matt or Tina, who switched off as attendants, to rush in. By the time she was ten minutes in, she'd kicked up the resistance and was focused on the TV screen to help her get through the workout.

When she hit the first mile, Quinn took a long gulp of water from the sports bottle she'd brought with her. As she started on mile two, she let her mind drift to what she hoped to accomplish that day. Research, the foundation of any project. And she wanted to draft what she thought would be the opening of her book. Writing it out might spark some idea. At some point, she wanted to walk around the town again, with Cybil—and Layla if she was up for it.

A visit to the cemetery was in order with Cybil in tow. Time to pay a call on Ann Hawkins.

Maybe Cal would have time to go with them. Needed to talk to him anyway, discuss how he felt, what he thought, about Gage—whom she wanted to get a look at—and Cybil's arrival. Mostly, she admitted, she just wanted to see him again. Show him off to Cybil.

Look! Isn't he cute? Maybe it was completely high school, but it didn't seem to matter. She wanted to touch him again, even if it was just a quick squeeze of hands. And she was looking forward to a hello kiss, and finding a way to turn that worried look in his eyes into a glint of amusement. She *loved* the way his eyes laughed before the rest of him did, and the way he . . .

Well. Well, well, well. She was absolutely gone over him, she realized. Seriously hooked on the hometown boy. That was kind of cute, too, she decided, except it made her stomach jitter. Still, the jitter wasn't altogether a bad thing.

It was a combination of *oh-oh* and *oh boy!*, and wasn't that interesting?

Quinn's falling in love, she thought, and hit mile two with a dopey smile on her face. She might've been puffing, sweat might have been dribbling down her temples, but she felt just as fresh and cheerful as a spring daisy.

Then the lights went out.

The machine stopped; the TV went blank and silent.

"Oh, shit." Her first reaction wasn't alarm as much as, what now? The dark was absolute, and though she could draw a reasonable picture in her mind where she was in relation to the outside door—and what was between her and the door—she was wary about making her way to it blind.

And then what? she wondered as she waited for her breathing to level. She couldn't possibly fumble her way to the locker room, to her locker and retrieve her clothes. So she'd have to go out in a damn sports bra and bike pants.

She heard the first thud; the chill washed over her skin. And she understood she had much bigger problems than skimpy attire.

She wasn't alone. As her pulse began to bang, she hoped desperately whatever was in the dark with her was human. But the sounds, that unholy thudding that shook the walls, the floor, the awful *scuttling* sounds creeping under it weren't those of a man. Gooseflesh pricked her skin, partly from fear, partly from the sudden and intense cold.

Keep your head, she ordered herself. For God's sake, keep your head. She gripped the water bottle—pitiful weapon, but all she had—and started to ease off the foot pads on the machine to the floor.

She went flying blindly in the black. She hit the floor, her shoulder and hip taking the brunt. Everything shook and rolled as she fought to scramble up. Disoriented, she had no idea which direction to run. There was a voice behind her, in front of her, inside her head—she couldn't tell—and it whispered gleefully of death.

She knew she screamed as she clawed her way across the quaking floor. Teeth chattering against terror and cold, she rapped her shoulder against another machine. Think, think, think! she told herself, because something was coming, something was coming in the dark. She ran her shaking hands over the machine—recumbent bike—and with every prayer she knew ringing in her head, used its placement in the room to angle toward the door.

There was a crash behind her, and something thudded against her foot. She jerked up, tripped, jerked up again. No longer caring what might stand between herself and the door, she flung herself toward where she hoped it would be. With her breath tearing out of her lungs, she ran her hands over the wall.

"Find it, goddamn it, Quinn. Find the goddamn door!"

Her hand bumped the hinges, and on a sob she found the knob. Turned, pulled.

The light burst in front of her eyes, and Cal's body—already in motion—rammed hers. If she'd had any breath left, she'd have lost it. Her knees didn't get a chance to buckle as he wrapped his arms around her, swung her around to use his body as a shield between hers and the room beyond.

"Hold on, now. Can you hold on to me?" His voice was eerily calm as he reached behind him and pulled the door closed. "Are you hurt? Tell me if you're hurt." His hands were already skimming over her, before they came up to her face, gripped it.

Before his mouth crushed down on hers.

"You're all right," he managed, propping her against the stone of the building as he dragged off his coat. "You're okay. Here, get into this. You're freezing."

"You were there." She stared up into his face. "You were there."

"Couldn't get the door open. Key wouldn't work." He took her hands, rubbed them warm between his. "My truck's right up there, okay. I want you to go up, sit in my truck. I left the keys in it. Turn on the heat. Sit in my truck and turn on the heat. Can you do that?"

She wanted to say yes. There was something in her that

wanted to say yes to anything he asked. But she saw, in his eyes, what he meant to do.

"You're going in there."

"That's what I have to do. What you have to do is go sit in the truck for a few minutes."

"If you go in, I go in."

"Quinn."

How, she wondered, did he manage to sound patient and annoyed at the same time? "I need to as much as you, and I'd hate myself if I huddled in your truck while you went in there. I don't want to hate myself. Besides, it's better if there's two of us. It's better. Let's just do it. Just do it, and argue later."

"Stay behind me, and if I say get out, you get out. That's the deal."

"Done. Believe me, I'm not ashamed to hide behind you."

She saw it then, just the faintest glimmer of a smile in his eyes. Seeing it settled her nerves better than a quick shot of brandy.

He turned his key again, keyed in the touch pad. Quinn held her breath. When Cal opened the door, the lights were on. Al Roker's voice cheerily announced the national weather forecast. The only sign anything had happened was her sports bottle under the rack of free weights.

"Cal, I swear, the power went out, then the room—"

"I saw it. It was pitch-black in here when you came through the door. Those weights were all over the floor. I could see them rolling around from the light coming in the door. The floor was heaving. I saw it, Quinn. And I heard it from outside the door."

He'd rammed that door twice, he remembered, put his full weight into it, because he'd heard her screaming, and it had sounded like the roof was caving in.

"Okay. My things are in the locker room. I really want to get my things out of the locker."

"Give me the key, and I'll—"

"Together." She gripped his hand. "There's a scent, can

you smell it? Over and above my workout and panic sweat."

"Yeah. I always thought it must be what brimstone smells like. It's fading." He smiled, just a little, as she stopped to pick up a ten-pound free weight, gripped it like a weapon.

He pushed open the door of the women's locker room. It was as ordered and normal as the gym. Still, he took her key, nudged her behind him before he opened her locker. Moving quickly, she dragged on her sweats, exchanged coats. "Let's get out of here."

He had her hand as they walked back out and Matt walked in.

He was young, the college-jock type, doing the part-time attendant, occasional personal trainer gig. A quick, inoffensive smirk curved on his lips as he saw them come out of the women's locker room together. Then he cleared his throat.

"Hey, sorry I'm late. Damnedest thing. First my alarm didn't go off, and I know how that sounds. Then my car wouldn't start. One of those mornings."

"Yeah," Quinn agreed as she put back the weight, retrieved her water bottle. "One of those. I'm done for the day." She tossed him the locker key. "See you later."

"Sure."

She waited until they were out of the building. "He thought we'd been—"

"Yeah, yeah."

"Ever do it in a locker room?"

"As that was actually my first foray into a girl's locker room, I have to say no."

"Me, either. Cal, have you got time to come over, have coffee—God, I'll even cook breakfast—and talk about this?"

"I'm making time."

SHE TOLD HIM EVERYTHING THAT HAD HAPPENED while she scrambled eggs. "I was scared out of my mind," she finished as she carried the coffee into the little dining room.

"No, you weren't." Cal set the plates of eggs and whole-wheat toast on the table. "You found the door, in the pitch-black, and with all that going on, you kept your head and found the door."

"Thanks." She sat. She wasn't shaking any longer, but the inside of her knees still felt like half-set Jell-O. "Thanks for saying that."

"It's the truth."

"You were there when I opened the door, and that was one of the best moments of my life. How did you know to be there?"

"I came in early because I wanted to swing by here, see how you were. Talk to you. Gage—"

"I know about that. Tell me the rest of this first."

"Okay. I turned off Main to come around the back way, come here, and I saw Ann Hawkins. I saw her standing in front of the door. I heard you screaming."

"From inside your truck, on the street. That far away—through stone walls, you heard me?"

"I heard you." It hadn't been one of the best moments of his life. "When I jumped out, ran toward the door, I heard crashing, thumping, God knows what from inside. I couldn't get the goddamn door open."

She heard it now, the emotion in his voice, the fear he hadn't let show while they were doing what needed doing. She rose, did them both a favor and crawled right into his lap.

She was still there, cradled in his arms, when Cybil strolled in.

"Hi. Don't get up." She took Quinn's chair. "Anyone eating this?" Studying them, Cybil took a forkful of eggs. "You must be Cal."

"Cybil Kinski, Caleb Hawkins. We had a rough morning."

Layla stepped in with a coffee mug and sleepy eyes that clouded with concern the minute she saw Quinn. "What happened?"

"Have a seat, and we'll run it through for both of you."

"I need to see the place," Cybil said as soon as the story was told. "And the room in the bowling alley, anyplace there's been an incident."

"Try the whole town," Quinn said dryly.

"And I need to see the clearing, this stone, as soon as possible."

"She's bossy," Quinn told Cal.

"I thought you were, but I think she beats you out. You can come into the bowling center anytime you like. Quinn can get you into the fitness center, but if I can't be there, I'll make sure either Fox or Gage is. Better, both of them. As far as the Pagan Stone goes, I talked with Fox and Gage about that last night. We're agreed that the next time we go, we all go. All of us. I can't make it today and neither can Fox. Sunday's going to be best."

"He's organized and take-charge," Cybil said to Quinn.

"Yes." She pressed a kiss to Cal's cheek. "Yes, he is. And I've made you let your eggs get cold."

"It was a worthwhile trade-off. I'd better get going."

"We still have a lot to talk about. Listen, maybe the three of you should come to dinner."

"Is someone cooking?" Cal asked.

"Cyb is."

"Hey!"

"You ate my breakfast. Plus you actually cook. But in the meantime, just one thing." She slid out of his lap so he could stand. "Would Fox hire Layla?"

"What? Who? Why?" Layla sputtered.

"Because you need a job," Quinn reminded her. "And he needs an office manager."

"I don't know anything about—you just can't—"

"You managed a boutique," Quinn reminded her, "so that's half the job. Managing. You're on the anal side of organized, Miss Colored Index Cards and Charts, so I say you can file, keep a calendar, and whatever with the best of them. Anything else, you'll pick up as you go. Ask Fox, okay, Cal?"

"Sure. No problem."

"She calls me bossy," Cybil commented as she finished Quinn's coffee.

"I call it creative thinking and leadership. Now, go fill that mug up again while I walk Cal to the door so I can give him a big, sloppy you're-my-hero kiss."

Cybil smiled after them as Quinn pulled Cal out of the room. "She's in love."

"Really?"

Now Cybil turned her smile on Layla. "That got your mind off taking a bite out of her for pushing that job in your face."

"I'll get back to that. Do you think she's in love with Cal—the uppercase *L*?"

"About to be all caps, in bold letters." She picked up the mug and rose. "Q likes to direct people," she said, "but she's careful to try to direct them toward something helpful, or at least interesting. She wouldn't push this job business if she didn't think you could handle it."

She blew out a breath as she walked back toward the kitchen. "What the hell am I supposed to fix for dinner?"

Fifteen

~⌇~

IT WAS HARD FOR CAL TO SEE BILL TURNER AND say nothing about Gage being in town. But Cal knew his friend. When and if Gage wanted his father to know, Gage would tell him. So Cal did his best to avoid Bill by closing himself in his office.

He dealt with orders, bills, reservations, contacted their arcade guy to discuss changing out one of their pinball machines for something jazzier.

Checking the time, he judged if Gage wasn't awake by now, he should be. And so picked up the phone.

Not awake, Cal decided, hearing the irritation in Gage's voice, hasn't had coffee. Ignoring all that, Cal launched into an explanation of what happened that morning, relayed the dinner plans, and hung up.

Now, rolling his eyes, Cal called Fox to run over the same information, and to tell Fox that Layla needed a job and he should hire her to replace Mrs. Hawbaker.

Fox said, "Huh?"

Cal said, "Gotta go," and hung up.

There, duty done, he considered. Satisfied, he turned to his computer and brought up the information on the automatic scoring systems he wanted to talk his father into installing.

It was past time for the center to do the upgrade. Maybe it was foolish to think about that kind of investment if everything was going to hell in a few months. But, if everything was going to hell in a few months, the investment wouldn't hurt a thing.

His father would say some of the old-timers would object, but Cal didn't think so. If they wanted to keep score by hand, the center would provide the paper score sheets and markers. But he thought if someone showed them how it worked, gave them a few free games to get used to the new system, they'd jump on.

They could get them used and reconditioned, which was part of the argument he was prepared to make. They had Bill onboard, and he could fix damn near anything.

It was one thing to be a little kitschy and traditional, another to be old-fashioned.

No, no, that wasn't the tack to take with his father. His father liked old-fashioned. Better to use figures. Bowling accounted for more than half, closer to sixty percent, of their revenue, so—

He broke off at the knock on his door and inwardly winced, thinking it was Bill Turner.

But it was Cal's mother who popped her head in. "Too busy for me?"

"Never. Here to bowl a few games before the morning league?"

"Absolutely not." Frannie loved her husband, but she liked to say she hadn't taken a vow to love, honor, and bowl. She came in to sit down, then angled her head so she could see his computer screen. Her lips twitched. "Good luck with that."

"Don't say anything to Dad, okay?"

"My lips are sealed."

"Who are you having lunch with?"

"How do you know I'm having lunch with anyone?"

He gestured to her pretty fitted jacket, trim pants, heeled boots. "Too fancy for shopping."

"Aren't you smart? I do have a few errands, then I'm meeting a friend for lunch. Joanne Barry."

Fox's mother, Cal thought, and just nodded.

"We have lunch now and then, but she called me yesterday, specifically to see if I could meet her today. She's worried. So I'm here to ask you if there's anything I should know, anything you want to tell me before I see her."

"Things are as under control as I can make them, Mom. I don't have the answers yet. But I have more questions, and I think that's progress. In fact, I have one you could ask Fox's mom for me."

"All right."

"You could ask if there's a way she could find out if any of her ancestors were Hawkins."

"You think we might be related somehow? Would it help if we are?"

"It would be good to know the answer."

"Then I'll ask the question. Now answer one for me. Are you all right? Just a yes or no is good enough."

"Yes."

"Okay then." She rose. "I have half a dozen things on my list before I meet Jo." She started for the door, said, *"Damn it"* very quietly under her breath, and turned back. "I wasn't going to ask, but I have no willpower over something like this. Are you and Quinn Black serious?"

"About what?"

"Caleb James Hawkins, don't be dense."

He would've laughed, but that tone brought on the Pavlovian response of hunched shoulders. "I don't exactly know the answer. And I'm not sure it's smart to get serious, in that way, with so much going on. With so much at stake."

"What better time?" Frannie replied. "My levelheaded

Cal." She put her hand on the knob, smiled at him. "Oh, and those fancy scoring systems? Try reminding your father how much his father resisted going to projection-screen scoreboards thirty-five years ago, give or take."

"I'll keep that in mind."

Alone, Cal printed out the information on the automatic systems, new and reconditioned, then shut down long enough to go downstairs and check in with the front desk, the grill, the play area during the morning leagues games.

The scents from the grill reminded him he'd missed breakfast, so he snagged a hot pretzel and a Coke before he headed back up to his office.

So armed, he decided since everything was running smoothly, he could afford to take a late-morning break. He wanted to dig a little deeper into Ann Hawkins.

She'd appeared to him twice in three days. Both times, Cal mused, had been a kind of warning. He'd seen her before, but only in dreams. He'd wanted her in dreams, Cal admitted—or Giles Dent had, working through him.

These incidents had been different, and his feelings different.

Still, that wasn't the purpose, that wasn't the point, he reminded himself as he gnawed off a bite of pretzel.

He was trusting Quinn's instincts about the journals. Somewhere, at some time, there had been more. Maybe they were in the old library. He certainly intended to get in there and search the place inch by inch. If, God, they'd somehow gotten transferred into the new space and mis-shelved or put in storage, the search could be a nightmare.

So he wanted to know more about Ann, to help lead him to the answers.

Where had she been for nearly two years? All the information, all the stories he'd heard or read indicated she'd vanished the night of the fire in the clearing and hadn't returned to the Hollow until her sons were almost two.

"Where did you go, Ann?"

Where would a woman, pregnant with triplets, go during the last weeks before their births? Traveling had to have been extremely difficult. Even for a woman without the pregnancy to weigh her down.

There had been other settlements, but nothing as far as he remembered for a woman in her condition to have walked or even ridden to. So logically, she'd had somewhere to go close by, and someone had taken her in.

Who was most likely to take a young, unmarried woman in? A relative would be his first guess.

Maybe a friend, maybe some kindly old widow, but odds were on family.

"That's where you went first, when there was trouble, wasn't it?"

While it wasn't easy to find specifics on Ann Hawkins, there was plenty of it on her father—the founder of the Hollow.

He'd read it, of course. He'd studied it, but he'd never read or studied it from this angle. Now, he brought up all the information he'd previously downloaded on his office computer relating to James Hawkins.

He took side trips, made notes on any mention of relatives, in-laws. The pickings were slim, but at least there was something to pick from. Cal was rolling with it when someone knocked on his door. He surfaced as Quinn poked her head in just as his mother had that morning.

"Working. I bet you hate to be interrupted. But . . ."

"It's okay." He glanced at the clock, saw with a twinge of guilt his break had lasted more than an hour. "I've been at it longer than I meant to."

"It's dog-eat-dog in the bowling business." She said it with a smile as she came in. "I just wanted you to know we were here. We took Cyb on a quick tour of the town. Do you know there's no place to buy shoes in Hawkins Hollow? Cyb's saddened by that, as she's always on the hunt. Now she's making noises about bowling. She has a vicious competitive streak. So I escaped up here before she drags me into that. The hope was to grab a quick bite at your grill—maybe you could join us—before Cyb . . ."

She trailed off. Not only hadn't he said a word, but he was staring at her. Just staring. "What?" She brushed a hand over her nose, then up over her hair. "Is it my hair?"

"That's part of it. Probably part of it."

He got up, came around the desk. He kept his eyes on her face as he moved past her. As he shut and locked the door.

"Oh. *Oh.* Really? Seriously? Here? Now?"

"Really, seriously. Here and now." She looked flustered, and that was a rare little treat. She looked, every inch of her, amazing. He couldn't say why he'd gone from pleased to see her to aroused in the snap of a finger, and he didn't much care. What he knew, without question, was he wanted to touch her, to draw in her scent, to feel her body go tight, go loose. Just go.

"You're not nearly as predictable as you should be." Watching him now, she pulled off her sweater, unbuttoned the shirt beneath it.

"I should be predictable?" Without bothering with buttons, he pulled his shirt over his head.

"Hometown boy from a nice, stable family, who runs a third-generation family business. You should be predictable, Caleb," she said as she unbuttoned her jeans. "I like that you're not. I don't mean just the sex, though major points there."

She bent down to pull off her boots, tossing her hair out of her eyes so she could look up at him. "You should be married," she decided, "or on your way to it with your college sweetheart. Thinking about 401(k)s."

"I think about 401(k)s. Just not right now. Right now, Quinn, all I can think about is you."

That gave her heart a bounce, even before he reached out, ran his hands down her bare arms. Even before he drew her to him and seduced her mouth with his.

She may have laughed when they lowered to the floor,

but her pulse was pounding. There was a different tone from when they were in bed. More urgency, a sense of recklessness as they tangled together in a giddy heap on the office floor. He tugged her bra down so he could use his lips, his teeth, his tongue on her breasts until her hips began to pump. She closed her hand around him, found him hard, made him groan.

He couldn't wait, not this time. He couldn't savor; needed to take. He rolled, dragging her over so she could straddle him. Even as he gripped her hips, she was rising. She was taking him in. When she leaned forward for a greedy kiss, her hair fell to curtain their faces. Surrounded by her, he thought. Her body, her scent, her energy. He stroked the line of her back, the curve of her hips as she rocked and rocked and rocked him through pleasure toward desperation.

Even when she arched back, even with his vision blurred, the shape of her, the tones of her enthralled him.

She let herself go, simply steeped herself in sensation. Hammering pulses and speed, slick bodies and dazzling friction. She felt him come, that sudden, sharp jerk of his hips, and was thrilled. She had driven him to lose control first, she had taken him over. And now she used that power, that thrill, to drive herself over that same edgy peak.

She slid down from it, and onto him so they could lie there, heated, a little stunned, until they got their breath back. And she began to laugh.

"God, we're like a couple of teenagers. Or rabbits."

"Teenage rabbits."

Amused, she levered up. "Do you often multitask in your office like this?"

"Ah . . ."

She gave him a little poke as she tugged her bra back in place. "See, unpredictable."

He held out her shirt. "It's the first time I've multitasked in this way during working hours."

Her lips curved as she buttoned her shirt. "That's nice."

"And I haven't felt like a teenage rabbit since I was."

She leaned over to give him a quick peck on the lips. "Even nicer." Still on the floor, she scooted into her pants as he did the same. "I should tell you something." She reached for her boots, pulled one on. "I think . . . No, saying 'I think' is a cop-out, it's the coward's way."

She took a deep breath, yanked on the other boot, then looked him dead in the eye. "I'm in love with you."

The shock came first—fast, arrow-point shock straight to the gut. Then the concern wrapped in a slippery fist of fear. "Quinn—"

"Don't waste your breath with the 'we've only known each other a couple of weeks' gambit. And I really don't want to hear the 'I'm flattered, but,' either. I didn't tell you so you could say anything. I told you because you should know. So first, it doesn't matter how long we've known each other. I've known me a long time, and I know me very well. I know what I feel when I feel it. Second, you should be flattered, goes without saying. And there's no need to freak out. You're not obligated or expected to feel what I feel."

"Quinn, we're—all of us—are under a lot of pressure. We don't even know if we'll make it through to August. We can't—"

"Exactly so. Nobody ever knows that, but we have more reason to worry about it. So, Cal." She framed his face with her hands. "The moment's important. The right-this-minute matters a whole hell of a lot. I doubt I'd have told you otherwise, though I can be impulsive. But I think, under other circumstances, I'd have waited for you to catch up. I hope you do, but in the meantime, things are just fine the way they are."

"You have to know I—"

"Don't, absolutely don't tell me you care about me." The first hint of anger stung her voice. "Your instinct is to say all the cliches people babble out in cases like this. They'll only piss me off."

"Okay, all right, let me just ask this, without you getting pissed off. Have you considered what you're feeling might be something like what happened in the clearing? That it's, say, a reflection of what Ann felt for Dent?"

"Yes, and it's not." She pushed to her feet, drew on her sweater. "Good question though. Good questions don't piss me off. What she felt, and I felt through that, was intense and consuming. I'm not going to say some of what I feel for you isn't like that. But it was also painful, and wrenching. Under the joy was grief. That's not this, Cal. This isn't painful. I don't feel sad. So . . . do you have time to come down and grab some lunch before Cyb and Layla and I head out?"

"Ah . . . sure."

"Great. Meet you down there. I'm going to pop in the bathroom and fix myself up a little."

"Quinn." He hesitated as she opened the door, turned back. "I've never felt like this about anyone before."

"Now that is a very acceptable thing to say."

She smiled as she strolled away. If he'd said it, he meant it, because that was the way he was. Poor guy, she thought. Didn't even know he was caught.

A THICK GROVE OF TREES SHIELDED THE OLD cemetery on the north side. It fanned out over bumpy ground, with hills rolling west, at the end of a dirt road barely wide enough for two cars to pass. A historical marker faded by weather stated the First Church of the Godly had once stood on the site, but had been destroyed when it had been struck by lightning and razed by fire on July 7, 1652.

Quinn had read that fact in her research, but it was different to stand here now, in the wind, in the chill, and imagine it. She'd read, too, as the plaque stated, that a small chapel had stood as a replacement until it was damaged during the Civil War, and gone to ruin.

Now, there were only the markers here, the stones, the winter-hardy weeds. Beyond a low stone wall were the graves of the newer dead. Here and there she saw bright blots of color from flowers that stood out like grief against the dull grays and winter browns.

"We should've brought flowers," Layla said quietly as she looked down at the simple and small stone that read only:

ANN HAWKINS

"She doesn't need them," Cybil told her. "Stones and flowers, they're for the living. The dead have other things to do."

"Cheery thought."

Cybil only shrugged at Quinn. "I think so, actually. No point in being dead *and* bored. It's interesting, don't you think, that there are no dates. Birth or death. No sentiment. She had three sons, but they didn't have anything but her name carved in her gravestone. Even though they're buried here, too, with their wives, and I imagine at least some of their children. Wherever they went in life, they came home to be buried with Ann."

"Maybe they knew, or believed, she'd be back. Maybe she told them death isn't the end." Quinn frowned at the stone. "Maybe they just wanted to keep it simple, but I wonder, now that you mention it, if it was deliberate. No beginning, no end. At least not until . . ."

"This July," Layla finished. "Another cheery thought."

"Well, while we're all getting cheered up, I'm going to get some pictures." Quinn pulled out her camera. "Maybe you two could write down some of the names here. We may want to check on them, see if any have any direct bearing on—"

She tripped while backing up to get a shot, fell hard on her ass. "Ouch, goddamn it! Shit. Right on the bruise I got this morning. Perfect."

Layla rushed over to help her up. Cybil did the same, even as she struggled with laughter.

"Just shut up," Quinn grumbled. "The ground's all bumpy here, and you can hardly see some of these stones popping out." She rubbed her hip, scowled down at the stone that had tripped her up. "Ha. That's funny. Joseph Black, died eighteen forty-three." The color annoyance brought to her face faded. "Same last name as mine. Common name Black, really. Until you consider it's here, and that I just happened to trip over his grave."

"Odds are he's one of yours," Cybil agreed.

"And one of Ann's?"

Quinn shook her head at Layla's suggestion. "I don't know. Cal's researched the Hawkins's family tree, and I've done a quick overview. I know some of the older records are lost, or just buried deeper than we've dug, but I don't see how we'd both have missed branches with my surname. So. I think we'd better see what we can find out about Joe."

HER FATHER WAS NO HELP, AND THE CALL HOME kept her on the phone for forty minutes, catching up on family gossip. She tried her grandmother next, who had a vague recollection about her mother-in-law mentioning an uncle, possibly a great-uncle, maybe a cousin, who'd been born in the hills of Maryland. Or it might've been Virginia. His claim to fame, family-wise, had been running off with a saloon singer, deserting his wife and four children and taking the family savings held inside a cookie tin with him.

"Nice guy, Joe," Quinn decided. "Should you be my Joe."

She decided, since it would get her out of any type of food preparation, she had enough time to make a trip to Town Hall, and start digging on Joseph Black. If he'd died here, maybe he'd been born here.

WHEN QUINN GOT HOME SHE WAS GLAD TO FIND the house full of people, sound, the scents of food. Cybil, being Cybil, had music on, candles lit, and wine poured. She had everyone piled in the kitchen, whetting appetites with marinated olives. Quinn popped one, took Cal's wine and washed it down.

"Are my eyes bleeding?" she asked.

"Not so far."

"I've been searching records for nearly three hours. I think I bruised my brain."

"Joseph Black." Fox got her a glass of wine for her own. "We've been filled in."

"Good, saves me. I could only trace him back to his grandfather—Quinton Black, born sixteen seventy-six. Nothing on record before that, not here anyway. And nothing after Joe, either. I went on side trips, looking for siblings or other relatives. He had three sisters, but I've got nothing on them but birth records. He had aunts, uncles, and so on, and not much more there. It appears the Blacks weren't a big presence in Hawkins Hollow."

"Name would've rung for me," Cal told her.

"Yeah. Still, I got my grandmother's curiosity up, and she's now on a hunt to track down the old family Bible. She called me on my cell. She thinks it went to her brother-in-law when his parents died. Maybe. Anyway, it's a line."

She focused on the man leaning back against the counter toying with a glass of wine. "Sorry? Gage, right?"

"That's right. Roadside service a specialty."

Quinn grinned as Cybil rolled her eyes and took a loaf of herbed bread out of the oven.

"So I hear, and that looks like dinner's ready. I'm starved. Nothing like searching through the births and deaths of Blacks, Robbits, Clarks to stir up the appetite."

"Clark." Layla lowered the plate she'd taken out to offer Cybil for the bread. "There were Clarks in the records?"

"Yeah, an Alma and a Richard Clark in there, as I remember. Need to check my notes. Why?"

"My grandmother's maiden name was Clark." Layla managed a wan smile. "That's probably not a coincidence either."

"Is she still living?" Quinn asked immediately. "Can you get in touch and—"

"We're going to eat while it's hot," Cybil interrupted. "Time enough to give family trees a good shake later. But when I cook—" She pushed the plate of hot bread into Gage's hand. "We eat."

Sixteen

$\sim\!\!\wedge\!\!\sim$

IT HAD TO BE IMPORTANT. IT HAD TO MATTER.
Cal rolled it over and over and over, carving time out of his
workday and his off time to research the Hawkins-Black
lineage himself. Here was something new, he thought,
some door they hadn't known existed, much less tried to
break down.

He told himself it was vital, and time-consuming work,
and that was why he and Quinn hadn't managed to really
connect for the last couple of days. He was busy; she was
busy. Couldn't be helped.

Besides, it was probably a good time for them to have
this break from each other. Let things just simmer down a
little. As he'd told his mother, this wasn't the time to get
serious, to think about falling in love. Because big, life-
altering things were supposed to happen after people fell
seriously in love. And he had enough, big, life-altering
things to worry about.

He dumped food in Lump's bowl as his dog waited for
breakfast with his usual unruffled patience. Because it was

Thursday, he'd tossed a load of laundry in the washer when he'd let Lump out for his morning plod and pee. He continued his habitual weekday morning routine, nursing his first cup of coffee while he got out a box of Chex.

But when he reached for the milk it made him think of Quinn. Two percent milk, he thought with a shake of his head. Maybe she was fixing her version of a bowl of cereal right now. Maybe she was standing in her kitchen with the smell of coffee in the air, thinking of him.

Because the idea of that held such appeal, he reached for the phone to call her, when he heard the sound behind him and turned.

Gage got the coffee mug out of the cupboard he opened. "Jumpy."

"No. I didn't hear you come in."

"You were mooning over a woman."

"I have a lot of things on my mind."

"Especially the woman. You've got tells, Hawkins. Starting with the wistful, cocker spaniel eyes."

"Up yours, Turner."

Gage merely grinned and poured coffee. "Then there's that fish hook in the corner of your mouth." He hooked his finger in his own, gave a tug. "Unmistakable."

"You're jealous because you're not getting laid regular."

"No question about that." Gage sipped his black coffee, used one bare foot to rub Lump's flank as the dog concentrated his entire being on his kibble. "She's not your usual type."

"Oh?" Irritation crawled up Cal's back like a lizard. "What's my usual type?"

"Pretty much same as mine. Keep it light, no deep thinking, no strings, no worries. Who could blame us, considering?" He picked up the cereal, dug right into the box. "But she breaks your mold. She's smart, she's steady, and she's got a big, fat ball of string in her back pocket. She's already started wrapping you in it."

"Does that cynicism you carry around everywhere ever get heavy?"

"Realism," Gage corrected as he munched on cereal. "And it keeps me light on my feet. I like her."

"I do, too." Cal forgot the milk and just took a handful of cereal out of the bowl he'd poured. "She . . . she told me she's in love with me."

"Fast work. And now she's suddenly pretty damn busy, and you're sleeping alone, pal. I said she was smart."

"Jesus, Gage." Insult bloomed on two stalks—one for himself, one for Quinn. "She's not like that. She doesn't use people like that."

"And you know this because you know her so well."

"I do." Any sign of irritation faded as that simple truth struck home. "That's just it. I do know her. There may be dozens, hell, hundreds of things I don't know, but I know who—how—she is. I don't know if some of that's because of this connection, because of what we're all tied to, but I know it's true. The first time I met her, things changed. I don't know. Something changed for me. So you can make cracks, but that's the way it is."

"I'm going to say you're lucky," Gage said after a moment. "That I hope it works out the way you want. I never figured any of us had a decent shot at normal." He shrugged. "Wouldn't mind being wrong. Besides, you look real cute with that hook in your mouth."

Cal lifted his middle finger off the bowl and into the air.

"Right back atcha," Fox said as he strolled in. He went straight to the refrigerator for a Coke. "What's up?"

"What's up is you're mooching my Cokes again, and you never bring any to replace them."

"I brought beer last week. Besides, Gage told me to come over this morning, and when I come over in the morning, I expect a damn Coke."

"You told him to come over?"

"Yeah. So, O'Dell, Cal's in love with the blonde."

"I didn't say I—"

"Tell me something I don't know." Fox popped the top on the can of Coke and gulped.

"I never said I was in love with anyone."

Fox merely shifted his gaze to Cal. "I've known you my whole life. I know what those shiny little hearts in your eyes mean. It's cool. She was, like, made for you."

"He says she's not my usual type, you say she's made for me."

"We're both right. She's not the type you usually fish for." Fox gulped down more soda, then took the box of cereal from Gage. "Because you didn't want to find the one who fit. She fits, but she was sort of a surprise. Practically an ambush. Did I get up an hour early to come over here before work so we could talk about Cal's love life?"

"No, it was just an interesting sidebar. I got some information when I was in the Czech Republic. Rumors, lore, mostly, which I followed up when I had time. I got a call from an expert last night, which is why I told you to come over this morning. I might have ID'd our Big Evil Bastard."

They sat down at the kitchen table with coffee and dry cereal—Fox in one of his lawyer suits, Gage in a black T-shirt and loose pants, Cal in jeans and a flannel shirt.

And spoke of demons.

"I toured some of the smaller and outlying villages," Gage began. "I always figure I might as well pick up some local color, maybe a local skirt while I'm stacking up poker chips and markers."

He'd been doing the same for years, Cal knew. Following any whiff of information about devils, demons, unexplained phenomenon. He always came back with stories, but nothing that had ever fit the, well, the profile, Cal supposed, of their particular problem.

"There was talk about this old demon who could take other forms. You get werewolf stuff over there, and initially, I figured that was this deal. But this wasn't about biting throats out and silver bullets. The talk was about how this thing hunted humans to enslave them, and feed off their . . . the translation was kind of vague, and the best I got was essence, or humanity."

"Feed how?"

"That's vague, too—or colorful as lore tends to be. Not on flesh and bone, not with fang and claw—that kind of thing. The legend is this demon, or creature, could take people's minds as well as their souls, and cause them to go mad, cause them to kill."

"Could be the root of ours," Fox decided.

"It rang close enough that I followed it up. It was a lot to wade through; that area's ripe with stories like this. But in this place in the hills, with this thick forest that reminded me of home, I hit something. Its name is *Tmavy*. Translates to Dark. The Dark."

He thought, they all thought of what had come out of the ground at the Pagan Stone. "It came like a man who wasn't a man, hunted like a wolf that wasn't a wolf. And sometimes it was a boy, a boy who lured women and children in particular into the forest. Most never came back, and those who did were mad. The families of those who did went mad, too. Killed each other, or themselves, their neighbors."

Gage paused, rose to get the coffeepot. "I got some of this when I was there, but I found a priest who gave me the name of a guy, a professor, who studied and publishes on Eastern European demonology. He got in touch last night. He claims this particular demon—and he isn't afraid to use the word—roamed Europe for centuries. He, in turn, was hunted by a man—some say another demon, or a wizard, or just a man with a mission. Legend has it that they battled in the forest, and the wizard was mortally wounded, left for dead. And that, according to Professor Linz, was its mistake. Someone came, a young boy, and the wizard passed the boy his power before he died."

"What happened?" Fox demanded.

"No one, including Linz, is sure. The stories claim the thing vanished, or moved on, or died, somewhere in the early- to mid-seventeenth century."

"When he hopped a goddamn boat for the New World," Cal added.

"Maybe. That may be."

"So did the boy," Cal continued, "or the man he'd become, or his descendent. But he nearly had him over there, nearly did at some point in time—that's something I've seen. I think. Him and the woman, a cabin. Him holding a bloody sword, and knowing nearly all were dead. He couldn't stop it there, so he passed what he had to Dent, and Dent tried again. Here."

"What did he pass to us?" Fox demanded. "What power? Not getting a freaking head cold, having a broken arm knit itself? What good does that do?"

"Keeps us healthy and whole when we face it down. And there's the glimmers I see, that we all see in different ways." Cal shoved at his hair. "I don't know. But it has to be something that matters. The three parts of the stone. They have to be. We've just never figured it out."

"And time's almost up."

Cal nodded at Gage. "We need to show the stones to the others. We took an oath, we all have to agree to that. If we hadn't, I'd have—"

"Shown yours to Quinn already," Fox finished. "And yeah, maybe you're right. It's worth a shot. It could be it needs all six of us to put it back together."

"Or it could be that when whatever happened at the Pagan Stone happened, the bloodstone split because its power was damaged. Destroyed."

"Your glass is always half empty, Turner," Fox commented. "Either way, it's worth the try. Agreed?"

"Agreed." Cal looked at Gage, who shrugged.

"What the hell."

CAL DEBATED WITH HIMSELF ALL THE WAY INTO town. He didn't need an excuse to stop by to see Quinn. For God's sake, they were sleeping together. It wasn't as if he needed an appointment or clearance or a specific reason to knock on her door, to see how she was doing. To ask what the hell was going on.

There was no question she'd been distracted every time he'd managed to reach her by phone the last couple of days. She hadn't dropped into the center since they'd rolled around his office floor.

And she'd told him she was in love with him.

That was the problem. The oil on the water, the sand in the shoe, or whatever goddamn analogy made the most sense. She'd told him she loved him, he hadn't said "me, too," which she claimed she didn't expect. But any guy who actually believed a woman always meant exactly what she said was deep in dangerous delusion.

Now, she was avoiding him.

They didn't have *time* for games, for bruised feelings and sulks. There were more important things at stake. Which, he was forced to admit, was why he shouldn't have touched her in the first place. By adding sex to the mix, they'd clouded and complicated the issue, and the issue was already clouded and complicated enough. They had to be practical; they had to be smart. Objective, he added as he pulled up in front of the rental house. Cold-blooded, clear-minded.

Nobody was any of those things when they were having sex. Not if they were having really good sex.

He jammed his hands in his pockets as he walked up to her door, then dragged one out to knock. The fact that he'd worked himself up to a mad might not have been objective or practical, but it felt absolutely right.

Until she opened the door.

Her hair was damp. She'd pulled it back from her face in a sleek tail, and he could see it wasn't quite dry. He could smell the girly shampoo and soap, and the scents wound their way into him until the muscle in his gut tightened in response.

She wore fuzzy purple socks, black flannel pants, and a hot pink sweatshirt that announced: T.G.I.F. THANK GOD I'M FEMALE.

He could add his own thanks.

"Hi!"

The idea she was sulking was hard to hang on to when he was blasted by her sunbeam smile and buzzing energy.

"I was just thinking about you. Come inside. Jesus, it's cold. I've so had it with winter. I was about to treat myself to a low-fat mug of hot chocolate. Want in on that?"

"Ah—I really don't."

"Well, come on back, because I've got the yen." She rose up on her toes to give him a long, solid kiss, then grabbed his hand to pull him back to the kitchen. "I nagged Cyb and Layla into going to the gym with me this morning. Took some doing with Cyb, but I figured safety in numbers. Nothing weird happened, unless you count watching Cyb twist herself into some advanced yoga positions. Which Matt did, let me tell you. Things have been quiet in the otherworldly sense the last couple days."

She got out a packet of powdered mix, slapped it against her hand a couple of times to settle it before ripping it open to pour it into a mug. "Sure you don't want some?"

"Yeah, go ahead."

"We've been a busy hive around here," she went on as she filled the mug, half with water, half with two percent milk. "I'm waiting to hear something about the family Bible, or whatever else my grandmother might dig up. Today, maybe, hopefully by tomorrow. Meanwhile, we've got charts of family trees as we know them, and Layla's trying to shake some ancestry out of her relatives."

She stirred up the liquid and mix, stuck it in the microwave. "I had to leave a lot of the research up to my partners in crime and finish an article for the magazine. Gotta pay the doorman, after all. So?" She turned back as the microwave hummed. "How about you?"

"I missed you." He hadn't planned to say it, certainly hadn't expected it to be the first thing out of his mouth. Then he realized, it was obviously the first thing on his mind.

Her eyes went soft; that sexy mouth curved up. "That's nice to hear. I missed you, too, especially last night when I crawled into bed about one in the morning. My cold, empty bed."

"I didn't just mean the sex, Quinn." And where had *that* come from?

"Neither did I." She angled her head, ignoring the beep of the microwave. "I missed having you around at the end of the day, when I could finally come down from having to hammer out that article, when I wanted to stop thinking about what I had to do, and what was going to happen. You're irritated about something. Why don't you tell me what it is?"

She turned toward the microwave as she spoke to get her mug out. Cal saw immediately she'd made the move as Cybil was stepping through the kitchen doorway. Quinn merely shook her head, and Cybil stepped back and retreated without a word.

"I don't know, exactly." He pulled off his coat now, tossed it over one of the chairs around a little cafe table that hadn't been there on his last visit. "I guess I thought, after the other day, after . . . what you said—"

"I said I was in love with you. That makes you quiver inside," she noted. "Men."

"I didn't start avoiding you."

"You think—" She took a deep inhale through her nose, exhaled in a huff. "Well, you have a really high opinion of yourself, and a crappy one of me."

"No, it's just—"

"I had things to do, I had work. I am not at your beck any more than you're at mine."

"That's not what I meant."

"You think I'd play games like that? Especially now?"

"Especially now's the point. This isn't the time for big personal issues."

"If not now, when?" she demanded. "Do you really, do you honestly think we can label and file all our personal business and close it in a drawer until it's *convenient*? I like things in their place, too. I want to know where things are, so I put them where I want or need them to be. But feelings and thoughts are different from the goddamn car keys, Cal."

"No argument, but—"

"And my feelings and thoughts are as cluttered and messy as Grandma's attic," she snapped out, far from winding down. "That's just the way I like it. If things were normal every day, bopping right along, I probably wouldn't have told you. Do you think this is my first cannonball into the Dating and Relationship Pool? I was engaged, for God's sake. I told you because—because I think, maybe *especially* now, that feelings are what matter most. If that screws you up, too damn bad."

"I wish you'd shut up for five damn minutes."

Her eyes went to slits. "Oh, really?"

"Yeah. The fact is I don't know how to react to all of this, because I never let myself consider being in this position. How could I, with this hanging over my head? Can't risk falling for someone. How much could I tell her? How much is too much? We're—Fox and Gage and I—we're used to holding back, to keeping big pieces of this to ourselves."

"Keeping secrets."

"That's right," he said equably. "That's exactly right. Because it's safer that way. How could I ever think about falling in love, getting married, having kids? Bringing a kid into this nightmare's out of the question."

Those slitted blue eyes went cold as winter. "I don't believe I've yet expressed the wish to bear your young."

"Remember who you're talking to," he said quietly. "You take this situation out of the equation you've got a normal guy from a normal family. The kind who gets married, raises a family, has a mortgage and a big sloppy dog. If I let myself fall in love with a woman, that's how it's going to work."

"I guess you told me."

"And it's irresponsible to even consider any of that."

"We disagree. I happen to think considering that, moving toward that, is shooting the bird at the dark. In the end, we're each entitled to our own take on it. But understand me, get this crystal, telling you I love you didn't mean I expected you to pop a ring on my finger."

"Because you've been there."

She nodded. "Yes, I have. And you're wondering about that."

"None of my business." Screw it. "Yes."

"Okay, it's simple enough. I was seeing Dirk—"

"Dirk—"

"Shut up." But her lips twitched. "I was seeing him exclusively for about six months. We enjoyed each other. I thought I was ready for the next stage in my life, so I said yes when he asked me to marry him. We were engaged for two months when I realized I'd made a mistake. I didn't love him. Liked him just fine. He didn't love me, either. He didn't really get me—not the whole of me, which was why he figured the ring on my finger meant he could begin to advise me on my work, on my wardrobe, habits, and career options. There were a lot of little things, and they're not really important. The fact was we weren't going to make it work, so I broke it off."

She blew out another breath because it wasn't pleasant to remember she'd made that big a mistake. That she'd failed at something she knew she'd be good at. "He was more annoyed than brokenhearted, which told me I'd done the right thing. And the truth is, it stung to know I'd done the right thing, because it meant I'd done the wrong thing first. When I suggested he tell his friends he'd been the one to end it, he felt better about it. I gave him back the ring, we each boxed up things we'd kept in each other's apartments, and we walked away."

"He didn't hurt you."

"Oh, Cal." She took a step closer so she could touch his face. "No, he didn't. The situation hurt me, but he didn't. Which is only one of the reasons I knew he wasn't the one. If you want me to reassure you that you can't, that you won't break my heart, I just can't do it. Because you can,

you might, and that's how I know you are. The one." She
slipped her arms around him, laid her lips on his. "That
must be scary for you."

"Terrifying." He pulled her against him, held her hard.
"I've never had another woman in my life who's given me
as many bad moments as you."

"I'm delighted to hear it."

"I thought you would be." He laid his cheek on top of
her head. "I'd like to stay here, just like this, for an hour or
two." He replaced his cheek with his lips, then eased back.
"But I've things I have to do, and so do you. Which I knew
before I walked in here and used it as an excuse to pick a
fight."

"I don't mind a fight. Not when the air's clear afterward."

He framed her face with his hands, kissed her softly.
"Your hot chocolate's getting cold."

"Chocolate's never the wrong temperature."

"The one thing I said before? Absolute truth. I missed
you."

"I believe I can arrange some free time in my busy
schedule."

"I have to work tonight. Maybe you could stop in. I'll
give you another bowling lesson."

"All right."

"Quinn, we—all of us—have to talk. About a lot of
things. As soon as we can."

"Yes, we do. One thing before you go. Is Fox going to
offer Layla a job?"

"I said something to him." Cal swore under his breath at
her expression. "I'll give him another push on it."

"Thanks."

Alone, Quinn picked up her mug, thoughtfully sipped at
her lukewarm chocolate. Men, she thought, were such interesting beings.

Cybil came in. "All clear?"

"Yeah, thanks."

"No problem." She opened a cupboard and chose a small tin of loose jasmine tea from her supply. "Discuss or mind my own?"

"Discuss. He was worked up because I told him I love him."

"Annoyed or panicked?"

"Some of both, I think. More worried because we've all got scary things to deal with, and this is another kind of scary thing."

"The scariest, when you come down to it." Cybil filled the teakettle with water. "How are you handling it?"

"It feels . . . great," she decided. "Energizing and bouncy and bright, then sort of rich and glimmering. You know, with Dirk it was all . . ." Quinn held out a hand, drawing it level through the air. "This was—" She shot her hand up, down, then up again. "Here's a thing. When he's telling me why this is crazy, he says how he's never been in a position—or so he thinks—to let himself think about love, marriage, family."

"Whoa, point A to Z in ten words or less."

"Exactly." Quinn gestured with her mug. "And he was rolling too fast to see that the *M* word gave me a serious jolt. I practically just jumped off that path, and whoops, there it is again, under my feet."

"Hence the jolt." Cybil measured out her tea. "But I don't see you jumping off."

"Because you know me. I like where my feet are, as it turns out. I like the idea of heading down that path with Cal, toward wherever it ends up. He's in trouble now," she murmured and took another sip.

"So are you, Q. But then trouble's always looked good on you."

"Better than a makeover at the Mac counter at Saks." Quinn answered the kitchen phone on its first ring. "Hello. Hello, Essie. Oh. Really? No, it's great. It's perfect. Thanks so much. I absolutely will. Thanks again. Bye." She hung up, grinned. "Essie Hawkins got us into the community center. No business there today on the main level. We can go in, poke around to our hearts' content."

"Won't that be fun?" Cybil said it dryly as she poured boiling water for her tea.

ARMED WITH THE KEY, CYBIL OPENED THE MAIN door of the old library. "We're here, on the surface, for research. One of the oldest buildings in town, home of the Hawkins family. But . . ." She switched on the lights. "Primarily we're looking for hidey-holes. A hiding place that was overlooked."

"For three and a half centuries," Cybil commented.

"If something's overlooked for five minutes, it can be overlooked forever." Quinn pursed her lips as she looked around. "They modernized it, so to speak, when they turned it into a library, but when they built the new one, they stripped out some of the newfangled details. It's not the way it was, but it's closer."

There were some tables and chairs set up, and someone had made an attempt at some old-timey decor in the antique old lamps, old pottery, and wood carvings on shelves. Quinn had been told groups like the Historical Society or the Garden Club could hold meetings or functions here. At election times it was a voting center.

"Stone fireplace," she said. "See, that's an excellent place to hide something." After crossing to it, she began to poke at the stones. "Plus there's an attic. Essie said they used it for storage. Still do. They keep the folding tables and chairs up there, and that kind of thing. Attics are treasure troves."

"Why is it buildings like this are so cold and creepy when no one's in them?" Layla wondered.

"We're in this one. Let's start at the top," Quinn suggested, "work our way down."

"ATTICS ARE TREASURE TROVES," CYBIL SAID twenty minutes later, "of dust and spiders."

"It's not that bad." Quinn crawled along, hoping for a loose floorboard.

"Not that good either." Courageously, Layla stood on a folding chair, checking rafters. "I don't understand why people don't think storage spaces shouldn't be cleaned as regularly as anyplace else."

"It was clean once. She kept it clean."

"Who—" Layla began, but Cybil waved a hand at her, frowned at Quinn.

"Ann Hawkins?"

"Ann and her boys. She brought them home, and shared the attic with them. Her three sons. Until they were old enough to have a room downstairs. But she stayed here. She wanted to be high, to be able to look out of her window. Even though she knew he wouldn't come, she wanted to look out for him. She was happy here, happy enough. And when she died here, she was ready to go."

Abruptly, Quinn sat back on her heels. "Holy shit, was that me?"

Cybil crouched down to study Quinn's face. "You tell us."

"I guess it was." She pressed her fingers to her forehead. "Damn, got one of those I-drank-my-frozen-margarita-too-fast-and-now-have-an-ice pick-through-my-brain headaches. I saw it, her, them, in my head. Just as clear. Everything moving, like a time-action camera. Years in seconds. But more, I felt it. That's the way it is for you, isn't it—going the other way?"

"Often," Cybil agreed.

"I saw her writing in her journal, and washing her sons' faces. I saw her laughing, or weeping. I saw her standing at the window looking into the dark. I felt . . ." Quinn laid a hand on her heart. "I felt her longing. It was . . . brutal."

"You don't look well." Layla touched her shoulder. "We should go downstairs, get you some water."

"Probably. Yeah." She took the hand Layla offered to help her up. "Maybe I should try it again. Try to bring it back, get more."

"You're awfully pale," Layla told her. "And, honey, your hand's like ice."

"Plenty for one day," Cybil agreed. "You don't want to push it."

"I didn't see where she put the journals. If she put anything here, I didn't see."

Seventeen

~⌣~

IT WASN'T THE TIME, CAL DETERMINED, TO TALK about a broken stone or property searches when Quinn was buzzed about her trip to the past with Ann Hawkins. In any case, the bowling center wasn't the place for that kind of exchange of information.

He considered bringing it up after closing when she dragged him into her home office to show him the new chart Layla had generated that listed the time, place, approximate duration, and involved parties in all known incidents since Quinn's arrival.

He forgot about it when he was in bed with her, when she was moving with him, when everything felt right again.

Then he told himself it was too late to bring it up, to give the topics the proper time when she was curled up warm with him.

Maybe it was avoidance, but he opted for the likelihood it was just his tendency to prefer things at the right time, in the right place. He'd arranged to take Sunday off so the entire group could hike to the Pagan Stone. That, to his mind, was the right time and place.

Then Nature screwed with his plans.

When forecasters began to predict an oncoming blizzard, he kept a jaundiced eye on the reports. They were, in his experience, wrong at least as often as they were right. Even when the first flakes began to fall midmorning, he remained unconvinced. It was the third blizzard hype of the year, and so far the biggest storm had dumped a reasonable eight inches.

He shrugged it off when the afternoon leagues canceled. It had gotten so people canceled everything at the first half inch, then went to war over bread and toilet paper in the supermarket. And since the powers-that-be canceled school before noon, the arcade and the grill were buzzing.

But when his father came in about two in the afternoon, looking like Sasquatch, Cal paid more attention.

"I think we're going to close up shop," Jim said in his easy way.

"It's not that bad. The arcade's drawing the usual suspects, the grill's been busy. We've had some lanes booked. A lot of towners will come in later in the afternoon, looking for something to do."

"It's bad enough, and it's getting worse." Jim shoved his gloves in the pocket of his parka. "We'll have a foot by sundown the way it's going. We need to send these kids home, haul them there if they don't live within easy walking distance. We'll close up, then you go on home, too. Or you get your dog and Gage and come on over and stay with us. Your mother'll worry sick if she thinks you're out driving in this at night."

He started to remind his father that he was thirty, had four-wheel drive, and had been driving nearly half his life. Knowing it was pointless, Cal just nodded. "We'll be fine. I've got plenty of supplies. I'll clear out the customers, close up, Dad. You go on home. She'll worry about you, too."

"There's time enough to close down and lock up." Jim glanced over at the lanes where a six-pack of teenagers sent off energy and hormones in equal measure. "Had a hell of a storm when I was a kid. Your grandfather kept her open. We stayed here for three days. Time of my life."

"I bet." Cal grinned. "Want to call Mom, say we're stuck? You and me can ride it out. Have a bowling marathon."

"Damned if I wouldn't." The lines around Jim's eyes crinkled at the idea. "Of course, she'll kick my ass for it and it'd be the last time I bowled."

"Better shut down then."

Though there were protests and moans, they moved customers along, arranging for rides when necessary with some of the staff. In the silence, Cal shut down the grill himself. He knew his father had gone back to check with Bill Turner. Not just to give instructions, he thought, but to make sure Bill had whatever he needed, to slip him a little extra cash if he didn't.

As he shut down, Cal pulled out his phone and called Fox's office. "Hey. Wondered if I'd catch you."

"Just. I'm closing. Already sent Mrs. H home. It's getting bad out there."

"Head over to my place. If this comes in like they're whining about, it might be a couple days before the roads are clear. No point wasting them. And maybe you should stop, pick up, you know, toilet paper, bread."

"Toilet . . . You're bringing the women?"

"Yeah." He'd made up his mind on that when he'd taken a look outside. "Get . . . stuff. Figure it out. I'll be home as soon as I can."

He clicked off, then shut down the alley lights as his father came out.

"Everything set?" Cal asked.

"Yep."

The way his father looked around the darkened alley told Cal he was thinking they weren't just going to lose their big Friday night, but likely the entire weekend.

"We'll make it up, Dad."

"That's right. We always do." He gave Cal a slap on the shoulder. "Let's get home."

QUINN WAS LAUGHING WHEN SHE OPENED THE door. "Isn't this great! They say we could get three feet, maybe more! Cyb's making goulash, and Layla went out and picked up extra batteries and candles in case we lose power."

"Good. Great." Cal stomped snow off his boots. "Pack it up and whatever else you all need. We're going to my place."

"Don't be silly. We're fine. You can stay, and we'll—"

As clear of snow as he could manage, he stepped in, shut the door behind him. "I have a small gas generator that'll run little things—such as the well, which means water to flush the toilets."

"Oh. Toilets. I hadn't thought of that one. But how are we all going to fit in your truck?"

"We'll manage. Get your stuff."

It took them half an hour, but he'd expected that. In the end, the bed of his truck was loaded with enough for a week's trek through the wilderness. And three women were jammed with him in the cab.

He should've had Fox swing by, get one of them, he realized. Then Fox could've hauled half the contents of their house in *his* truck. And it was too late now.

"It's gorgeous." Layla perched on Quinn's lap, bracing a hand on the dash while the Chevy's windshield wipers worked overtime to clear the snow from the glass. "I know it's going to be a big mess, but it's so beautiful, so different than it is in the city."

"Remember that when we're competing for bathroom time with three men," Cybil warned her. "And let me say right now, I refuse to be responsible for all meals just because I know how to turn on the stove."

"So noted," Cal muttered.

"It *is* gorgeous," Quinn agreed, shifting her head from side to side to see around Layla. "Oh, I forgot. I heard from my grandmother. She tracked down the Bible. She's having her sister-in-law's granddaughter copy and scan the appropriate pages, and e-mail them to me." Quinn wiggled to try for more room. "At least that's the plan, as the granddaughter's the only one of them who understands how to scan and attach files. E-mail and online poker's as far as Grandma goes on the Internet. I hope to have the information by tomorrow. Isn't this great?"

Wedged between Quinn's butt and the door, Cybil dug in to protect her corner of the seat. "It'd be better if you'd move your ass over."

"I've got Layla's space, too, so I get more room. I want popcorn," Quinn decided. "Doesn't all this snow make everyone want popcorn? Did we pack any? Do you have any?" she asked Cal. "Maybe we could stop and buy some Orville's."

He kept his mouth shut, and concentrated on surviving what he thought might be the longest drive of his life.

He plowed his way down the side roads, and though he trusted the truck and his own driving, was relieved when he turned onto his lane. As he'd been outvoted about the heat setting, the cab of the truck was like a sauna.

Even under the circumstances, Cal had to admit his place, his woods, did look like a picture. The snow-banked terraces, the white-decked trees and huddles of shrubs framed the house where smoke was pumping from the chimney, and the lights were already gleaming against the windows.

He followed the tracks of Fox's tires across the little bridge over his snow- and ice-crusted curve of the creek.

Lump padded toward the house from the direction of the winter-postcard woods, leaving deep prints behind him. His tail swished once as he let out a single, hollow bark.

"Wow, look at Lump." Quinn managed to poke Cal with her elbow as the truck shoved its way along the lane. "He's positively frisky."

"Snow gets him going." Cal pulled behind Fox's truck, smirked at the Ferrari, slowly being buried, then laid on the horn. He'd be damned if he was going to haul the bulk of what three women deemed impossible to live without for a night or two.

He dragged bags out of the bed.

"It's a beautiful spot, Cal." Layla took the first out of his hands. "Currier and Ives for the twenty-first century. Is it all right if I go right in?"

"Sure."

"Pretty as a picture." Cybil scanned the bags and boxes, chose one for herself. "Especially if you don't mind being isolated."

"I don't."

She glanced over as Gage and Fox came out of the house. "I hope you don't mind crowds either."

They got everything inside, trailing snow everywhere. Cal decided it must have been some sort of female telepathy that divided them all into chores without discussion. Layla asked him for rags or old towels and proceeded to mop up the wet, Cybil took over the kitchen with her stew pot and bag of kitchen ingredients. And Quinn dug into his linen closet, such as it was, and began assigning beds, and ordering various bags carried to various rooms.

There wasn't anything for him to do, really, but have a beer.

Gage strode in as Cal poked at the fire. "There are bottles of girl stuff all over both bathrooms up there." Gage jerked a thumb at the ceiling. "What have you done?"

"What had to be done. I couldn't leave them. They could've been cut off for a couple of days."

"And what, turned into the next Donner Party? Your woman has Fox making my bed, which is now the pullout in your office. And which I'm apparently supposed to share with him. You know that son of a bitch is a bed hog."

"Can't be helped."

"Easy for you to say, seeing as you'll be sharing yours with the blonde."

This time Cal grinned, smugly. "Can't be helped."

"Esmerelda's brewing up something in the kitchen."

"Goulash—and it's Cybil."

"Whatever, it smells good, I'll give her that. She smells better. But the point is I got the heave-ho when I tried to get a damn bag of chips to go with the beer."

"You want to cook for six people?"

Gage only grunted, sat, propped his feet on the coffee table. "How much are they calling for?"

"About three feet." Cal dropped down beside him, mirrored his pose. "Used to be we liked nothing better. No school, haul out the sleds. Snowball wars."

"Those were the days, my friend."

"Now we're priming the generator, loading in firewood, buying extra batteries and toilet paper."

"Sucks to be grown up."

Still, it was warm, and while the snow fell in sheets outside, there was light, and there was food. It was hard to complain, Cal decided, when he was digging into a bowl of hot, spicy stew he had nothing to do with preparing. Plus, there were dumplings, and he was weak when it came to dumplings.

"I was in Budapest not that long ago." Gage spooned up goulash as he studied Cybil. "This is as good as any I got there."

"Actually, this isn't Hungarian goulash. It's a Serbo-Croatian base."

"Damn good stew," Fox commented, "wherever it's based."

"Cybil's an Eastern European stew herself." Quinn savored the half dumpling she'd allowed herself. "Croatian, Ukrainian, Polish—with a dash of French for fashion sense and snottiness."

"When did your family come over?" Cal wondered.

"As early as the seventeen hundreds, as late as just before World War Two, depending on the line." But she understood the reason for the question. "I don't know if there is a connection to Quinn or Layla, or any of this, where it might root from. I'm looking into it."

"We had a connection," Quinn said, "straight off."

"We did."

Cal understood that kind of friendship, the kind he saw when the two women looked at each other. It had little to do with blood, and everything to do with the heart.

"We hooked up the first day—evening really—of college." Quinn spooned off another minuscule piece of dumpling with the stew. "Met in the hall of the dorm. We were across from each other. Within two days, we'd switched. Our respective roommates didn't care. We bunked together right through college."

"And apparently still are," Cybil commented.

"Remember you read my palm that first night?"

"You read palms?" Fox asked.

"When the mood strikes. My gypsy heritage," Cybil added with a flourishing gesture of her hands.

And Cal felt a knot form in his belly. "There were gypsies in the Hollow."

"Really?" Carefully, Cybil lifted her wineglass, sipped. "When?"

"I'd have to check to be sure. This is from stories my gran told me that her grandmother told her. Like that. About how gypsies came one summer and set up camp."

"Interesting. Potentially," Quinn mused, "someone local could get cozy with one of those dark-eyed beauties or hunks, and nine months later, oops. Could lead right to you, Cyb."

"Just one big, happy family," Cybil muttered.

After the meal, chores were divvied up again. Wood needed to be brought in, the dog let out, the table cleared, dishes dealt with.

"Who else cooks?" Cybil demanded.

"Gage does," Cal and Fox said together.

"Hey."

"Good." Cybil sized him up. "If there's a group breakfast on the slate, you're in charge. Now—"

"Before we . . . whatever," Cal decided, "there's something we have to go over. Might as well stick to the dining room. We have to get something," he added, looking at Fox and Gage. "You might want to open another bottle of wine."

"What's all this?" Quinn frowned as the men retreated. "What are they up to?"

"It's more what haven't they told us," Layla said. "Guilt and reluctance, that's what I'm picking up. Not that I know any of them that well."

"You know what you know," Cybil told her. "Get another bottle, Q." She gave a little shudder. "Maybe we should light a couple more candles while we're at it, just in case. It already feels . . . dark."

T HEY LEFT IT TO HIM, CAL SUPPOSED, BECAUSE IT was his house. When they were all back around the table, he tried to find the best way to begin.

"We've gone over what happened that night in the clearing when we were kids, and what started happening after. Quinn, you got some of it yourself when we hiked there a couple weeks ago."

"Yeah. Cyb and Layla need to see it, as soon as the snow's cleared enough for us to make the hike."

He hesitated only a beat. "Agreed."

"It ain't a stroll down the Champs Élysées," Gage commented, and Cybil cocked an eyebrow at him.

"We'll manage."

"There was another element that night, another aspect we haven't talked about with you."

"With anyone," Fox added.

"It's hard to explain why. We were ten, everything went

to hell, and . . . Well." Cal set his part of the stone on the table.

"A piece of rock?" Layla said.

"Bloodstone." Cybil pursed her lips, started to reach for it, stopped. "May I?"

Gage and Fox set theirs down beside Cal's. "Take your pick," Gage invited.

"Three parts of one." Quinn picked up the one closest to her. "Isn't that right? These are three parts of one stone."

"One that had been rounded, tumbled, polished," Cybil continued. "Where did you get the pieces?"

"We were holding them," Cal told her. "After the light, after the dark, when the ground stopped shaking, each one of us was holding his part of this stone." He studied his own hand, remembering how his fist had clenched around the stone as if his life depended on it.

"We didn't know what they were. Fox looked it up. His mother had books on rocks and crystals, and he looked it up. Bloodstone," Cal repeated. "It fit."

"It needs to be put back together," Layla said. "Doesn't it? It needs to be whole again."

"We've tried. The breaks are clean," Fox explained. "They fit together like a puzzle." He gestured, and Cal took the pieces, fit them into a round.

"But it doesn't do anything."

"Because you're holding them together?" Curious, Quinn held out her hand until Cal put the three pieces into it. "They're not . . . fused would be the word, I guess."

"Tried that, too. MacGyver over there tried superglue."

Cal sent Gage a bland stare. "Which should've worked— at least as far as holding the pieces together. But I might as well have used water. No stick. We've tried banding them, heating them, freezing them. No dice. In fact, they don't even change temperature."

"Except—" Fox broke off, got the go-ahead nod. "During the Seven, they heat up. Not too hot to hold, but right on the edge."

"Have you tried putting them back together during that week?" Quinn demanded.

"Yeah. No luck. The one thing we know is that Giles Dent was wearing this, like an amulet around his neck, the night Lazarus Twisse led that mob into the clearing. I saw it. Now we have it."

"Have you tried magickal means?" Cybil asked.

Cal squirmed a little, cleared his throat.

"Jesus, Cal, loosen up." Fox shook his head. "Sure. I got some books on spells, and we gave that a try. Down the road, Gage has talked to some practicing witches, and we've tried other rites and so on."

"But you never showed them to anyone." Quinn set the pieces down carefully before picking up her wine. "Anyone who might have been able to work with them, or understand the purpose. Maybe the history."

"We weren't meant to." Fox lifted his shoulders. "I know how it sounds, but I knew we weren't supposed to take it to, what, a geologist or some Wiccan high priestess, or the damn Pentagon. I just . . . Cal voted for the science angle right off."

"MacGyver," Gage repeated.

"Fox was sure that was off-limits, and that was good enough. That was good enough for the three of us." Cal looked at his friends. "It's been the way we've handled it, up till now. If Fox felt we shouldn't show you, we wouldn't be."

"Because you feel it the strongest?" Layla asked Fox.

"I don't know. Maybe. I know I believed—I believe—we survived that night, that we came out of it the way we came out of it because we each had a piece of that stone. And as long as we do, we've got a chance. It's just something I know, the same way Cal saw it, that he recognized it as the amulet Dent wore."

"How about you?" Cybil asked Gage. "What do you know? What do you see?"

His eyes met hers. "I see it whole, on top of the Pagan

Stone. The stone on the stone. And the flames flick up from it, kindling in the blood spots. Then they consume it, ride over the flat, down the pedestal like a sheath of fire. I see the fire race across the ground, fly into the trees until they burst from the heat. And the clearing's a holocaust even the devil himself couldn't survive."

He took a drink of wine. "That's what I see when it's whole again, so I'm in no big hurry to get there."

"Maybe that's how it was formed," Layla began.

"I don't see back. That's Cal's gig. I see what might be coming."

"That'd be handy in your profession."

Gage shifted his gaze back to Cybil, smiled slowly. "It doesn't hurt." He picked up his stone, tossed it lightly in his hand. "Anyone interested in a little five-card draw?"

As soon as he spoke, the light snapped off.

Rather than romance or charm, the flickering candles they'd lit as backup lent an eeriness to the room. "I'll go fire up the generator." Cal pushed up. "Water, refrigerator, and stove for now."

"Don't go out alone." Layla blinked as if surprised the words had come out of her mouth. "I mean—"

"I'm going with you."

As Fox rose, something howled in the dark.

"Lump." Cal was out of the room, through the kitchen, and out the back door like a bullet. He barely broke stride to grab the flashlight off the wall, punch it on.

He swept it toward the sound. The beam struggled against the thick, moving curtain of snow, did little but bounce the light back at him.

The blanket had become a wall that rose past his knees. Calling his dog, Cal pushed through it, trying to pinpoint the direction of the howling. It seemed to come from everywhere, from nowhere.

As he heard sounds behind him, he whirled, gripping the flashlight like a weapon.

"Don't clock the reinforcements," Fox shouted. "Christ,

it's insane out here." He gripped Cal's arm as Gage moved to Cal's other side. "Hey, Lump! Come on, Lump! I've never heard him like that."

"How do you know it's the dog?" Gage asked quietly.

"Get back inside," Cal said grimly. "We can't leave the women alone. I'm going to find my dog."

"Oh yeah, we'll just leave you out here, stumbling around in a fucking blizzard." Gage jammed his freezing hands in his pockets, glanced back. "Besides."

They came, arms linked and gripping flashlights. Which showed sense, Cal was forced to admit. And they'd taken the time to put on coats, probably boots as well, which is more than he or his friends had done.

"Go back in." He had to shout now, over the rising wind. "We're just going to round up Lump. Be right there."

"We all go in or nobody does." Quinn unhooked her arm from Layla's, hooked it to Cal's. "That includes Lump. Don't waste time," she said before he could argue. "We should spread out, shouldn't we?"

"In pairs. Fox, you and Layla try that way, Quinn and I'll take this way. Gage and Cybil toward the back. He's got to be close. He never goes far."

He sounded scared, that's what Cal didn't want to say out loud. His stupid, lazy dog sounded scared. "Hook your hand in my pants—the waistband. Keep a good hold."

He hissed against the cold as her gloves hit his skin, then began to trudge forward. He'd barely made it two feet when he heard something under the howls.

"You catch that?"

"Yes. Laughing. The way a nasty little boy might laugh."

"Go—"

"I'm not leaving that dog out here any more than you are."

A vicious gush of wind rose up like a tidal wave, spewing huge clumps of snow, and what felt like pellets of ice. Cal heard branches cracking, like gunfire in the dark. Behind him, Quinn lost her footing in the force of the wind and nearly took them both down.

He'd get Quinn back into the house, he decided. Get her the hell in, lock her in a damn closet if necessary, then come back out and find his dog.

Even as he turned to get a grip on her arm, he saw them.

His dog sat on his haunches, half buried in the snow, his head lifted as those long, desperate howls worked his throat.

The boy floated an inch above the surface of the snow. Chortling, Cal thought. There was a word you didn't use every day, but it sure as hell fit the filthy sound it made.

It grinned as the wind blasted again. Now Lump was buried to his shoulders.

"Get the fuck away from my dog."

Cal lurched forward; the wind knocked him back so that both he and Quinn went sprawling.

"Call him," Quinn shouted. "Call him, make him come!" She dragged off her gloves as she spoke. Using her fingers to form a circle between her lips, she whistled shrilly as Cal yelled at Lump.

Lump quivered; the thing laughed.

Cal continued to call, to curse now, to crawl while the snow flew into his eyes, numbed his hands. He heard shouting behind him, but he focused everything he had on pushing ahead, on getting there before the next gust of wind put the dog under.

He'd drown, Cal thought as he pushed, shoved, slid forward. If he didn't get to Lump, his dog would drown in that ocean of snow.

He felt a hand lock on his ankle, but kept dragging himself forward.

Gritting his teeth, he flailed out, got a slippery hold on Lump's collar. Braced, he looked up into eyes that glittered an unholy green rimmed with red. "You can't have him."

Cal yanked. Ignoring Lump's yelp, he yanked again, viciously, desperately. Though Lump howled, whimpered, it was as if his body was sunk in hardened cement.

And Quinn was beside him, belly down, digging at the snow with her hands.

Fox skidded down, shooting snow like shrapnel. Cal gathered everything he had, looked once more into those monstrous eyes in the face of a young boy. "I said you can't have him."

With the next pull, Cal's arms were full of quivering, whimpering dog.

"It's okay, it's okay." He pressed his face against cold, wet fur. "Let's get the hell out of here."

"Get him in by the fire." Layla struggled to help Quinn up as Cybil pushed up from her knees. Shoving the butt of a flashlight in his back pocket, Gage pulled Cybil to her feet, then plucked Quinn out of the snow.

"Can you walk?" he asked her.

"Yeah, yeah. Let's get in, let's get inside, before somebody ends up with frostbite."

Towels and blankets, dry clothes, hot coffee. Brandy—even for Lump—warmed chilled bones and numbed flesh. Fresh logs had the fire blazing.

"It was holding him. He couldn't get away." Cal sat on the floor, the dog's head in his lap. "He couldn't get away. It was going to bury him in the snow. A stupid, harmless dog."

"Has this happened before?" Quinn asked him. "Has it gone after animals this way?"

"A few weeks before the Seven, animals might drown, or there's more roadkill. Sometimes pets turn mean. But not like this. This was—"

"A demonstration." Cybil tucked the blanket more securely around Quinn's feet. "He wanted us to see what he could do."

"Maybe wanted to see what we could do," Gage countered, and earned a speculative glance from Cybil.

"That may be more accurate. That may be more to the point. Could we break the hold? A dog's not a person, has to be easier to control. No offense, Cal, but your dog's brainpower isn't as high as most toddlers'."

Gently, affectionately, Cal pulled on one of Lump's floppy ears. "He's thick as a brick."

"So it was showing off. It hurt this poor dog for sport."
Layla knelt down and stroked Lump's side. "That deserves
some payback."

Intrigued, Quinn cocked her head. "What do you have
in mind?"

"I don't know yet, but it's something to think about."

Eighteen

CAL DIDN'T KNOW WHAT TIME THEY'D FALLEN into bed. But when he opened his eyes the thin winter light eked through the window. Through it, he saw the snow was still falling in the perfect, fat, white flakes of a Hollywood Christmas movie.

In the hush only a snowfall could create was steady and somehow satisfied snoring. It came from Lump, who was stretched over the foot of the bed like a canine blanket. That was something Cal generally discouraged, but right now, the sound, the weight, the warmth were exactly right.

From now on, he determined, the damn dog was going everywhere with him.

Because his foot and ankle were currently under the bulk of the dog, Cal shifted to pull free. The movement had Quinn stirring, giving a little sigh as she wiggled closer and managed to wedge her leg between his. She wore flannel, which shouldn't have been remotely sexy, and she'd managed to pin his arm during the night so it was now alive with needles and pins. And that should've been, at least mildly, annoying.

Instead, it was exactly right, too.

Since it was, since they were cuddled up together in bed with Hollywood snow falling outside the window, he couldn't think of a single reason not to take advantage of it.

Smiling, he slid a hand under her T-shirt, over warm, smooth flesh. When he cupped her breast he felt her heart beat under his palm, slow and steady as Lump's snoring. He stroked, a lazy play of fingertips as he watched her face. Lightly, gently, he teased her nipple, arousing himself as he imagined taking it into his mouth, sliding his tongue over her.

She sighed again.

He trailed his hand down, tracing those fingertips over her belly, under the flannel to skim down her thigh. Up again. Down, then up, a whispering touch that eased closer, closer to her center.

And the sound she made in sleep was soft and helpless.

She was wet when he brushed over her, hot when he dipped inside her. When he pressed, he lowered his mouth to hers to take her gasp.

She came as she woke, her body simply erupting as her mind leaped out of sleep and into shock and pleasure.

"Oh God!"

"Shh." He laughed against her lips. "You'll wake the dog."

He tugged down her pants as he rolled. Before she could clear her mind, he pinned her, and he filled her.

"Oh. Well. Jesus." The words hitched and shook. "Good morning."

He laughed again, and bracing himself, set a slow and torturous pace. She fought to match it, to hold back and take that slow climb with him, but it flashed through her again, and flung her up.

"God. God. God. I don't think I can—"

"Shh, shh," he repeated, and brought his mouth down to toy with hers. "I'll go slow," he whispered. "You just go."

She could do nothing else. Her system was already wrecked, her body already his. Utterly his. When he took her up again, she was too breathless to cry out.

THOROUGHLY PLEASURED, THOROUGHLY USED, Quinn lay under Cal's weight. He'd eased down so that his head rested between her breasts, and she could play with his hair. She imagined it was some faraway Sunday morning where they had nothing more pressing to worry about than if they'd make love again before breakfast, or make love after.

"Do you take some kind of special vitamin?" she wondered.

"Hmm?"

"I mean, you've got some pretty impressive stamina going for you."

She felt his lips curve against her. "Just clean living, Blondie."

"Maybe it's the bowling. Maybe bowling . . . Where's Lump?"

"He got embarrassed about halfway through the show." Cal turned his head, gestured. "Over there."

Quinn looked, saw the dog on the floor, his face wedged in the corner. She laughed till her sides ached. "We embarrassed the dog. That's a first for me. God! I feel good. How can I feel so good after last night?" Then she shook her head, stretched up her arms before wrapping them around Cal. "I guess that's the point, isn't it? Even in a world gone to hell, there's still this."

"Yeah." He sat up then, reached down to brush her tumbled hair as he studied her. "Quinn." He took her hand now, played with her fingers.

"Cal," she said, imitating his serious tone.

"You crawled through a blizzard to help save my dog."

"He's a good dog. Anyone would have done the same."

"No. You're not naive enough to think that. Fox and Gage, yeah. For the dog, and for me. Layla and Cybil, maybe. Maybe it was being caught in the moment, or maybe they're built that way."

She touched his face, skimmed her fingers under those patient gray eyes. "No one was going to leave that dog out there, Cal."

"Then I'd say that dog is pretty lucky to have people like you around. So am I. You crawled through the snow, toward that thing. You dug in the snow with your bare hands."

"If you're trying to make a hero out of me . . . Go ahead," she decided. "I think I like the fit."

"You whistled with your fingers."

Now she grinned. "Just a little something I picked up along the way. I can actually whistle a lot louder than that, when I'm not out of breath, freezing, and quivering with terror."

"I love you."

"I'll demonstrate sometime when . . . What?"

"I never thought to say those words to any woman I wasn't related to. I was just never going to go there."

If she'd been given a hard, direct jolt of electricity to her heart, it couldn't have leaped any higher. "Would you mind saying them again, while I'm paying better attention?"

"I love you."

There it went again, she thought. Leaps and bounds. "Because I can whistle with my fingers?"

"That might've been the money shot."

"God." She shut her eyes. "I want you to love me, and I really like to get what I want. But." She took a breath. "Cal, if this is because of last night, because I helped get Lump, then—"

"This is because you think if you eat half my slice of pizza it doesn't count."

"Well, it doesn't, technically."

"Because you always know where your keys are, and you can think about ten things at the same time. Because you don't back down, and your hair's like sunlight. Because you tell the truth and you know how to be a friend. And for dozens of reasons I haven't figured out yet. Dozens more I may never figure out. But I know I can say to you what I never thought to say to anyone."

She hooked her arms around his neck, rested her forehead on his. She had to just breathe for a moment, just breathe her way through the beauty of it as she often did with a great work of art or a song that brought tears to her throat.

"This is a really good day." She touched her lips to his. "This is a truly excellent day."

They sat for a while, holding each other while the dog snored in the corner, and the snow fell outside the windows.

When Cal went downstairs, he followed the scent of coffee into the kitchen, and found Gage scowling as he slapped a skillet onto the stove. They grunted at each other as Cal got a clean mug out of the dishwasher.

"Looks like close to three out there already, and it's still coming."

"I got eyes." Gage ripped open a pound of bacon. "You sound chipper about it."

"It's a really good day."

"I'd probably think so, too, if I started it off with some morning nookie."

"God, men are crude." Cybil strolled in, her dark eyes bleary.

"Then you ought to plug your ears when you're around our kind. Bacon gets fried, eggs get scrambled," Gage told them. "Anybody doesn't like the options should try another restaurant."

Cybil poured her coffee, stood studying him over the rim as she took the first sip. He hadn't shaved or combed that dark mass of hair. He was obviously morning irritable, and none of that, she mused, made him any less attractive.

Too bad.

"You know what I've noticed about you, Gage?"

"What's that?"

"You've got a great ass, and a crappy attitude. Let me

know when breakfast is ready," she added as she strolled out of the kitchen.

"She's right. I've often said that about your ass and attitude."

"Phones are out," Fox announced as he came in, yanked open the refrigerator and pounced on a Coke. "Got ahold of my mother by cell. They're okay over there."

"Knowing your parents, they probably just had sex," Gage commented.

"Hey! True," Fox said after a moment, "but, hey."

"He's got sex on the brain."

"Why wouldn't he? He's not sick or watching sports, the only two circumstances men don't necessarily have sex on the brain."

Gage laid bacon in the heated skillet. "Somebody make some toast or something. And we're going to need another pot of coffee."

"I've got to take Lump out. I'm not just letting him out on his own."

"I'll take him." Fox leaned down to scratch Lump's head. "I want to walk around anyway." He turned, nearly walked into Layla. "Hi, sorry. Ah . . . I'm going to take Lump out. Why don't you come along?"

"Oh. I guess. Sure. I'll just get my things."

"Smooth," Gage commented when Layla left. "You're a smooth one, Fox."

"What?"

"Good morning, really attractive woman. How would you like to trudge around with me in three feet of snow and watch a dog piss on a few trees? Before you've even had your coffee?"

"It was just a suggestion. She could've said no."

"I'm sure she would have if she'd had a hit of caffeine so her brain was in gear."

"That must be why you only get lucky with women without brains."

"You're just spreading sunshine," Cal commented when Fox steamed out.

"Make another damn pot of coffee."

"I need to bring in some wood, feed the generator, and start shoveling three feet of snow off the decks. Let me know when breakfast is ready."

Alone, Gage snarled, and turned the bacon. He still had the snarl when Quinn came in.

"I thought I'd find everyone in here, but they're all scattered." She got out a mug. "Looks like we need another pot of coffee."

Because she got the coffee down, Gage didn't have time to snap at her.

"I'll take care of that. Anything else I can do to help?"

He turned his head to look at her. "Why?"

"Because I figure if I help you with breakfast, it takes us both off the cooking rotation for the next couple of meals."

He nodded, appreciating the logic. "Smart. You're the toast and additional coffee."

"Check."

He beat a dozen eggs while she got to work. She had a quick, efficient way about her, Gage noted. The quick wouldn't matter so much to Cal, but the efficient would be a serious plus. She was built, she was bright, and as he'd seen for himself last night, she had a wide streak of brave.

"You're making him happy."

Quinn stopped, looked over. "Good, because he's making me happy."

"One thing, if you haven't figured it out by now. He's rooted here. This is his place. Whatever happens, the Hollow's always going to be Cal's place."

"I figured that out." She plucked toast when it popped, dropped more bread in. "All things considered, it's a nice town."

"All things considered," Gage agreed, then poured the eggs into the second skillet.

OUTSIDE, AS GAGE PREDICTED, FOX WATCHED Lump piss on trees. More entertaining, he supposed, had been watching the dog wade, trudge, and occasionally leap through the waist-high snow. It was the waist-high factor that had Fox and Layla stopping on the front deck, and Fox going to work with the shovel Cal had shoved into his hands on their way out.

Still, it was great to be out in the snow globe of the morning, tossing the white stuff around while more of it pumped out of the sky.

"Maybe I should go down, knock the snow off some of Cal's shrubs."

Fox glanced over at her. She had a ski cap pulled over her head, a scarf wrapped around her neck. Both had already picked up a layer of white. "You'll sink, then we'll be tossing you a lifeline to get you back. We'll dig out a path eventually."

"He doesn't seem to be spooked." She kept an eagle eye on Lump. "I thought, after last night, he'd be skittish about going out."

"Short-term doggie memory. Probably for the best."

"I won't forget it."

"No." He shouldn't have asked her to come out, Fox realized. Especially since he couldn't quite figure out how to broach the whole job deal, which had been part of the idea for having her tag along.

He was usually better at this stuff, dealing with people. Dealing with women. Now, he worked on carving down a shovel-width path across the deck to the steps, and just jumped in.

"So, Cal said you're looking for a job."

"Not exactly. I mean I'm going to have to find some work, but I haven't been looking."

"My secretary—office manager—assistant." He dumped snow, dug the shovel back down. "We never settled on a title, now that I think about it. Anyway, she's moving to Minneapolis. I need somebody to do the stuff she does."

Damn Quinn, she thought. "The stuff."

It occurred to Fox that he was considered fairly articulate in court. "Filing, billing, answering phones, keeping the calendar, rescheduling when necessary, handling clients, typing documents and correspondence. She's a notary, too, but that's not a necessity right off."

"What software does she use?"

"I don't know. I'd have to ask her." Did she use any software? How was he supposed to know?

"I don't know anything about secretarial work, or office management. I don't know anything about the law."

Fox knew tones, and hers was defensive. He kept shoveling. "Do you know the alphabet?"

"Of course I know the alphabet, but the point—"

"Would be," he interrupted, "if you know the alphabet you can probably figure out how to file. And you know how to use a phone, which means you can answer one and make calls from one. Those would be essential job skills for this position. Can you use a keyboard?"

"Yes, but it depends on—"

"She can show you whatever the hell she does in that area."

"It doesn't sound as if you know a lot about what she does."

He also knew disapproval when he heard it. "Okay." He straightened, leaned on the shovel, and looked dead into her eyes. "She's been with me since I set up. I'm going to miss her like I'd miss my arm. But people move on, and the rest of us have to deal. I need somebody to put papers where they belong and find them when I need to have them, to send out bills so I can pay mine, to tell me when I'm due in court, to answer the phone we hope rings so I'll have somebody to bill, and basically maintain some kind of order so I can practice law. You need a job and a paycheck. I think we could help each other out."

"Cal asked you to offer me a job because Quinn asked him to ask you."

"That would be right. Doesn't change the bottom line."

No, it didn't, she supposed. But it still griped. "It wouldn't be permanent. I'm only looking for something to fill in until . . ."

"You move on." Fox nodded. "Works for me. That way, neither of us are stuck. We're just helping each other out for a while." He shoveled off two more blades of snow, then stopped just to lean on it with his eyes on hers.

"Besides, you knew I was going to offer you the job because you pick up that sort of thing."

"Quinn asked Cal to ask you to offer it to me right in front of me."

"You pick up on that sort of thing," he repeated. "That's your part in this, or part of your part. You get a sense of people, of situations."

"I'm not psychic, if that's what you're saying." The defensive was back in her tone.

"You drove to the Hollow, when you'd never been here before. You knew where to go, what roads to take."

"I don't know what that was." She crossed her arms, and the move wasn't just defensive, Fox thought. It was stubborn.

"Sure you do, it just freaks you. You took off with Quinn that first night, went with her, a woman you'd never met."

"She was a sane alternative to a big, evil slug," Layla said dryly.

"You didn't just run, didn't haul ass to your room and lock the door. You got in her car with her, came with her out here—where you'd also never been, and walked into a house with two strange men in it."

"*Strange* might be the operative word. I was scared, confused, and running on adrenaline." She looked away from him, toward where Lump was rolling in the snow as if it were a meadow of daisies. "I trusted my instincts."

"Instincts is one word for it. I bet when you were working in that clothes shop you had really good instincts about what your customers wanted, what they'd buy. Bet you're damn good at that."

He went back to shoveling when she said nothing. "Bet you've always been good at that sort of thing. Quinn gets flashes from the past, like Cal. Apparently Cybil gets them of possible future events. I'd say you're stuck with me, Layla, in the now."

"I can't read minds, and I don't want anyone reading mine."

"It's not like that, exactly." He was going to have to work with her, he decided. Help her figure out what she had and how to use it. And he was going to have to give her some time and some space to get used to the idea.

"Anyway, we're probably going to be snowed in here for the weekend. I've got stuff next week, but when we can get back to town, you could come in when it suits you, let Mrs. H show you the ropes. We'll see how you feel about the job then."

"Look, I'm grateful you'd offer—"

"No, you're not." Now he smiled and tossed another shovel of snow off the deck. "Not so much. I've got instincts, too."

It wasn't just humor, but understanding. The stiffness went out of her as she kicked at the snow. "There's gratitude, it's just buried under the annoyance."

Cocking his head, he held out the shovel. "Want to dig it out?"

And she laughed. "Let's try this. If I do come in, and do decide to take the job, it's with the stipulation that if either of us decides it's not working, we just say so. No hard feelings."

"That's a deal." He held out a hand, took hers to seal it. Then just held it while the snow swirled around them.

She had to feel it, he thought, had to feel that immediate and tangible link. That recognition.

Cybil cracked the door an inch. "Breakfast is ready."

Fox released Layla's hand, turned. He let out a quiet breath before calling the dog home.

PRACTICAL MATTERS HAD TO BE SEEN TO. SNOW needed to be shoveled, firewood hauled and stacked. Dishes had to be washed and food prepared. Cal might have felt like the house, which had always seemed roomy, grew increasingly tight with six people and one dog stuck inside it. But he knew they were safer together.

"Not just safer." Quinn took her turn plying the shovel. She considered digging out a path to Cal's storage shed solid exercise in lieu of a formal workout. "I think all this is meant. This enforced community. It's giving us time to get used to each other, to learn how to function as a group."

"Here, let me take over there." Cal set aside the gas can he'd used to top off the generator.

"No, see, that's not working as a group. You guys have to learn to trust the females to carry their load. Gage being drafted to make breakfast today is an example of the basics in non-gender-specific teamwork."

Non-gender-specific teamwork, he thought. How could he not love a woman who'd use a term like that?

"We can all cook," she went on. "We can all shovel snow, haul firewood, make beds. We can all do what we have to do—play to our strengths, okay, but so far it's pretty much been like a middle school dance."

"How?"

"Boys on one side, girls on the other, and nobody quite sure how to get everyone together. Now we are." She stopped, rolled her shoulders. "And we have to figure it out. Even with us, Cal, even with how we feel about each other, we're still figuring each other out, learning how to trust each other."

"If this is about the stone, I understand you might be annoyed I didn't tell you sooner."

"No, I'm really not." She shoveled a bit more, but it was mostly for form now. Her arms were *killing* her. "I started to be, even wanted to be, but I couldn't stir it up. Because I get that the three of you have been a unit all your lives. I don't imagine you remember a time when you weren't. Added to that you went through together—I don't think it's an exaggeration to say an earth-shattering experience. The three of you are like a . . . a body with three heads isn't right," she said and passed off the shovel.

"We're not the damn Borg."

"No, but that's closer. You're a fist, tight, even closed off to a certain extent, but—" She wiggled her gloved fingers. "Individual. You work together, it's instinctive. And now." She held up her other hand. "This other part comes along. So we're figuring out how to make them mesh." She brought her hands together, fingers linked.

"That actually makes sense." And brought on a slight twinge of guilt. "I've been doing a little digging on my own."

"You don't mean in the snow. And on your own equals you've told Fox and Gage."

"I probably mentioned it. We don't know where Ann Hawkins was for a couple of years, where she gave birth to her sons, where she stayed before she came back to the Hollow—to her parents' house. So I was thinking about extended family. Cousins, aunts, uncles. And figuring a woman that pregnant might not be able to travel very far, not back then. So maybe she'd have been in the general area. Ten, twenty miles in the sixteen hundreds was a hell of a lot farther than ten or twenty miles is today."

"That's a good idea. I should have had it."

"And I should've brought it up before."

"Yeah. Now that you have, you should give it to Cyb, give her whatever information you have. She's the research queen. I'm good, she's better."

"And I'm a rank amateur."

"Nothing rank about you." Grinning, she took a leap, bounced up into his arms. The momentum had him skidding. She squealed, as much with laughter as alarm as he tipped backward. He flopped; she landed face-first.

Breathless, she dug in, got two handfuls of snow to mash into his face before she tried to roll away. He caught her at the waist, dragged her back while she screamed with helpless laughter.

"I'm a champion snow wrestler," he warned her. "You're out of your league, Blondie. So—"

She managed to get a hand between his legs for a nice,

firm stroke. Then taking advantage of the sudden and dramatic dip of his IQ, shoved a messy ball of snow down the back of his neck.

"Those moves are against the rules of the SWF."

"Check the book, buddy. This is intergender play."

She tried to scramble up, fell, then whooshed out a breath when his weight pinned her. "And still champion," he announced, and was about to lower his mouth to hers when the door opened.

"Kids," Cybil told them, "there's a nice warm bed upstairs if you want to play. And FYI? The power just came back on." She glanced back over her shoulder. "Apparently the phones are up, too."

"Phones, electricity. Computer." Quinn wiggled out from under Cal. "I have to check my e-mail."

CYBIL LEANED ON THE DRYER AS LAYLA LOADED towels into the washing machine in Cal's laundry room. "They looked like a couple of horny snow people. Covered, crusted, pink-cheeked, and groping."

"Young love is immune to climatic conditions."

Cybil chuckled. "You know, you don't have to take on the laundry detail."

"Clean towels are a memory at this point, and the power may not stay on. Besides, I'd rather be warm and dry in here washing towels than cold and wet out there shoveling snow." She tossed back her hair. "Especially since no one's groping me."

"Good point. But I was bringing that up as, by my calculations, you and Fox are going to have to flip for cooking detail tonight."

"Quinn hasn't cooked yet, or Cal."

"Quinn helped with breakfast. It's Cal's house."

Defeated, Layla stared at the machine. "Hell. I'll take dinner."

"You can dump it on Fox, using laundry detail as leverage."

"No, we don't know if he can cook, and I can."

Cybil narrowed her eyes. "You can cook? This hasn't been mentioned before."

"If I'd mentioned it, I'd have had to cook."

Lips pursed, Cybil nodded slowly. "Diabolical and self-serving logic. I like it."

"I'll check the supplies, see what I can come up with. Something—" She broke off, stepped forward. "Quinn? What is it?"

"We have to talk. All of us." So pale her eyes looked bruised, Quinn stood in the doorway.

"Q? Honey." Cybil reached out in support. "What's happened?" She remembered Quinn's dash to the computer for e-mail. "Is everyone all right? Your parents?"

"Yes. Yes. I want to tell it all at once, to everyone. We need to get everyone."

She sat in the living room with Cybil perched on the arm of her chair for comfort. Quinn wanted to curl up in Cal's lap as she'd done once before. But it seemed wrong.

It all seemed wrong now.

She wished the power had stayed off forever. She wished she hadn't contacted her grandmother and prodded her into seeking out family history.

She didn't want to know what she knew now.

No going back, she reminded herself. And what she had to say could change everything that was to come.

She glanced at Cal. She knew she had him worried. It wasn't fair to drag it out. How would he look at her afterward? she wondered.

Yank off the bandage, Quinn told herself, and get it over with.

"My grandmother got the information I'd asked her about. Pages from the family Bible. There were even some records put together by a family historian in the late eighteen hundreds. I, ah, have some information on the Clark branch, Layla, that may help you. No one ever pursued that end very far, but you may be able to track back, or out from what I have now."

"Okay."

"The thing is, it looks like the family was, we'll say, pretty religious about their own tracking back. My grandfather, not so much, but his sister, a couple of cousins, they were more into it. They, apparently, get a lot of play out of the fact their ancestors were among the early Pilgrims who settled in the New World. So there isn't just the Bible, and the pages added to that over time. They've had genealogies done tracing roots back to England and Ireland in the fifteen hundreds. But what applies to us, to this, is the branch that came over here. Here to Hawkins Hollow," she said to Cal.

She braced herself. "Sebastian Deale brought his wife and three daughters to the settlement here in sixteen fifty-one. His eldest daughter's name was Hester. Hester Deale."

"Hester's Pool," Fox murmured. "She's yours."

"That's right. Hester Deale, who according to town lore denounced Giles Dent as a witch on the night of July seventh, sixteen fifty-two. Who eight months later delivered a daughter, and when that daughter was two weeks old, drowned herself in the pond in Hawkins Wood. There's no father documented, nothing on record. But we know who fathered her child. We know what fathered her child."

"We can't be sure of that."

"We know it, Caleb." However much it tore inside her, Quinn knew it. "We've seen it, you and I. And Layla, Layla experienced it. He raped her. She was barely sixteen. He lured her, he overpowered her—mind and body, and he got her with child. One that carried his blood." To keep them still, Quinn gripped her hands together. "A half-demon child. She couldn't live with it, with what had been done to her, with what she'd brought into the world. So she filled her pockets with stones and went into the water to drown."

"What happened to her daughter?" Layla asked.

"She died at twenty, after having two daughters of her own. One of them died before her third birthday, the other went on to marry a man named Duncan Clark. They had three sons and a daughter. Both she, her husband, and her youngest son were killed when their house burned down. The other children escaped."

"Duncan Clark must be where I come in," Layla said.

"And somewhere along the line, one of them hooked up with a gypsy from the Old World," Cybil finished. "Hardly seems fair. They get to descend from a heroic white witch, and we get the demon seed."

"It's not a joke," Quinn snapped.

"No, and it's not a tragedy. It just is."

"Damn it, Cybil, don't you see what this means? That *thing* out there is my—probably our—great-grandfather times a dozen generations. It means we're carrying some part of that in us."

"And if I start to sprout horns and a tail in the next few weeks, I'm going to be very pissed off."

"Oh, fuck that!" Quinn pushed up, rounded on her friend. "Fuck the Cybilese. He raped that girl to get to us, three and a half centuries ago, but what he planted led to this. What if we're not here to stop it, not here to help this end? What if we're here to see that it doesn't stop? To play some part in hurting them?"

"If your brain wasn't mushy with love you'd see that's a bullshit theory. Panic reaction with a heavy dose of self-pity to spice it up." Cybil's voice was brutally cool. "We're not under some demon's thumb. We're not going to suddenly jump sides and put on the uniform of some *dark entity* who tries to kill a dog to get his rocks off. We're exactly who we were five minutes ago, so stop being stupid, and pull yourself together."

"She's right. Not about being stupid," Layla qualified. "But about being who we are. If all this is part of it, then we have to find a way to use it."

"Fine. I'll practice getting my head to do three-sixties."

"Lame," Cybil decided. "You'd do better with the sarcasm, Q, if you weren't so worried Cal's going to dump you because of the big *D* for demon on your forehead."

"Cut it out," Layla commanded, and Cybil only shrugged.

"If he does," Cybil continued equably, "he's not worth your time anyway."

In the sudden, thundering silence a log fell in the grate and shot sparks.

"Did you print out the attachment?" Cal asked.

"No, I . . ." Quinn trailed off, shook her head.

"Let's go do that now, then we can take a look." He rose, put a hand on Quinn's arm, and drew her from the room.

"Nice job," Gage commented to Cybil. Before she could snarl, he angled his head. "That wasn't sarcasm. It was either literally or verbally give her a slap across the face. Verbally's trickier, but a lot less messy."

"Both are painful." Cybil pushed to her feet. "If he hurts her, I'll twist off his dick and feed it to his dog." With that, she stormed out of the room.

"She's a little scary," Fox decided.

"She's not the only one. I'm the one who'll be roasting his balls for dessert." Layla headed out behind Cybil. "I have to find something to make for dinner."

"Oddly, I don't have much of an appetite right now." Fox glanced at Gage. "How about you?"

Upstairs, Cal waited until they'd stepped into the office currently serving as the men's dorm. He pushed Quinn's back to the door. The first kiss was hard, with sharp edges of anger. The second frustrated. And the last soft.

"Whatever's in your head about you and me, because of this, get it out. Now. Understand?"

"Cal—"

"It's taken me my whole life to say what I said to you this morning. I love you. This doesn't change that. So pitch that out, Quinn, or you're going to piss me off."

"It wasn't—that isn't . . ." She closed her eyes as a storm of emotions blew through her. "All right, that was in there, part of it, but it's all of it, the whole. When I read the file she sent, it just . . ."

"It kicked your feet out from under you. I get that. But you know what? I'm right here to help you up." He lifted a hand, made a fist, then opened it.

Understanding, she fought back tears. Understanding, she put her palm to his, interlaced fingers.

"Okay?"

"Not okay," she corrected. "Thank God about covers it."

"Let's print it out, see what we've got."

"Yeah." Steadier, she glanced at the room. The messy, unmade pullout, the piles of clothes. "Your friends are slobs."

"Yes. Yes, they are."

Together, they picked their way through the mess to the computer.

Nineteen

～～

IN THE DINING ROOM, QUINN SET COPIES OF THE printouts in front of everyone. There were bowls of popcorn on the table, she noted, a bottle of wine, glasses, and paper towels folded into triangles. Which would all be Cybil's doing, she knew.

Just as she knew Cybil had made the popcorn for her. Not a peace offering; they didn't need peace offerings between them. It was just because.

She touched a hand to Cybil's shoulder before she took her seat.

"Apologies for big drama," Quinn began.

"If you think that was drama, you need to come over to my parents' house during one of the family gatherings." Fox gave her a smile as he took a handful of popcorn. "The Barry-O'Dells don't need demon blood to raise hell."

"We'll all accept the demon thing is going to be a running gag from now on." Quinn poured a glass of wine. "I don't know how much all this will tell everyone, but it's more than we had before. It shows a direct line from the other side."

"Are you sure Twisse is the one who raped Hester Deale?" Gage asked. "Certain he's the one who knocked her up?"

Quinn nodded. "Believe me."

"I experienced it." Layla twisted the paper towel in her hands as she spoke. "It wasn't like the flashes Cal and Quinn get, but . . . Maybe the blood tie explains it. I don't know. But I know what he did to her. And I know she was a virgin before he—it—raped her."

Gently, Fox took the pieces of the paper towel she'd torn, gave her his.

"Okay," Gage continued, "are we sure Twisse is what we're calling the demon for lack of better?"

"He never liked that term," Cal put in. "I think we can go affirmative on that."

"So, Twisse uses Hester to sire a child, to extend his line. If he's been around as long as we think—going off some of the stuff Cal's seen and related, it's likely he'd done the same before."

"Right," Cybil acknowledged. "Maybe that's where we get people like Hitler or Osama bin Laden, Jack the Ripper, child abusers, serial killers."

"If you look at the lineage, you'll see there were a lot of suicides and violent deaths, especially in the first hundred, hundred and twenty years after Hester. I think," Quinn said slowly, "if we're able to dig a little deeper on individuals, we might find more than the average family share of murder, insanity."

"Anything that stands out in recent memory?" Fox asked. "Major family skeletons?"

"Not that I know of. I have the usual share of kooky or annoying relatives, but nobody's been incarcerated or institutionalized."

"It dilutes." Fox narrowed his eyes as he paged through the printouts. "This wasn't his plan, wasn't his strategy. I know strategy. Consider. Twisse doesn't know what Dent's got cooking that night. He's got Hester—got her mind under control, got the demon bun in the oven, but he doesn't know that's going to be it."

"That Dent's ready for him, and has his own plans," Layla continued. "I see where you're going. He thought—planned—to destroy Dent that night, or at least damage him, drive him away."

"Then he gets the town," Fox continued, "uses it up, moves on. Leaves progeny, before he finds the next spot that suits him to do the same."

"Instead Dent takes him down, holds him down until . . ." Cal turned over his hand, exposed the thin scar on his wrist. "Until Dent's progeny let him out. Why would he want that? Why would he allow it?"

"Could be Dent figured keeping a demon in a headlock for three centuries was long enough." Gage helped himself to popcorn. "Or that's as long as he could hold him, and he called out some reinforcements."

"Ten-year-old boys," Cal said in disgust.

"Children are more likely to believe, to accept what adults can't. Or won't," Cybil added. "And hell, nobody said any of this was fair. He gave you what he could. Your ability to heal quickly, your insights into what was, is, will be. He gave you the stone, in three parts."

"And time to grow up," Layla added. "Twenty-one years. Maybe he found the way to bring us here. Quinn, Cybil, and me. Because I can't see the logic, the purpose of having me compelled to come here, then trying to scare me away."

"Good point." And it loosened something inside Quinn's belly. "That's a damn good point. Why scare if he could seduce? Really good point."

"I can look deeper into the family tree for you, Q. And I'll see what I can find on Layla's and my own. But that's just busywork at this point. We know the root."

Cybil turned one of the pages over, used a pencil on the back. She drew two horizontal lines at the bottom. "Giles Dent and Ann Hawkins here, Lazarus Twisse and the doomed Hester here. Each root sends up a tree, and the trees their branches." She drew quickly, simply. "And at the right point, branches from each tree cross each other. In palmistry the crossing of lines is a sign of power."

She completed the sketch, three branches, crossing three branches. "So we have to find the power, and use it."

THAT EVENING, LAYLA DID SOMETHING FAIRLY tasty with chicken breasts, stewed tomatoes, and white beans. By mutual agreement they channeled the conversation into other areas. Normal, Quinn thought as it ranged from dissecting recent movies to bad jokes to travel. They all needed a good dose of normal.

"Gage is the one with itchy feet," Cal commented. "He's been traveling that long, lonesome highway since he hit eighteen."

"It's not always lonesome."

"Cal said you were in Prague." Quinn considered. "I think I'd like to see Prague."

"I thought it was Budapest."

Gage glanced at Cybil. "There, too. Prague was the last stop before heading back."

"Is it fabulous?" Layla wondered. "The art, the architecture, the food?"

"It's got all that. The palace, the river, the opera. I got a taste of it, but mostly I was working. Flew in from Budapest for a poker game."

"You spent your time in—what do they call it—the Paris of Eastern Europe playing poker?" Quinn demanded.

"Not all of it, just the lion's share. The game went for just over seventy-three hours."

"Three days, playing poker?" Cybil's eyebrow winged up. "Wouldn't that be a little obsessive?"

"Depends on where you stand, doesn't it?"

"But don't you need to sleep, eat? Pee?" Layla wondered.

"Breaks are worked in. The seventy-three hours was

actual game time. This was a private game, private home. Serious money, serious security."

"Win or lose?" Quinn asked him with a grin.

"I did okay."

"Do you use your precognition to help you do okay?" Cybil asked.

"That would be cheating."

"Yes, it would, but that didn't answer the question."

He picked up his wine, kept his eyes on hers. "If I had to cheat to win at poker, I should be selling insurance. I don't have to cheat."

"We took an oath." Fox held up his hands when Gage scowled at him. "We're in this together now. They should understand how it works for us. We took an oath when we realized we all had something extra. We wouldn't use it against anyone, or to hurt anyone, or, well, to screw anyone. We don't break our word to each other."

"In that case," Cybil said to Gage, "you ought to be playing the ponies instead of cards."

He flashed a grin. "Been known to, but I like cards. Wanna play?"

"Maybe later."

When Cybil glanced at Quinn with a look of apology, Quinn knew what was coming. "I guess we should get back to it," Cybil began. "I have a question, a place I'd like to start."

"Let's take fifteen." Quinn pushed to her feet. "Get the table cleared off, take the dog out. Just move a little. Fifteen."

Cal brushed a hand over her arm as he rose with her. "I need to check the fire anyway, probably bring in more wood. Let's do this in the living room when we're finished up."

THEY LOOKED LIKE ORDINARY PEOPLE, CAL thought. Just a group of friends hanging out on a winter night. Gage had switched to coffee, and that was usual. Cal hadn't known Gage to indulge in more than a couple drinks at a time since the summer they'd been seventeen. Fox was back on Coke, and he himself had opted for water.

Clear heads, he mused. They wanted clear heads if there were questions to be answered.

They'd gone back to gender groups. Had that been automatic, even intrinsic? he wondered. The three women on the couch, Fox on the floor with Lump. He'd taken a chair, and Gage stood by the fire as if he might just walk out if the topic didn't suit his mood.

"So." Cybil tucked her legs under her, let her dark eyes scan the room. "I'm wondering what was the first thing, event, instance, the first happening, we'll say, that alerted you something was wrong in town. After your night in the clearing, after you went home."

"Mr. Guthrie and the fork." Fox stretched out, propped his head on Lump's belly. "That was a big clue."

"Sounds like the title of a kid's book." Quinn made a note on her pad. "Why don't you fill us in?"

"You take it, Cal," Fox suggested.

"It would've been our birthday—the night, or really the evening of it. We were all pretty spooked. It was worse being separated, each of us in our own place. I talked my mother into letting me go in to the bowling center, so I'd have something to do, and Gage would be there. She couldn't figure out whether to ground me or not," he said with a half smile. "First and last time I remember her being undecided on that kind of issue. So she let me go in with my father. Gage?"

"I was working. Mr. Hawkins let me earn some spending money at the center, mopping up spills or carrying grill orders out to tables. I know I felt a hell of a lot better when Cal came in. Then Fox."

"I nagged my parents brainless to let me go in. My father finally caved, took me. I think he wanted to have a confab with Cal's dad, and Gage's if he could."

"So, Brian—Mr. O'Dell—and my dad sat down at the

end of the counter, having coffee. They didn't bring Bill, Gage's father, into it at that point."

"Because he didn't know I'd been gone in the first place," Gage said. "No point getting me in trouble until they'd decided what to do."

"Where was your father?" Cybil asked.

"Around. Behind the pins. He was having a few sober hours, so Mr. Hawkins had him working on something."

"Ball return, lane two," Cal murmured. "I remember. It seemed like an ordinary summer night. Teenagers, some college types on the pinballs and video games. Grill smoking, pins crashing. There was a kid—two or three years old, I guess—with a family in the four lane. Major tantrum. The mother hauled him outside right before it happened."

He took a swig of water. He could see it, bell clear. "Mr. Guthrie was at the counter, drinking a beer, eating a dog and fries. He came in once a week. Nice enough guy. Sold flooring, had a couple of kids in high school. Once a week, he came in when his wife went to the movies with girlfriends. It was clockwork. And Mr. Guthrie would order a dog and fries, and get steadily trashed. My dad used to say he did his drinking there because he could tell himself it wasn't real drinking if he wasn't in a bar."

"Troublemaker?" Quinn asked as she made another note.

"Anything but. He was what my dad called an affable drunk. He never got mean, or even sloppy. Tuesday nights, Mr. Guthrie came in, got a dog and fries, drank four or five beers, watched some games, talked to whoever was around. Somewhere around eleven, he'd leave a five-dollar tip on the grill and walk home. Far as I know he didn't so much as crack a Bud otherwise. It was a Tuesday night deal."

"He used to buy eggs from us," Fox remembered. "A dozen brown eggs, every Saturday morning. Anyway."

"It was nearly ten, and Mr. Guthrie was having another beer. He was walking by the tables with it," Cal said.

"Probably going to take it and stand behind the lanes, watch some of the action. Some guys were having burgers. Frank Dibbs was one of them—held his league's record for high game, coached Little League. We were sitting at the next table, eating pizza. Dad told us to take a break, so we were splitting a pizza. Dibbs said, 'Hey, Guth, the wife wants new vinyl in the kitchen. What kind of deal can you give me?'

"And Guthrie, he just smiles. One of those tight-lipped smiles that don't show any teeth. He picks up one of the forks sitting on the table. He jammed it into Dibbs's cheek, just stabbed it into his face, and kept walking. People are screaming and running, and, Christ, that fork is just sticking out of Mr. Dibbs's cheek, and blood's sliding down his face. And Mr. Guthrie strolls over behind lane two, and drinks his beer."

To give himself a moment, Cal took a long drink. "My dad wanted us out. Everything was going crazy, except Guthrie, who apparently *was* crazy. Your dad took care of Dibbs," Cal said to Fox. "I remember how he kept his head. Dibbs had already yanked the fork out, and your father grabbed this stack of napkins and got the bleeding stopped. There was blood on his hands when he drove us home."

Cal shook his head. "Not the point. Fox's dad took us home. Gage came with me—my father took care of that. He didn't get home until it was light out. I heard him come home; my mother had waited for him. I heard him tell her they had Guthrie locked up, and he was just sitting in his cell laughing. Laughing like it was all a big joke. Later, when it was all over, he didn't even remember. Nobody remembered much of what went on that week, or if they did, they put it away. He never came in the center again. They moved away the next winter."

"Was that the only thing that happened that night?" Cybil asked after a moment.

"Girl was raped." Gage set his empty mug on the mantel. "Making out with her boyfriend out on Dog Street. He didn't stop when she said stop, didn't stop when she started to cry, to scream. He raped her in the backseat of his secondhand Buick, then shoved her out on the side of the road and drove off. Wrapped his car around a tree a couple hours later. Ended up in the same hospital as she did. Only he didn't make it."

"Family mutt attacked an eight-year-old boy," Fox added. "Middle of that night. The dog had slept with the kid every night for three years. The parents woke up hearing the kid screaming, and when they got to the bedroom, the dog went for them, too. The father had to beat it off with the kid's baseball bat."

"It just got worse from there. That night, the next night." Cal took a long breath. "Then it didn't always wait for night. Not always."

"There's a pattern to it." Quinn spoke quietly, then glanced up when Cal's voice cut through her thoughts.

"Where? Other than ordinary people turn violent or psychotic?"

"We saw what happened with Lump. You've just told us about another family pet. There have been other incidents like that. Now you've said the first overt incident all of you witnessed involved a man who'd had several beers. His alcohol level was probably over the legal limit, meaning he was impaired. Mind's not sharp after drinking like that. You're more susceptible."

"So Guthrie was easier to influence or infect because he was drunk or well on the way?" Fox pushed up to sitting. "That's good. That makes good sense."

"The boy who raped his girlfriend of three months then drove into a tree hadn't been drinking." Gage shook his head. "Where's that in the pattern?"

"Sexual arousal and frustration tend to impair the brain." Quinn tapped her pencil on her pad. "Put those into a teenage boy, and that says susceptible to me."

"It's a valid point." Cal shoved his hand through his hair. Why hadn't they seen it themselves? "The dead crows. There were a couple dozen dead crows all over Main Street the morning of our birthday that year. Some broken windows where they'd repeatedly flown into the glass. We always figured that was part of it. But nobody got hurt."

"Does it always start that way?" Layla asked. "Can you pinpoint it?"

"The first I remember from the next time was when the Myerses found their neighbor's dog drowned in a backyard swimming pool. There was the woman who left her kid locked in the car and went into the beauty salon, got a manicure and so on. It was in the nineties that day," Fox added. "Somebody heard the kid crying, called the cops. They got the kid out, but when they went in to get the woman, she said she didn't have a baby. Didn't know what they were talking about. It came out she'd been up two nights running because the baby had colic."

"Sleep deprivation." Quinn wrote it down.

"But we knew it was happening again," Cal said slowly, "we knew for sure on the night of our seventeenth when Lisa Hodges walked out of the bar at Main and Battlefield, stripped down naked, and started shooting at passing cars with the twenty-two she had in her purse."

"We were one of the cars," Gage added. "Good thing for all concerned her aim was lousy."

"She caught your shoulder," Fox reminded him.

"She *shot* you?"

Gage smiled easily at Cybil. "Grazed me, and we heal fast. We managed to get the gun from her before she shot anyone else, or got hit by a car as she was standing buck naked in the middle of the street. Then she offered us blow jobs. Rumor was she gave a doozy, but we weren't much in the mood to find out."

"All right, from pattern to theory." Quinn rose to her feet to work it out. "The thing we'll call Twisse, because it's better to have a name for it, requires energy. We're all made up of energy, and Twisse needs it to manifest, to work. When he's out, during this time Dent is unable to hold him, he seeks out the easiest sources of energy first.

Birds and animals, people who are most vulnerable. As he gets stronger, he's able to move up the chain."

"I don't think the way to stop him is to clear out all the pets," Gage began, "ban alcohol, drugs, and sex and make sure everyone gets a good night's sleep."

"Too bad," Cybil tossed back, "because it might buy us some time. Keep going, Q."

"Next question would be, how does he generate the energy he needs?"

"Fear, hate, violence." Cal nodded. "We've got that. We can't cut off his supply because you can't block those emotions out of the population. They exist."

"So do their counterparts, so we can hypothesize that those are weapons or countermeasures against him. You've all gotten stronger over time, and so has he. Maybe he's able to store some of this energy he pulls in during the dormant period."

"And so he's able to start sooner, start stronger the next time. Okay," Cal decided. "Okay, it makes sense."

"He's using some of that store now," Layla put in, "because he doesn't want all six of us to stick this out. He wants to fracture the group before July."

"He must be disappointed." Cybil picked up the wine she'd nursed throughout the discussion. "Knowledge is power and all that, and it's good to have logical theories, more areas to research. But it seems to be we need to move. We need a strategy. Got any, Mr. Strategy?"

From his spot on the floor, Fox grinned. "Yeah. I say as soon as the snow melts enough for us to get through it, we go to the clearing. We go to the Pagan Stone, all of us together. And we double-dog dare the son of a bitch."

IT SOUNDED GOOD IN THEORY. IT WAS A DIFFER-ent matter, in Cal's mind, when you added the human factor. When you added Quinn. He'd taken her there once before, and he'd zoned out, leaving her alone and vulnerable.

And he hadn't loved her then.

He knew there was no choice, that there were bigger stakes involved. But the idea of putting her at risk, at deliberately putting her at the center of it with him, kept him awake and restless.

He wandered the house, checking locks, staring out windows for any glimpse of the thing that stalked them. The moon was out, and the snow tinted blue under it. They'd be able to shovel their way out the next day, he thought, dig out the cars. Get back to what passed for normal within a day or two.

He already knew if he asked her to stay, just stay, she'd tell him she couldn't leave Layla and Cybil on their own. He already knew he'd have to let her go.

He couldn't protect her every hour of every day, and if he tried, they'd end up smothering each other.

As he moved through the living room, he saw the glow of the kitchen lights. He headed back to turn them off and check locks. And there was Gage, sitting at the counter playing solitaire with a mug of coffee steaming beside the discard pile.

"A guy who drinks black coffee at one a.m. is going to be awake all night."

"It never keeps me up." Gage flipped a card, made his play. "When I want to sleep, I sleep. You know that. What's your excuse?"

"I'm thinking it's going to be a long, hard, messy hike into the woods even if we wait a month. Which we probably should."

"No. Red six on black seven. You're trying to come up with a way to go in without Quinn. Without any of them, really, but especially the blonde."

"I told you how it was when we went in before."

"And she walked out again on her own two sexy legs. Jack of clubs on queen of diamonds. I'm not worried about her. I'm worried about you."

Cal's back went up. "Is there a time I didn't handle myself?"

"Not up until now. But you've got it bad, Hawkins. You've got it bad for the blonde, and being you, your first and last instinct is going to be to cover her ass if anything goes down."

"Shouldn't it be?" He didn't want any damn coffee, but since he doubted he'd sleep anyway, he poured some. "Why wouldn't it be?"

"I'd lay money that your blonde can handle herself. Doesn't mean you're wrong, Cal. I imagine if I had a woman inside me the way she's inside you, I wouldn't want to put how she handled herself to the test. The trouble is, you're going to have to."

"I never wanted to feel this way," Cal said after a moment. "This is a good part of the reason why. We're good together, Gage."

"I can see that for myself. Don't know what she sees in a loser like you, but it's working for her."

"We could get better. I can feel we'd just get better, make something real and solid. If we had the chance, if we had the time, we'd make something together."

Casually, Gage gathered up the cards, shuffled them with a blur of speed. "You think we're going down this time."

"Yeah." Cal looked out the window at the cold, blue moonlight. "I think we're going down. Don't you?"

"Odds are." Gage dealt them both a hand of blackjack. "But hell, who wants to live forever?"

"That's the problem. Now that I've found Quinn, forever sounds pretty damn good." Cal glanced at his hole card, noted the king to go with his three. "Hit me."

With a grin, Gage flipped over a nine. "Sucker."

Twenty

~⌐~

CAL HOPED FOR A WEEK, TWO IF HE COULD MAN-
age it. And got three days. Nature screwed his plans again,
this time shooting temperatures up into the fifties. Mountains of snow melted into hills while the February thaw
brought the fun of flash flooding, swollen creeks, and black
ice when the thermometer dropped to freezing each night.

But three days after he'd had his lane plowed and the
women were back in the house on High Street, the weather
stabilized. Creeks ran high, but the ground sucked up most
of the runoff. And he was coming up short on excuses to
put off the hike to the Pagan Stone.

At his desk, with Lump contentedly sprawled on his
back in the doorway, feet in the air, Cal put his mind into
work. The winter leagues were winding up, and the spring
groups would go into gear shortly. He knew he was on the
edge of convincing his father the center would profit from
the automatic scoring systems, and wanted to give it one
more solid push. If they moved on it soon, they could have
the systems up and running for the spring leagues.

They'd want to advertise, run a few specials. They'd have to train the staff, which meant training themselves.

He brought up the spreadsheet for February, noted that the month so far had been solid, even up a bit from last year. He'd use that as more ammunition. Which, of course, his father could and would counter that if they were up the way things were, why change it?

As he was holding the conversation in his head, Cal heard the click that meant a new e-mail had come in. He toggled over, saw Quinn's address.

Hi, Love of My Life,

I didn't want to call in case you were knee-deep in whatever requires you to be knee-deep. Let me know when you're not.

Meanwhile, this is Black's Local Weather Service reporting: Temperatures today should reach a high of forty-eight under partly sunny skies. Lows in the upper thirties. No precipitation is expected. Tomorrow's forecast is for sunny with a high of fifty.

Adding the visual, I can see widening patches of grass in both the front and backyard. Realistically, there's probably more snow, more mud in the woods, but, baby, it's time to saddle up and move out.

My team can be ready bright and early tomorrow and will bring suitable provisions.

Also, Cyb's confirmed the Clark branch connection, and is currently climbing out on some Kinski limbs to verify that. She thinks she may have a line on a couple of possibilities where Ann Hawkins stayed, or at least where she might have gone to give birth. I'll fill you in when I see you.

Let me know, soon as you can, if tomorrow works.

XXOO Quinn.

(I know that whole XXOO thing is dopey, but it seemed more refined than signing off with: I wish you could come over and do me. Even though I do.)

The last part made him smile even though the text of the post had a headache sneaking up the back of his skull.

He could put her off a day or two, and put her off honestly. He couldn't expect Fox to dump his scheduled clients or any court appearances at the snap of a finger, and she'd understand that. But if he were to use that, and his own schedule, he had to do it straight.

With some annoyance, he shot an e-mail to Fox, asking when he could clear time for the trip to the clearing. The annoyance increased when Fox answered back immediately.

Fri's good. Morning's clear, can clear full day if nec.

"Well, fuck." Cal pushed on the ache at the back of his head. Since e-mail wasn't bringing him any luck, he'd go see Quinn in person when he broke for lunch.

AS CAL PREPARED TO CLOSE OUT FOR THE MORN-ing, Bill Turner stopped in the office doorway.

"Ah, got that toilet fixed in the ladies' room downstairs, and the leak in the freezer was just a hose needed replacing."

"Thanks, Bill." He swung his coat on as he spoke. "I've got a couple of things to do in town. Shouldn't be above an hour."

"Okay, then. I was wondering if, ah . . ." Bill rubbed a hand over his chin, let it drop. "I was wondering if you think Gage'll be coming in, maybe the next day or two. Or if maybe I could, maybe I could run over to your place to have a word with him."

Rock and a hard place, Cal thought, and bought himself some time by adjusting his jacket. "I don't know if he's thinking about dropping by, Bill. He hasn't mentioned it. I think . . . Okay, look, I'd give him some time. I'd just give it some time before you made that first move. I know you want—"

"It's okay. That's okay. Appreciate it."

"Shit," Cal said under his breath as Bill walked away. Then, "Shit, shit, shit," as he headed out himself.

He had to take Gage's side in this, how could he not? He'd seen firsthand what Bill's belt had done to Gage when they'd been kids. And yet, he'd also witnessed, firsthand, the dozens of ways Bill had turned himself around in the last few years.

And, hadn't he just seen the pain, guilt, even the grief on Bill's face just now? So either way he went, Cal knew he was going to feel guilty and annoyed.

He walked straight out and over to Quinn's.

She pulled open the door, yanked him in. Before he could say a word her arms were locked around his neck and her mouth was very busy on his. "I was hoping that was you."

"Good thing it was, because Greg, the UPS guy on this route, might get the wrong idea if you greeted him that way."

"He is kind of cute. Come on back to the kitchen. I'd just come down to do a coffee run. We're all working on various projects upstairs. Did you get my e-mail?"

"Yeah."

"So, we're all set for tomorrow?" She glanced back as she reached up for the coffee.

"No, tomorrow's no good. Fox can't clear his slate until Friday."

"Oh." Her lips moved into a pout, quickly gone. "Okay then, Friday it is. Meanwhile we'll keep reading, research-ing, working. Cyb thinks she's got a couple of good possi-bilities on . . . What?" she asked when she got a good look at his face. "What's going on?"

"Okay." He took a couple paces away, then back. "Okay, I'm just going to say it. I don't want you going back in there. Just be quiet a minute, will you?" he said when he saw the retort forming. "I wish there was a way I could stop you from going, that there was a way I could ignore the fact that we all need to go. I know you're a part of this, and I know you have to go back to the Pagan Stone. I know there's going to be more you have to be a part of than I'd wish otherwise. But I can wish you weren't part of this, Quinn, and that you were somewhere safe until this is over. I can want that, just as I know I can't have what I want.

"If you want to be pissed off about that, you'll have to be pissed off."

She waited a beat. "Have you had lunch?"

"No. What does that have to do with anything?"

"I'm going to make you a sandwich—an offer I never make lightly."

"Why are you making it now?"

"Because I love you. Take off your coat. I love that you'd say all that to me," she began as she opened the refrigerator for fixings. "That you'd need to let me know how you felt about it. Now if you'd tried ordering me to stay out of it, if you'd lied or tried to do some sort of end-run around me, I'd feel different. I'd still love you, because that sort of thing sticks with me, but I'd be mad, and more, I'd be disappointed in you. As it is, Cal, I'm finding myself pretty damn pleased and a hell of a lot smug that my head and heart worked so well together and picked the perfect guy for me."

She cut the sandwich into two tidy triangles, offered it. "Do you want coffee or milk?"

"You don't have milk, you have white water. Coffee'd be fine, thanks." He took a bite of the turkey and Swiss with alfalfa on whole wheat. "Pretty good sandwich."

"Don't get used to the service." She glanced over as she poured out coffee. "We should get an early start on Friday, don't you think? Like dawn?"

"Yeah." He touched her cheek with his free hand. "We'll head in at first light."

SINCE HE'D HAD GOOD LUCK WITH QUINN, AND gotten lunch out of it, Cal decided he was going to speak his mind to Gage next. The minute he and Lump stepped into the house, he smelled food. And when they wandered back, Cal found Gage in the kitchen, taking a pull off a beer as he stirred something in a pot.

"You made food."

"Chili. I was hungry. Fox called. He tells me we're taking the ladies for a hike Friday."

"Yeah. First light."

"Should be interesting."

"Has to be done." Cal dumped out food for Lump before getting a beer of his own. And so, he thought, did this have to be done. "I need to talk to you about your father."

Cal saw Gage close off. Like a switch flipped, a finger snapped, his face simply blanked out. "He works for you; that's your business. I've got nothing to say."

"You've got every right to shut him out. I'm not saying different. I'm letting you know he asks about you. He wants to see you. Look, he's been sober five years now, and if he'd been sober fifty it wouldn't change the way he treated you. But this is a small town, Gage, and you can't dodge him forever. My sense is he's got things to say to you, and you may want to get it done, put it behind you. That's it."

There was a reason Gage made his living at poker. It showed now in a face, a voice, completely devoid of expression. "My sense is you should take yourself out of the middle. I haven't asked you to stand there."

Cal held up a hand for peace. "Fine."

"Sounds like the old man's stuck on Steps Eight and Nine with me. He can't make amends on this, Cal. I don't give a damn about his amends."

"Okay. I'm not trying to convince you otherwise. Just letting you know."

"Now I know."

IT OCCURRED TO CAL WHEN HE STOOD AT THE window on Friday morning, watching the headlights cut through the dim predawn, that it had been almost a month exactly since Quinn had first driven up to his house.

How could so much have happened? How could so much have changed in such a short time?

It had been slightly less than that month since he'd led her into the woods the first time. When he'd led her to the Pagan Stone.

In those short weeks of the shortest month he'd learned it wasn't only himself and his two blood brothers who were destined to face this threat. There were three women now, equally involved.

And he was completely in love with one of them.

He stood just as he was to watch her climb out of Fox's truck. Her bright hair spilled out from under the dark watch cap. She wore a bold red jacket and scarred hiking boots. He could see the laugh on her face as she said something to Cybil, and her breath whisked out in clouds in the early morning chill.

She knew enough to be afraid, he understood that. But she refused to allow fear to dictate her moves. He hoped he could say the same as he had more to risk now. He had her.

He stood watch until he heard Fox use his key to unlock the front door, then Cal went down to join them, and to gather his things for the day.

Fog smoked the ground that the cold had hardened like stone overnight. By midday, Cal knew the path would be sloppy again, but for now it was quick and easy going.

There were still pockets and lumpy hills of snow, and he identified the hoofprints of the deer that roamed the woods, to Layla's delight. If any of them were nervous, they hid it well, at least on this first leg of the hike.

It was so different from that long-ago day in July when he and Fox and Gage had made this trip. No boom box pumping out rap or heavy metal, no snacks of Little Debbies, no innocent, youthful excitement of a stolen day, and the night to come.

None of them had ever been so innocent again.

He caught himself lifting a hand to his face, where his glasses used to slide down the bridge of his nose.

"How you doing, Captain?" Quinn stepped up to match her pace to his, gave him a light arm bump.

"Okay. I was just thinking about that day. Everything hot and green, Fox hauling that stupid boom box. My mother's lemonade, snack cakes."

"Sweat rolling," Fox continued from just behind him.

"We're coming up on Hester's Pool," Gage said, breaking the memory.

The water made Cal think of quicksand rather than the cool and forbidden pool he and his friends had leaped into so long ago. He could imagine going in now, being sucked in, deeper and deeper until he never saw light again.

They stopped as they had before, but now it was coffee instead of lemonade.

"There's been deer here, too." Layla pointed at the ground. "Those are deer prints, right?"

"Some deer," Fox confirmed. "Raccoon." He took her arm to turn her, pointed to the prints on the ground.

"Raccoons?" Grinning, she bent to take a closer look. "What else might be in here?"

"Some of my namesakes, wild turkey, now and then— though mostly north of here—you might see bear."

She straightened quickly. "Bear."

"Mostly north," he repeated, but found it as good an excuse as any to take her hand.

Cybil crouched by the edge of the pool, stared at the water.

"A little cold to think about taking a dip," Gage told her.

"Hester drowned herself here." She glanced up, then looked over at Cal. "And when you went in that day, you saw her."

"Yeah. Yeah, I saw her."

"And you and Quinn have both seen her in your heads. Layla's dreamed of her, vividly. So . . . maybe I can get something."

"I thought yours was precog, not the past," Cal began.

"It is, but I still get vibes from people, from places that

are strong enough to send them out. How about you?" She looked back at Gage. "We might stir up more in tandem. Are you up for that?"

Saying nothing, he held out a hand. She took it, rose to her feet. Together, they stared at that still, brown surface.

The water began to beat and froth. It began to spin, to spew up white-tipped waves. It roared like a sea mating with a wild and vicious storm.

And a hand shot out to claw at the ground.

Hester pulled herself out of that churning water—bone white skin, a mass of wet, tangled hair, dark, glassy eyes. The effort, or her madness, peeled her lips back from her teeth.

Cybil heard herself scream as Hester Deale's arms opened, as they locked around her and dragged her toward that swirling brown pool.

"Cyb! Cyb! Cybil!"

She came back struggling, and found herself locked not in Hester's arms, but Gage's. "What the hell was that?"

"You were going in."

She stayed where she was, feeling her heart hammer against his as Quinn gripped her shoulder. Cybil took another look at the still surface of the pool. "That would've been really unpleasant."

She was trembling, one hard jolt after the next, but Gage had to give her points for keeping her voice even.

"Did you get anything?" she asked him.

"Water kicked up; she came up. You started to tip."

"She grabbed me. She . . . embraced me. That's what I think, but I wasn't focused enough to feel or sense what she felt. Maybe if we tried it again—"

"We've got to get moving now," Cal interrupted.

"It only took a minute."

"Try nearly fifteen," Fox corrected.

"But . . ." Cybil eased back from Gage when she realized she was still in his arms. "Did it seem that long to you?"

"No. It was immediate."

"It wasn't." Layla held out another thermos lid of coffee. "We were arguing about whether we should pull you back, and how we should if we did. Quinn said to leave you be for another few minutes, that sometimes it took you a while to warm up."

"Well, it felt like a minute, no more than, for the whole deal. And it didn't feel like something from before." Again, Cybil looked at Gage.

"No, it didn't. So if I were you, I wouldn't think about taking a dip anytime soon."

"I prefer a nice blue pool, with a swim-up bar."

"Bikini margaritas." Quinn rubbed her hand up and down Cybil's arm.

"Spring break, two thousand." Cybil caught Quinn's hand, squeezed. "I'm fine, Q."

"I'll buy the first round of those margaritas when this is done. Ready to move on?" Cal asked.

He hitched up his pack, turned. Then shook his head. "This isn't right."

"We're leaving the haunted pool to walk through the demonic woods." Quinn worked up a smile. "What could be wrong?"

"That's not the path." He gestured toward the thawing track. "That's not the direction." He squinted up at the sun as he pulled his old Boy Scout compass out of his pocket.

"Ever thought about upgrading to a GPS?" Gage asked him.

"This does the job. See, we need to head west from here. That trail's leading north. That trail shouldn't even be there."

"It's not there." Fox's eyes narrowed, darkened. "There's no trail, just underbrush, a thicket of wild blackberries. It's not real." He shifted, angled himself. "It's that way." He gestured west. "It's hard to see, it's like looking through mud, but . . ."

Layla stepped forward, took his hand.

"Okay, yeah. That's better."

"You're pointing at a really big-ass tree," Cybil told him.

"That isn't there." Still holding Layla's hand, Fox walked forward. The image of the large oak broke apart as he walked through it.

"Nice trick." Quinn let out a breath. "So, Twisse doesn't want us to go to the clearing. I'll take point."

"I'll take point." Cal took her arm to tug her behind him. "I've got the compass." He had only to glance back at his friends to have them falling in line. Fox taking center, Gage the rear with the women between.

As soon as the track widened enough to allow it, Quinn moved up beside Cal. "This is the way it has to work." She glanced back to see the other women had followed her lead, and now walked abreast with their partners. "We're linked up this way, Cal. Two-by-two, trios, the group of six. Whatever the reasons are, that's the way it is."

"We're walking into something. I can't see what it is, but I'm walking you and the others right into it."

"We're all on our own two feet, Cal." She passed him the bottle of water she carried in her coat pocket. "I don't know if I love you because you're Mr. Responsibility or in spite of it."

"As long as you do. And since you do, maybe we should think about the idea of getting married."

"I like the idea," she said after a moment. "If you want my thoughts on it."

"I do." Stupid, he thought, stupid way to propose, and a ridiculous place for it, too. Then again, when they couldn't be sure what was around the bend, it made sense to grab what you did now, tight and quick. "As it happens, I agree with you. More thoughts on the idea would be that my mother, especially, will want the splash—big deal, big party, bells and whistles."

"I happen to agree with that, too. How is she with communication by phone and/or e-mail?"

"She's all about that."

"Great. I'll hook her up with my mother and they can go for it. How's your September schedule?"

"September?"

She studied the winter woods, watched a squirrel scamper up a tree and across a thick branch. "I bet the Hollow's beautiful in September. Still green, but with just a hint of the color to come."

"I was thinking sooner. Like April, or May." Before, Cal thought. Before July, and what might be the end of everything he knew and loved.

"It takes a while to organize those bells and whistles." When she looked at him he understood she read him clearly. "After, Cal, after we've won. One more thing to celebrate. When we're—"

She broke off when he touched a finger to her lips.

The sound came clearly now as all movement and conversation stopped. The wet and throaty snarl rolled across the air, and shot cold down the spine. Lump curled down on his haunches and whined.

"He hears it, too, this time." Cal shifted, and though the movement was slight, it put Quinn between him and Fox.

"I don't guess we could be lucky, and that's just a bear." Layla cleared her throat. "Either way, I think we should keep moving. Whatever it is doesn't want us to, so . . ."

"We're here to flip it the bird," Fox finished.

"Come on, Lump, come on with me."

The dog shivered at Cal's command, but rose, and with its side pressed to Cal's legs, walked down the trail toward the Pagan Stone.

The wolf—Cal would never have referred to the thing as a dog—stood at the mouth of the clearing. It was huge and black, with eyes that were somehow human. Lump tried a halfhearted snarl in answer to the low, warning growl, then cowered against Cal.

"Are we going to walk through that, too?" Gage asked from the rear.

"It's not like the false trail." Fox shook his head. "It's not real, but it's there."

"Okay." Gage started to pull off his pack.

And the thing leaped.

It seemed to fly, Cal thought, a mass of muscle and teeth. He fisted his hands to defend, but there was nothing to fight.

"I felt . . ." Slowly, Quinn lowered the arms she'd thrown up to protect her face.

"Yeah. Not just the cold, not that time." Cal gripped her arm to keep her close. "There was weight, just for a second, and there was substance."

"We never had that before, not even during the Seven." Fox scanned the woods on both sides. "Whatever form Twisse took, whatever we saw, it wasn't really *there*. It's always been mind games."

"If it can solidify, it can hurt us directly," Layla pointed out.

"And be hurt." From behind her Gage pulled a 9mm Glock out of his pack.

"Good thinking," was Cybil's cool opinion.

"Jesus Christ, Gage, where the hell did you get that?"

Gage lifted his eyebrows at Fox. "Guy I know down in D.C. Are we going to stand here in a huddle, or are we going in?"

"Don't point that at anybody," Fox demanded.

"Safety's on."

"That's what they always say before they accidentally blow a hole in the best friend."

They stepped into the clearing, and the stone.

"My God, it's beautiful." Cybil breathed the words reverently as she moved toward it. "It can't possibly be a natural formation, it's too perfect. It's designed, and for worship, I'd think. And it's warm. Feel it. The stone's warm." She circled it. "Anyone with any sensitivity has to feel, has to know this is sacred ground."

"Sacred to who?" Gage countered. "Because what came up out of here twenty-one years ago wasn't all bright and friendly."

"It wasn't all dark either. We felt both." Cal looked at Fox. "We saw both."

"Yeah. It's just the big, black scary mass got most of our attention while we were being blasted off our feet."

"But the other gave us most of his, that's what I think. I walked out of here not only without a scratch, but with twenty-twenty vision and a hell of an immune system."

"The scratches on my arms had healed up, and the bruises from my most recent tussle with Napper." Fox shrugged. "Never been sick a day since."

"How about you?" Cybil asked Gage. "Any miraculous healing?"

"None of us had a mark on him after the blast," Cal began.

"It's no deal, Cal. No secrets from the team. My old man used his belt on me the night before we were heading in here. A habit of his when he'd get a drunk on. I was carrying the welts when I came in, but not when I walked out."

"I see." Cybil held Gage's eyes for several beats. "The fact that you were given protection, and your specific abilities, enabled you to defend your ground, so to speak. Otherwise, you'd have been three helpless little boys."

"It's clean." Layla's comment had everyone turning to where she stood by the stone. "That's what comes to my mind. I don't think it was ever used for sacrifice. Not blood and death, not for the dark. It feels clean."

"I've seen the blood on it," Gage said. "I've seen it burn. I've heard the screams."

"That's not its purpose. Maybe that's what Twisse wants." Quinn laid her palm on the stone. "To defile it, to twist its power. If he can, well, he'll own it, won't he? Cal?"

"Okay." His hand hovered over hers. "Ready?" At her nod, he joined his hand to hers on the stone.

At first there was only her, only Quinn. Only the courage in her eyes. Then the world tumbled back, five years, twenty, so that he saw the boy he'd been with his friends, scoring his knife over their wrists to bind them together. Then rushing back, decades, centuries, to the blaze and the screams while the stone stood cool and white in the midst of hell.

Back to another waning winter where Giles Dent stood with Ann Hawkins as he stood with Quinn now. Dent's words came from his lips.

"We have only until summer. This I cannot change, even for you. Duty outstrips even my love for you, and for the lives we have made." He touched a hand to her belly. "I wish, above all, that I could be with you when they come into the world."

"Let me stay. Beloved."

"I am the guardian. You are the hope. I cannot destroy the beast, only chain it for a time. Still, I do not leave you. It is not death, but an endless struggle, a war only I can wage. Until what comes from us makes the end. They will have all I can give, this I swear to you. If they are victorious in their time, I will be with you again."

"What will I tell them of their father?"

"That he loved their mother, and them, with the whole of his heart."

"Giles, it has a man's form. A man can bleed, a man can die."

"It is not a man, and it is not in my power to destroy it. That will be for those who come after us both. It, too, will make its own. Not through love. They will not be what it intends. It cannot own them if they are beyond its reach, even its ken. This is for me to do. I am not the first, Ann, only the last. What comes from us is the future."

She pressed a hand to her side. "They quicken," she whispered. "When, Giles, when will it end? All the lives we have lived before, all the joy and the pain we have known? When will there be peace for us?"

"Be my heart." He lifted her hands to his lips. "I will be your courage. And we will find each other once more."

Tears slid down Quinn's cheeks even as she felt the images fade. "We're all they have. If we don't find the way, they're lost to each other. I felt her heart breaking inside me."

"He believed in what he'd done, what he had to do. He believed in us, though he couldn't see it clearly. I don't think he could see us, all of us," Cal said as he looked around. "Not clearly. He took it on faith."

"Fine for him." Gage shifted his weight. "But I put a little more of mine in this Glock."

It wasn't the wolf, but the boy that stood on the edge of the clearing. Grinning, grinning. He lifted his hands, showed fingernails that were sharpened to claws.

The sun dimmed from midday to twilight; the air from cool to frigid. And thunder rumbled in the late winter sky.

In a lightning move so unexpected Cal couldn't prevent it, Lump sprang. The thing who masked as a boy squealed with laughter, shinnied up a tree like a monkey.

But Cal had seen it, in a flash of an instant. He'd seen the shock, and what might have been fear.

"Shoot it," Cal shouted to Gage, even as he dashed forward to grab Lump's collar. "Shoot the son of a bitch."

"Jesus, you don't actually think a bullet's going to—"

Over Fox's objection, Gage fired. Without hesitation, he aimed for the boy's heart.

The bullet cracked the air, struck the tree. This time no one could miss the look of shock on the boy's face. His howl of pain and fury gushed across the clearing and shook the ground.

With ruthless purpose, Gage emptied the clip into it.

It changed. It grew. It twisted itself into something massive and black and sinuous that rose over Cal as he stood his ground, fighting to hold back his dog, who strained and barked like a mad thing.

The stench of it, the *cold* of it hammered down on him like stones. "We're still here," Cal shouted. "This is our place, and you can go to hell."

He staggered against a blast of sound and slapping air.

"Better reload, Deadeye," Cybil commanded.

"Knew I should've bought a howitzer." But Gage slapped in a full clip.

"This isn't your place," Cal shouted again. The wind threatened to knock him off his feet, seemed to tear at his clothes and his skin like a thousand knives. Through the scream of it, he heard the crack of gunfire, and the rage it spewed out clamped on his throat like claws.

Then Quinn braced against his side. And Fox shouldered in at his other. They formed a line, all six.

"This," Cal called out, "is ours. Our place and our time. You couldn't have my dog, and you can't have my town."

"So fuck off," Fox suggested, and bending picked up a rock. He hurled it, a straightaway fast ball.

"Hello, got a gun here."

Fox's grin at Gage was wild and wide as the feral wind battered them. "Throwing rocks is an insult. It'll undermine its confidence."

Die here!

It wasn't a voice, but a tidal wave of sound and wind that knocked them to the ground, scattered them like bowling pins.

"Undermine, my ass." Gage shoved to his knees and began firing again.

"You'll die here." Cal spoke coolly as the others took Fox's tack and began to hurl stones and sticks.

Fire swept across the clearing, its flames like shards of ice. Smoke belched up in fetid clouds as it roared its outrage.

"You'll die here," Cal repeated. Pulling his knife from its sheath, he rushed forward to plunge it into the boiling black mass.

It screamed. He thought it screamed, thought the sound held something of pain as well as fury. The shock of power sang up his arm, stabbed through him like a blade, twin edges of scorching heat and impossible cold. It flung him away, sent him flying through the smoke like a pebble from a sling. Breathless, bones jarred from the fall, Cal scrambled to his feet.

"You'll die here!" This time he shouted it as he gripped the knife, as he charged forward.

The thing that was a wolf, a boy, a man, a demon looked at him with eyes of hate.

And vanished.

"But not today." The fire died, the smoke cleared as he bent over to suck in air. "Anybody hurt? Is everybody okay? Quinn. Hey, Lump, hey." He nearly toppled backward when Lump leaped up, paws on shoulders to lap his face.

"Your nose is bleeding." Scurrying over on her hands and knees, Quinn gripped his arm to pull herself to her feet. "Cal." Her hands rushed over his face, his body. "Oh God, Cal. I've never seen anything so brave, or so goddamn stupid."

"Yeah, well." In a defiant move, he swiped at the blood. "It pissed me off. If that was its best shot, it fell way short."

"It didn't dish out anything a really big drink and a long hot bath won't cure," Cybil decided. "Layla? Okay?"

"Okay." Face fierce, Layla brushed at her stinging cheeks. "Okay." She took Fox's outstretched hand and got to her feet. "We scared it. We scared it, and it ran away."

"Even better. We hurt it." Quinn took a couple shuddering breaths, then much as Lump had, leaped at Cal. "We're all right. We're all okay. You were amazing. You were beyond belief. Oh God, God, give me a really big kiss."

As she laughed and wept, he took her mouth. He held her close, understanding that of all the answers they needed, for him she was the first.

They weren't going down this time, he realized.

"We're going to win this." He drew her away so he could look into her eyes. His were calm, steady, and clear. "I never believed it before, not really. But I do now. I know it now. Quinn." He pressed his lips to her forehead. "We're going to win this, and we're getting married in September."

"Damn straight."

When she wrapped around him again, it was victory enough for now. It was enough to stand on until the next time. And the next time, he determined, they'd be better armed.

"Let's go home. It's a long walk back, and we've got a hell of a lot to do."

She held on another moment, held tight while he looked over her head into the eyes of his brothers. Gage nodded, then shoved the gun back in his pack. Swinging it on, he crossed the clearing to the path beyond.

The sun bloomed overhead, and the wind died. They walked out of the clearing, through the winter woods, three men, three women, and a dog.

On its ground the Pagan Stone stood silent, waiting for their return.

Turn the page for a look at

THE HOLLOW

the second book in the
Sign of Seven Trilogy.

Now available from Jove Books.

Hawkins Hollow
June 1994

ON A BRIGHT SUMMER MORNING, A TEACUP poodle drowned in the Bestlers' backyard swimming pool. At first, Lynne Bestler, who'd gone out to sneak in a solitary swim before her kids woke, thought it was a dead squirrel. Which would've been bad enough. But when she steeled herself to scoop out the tangle of fur with the net, she recognized her neighbor's beloved Marcell.

Her shouts, and the splash as Lynne tossed the hapless dog, net and all, back into the pool, brought Lynne's husband rushing out in his boxers. Their mother's sobs and their father's curses as he jumped in to grab the pole and tow the body to the side, woke the Bestler twins, who stood screaming in their matching My Little Pony nightgowns. Within moments, the backyard hysteria had neighbors hurrying to fences just as Bestler dragged himself and his burden out of the water. As, like many men, Bestler had developed an attachment to ancient underwear, the weight of the water was too much for the worn elastic.

So Bestler came out of his pool with a dead dog, and no boxers.

The bright summer morning in the little town of Hawkins Hollow began with shock, grief, farce, and drama.

Fox learned of Marcell's untimely death minutes after he stepped into Ma's Pantry to pick up a sixteen-ounce bottle of Coke and a couple of Slim Jims.

He'd copped a quick break from working with his father on a kitchen remodel down Main Street. Mrs. Larson wanted new countertops, cabinet doors, new floors, new paint. She called it freshening things up, and Fox called it a way to earn enough money to take Allyson Brendon out for pizza and the movies on Saturday night. He hoped to use that gateway to talk her into the backseat of his ancient VW Bug.

He didn't mind working with his dad. He hoped to hell he wouldn't spend the rest of his life swinging a hammer or running a power saw, but he didn't mind it. His father's company was always easy, and the job got Fox out of gardening and animal duty on their little farm. It also provided easy access to Cokes and Slim Jims—two items which would never, never be found in the O'Dell-Barry household.

His mother ruled there.

So he heard about the dog from Susan Keefaffer, who rang up his purchases while a few people with nothing better to do on a June afternoon sat at the counter over coffee and gossip.

He didn't know Marcell, but Fox had a soft spot for animals, so he suffered a twist of grief for the unfortunate poodle. That was leavened somewhat by the idea of Mr. Bestler, whom he *did* know, standing "naked as a jaybird," in Susan Keefaffer's words, beside his backyard pool.

While it made Fox sad to imagine some poor dog drowning in a swimming pool, he didn't connect it—not then—to the nightmare he and his two closest friends had lived through seven years before.

He'd had a dream the night before, a dream of blood

and fire, of voices chanting in a language he didn't understand. But then he'd watched a double feature of videos— *The Night of the Living Dead* and *The Texas Chainsaw Massacre*—with his friends Cal and Gage.

He didn't connect a dead French poodle with the dream, or with what had burned through Hawkins Hollow for a week after his tenth birthday. After the night he and Cal and Gage had spent at the Pagan Stone in Hawkins Wood—and everything had changed for them, and for the Hollow.

In a few weeks he and Cal and Gage would all turn seventeen—and that was on his mind. Baltimore had a damn good chance at a pennant this year, so that was on his mind. He'd be going back to high school as a senior, which meant top of the food chain at last, and planning for college.

What occupied a sixteen-year-old boy was considerably different than what occupied a ten-year-old. Including rounding third and heading for home with Allyson Brendon.

So when he walked back down the street, a lean boy not quite beyond the gangly stage of adolescence, his dense brown hair tied back in a stubby tail, golden brown eyes shaded with Oakleys, it was, for him, just another ordinary day.

The town looked as it always did. Tidy, a little old-timey, with the old stone townhouses or shops, the painted porches, the high curbs. He glanced back over his shoulder toward the Bowl-a-Rama on the square. It was the biggest building in town, and where Cal and Gage were both working.

When he and his father knocked off for the day, he thought, he'd head on up, see what was happening.

He crossed over to the Larson place, walked into the unlocked house where Bonnie Raitt's smooth Delta blues slid smoothly out of the kitchen. His father sang along with her in his clear and easy voice as he checked the level on the shelves Mrs. Larson wanted in her utility closet. Though the windows and back door were open to their screens, the room smelled of sawdust, sweat, and the glue they'd used that morning to lay the new Formica.

His father worked in old Levi's and his Give Peace a Chance T-shirt. His hair was six inches longer than Fox's, worn in a tail under a blue bandanna. He'd shaved off the beard and mustache he'd had as long as Fox remembered. Fox still wasn't quite used to seeing so much of his father's face—or so much of himself in it.

"A dog drowned in the Bestlers' swimming pool over on Laurel Lane," Fox told him, and Brian stopped working to turn.

"That's a damn shame. Anybody know how it happened?"

"Not really. It was one of those little poodles, so think it must've fallen in, then it couldn't get out again."

"You'd think somebody would've heard it barking. That's a lousy way to go." Brian set down his tools, smiled at his boy. "Gimme one of those Slim Jims."

"What Slim Jims?"

"The ones you've got in your back pocket. You're not carrying a bag, and you weren't gone long enough to scarf down Hostess Pies or Twinkies. I'm betting you're packing the Jims. I get one, and your mom never has to know we ate chemicals and meat by-products. It's called blackmail, kid of mine."

Fox snorted, pulled them out. He'd bought two for just this purpose. Father and son unwrapped, bit off, chewed in perfect harmony. "The counter looks good, Dad."

"Yeah, it does." Brian ran a hand over the smooth, eggshell surface. "Mrs. Larson's not much for color, but it's good work. I don't know who I'm going to get to be my lapdog when you head off to college."

"Ridge is next in line," Fox said, thinking of his younger brother.

"Ridge wouldn't keep measurements in his head for two minutes running, and he'd probably cut off a finger dreaming while he was using a band saw. No." Brian smiled, shrugged. "This kind of work isn't for Ridge, or for you, for that matter. Or either of your sisters. I guess I'm going to have to rent a kid to get one who wants to work with wood."

"I never said I didn't want to." Not out loud.

His father looked at him the way he sometimes did, as if he saw more than what was there. "You've got a good eye, you've got good hands. You'll be handy around your own house once you get one. But you won't be strapping on a tool belt to make a living. Until you figure out just what it is you want, you can haul these scraps on out to the Dumpster."

"Sure." Fox gathered up scraps, trash, began to cart them out the back, across the narrow yard to the Dumpster the Larsons had rented for the duration of the remodel.

He glanced toward the adjoining yard and the sound of kids playing. And the armload he carried thumped and bounced on the ground as his body went numb.

The little boys played with trucks and shovels and pails in a bright blue sandbox. But it wasn't filled with sand. Blood covered their bare arms as they pushed their Tonka trucks through the muck inside the box. He stumbled back as the boys made engine sounds, as red lapped over the bright blue sides and dripped onto the green grass.

On the fence between the yards, where hydrangeas headed up toward bloom, crouched a boy that wasn't a boy. He bared its teeth in a grin as Fox backed toward the house.

"Dad! Dad!"

The tone, the breathless fear had Brian rushing outside. "What? What is it?"

"Don't you—can't you see?" But even as he said it, as he pointed, something inside Fox knew. It wasn't real.

"What?" Firmly now, Brian took his son's shoulders. "What do you see?"

The boy that wasn't a boy danced along the top of the chain-link fence while flames spurted up below and burned the hydrangeas to cinders.

"I have to go. I have to go see Cal and Gage. Right now, Dad. I have to—"

"Go." Brian released his hold on Fox, stepped back. He didn't question. "Go."

He all but flew through the house and out again, up the sidewalk to the square. The town no longer looked as it usually did to him. In his mind's eye Fox could see it as it had been that horrible week in July seven years before.

Fire and blood, he remembered, thinking of the dream.

He burst into the Bowl-a-Rama, where the summer afternoon leagues were in full swing. The thunder of balls, the crash of pins pounded in his head as he ran straight to the front desk where Cal worked.

"Where's Gage?" Fox demanded.

"Jesus, what's up with you?"

"Where's Gage?" Fox repeated, and Cal's amused gray eyes sobered. "Working the arcade. He's . . . he's coming out now."

At Cal's quick signal, Gage sauntered over. "Hello, ladies. What . . ." The smirk died after one look at Fox's face. "What happened?"

"It's back," Fox said. "It's come back."

NORA ROBERTS

"You can't bottle wish fulfillment,
but Ms. Roberts certainly knows
how to put it on the page."

—*The New York Times*

For a complete list of titles,
please visit prh.com/noraroberts